A Soul to Steal

Duskwalker Brides

Book Six

Opal Reyne

ISBN: 978-0-6458301-6-3

Cover art: Sam Griffin
Editing/Proofreader: Messenger's Memos

Author's note on language

I'm from AUSTRALIA.

My English is not the same as American English.
I love my American English spoken readers to bits.
You're cute, you all make me giggle, and I just wanna give you a big ol' hug. However, there are many of you who don't seem to realise that your English was born from British English, which is what I use (although a bastardised version since Australians like to take all language and strangle it until it's a ruined carcass of slang, missing letters, and randomly added o's).

We don't seem to like the letter z.

We write colour instead of color. Recognise instead of recognise. Travelling instead of traveling. Skilful instead of skillful. Mum instead of mom. Smelt is a past participle of smell. We omit the full-stop in Mr. Name, so it's Mr Name. Aussies cradle the word cunt like it's a sweet little puppy, rather than an insult to be launched at your face.

Anyway, happy reading!

P.S. Our seasons in the southern hemisphere are opposite to those in the northern hemisphere.

Trigger Warning
Major spoiler below

Please only read further if you have triggers, otherwise you will seriously spoil the book for yourself.

Firstly, I will list what triggers **AREN'T** in the book so you can stop reading in order not to spoil it: No rape, non-con, dub-con, purposeful harm done between the MMCs, torture, physical abuse, cheating, suicide/self-harm, abortion, pregnancy, incest, drug/alcohol abuse, or child harm.

Please consider stopping here if your trigger has been detailed above as the rest are major spoilers.

This book has depictions of depression, hopelessness, and trauma. There are topics of death, of dying, and the memories associated with them. Grief and loss. Both characters are dealing with internal struggles, and the human becomes rather volatile part way through, but he deeply regrets it shortly after.

Memory loss that may be unsettling for those who have trauma around dementia.

There is a memory of coming out as gay to his family that may be uncomfortable for some, but please be reassured that the memory does have a very happy ending.

There is OM drama relating to a past relationship from before they met, which our human battles letting go of while having little closure. He died, and everyone and everything he knew is gone in the blink of an eye.

Minor implied soft vore – vorarephilia trigger. As always with my books, there is gore.

Are you new to the Duskwalker Brides series?

This book absolutely **cannot be read** before previous books in the series. A Soul to Guide has important information pertaining to this book, so you will be very lost and confused while reading if you don't have it. A Soul to Revive is directly tied to this one. Aleron is a twin, and Ingram's book is A Soul to Revive.

Please consider reading the other books, as the Duskwalker Brides series has an overarching plot arc and we are most of the way through it. You will also spoil the entire series for yourself if you do end up enjoying this book and wish to read it from the very beginning.

Many people come for the spice, but stay for plot.

You have been warned.

To all the male queer MonsterFuckers out there,

this book is for you.

My Duskwalkers love everyone, no matter their gender. So come enjoy their touch, their sweet words, and let this loving monster show you what it means to be adored unconditionally... while also getting railed hard and fast within an inch of your life.

I know you've all been hoping for this book.

I would like to give a big shoutout to the wonderful **sensitivity readers** who helped to make this book a safe place for those I am trying to positively represent. As you all know, representation is a big part of what I want to do, but I want to do so in a way that isn't harmful.

Thank you to Bryus, Wolfgang, Marco, Jakob, Alexx, and Jonah for your contribution towards M/M sensitivity.

I would also like to give a special thank you to Crystal for your contribution towards POC sensitivity.

I appreciate all the time and effort you put into helping me with this book. You will forever have a place in my heart.

ONE

Curiously staring up at his kindred, who cast a shadow over him from the false sun, Aleron knew there was a distinct difference between them.

One that had not existed before Aleron died.

It wasn't the fact that Ingram was now a purple spectre – a Ghost of himself that mirrored the colour of his orbs. It was that he now stood tall on two legs, rather than on all fours, like Aleron. His kindred also spoke... *differently*. Ingram sounded more human, like his thoughts were better collected than Aleron's own.

Although Aleron had obtained a decent amount of humanity by eating souls here in Tenebris, the afterworld, even he could tell his level didn't compare to Ingram's.

They had once been two inseparable souls, their shadows constantly overlapping and entwining. One being split into two. A unit, defined not by their different exteriors, but by their collective desires. They had been able to read each other's thoughts, as though they shared a single conscience. Their hopes, their dreams, their wants, and fears had been exactly the same.

The missing piece of himself, his other half, now stood before him, yet they felt miles and decades apart.

As he drifted his bat skull to the pretty female at his kindred's side, he knew they were truly beginning to walk different paths.

Unlike Ingram, who appeared ghostly and intangible, Emerie looked normal. In this world, it was as if they were the ones who lived and could touch, and it'd been his kindred who had passed. They existed on this plane, and him on another: the living world.

She looked dirty, with spots all over her cheeks, nose, and forehead, but her features were... delicate. The scarring on the left side of her face was noticeable to a Mavka's sensitive sight, but it meant little to him or Ingram. It was pale and red in places, whereas the rest of her skin was lightly tanned from the sun.

Although Ingram claimed that her hair was orange, in the current light, Aleron could only see it as red. Red like flames, like a rose, like the rage of their orbs. Her eyes were a cold, watery blue, but the warmth she shined through them in Aleron's direction held unmistakable kindness.

He was put off by it, by her.

Why does she get to go back with Ingram, and I cannot?

Aleron's sight changed from its usual pink to a bright green, as a terrible emotion rotated like a sharp rock within his chest. He wanted to be with Ingram, his kindred, his... *twin* brother. Ingram had tried his hardest to explain the connection of this familial bond in the limited time they'd had here in Tenebris, but Aleron was still a little shaky on the details.

However, as he stared at the female, alongside that nasty little rock of loathing was a swell of tenderness that outshined it.

Despite Aleron's disgruntled, envious feelings towards Emerie, and the fact she was allowed to be taken from the afterworld to be Ingram's little bride, he was awash in happiness. Neither had sought a bride, but in his absence within the living world, Aleron was thankful Ingram had someone.

She was very kind to me.

In just a small amount of time, she had managed to win Aleron over. Her soft, understanding voice, her welcoming smiles in his direction, and the comfort of a hug, during which they shared many private words.

She said they will be waiting for me. Which meant Emerie had no intention of getting in the way of Ingram and himself reuniting. Actually, it sounded as though she intended to openly accept it.

Ingram was obviously obsessed with the little female, considering he constantly tried to touch her with his intangible form. He'd huff with annoyance, and just hover his palm around any part of her he could. His kindred had only craved a physical link like this with him. It brought Aleron great contentment to know he desired that touch from her, and that he had someone to dote on.

A quiet chuckle rumbled from him when Ingram tried putting his hand on her side, only for it to flow through her.

Weldir – the spirit of the void and their male creator – stood quietly beside Ingram. He had very little intention of interfering with their discussions, seemingly satisfied to be a spectator.

The ribbon-like visibility to his form was the smallest Aleron had ever seen of him.

He knew, after being here for so long, that Weldir's magical essence was draining faster and faster by the second. Aleron was unsure what would happen when his power ran out and his form fully disappeared, but it couldn't be a good thing.

Will he stop visiting me?

Weldir was the only one who was able to give Aleron attention, and he gave it as often as possible. He'd spent many hours, days, possibly weeks, venturing through Tenebris at Weldir's side.

The serpent Mavka will not speak to me.

He didn't know why, only that he often spent his time in

the sun upon a certain rock, and stared out at the expanse of fields and nothingness beyond them. Was his mind lost? All attempts at conversing with him had fallen on unlistening ears.

If Weldir stopped visiting him, he would be... *alone* again. Truly alone in this world.

The human souls here, if disturbed by his touch, would scream in fright and flee. It's why he'd eaten a few, having chased them for fun before, unfortunately, consuming them.

Despite his lack of insatiable hunger, it appeared his instincts to destroy weren't settled simply because he died. As like with any living Mavka, he still needed to chase, play with, and hunt escaping prey. Their screams and fear only worsened and caused him to froth at the maw in glee.

They weren't good company for this reason.

"I wish you could come with us," Emerie sadly grumbled, bringing Aleron out of his thoughts, as she nibbled at her pink bottom lip.

She didn't just say this to him, but another who was with them. A fifth person.

Aleron peeked at the male human at his side.

No, not alone. This one is not screaming in terror and trying to flee.

His hair was relatively short, about the length of Aleron's little finger – since he didn't know how to count properly – yet messily swept back. It was a light brown and had the oddest orange to it in the false sun. That same shade of brown had grown as very short hairs upon his cheeks, jaw, and neck. His skin was tanned but lacked any of the spots the female had upon her.

He was much taller than his female companion, surpassing her by over a head. He was also much wider in his shoulders and thighs, holding strong muscles for a human – not the biggest he'd seen, but enough for Aleron to know he wasn't small and feeble.

Aleron had taken in his intensely piercing green eyes

from the few fleeting moments they'd shared a wary look upon each other, but he'd noticed they were... sparkly. They were light in colour, like a brightly lit forest and the sparkling gemstones he'd seen in the dirt and some caves.

However, he was just a human – someone who meant very little to him in comparison to his kindred and his bride before him.

Gideon, the brother to this female, rubbed at his short-hair-covered cheek with the heel of his palm.

"It's fine, Emerie," Gideon mumbled back, raising his green eyes to the false blue sky.

He did have a nice, deep voice when he spoke, Aleron decided. It was the most enjoyable quality of the male so far.

"There's no point in wishing for things that can't change." Then he pulled his hand away as he chuckled, making two little indented dots form in his cheeks. His tone was coy, aloof, and playful as he continued, "Who says I want to go with you and this Duskwalker anyway? I don't want to be a witness to anything possibly... *unseemly*."

Emerie's bottom lip fell in disbelief of what he'd said, only for her to launch forward into an attack.

"You're still a big jerk!" she squealed, punching the bottom of her fists against the tops of his shoulders before yanking on his hair. "You know what? I'm glad you're not coming. I don't have to hear you sing another lame ballad and mangle a guitar anymore."

"I'll give you a lame ballad."

Within seconds, the female let out a shriek as he curled his arm around the back of her neck, tucked her head against the side of his chest, and ran his knuckles back and forth over the top of her head. She fought him, even tried to pull away by pushing back with her feet, which only caused them to go in a circle.

With a growl, Ingram attempted to interfere, only to

shove his grasping, intangible claws through their bodies. Aleron worried if he tried to assist, he'd hurt his kindred's bride-to-be.

"Ow! Stop it!"

When Gideon let her go, her long, wavy hair looped in a nest of tangled strands. Her face had flushed deeply, and her lips tightened in annoyance – only to vibrate as she let out a 'pfft' and a giggle.

Just as she opened her mouth, Gideon pulled her in for a tight hug before she could speak. She immediately put her arms around him to return it, and clawed at the back of his sleeveless grey shirt.

Aleron faced his skull towards Ingram's ghostly raven one to gauge if he was bothered by this open affection.

He wasn't, from what he could tell.

Instead, he crouched to be at the same level and leaned forward, and Aleron mimicked the action. They pretended to nuzzle skulls.

"We will try to figure out a way to bring you back to the living world," Ingram stated quietly. "If Emerie can come back, there must be a way for you as well."

Ever since Aleron had arrived in the afterworld, he hadn't had much hope of returning to Ingram's side. However, Ingram's belief and determination lifted Aleron's spirit, alongside Weldir's earlier mention that not all hope may be lost for him.

"I will do the same from here," Aleron answered, his voice more guttural in comparison to Ingram's – likely due to still being in his monstrous form. *"Then I will not stop until I find you."*

Finding Ingram and Emerie would be the first thing Aleron would do if he were to be revived. He would never rest, nor deviate from this task. He would allow nothing to get in the way.

As Ingram stood, and Emerie let go of her brother, they both backed up. After staring at each other for a long while,

Ingram dipped his head towards Weldir.

His voice came out strained and thick with emotion as he stated, "We are ready."

Ingram reached his hand out to the little female, and Aleron sensed she was the only reason Ingram had the strength to leave him.

His chest warmed when she came closer and reached out her palm to pretend to hold it, her features softening into a lovely expression up at his kindred. Just like that, she'd stolen a little more of Aleron's heart at seeing how much she adored Ingram.

"Good, because you are almost out of time," Weldir stated, what remained of his face dropping to Ingram's chest, examining something upon it Aleron couldn't see.

"Actually, I do have one question for you," Emerie said, turning to Weldir. "Did I do it? Did I destroy the Demon King?"

Weldir was silent for a moment, which Aleron had discovered wasn't uncommon for him. He was often stoic and silent. His only visible fist tightened, and Aleron tilted his head at the action. "I am not sure."

Her brows furrowed deeply. "What do you mean, you're not sure?"

A small discussion started about the likelihood of the Demon King's death, but Weldir explained that, although he could not sense his magic, he had not consumed his soul. All were worried about the spirit of the void being so unsure, and that uncertainty rested heavily between them.

No one was given time to digest this, as Weldir shoved his hand into Emerie's sternum. A gasp tore from her as her essence waved like rippling water. Her body disappeared, sucking towards his hand as he pulled back, until he held a small, flaming white soul.

Ingram, eager to hold it, was denied.

They had already shared many goodbyes, and they

weren't given anymore.

Weldir disappeared with Emerie's soul without saying a word. A moment later, Ingram, scratching at nothing with the claws of his hands and feet, lifted off the ground and floated towards the sky.

His heart gouged in loss, in heartache, as his sight turned blue with sorrow. A whine broke from his chest. *Come back.* He didn't want to be... abandoned again.

Watching his kindred leaving, his body rotating and spinning, he considered lifting off with his wings. He would chase him to the ends of the world, desperate to be with him, to follow him wherever he went.

His feathers shifted as he spread them to do just that.

"Guess it's just us now," Gideon grumbled with a shrug, catching his attention instead. All cheer from earlier had fallen from his face.

Aleron had almost forgotten he stood there, too consumed by the weight of his emotions.

"Us?" he asked, leaping back and tucking his chest down, his tail feathers flaring wide.

He said us! That meant he didn't have to be alone. He'd found a companion here after all, and it was the *human* who stated it!

"Well, yeah. If my parents died when I was young, and my adopted parents died due to a fire, I don't think they'll be here. They had to be eaten to come here, right? And, to be honest, the idea of falling back into a dream state feels... weird. I'd rather remain conscious." Rubbing at the side of his neck, he turned his gaze towards the sky, and a sad smile lifted his features. "I'm just glad I got to see Emerie, and know that she's happy, safe, and has someone who will love her. It's more reassurance than anyone else here in the afterlife would get. Does that make sense?"

He turned his face down from looking above, and his green eyes fell upon Aleron's bat skull expectantly.

Aleron raised himself from his curious stance, then lifted

his sight to the sky. His orbs turned blue once more, but the sadness that swallowed him wasn't as prevalent as it could have been.

"Yes, I understand how you feel. It brings me comfort to know that Ingram has a bride and is not alone. I will miss him, though."

He wished he could have gone with him. Even if he were to fly now, it was impossible, no matter how hard he chased. He was here, *for now.*

"You know what?" Gideon stated. "I never expected your kind to be so... I don't know, caring?"

Aleron lowered his skull to the male next to him. *He thinks I am caring?*

"We, Mavka, can feel many things. I... love Ingram, and always have." Glad Ingram had explained what the word 'love' meant, he now understood the significance of it. How it could be shared among many people, and not just between their kindred bond. *"I love Emerie, too, as she is important to my kindred, who is special to me."*

"You're known to be violent, human-eating entities. We never knew you could care for one another, or even a human." Gideon averted his gaze, inspecting a stray human Ghost who was lost in their memory dreams. "If I hadn't witnessed it myself between Emerie and your... twin, was it? I wouldn't have believed it."

The male stilled.

Before Aleron could answer, the human's sharp features fell and his eyes dazed. He became lifeless within the breath of a second. The only sign of life came from his hair and clothes billowing, but even his tanned face paled slightly.

"Gideon?" Aleron hesitantly stepped forward as he dipped his body in uncertainty.

When he didn't respond, Aleron gently raised his hand from the ground so he could brush his knuckles against the side of his elbow.

Gideon sprung to life, tearing his arm away as though he'd been startled. Aleron stepped back and lowered further until even his wings had sunk to the ground submissively. He didn't wish to frighten the little male.

The human paused when he looked upon his skull, and for a few heartbeats, Aleron feared the worst. Especially since Gideon's expression looked bewildered and distant.

Did I touch him too late?

Weldir warned him if he didn't touch the humans within an hour, they would fall back into their dream states and... forget their most recent memories.

"Fuck," Gideon spat out, combing his fingers through his hair. He turned fully to Aleron. "What the hell just happened to me? A whole chunk of my memories just disappeared." Then he rubbed at his eyes before moving his hands away to blink at them, as if trying to regain them through sheer force of will. "I remember nothing from before Ingram confessed to Emerie and asked her to go back to Earth with him."

"But you remember everything after that?" Aleron asked, twisting his head as he straightened on all fours.

"Yeah," he grumbled, his eyes slitting with annoyance. "But it's still shit to only remember half a conversation that only *just* happened."

The initial introduction to them all meant little to Aleron, so long as Gideon retained everything else – which was much more important. For example, when he'd called Mavka caring, or when they'd shaken hands in their human custom of greeting. That was all this human needed, because Aleron understood it would be what kept him as his companion.

Without it, he'd be alone in this world again.

I must not let him forget... me.

TWO

How did I end up in this predicament? Gideon thought, then a better question came to mind. *No. Why... am I in this predicament?*

One minute he'd been talking to Aleron, trying his hardest to not be freaked out about everything, and then suddenly the Duskwalker *pounced*.

Coiling lean, elongated arms around his body, Aleron tackled Gideon to the ground so swiftly it was like he turned into a striking snake. With both of them ending up on the ground, Gideon forced to be seated between the Duskwalker's knees that came to his shoulder height, he found himself trapped.

Struggling had meant very little, as Aleron didn't seem to feel it, notice it, or care.

"Some space, Aleron," Gideon demanded, whilst trying to not upset the Duskwalker he hadn't known before this very day.

He had no idea what his temperament was like, if the caring nature of him was only temporary and he was actually mercilessly violent. He may not tolerate being told what to do.

Gideon wrestled both his arms until one was freed. The rounded ball joint of his shoulder pressed firmly against his ear as he stuck his arm straight up through a small pocket.

He let his forearm flop onto his head to relax.

Fuck, I made it worse. He couldn't fight with his left arm anymore. He swung it around uselessly.

"Stay," Aleron gruffed out, tightening his arms.

Just remain calm. Figure out what he wants and then find out a way to get away from him. That didn't look quite possible right now, but Gideon had every intention of ditching this clingy Duskwalker the first chance he got.

Will he eat me if I anger him? Gideon's somewhat thick brows drew together. *Can he kill me if I'm already dead?*

Honestly, the fact he technically wasn't alive anymore was the only reason he hadn't lost his shit already. It helped that he'd had some positive – because he couldn't say truly pleasant – conversations with this Duskwalker.

Meeting Emerie in the afterlife... then watching her be taken away to be some raven-skulled Duskwalker's bride or wife – whatever that truly entailed – was a lot to wrap his mind around. Being stuck here also meant that anything and everything he did became fucking *pointless*.

Even the air here feels stale and wrong.

Breathing didn't feel natural. He stilled his lungs to test if he needed to at all. He didn't. No tickle or burning sensation radiated in his chest, demanding he desperately took another breath.

He still did, because it felt unnatural not to, but it just proved how utterly futile everything was.

He pulled on the grey collar of the sleeveless tunic clothing him, before looking down at his plain-brown trousers and boots through the crevice of their bodies. *I don't think I was wearing this when I died.* It looked familiar, perhaps one of his favourite summer shirts, but he was sure he'd been wearing a jacket the night he perished.

He could feel the weight of his gold hooped earrings dangling from both of his lobes. They were cold when they should be warm from his body temperature.

I still can't believe I'm dead.

He remembered his death, like it was only yesterday. Then again, it *was* only yesterday to him when, in reality, it'd been eight years!

Eight years, and the world moved on without him as if he hadn't mattered at all. Like Gideon's existence was unimportant in the flow of time.

He eventually relaxed in Aleron's hold, his thoughts turning remorseful. *That's not true. Emerie... she missed me. She must have suffered so much since that night.* A fuzziness assaulted his sinuses, as if the urge to cry tickled his face. He quickly hardened his expression and stemmed any liquid from escaping his eyes. *She lost me, our parents, her face... her beautiful, pretty face – all in one night.*

All because of some fuckwit of a guy who didn't know how to keep her safe. What good is a partner if they won't make you see sense in order to keep you alive?

Instead, Declan, the limp noodle of a man, barely in his twenties, had let Emerie out of his house like an unprotected baby bird. In the middle of the damn night. Fewer instances of Demons in the southland region made people complacent and stupid.

And that's what caused... everything.

Not only did Gideon have to digest he'd died that night, but he'd learnt how much Emerie had suffered in only a few words. Just looking upon her showed the scars she'd physically endured, but the lack of sweet innocence and naivety in her gaze was what truly crushed him.

His little sister, no matter that she wasn't blood-related, was one of the most important people to Gideon. And, because of her own silliness and Declan's stupidity, it'd ended lives and broken one of the sweetest people he'd ever known.

Sure, she also *used* to have a horrible, snarky temper. He knew what her final unpleasant words to him were; she'd told him to fuck off in front of their home. Apparently, he'd been 'meddling' in her affairs, but he'd been so angry that she was acting foolishly – childishly even.

I can't imagine how much that must have weighed on her.

And yet, his fears had been proven right.

Of course the winged Demon who had swept Emerie off her feet had some part to blame in all this.

Gideon could still remember jumping for her legs, tearing at her dress to keep her on the ground just after they'd been arguing. Her scream would likely have given him nightmares here in the afterlife, but the pain he recalled would be something he could never, *ever* forget.

After he fumbled and swiped his dagger from his belt, he'd stabbed it into the Demon's thigh to make it let go of her. It'd given up on Emerie. Instead, making Gideon its target.

He touched his abdomen, and through the light material shirt, the horrible, raised scars marring him abraded his fingertips.

From the right side of his chest to his left hip were four long claw marks. The second swipe, which spanned in the opposite direction, was shorter yet deeper in its scarring. Gideon remembered very little after that, except maybe some of his internal organs slipping out of him right as his heart gave out.

He hadn't lived long enough to be flown past the town's protective walls.

He didn't even see his home had been on fire, with his adoptive parents – Emerie's parents – still inside it.

Part of him wanted to blame her, but it was hard to. It happened, and nothing they did could change it. He wouldn't torment himself or taint his memory of his little sister – who was technically his older sibling now.

She's twenty-seven while I'm stuck at twenty-three. His expression turned into a grimace. *And what about Beau? Fuck! Beau would have been devastated.*

Tears welled in his eyes, and he didn't know if he had

A Soul to Steal   15

the strength to stem them this time. Beau Parker had been one of the most cherished people in his life, other than his parents and Emerie, of course.

Knowing that Beau would have suffered immense grief and loss at Gideon's death was almost impossible to bear. Gideon also, just now, had to grieve the loss of a future.

I was going to ask him to marry me that coming autumn. We were going to start a family together, adopt a bunch of kids from the poor side of Fishket. I wanted us to buy our own house, and I would watch him cook for me every night after we both worked throughout the day.

His future, his life, and all the people he loved had been taken away from him.

Despite the constricting hold, he grew thankful the Duskwalker gave him time to process everything he'd lost. In some ways, it was comforting to have someone or something steadying him through this. It was nice to not be alone as he digested the finality of his life. He'd become obsolete, and his existence consisted of the nothingness of this weird, freakish afterlife he found himself in.

Quietly staring at the grass, he noticed it had the strangest blue tinge to it, once more solidifying he wasn't on Earth.

He was also thankful the monster clutching him didn't seem to notice the emotional anguish Gideon was currently going through. Or maybe Aleron just didn't care about his pain, which was actually rather rude and hurtful when he thought about it.

The least he could do was give Gideon a reassuring head pat in sympathy or something.

However, as time passed, the hold loosened until he was able to bring his arm back down. He shoved the pads of his thumbs and fingers into his closed eyes, wishing the pressure would stop the tears of internal agony from falling.

Why is it possible to cry in the afterlife? Why could he

feel pain in his chest and gut? Why did his face tingle and feel warm? What use was there in feeling these things when he was dead and, thus, inconsequential?

What use was there having human emotions and physical pain when he was nothing but a Ghost?

Fuck, Beau, I'm so sorry. I'm so sorry I left you behind. Gosh, is my dog still alive? Gideon had no doubt that Beau, who worked in the same profession, would have taken his dog as his own.

Dex, his three-year-old Cattle dog, had been the sweetest, most loving boy.

He'd been trained to alert them of incoming Demons. Many of those who worked outside the town's protective walls kept dogs, and Gideon had been no different. Dex had saved his life, and his fellow woodcutters', twice.

Are you having a nice life, boy? Does Beau feed you well and scratch your cheeks for being a good dog? Despite knowing he was likely being cared for, it still hurt that he wasn't the one to do so.

Gideon didn't realise how badly his thoughts had spiralled until the Duskwalker retracted his arms.

"Am I causing you to be afraid?" Aleron asked quietly, as though truly concerned by that possibility.

"What?" Gideon choked. "Why would I be afraid?"

He was dead! How could he be afraid of anything now?

"I cannot smell anything, not even your scent, but you are shaking." Aleron said this, yet he didn't fully pull away. Both of his long legs were still bent and resting against Gideon's sides. *"I did not mean to make you uncomfortable."*

What made him uncomfortable was how *gruff* and pleasant he found his voice just next to his ear.

The hell? Why is he being so damn nice? How could a monster be this considerate? It made little sense.

Still, the gentler side of Gideon said, "No, this isn't because of you." He palmed his cheeks, attempting to remove the evidence of his tears, before swiping the back of his wrist against his nose. "I just... I have a lot on my mind. A lot to absorb."

"What are these then?" The back of a long, sharp, and glossy black claw swiped just below his eye, stealing a fresh teardrop. *"I thought humans only produced liquid from their eyes when they are afraid."*

"I'm guessing you've only seen humans when they are afraid, then," Gideon grumbled, before finally turning to look at the creature trapping him.

His long, spiral goat horns stuck up from his head, reminding him of a sketch of an evil devil he'd once seen. Aleron's bat skull tilted as Gideon stared at them. In his empty, bony eye sockets, glowing orbs shone dark yellow at him – not that Gideon knew what it signified.

"This is true," he replied honestly, without a shred of negative infliction. Aleron never opened his fangs to speak, and it made him wonder where his voice came from. *"Why do you produce this liquid then, if you are not afraid?"*

"We cry because we are sad too. Sometimes when we're happy, but it's usually because we are upset."

Gideon could count how many times he'd cried as an adult on one hand, but he didn't think he'd ever been this shocked or upset before in his life. Maybe it would have been best if he hadn't awoken at all in this world.

"But you are not upset because of me. What is causing you to cry *then, little human?"*

Gideon opened his mouth to yell at him in outrage at his question. Wasn't it fucking obvious? What person wouldn't undoubtably be upset that they were no longer alive?

However, he quickly shut his mouth when he realised he wasn't talking to a human. What would a monster know?

He gave a sigh and dropped his head. He only raised it when he answered, peering out at this world.

He doesn't even know what crying is. I bet his kind can't

even cry.

"I've lost... everything. I had my whole life ahead of me, and now I have nothing. I want to go home. I miss my friends, my partner, my family, my dog. I miss the house I was renting and how it smelled like burnt wood from the fireplace. I'm upset because I left all that too early, and there are likely people who suffered because of that. I'm crying because my chest hurts, and I don't know how else to ease it when there is nothing I can do from here." Gideon's eyes bowed when he realised he was explaining all this to a creature who didn't have any of this. "You probably don't understand, so don't worry about it."

The silence from the Duskwalker was telling.

He probably lived in the forest like an animal, hunting for food. He wouldn't have had a partner, a pet, a home to miss.

Gideon knew he had a brother, but he'd gotten the chance to meet him after only being separated for what... a month? That wasn't the same as the eight years he'd lost, and the people he'd left behind that wouldn't get any closure.

He felt for those people, and everything they had suffered in his absence.

Once more, the back of Aleron's cool claw stole another stray tear. In his peripheral, Gideon watched him inspect it as it slid down the curve of his claw.

"You cry because you are upset... in pain. So that is what I saw when I first came here."

The saliva in his mouth grew sticky as he rasped, "Pardon?"

The teardrop clung to the sharp point of his claw a moment before it dropped to the ground. At the same time, his yellow orbs turned a dark blue.

"Tears. When I first came here, I produced something similar. However, they were not wet like this, but rather came from my skull like floating drops. They were such a

deep colour of blue that it hurt even more seeing them." Aleron finally looked away from his own claw to face his skull towards Gideon. Those blue orbs seemed to absorb Gideon's face like a swirling vortex of anguish. *"Thank you for giving me the name for them."*

"You cried?" Gideon asked, his deep voice cracking an octave.

Within seconds, a cold wash of shame rolled over him like a wave. Although he hadn't rudely said it aloud, his thoughts had not been kind. He couldn't believe his assumption that Duskwalkers didn't cry had been so wrong.

"Yes. I missed Ingram. I was sad because I knew I could no longer be with him, and I worried about how he must be feeling. I searched for him, hoping I would find him among the humans here, but Weldir explained that Ingram had not come with me. I did not want to be alone. I was... scared."

As Gideon listened, his tears began to ease.

"Scared?" he asked in disbelief. "Why were you scared?"

"For Ingram. If I was alone, then so was he. It meant I could no longer protect him, and that distressed me. I am now safe from the Demons, and my life started anew here, but who would keep him warm or play with him if not me? Who would do that for me? I tried to befriend the humans here, but they only screamed when I touched them, and the other Mavka will not speak to me. I was scared that I would suffer alone in this world I do not know or understand... forever."

"You wanted Ingram to die with you? Most would consider that pretty selfish," Gideon said honestly.

"Why would this be selfish? Ingram and I are one, and we were better together."

"Because he still has the potential to have a happy life, even if it is without you."

"I guess this is true," Aleron grumbled as he lifted his

head to look at the world stretching before them. *"He did find a bride without me."*

Now that Aleron's wings were no longer blocking his vision, Gideon looked out as well. There wasn't much to see, except for a grassy field with a mountain range just beyond it. There were trees to the right of them some distance away, whereas to their left was Fishket – or rather, an incorrect replica of it.

It lacked its protective wooden stake wall, and a few houses were duplicates – as if to house people from different eras and times.

"Weldir helped me. He made sure I was not completely alone and has often been by my side. Yet, that did not stop my fear for Ingram. Only now... has it settled."

Gideon's brows creased. "Because of Emerie?"

"I am happy he is not alone, even if it hurts that I cannot go to him." Aleron's inhuman, deep baritone darkened with sorrow. *"So do not cry. They are safe together."*

"It's not just Emerie, though," Gideon stated with a sigh. He brought his knees up so he could wrap his arms around his legs and placed his chin on top of them. "I had so many people in my life. I had hopes, dreams, and plans, and I never got to see a single one of them come to fruition. I should have died an old man."

"I do not know what being an old man is, but I do know we, Mavka, can live forever unless killed. A horde of Demons attacked us and they crushed my skull before I could escape. How did you die then?"

Gideon's head bounced as he spoke with his chin firmly on his knees. "In the middle of the night, Emerie and I were outside when we shouldn't have been. A winged Demon tried to fly off with her, but I grabbed her to keep her on the ground and it took me instead."

"You saved her life by sacrificing your own? Is this not a good thing to do? I would have done this for my kindred."

"I would much rather it not have been needed at all," he

answered honestly. "It would've been so easily avoided. Yeah, if I could go back in time knowing what I do now, I would absolutely do it again if I was given a choice between me and her, but I wish..."

What point was there in wishing or thinking about the 'what ifs'? They only made tears well in his eyes again.

"I don't want to be here," Gideon stated. "It's not fair that my life was ended short because of others, or that Demons exist in the first place. I hate that I missed out on everything." Then Gideon reached down to grab a fistful of grass from the dirt. "I hate that I'm here. This world doesn't even look right, like the person who created it never truly understood Earth. The grass even has a blue tinge to it, and the sky is the wrong fucking colour of blue, and why does everything smell like it has vinegar in it? The wind doesn't have a temperature, and the sun doesn't even feel warm. It's like they wanted to trick us into believing its real when it's so obviously not. I want to feel... human, like I *exist*."

Gideon winced in surprise when he was shoved into darkness.

The whoosh that accompanied it informed him the Duskwalker had covered them both totally in his wings. Gideon's breaths didn't even echo or reverberate against his feathers, reminding him they were needless. The only light came from Aleron's blue orbs floating in nothingness.

"Is this better?" Somehow, Aleron's voice sounded louder than before.

At first, no. Being hidden away in Aleron's wings only brought on the choking fear of the dark that had been ingrained into all humans from a young age. That was quickly eaten away by the reminder that he no longer needed to be terrified of the dark and the Demons that could possibly be lingering in it.

For a few moments, he just... listened as he tried to make up his mind.

His own breaths sounded much quieter than Aleron's more substantial ones. With how big the Duskwalker was, he expected to hear a heartbeat.

He never did, even when he subtly closed the space between them so he could place his head near Aleron's chest.

He couldn't sense Aleron's heart, and he eventually realised he couldn't truly hear his own. There was a pulsing from within, like the familiar circulation of blood. Yet, when he pressed into his jugular, it pumped faintly. Once more, it felt false.

Not being able to see the world that Gideon had been thrust into was actually... soothing.

"Yeah, I guess that's better," Gideon finally answered as he straightened up – only for the Duskwalker to wrap his arms around him once more and shove his head against his torso again. "Why are you even doing this?"

"You said you did not like–"

"Not the wing thing," Gideon cut in. "You've been holding and touching me since Ingram and Emerie left. Why? It's not like I can run from you. I doubt I'd get far."

"If I do not touch you for a long period of time, you will eventually fall back asleep like the other humans here. I am trying to prevent that."

"Then just wake me again, like you did before."

"You will forget everything you have learned here if I am too late."

Oh, Gideon thought, his brows furrowing deeply.

He didn't want to go back to sleep before, but after realising everything... would that actually be better? He'd no longer have to bear the reality before him if he did. Yet...

I will forget Emerie is happy.

"So that's what happened before." He'd fallen back asleep and had begun to lose his memories. He shuddered at the thought. "As much as it hurts learning that I died, I still don't think I want to go back to sleep."

"I will make sure you do not," Aleron stated firmly, his orbs shifting to a light pink – one which Gideon had already seen many times from him.

It wasn't as bright as the pink he'd shone at Ingram a few times.

The laugh that came from Gideon was as hollow as he felt inside. "Guess I'm stuck with you."

There go my plans for getting away from him. He now needed Aleron if he wanted to stay conscious. *Then again, it could be worse.*

He wasn't quite sure *how*, only that it probably could be.

For a long while, they sat together in the darkness. Neither spoke, and neither moved, yet Gideon often peeked at Aleron from the corner of his eye. Barely two inches away, the Duskwalker never seemed to drift his gaze away, his imposing bat skull and weird orbs staring at him all the way to the pit of his soul. It had been uncomfortable at first, creepy almost, but those feelings eventually settled as he just quietly worked through his thoughts.

His eyes never drooped, instead blinking with constant alertness.

Eventually, he felt calm within the swirling storm of his unpleasant thoughts. The darkness helped, allowing him to fully settle into the reality of his new life without the unbearable oddity of the bright world around him. He also wasn't alone, even though he would have preferred to not cry in front of someone he considered a stranger.

He attempted to remain pragmatic about everything but found that a little too difficult with the unknowns before him.

I feel restless. Not physically – he lacked the itch to move from the cramping of muscles – but mentally.

"Could you open your wings?" he asked.

With a whoosh, Aleron parted his dark, feathered wings and allowed the world back into their senses. Gideon had

expected the light to burn his eyes after so long, but it
didn't, and he kind of hated that the sting was missing. It
was as though he'd just been suspended in a long blink.

He attempted to get up, but only made it halfway to his
feet before the Duskwalker stopped him by grabbing his
forearm. The grip wasn't tight, or rather didn't feel tight, but
it was firm and unbreakable.

"Where are you going?" Gideon raised a brow at the
slight panic in Aleron's tone.

"I'm just getting up. I don't want to sit anymore."

Aleron let him go, but his orbs shifted to white – a colour
he hadn't seen him produce before. *"Have I upset you?"*

His question left Gideon with many of his own. Why
was the Duskwalker so panicked to keep ahold of Gideon
when he should only need to touch him periodically? Why
would Gideon be upset with him when they had literally
been doing nothing? Wasn't he bored of sitting here as well?

Instead of asking any of them, he just turned to the
Duskwalker to truly take in what he had been technically
cuddling.

Although Ingram had been nothing but a giant purple
ghostly creature, Aleron was solid and appeared as real as
life.

His white skull looked like one that belonged to a fruit
bat, and yet the dark-brown horns on his head reminded him
of a goat's. They twisted and spiralled backwards twice and
were oval in shape rather than round. At the base of his skull
was a big, fluffy collar of black fur, making his neck appear
thicker than it likely was. Fur covered the entire front and
sides of his torso, arms, and legs, while most of his back
appeared to be long, sleek feathers.

Gideon didn't know what part of him he found strangest:
Aleron's skull, his claws that looked too sharp, his bird-like,
four-toed feet with talons, or his wings and tail. His tail was
like that of a raven's and appeared to be as long as Gideon
was tall. Many of his wing feathers were similar.

He was entirely black, with a slight glint of blue where the sun shone on him. A small patch of lizard scales was visible on his stomach, and on the inside of his knees and elbows. It seemed to match where the skin was thinner on a human.

Ingram had been covered from head to toe in bones protruding past his flesh. It was difficult to see what bones protruded outside of Aleron's skin, but they peeked out from the mass of his feathers and fur. Most were visible, similar to his twin, but the most noticeable ones were on the backs of his hands, wrists, feet, and ankles.

His orbs were a light pink, almost pastel.

Everything about him looked wrong, monstrous, freaky. He had a bite that could kill, likely *had* killed.

And yet, after rubbing the back of his head as he warily inspected the creature before him, Gideon eventually held out his hand to him.

"Come on, let's go," Gideon said, making an official offering to the Duskwalker to become his friend.

Aleron reached his hand out as well, grasped Gideon's, and shook it.

When Gideon had first introduced himself to Aleron, they shook hands. Gideon had put all his might into that handshake, only for Aleron to yank downwards on his arm so hard he faceplanted on the ground. If he had been alive, he would have broken his nose in the process.

For the first time since Emerie had left, Gideon let out a genuine smile and a small chuckle.

"I didn't mean for you to shake my hand," Gideon said, shaking his head as his chuckle deepened. "I'm trying to help you to your feet so we can move on *together*."

"Oh," Aleron rasped, his orbs turning reddish pink.

"Hold it, and I'll pull you up?" He found it funny that a situation that would've been so natural between two humans was apparently rather complicated between them.

Aleron grabbed his hand, and Gideon pulled... and pulled, to no avail. He eventually clasped both his hands around Aleron's massive fist and dug his heels into the ground to kick off and pull him up.

"You're supposed to help," Gideon said with a grunt.

He went flying backwards when Aleron stood completely on his own. He fell to his arse with an *oomph*.

Before he could get his bearings, Aleron shoved his hand near his face. Without needing to think about it, although grumbling in annoyance, Gideon grabbed it and let Aleron help him to his feet. His legs kicked before he actually touched the ground; he'd been tossed like a rag doll.

"Alright," he mumbled, dusting off his clean pants as a way to hide his irritation at not being able to pick the Duskwalker up. "I've always had an itch to go on an adventure."

He'd rather explore this place than sit and dwell on the past. It was what it was; nothing could change it or bring him back to life, and he'd rather give himself a reason to exist.

Aleron had been awake longer than him, since Gideon had been in limbo for eight years. The Duskwalker could be his guide in this world.

We might as well make the most of what we have.

THREE

Walking on all fours, Aleron followed the human while staring in blatant awe.

He'd made his first real human companion, and he was excited the male had made the offer himself! He wasn't afraid of Aleron, nor did he seem deterred by their differences.

Giddiness added bounce to each of his steps, despite the pervading anxiety that constantly made him brush against him – whether it be his shoulder or wing.

He let me hold him. Hehe! Bright yellow filled his vision as he swayed his head, rather pleased about all this. *He even let me put my wings around him.* And he hadn't seemed to mind Aleron staring at him the entire time they had been encased in the feathery blanket.

I made a friend here. One that wants me to join him on his adventure.

He wasn't afraid or attempting to run away. He wasn't screaming upon seeing his skull like the other humans here. He wasn't being mean and growling at him.

Aleron truly thought he would be alone here forever.

Well, not particularly true, since Weldir often came to his side, but the spirit of the void was... busy. He had tasks or needed to be elsewhere, leaving Aleron to chase after and find him when he felt his presence within Tenebris.

He could always feel Weldir when he was nearby.

But now he had Gideon, someone who *needed* him. Aleron wanted to be needed, wanted to be useful to someone in the way he had been vital for his dear kindred. He wanted someone to give him meaning. If this human wished to remain conscious within Tenebris, Aleron would happily touch him in order to do so.

Weldir had once stated that hope wasn't lost for Aleron. Although that had been rather cryptic, he pondered whether this meant he could be brought back to life. If so, did that mean he could bring Gideon with him in the same way Ingram had done so for Emerie?

Weldir said I may yet steal another soul from him, and that my bride could already be within Tenebris. Could that be Gideon? Had his bride been here all along, or was he being foolishly hopeful?

He liked the male enough.

Before he'd died, Aleron and Ingram hadn't particularly thought any humans were attractive.

To Aleron, Emerie had just been another person, and he felt this way about Gideon as well. He'd also held nothing but friendship towards the pointy-eared Elven female he'd once met, with her hair as white as snow and her skin a strange, inhuman brown due to its grey undertone.

Something must have won over the heart of his kindred for him to travel all the way to the afterlife simply for Emerie.

Ingram told me their beginning had not been easy. He raked his gaze down Gideon again. *Did he grow to care for her, or did he know straight away?*

Aleron didn't know if it was supposed to be instantaneous or if it was something he needed to work on to decide.

Should I try with Gideon? How would he even begin to do that?

Apparently, Emerie had been kind. Since Gideon had not

been rude towards Aleron, he wondered if this was a trait shared between them.

He didn't know what he desired in a bride. He would like them to be kind to him, warm towards him. *I would like them to cuddle with me and enjoy being within my wings.* He wanted them to... be at ease and find comfort within his embrace.

He said he felt better when I hid him from the world.

Just remembering that had his wings flapping against his back in joy.

He decided then that he would try. If not, then he could find a different human to be his bride.

But he must admit... he did like the look of this one.

His light-brown hair was a nice colour. His skin was tan, and his body looked sturdy enough. He would need to be sturdy if he wished to be Aleron's companion, since he often liked to play and would squeeze Ingram in the process.

I also find his eyes... pretty. They were such a light, but intense green that they seemed piercing each time they briefly flicked to him. He liked them the most, although his deep voice did tingle his ear holes.

As they walked together, Aleron thought back on everything his kindred had taught him in the short amount of time they'd shared. Their reunion hadn't been as long as Aleron would have preferred, but then again... he'd wished Ingram hadn't left at all.

He said changing forms and standing on two legs seems to help. That I must act and appear more human. He looked down at his hands as he placed them against the grass, noting his claws. Humans didn't have them. They also didn't have fur like he did, nor wings and a tail.

How am I supposed to be like them when Mavka cannot change their outsides? He'd never seen Kitty, the feline-skulled Mavka, or any other Mavka, look completely human.

Even Ingram hadn't magically transformed for Emerie. He'd just... stood on two legs and hid his claws.

Aleron bumped Gideon with his shoulder and initiated contact to ensure he didn't forget. He winced when the male almost fell to the ground, since he'd done it a little harder than he intended.

"Bloody hell, you're strong," Gideon grumbled as he quickly righted himself. He whipped his face towards Aleron's skull, before drifting it forward to watch where he stepped as he led them up an incline.

"I am sorry," Aleron said, lowering his head as his orbs slowly turned white.

He grew nervous, as he lacked knowledge of what it meant to have a human companion. He didn't wish to do something wrong.

"I didn't mean it as a bad thing." He rubbed the side of his neck before shaking his head, making the front strands of hair fall down over his forehead. "It just keeps surprising me. You can't hurt me here, though, so I don't think it matters."

He shined Aleron a smile, flashing his teeth, and the little dots sunk in his cheeks, his apprehension dissipating. His sight returned to its usual pink colouring.

"I can hurt you, though," Aleron corrected.

Gideon halted. With his brows drawn and his lips thinning, he turned to him. "What do you mean, you can hurt me? I'm dead."

"Yes, but I can injure your soul."

Aleron had eaten a few and knew that it could be devastating to the human. They would obliterate completely, fading from every existence with no chance at all of being returned.

Weldir had been furious when he discovered it. He hadn't managed to stop Aleron from eating a few, which had seemed to gift him more humanity than when he ate their flesh. Not only had it weakened his father creator, but it'd caused Aleron to have distressing memories that didn't belong to him.

Weldir had managed to remove those memories from him, as they had been confusing and disorientating. It had also been haunting reliving the painful deaths of those humans.

He often shuddered at the echo of their screams that lingered.

Gideon slapped his face into one of his hands. "Great. So you're telling me that, although I'm dead, I can die again. What point is there to any of this then?"

Aleron waved his hand at their surroundings. *"It is not that you will die again, but you will cease to exist entirely. There is no other afterworld."*

"That feels like the same thing," he stated, as he lowered his hand to peek at Aleron from the side. "You know what? Never mind. It's fine. Just don't go chewing on my leg because you're hungry."

He tilted his skull at him. *"I do not feel hunger anymore. You do not need to fear this from me."*

"That's good. Does that mean I'll 'cease to exist' if I fall off a cliff or drown here?"

"No. Only Mavka or Weldir can destroy the souls here."

"Ah," he said, nodding like he understood. "So you're the final grim reapers." Then he pointed to his green eyes with two fingers before jabbing those fingers at Aleron. "I'm watching you, Duskwalker."

He tilted his skull the other way. *"I am watching you as well, human."*

"Not what I meant," Gideon said, once more shaking his head. Gideon let out a laugh that sounded rather... empty. "You're actually pretty funny. I can tell you aren't very smart, but I guess that makes you charming in your own way."

Until now, Aleron didn't know it was possible to be both

offended and complimented at the same time.

His orbs turned a reddish pink in embarrassment. Only to morph to yellow because Gideon called him funny and charming.

"I do not have much humanity," Aleron admitted. *"I did not eat enough humans."*

His companion's features paled, and Aleron lowered his body slightly when he realised he must have said the wrong thing. *Should I not speak of my humanity or eating humans?*

Gideon looked away from him while rubbing the side of his head. Aleron wondered if he did this because he no longer felt comfortable looking upon him, or if he just wished to inspect the brightly lit forest around them.

"Eating humans is how you gain intelligence, huh? Does that mean you can become human?"

"No. What animals I first ate dictate what form I have. What I am now is what I will always be. Does this bother you?"

Could Aleron's hopes for a bride be squashed within seconds of playing with the thought?

"Hmm. Not really." He shrugged his lithe, muscular shoulders. "You look fluffy and soft, like a big puppy with wings. It did take me a bit to adjust to both you and Ingram having skulls and looking so different, but I saw the way he treated Emerie. She also said he was a good guy. I care more about a person's heart than their face, and you both seemed to be alright." He shrugged a second time, before sliding his hands into his pockets as though to hide them. Then, he tossed his face in Aleron's direction, and his green eyes fell on his skull. "Plus, I'm a Ghost now. Can't really be picky about my friends anymore, and I think... I'd rather not be alone here. You're willing to come on this journey with me and help me stay awake, and I'm really appreciative of you for that. I'm a stranger; there is no reason for you to show me such kindness."

"But we are friends now. That no longer makes us

strangers, yes?" Aleron asked, hoping for clarification.

The corners of Gideon's eyes crinkled, making them shine when he gave Aleron a small smile. "I guess that's true." Then, with his hands remaining in his pockets, he bent forward slightly to be the same height as Aleron on all fours. "So, *friend.* Where are you going to take me?"

"Take you? I thought you were leading the way."

Gideon straightened up. "Why would I be leading the way? I don't know where we are or what this place is like. I remember someone mentioning you've been here for a month, and I only just woke up. Why don't you show me what's here? I'll happily follow your lead."

Aleron nodded, despite his shoulders turning inward self-consciously. He didn't know where to take the human, since he didn't know what he'd like to see.

There were many places within Tenebris.

"I could... take you to the other Mavka who lives here." Aleron couldn't think of anywhere else to take the little human, and perhaps he could help get the silent serpent Mavka to talk. If so, then Aleron may no longer need Gideon's presence so desperately. *"It is far, though."*

"The further, the better." Gideon pointed with his head and, with a spike of humour in his tone, stated, "Lead on, Captain."

Aleron hesitantly stepped forward, only to turn right when he remembered it was in the other direction. *I hope we do not get lost.* He was used to flying across Tenebris.

Then again, he always seemed to head the correct way no matter what he did, as though he instinctually knew the way.

"I could fly us both there," Aleron offered, dipping his skull to the side when the human came to walk next to his right shoulder. *"It would be faster."*

Gideon's firm lips tightened as his eyes drifted over their surroundings. There wasn't much to see, as a mist constantly overshadowed the land like a barrier between towns and forests. Most of what was around them consisted of hills and valleys of densely packed trees. Only where they walked the sun appeared, as if it followed them – although Aleron knew that wasn't true, just the perspective of walking across the ground.

"No offense, but I don't know how I feel about flying." He shot Aleron a twisted expression. "The southlands, which is where I'm from, doesn't have many mountain ranges. I've never been up high, so I don't know if I'd be comfortable with that."

"You do not know until you try," Aleron responded, confused about his hesitancy.

Now that Aleron knew how to fly, it felt so... natural. He hadn't known how to before he came to the afterworld.

"That's true, but..." He cast Aleron an odd smile. Why did it seem like the more he did it, the less genuine it felt? "We have no reason to rush. I'm guessing time is meaningless here. This is forever, so why rush through it when we can just take our time? Is there an end to this world?"

Aleron drifted his sight to the sky. *"I have not found an end, but all I know is that it is round."*

"Aren't most worlds round? We knew enough to understand that about Earth, and that there are other planets somewhere out there. Even the stars are round."

The Earth is round? Aleron had not known this.

"You know a lot. Could you teach me more?"

"Sure, I can teach you all I know, but it's actually not that much since there were many books I never had the chance to finish reading. It was just some shit I learned in school and at the library. I enjoyed reading texts rather than fiction."

About half of what Gideon said was coherent to him. *"What is a library?"*

"It's a place you can go to borrow books. Ashpine City,

which is about a five-day walk from where I grew up, had the biggest library in the region, but Fishket's was pretty big. I used to help volunteer as a scribe in my free time, since many of the books were decaying. Since I liked reading about astrology, psychology, and philosophy, and most people don't, I was able to choose the books I'd like to scribe and learnt a bit. I'm not that smart, though, so not all of it sunk in."

"You seem pretty smart to me," Aleron grumbled, unsure of what was required to be deemed 'smart.'

His own mind felt like a lost cause, especially the more the human spoke. A graininess lingered – like his thoughts and his ability to piece things together were broken.

An odd, yet subtle, pinkness lifted into the high ridge of Gideon's cheeks. "Thanks. I tried really hard to learn, especially for my parents. My birth parents died when I was really young, but I knew we were poor since they weren't able to enrol me in school. My adopted parents enrolled me, but I was already behind, and the other kids made fun of me. I wanted to do well with the opportunity given to me and make my new parents proud, so I studied hard and tried to be an information sponge."

"Your learning was stunted because you were not enrolled *early enough?"* Aleron asked, curiosity lacing his tone.

"Well, of course," he responded, lifting an arm to shrug with it. "How the fuck are you supposed to learn anything if no one teaches you? Half the time people come across as idiots because no one gave them a chance to learn. We judge people for being uneducated, when really it's the way society is that fails them. They aren't stupid; they just aren't able to reach their true potential."

"I see..." Aleron's wings dipped as his sight turned blue, and he looked at the ground. *"I do not think this is the same for Mavka. Much of what you have said I do not understand,*

but I can also tell that I am not able to properly absorb it either. There is a blankness in my mind. I do not think a library will be useful for me."

"I'm guessing Mavka is the term you Duskwalkers use to call each other?"

"It is what the Demons call us. I believe it means 'forest creature.'"

He ducked his blue sight to Gideon, whose head had dipped forward to look upon Aleron's skull better.

"Well, I guess my first question for you would be... do you know how to read?"

"Read? I do not know what that is."

"To read is to look at words on a page and know what they say." He lifted his hand, this time with one finger visible. "You wouldn't be able to use a library because you can't read, but that isn't your fault. No one has taught you yet, and that is just the first step. No one learns how to read in a day, and it can take years to be truly adept at it. It's not that you have blank spaces, but that the equation for thought hasn't been formulated yet. Your mind would eventually figure out a solution, even if it's out of the box of normal. You would eventually learn and understand through repetition. At least, I think so."

Aleron's wings rose in renewed confidence, just as a strange warmth tingled his chest. Once more, he didn't truly understand everything the male said, but it sounded like... he believed Aleron had *potential*. He liked this, would like to be smarter, and would like others to see him as such.

And it was true he was learning. Even this conversation brought to light many aspects, and gave names for tasks and activities he'd seen in humans. He knew what a book was, as the Witch Owl had once shown him and Ingram. He'd seen wiggly lines on those pages, but neither of them had been interested in learning at the time.

But that memory and Gideon's information helped create a link of knowledge he'd lacked.

He rolled his shoulders and wings back, consciously brushing one against Gideon's side to create the brief contact, before a spring entered his steps.

"Since we're on the subject of learning," Gideon said as they climbed over an incline with many large boulders – a hill made of rock rather than dirt, "could you tell me more about this world? Who created it?"

"Weldir, the spirit of the void, created this place," Aleron answered, having no issues climbing whereas the human appeared to struggle due to the sharp, rocky inclines. Gideon often used his hands to steady or pull himself up, and lacked claws that Aleron had used to latch on and climb with.

"Was that the weird guy made up of black floating ribbon I saw earlier? The one who took Emerie's soul?"

"Yes, but he does not always look like that. Usually I am able to see more of his form. He is weak currently."

Weldir, when he often appeared to Aleron, had consisted of many forms. Sometimes a chalky mist all over, but if that mist disappeared, he would begin to appear as Gideon described. Sometimes Aleron could only see patches of his body, like a horn and opposing cheek, half his chest with no legs, or the opposite.

His form could be sporadic.

"Who is he? Some kind of reaper or god of the afterlife?"

When Aleron made it to the top of the hill that had become rather sharp in its incline, he reached down to grab the male's fumbling hand as he tried to find purchase. He easily yanked him up until his feet were dangling in the air before setting them to the rocky ground.

"Thanks," he bit out, looking down at his pants and wiping at them, despite their clean appearance. A muscled knot in his jaw pulsed.

He didn't appear to like being picked up as though he

weighed nothing.

"Weldir is a demi-god. His name means Warden of Shadows, and he is from the Elven world. He is also my creator – father."

Gideon's face shot up, his lips parted and his eyes wide. "Your father was that guy? What is your mother then? A skeleton?" Then, his features twisted up as he loudly blurted out, "An Elf? Elves are real?!"

Aleron tilted his head at his surprise.

"No, my mother creator is a Phantom. She was once human, and she is what Emerie will become. They both will have the ability to turn from physical into a Ghost at will." When his mouth fell impossibly lower, Aleron chuckled at him for it. *"Mavka are part spirit like Weldir and part human like the Witch Owl. When a human bonds with us, they become like us. And yes, Elves are real – I have met one. I thought you were smart, so how can you not know this?"*

Aleron's orbs turned bright yellow in joy.

He found it entertaining to know more than the human who had, just moments before, made him feel inadequate with his big human words. It felt nice to know that Aleron wasn't as unknowledgeable as he originally thought.

"Ooft," Gideon said with a wince. "What a way to take back a compliment." He placed his hand over his chest as though wounded. "That stings, Aleron. I was being so nice to you."

His wings drooped suddenly, as a coldness pierced his gut. His orbs turned a stark white, and he dipped his head in a submissive stance.

"I am sorry. I did not mean to cause you to sting." His apology was sincere, and he feared that Gideon would no longer want to 'go on an adventure' with him.

I made a mistake.

The laugh that burst out of the human startled him, causing him to step back warily.

"I'm joking, Aleron! Jeez, man." His elbow went high as he rubbed the side of his neck and then his nape. "I guess I better teach you sarcasm first before anything else. I use sarcasm as a way to play and joke around with people, but I'm pretty straight forward with it and it's obvious."

Aleron stepped forward as his sight returned to its normal pink. *"You were playing with me?"*

He offered Aleron another smile, but it didn't feel as genuine as the others before it. Still, it was pleasant enough that his green eyes glinted, and Aleron's wings tightened against his back pleasantly for being gifted it.

Humans had never given Aleron smiles. Emerie had offered a few, but they had seemed to be tangled in sadness. Raewyn, his Elven friend, she had gifted him many, but it didn't feel like this male's.

It did not make pleasure ripple down his spine.

Perhaps it was due to them just being for Aleron, rather than shared between him and his kindred.

"Yeah, I was." His expression softened, before falling away into a relaxed state. "I'll teach you some sarcasm, so it doesn't come across so shocking in the future, and maybe you can do it to me. Since you have a skull, it'll be even harder to gauge if it's true or not. Think of it as a game."

His feathers puffed. *"Yes, I would like to play a game."*

"But first," Gideon stated while holding a finger up. "Tell me more about Weldir and this world. Does it have a name?"

Aleron turned to stare at the direction they just came from, seeing the mist below them and the way it danced throughout the horizon. When higher up, it became possible to see the world further beyond, as if only what surrounded them was shrouded in a veil.

"This place is called Tenebris, and it is where all those eaten by Demons and Mavka come to spend their deaths."

"You said it was round, round how?" Gideon asked,

turning to look in the same direction as Aleron. He gasped and stepped back in surprise. "Wow. That's actually remarkably beautiful."

His orbs flared yellow. *I think so, too.*

Although before them was shrouded in mist, the tops of trees were visible throughout the many valleys. The mist frolicked heaviest where there were many active souls, so they could just barely see the tops of houses from where they'd come – the town of Fishket, as Aleron had been informed.

But beyond that lay a clear view.

Just after Fishket, a cliff side opened up into a vast area of meadows, hills, and then further on, a mountain. A gigantic waterfall glittered in a shroud of its spray, and Aleron had once dipped his wing through its fall whilst passing by. A rainbow shone just in front of its streaming fall, which is what had once caught Aleron's attention and brought him there.

Everything was bright, green, and looked alive.

Birds above swooped and dived, and he knew without a doubt they were the souls of birds that had been eaten by Demons. He'd seen many, many other animals here, who were skittish and didn't seem to be in a dream state. They were at peace, happy even, whenever he wasn't nearby.

However, not all of Tenebris was this... beautiful – as Gideon had called it.

He lifted his gaze to the misted sky.

"You cannot see it from here, but if we were to fly directly up, we would find more of this world, more land. It is round, like everything is contained within something." He lowered his skull back to Gideon, to find his expression had once more fallen in surprise. *"That something is Weldir's stomach."*

The human paled.

FOUR

Gideon lifted his uncertain gaze to the sky, wondering how the *fuck* he was supposed to be in someone's stomach. Considering *Tenebris* looked like Earth, it was difficult to swallow such a horrifying thought.

Not particularly into vore – a desire to be consumed or to consume another – a cold shiver ran down his spine.

How could a stomach hold trees, houses, people? He found the idea startling. If none of this was here, would it look like the inside of an organ? Was it all just some kind of mystical mirage that could be touched?

Holy shit, am I being digested right now?

No, that couldn't be it, considering he'd been here for years. The ground wasn't mushy or wet beneath his boots, like he was standing in stomach acid.

Peering up at the blue sky, the bright-yellow sun, and white clouds, he realised it actually appeared *before* the mist. Like a refraction – a projected image.

However, as he lowered his face to take in the oddly serene landscape, it was obvious the person who created it did so with care. Sure, there was a blurriness to it that, once he became aware of these details, made it even more obvious it was nothing but an illusion.

"What's the point in creating all this if Weldir can just

Aleron's head swayed, his glowing orbs shifting to a dark yellow. The more Gideon looked upon him, spoke to him, the more at ease he felt with the Duskwalker.

He didn't look too bad, and Gideon had been honest when he stated that he cared more about a person's heart. There was nothing worse than a pretty face and a rotten heart – he'd much prefer the opposite.

"I am not fully sure. Although not everywhere is like the Fishket town where I met you. He claimed it is because the humans wake too easily." He stepped off, leading them away from the rocky, mountainous hill they'd been climbing. *"Allowing the spirits here to roam in a half-awake state, interacting with their memories and a world that is similar, keeps them docile. Interacting with others allows for it to feel real."*

"It's obviously not, though." As Aleron took them into a forest, Gideon yanked an abnormally vibrant leaf from a low-hanging branch. "Everything feels off."

Even just walking was wrong.

He'd been hoping for the huffing, the puffing, and the strain of movement. Other than climbing the near-vertical incline, everything had been as effortless as air, like he weighed nothing. Sometimes, it felt like they were gliding over water.

Gideon rubbed the pad of his thumb over the leaf, inspecting its weird, woolly texture. It felt wrong. Then he brought it to his nose, and the smell of vinegar and a collision of every leaf he'd ever scented bombarded him all at once.

"Nothing looks, feels, or smells right. It's like he's never been to Earth."

"I asked Weldir about this as well," Aleron stated, casting him a glance. His wing slipped over the side of Gideon's hip, creating that much needed contact. *"Weldir cannot smell or touch anything from Earth. Everything he has created was designed by memory – whether it was his*

own or from the minds of humans he delved into. Much of this is also influenced by our own memories."

Ah, so that's why everything looked... fuzzy or covered in a layer of fur. He still didn't understand why everything had a vinegar smell to it, though.

Gideon sniffed his own arm. "I wonder if I smell wrong."

"You do not smell like anything."

"Really?" he asked, dropping the leaf to cover his mouth and tap at his cheek. "Maybe that's because we can't smell our own scent? If we influence our perception of the world, then that would make the most sense."

Just at that moment, a sharp, thorny branch cut across his arm, and he hissed in a breath. He recoiled away from it before cupping his forearm. Blood welled, but faded almost instantly, as did the wound.

"I'm guessing sensation is another part of his design to trick us." He wasn't particularly pleased about that. "But that does leave me wondering what else I can feel."

He knew he could feel emotions and their physical aspects within, could cry and have his face feel tingly with tears. What about tiredness, the feel of water, or perhaps even... pleasure?

His gaze drifted to the Duskwalker. With Aleron around, he refused to tug on his dick to find out if that last one was possible.

Does that mean if I drown or am crushed beneath something, I would be stuck? Would I heal only to suffer the same fate over and over again? That meant this paradise could potentially become a form of hell.

He shuddered at the thought.

Thankfully the demi-god in charge was benevolent.

"You said that only your kind and him could fully extinguish my soul. How is that possible if I'll just heal?" Gideon would rather know what future he could potentially be faced with. He was also rather curious about this place.

It was helping to ease his painful pondering.

As much as he was attempting to hide it, he still struggled to adjust to all this. He forced his smiles, hoping they would eventually feel real – like he could force happiness and calm. He also thought it best that he didn't let Aleron know he wasn't coping. He didn't want to have to talk about his sorrow and grief. Not just with him, but in general, hoping he'd eventually forget.

He had plenty of time – the rest of eternity – to heal from this. Hopefully one day, he would.

"The body you are looking upon is not your soul," the Duskwalker answered.

He moved through the forest environment, which grew more intense with every step, with ease. He barrelled his way through shrubbery, whereas Gideon had to constantly pause and shove it away to make his way through. He often had to jog a few steps to catch back up when there was a break in density.

"What do you mean?" Gideon asked, shoving a branch away.

Aleron paused and turned to him. Balancing on three limbs, he reached out.

"This is just a husk, a projection. For me, I can eat this like it is flesh – I can even harm it."

To give a demonstration, he grabbed his hair-dusted arm. With little understanding or care as to how Gideon may react, he sunk the claw of his thumb all the way into his skin and muscle until he'd buried it to the fleshy tip of his finger.

"Ow! Fuck, man!" he roared, yanking his arm away only for the Duskwalker to hold him tight. Then he drew his claw down, cutting a slice into his flesh. Gideon gripped his wrist, trying to ease the pain that felt like it was scratching against his *bone*. "Stop!"

Aleron let go. Since the wound was deeper than the thorn scratch, the pain and puncture took a few seconds longer to fade. No scar remained, as if the interaction had been nothing but a figment of his imagination.

Before the betrayal could truly settle in his chest, he gasped in surprise.

"But this." Aleron shoved his clawed hand, covered in dark-grey skin and protruding knuckle bones, straight into his chest. He expected to feel pain, but there was no sensation as his body rippled like water. *"If I was to damage any part of this, it would be permanent."*

Gideon looked down to see his torso had turned transparent, and Aleron held a floating white flame within him. No, it wasn't a flame, but a human – that looked strangely like him – covered in fire.

Then, the weirdest fucking sensation abraded him.

From his groin, over his navel, and all the way up his chest, he *felt* a large and imposing thumb rub over him. It was warm, calloused, and left his entire body tingling. Shit, even his cock *jerked,* excited by the most intimate touch he'd ever received.

Leaping back in surprise, Gideon self-consciously covered his groin in reaction.

That did not just happen. There was a stiffness within his pants, an unwelcome one. He was semi-hard because of what this Duskwalker had just done to him, or his soul, rather.

Well... that answered his earlier musings on whether or not he could feel pleasure, and if his dick was active in the afterlife! Not how he would have liked to discover that.

Even now, the stroke of Aleron's thumb against his entire body still tingled.

"Are you okay?" Aleron asked, lowering his head and shoulders as he reached out to Gideon's face. He brushed the backs of his curled claws over one of his cheeks. *"Your face has turned all red."*

He darted away from his tender caress and awkwardly

covered his mouth and nose. He was *not* blushing because of this monster. He wasn't – he refused to believe it.

"It's nothing. Don't worry about it," he choked out, his words muffled behind his hand. He wished his face would stop feeling hot, or that his ears didn't burn, and he muttered to himself quietly, "Bloody hell. How much am I going to learn in just one day?"

Aleron's bat skull tilted sharply. *"It has not been one day, little human. It has been many."*

Gideon froze, and the embarrassed and aroused flush swiftly fled from him. "What do you mean, it's been many?" He turned his gaze to the false sky as he lowered his hand. "But the sun hasn't gone down."

"It never does. It is always day here."

"But... how am I not tired? I haven't slept or anything." He wasn't even hungry!

Aleron's head tilted the other way, like he didn't understand why he was so shocked about this. *"I am tired, though. Although we are both Ghosts, this is a second life for Mavka. We are a part of life and death, and so we exist in both worlds – just separately."* Then he reared back to sit on his hind legs, his tail splaying behind him against the ground. *"Unlike you, what you see before you is my entire essence. I do not have an inner soul. I am truly physical here, and I must rest. The only difference is I no longer hunger, and that I can truly be harmed."*

His eyes grew wide with alarm. "Harmed? So you can't heal like me?"

"Yes, this. I have a mortal form here, despite living forever in this world." He touched a foreclaw to his chest. *"If I am hurt, it will heal slowly, painfully, and will scar."*

"Doesn't that... worry you?" Gideon asked, unsure of how he would have felt if their positions were reversed.

Was Aleron afraid? Why did that make his chest pang? At least Gideon no longer had a need for fear.

"No," he answered. *"Nothing here wishes to harm me*

*besides the environment, and it takes much to do so. I only
know this because I hurt myself and Weldir needed to heal
me."*

Poor guy. He couldn't imagine dying, only to find out
the afterlife could be lastingly painful.

He reached out and patted the Duskwalkers big, rounded
shoulder. "Guess we better look out for you, then."

Gideon's brows twitched as he frowned when Aleron's
feathers puffed and his orbs turned a bright yellow. He
found he liked their colourful glow; it made it easy to read
that Aleron had gone through an emotional change. Figuring
out what they meant had quickly become a secret game and
a main point of interest for him.

"You wish to... protect me?" He said it as though he was
truly perplexed.

"Well, yeah," Gideon grumbled, slipping his hand over
his mouth as he averted his gaze. He didn't like the relieved
undertone in Aleron's response, and how it made pity swell.
He doubted any humans had been kind to this Duskwalker.
"I take care of my friends."

*"I am surprised you do not wish to harm me, but this
makes me happy."*

A coldness ran through his body and created a steel knot
in his gut. He imagined many humans had attacked Aleron
to make him feel that way, and after speaking with him... he
wondered if it had even been deserved. *I know
Demonslayers will attack a Demon even if it's not one
they're hunting.*

They likely would unfairly attack a Duskwalker who was
just moseying through the forest.

If all Duskwalkers could be this... kind, and perhaps not
always bloodthirsty monsters, would the relationship
between their species be more friendly? It would have been
nice if they could have worked together. Gideon winced,
knowing humans were violent towards anything that

frightened or confused them.

"I would never do that," Gideon said, unsure if that was a lie or not. Had he been alive, he may have reacted differently to all this. He gave Aleron's shoulder a harder pat before walking forward to restart their journey. "So, how did you hurt yourself? Just so I can keep it in mind."

"Weldir threw me off a cliff."

Gideon almost tripped over his own feet in shock; it didn't help a random fallen stick twisted between his ankles. With his eyes wide and his lips parted in disbelief, he turned his gawking expression to Aleron.

"He fucking did *what*?!"

Unsure why the male shouted with outrage, Aleron tilted his head at him like he often did. Especially since Aleron knew Weldir had done it with good intentions, despite what happened afterwards.

Gideon's hands clenched into tight fists, like he was truly enraged on his behalf. That elated him to no end, and he almost hummed contentedly. *That must mean the human cares for me.* This was, at least, what he told himself.

I will protect Gideon, too. I will make sure nothing happens to his soul. He would even fight with Weldir or the other Mavka here if they tried to touch it.

He would be fierce about it and safeguard it with all his might. He would protect his little human companion.

"Why would he do that if he knew you could be harmed?" Gideon gritted out, gripping at his fringe that nearly came to his eyes, before swiping his hair back. "That sounds... cruel. How could a father do that to their child?"

Although Aleron knew to call his creators mother and father, the bond, in his mind, was still disjointed. He understood a little of it, that he was supposed to care for them, but not why it would make the human so upset about learning this.

Weldir was his... friend. That's what he saw in his creator.

"He did not mean to hurt me," Aleron stated in his defence, snorting through his nose hole. *"He was teaching me to fly."*

He let out a huffing laugh, remembering the day he'd acted rather foolish and skittish. Even his orbs brightened to a joyous yellow at what Weldir had gifted him in doing something this human deemed callous.

Weldir had led him to a cliff and told him to spread his wings and leap. Of course, wary about falling, Aleron had shaken his head. Then, lowering himself so his bowed chest was rubbing across the ground, he backed up in fear.

When his command was denied, enough of Weldir's patchy form was visible to reveal an annoyed frown. When he stepped forward, Aleron attempted to bolt.

He didn't make it far before his tail feathers were grabbed. Then he was flipped onto his back and lifted off the ground. With his legs flailing above him, whining and whimpering, Weldir held him above his head like he weighed absolutely nothing. The closer he got to the edge, the more Aleron panicked.

Only to roar when he'd been... *tossed.*

At first, he fell, then he spun in the air so he could uselessly land on his feet, knowing he'd probably break all his legs when he hit the ground. But as he plummeted, his arms, legs, and wings twisting and moving, wind caught underneath his feathers.

His descent felt endless, but it gave him enough time to spread his wings and try to flap them. At first, he moved them one at a time, then eventually caught more wind and steadied them.

Just as he was close to the ground, he began to glide.

He looked down in surprise. At himself, and because Weldir was on the ground, ready to catch him in case he hadn't figured it out.

Unfortunately, just because he'd gotten the hang of gliding and flapping his wings, it didn't mean he knew how to steer. He ran into a tall tree, breaking his right arm and wing in the process.

There was no laughter from Weldir as he reappeared at Aleron's side. Instead, he apologised, explaining how he thought Aleron would make it past the tree line since he'd started flying upwards. Weldir immediately healed him, and he suffered no ill effects from the damage, nor any scarring.

If he was left to heal on his own, it could have been different.

Despite the pain, those few seconds of flying were exhilarating. He begged Weldir to take him to the top of the cliff so he could leap off the edge himself. He bounced on all four limbs, practically *begging* for it.

And, once Aleron flew confidently in the sky, safely away from the trees, he discovered Weldir could change his form at will. His creator came up beside him with his own set of wings, their bat-like tips flicking against his feathered ones.

He didn't know how long they'd flown together, but after a long length of sadness and sorrow, it was the first time he'd... laughed. It was the first time he'd been able to forget and just enjoy his presence in this new world.

He didn't know if it was true, or just something he wished to tell himself, but he wanted to believe his creator had done this in order to help him. Not just to teach him, but also to give Aleron that freedom. To help... ease him, heal him, be there for him in his own way.

He is a good creator. He cares.

He chose to believe this, just as he chose to believe in most – even if they hurt him. Like Merikh, the bear-skulled Mavka, who often acted mean to him and his kindred; he believed this about him too. Why else would he have allowed Aleron and his kindred to rest under his protective ward?

Perhaps Aleron was too trusting and forgiving, but he wanted to see pleasantness in the world. He wanted to think it could be kind, even to a monster like him.

"What do you mean 'to teach you to fly'?" Gideon asked with a frown in his voice, and Aleron glanced at the expression on the human's face. "You didn't know how to before?"

He shook his skull. *"I never needed to before."* Then he looked at the ground as they walked through the heavily misted forest. *"If I am being honest, I had seen birds do it and knew their wings were like mine. I think I may have been able to before, but I did not want to."*

"Why not?"

"Ingram," he stated softly, just as his sight faded to blue. *"He could not fly with me. I did not wish to part from him."*

"So your love for your brother held you back and kept you on the ground?"

When Aleron once more glanced at the human, he'd only been intending to peek at him briefly. Instead, he lifted his head as warmth lashed across his torso in a mixture of pleasantness and curiosity.

Gideon's expression had become so soft that it bruised his chest. His eyes had not only crinkled, but they'd bowed, and held a sincere and gentle emotion – one which he'd never seen before. His lips were curled in a subtle smile, more vulnerable than any other he'd shone at him.

It almost looked like Gideon was hurting. A happy hurt that radiated a tender, painful, yet lovely ache through his chest.

"Pretty," he rasped without meaning to, just as his hand lifted of its own accord. He brushed the back of his foreclaw below one of Gideon's green eyes without thinking.

The male's eyes widened, his face fell, and his entire body stiffened. His gaze darted to the sharp point right near his eye.

Aleron broke contact, realising he'd ruined the expression by touching it.

Gideon's stare followed Aleron's hand as he pulled away, then it darted to his skull. His eyes grew wider before he averted his gaze to the side and covered his mouth and nose. The tips of his ears darkened a few shades, nearing on pink, as he quietly muttered to himself.

"We should keep moving," Gideon eventually blurted out, his deep voice thick and cracked.

As Aleron moved to follow, he wondered about the expression the male had just tried to hide. Was it of distaste that Aleron had touched him too affectionately? He hadn't meant to, but the action was pulled out of him against his will.

He didn't know why he'd done it, and he stared at the back of the human as he pondered it.

He pondered many things.

I would like for him to share that expression with me again. The sincere one that had caused him to reach out. *Should I talk more about my kindred?* Every time he did, it seem to disarm Gideon.

Ingram said I must change in order to make humans like me. And, right now, he very much wanted this human to like him. *Hmm. I must stand tall...*

He watched how the human walked on two legs, then tried to sniff his feet like that would teach him how. He smelled nothing and was rather disappointed. He would like to know what the human smelt like – would it be pleasant, like his kindred, or something nasty?

He is nice. He bet Gideon would have a nice smell as well.

His jumbled thoughts moved back to what he'd been lingering on.

Oddly enough, he closed his sight as he concentrated on changing, shifting. He tried to remember how Ingram had demonstrated the process for him.

Just like flying, it was almost effortless. As soon as he desired it, his body clicked and clacked as it altered. The moment the change was complete, his gait felt... wrong.

His arms had shortened and put a strain on his legs, which now bowed differently. It even hurt his back, as his hips swivelled drastically to compensate. He winced and stood.

He expected to be wobbly or fall, but he remained steady as though he'd always stood like this. Even following Gideon was effortless, his bird-like legs easily stepping after him. He did notice he swayed side to side slightly as he got used to it, but eventually held himself perfectly straight.

He figured this was likely due to being in Tenebris. He found everything he attempted here to be much easier, as if he weighed less.

"I was wondering when you would do that," Gideon stated quietly.

"You knew I could?" Aleron asked with a note of surprise, yet it didn't sound as deep and brutal like how he normally spoke.

My voice changed as well, just like Ingram's did.

"Well, yeah. We both watched Ingram do it, so I suspected you could as well." Gideon slowed, allowing Aleron to catch up, and turned his face up to him. His features lacked wariness or concern, but his lips did thin momentarily. "Your kind really knows how to make us feel short."

"What do you mean?"

Admittedly, once he paid attention, the human looked much smaller than before. If Aleron had wanted to, he could have placed his elbow on his little head – especially since it only came to the centre of his sternum.

"I'm pretty tall. I was happy when I hit five foot eleven, even though I didn't grow any taller." His lips pushed forward as they stiffened, before he tilted his head side to side, making his fringe sway. "But standing next to you, when you're at least a foot and a half taller than me? I'll have to crane my neck while talking to you."

Aleron dipped his head forward to inspect Gideon's expression. He didn't understand enough about humans to accurately decipher it. "Is this a bad thing? I can change back."

"You can do what you like. It doesn't bother me." The male cast him a smile, and he was unsure if it was sincere or not. Then he folded his arms, only to lift one hand and tap a knuckle against his chin. "Have to ask, though. What's the weather like up there?"

"The weather?" Aleron sharply reared his head back so he could dart it around the dense but sunny patch of forest. "It is the same as before."

"Really?" Gideon's brows furrowed deeply, as though troubled. "It's pouring down here."

Aleron's sight shifted to white when a distressing tangle of emotions coiled in his chest. He didn't understand what he was talking about, as he saw no rain clouds floating around his head. He even released a small whimper, unsure of why he couldn't see them.

The laugh that exploded from the human was deep, loud, and sounded more like a cackle. "I'm joking, Aleron! Remember when I told you of sarcasm? If it doesn't make sense, then I'm probably being sarcastic."

All Aleron could do was give a fake chuckle to hide his embarrassment, his orbs morphing to a reddish pink because of it. His wings drew in tight against his back in apprehension, the very tips of them dancing against the leafy dirt.

The negative swell of emotions dispersed when Gideon reached up to pat his biceps. "Don't worry about it. I'll get you used to it."

He hoped so, and soon, if he continued to do it.

Gideon silently mulled over everything he'd learned as he sat back against Aleron's side. He glanced over his shoulder to take in the sleeping Duskwalker, whose quiet but deep snores were tranquil and oddly calming. His massive lungs slowly waved Gideon's entire body back and forth.

He found the repetitive motion and noise... soothing.

He wished they would make his own eyes droop and lull him into sleep, but they didn't. Not once did tiredness or exhaustion come over him. His lack of needing to truly breathe, or eat, or have any normal human functions bothered him at first and made him feel morose. It was just further proof that everything he did, everything he thought, his entire existence... was pointless.

That had faded over the many... Fuck, had it been days or perhaps weeks since he'd woken up? He wished the sun would move, would rotate, would do anything but just sit there in the sky like a useless, taunting ball of nothingness.

This was Aleron's second time resting, and he knew the big guy had truly exhausted himself. It seemed the longer they travelled together, the more... anxious the Duskwalker became of sleeping.

He eventually sat in the middle of the forest, and just claimed he couldn't move anymore. The Duskwalker's body quaked, but he forced himself to kneel rather than truly collapse.

"Do not leave without me. Do not fall back asleep. Do not... forget me." Those were the words he'd uttered.

It was only once Gideon promised he'd lean against him the entire time that he laid down and *immediately* passed out.

I'm a little jealous of him right now, Gideon thought, despite lacking any envy in his chest. *What I wouldn't give to be able to have a nap and just blank out for a few hours.*

His mind constantly working, looping back on itself as he replayed his life and what was currently happening to him, was... bothersome.

There was a lot of good there too, but the fact that everything he once knew was gone overshadowed it. He would have been content with being in the afterlife if he'd been given the opportunity to live life to the fullest. To have met his goals or learn the answers to the many questions he'd had.

But... He peeked at the Duskwalker's sleeping form, taking in his bat skull, his twisting horns, and his blackened orbs, watching them swirl like vortexes. *I guess it's not too bad here.*

The world sucked, but at least his companion was agreeable.

He snorted a silent laugh. *I'm pretty, huh?*

He fingered where Aleron had caressed his cheek with the back of his glossy, curved claw.

Gideon was used to such a compliment. He knew what his face looked like, as well as his physique. He was broad, but not overly muscular. He became strong from years of hard labour, and much of him was covered in a bronze tan due to extensive exposure to the sun.

He'd been called pretty, handsome, beautiful, and even lovely. His features, despite them being quite masculine, were soft. His lips weren't full, but his nose, cheeks, and jaw were sculpted in pleasing curves and angles. Even his full eyebrows added to his charm. Most people complimented the light colour of his green eyes, comparing them to emeralds.

Gideon had received attention from women and men alike; he only found it strange because a monster had uttered it.

He half expected Aleron to say blood and entrails were pretty, not his face. He also didn't know *why* he'd suddenly uttered it.

He leant forward with his knees up – making sure his lower back stayed pressed against Aleron's wing – then rested his elbow on his knee and covered his mouth. Like he couldn't help himself, his eyes drifted to his skull.

You're not too bad, yourself.

Conventionally, Aleron was... well, he was ugly. He had a skull for a face. Then there were all the other animalistic aspects about him.

However, when one looked past the veil of normality and human ideology, there was definitely much more to be seen. Sure, he looked like a deity of death, but there was beauty in dying. There was beauty in decay and rot.

Aleron radiated magnificence.

It was easy for Gideon to shine a different perspective on the way Aleron appeared. His monstrous form had been more frightening, but it wasn't any less agreeable than the humanoid version he'd finally turned into.

He still appeared masculine, brutish, and charming, even when all his fur hid his physique and his orbs stayed pink.

I bet you don't know this, but you're kind of cool.

Already he could tell that Aleron's monstrous outsides absolutely did not reflect the tenderness in his heart. Just by observing him, what he said, and how readily he was able to adjust to Gideon's quirks, revealed he likely had a rich personality.

He'd shown great kindness and had listened to Gideon intently in the rare moments he wished to reveal information about his past. Never too much regarding what bothered him, as he didn't want to divulge too deeply nor burden the Duskwalker, but it was nice to openly share and know he would be heard.

Aleron always asked him questions about his stories. He also asked about their environment, the strange animals they passed. He often pointed to flowers and herbs they passed with curiosity, asking for their names. Every minute together, Gideon could tell he was learning – a slow sponge, but one that was rather... cute at times because of it. Too cute, perhaps, but that was fine.

As time went on, Gideon found himself becoming more and more drawn to the menacing-looking creature beside him.

If he ignored that Aleron had eaten people, everything else about him was... calm. *It's rare to find a heart of gold within the world* – there was usually an underlying goal to it. Whether it be the self-servicing pleasure of being thanked, the vain or anxious desire to be liked by all, or something more morbid, usually kindness could be false.

There was no need for that from either of them.

What they were doing here, together, this silly adventure, was fruitless – which made it all the more real. Aleron had already mentioned he could spend time with Weldir or this other Duskwalker they were venturing towards. There was absolutely no need for Aleron to take pity on Gideon, who, without a doubt, knew he would be alone in this world.

And he was taking that task very, very seriously. Aleron constantly brushed up against him, never forgetting.

I wonder if there is a way we can quell that anxiety of his about it. Gideon had an idea, but wasn't sure if he was willing to impose on his own personal space to do it. He'd consider it later.

I miss my guitar, he thought as he drifted his gaze around the foreboding, but always brightly lit forest around them.

What he wouldn't give to be able to lose himself in music. It'd be therapeutic to push out all his emotions in a rambling song that made no sense since he'd come up with it on the spot.

It would have helped to pass the endless time.

A weird smile pestered his lips, as his cheeks mildly warmed. *I wonder if Aleron would like it.*

FIVE

'Well, aren't you just handsome?" With his hands on his hips, and a grin plastered across his face, Gideon stared down at the cat before him.

Unsure what breed it was, its bright orange-and-red striped fur reminded him of Emerie. Its eyes were such a vibrant yellow, it appeared to be looking up at him with a set of moons.

And it was definitely staring at him, just as conscious and aware as he was.

He crouched down with the intention of petting it. He'd never owned a cat, but he'd always been fond of them. He was able to get in about three neck scratches, eliciting loud purring as it rubbed against his fingertips in welcome, before Aleron stepped closer. That spooked it. With a loud *meow*, it ran off between two buildings.

Gideon sighed. Feeling bad for Aleron, whose orbs had turned blue, he continued down the dirt footpath.

Still trying to figure out the Duskwalker's orb changes he knew what blue meant, but remained uncertain about yellow – especially since it could be two different hues. It was either curiosity or happiness. He'd already surmised pale pink to be his natural colouring.

They'd been white when they entered this unfamiliar village. Aleron likely hesitant. That had quickly dissolved considering the sparsity of people.

One thing Gideon knew with absolute certainty: this village had not been situated on Austrális.

Those they did pass spoke a foreign language, and even the wood they used in their buildings was a deep hue of red. He'd never seen or heard of trees like that before.

When he questioned Aleron about it, he claimed he didn't know. *Did Weldir possibly take souls from all over Earth?* He couldn't imagine having that much power or reach to claim an entire planet.

Gideon wasn't too keen on geography, and many of the world maps he'd seen were obviously unfinished. There were texts about people from foreign lands, with descriptions of them, but it was impossible to explore the world. Demons would sink their ships before they even made it out of the decaying docks.

As they passed house after house, most made of brick, clay, or that red timber, he'd begun to notice a pattern. Quite a few of the homes repeated, as if they had been duplicated for those who inhabited them in different eras.

There were also dozens, if not hundreds, of cats. Their little eyes watched them walk down the main street path from windows, rooftops, and alleys.

They both dodged a Ghost walking towards them, as Aleron fretted his touch to the human could wake her from her memory sleep. They could have gone around the village, but Gideon had been rather curious about it when he'd seen it.

The idea is to explore Tenebris. Hopefully he could show Aleron a library. Even if they were alive, the big Duskwalker's feathered butt wouldn't be able to merrily waltz through a town without someone bringing out a pitchfork.

They passed a market that had many wagons with false food but no salesperson. Gideon attempted to take a carrot, apparently a universal food, but it disappeared the moment he picked it up.

Aleron asked him a handful of questions about the people they saw, what they were doing, and why they were doing it. Gideon gave as many answers as he could to the best of his ability, detailing the way humankind often lived.

The more he did, the more at ease the Duskwalker became.

Actually, at ease likely wasn't the right way to describe Aleron's current jumping, chaotic behaviour. A warm smile curled Gideon's lips at his bristling excitement, finding it contagious. *Why the hell do I think that's cute?* He figured it was because he never expected a huge monster to be so sweetly inquisitive about the very world around him.

Aleron bounced one way and then the other as he turned his skull in every direction, some movements reminiscent of an owl. He pointed a claw at anything that took his interest, and even dragged Gideon over to a flowerpot or a shrine sitting on a windowsill.

"What are these ones?" Aleron asked, pointing to different herbs from a stall cart.

Gideon looked over his thick arm to check before taking a whiff. "I think that's mint. It's really nice in tea." He pointed to another. "That one is patchouli, maybe? It's a shame the vinegar smell ruins it, as it's usually really nice."

He held the end of his snout as he hummed. "I see." Then he picked it up by its tiny stem and twirled it. It didn't disappear like the carrot had for Gideon. "It has a pretty purple flower. I like it."

Gideon's eyes softened, finding that quite endearing.

Even when they moved on, the soft expression never fell.

Aleron darted to the side to look at something else, and Gideon shrugged when he returned. He did it a few times. Thankfully, if Aleron did fall behind by inspecting something, he always came back to Gideon's side with a subtle brush of contact.

At least, that was until he didn't feel it again, and silence fell over him. The only things he could hear were the mild chattering from strangers and the bustle of a mostly empty street.

Gideon turned with his brows furrowing when he realised the Duskwalker hadn't come to him for a little while. A small amount of dread struck him, unsure of how they were supposed to find each other again in this weird world.

Aleron couldn't track Gideon by scent.

Shit, Aleron. Where'd you go? His thoughts were panicked as he sprinted to search down other intersecting streets and between houses. He doubled back the way they came, hoping to find him.

His sudden fear didn't last long.

As he rounded a bend, he noticed Aleron's big, feathered backside and wings straight away. The upper half of his torso was jammed inside a window like he'd been attempting to climb inside but couldn't fit.

Whatever had grabbed his attention, it had done so fiercely. Enough to forget his duty to Gideon.

With a laugh to mask just how stressed he'd been, he swiped back his fallen fringe. "What the hell are you doing, Aleron?"

"I am watching," he answered without backing out. "There are strange noises coming from inside this human hut. I have never heard anything like them before."

Excited curiosity was evident in his tone, but also in the way his tail feathers had splayed and almost seemed to vibrate.

It piqued Gideon's own curiosity, and he shouldered the big Duskwalker over so he could slot himself between the window frame and his towering body. He only gained room when Aleron retracted himself until just his head was sticking inside.

His back stiffened when a warm and imposing clawed hand wrapped around his left hip and side as Aleron let him into the pocket of space he'd created.

Before he could even see, the noises coming from within were obvious. The creaking of a squeaky bed, a headboard lightly bashing against a hard wall, the fwapping noise of two sweating bodies joining. There were soft moans and hard grunts.

Inside the room, a man lay on his back while he gripped the hipbones of a fully naked woman who bounced on his cock. Her short hair danced around her shoulders as she leaned her head back. While her small breasts jiggled and bounced along with the speed of her hips, she dug her nails into her partner's lean chest.

His groin spread with tingling warmth, and suddenly the hand on his side became more noticeable, the heat of it causing a shiver up his spine. Despite not finding it particularly arousing, his body reacted to viewing an erotic scene no matter who was involved due to its sexual nature, and it made him hyperaware of the person next to him.

Aleron then asked him the most *absurd* question.

"Why are they hurting each other?"

Gideon couldn't help chuckling at the naïve Duskwalker. "They're not hurting each other," he answered, shaking his head in disbelief. At least that informed him Aleron was, in fact, a virgin.

Then again, he'd never seen any genitalia on him. *Maybe Duskwalkers don't experience desire?*

"But their faces show pain." Aleron dipped back just enough so he could direct his skull to Gideon. "They look like they are fighting with their hips. Is this a human custom?"

Once more, he laughed at the Duskwalker, which caused his orbs to whiten. He hid his expression by returning to watch the couple, just as the woman began to scream. He winced, the sound likely confusing Aleron even more.

"Pain and pleasure often have similar expressions. This is sex. They are fucking, and rather hard, if I may add. It's a good thing, and it feels nice. We do this to relieve ourselves of pent-up lust, or to be closer to our partner."

"I... see," Aleron mumbled, tilting his head at the couple. "I can see they are connected."

Then, he cupped the end of his snout and rubbed at his fangs as he watched while deep in thought. His claws dug into Gideon's hip a little deeper, like Aleron wanted to clutch him, but it was the one that tickled into the muscled vee of his pelvis that caused him to flinch.

Gideon stepped back and out of his reach, since his ears were a little too warm for comfort. He just put it up to suddenly becoming sensitive due to what they'd been witnessing.

"We probably should leave. It's not polite to watch two people in the middle of sex without their permission."

"No," Aleron rejected. Rolling his eyes, he tried to yank on Aleron's arm, but the big Duskwalker only pushed him away. "I want to see what happens."

Throwing his hands into the air, he gave up, doubtful he'd be able to change his mind. He was fascinated in his peeping, and far too strong for Gideon to have a hope of forcibly controlling.

Instead, he turned, sat on the ground, and leant his back against the brick exterior of the house. *They should stop soon, then we can move on.*

"Oh! Oh!" Aleron exclaimed as he bounced from foot to foot. His bird-like feet patted the dirt and crushed the poor, unsuspecting garden of flowers and overgrown grass. "Ingram told me about this! He is putting his cock inside her pussy. Yes, now I understand. He did say it feels wonderful."

At least he's learned something new. Something Gideon didn't need to further explain. However, his head shot back as realisation dawned. *Ingram... said it feels wonderful?*

Horror drained the heat straight from his face right before he scrunched it up in disgust. *Oh! Ew! That means he... she... they probably fucked.*

And he did *not* want to think about his little sister in this light. He shuddered at the image that materialised in his head. When he'd insinuated it with Emerie, he'd only been joking!

That means their kind do feel desire. How would it even fit? Another question he didn't wish to know.

Gideon palmed his face before twisting his head to Aleron beside him. *Guess he'll go find himself his own woman at some point.* His brows drew together tightly. *Wait... can Aleron even have a partner now that he's dead?*

He mentally threw his hands up. He didn't know, and he doubted Aleron would either.

Thankfully Aleron wasn't getting hard. He was purely watching out of gross inquisitiveness rather than being a creep, peeping through a window and jerking off.

Still, it's kind of saddening that he may not be able to have a... what did they call it? A bride? His gaze slipped to his wing resting over Gideon's shoulder, watching as it brushed up and down with his bounces. *Then again... doesn't look like he really cares.*

"The male is touching the flesh on her chest – why?"

Gideon blew a few strands of hair that had fallen across his brow, wishing it would just stay back. He usually would have used some kind of paste to slick his hair back.

"Her breasts?" While keeping one leg straight, he drew up the knee of the other and rested his forearm across it. "Nipples are sensitive. It generally feels nice when someone touches your chest."

"It does? So I should do this?"

"Don't go touching my nipples, Duskwalker," Gideon warned half-heartedly.

To be honest, he found the whole conversation awkward,

but it couldn't be helped. Aleron was probably getting the best demonstration he could, and it would only make everything easier for the Duskwalker that he had someone to explain it.

Gideon wished sex education had been so easy for him.

Shit. If someone had just explained it all to me...

He may not have lived with regret and shame.

Chewing on the inside of his cheek, he wondered if it was... okay to let those feelings go now. Why should he be burdened by the actions of his past when he no longer lived?

This current situation, having to listen to those people enjoy themselves while Gideon answered whatever question Aleron had, only made him remember. Reflecting on his past made him wince, and cringe, and wish he could go back in time and change things.

He wouldn't have made so many mistakes. *I wish I could have told my younger self that it would all be okay.*

Losing his virginity had been unpleasant. *The only person I ever told was Beau.* His partner – ex-partner, really – had been the only person he gained enough courage to tell.

It wasn't my fault, though. And, if he'd just known the truth about himself, and revealed that truth to his parents, they wouldn't have made him feel cornered. It wasn't their fault either.

In reality, it was no one's fault. Just a string of events that led him to a brothel on his eighteenth birthday.

But... he could still remember that stifling chokehold his fears had on him. They refused to dissipate, no matter how much he tried to let them go. The bridge of his nose bunched as he cringed once more.

Before his birth parents had died from a disease when he'd been eight, they'd been close friends with Emerie's. There had been talks of an arranged marriage, so long as both he and Emerie agreed to it when they were older. She was only five at the time, but he often played with her at their house because it was in a nicer part of Fishket. They'd known each other basically her whole life.

The moment she could confidently walk, he had this little girl following him everywhere. With big, round blue eyes of awe, he'd been helpless but to befriend her.

Until one unfortunate day, she became his little sister. Not by blood, or relation, but due to him being adopted into their family. They were *his* family for sixteen years.

I barely remember my birth parents.

Although there hadn't truly been any pressure from their parents from then on that they would marry, Emerie had it stuck in her head. She'd grown up loving him, but his feelings towards her grew platonic – or rather, had always been innocent.

He'd tried. With all his might, he'd tried to see her in the same way she did him, but just... *couldn't.*

He grew older, became a teenager, and her fantasies became more stifling for him. The more this little girl kept telling him about her wishes, their wedding, and how happy she knew she would be with him, the more he felt like he was being strangled with a leash.

He thought something was wrong with him.

Yet, it wasn't only Emerie he couldn't love. Although he'd found women beautiful for the alluring creatures they were, none of them... enticed him.

So, on a mission to change that and kindle his desires, on the week of his eighteenth birthday, he'd walked himself to a brothel. His friends had all slapped him on the back as they walked him inside.

He'd gotten hard simply because the situation was sexual, and the woman knew her way around a man's body better than he did, so he came. Yet, a ball of disgust at his actions had firmly lodged itself into his gut. He'd hated what he'd done, hadn't truly enjoyed it, and he'd just grown more confused than ever.

He felt like he'd betrayed Emerie... and himself.

He didn't know why.

For a long while, he'd contemplated if perhaps he was just asexual. It explained a lot of how he felt, or rather, *didn't*. Which only made self-loathing eat at him. Emerie deserved someone who could fully love her, in all ways, and not someone who would be forcing themselves to shape to her will. She deserved someone who could give their entire heart.

She was beautiful, kind, a bit of a brat – which just made her fun – and she would have made a wonderful wife. So, who was he to be a shell of a husband, just playing pretend?

He'd considered it, hoping he would fall in love with her when she came of age. He'd wondered if the problem was simply because she was just too young at the time. Any time he tried to look at her in that light, she'd still been a teenager and he'd felt like a creep.

Even now, it gave him repulsive shivers.

That all changed when she turned sixteen and he was well into his nineteenth year.

While drinking alone at a tavern because all his adult friends had gone home, someone had approached Gideon at the bar.

He had been mesmerised by the man before him. His features were gentle to the point he almost looked like an angel. Perhaps, because his features had a more feminine aspect to them, it was easier to make that leap when his mind had never dreamed of considering it.

Only another drink, and Gideon's feet unwittingly followed him to one of the rooms above. He wasn't drunk, or even tipsy. He was basically stone-cold sober as he followed him.

And he enjoyed every second, every touch that came from it. Despite it being Gideon's first time with a man, and he was the one on his back being thrusted into, his nails clawed for more.

When he woke, Raphael was gone, but the startling realisation of what he learned never faded. The reason he was never able to reciprocate Emerie's affection, why the prostitute left him feeling sick, why he wasn't able to make himself hard, was because he thought he was destined to be with a woman.

Even though the bed beside him was empty, the emotions that spiralled within were enlightening, heavy, freeing, but also damning.

Once more, he'd betrayed Emerie, her parents. Yet, the relief that he hadn't betrayed himself allowed him to lift his head up high.

But he was too afraid of disappointing everyone, so he remained... silent. He worried they'd come to resent him if he told the truth. That they would kick him out, and he'd lose the only family he had left.

It weighed on him every single *fucking* day, and it was tiring being in that loving home and feeling like an imposter.

After that night, he sought a boyfriend while trying to save as much coin as he could to rent his first home. He wanted someone to hold his hand for when he revealed who he really was, what he wanted, so they could help him bear the pain of what was to come. Someone who could help him suddenly and swiftly move his stuff, and protect him as he did so.

They didn't need to be strong; they just needed to be *there*.

Which led Gideon to the biggest regret of his life.

Thomas was handsome, and kind when he wanted to be, but he was really a self-serving prick. Or maybe Gideon just saw him like this because their breakup led to one of the most painful memories he had.

He shouldn't have allowed the man to convince him to mess around in his home. But Thomas' parents had been home, his own vacant since everyone was at work, and they'd both thought it would be okay.

Gideon had the day off, and he'd never expected Emerie to come home early from working the farmlands.

He still remembered the haunting betrayal in her eyes when she found him in bed with his boyfriend. It wasn't the way he wanted to reveal his truth, and to this day, it made him sick to his stomach.

Her scream, tears, and destruction still gave him nightmares. Especially since he'd taken it all while buck-naked, a pillow covering his groin, as Thomas bolted out the window to escape. *Coward.*

She'd locked herself in her room after that, and he'd paced his own while panicking. He'd packed his bag, preparing himself to be kicked out when their parents came home and she told them what she'd discovered.

The thoughts he'd contemplated that day had been unpleasant, and *dark*. He was about to lose the people he loved most in the world.

But he'd wanted to brave the conversation so he could explain and get closure. He'd had enough money to rent a cheap hotel in the poorer part of Fishket, and he would just work harder.

Crap. My chest hurts again. Just like that night, it seemed to burn.

He'd clenched his trouser legs, head hung low so he could stare at the ground between his knees while he and his parents sat at the dining table. He'd bitten his lips so hard he thought he'd draw blood. The air between himself and his adopted parents had felt so heavy and suffocating that he'd been rendered incapable of speaking.

Every quiet minute was made worse by the fact that, from the second level of their home above, he was able to hear Emerie crying.

The moment he thought he finally gained the courage to open his mouth and apologise, he clenched his eyes shut because he started to cry.

But it was the warmth of his mother's hand on his own, and the way she gently lifted his chin to face them, that startled him. Her brown eyes were brimming with tears, and instead of him uttering an apology, it was her.

All his fears, his worries, his self-loathing unravelled when she explained that it was okay. With her nimble thumb, she wiped away his tears as she took charge of the conversation he was frightened of having.

She told him there was nothing wrong with him. That they were sorry they didn't realise sooner, and they shouldn't have pushed the idea of marrying their daughter on him – despite them really never doing so. They explained that they thought it was what *he* wanted, so they never stopped Emerie's fantasies. They thought he shared them since he never stated otherwise.

His heart nearly burst out of his chest when they said they loved him exactly as he was, and that he was their son, no matter who he loved. That any partner he found would be lucky to have him because they knew he was good inside and deserved the absolute best.

They just wanted him to be happy.

It's all they'd ever wanted.

I was scared for no reason. He never needed to hide anything, and all his wild fantasies of being kicked out were unnecessary.

The hug they'd shared after the truth came to light had been filled with sobs, not just from him and his mother, but his father as well – who had been the biggest instigator for their group cuddle.

And rather than making Gideon face Emerie, they did it.

He wished he just had faith in them and had come forward in the beginning, but he heard a few horror stories and just wasn't able to. When he finally did, it was the most agonisingly stressful day of his life, but it was also the day he was able to truly step into it.

It reshaped him.

Emerie, however, was hit hard by it all, and she was sour with him for quite a few weeks – especially since she felt like he just ripped her whole life away from her. She had plans, and him leading her on only solidified them.

However, what blossomed between them afterwards was powerful. They truly became brother and sister, and their relationship grew strong. She became his best friend, and Gideon hers, and they were there for each other through tough times.

She was also the first person he'd introduced Beau to a few months later since he'd broken up with Thomas. Gideon just couldn't look at Thomas the same way after he'd ditched him when Gideon needed him most.

A small, sad smile curled his lips, only for them to twitch with humour.

Gideon had never seen Beau coming. Especially since he'd been working alongside the man for two years.

Once the truth was revealed to his parents, Gideon did not give a single fuck who found out afterwards. Why should he when he was accepted by the people who mattered most to him in the world? Word slowly spread, especially between those who knew him.

Beau was tall, large, heavily muscled, covered in hair, and much older than him. Yet, he was so shy and awkward in his attempts to get closer to Gideon, even just by proximity. He was a quiet man, who didn't share about himself with anyone, to the point he often became an invisible bystander despite his overbearing size. It was no wonder Gideon didn't realise he was attracted to men, or that Beau secretly had a crush on him.

One thing eventually led to another, and they formed a really healthy, strong, and loving relationship with each other. One that had persisted for nearly four years.

There were some awkward encounters with others.

People had a tendency to pry in such rude ways that it made him want to be violent.

Everyone assumed Gideon was the one often on his back since he was the smaller one of them, when that couldn't have been further from the truth. Gideon liked to conform to his partner and their desires, since he found pleasure in both receiving and giving.

So many times he wanted to punch the daylights out of someone who asked them who was the top and the bottom, but his follow through only remained at zero because Beau would hold him back with a mature chuckle. He never understood why Beau didn't get angry by people's rudeness, especially since it was the equivalent of asking a straight couple about their sex life.

Their private life was no one's business, and he wished others would give him the same respect he gave them.

Still, regardless of any ups and downs, he'd been happy the day they moved in together. He'd even made plans for the coming autumn to get down on one knee and ask the man to marry him.

Emerie had been helping him plan the perfect proposal with all her heart.

I really hope he found someone after I died. Someone who treats him well, makes him happy, knows that he likes the colder months because he runs so hot, and that he absolutely hates tomatoes.

Even though his thoughts had sunk to a darker place, they weren't as... hurtful as before. Pain lingered, but it didn't feel anywhere near as hollowing or despondent. Instead, a small smile curled his lips.

He probably did. Beau is a good guy, and someone else will have seen that.

His love for the man had ebbed in the wake of realising that they probably just weren't meant for each other. Gideon didn't know if he believed in fate, but if it truly was his time to die, he hoped there was a damn good reason for it. He wanted there to be, simply because it made him at ease with all this.

Maybe he was always meant to be Aleron's friend, in the same way it had all happened so that Ingram and Emerie could meet.

That tickled his chest with relief.

"Gideon?" Aleron asked, tilting his head as he crouched over him.

Shit, he thought, thankful that Aleron had yanked him from his barrage of thoughts. Although, he had to admit he was pleased he was beginning to truly let go of the past.

He cracked the best smile he could muster, only for it to fall when he saw white orbs staring down at him. His features wrinkled into a deep frown. "What's wrong?"

"I asked you what they are doing now, and you did not answer. I thought... I grew worried that you had faded."

He scratched at the side of his neck. "Sorry about that." He tried to laugh it off. "Are they done yet?"

Gideon stood and peered inside the house. The couple were done, made evident by the woman sprawled on the bed as the man used a wet cloth to clean between her legs.

"Hmm, I'm not sure what they're doing. Maybe he's giving her aftercare?" When Aleron tilted his head like he often did, his own way of asking a silent question, he rolled his eyes. "He's cleaning her, soothing her, and making sure she's okay. It's a way to show he cares."

A sincere smile filled his features when the man, once he had completed this task, leapt onto the bed to tackle the woman and bring her in for a hug. She squealed out her laughter. No wonder this memory dream was being played to them.

They appeared happy, especially with the way they began chatting and touching, with the intention of just being close. It didn't matter that a foreign language was being quietly and lovingly uttered; the emotions were apparent.

"This *aftercare*. Is this important?" Aleron asked, watching as well.

"I'd say it's the most important part. No one likes to feel used." Unless that was a playful, consensual kink – but Gideon wasn't going to tell Aleron that.

I probably shouldn't give him details that'll just confuse him.

If there was a way for Aleron to have a bride, this couple was perfect for demonstrating a healthy, caring relationship.

"I... see." His skull jerked, almost going upside down. "They are connected again."

Humour flared in his chest, but so did a strange emotion. "They're just holding each other's hand."

Aleron attempted to mimic them before interlacing his fingers together, creating a giant fist of two hands. Why did Gideon find that... sweet?

"Come on," Gideon said as he slapped his back. "Let's move on. The sun is going down and we don't want to be out after curfew." The sun never went down.

Aleron unlatched his fingers and turned his skull to him sharply. "Then we best leave before a Demon comes and eats us." Demons didn't exist here.

The laugh that burst from Gideon shook his entire being. "Good job. You're starting to get the hang of it."

The Duskwalker's feathers puffed in obvious delight. His tail quivered as his orbs turned a bright yellow.

But something about the way he'd laced his hands together had snagged Gideon's thoughts. He rubbed the short stubble on his cheek, grumbling to himself. *How bad could it be?*

Finally making his decision when they started walking, he reached his hand back. When nothing happened, he braved looking back to meet Aleron's pale-pink orbs. He waved it at him.

"Take it."

"You wish to hold hands with me?" His tone was high,

full of surprise, and perhaps even a little uncertain.

"It'll help with your anxiety regarding your need to touch me so I don't forget." This was true, and partly the reason he was even offering it. "It also means I won't lose you again."

If Aleron suddenly ran off to investigate something, he'd just unwittingly drag him with him.

Yet, the moment he placed his massive hand around Gideon's much smaller one, his ears became so hot he was sure they would disintegrate from the sides of his head. It wasn't something he was used to doing, holding another's hand, unless it was an intimate moment.

It was usually reserved for lovers, which made the strange pulsing he could feel within suddenly turn rapid.

Aleron's hand dominated his and was far too big for Gideon to hold. He basically disappeared within the depths of his rough, calloused palm. Yet, it was... warm. Even though his arms were slightly elongated, he leaned forward for Gideon's comfort, meeting his height rather than the other way around.

"Thank you," Aleron said sincerely, his orbs turning a bright yellow in Gideon's peripheral. "Does this mean you wish to do the sex action with me as well, like that male and female?"

Gideon nearly tripped over his own feet in shock. He attempted to rip his hand away, but Aleron's light grip tightened and threatened to crush him.

"N-no," he stuttered out, turning his head away to hide how embarrassed he was about that prospect. "I was trying to make life easier."

"Why not?" Aleron grumbled. "I would like to try this with you."

He turned to face Aleron with his jaw threatening to unhinge and his eyes wide in disbelief. The Duskwalker looked up and to the side, scratching at the side of his bony snout almost bashfully.

What the hell did I just do?

SIX

Aleron didn't understand how or why the human appeared perplexed and troubled at the same time.

He even stopped leading Aleron forward, halting their walk to gawk up at him. He couldn't help turning his skull away, scratching at his snout from the shy, fluffy feeling sprouting in his chest.

Is it not normal to ask such a question? How else was he supposed to instigate touch such as this? Aleron would like to try this sex act with Gideon.

He had many reasons for this.

He was intrigued by the physical connection, and what it could possibly mean. His kindred had explained that it was pleasurable, not just in body but also in heart. Ingram said it made him feel closer to Emerie, and he described how he'd been obsessed with touching, tasting, and feeling her essence against his own.

Unfortunately, just as he was explaining the act to Aleron, Emerie had shouted at Ingram to stop. Apparently, it was a private thing they shouldn't be discussing with each other?

But private meant... intimate, didn't it? A special act that should be shared only with themselves.

He wanted to try this special act with Gideon.

Especially since the more time he spent with the human

the more obsessed Aleron became with him.

It'd started off small.

The wind would shift his short, brow-length hair slightly to the side, or the tips of strands would catch behind one ear. Ears that Aleron examined constantly, wondering why they turned pink and how he could make them do so – especially since Gideon's green eyes would sparkle at the same time. His eyes were two pools of forest saturated in sunshine; their brightness was warm and welcomed a creature such as him deeper into their depths. His golden skin was starting to look tasty for some strange reason. Aleron knew by the lack of scent coming from Gideon that he'd taste of nothing, which had begun to bother him.

He wanted to know what he smelt like, tasted like. His desire to lick had come from Ingram explaining that Emerie's scent was naughty and delicious. It made his kindred want to lick her all over.

I often licked Ingram's face with affection. Is this why he suddenly craved doing it to Gideon?

He had muscles that Aleron was now aware he himself lacked. He looked stronger than Aleron and yet was undeniably weaker in strength. Despite this, Gideon had offered to protect him.

It had made his chest hurt so much with joy, he'd almost clawed at it.

The only people who had offered or even tried to protect him were his kindred and the Witch Owl. Although he didn't want to need protecting, it was nice that Gideon was willing to fight for his sake – just as Aleron was now willing to do so for him.

Even the way the male's clothing rustled around his body was like an intimate dance, occasionally revealing hair that covered his chest. He also noted hair on the backs of his hands, wrists, and forearms. It often made him cheerful that he and Gideon were furry like each other – perhaps it meant he wouldn't mind Aleron's fur and feathers.

Even the ball at the centre of his throat, which bobbed up and down regularly, stole his attention.

And his voice... he had a wonderful voice that often soothed Aleron's mind. He'd been alarmed by this at first, wondering if the human held tricksy magic like the Witch Owl, but he'd long ago discovered the truth. He just liked it whenever he spoke, and the subtle depth in his voice was perfect. It didn't grate on his nerves. It wasn't truly deep, but it lacked the higher pitch that Emerie's held.

Gideon's height was also greater than that female, which pleased him. He was easier to speak to and stare at, despite only coming to the centre of Aleron's chest.

What he didn't like was how Gideon tried to pull his hand from his own when he'd just offered it. Annoyed, he refused to relinquish his prize.

Gideon eventually sighed, realising it was useless, and he tugged his arm to move them on.

They were almost at the other side of this village. What had once taken all of Aleron's short attention span had been completely and utterly stolen by this male. Even just the top of his head, and how his hair flopped over, took his interest.

After many moments of him having a very pensive expression, his lips tight and his eyes narrowed, he finally glanced to his right. Aleron's chest sprouted little tickly fluff balls from just this male's gaze on him.

"Okay. I guess I should ask *why* you would want to have sex with me?" Even though his question was stern, there was a quietness to it.

Aleron's tail feathers spread slightly, his wings shifting in delight, when the human's little ears pinkened. Finally giving into his craving, he reached forward with his free hand so he could brush the back of his foreclaw against one of the arches.

"Because I like you." It was the best he could do to describe the way he felt. There wasn't a single thing he disliked.

Gideon gasped and slapped his free hand over the ear he'd caressed, incidentally crossing his arm over his neck. His eyes grew wide, as though startled, just as his cheeks pinkened as well.

Realising his touch had elicited a stronger response, Aleron wondered if it were possible to make the male's entire body flush. Was this provoking enjoyable? And just where else on his body could Aleron touch that could deepen the colourful reaction?

He very much wanted to find out.

"*Why* do you like me then, Aleron?" Gideon asked, covering his mouth and looking off to the side.

Aleron leaned forward so he could examine his expression, but it was too hidden away for him to even attempt to decipher it. Instead, he tilted his head at him.

"I do not know why, only that I do. Must there be a reason?" His question was sincere, as he didn't see the need for an explanation. His chest did strange things, and he'd developed an intense desire to be closer to this male.

Their unity of hand holding was just the beginning, one which he didn't know he could instigate. He would do it often in the future, ensuring a physical connection with him – so long as he did not protest it. Not because he needed to alleviate his worries, but because he liked the way Gideon's hand felt in his own, secured within his strength.

Gideon whipped his face to him, his strong brows drawing together like he wasn't expecting such a rebuff. He eventually lowered his hand from his mouth.

"I guess you don't particularly need a reason," Gideon grumbled, the pinkness fading as he rubbed the side of his hair-covered neck. "I think what I'm trying to say is that I don't understand. Wouldn't you want to do this with a woman?"

Aleron reared his head back, only to tilt it until it threatened to turn upside down in surprise.

"This is only something that can be done between a male and a female?" Suddenly, his sight shifted to a deep blue, not liking this at all. He hadn't known this was a strict action that could only be performed between two opposing genders.

Does this mean I also cannot have Gideon as my bride? The fluffy balls that had been bouncing around in his chest earlier stilled and grew weighted, like they wanted to sink to his stomach. *But I like this human. I would like to protect him.*

"Well, no," he grumbled, once more looking away. This perked Aleron's head up, his tail feathers vibrating again, but in hope. "It's absolutely possible between two guys, but I thought you would want to fuck a woman, not me. Your kind seek a bride, right? Well, the term 'bride' is generally given to a woman getting married, not a man."

"It is?" He didn't know this, nor did he understand why it mattered.

"I guess I just assumed..." he trailed off, before quietly muttering, "I just don't want to confuse you, is all."

"'Bride' is only for females? Why? I thought it just meant the person who I bond with. You could be my bride."

Again, Gideon's ears pinkened. However, this time he didn't cover his face even though it also darkened in colour. His lips parted.

Gideon turned his gaze to the ground. "Have you been thinking about this with me?"

He then began to rub at his neck, the side of his face, and even ran his fingers through his fringe to push it back. Even though he appeared panicked, not once did he try to take his hand from Aleron's, which allowed the flare of hope to burn hotter.

"Are... you against this with me?" Aleron asked instead, his way of answering affirmatively. "I am not a human, and I am a male. Do you not like me because of these things?"

"You being a male is absolutely not the problem," Gideon stated. "I guess I never told you, since it's not usually anyone's business, but I'm gay." Like he'd know Aleron didn't understand what the term meant, he briefly peeked at him as he said, "It means I like men, not women. And, to be honest, I'm realising you being a Duskwalker isn't actually a problem for me. I just... like I said, I don't want to confuse you. I also don't know how I feel about being an experiment for you. Discovering my own sexuality wasn't entirely pleasant, and I'm worried that helping you with this might make things harder for you in the future. I also don't want to be a source of unpleasantness for you. We're friends, and I don't want that to change negatively."

He does not want to be a source of unpleasantness for me? But Ingram said doing this feels wonderful. The human was making it more complicated than it seemed.

Then Gideon turned to him with a beseeching frown crinkling his brow and the corners of his eyes. "You're... you're the only one I have here, Aleron."

Too distracted by this pretty human's expressions, Aleron didn't realise they'd passed through a gate. They'd even wandered across a meadow.

He stopped them by yanking on Gideon's hand.

"I do not care about the gender of my partner, only that they make me feel warm here." He pointed to his chest, to the place Ingram had told him his desired partner should move him.

Currently, it felt like a mess, and he was rather liking that mixed-up, chaotic feeling within. Its uncomfortableness sprouted confusing pleasure behind his sternum.

"You do this for me, and I would like to touch you in return. But I do not know how to do this. I do not know how or where to touch, which is why I have not done so."

When Gideon pulled on his arm, wanting freedom, Aleron relinquished their connection for his comfort. Gideon stepped back from him, putting unwanted space between them.

The male put his hands up, as if to ward him away. Aleron let out a snorting huff of irritation at him for it.

"Isn't this a little too fast?" With his shoulders tucked up, and his face averted, he stated, "You only learned what sex was like a few minutes ago, man. Now you're spouting all this other stuff, but how the hell are we supposed to know if that's truly how you feel or if it's because I'm the only one here? I don't want to just say yes because I'm curious about you."

Aleron tilted his head. "Why not? I am also curious about you – and this *sex*."

"Because I'm not a woman, Aleron. I wouldn't be a 'bride' but a 'groom,' and sex is different for each kind of pairing."

"I told you. The gender of my partner does not matter to me." When Gideon's brows narrowed in obvious disapproval, he couldn't help the chuckle that rumbled from him. "I know what I want, little human. I feel it in here."

He indicated to his chest again.

Gideon rolled his eyes. "Well, you're supposed to feel it there." He pointed to the fur covering Aleron's groin. "Where even is your dick? If you were horny, it would be hard, and considering the size of you, it should be very noticeable right now if you wanted me."

That was... an excellent point. *Where is my cock?* He touched at his torso and then groin, wondering where it was. He didn't know a cock would harden, so did that mean it was currently soft?

"Horny... does this mean desire?" Gideon nodded, which made him cover the end of his bony snout in thought. "I have never felt *horny* before. I did not even know what any of this was, even when Ingram explained it to me." Aleron eventually shrugged. "I was hoping you would teach me, show me where it is and how to use it."

He didn't know whether to laugh or if his orbs wanted to shift back to a reddish pink when Gideon slapped one of his hands over his face. He drew it down, sternly eyeing his bony skull with a conflicted gawk. Then he crossed his arms over his broad chest and tapped his fingers on his biceps.

"If," he started, before his lips drew into a hard line. "*If* I agree to help you with this, I want to state a few conditions."

When Aleron's orbs turned bright yellow, Gideon sighed and lifted a single finger.

"Wait a second before you get all happy on me. Firstly, we won't be having sex. I'll show you how to touch someone to entice them, and hopefully we can get your dick to harden so you can learn about that part of yourself. Secondly, the moment you or I feel uncomfortable, I want to stop – especially you. Touching should be pleasurable, so if you don't like something about it, anything, I want you to tell me. Lastly, communication and consent are very important. If you say you don't like something, I will try something else. If you say stop, that will be the end of this and it's likely best we don't try again."

These were the conditions? The only truly disheartening part was the restriction on sex.

"Why no sex?" Aleron asked, genuinely puzzled. What else were they supposed to do then? "Is this not the point?"

Like the male couldn't help himself, his eyes lifted up and then away. "It feels like a bit much. You should have a more solid understanding after this, and can make a better, more informed choice. Plus, I don't know how I'll truly feel during it, and I must also be aroused for sex."

Aleron wanted to argue, but didn't. Instead, a naughty, evil little emotion played within his torso.

If Gideon taught him how to entice another, then he could take all he learned and eventually use it on him later. Once he gained the power of this newfound knowledge, he could wield it with his claw tips.

"Okay, little human," Aleron conceded with a purring rumble, excitement swelling within. He reached forward to curl his claw behind the shell of Gideon's ear, knowing it would make it turn pink and he'd get all cute and jittery again. "I agree to your *conditions*."

I can't believe I'm doing this, Gideon internally grumbled.

Both he and Aleron knelt upon the ground, facing each other, as dappled sunlight played over them through the forest canopy. He'd wanted them as far away from that human village as possible. He didn't want anyone to see the deplorable things he was about to do with this Duskwalker, even through a blurry, dream-like haze.

He couldn't help turning his gaze to the side while scratching at the stretched side of his neck. At this point, if he kept doing this action, he was going to scratch a hole into himself permanently.

The whole situation was fucking *awkward*.

It feels like a first date. No, it was *worse* than that.

Rather than trying to find the most appropriate moment to lean in for a kiss, uncertain if the other person felt the same way, he was about to roam his hands over this Duskwalker's body.

Sex, for Gideon, didn't always come later. Sometimes his chance meeting with a person could have them rolling around in bed together. A spark could be wild and passionate when shared with the right stranger, but that wasn't very common.

There was usually a natural lead up. A warm hug that could turn into a lock of lips before someone was pushed up against a wall, or the back of their chair. There was usually a story written in body language, a call to be closer and closer until they were both lost in each other.

This? They were kneeling here, and he was acutely aware it was because Aleron had no idea what to do.

I wish my fucking face would stop feeling warm. He only blushed when truly awkward and out of depth within a situation. He hated how his face gave away his emotions, which only worsened the more he wished to hide them.

It didn't help that every time Aleron touched his damn ear, his cock jerked. Very few knew his ears were particularly sensitive – to pain, pleasure, the heat, and the cold.

He didn't even know if he was horny or not. The confusing tingle in his groin only felt strange because it was for Aleron, and the fact that a sexual situation was about to occur.

What if he hated it, or Aleron did? How would their already uncertain friendship recover? Would this be blurring the lines between them too much?

He'd struggled just to hold his hand, and now he was supposed to give his dick a handshake?

Then there was the issue of what to do if they both... enjoyed it. Gideon would then need to think long and hard about what that meant, and they'd really only just met.

Well, that wasn't entirely true. Neither knew how long they'd been stuck in Tenebris with each other. It'd seemed like a sleepless forever. *Maybe it's been two or three weeks?* Then again, the passage of time in Tenebris felt wonky, and his estimation could be grossly inaccurate.

He said he was curious, and Gideon was too. He'd been intrigued about this Duskwalker for a while now, their prolonged, uninterrupted companionship giving him thoughts and feelings he probably shouldn't be considering. He just hadn't wanted to act on them since he thought Aleron wouldn't want it.

Gideon decided to try and let go of the past. He could have a future here, and the idea of having Aleron in it permanently was starting to bring him contentment.

Let's just get this over and done with. His cock throbbed at the thought. *Shit. Stop that!* The idea of getting hard when Aleron may grow uncomfortable only caused mortification to singe his nape.

Gideon raised his right hand, unable to deny how much it shook in nervousness, and reached it towards Aleron's neck. *Just go slow.* Sometimes relationships could start off weird and uncomfortable. *I gave him my conditions, so hopefully he'll tell me to stop if he doesn't like something.*

"You should start in places that aren't intimate and work your way from there. Sometimes those touches can matter more."

The moment his fingertips brushed *into* the long, furry collar surrounding Aleron's neck, his lips parted on a gasp. Although it was fluffy and undeniably soft, it didn't feel fuzzy like every other fabricated thing here in this false world. The strands were fibrous, but silky. *It feels real.* He should have known that by the scraping roughness of Aleron's palm.

Trying to watch out for anything negative in Aleron's body signals, he dug his fingers deeper until he was able to caress down to the root of his fur. He touched lightly, and Aleron leaned into it, the arches of his wings twitching. When Gideon scratched his nails into him instead, wondering if more pressure felt better, his orbs turned black and Aleron stretched his neck out for him.

Okay, that's a good sign.

Gideon pushed his other hand into the fur of his chest, only to pause the moment his fingertips caressed something hard. Parting his black fur just enough to peek through, he discovered he'd touched a protruding rib bone. He continued to search, moving fibres to the side, until he found his sternum – stark white and protruding as well.

The strangeness of bone on the outside of his body

should have been off-putting, but Gideon found he kind of liked it. Silkiness surrounded his fingertips from the fur, the bone just as nice, but the flesh surrounding it was hot. Even his other hand felt heat when he glided it to the back of Aleron's neck so he could scratch down the nape of it and over his shoulder, causing his wings to twitch even more.

"Is this alright?" Gideon asked, touching at the bone.

Oddly enough, his mouth grew parched, when not once since waking up in this world had he felt thirsty or even hungry. *I guess I've grown used to all his features.* Not even the new ones were truly startling to him; they were just another fascinating aspect of this monster.

Aleron nodded, and he allowed himself to be more confident. He shoved his hand to the side, trying to figure out if he had nipples under all this fur to play with.

Just as the pad of his middle finger grazed something small and firm, Aleron's chest dipped forward. The tiniest *growl* radiated from between his fangs. He paused, his eyes widening since it was the first time, other than when they'd met... that Aleron had growled.

The hairs on the back of his neck stood on end at the same time a tingle raced down his spine.

"Yes, still fine," Aleron rasped, and he wasn't sure if it was huskier or not. He gripped Gideon's hand to press it firmly against his chest. "I was surprised."

Who the fuck growls because something surprises them?

Yet, when Gideon grazed his nipple again, another rumble vibrated from Aleron.

"Aleron," Gideon warned.

"Leave me be, human. I do not know why I am reacting this way," Aleron answered curtly. "You gave me your conditions, and I have not said 'stop,' as you have asked of me."

So, he was supposed to just go against his human instincts when something was snarling at him to stop irritating it? He almost wanted to roll his eyes, but he decided he would try to ignore Aleron's unnerving response.

He slipped his other hand down so it could join the first in fumbling around his furry chest. He attempted to grip around the hardness of rib bones in order to squish whatever muscle Aleron had beneath his flesh. He wasn't as plump as Gideon's muscles made him, but there was some softness there. It elicited a warmer response, as a contented 'hum' came from his throat.

"Anything?" Gideon asked as he flicked his thumb over his nipple again, gaining a less feral growl, while his other hand descended slowly down his hard body.

Lustrous fur greeted him everywhere he went, and it didn't take him long to admit that he enjoyed the feel of it slipping through his fingers. It disappeared around his navel, until he eventually brushed over scales. Even they were nice to touch, lightly textured.

"I am... unsure."

Gideon wished he could say the same thing. The more he touched Aleron, the stiffer his own dick grew. It was only semi-hard, though; the thing stopping him from truly growing erect was the shaky uncertainty of this.

The moment Gideon glided the pads of his fingers down a seam of fur at Aleron's pelvis, his orbs flickered purple. His fangs parted slightly to let out a gruff exhale as his entire abdomen clenched.

Not once since they'd met had Aleron's orbs morphed to purple. He decided to make an assumption on the colour's meaning.

"Here?" he asked, tickling that seam with an up and down motion. Bright purple persistently flickered, and Aleron's maw parted further. "Considering I've never seen it, I figured it could be hidden inside you or something."

Gideon tried to wrap his head around that revelation, but eventually shrugged. Aleron wasn't human. He was a monster, and apparently this monster's cock had an inhuman sexual function, like a weird seam or slit.

Am I supposed to... push into it?

Rather than doing so, he firmly glided his entire palm over it. As much as he wanted to get this over with, this was more than just getting Aleron off. He was supposed to be teaching him to touch, and there were many places he could caress first. Hopefully something would make it come out on its own.

Oh, right... the teaching. He'd forgotten and had just been enthusiastically exploring.

"Since you don't have lips, you can't really kiss, but licking someone's neck or chest can help to elicit desire. It feels nice to have your body petted." He licked at his lips, considering leaning in to demonstrate. Where he could kiss, he didn't know, but his skull looked kissable right now. "You can go slow or fast, but I've found that creating build-up and anticipation makes everything more sensual and exciting."

Gideon palmed his hand down the Duskwalker's thigh, only to drag his nails up the sensitive inner line. Aleron's hand shot forward to grasp Gideon's shoulder, just as his thighs twitched and his feathers – from wings to tail – flared.

He thumbed Aleron's nipple, grasped his chest, then slid his hand up to dig into the furry collar around his neck. From there he touched his bony jaw, following the length of his snout, before going down his throat. In his own way, he was attempting to show his acceptance of it, and how a partner *should* greet him.

There should be no hesitancy regarding his body, only the shy nervousness of being intimate.

When his orbs turned bright purple and remained there, Gideon was sure of the meaning.

"You like your thighs being touched?" He drew his hand down a little, only to come back up and rub the pad of his thumb over his protruding hip bone.

"Gideon," Aleron rasped with an obvious wince before he clawed low on his stomach. "It feels strange, like there is pressure."

But his cock hasn't come out.

Deciding to just... brave it, Gideon slipped his fingers over the seam of fur and pushed in. He wished he hadn't. Not only because Aleron hissed out a concerning sharp breath like he'd potentially hurt him, but because it had his hardening cock quickly deflating.

Although he'd only had one sexual situation with a woman, he knew what the inside of a pussy felt like, and found it remarkably similar in its warmth, wetness, and softness. Much about it was very different, like the textures that made little sense to him, but the similarity was off-putting.

It also brought up memories he wasn't fond of.

Still, since Aleron hadn't asked him to stop, he gritted his teeth through it and reminded himself this was for the Duskwalker. He pushed further in with the knowledge he'd lost his own heated edge for this, which made it a little easier.

With all four knuckles deep inside, he frowned when he swore something gripped all his fingers. Aleron grasped his wrist tightly to halt him.

He lifted his head to stare up at black orbs, and the big Duskwalker deeply shuddering. Groaning, Aleron's claws dug into his shoulder as he pushed some of his weight onto him.

"Are you alright?" Gideon asked.

"Feels. Weird." He shook his bony skull. "Too good, too much, all at the same time."

Fair enough. At least that meant Gideon could pull away, or rather, *try* to. When he yanked his hand back, whatever had gripped him inside yanked back! A small tug-o-war happened between his hand and the inside of Aleron's seam.

Gideon panicked, pulling back harder and harder, fretting to be let go.

When he eventually gained freedom, he incidentally pulled everything with him.

Unable to help it, his eyes grew wide and his jaw slackened at what came from Aleron's body. *Whoa! That's a freaky dick.*

Four dark-purple tentacles writhed, their ends curling inwards on themselves like little seekers. That wasn't even the strangest part. Aleron had the fattest and biggest cock he'd ever seen, and the fact it was bright purple was just as startling.

Two dark-purple braided rings were thick and sat low, roughly three-quarters of the way down. The braids also knotted up three sides of him, giving him a strange texture on the top and sides. Overlubricated to the point it constantly dripped, his erection was fierce and visibly throbbing. Even the groove underneath the length of it looked swollen and uncomfortable – or rather, he assumed so.

Had... had it been stuck? This was *not* a soft dick!

A nudge at his temple snapped him from his ogling stare, and he turned it up to Aleron's bat skull instead. He continuously bumped the blunted tip of his snout and fangs against Gideon, almost with encouragement.

"More," Aleron purred, confirming his guess, as he grasped one of Gideon's hands and placed it against his cock. "Touch."

Gideon wasn't unfamiliar with a wetted cock, having used lubricant in the past. The more the better was often his opinion on the matter, so the fact the Duskwalker was dripping with it wasn't unwelcome. He was surprised by just how hot, hard, and velvety it felt, and even the braids on the sides of him were actually a nice texture against his rough, calloused palms.

As freaky and unusual as it was, Gideon's earlier semierection not only returned, but instead engorged fully. The pressure within his pants became uncomfortable, but he ignored it as he stroked Aleron's cock in wonder.

Heavy as he weighed it in his palm, his decently sized hand was only able to wrap three-quarters of the way around it. Gideon liked the colour, and only realised it matched his long, thick, yet thin-in-width tongue when he licked over his snout.

A soft growl constantly rumbled from Aleron, and the sound of it vibrated in his ears. It was loud to him, despite its subtleness.

Real. Everything about this felt *real*. From Aleron's sounds, to the way his fur and little nipple felt against his other hand, to the balmy hardness he was stroking. Nothing about this felt false, like the world around them.

However, his breaths weren't rapid. Only Aleron was gasping for air against Gideon's rough ministrations, especially when he tightened his grip and started truly playing with his cock with enthusiasm. How could the Duskwalker come across as needy like this? Even his unhidden pants became cute and shallow.

Staring down with eyes riveted to the massive cock he was petting, he explored it.

With a deep stroke, he delved into his tentacles to see what they would do, what their function was.

They clasped to his forearm, and pulled, yanking his hand all the way down. Two ovals, similar to his own balls but embedded in the base rather than a pendulum sac, greeted his fingertips. The quaking whine that escaped Aleron reminded him of the times his own sac had been played with, and how it would make his thighs twitch and draw a nose-crinkling groan from his parted lips.

Gideon attempted to grasp them in some form, and only managed to fondle them instead. Still, Aleron's intense reaction, how he continued to shake, how his back arched, and the menacing growl that burst from him meant he fiercely enjoyed it. Gideon only pulled away because Aleron started thrusting his engorged cock through the air, like it sought the friction Gideon currently wasn't giving it.

Needing to use strength, he freed his arm from Aleron's tentacles and slipped up the length of him. The two close-together, braided rings wrapping low on his shaft didn't elicit a powerful response, but Gideon couldn't help playing with them.

He grew more infatuated and curious with every transfixed stroke.

His gaze was forcibly taken away when Aleron clasped the underside of his jaw and lifted. Purple orbs peered into his very being as he towered over him on his knees. The other hand, which was still steadying much of his weight on Gideon's shoulder, dug its sharp claws into his false flesh.

The small bite of pain was welcome.

Aleron leaned closer, only to let out a grated moan when Gideon stroked back and forth over the flare of his cock head. He noted how sensitive it was, so he flicked repeatedly over its plush, spongy rim.

"I have this craving to... lick you right now. Is this wrong?"

How the fuck would he know?

"No?" he answered, his voice laden with uncertainty – or was it excitement? Gideon no longer knew what had come over him, only that something had started nibbling at him from the inside, making his shaft throb. "Whatever makes you feel good, I guess. That's the point of this."

Right. Whatever made Aleron feel good was the point, so why the hell did he have a raging boner desperately trying to tear its way through his damn pants right now? He hadn't expected to be this turned on just by the sight of his cock, and even more so by stroking the damn thing.

His balls clenched, his cock jerking along with them, when Aleron leaned forward even more. He hadn't even licked him yet, and he was already reacting! And the sound that fell from Gideon when the Duskwalker's long, nearly round tongue slipped across his cheek, scraping the short hair there, was almost too lewd to be called a groan.

His response grew breathier when that flexible appendage messily swirled in and around his ear at the same time. Rather than seeking air, his lungs shuddered from the shivering goosebumps that cascaded across his skin.

His knees turned inwards, as different places upon his body reacted. His nipples, already hard, throbbed, as did his ass and cock.

Everything about this world had felt so weak up until now. Even the wind, that usually had no temperature, felt cool against his flesh. Was it because he was directly touching Aleron, like some kind of physical anchor in this pretend world?

He didn't even realise he was getting foolishly swept away in his own reaction, confused, concerned, and so deeply aroused, until he parted his lips. He let Aleron's tongue sweep inside it. Before he could dart his head away at the unfamiliar experience of something like a flexible limb swirling within the cavity of his mouth, Aleron cupped the back of his head.

Drawing him closer, he shoved deeper with a sharp growl, his cock thickening under Gideon's palm. The hand on Gideon's shoulder darted down to grip one of his thighs, Aleron leaning over him as he pushed his tongue further inside.

"So I touch like this?"

Before Gideon could wrap his head around Aleron talking with his damn tongue in his mouth, the thought unravelled when the Duskwalker roughly glided his hand up his inner thigh. His cock jerked, and his nose wrinkled with a light groan – until he realised his likely destination.

Before Gideon could stop him from going any higher, his

free hand gripping the back of the Duskwalker's, Aleron had already brushed his entire palm over his cock resting over his left hip. Then he tentatively squeezed it with his large, thick fingers.

Unsure as to why his face heated in embarrassment, likely because he was caught cock-hard in a situation he'd truly thought he wouldn't be aroused by, he clenched his eyes shut. Thankfully Aleron pulled his tongue away, so he could point his skull downwards.

Gideon opened his eyes to do the same, wishing his mouth would move when it refused. His eyes crinkled with an array of conflicting emotions when he noticed his hand still gripping the giant, tentacled, purple monster cock jutting between them.

I forgot how damn big it is. The moment he took his eyes from it, suddenly it got bigger.

"You are hard, like me." Aleron petted Gideon's cock with inexperienced fumbles before digging his claws into the edge of his trousers. "I would like to touch."

"I don't think that's a good–" Gideon's words cut short when Aleron lifted his skull, and for the first time, his orbs *reddened* as a light snarl burst from him.

They swiftly turned back to purple, but a darker shade this time. Then he licked across Gideon's mouth, swiping each of his cheeks before nuzzling the hair hanging over his temple.

"This," he started, wrapping his hand around Gideon's and his cock, tightening the hold so he could thrust into it. "This feels *very* good. I would like for you to feel good with me."

Gideon averted his gaze to the side as he thought. Well, tried to, since Aleron gripped his jaw again to steer his face forward. Taking the opportunity when it was present, the Duskwalker shoved his flexible tongue past his lips and teeth once more, and this time Gideon melted for it.

Screw it. There was nothing wrong with his own desire.

If Aleron was consenting to it, then there was nothing wrong with him getting off either. Hell, the Duskwalker even *asked* for it.

Stroking Aleron's cock with renewed conviction and pressing his thumb into the deep groove where the frenulum on a human would be – right behind the head – he reached down with his free hand. The buttons of his trousers opened easily when he pulled the material to the side, and it allowed him plenty of room to yank his cock free.

His erection jutted forward, and he stroked it to see how it would feel in this world.

Unfortunately, it did feel muted, until Aleron attempted to take over. The strange warmth and roughness of his hand made him groan, and the contact was somehow stronger than his own. His hips even jerked forward into his hold. The size of Aleron's hand against the girth and length of his human cock meant he'd enveloped most of it, but Gideon wasn't ashamed of that at all.

He was average for a human, from what he'd gathered, and he knew it didn't matter anyway. A dick was great, regardless of its length or girth.

Aleron was also unnaturally bigger than him in every aspect.

Rather than feeling any negativity, he just swelled within the pleasure of his palm, as Aleron's did the same within his.

Their tongues lashed at each other, trying to find a rhythm within the confusing clashes and slips. Gideon eventually pulled away, just so he could bite out a heated, *"Fuck."*

He turned his gaze down to watch his light-pink cockhead disappearing and reappearing within the ring of Aleron's dark-grey fingers. Both their arms were moving, Aleron's subtle, but more than enough to make his spine tingle. Then, his eyes flicked to what his own hand was stroking.

Shit. I'm so horny right now. It looked so wet and slippery. Overwhelming desire struck Gideon, his mind and body now fixated on the unbearable need to come.

He didn't even truly register what the intense reaction coming from Aleron meant.

Aleron's purple cock thickened in waves, swelling over and over again as he rocked harder into Gideon's hold. He shuddered and his wings kinked in on themselves, while his entire body fluffed up, his fur and feathers standing on end.

"Gideon," Aleron groaned, the hint of a whimper tangling with it.

When Aleron's shaken grip on his cock loosened and pulled away, Gideon rose to his knees. He dug his fingers into the fur of the Duskwalker's chest to balance himself, then shoved the undersides of their cocks together. Just the wet touch against the underside of his erection spread desirous heat throughout his groin.

He tried to keep them together with one hand but found it too difficult.

"Can I have your hand, Aleron?" Gideon asked, noticing his chest and shoulders rising and falling rapidly.

Silently obeying, he reached forward.

Gideon brought it to both their cocks pressed together and made him grip them until they were tightly meshed, holding onto the back of it to guide him to stroke. Thankfully, Aleron was resting back on his calves while Gideon was raised fully on his knees, making them line up perfectly. The flared rim of their heads could rub over each other's when Gideon began to thrust.

Right now, he didn't care what he did, or how wildly he moved, since it brought them both pleasure. Aleron's groans were constant, unhidden, and they only made his own fall from his lips more eagerly.

His eyes and nose crinkled in bliss as he stared down to watch what they were doing together.

Fucking hell, that feels so damn good. The hardness and roughness of Aleron's fingers against the top of his shaft, combined with the slippery, hot, and nuzzling groove of his giant cock gliding over him from underneath. Both were such intense, conflicting textures that they felt amazing.

Squished together, he thrust harder and made Aleron tighten his hold. Just as his eyes were rolling and his balls clenched hard, he noticed Aleron watching. He began to thrust as well, uncertain and cautious, but the more he got used to it, to all of this, the more confident he became.

Gideon fisted the fur of Aleron's chest just as his head fell back.

"*Fuck.* I think I'm about to come." He didn't know why he told Aleron; he doubted he would care.

Yet, Aleron's thrusts became harder, faster, and longer. His hand only worked to keep them together at this point. Before he knew it, Gideon was forced to rest back on his calves as Aleron pushed forward to thrust wildly.

His big, heavy wings whooshed and fluttered against the ground, right as a growl grew violent, only to die. Aleron's following groan was so deep that it sent a wave of goosebumps across his skin.

He slowed; they both did. Gideon was thankful for it when his spine tingled, his balls clenched upwards, and his cock began pulsating along with thick swells from Aleron's.

But Gideon darted his head forward when the ease of pressure was completely and utterly *missing.*

He hissed in a breath of annoyance. Despite the fact that they were both coming, neither one of them was producing cum. Their orgasms were dry, likely some messed-up byproduct of doing this in the afterlife. It ripped away the blissful intensity that was supposed to shoot them to rapture.

It still felt good, but Gideon knew what a true orgasm was supposed to be like, and this wasn't it. It also dawned on him that this wasn't Aleron's first time coming during this.

Did my excitement keep him hard? At least that was a good sign.

He would have been disappointed by their muted orgasms if Aleron didn't plop his bony forehead against the top of his shoulder. Gideon quickly ducked his head sideways so his long, twisting horn didn't slam into his forehead. His entire body was still puffed and jerking with aftershocks, as he slowly thrust his hard cock against Gideon's softening one like he couldn't help himself.

Pressing his fingertips against the ground, Aleron attempted to take the worst of his weight from Gideon, like he understood he would snap his spine in half otherwise.

"More," he grated, continuing to thrust. "Again."

"I think this is enough," Gideon mumbled, pleased that Aleron had enjoyed this, and they both had received satisfaction.

His growl was light, but so half-hearted it barely counted as threatening. "Okay. Only because I am tired now, little human."

Gideon chuckled at that.

Considering Aleron pushed himself, refusing to sleep, it was no surprise he was exhausted. *At least there is nothing to clean up.* No cum, no sweat, and even Aleron's lubricant didn't linger once Gideon tucked his dick back into his trousers.

Within what could only be seconds, a soft snore vibrated from Aleron, whose skull was still pressed into his shoulder. Only then did his jumping erection start to sag, and Gideon only knew that because it flopped onto his knee like a snake falling from a tree.

Holy hell, what did we just do together? He lifted his eyes to the canopy of leaves above, surprised to find he wasn't all that beaten up about it. *It felt great.* That's all that needed to matter.

Aleron fell further forward, pressing more of his weight

on him as his snores continued.

"Yo," Gideon said firmly, shaking the Duskwalker's shoulder. "Don't fall asleep on me like that."

Aleron jerked and leaned back.

Then he practically dived at him, causing Gideon to squawk in shock as large, dense arms wrapped around him. Even Aleron's wings encircled him so their torsos were meshed. The big, heavy Duskwalker rolled them onto their sides and wriggled until he was comfortable, which thankfully stopped Gideon from being crushed. Darkness surrounded them, but it didn't bother nor frighten him. Instead, he found it soothing in comparison to the incessant light that always shined in Tenebris.

Fighting a mouth and face full of soft, fluffy fur, he wasn't able to get his arms up through the Duskwalker's tight hold.

"What's the big idea?" Gideon exclaimed, wiggling to get an inch of room and failing. "You didn't do this the last two times you slept."

"My heart is telling me to hold you," Aleron softly stated in return, nuzzling the jaw of his skull against his temple. "My wings are precious to me, but they ached to bring you into their close and protective hold. I have never felt this for anyone but my kindred. It means much to me to feel this for you."

He opened his mouth to refute this intimate cuddle, not wanting to add confusion to what they'd just done together, but quickly shut his lips. Aleron had darted his head back and was peering down at him within the comforting darkness that belonged to the shelter of his wings.

He couldn't help but frown up at him. *Are his orbs a brighter pink than usual?* He'd never seen them this intense colour of pink before, at least not towards his face. Ingram, yes.

He put it up to a trick, due to the lack of light, since his orbs would naturally look brighter in the dark, right?

Still, they were kind of... handsome.

It didn't help he was acutely aware they'd just rubbed their dicks together, and that Gideon had gotten swept up in an intensely intimate moment with Aleron when he probably shouldn't have. Hell, Aleron's cock was still nestled between them. He'd never intended for things to go that far, or to find his own release, but his body had just taken ahold of his thoughts.

I guess I'm attracted to him, and I really did like doing that. Just thinking about it made his dick twitch, like it wanted a second round. Once was enough.

It had all been to teach Aleron so he could figure out what he wanted, how to touch himself, and how to pleasure someone. Although, he hadn't really intended for that someone to be another guy. *Fuck. I forgot that was the entire point.*

So why didn't he wish to pull away?

Annoyingly, his ears grew hot. He rolled his eyes away to inspect the only sliver of light cascading within from Aleron loosening his wings.

His furry arms were comfortable, and his feathers cushioned him from all sides. He didn't mind being held by Aleron, even though he'd be awake the entire time the Duskwalker slept.

However, he was incapable of looking upon Aleron's oddly alluring face right then. "Nah. It's fine, I guess," he grumbled out awkwardly.

Aleron shifted his wings, and the gap of light closed.

SEVEN

Standing on the edge of a shallow, shady canyon, Gideon narrowed his brows and his lips pulled tight. His chest flooded with a sickening, dreadful ache, like his lungs were filled with thick oil. He should have known the afterlife couldn't be entirely pleasant at every corner.

"What is this?" Gideon asked in disbelief.

His eyes roamed over what had to be thousands of people just... *standing* there. Standing there, doing nothing! Most of their heads were forward facing, and their expressions were truly blank of emotion. Their eyes were closed, as though peacefully sleeping.

With the canyon and mountains in the distance, most people were shaded. Mist danced all throughout, making it even more eerie. It looked like a valley of the dead and forgotten.

Another disturbing aspect was the different styles of clothing they all wore. Some women were dressed in elegant and outdated ballgowns, with men wearing intricate suits that matched. Many wore robes and outfits that must be from other lands, while even fewer were dressed similarly to how he was.

Thousands of people from different eras were all cluttered together in this sad canyon. He tried to ignore the different ages, from young children all the way to those who were old and needed to wield a cane.

Such devastation upon humankind, such sorrow and sadness to be witnessed here.

All of it unnecessary – if it weren't for the Demons who plagued the world.

Aleron's hand clasped his tighter. That shouldn't have comforted him as much as it did, but it felt like he'd spoken a dozen easing words by doing so.

"These are the humans who have no ties here, or do not have pleasant memories with the others here they know," Aleron stated quietly, as though also unnerved. When Gideon turned his head to look up at his skull, Aleron dipped his head forward and to the side. "Only those who have strong bonded strings are able to be active in their memories. Otherwise, Weldir told me they come here, and play any and all happy memories."

"Shit," Gideon rasped, wishing the despondent emotion gripping his throat actually felt physical. He couldn't help bringing his gaze back to the vacant humans, his eyes crinkling in remorse, pity, and *fear*. "Is this... Is this where I was before Emerie came here? Is this where I'll go if we get separated?"

Neither set of his parents would be here, since they hadn't been killed by Demons or Duskwalkers. Beau should have been a part of his happiest memories if he'd been eaten, and Emerie... she was with Ingram now. As much as the other people in his life had been precious to him, he doubted he would have been included in their happiest memories.

Just as his thoughts began to spiral, a heavy, feathered black wing encompassed his back and opposing side. Aleron drew him closer with it, and his shoulder bumped against his furry torso.

"I do not know where you were before I met you, but I will not let you go," Aleron stated, his tone holding confidence in his promise. "I will stay by your side, always."

Gideon lifted a weak but appreciative smile to him. "Thanks for saying that."

He had his doubts.

Aleron had yet to meet a woman here, which could be more in tune with his desires. Regardless of any emotions, Gideon didn't have a pussy and couldn't produce children – assuming reproduction was a large part of what Duskwalkers sought. Why else would they seek a bride, if not for this?

Humans didn't always desire a child; sex was more about pleasure and connecting with the one they loved. But it'd already become apparent that Duskwalkers in general seemed to be more animalistic in their thoughts and behaviour. Even Aleron acted on instinct much of the time.

Then again... Ingram didn't seem to mind that Emerie is infertile. Overhearing that Emerie had chosen to do that to herself to climb the Demonslayer ranks had been... saddening. Only because it was obvious she regretted it.

It was the moment that he truly accepted Ingram as his 'brother-in-law,' technically speaking. With a full heart and absolute confidence, he'd stated he didn't mind so long as he had Emerie.

It was love in its purest form, in Gideon's eyes. The same kind of love he saw within same-sex couples.

Humans could adopt, but it was with a drive to extend their family through unrelated bonds, share an unconditional love that wasn't a 'requirement' because of blood. A chosen family that held no accidents. Every step on that journey was planned, and arms were opened willingly.

If that pure, chosen love could be accepted by Ingram, then it *did* mean it was possible between him and Aleron. That's even if Aleron could have a bride now that he was dead.

But... would I even want that? A bride seemed like a

massive, unbreakable, binding relationship. Would it be a heavy burden to bear, being the human within a Duskwalker pairing, or would it be enlightening? Especially with one that had so little humanity?

He wouldn't make the decision solely based on not wanting to turn into the humans before him. In this world, there was absolutely no reason for Gideon to bond with anyone. His existence was entirely pointless – neither of them were alive.

Aleron would also have to choose Gideon. *With what he said yesterday, it seems like he's already been thinking about it.* But Gideon was the first human he'd truly befriended here in this realm.

Part of him wanted to march down into this horrible canyon of lost souls, shake a woman from her slumber, and tell her to fall in love with this big goofball. He would have even assisted, spouting on about how amazing Aleron was, that he was sweet, thoughtful, and charming in all his oddities. He could be Aleron's knight in shining armour, his bride matchmaker, his wingman. Every step of the way, he would have his fist in the air, rooting for him.

However, the thought hollowed out his heart.

Gideon would have to wave goodbye to Aleron and his woman as he watched them hold hands and skip off into the fake sunset, leaving him to fade into nothing but a sleeping Ghost. It would also mean... he would no longer be by Aleron's side.

I... wouldn't even remember him. For some reason, that stung all the way to the soul floating inside his chest. *I don't want to forget him or everything we've done here, everything I've learned about him and this world.*

Say we both could just magically come to life... He almost wanted to slap his face into his palm in mortification. *He'd break my ass.*

Although Gideon was happy to conform to his partner's desires, he just couldn't see that working out for them without a hell of a lot of patience. Aleron would have to learn by taking first, so he wouldn't tear Gideon in half. Sure, an asshole could take a lot more than a woman's pussy, could heal and be quite stretchy, but there were limits.

Aleron's dick *might* extend past those limits.

Fucking hell. If Ingram is similar in size to Aleron, how can they be compatible? Although the thought of Emerie getting it on with *anyone* made him want to dry retch, he still wondered, especially after what happened earlier between himself and the monster currently clasping his hand.

Just thinking of their combined petting experience kept making his dick jerk in his pants.

When Aleron had woken up, he'd begun licking at Gideon's neck. Just constant, incessant licking. He'd squirmed because it tickled, especially when that long purple tongue brushed his ear here and there, but that was only until he'd started getting... hard. Unbearably so.

The moment the Duskwalker started thrusting against him, he quickly pushed at Aleron's chest to separate them. His thoughts during the hours Aleron slept had been rapid and conflicting. Shame had never registered within his conscience, but embarrassment at his own behaviour, as well as some bashfulness, had sucker-punched him repeatedly. So did arousal, and the cold and warm tangle of tender feelings. Worried and confused. Joyful and satisfied.

How did one person experience so many emotions all at once? When did their meaningless lives become an exciting thing?

It didn't help that the entire time, he'd considered petting Aleron's seam to make his dick come out for them to do it again. Maybe the second time around, they may have actually produced semen. Rather than being cock-blocked, they'd been cum blocked by this world.

At least desire and lust were possible between them, but he didn't think that would be enough for them to have a future.

Why am I even thinking about this right now?

Freaked out about all the possibilities that lay before him, and his unknown future, he eventually stepped away from the safe blanket of Aleron's wing. Then he tugged the Duskwalker's hand.

"Come on, let's move on." He pointed to the distance, in the gap between a set of mountains that were misty and difficult to see. "Didn't you say we're almost there?"

I wonder where he'll take me after this.

Gideon avoided looking at the woeful canyon of humans they walked next to. He hated that it appeared miles long, and mentally crossed his fingers there wasn't anything else this *depressing* along their travels.

I hope this other Duskwalker is as nice as Aleron.

Aleron paused, and with a disgruntled huff, released Gideon's hand when he told him to stay put. *I do not want to let his hand go.* He liked holding it. It felt nice.

The human sunk low to the ground, crouch-walked forward on one hand like a Mavka, then reached out to the animal before them. It stepped back, hooves crossing, with its body language wary and guarded. Bucking its head with lowing snorts, it eyed Gideon as he kept inching closer.

Finally, he managed to place his palm on the side of the creature's neck. His *handsome* features, as Aleron learned was an appropriate word to describe a male's beauty, melted into an expression of radiant awe. His green eyes widened, like he simply couldn't believe he'd touched this animal. Even his cheeks pinkened with glee.

Aleron, unsure as to why, experienced a wildly

unpleasant emotion within the pit of his gut. His sight shifted to green, a colour he wasn't familiar seeing and was uncommon for him. He didn't exactly know the name of the emotion, but it sunk into him like the fangs of a venomous snake.

I wish he would look at me with such an expression. Aleron may have seen something similar directed towards him, but not to this intensity. *He should only look at me like that.*

He wanted that radiating awe and the loveliness directed upon his own skull. He was better than this creature, surely.

His fur was longer and fluffier than its coarse brown. His horns were also thicker, although not longer. He also had pretty wings and could stand on two legs. Aleron was stronger, bigger, smarter, and better than this small *thing*.

"This is so cool," Gideon quietly uttered, as he stroked the short fur on its neck.

He directed his beaming face at Aleron, his smile growing so wide the dimples within his cheeks deepened and became more prominent. Somehow, some of his petty annoyance deflated out of him.

"Come," he whispered, reaching his other hand out and waving his fingers at him beckoningly. "Slowly, though. Don't spook it like that cat from the village."

With the nasty venom coursing through him, it likely wasn't safe for this creature if he were to come closer. He had half a mind to pick it up, lift it above his head, and *fucking* toss it, much like how Weldir had tossed him off a cliff.

He'd learned all kinds of exciting words from Gideon, and was rather pleased that he now had something to show the power of what he wanted to convey. *Fucking, fuck, shit, damn.* They were harsh, but they could convey much, both negative and positive.

Despite his reservations, Aleron cautiously approached

because that was what Gideon wanted from him, and he desired to keep this little human happy. He was beginning to obsess about how he could make Gideon content, and wipe away the often despondent, solemn expression that washed over his features.

He wanted him to associate Aleron with joy, so that he could convince this male to become his bride. Or groom. Or whatever he wanted to be called.

When Aleron crawled closer, lowering, the herd beyond Gideon backed up. Surprisingly, the animal he petted seemed as mesmerised by his companion as much as Aleron often was, staying put.

It wanted to fight with Aleron for Gideon's affection by being just as obedient. His orbs flared red at it.

"What is it?" Aleron asked in a low tone, wanting the name of it so he could solidify it within his mind as his least favourite beast.

There were many creatures here who had likely been eaten by Demons. This wasn't his first time seeing these ones in particular.

Like him, it couldn't scent anything. Aleron couldn't smell its fear, and it likely couldn't smell any hostility on his approach.

"I think they're impala antelope," Gideon said in a cooing and calm voice, trying to settle the antelope as Aleron came upon them. He gave it a scratch under its chin, and all Aleron could think was how he wanted him to do that to his bony one. "I've read about them, but as far as we know, they're extinct in Austrális. They were one of the first animals the Demons eradicated when they arrived."

As he spoke, he slipped his other hand over the back of Aleron's protruding white knuckle bones and directed him towards the beast's neck. With Gideon's guidance, he stroked it.

At first, disdain caused his fur and feathers to puff, but it was quickly overshadowed by his own unwitting awe. The green in his sight faded to bright yellow, and he began to enthusiastically stroke the creature as well.

Despite its size, it felt strong, its fur rough, and yet there was a sense of... elegance in the way it held itself. Meekly, it bucked its head, but eventually settled when it must have understood that Aleron intended no harm... for now.

Graceful – that's how he saw it.

"There is a Mavka who shares the same horns as this antelope," Aleron explained, eyeing the long, spiralling horns that were similar to his own. However, they were rounder and thinner compared to his, and small, bumpy rings went up their lengths.

"You said you get your characteristics from what you first ate, right?" Gideon whispered as he pet its back, and its short, upward-curling tail flickered with delight. "That Duskwalker must be pretty old then, since they haven't been around for a long while."

"I am unsure." Aleron didn't even know how old he was.

Aleron's entire essence wanted to melt when Gideon directed a strange but tender smile towards him. It was so strong that his dimples became prominent once more, and even the tops of his cheeks bunched his eyes.

With a gentle and sincere voice, Gideon said, "I know it's probably weird to say, but thank you for this."

His skull tilted sharply. "But I did not do anything."

"I never would have been able to pet a wild animal if it wasn't for you allowing me to stay by your side here in Tenebris. I never would have gotten to experience this, and it's really surreal." His expression softened to something that made Aleron's heart swell before Gideon gazed at the creature once more. "It's pretty rare. You really have to venture away from a village, but I've seen a deer before. I couldn't get close to it, let alone touch it, since they are really skittish towards anything. It would have been even cooler if it was a wolf or a mountain cat – since they're really dangerous."

"I do not know these names," Aleron admitted, but he didn't feel embarrassed by his lack of knowledge.

Gideon had been very understanding and welcoming of this, and he'd grown increasingly comfortable stating when he was uncertain.

Perhaps it was due to their very limited time together, but Ingram had incidentally made him feel... inadequate. It wasn't on purpose – his kindred had only wanted to share as much information as he could with him, excitedly explaining everything he'd learned. Yet, he'd realised there was a giant gap of humanity between them.

They were no longer one being split into two. Ingram had become his own person, and in some ways, Aleron had felt left behind. He'd felt inferior.

His other half had changed so much that his inner self almost seemed unrecognisable.

Over the course of their time together, Gideon had managed to erase those insecurities within him. He told Aleron it wasn't his fault, and that he had potential – he just had to learn it first. Gideon accepted him, from his mind to his heart, and even his body.

He welcomed everything Aleron felt he lacked and then threw it back to him with an evolved version of encouragement. It allowed him the freedom to state his broken and disjointed thoughts, without the shadow of judgement looming over him.

Aleron appreciated that, and it was a large part of the reason why he'd grown to care for the little human so deeply.

I even asked him to teach me about my body, and he agreed to it. His orbs flickered purple at the back of his head. *And he became aroused as well.*

The glee of that often sent thrills down his limbs, flexing his fingers with the urge to touch again.

"I'll point them out to you if we see them," Gideon

offered, once more showing that unconditional acceptance. "I'm sure you've seen them before. Wolves are still pretty common, since they kill Demons." Then he shrugged and stood, causing the antelope to startle and shy away. "To be honest with you, the only reason I know what these guys are called is because I copied a book on them. I had to trace the sketch of one, which is why it's probably stuck with me."

Aleron stood as well, following Gideon's lead. He offered his hand to the human, and a tickling warmth sprouted in his chest when he willingly took it.

Aleron always felt that way, adoring how his small hand felt within the crease of his own. His anxieties about Gideon's potential fading memory became instantly non-existent in the process.

"Come on," Gideon commanded, pulling just enough to stir him into moving.

The gentle tug was unnecessary; he'd already begun to realise he might just follow him anywhere. So long as Gideon remained by his side, he wouldn't mind where they were taken.

"I'm glad we finally passed that creepy canyon, but we still have to go meet your friend, yeah? Well... brother, really."

When Gideon peeked at him, and his green eyes connected with his pale-pink orbs, looking at him without any fear or timidness in those piercing depths, something startling dawned on him with absolute certainty.

He wouldn't just follow him anywhere; he'd happily let Gideon escort him to his own demise.

EIGHT

As they arrived at a cliff wall with a lake next to it, Aleron always thought it looked very similar to the home of the bull-horned, bear-skulled Mavka, Merikh.

However, it didn't have a large, cascading waterfall – the lake water seeming to come from nowhere – and there was a giant slab of flat rock right next to a sandy bank. There were no trees, no cave entrance, and cliff walls encompassed the area much more tightly and in a vee shape.

The water within Tenebris didn't linger on one's body once they left it, nor did it have a scent. It lacked any form of nutrition, and its temperature was the same as the air surrounding them.

Gideon never walked over to its sandy shore, seeking to desperately drink from it like he'd seen many humans do. He never needed to drink, eat, or sleep.

"We are here," Aleron explained, gesturing to the Mavka curled up on the slab of flat rock.

The rock itself was a dark grey, but the coiled up Mavka was as black as the night sky. His scales didn't have a blue glint to them like Ingram's, but rather a glistening rainbow sheen instead.

Gideon placed his hands on his slim waist, causing his grey tunic to bunch around his fingers, and drifted his gaze across the area with a deep frown. A small flurry of wind caused the short lengths of his light-brown hair to flick to the right, dancing against the edge of his brow.

"Am I missing something?" Gideon stated, eventually letting his gaze fall on him. "I don–"

He gasped and shuffled back, his lips parting as the Mavka moved.

Since they were behind the Mavka, he pulled himself backwards while lifting his tail, so he could uncoil his own waist from on top of himself. As though he was entirely flexible, he twisted in order to face them, walking with his hands to steady his upper body weight.

Inspecting those who had disturbed him with white orbs, they shone bright against the bone of his snake skull. With his horns black, the only true colour on him was the tiny glints of rainbows dancing where the sunlight hit him. His horns were round in shape but curved backwards like a hook that pointed down.

Aleron didn't know what animal they were from, only that his skull – and most of his body – was serpent in nature.

A strong, humanoid torso flexed with muscle similar to his own body, much wider than his, but still lean. His collarbones, hips, and rib bones were visible, although most of his sternum was sunken beneath his flesh. However, most of his spine was exposed except for the last few feet of his exceptionally long tail.

Fish fins ruffled along his tail, starting from the middle of his back and continuing all the way down. He also had them going down the entire length of his arms, but they looked different here – like spined fins instead of ruffles. They were grey, similar to the softer underbelly of his human-like torso.

As far as Aleron knew, he was the only Mavka without legs. He may also be the only one who had gills down his neck.

After assessing who had come to disturb his constant slumber, the Mavka's orbs eventually settled from white to orange – his natural colouring. He didn't come closer, remaining on the slab of rock and leaning upon his hands, but did tilt his snake skull towards Gideon.

His orbs then shifted to a dark yellow in curiosity, likely confused as to why the human didn't flee. Then his skull darted towards Aleron.

"Holy shit," Gideon grated. "You could have warned me he was huge."

Due to his astonishment, Aleron first thought he'd upset the human. Only when he looked upon Gideon and noticed his features had cooled, and he was examining the Mavka like how he did the world, did it reveal he was just speaking his mind. He did this a lot, spoke his thoughts aloud, sharing them with Aleron in order to fill the silence often between them.

Aleron appreciated this, as he didn't always know how to start up a conversation.

"He is not that big," Aleron said before sighing and stepping closer to demonstrate it was safe. Although the Mavka had never shown even a hint of aggression, he wouldn't let him hurt his little human either way. "He just has a long tail."

"Uh huh, sure." Gideon nodded as he drew close enough to put his hand out in greeting. "Hey there. My name is Gideon. It's a pleasure to meet you."

The Mavka turned his skull down to inspect Gideon's hand, twisting his head one way and then the other, which produced a quiet rattling noise. His yellow orbs darkened even further.

He said nothing, and his head movements were the most interaction Aleron had ever received from him. Usually, the Mavka would silently stare upon him, only to eventually retreat into the cocoon of his tail.

"You are supposed to shake it. It is a human greeting." Aleron's shoulders rounded back, making his wings flap slightly, as pride swelled within his chest. He knew something this Mavka didn't. He assumed that made him more intelligent. "I will show you."

He clasped Gideon's hand, and *veeery* carefully shook it.

Gideon's eyes glinted with humour, the memory of them first doing this radiating between them. Then, he offered his hand to the Mavka once more, nudging it closer with a welcoming expression.

"Gently, though," Aleron demanded softly.

Surprisingly, the Mavka reached out. Like Aleron, his large hand swallowed up Gideon's as he clasped it. The Mavka shook up, and then down, yanking Gideon off his feet until his face crashed into the dirt. At the unsettling thwap of him hitting the ground, Aleron's entire body puffed in rage.

"I said gently!" He roared, his sight shifting to deep crimson.

In the corner of his sight, the Mavka's orbs flared a brighter orange than normal as he shrunk away. Aleron didn't care about his wariness, or his feelings of guilt. Not when he had to carefully assist Gideon to his feet, and not just pick him up like he weighed nothing.

"Are you o–" Before he could finish checking on his wellbeing, Gideon burst into a roaring laugh.

"I can't believe I fell for that a second time!" Once he was on his feet, his lips curled up in a bright grin. He brushed his pants of dirt that didn't exist. "You would have thought I'd learned the first time that you guys don't know how to control your strength." His green eyes took in Aleron's orbs, and then the Mavka's, which only seemed to make him laugh harder. "Hey, don't worry about it. It only hurt for like... a second. Like I said, my name's Gideon. What's yours?"

Gideon turned to the Mavka once more, his smile remaining. He was much quicker to adjust to this situation, and he seemed to have the kind of personality that was easily adaptable. He'd taken learning about Emerie, Mavka, and this world with such strength.

His wings tightened against his back as a contented thrill ruffled his feathers. Gideon would fit *perfectly* into the often chaotic and sporadic nature of his kindred bond.

When the Mavka didn't respond, Aleron reluctantly drew his gaze away from the pretty human. Despite recoiling back as though he'd intended to hide within his tail, the Mavka did eventually slither forward. Perhaps captivated by Gideon's warm and welcoming expression, as Aleron often was, or perhaps it was the male's beauty he was drawn to, he slowly extended himself.

"He may not have a name," Aleron stated, since he and his kindred had only obtained their names through the kindness of Raewyn – a female Elf he'd met on Earth – and Merikh.

He hissed at Aleron.

"So, you do have a name?" Gideon asked, one of his brows arching higher, and he nodded in response. "Then why won't you..." Gideon trailed off, as did his gaze. Then his eyes narrowed with deep thought and almost... suspicion? "You... you can't speak, can you?"

With orbs turning bright yellow, the serpent Mavka closed the distance so swiftly that it even surprised Aleron. Gideon didn't have a chance to stop him, his human reflexes slow in comparison.

The Mavka grabbed his hand and cupped the underside of it, while he used the other to pat the top of it.

None of them moved as he towered over Gideon, holding his hand with both of his as his tail slithered underneath his body to support his torso. The moment seemed intimate, as though they were having a private, unspoken conversation without Aleron.

He didn't like that one bit, nor how it made his sight turn dark green. The nasty little emotion that had coiled in his chest with the impala antelope nipped again, this time taking on the form of a serpent within him.

He quickly attempted to insert himself between them, disliking that the Mavka seemed to purposefully leave him out of their silent conversation.

Aleron growled, only for it to choke in the back of his throat when the Mavka grabbed his hand instead. Just like with Gideon's, he clutched it in both of his own, cradling it with a gentleness that conveyed many unnameable but weighty emotions.

He was quick to release Aleron though, but his orbs were bright yellow. It was the first time he'd seen the serpent Mavka produce a positive colour. Usually, he could be quite shy and reserved, even for one of their kind. It was obvious he preferred to be alone, whereas Aleron craved company.

A stifled chuckle caught his attention, and he darted his skull to the sound. As embarrassment flushed his sight, Aleron parted his fangs just so he could clip them menacingly at the human.

Thankfully the serpent Mavka retreated of his own volition, allowing his tail to curl and twist over himself until he was lying down. He kept his head and shoulders free so he could observe them.

"Don't you get snappy with me." Gideon rolled his eyes before stepping closer. "Did you really just growl like some jealous, possessive, Duskwalker-equivalent asshole? He was saying hello, I think."

Jealousy? Was this what he'd been feeling?

"No," Aleron lied, lifting his skull to the sky as he attempted to whistle like Gideon did when obviously caught out. However, he didn't whistle at all, as he didn't have lips and couldn't figure out how else to produce such a noise other than humming. "You must have misheard me with your little human ears."

Gideon turned to the Mavka with one side of his nose wrinkled, a deep furrow of his brows, and his upper lip twisted. He jerked his thumb towards Aleron as he said, "Get a load of this guy. He can't lie for shit."

A hissing snicker came from the snake.

With a playful snarl, Aleron wound his arm around Gideon's side, dragged him against the side of his chest, and wrapped his wings around him. Within his arms, the weak human wrestled to free himself, which only made him tighten all his limbs until he was truly stuck.

Aleron let out a chuckle. "I may not be able to lie well, but I can trap you forever."

Gideon managed to squeeze out a single hand and cupped the end of Aleron's bony snout. Then he latched onto a few of his bottom fangs and parted his jaw slightly as he pulled down.

"Let me go, or I'll show you what it's like when a human unhinges your jaw." In retaliation, Aleron bit down on his entire hand, not hard enough to hurt him, but enough to capture that as well. "Fuck. It's not fair that you're way stronger than me."

The weird argument between them only highlighted just how comfortable Aleron was with this little human. Gideon often liked to tease him, and even though he was new to this kind of human banter, Aleron was swiftly learning so he could do it back – but in his own way.

Gideon was smarter, Aleron was stronger, so he fought his brains with his brawn. Along their travels, he'd thrown Gideon over his shoulder when he needled him just a little too much. Aleron always enjoyed how the little male fought him the entire time they strolled through whatever forest or meadow they were crossing.

He reminds me of Ingram. Of my kindred bond. But in a dissimilar way – one that wholly reshaped him. He was learning all these new, unique facets of his personality, and he was delighted to dole them out on the one who showed them to him.

Aleron felt like he was being rebirthed in his death.

"Okay, okay, I concede," Gideon eventually sighed. "You win. You always fucking win."

This is fun. With a chuckle, he loosened his hold.

One minute he was holding Gideon, the next he just… wasn't.

With a yell, the human was yanked from his arms and across the ground. With the serpent Mavka's tail securely wrapped around his ankle, he was lifted into the air. Dangling upside down with his arms flailing beneath him, he swung back and forth.

"Whoa, big fella!" Gideon exclaimed, twisting to search for Aleron. The fact he'd look for him at all, as though he was a pillar of safety and protection, meant much.

With his sight darkening to crimson, Aleron immediately leapt to his feet and charged forward. The Mavka jerked Gideon back when he came too close.

"Put him down!"

"Watch what you say!" Gideon yelped back. "He might take that literally and drop me."

Aleron didn't see why this would be an issue. Gideon wouldn't be hurt, since he'd heal near instantly, and Aleron would likely catch him before he hit the ground.

The Mavka's orbs had turned a bright yellow, hinting at how much fun he was having. Balancing on his lengthy tail, the serpent Mavka brought Gideon forward and dangled him above Aleron's head, and his anger quickly began to settle. He thought he was going to give the human back by slowly lowering him, but when Aleron opened his arms, the Mavka yanked back.

The snicker that came from him caused rage to hold Aleron's throat in a vice grip. A vicious snarl, promising pain, tore from him.

And in Tenebris, that would be *lasting* pain.

Whoa, this is weird, Gideon thought, attempting to adjust

to being upside down.

He wasn't really afraid, since being hurt wouldn't last for long.

No dizziness from blood and heat rushing to his head came, since he technically didn't have blood. It was just uncomfortable. He preferred to have his two feet firmly on the ground.

He wasn't much of a swimmer either, since he didn't know how to. Just one of the many things he'd meant to change, but never got the chance before he stopped existing.

The only worrisome thing about this was why the Duskwalker even started this, and how much it seemed to upset Aleron.

"Give. Him. Back," Aleron slowly, and ominously snarled, his voice monstrous and reverberating like when they'd first met.

The goosebumps cascading across his skin were more impactful than this whole situation. Gideon subconsciously covered his groin, wondering how the fuck that made his shaft surge. He stopped trying to twist to see Aleron.

I must be going insane. I touch his dick and now I seem to have no control of my own. That wasn't true, but his attraction to the handsome Duskwalker, with his mesmerising skull of death, had grown tenfold.

Even more so after watching him pat that stupid antelope.

A snicker drew louder, more noticeable on purpose. Gideon had to stifle any yells of surprise when tossed about through the air suddenly.

At this rate, his neck would snap from whiplash.

The cause of the serpent Duskwalker's erratic actions was something fluttering before them. The moment Gideon properly caught a glimpse of Aleron, his false breath left him and his lips parted.

"Holy shit," Gideon rasped out. "He's magnificent."

Hovering in the air, Aleron had fully extended his wings

for the very first time. Considering his height, he shouldn't have been so surprised that they would be humongous. His wingspan had to be at least twenty feet, if not more.

No wonder they'd felt like a blanket that had the capability to completely and utterly block out the world.

And he was... *graceful* in the air.

The subtle, deep whooshing blasted infrequently, steadily, and sparsely. It highlighted just how strong they were, his feathers ruffling as he flapped to keep himself afloat.

Every chance he got, Gideon attempted to watch him in awe, uncaring of the predicament he found himself in. Why should he care when he was witnessing one of the most impressive things he'd ever seen?

Then, Aleron dived straight for him with his talons and claws at the ready, his orbs an angry colour of red. It should have been terrifying. It should have reminded him of how he died. It should have, at least, been off-putting.

It absolutely wasn't. Perhaps due to Gideon thinking of him fondly, and trusting him deeply, he couldn't help seeing him as anything but some kind of weird knight in shining feathers.

Not that he thought he needed one.

Despite his massive wings, Aleron was agile and swift. Yet, he still couldn't catch Gideon, which only angered him more by the second. The serpent Duskwalker snickering and chuckling only worsened his erratic attempts at rescue.

Gideon felt for him, unsure of why he was so upset.

When purposefully brought closer to Aleron and bounced up and down at him, as though to taunt, something became startlingly clear.

I figured out what he's doing.

"Hey!" Gideon shouted, waving his arms to gain Aleron's attention. "Stop trying to get me."

"But–" Aleron started.

"He's just teasing you!"

Gideon tried to stop himself from laughing, he truly did, but he just couldn't help seeing the humour in this. *He saw how much Aleron is attached to me and decided to steal me.* Like a toy, the two brothers were fighting over him.

"If you stop trying to grab me, he'll get bored."

Gideon should know. He'd done this to Emerie many times. Since he was three years older than her, and therefore taller than her, when he wanted to bully his little sister, he'd dangle whatever she wanted above her head. She would jump for it, crying and screaming to have it back, while he mocked her diminutive height.

He was a good brother, loved her dearly, but he enjoyed needling her any chance he got. Unfortunately, that had seen him many times tackled to the ground and bashed in the nose by her fists – her own version of karma.

As if to demonstrate the truth of Gideon's words, the Duskwalker turned his snake skull towards him and gave a little growl.

Gideon did the only thing he could think of. He laughed as he gave him the middle finger with his tongue sticking out.

Oh yeah, dude. As an older brother myself, I've got you pinned.

Aleron stopped reaching for him and instead waited. He even crossed his arms over his chest, likely mimicking what Gideon had done a few times. He just watched as the serpent Duskwalker dangled and bounced Gideon around.

His heart nearly leapt out of his chest when the Duskwalker then opened his jaw, dislodged it, and hovered Gideon above his massive maw.

Oh shit! Oh fuck! Gideon prepared his hands to grab hold of something, like the side of his mouth, so he could stop himself from being swallowed.

The back of his throat was pitch black, like a narrow, claustrophobic abyss.

Now *that* was terrifying.

I'm still not into vore!

He tossed Gideon sideways through the air, somewhat in Aleron's direction, but he still had to dive to catch him. With an oomph, he fell into his strong, meaty arms.

"Nice catch," Gideon stated, giving him a reassuring thumbs up.

Apparently, that didn't placate Aleron, as he gave a deep, growling huff. Rather than dropping to the ground, he flew upwards to leave.

Gideon only had just enough freedom to look over Aleron's arm to check on the Duskwalker below. His orbs were still bright yellow, and they finally revealed what the colour meant – joy.

He'd been playing with them, picking on his sibling, and he couldn't help finding that… touching. He never expected such a human trait. It further solidified that, despite their monstrous outsides and behaviour, they were rather cute.

Especially Aleron, who currently sulked.

Then he watched the serpent Duskwalker fully uncoil himself as he used his hands to step down from the flat rock he'd been resting upon. With the use of his tail wiggling side to side, his hands pushed off to keep his torso off the ground until his tail slid from the rock. Upright as he moved, he eventually slithered into the water and disappeared into its depths.

I knew he had gills for a reason.

"Are we really going to leave because you're upset?" Gideon gave a dull look to show he wasn't impressed.

"Yes," Aleron answered curtly, banking left to go over the mountains.

Gideon wished his clothes rustled as though he truly flew, or that his hair at least rushed back rather than gently swaying. Considering this was the first time he'd ever flown, he would have preferred to have a slight kick of adrenaline.

It just felt like being carried by someone walking.

The only difference was that they were high in the air, but the constant mist made it difficult to see anything directly below them. Only in the distance could he truly make out more details, like the world suddenly opened up.

"But we came all this way," he said with a sigh.

Aleron stopping moving forward to hover them in the air, his massive wings stealing his attention now that he was able to see them up close. His wings looked even fluffier than usual, and yet so sleek that he wanted to reach out and touch the closest one.

He didn't, only because Aleron dipped his skull forward with his orbs flaring to a dark green. His fingers curled around Gideon's outer leg and arm more tightly, causing his claw tips to stab into his flesh.

"Would you prefer to go back and be with that Mavka instead?" The tone of his voice was rather dark and unnerving.

Gideon opened his mouth to stupidly utter something sarcastic, but then immediately shut it. It didn't take a genius to figure out now may not be the right time for something idiotic to come from his mouth.

He didn't wish to further upset the Duskwalker.

"I'm pretty content with where I am right now," Gideon answered honestly, wiggling down to show just how much trust he had for him right then. "I just thought we came here because you wanted to hang out with him."

"I just gave us a direction." Aleron's hold loosened, but the edge in his tone didn't settle. "I would not have come here had I known he would do this."

"You're acting really overprotective right now."

Gideon teasingly flicked Aleron on his bony forehead, only to instantly regret it. *Motherfucker. That hurt!* He shook his hand to ease the ache radiating down his middle finger.

"You are mine," Aleron growled, his hands tightening once more.

Gideon reared his head back in surprise, not expecting such a proclamation. *What is that supposed to mean?* And why the hell did it make his stomach flutter?

Ugh. My head is a mess.

"Could you put me down?" Gideon looked beyond his cradle to observe their surroundings. He pointed to a clearing situated on top of the mountain the lake had been next to. "How about over there? There looks to be a cave."

"I thought you said you were 'content' with where you are right now?" Then, his orbs finally shifted back to normal. "I like holding you like this. I have been wanting to fly with you."

"To be honest, I thought it would be... scarier. I've never flown before." Gideon cast him a large grin. "But it's actually not that bad, and I trust you now. Why don't you let me down first? I'd like to deal with the fact I thought I was going to be swallowed whole by a snake, then we can check out that cave."

The mouth of the cave was the first time Gideon had seen anywhere that wasn't showered in light. Now that he was constantly in brightness, he sought the darkness.

Funny that, considering humankind totally lived with the opposite desire due to Demons.

Aleron's head cocked, and his voice softened exponentially. "You... trust me?"

A laugh burst out of him. "Of course I do. What kind of question is that?"

They lost a little height when Aleron's wings shuddered slightly. He quickly righted them and then held Gideon tighter to hug him close. He even buried the length of his bat skull against the side of his head.

"I trust you too." It took him a moment, but Gideon eventually returned the nuzzle. Then Aleron pulled back and shone bright-pink orbs at him. "Before we land, can I fly you around the mountain first? I am rather content like this right now."

Gideon's gaze softened at his honesty. Suddenly, he didn't mind the idea.

"Sure. If that's what you really want."

NINE

After they landed on a field of plush grass, Gideon noticed Aleron seemed reluctant to put him down. Unsure if he appreciated being held as though severely wounded or a bride being carried over the threshold, he didn't fight to get free of his arms.

Aleron would put him down when he was ready, and he saw no reason to rush him.

It's so easy to make him happy. Gideon almost chuckled. *Just saying I trusted him turned him into a big puppy.* He was growing fond of this side of Aleron's personality.

He'd always liked it when people were upfront with their feelings. It made them easy to read and allowed Gideon to know what limitations he needed to put on himself. He could be rather free spirited when not despondent.

He laughed when he wanted to, cried when he was comfortable with the person, sang, danced, played guitar, and got drunk and rowdy for fun.

If the person within his company was honest, it let him know how to best entertain and ease them. He wanted to be seen as a pillar of comfort for others.

With Aleron, due to the difference in species, he'd been finding it difficult to figure out how he should act. He'd learned that being himself was absolutely best, and being as forward as he could would benefit Aleron most.

The only person he'd ever been free like that with was…
Beau. Although Emerie came in close second, the slight
barrier of them being siblings sometimes got in the way. The
fact that he'd grown more comfortable in Aleron's presence
than even Emerie's was startling.

It also brought on a whole bunch of emotions he grew
unsure about. The level of trust he'd started to develop for
the Duskwalker was dangerous for his heart.

"The hair on your face is scratchy," Aleron commented,
nuzzling his bony bat cheek against it.

"Yeah, I need to shave my beard," Gideon grumbled, a
little disgruntled that it wasn't clean shaven. He rubbed at
the slight stubble on his jaw and cheek; two days' worth of
growth. "I'm glad it hasn't grown, though. Then again, I
don't like that if I ever want to grow it out, I literally can't."

"I like it." As if to demonstrate that, the Duskwalker
licked at his jaw, making him tense up in surprise. "Do not
do this *shave* thing."

Finally, Aleron put him down of his own accord.

Gideon covered his cheek with a fist, hiding where he'd
just been licked. *It's weird when he does that.* It almost felt
like his own version of a kiss.

"Come on." Feeling a little bashful, he waved for Aleron
to follow. "Let's go check out this cave."

The fact he led the Duskwalker to a dark and secluded
location didn't escape his notice. It could even be… oddly
romantic inside. He wondered what Aleron would look like
with natural crystals surrounding him, with just the
illumination of firelight.

If his mouth could have truly gone dry, it would have in
that moment. He bet Aleron would have looked spectacular,
especially if rainbows refracted onto the white canvas of his
skull.

His thoughts often turned twisted and slightly perverse
as of late. When Aleron reached for his hand to hold it, and
Gideon peeked back at his bat skull, he knew why.

I'm attracted to him. Not just a little, but a whole lot.

Ever since their sexual interlude within the forest, he hadn't been able to stop thinking about it. What Gideon thought would be a deterrent had done the complete and utter opposite. Rather than being disturbed, he was intrigued, curious, and... desired him. He didn't know if Aleron wanted more, but he wanted to touch him again.

Gideon wanted to try other things too.

He healed near instantly in this world, which would likely make it pain-free – allowing him to just enjoy it.

But long before that moment in the forest, something about Aleron's heart had begun calling to him.

He'd never really been a cutesy sort of guy, but he did like nice people. Aleron was sometimes cute, especially when he was excited or jealous. His heart of gold easily touched at Gideon's own, and Aleron's open mind meant he was accepting of everything. Other than the violent tendencies he already learned from Aleron's past, which seemed more animalistic than malicious, he thought... perhaps... Aleron had more pureness than anyone he'd ever met.

Aleron's naïveté sometimes made him come across as really sweet and innocent, which was making Gideon want to corrupt him.

Rather than a murdering, human-eating entity that caused people's hearts to stop in fear, he had this growing, deranged desire to make him a sexual deviant. One who would punish Gideon with his newly discovered powers of eroticism and sensuality.

Just the thought made a thrilling tingle race down his spine.

Fucking hell, what's wrong with me? I've never had thoughts about anyone like that. Then again, most of his partners had been experienced. A preference, he'd thought.

Aleron was a Duskwalker. The fact he *should* be far more dominant than him – a measly human – but wasn't, was damn near so erotic it had him ravenous.

However, Gideon decided to wait on him.

Other than that one moment of petting, Aleron never approached a similar subject. Days must have passed since then.

He'd shown Aleron how to wield his body, taught him about it, and had inadvertently revealed his own desire in the process. From here on out, it would have to be Aleron's decision – and whatever that ended up being, Gideon would just help support him.

His own discovery of sexuality and sex in general hadn't been easy. He imagined that to be a tougher battle for a Duskwalker who didn't have a deep understanding of anything regarding lust.

I have faith that he'll figure it out.

As they passed through the threshold of the cave's entrance, darkness descended upon them.

Gideon let out an awkward laugh. "I just realised that we won't be able to see without a torch."

He'd been absentminded about not being able to see in the dark due to Tenebris' constant brightness.

Just as he halted with the intention of turning back, a strange, dim light slowly spread just further down the large tunnel. It didn't come up to their path, but rather grew within the distance to highlight a potential area. The light appeared to be artificial; not like how Tenebris was unnatural, but like nothing he'd ever seen.

Hesitantly, he dragged Aleron deep within the tunnel, and the light expanded.

Just beyond, the area opened up into a daunting and massive cavern.

He paused once more and blinked rapidly at what floated in the air at chest height. A little ball, no bigger than the palm of his hand, glowed. It was one of the oddest things he'd ever seen.

Black in the centre, the silhouette of it glowed with

tendrils of rainbows. The light it produced was white and entirely absent of colour. It was everything and nothing all at once.

There appeared to be hundreds of them floating at different heights within the cavern.

He moved forward. Just as he intended to go around it, the presence of his body repelled it to the side, and it darted out of reach.

Those little lights revealed what lay within the cavern.

Once more, his feet halted as he took everything in. Due to its overbearing size, the first thing that caught his eye was a stone statue situated within the very centre.

It was an effigy of a woman, reaching at least four times his five-foot-eleven height. Long hair, with loose corkscrew curls, framed a feminine face with strong features. Her brows were high, her cheeks prominent, and even her jaw and chin were stern. However, her nose, full and pouted lips, and the shape of her eyes were utterly feminine and soft.

Just her face alone was breathtaking, and the person who carved it did so with care and affection, noting even the tiniest of details. Long, uneven lashes, a cowlick curl that stuck up just a little higher than the others, and a natural wrinkle that formed at the outer crease of her right eye.

Even the cloak of feathers that rested over her shoulders, the hood back but crumpled around her neck, had intricate details. The parted front allowed all those viewing it to map out the line of her body, her breasts full, her waist curved, and her hips wide. The modest dress she wore revealed only a small amount of cleavage and the long length of her left leg from just above the knee down.

Gideon's gaze softened as he took in her expression. Despite the sternness within the hard line of her mouth, the artist had managed to capture her eyes in a tender way.

Aleron came up beside him and then pointed. "That is the Witch Owl," he explained. "This is how she appears when in human form."

"The Witch Owl?" *Aleron spoke of her.*

"She once called herself mother. I only understood what that meant when Weldir explained it to me."

"She's beautiful," Gideon complimented, taking in the grey stone.

"Really?" Aleron tilted his head, his orbs turning dark yellow. He shined them down at Gideon. "I think you are more so."

An embarrassed, awkward chuckle came from him. *Cute, Aleron.*

He averted his gaze to the side to check out the rest of the chamber, noting other statues. He pulled Aleron over to them.

Each statue appeared to be a Duskwalker in their more monstrous form.

"Hey, it's you." Gideon pointed to the statue of Aleron. It had to be him, considering it had a bat skull, long twisting horns like a goat, and was the only one with massive wings. "And that's Ingram, correct?"

He gestured to Ingram's raven skull and short, upward-jutting goat horns. Intricate scales had been carved, with protruding bones on the outside of most of him. He'd also seen that long lizard tail before.

On the right of Ingram were two little creatures he couldn't even begin to name. He let go of Aleron's hand so he could crouch down and inspect them. They appeared to be crawling over each other, one with no distinct shape other than a blobby baby body that had a featureless oval for a face, and the other with some kind of animal skull – a wolf or a fox of some sort.

"Do you know what these are?" Gideon asked.

"No. I have never seen them before," Aleron answered, an obvious shrug in his voice.

"Fair enough." He stood and subconsciously reached out without even thinking about it, only to flinch when Aleron suddenly wrapped his large hand around his own, but his surprise faded quickly. "Who's this then?"

Moving to a Duskwalker who stood taller than all the others at their skull height, he thought their impressive antlers made them even more formidable. A fox skull was collared by large feathers covering the upper part of their torso, as well as the backs of their forearms and calves. The rest of them wasn't fluffy, like Aleron, except for their long fox tail.

"I do not know if he has a name, but we called him the fox Mavka." He pointed to the next Duskwalker. "That is Kitty, or Faunus. He has two names; I am unsure why. He is nice – we like him."

"Kitty? What kind of name is that?" Gideon shook his head as he took in his feline skull and the ram horns that curled backwards before going forwards, so the ends could jut out near his cheeks. Although fluffy all over, his tail was long and thin like a cat's. "What's up with his face, though?"

A crack filled in with some kind of molten material lined the left of his skull. It surrounded the entire horn on that side as it went down over his eye before going over his cheek.

"The Demon King hurt him. His skull broke completely, but he was put back together. We were not sure how he did this." He covered his fangs with a hand and tapped a claw at the side of his bony face in thought. "Perhaps I can be put together the same way?"

Gideon peeked at Aleron as he leaned forward to take a closer look. Aleron didn't hold a hint of sadness or pain in his voice, only thoughtfulness, nor had his orbs changed colour. Still, he decided to move on from 'Kitty/Faunus' so Aleron didn't dwell on it.

"This is Orpheus," Aleron stated when they came to a wolf-skulled Duskwalker with twisting horns like the impala they saw recently.

Fur covered most of his body, while long fish fins went down his back, forearms, and calves. He looked strong and seemed to have the least amount of bones protruding on the outside of his body so far. He had a small, upward-curling deer tail.

"We... we were not kind to him," Aleron admitted. In his peripheral, Gideon noted his orbs morphed to a reddish pink. "We hurt him and destroyed part of his home where he kept humans. He was very untrusting of us after that, although he *used* to let us rest within his salt circle."

"He had a home and kept humans?" Gideon asked, surprised to learn a Duskwalker would do this.

Somehow, Aleron's orbs brightened in their hue. It didn't seem like embarrassment, but rather... in *shame*.

"He became rather angry when we tried to eat one," he stated honestly. "He refused to allow us anywhere near his territory after this. It is hard to remember, as I fell into a bloodlust and my memories are often fragmented when like this. I only just remembered now because I am looking at him. But... I think we hurt him very deeply."

"You tried to kill his friend?" Gideon asked, narrowing his brows in disappointment. "I would have been furious with you too."

"I am sorry," Aleron whimpered.

"I'm not the one you need to apologise to," Gideon grumbled, turning away while rubbing at the side of his neck. He hadn't meant to upset Aleron, and now felt rather bad about it. "Who is this one?"

He gestured to a Duskwalker with a bear skull and bull horns on his head. Although shorter than the other Duskwalkers, he appeared to be much larger in terms of muscle and... fat content? His stomach was rounded, his thighs thick like tree trunks. There were no bones protruding from the outside of his body, and he looked like he'd snap the other Duskwalkers in half with his meaty hands.

His fur was short, barely noticeable, and the only things

that truly made him appear like a Duskwalker were his skull, horns, claws, and long bull tail. He noted the echidna spikes going down his back, forearms, and calves, and they were what made him appear truly dangerous in comparison to the others. Just one throw of his arm, and he'd pulverise and pierce anything that came near him.

There were also claw marks going down his right eye hole, and what appeared to be a sword slash over the top of his snout. He was the only one with any kind of real 'scarring' upon his skull.

"This is Merikh. He is... strange. I do not know how to describe him."

Gideon furrowed his brows. "What do you mean?"

"Is it possible for someone to be mean, yet kind at the same time? He did not like us, refused to play with or talk to us, but he would allow us to rest within his ward. He never turned us away, no matter how much we annoyed him or how many times we fought. He even named us."

"You're all related, right? Brothers?" Gideon's gaze flicked to Aleron as he nodded. "Sounds like he cared about you, but maybe he just wanted to be left alone? Like a big brother that wants to protect his siblings, while keeping distance from his family. I was never mean to Emerie, but I felt like I had to keep her and our parents at arm's length before I was able to tell them the truth about myself. It was too painful, otherwise."

Aleron cupped the tip of his snout again. "I see."

Then Gideon, with his feet wide, placed his hands on his hips – as well as Aleron's hand he was holding – and stood in front of one last Duskwalker.

The serpent one he'd met earlier didn't look any different.

"Still fucking massive." Gideon turned to Aleron while hiking his thumb at his snake skull. "You know he's the creepiest looking one out of the lot of you, right? I'm not afraid of snakes, but he makes me question that."

Aleron shot his free hand up to his chest, placing his claws over his heart. "We're... creepy?"

Gideon winced. *Shit, I shouldn't have said it like that.*

"Yeah, but in a way that's also really cool," Gideon fumbled, hoping to ease whatever hurt he'd just caused. "Maybe I'm biased, but I think your skulls are awesome. You Duskwalkers all have this supernatural beauty about you. Especially you, Aleron."

That perked up the Duskwalker, and his lowering head jerked upwards. "Especially me?"

Gideon, relieved by the cheerful note in his question, beamed. "Well, yeah. Your wings are badass, and you're the only one with them. That makes you special, even within your own family. Now that you've taken me for a flight, I'm kind of jealous I don't have any."

This time, the yellow in his orbs turned bright, highlighting his joy. *I really like how easy it is to read him now, since I've pretty much figured out what all the colours mean. It makes him so honest.*

He didn't have time to register anything before Aleron wrapped his arms around Gideon's torso and lifted him off the ground in a giant hug.

"I can be your wings, Gideon." His wings twitched back and forth, and even his tail fluffed and vibrated. "I am glad you see me as special and beautiful. I like this."

Once the surprised tension eased out of him, the laugh that came from Gideon was warm, tender, and quiet. He attempted to hug him back, despite his arms being trapped at his sides.

"I'm sorry if I hurt your feelings," Gideon mumbled into his fluffy chest. "I hope you know I didn't mean anything negative by it."

The strong arms around him tightened, just as Aleron's wings came around to envelop him in a feathery cocoon. "It is fine. I do not mind if I am creepy, so long as you are not bothered. You are beautiful as well. Pretty for a human."

Gideon snorted. "Are you saying most humans aren't pretty, then?"

"You are all squishy and weak. I do not mind this about you, though."

Humour curled his lips. "Ouch. That cuts deep, Aleron."

"Then perhaps you should not cut yourself on the truth, yes?"

"Oooh! You're getting good at this."

If Aleron started doing it back to him, and managed to confuse Gideon, there was no hope for his sanity. He loved it when a person knew how to play with him just right.

A little chuckle rumbled out of Aleron as he placed him back on his feet. "You are a good teacher." He then proceeded to pat Gideon on the top of his head. "It makes me wish to listen and learn, so I can become something you want."

Gideon's brows drew together to crease his forehead just as Aleron dragged him to a bunch of other statues.

"Something I want?" he couldn't help asking.

"I am different to you. You have already shown that you are hesitant and unsure of me. I wish to make you comfortable, so that you will feel the tenderness towards me as I do for you."

Gideon didn't quite understand. *But I've been trying to make him comfortable!* He thought he'd been welcoming and open-minded towards Aleron. Hell, he'd even jerked the guy off. What more could he do?

Before he could ask Aleron to divulge on what he'd just said, and the many things Gideon needed clarification on, he was taken to another Duskwalker. They had a rabbit skull with large antlers on top of their head, but he'd stopped paying attention. Even the three little featureless creatures next to it, sitting in a row, didn't even draw Gideon's gaze – although they did resemble the two blobby creatures he'd seen beside the other Duskwalker statues.

Instead, his eyes kept straying to Aleron.

He feels a tenderness towards me? What kind, though? Friendship, or more? What did he want? *Is there any point to us having any kind of feelings towards each other in the afterlife?*

As he pondered, Gideon was dragged to the back of this cavern's chamber, which narrowed into another tunnel. Darkness surrounded them as Aleron led them down it.

Could... he be waiting on me instead? If so, he found that infuriating.

Then again, there had never been a situation since the forest that really allowed anything romantic or sexual to happen between them. Those scenarios often happened around food, or when two people laid down to sleep in a fond embrace.

Aleron kept pushing himself, going without sleep for what had to be many Earth days. Neither one had a desire to eat. In reality, besides each other's company, the world was lifeless. The only warmth was shared during their light-hearted conversations, in which Gideon tried to teach Aleron everything he'd learned from the books he'd read, or what life was like for a human – which could often be a dreary subject.

Whenever Aleron shared about himself, it usually consisted of Demons who had been unkind to him, the other Duskwalkers who he had minimal contact with, and Ingram.

Ingram invaded Aleron's thoughts constantly, and he often reminisced about his twin. The love and affection he had for his kindred was wrapped in humour, playfulness, and special embraces that touched Gideon deeply. However, those same things were imbued with the overshadowing sadness and loneliness residing deep within Aleron.

He tried to hide it.

Gideon had come to learn that Weldir helped him through the hardest and roughest part of his adjustment. He'd remained by his child's side, never leaving him. He let Aleron take his pain out on him, no matter if it was sadness or rage, bearing the weight of it all while knowing there was little Weldir could do to change it.

It'd taken Aleron a while to realise this, but when he did, he started to trust him. He began to see the spirit of the void as a supportive place he could lay his skull, fears, and pain on.

It did mean that Gideon didn't have to wear the brunt of it, and he didn't know if he would have been able to. Not because he was unfeeling towards Aleron's plight, but because they were facing the same problem.

He has been my rock here.

Even though Gideon hadn't fully shared all of his longing for the life he'd left behind, Aleron had been by his side. Patiently, he let Gideon absorb... everything. He'd needed that more than anything.

He needed someone to just let him silently cry without asking him why he was upset. Gideon needed someone to be strong by leading him forward when there were times he just wanted to sit on the ground and dwell on every painful memory with his face buried against his knees.

Until Gideon had initiated it, he hadn't realised he needed someone to squeeze his hand back in an almost comforting way. Even when Gideon's grip would tighten because of the rage and hurt that tensed his entire being, Aleron shared a look with him, but never questioned it.

Aleron had been his rock, in a world where he felt hopelessly lost. Then Aleron allowed him to feel empowered by sometimes needing him in return.

Their frequent bouts of silence were heavy with loss and sadness from both sides, but never emanated loneliness. It wasn't suffocating. Sometimes Gideon wondered if their palms touching was the only thing stopping him from turning cold like a real Ghost.

So, during all this, how were they supposed to physically get closer? Maybe it was stupid of Gideon, but he often thought moments should be special.

A first kiss. A first intimate touch. Even the first reveal of deeper, coy, and secretive feelings being shared... all these things should have a lead up. They should be a product of a perfect environment that spun out of control and heated him from within.

With Aleron, these things were difficult.

He had no lips to kiss, never mind the fact he was nearly a foot and a half taller than Gideon, so reaching him was difficult. Their first intimate touch had been more of an educational lesson that had spun out of control. And the sharing of deeper feelings was disjointed due to everything about this being confusing – for both of them.

He wasn't even sure why he wanted to do these things with a monster, only that he did. And, little by little, Beau left his heart only for Aleron to take it over. He'd stopped seeing the big, burly man as his partner; instead, he had become a stranger.

That should be painful, but it didn't *hurt* anymore.

Gideon never thought he could be happy here in the afterlife, only tolerant. With Aleron, contentment and joy had taken over.

Did he potentially want to ruin that by making it complicated? The answer should have been no. This friendship should be enough. Instead, he found himself wanting to take things further. To see what could happen between them, where it may lead them, and what was truly possible.

This was all born from Aleron's heart.

The Duskwalker had more gentleness and compassion in it than Gideon thought he could ever have. His intelligence may truly be low, but his understanding of how to treat someone was deep – likely a byproduct of his bond with Ingram.

Gideon wished he could say he had that same emotional intelligence, but he didn't. Although he'd had many friends, a relationship that had been healthy, and a family that loved and accepted him, he didn't have most of those things until his later years of life.

Before that, he'd been secretive, reserved, and almost shy. He'd found it hard to be forthcoming when he didn't even understand a large part of who he was.

Should I reach out to Aleron more? Despite the conflicting and puzzling nature of the feelings growing within, they were there.

His eyes crinkled when he worried it was due to him being completely dependent on Aleron. Yet, somehow, he knew deep within that what he felt was real. It was the most real thing within this false, messed-up world. But the worrying question was: what if Aleron was only attaching himself to Gideon for that reason? His feelings could be muddled by him being the only friendly human he'd ever met.

That thought burned a hole in his chest, right where Aleron had literally touched his soul.

Which meant he came straight back to the conundrum of why he'd been waiting on Aleron this entire time. He wanted Aleron to make the first move – or, rather, any move – to show Gideon he felt a fondness that went beyond simple companionship.

Love, lust, a craving to be closer. Something, *anything* to indicate a potential for there to be a place within his big monster heart for Gideon.

He needed to show him that his feelings weren't influenced by Gideon's and were his own. *Then why did he say he felt a tenderness towards me? Dammit! Could this be any more confusing?*

Gideon would be damned if he allowed this to pester him any longer.

"Hey," he said, hoping to gain Aleron's attention as he pulled back on his arm. "When you said you felt a tenderness..." His voice died off completely.

When he came back to reality and took in their

environment, which had fully opened back up to a different chamber, his jaw fell.

More of those small lights floated, brightening a room completely.

A chilly creep of disturbed dread slid down his side.

Letting go of Aleron's hand, he jumped onto his back. He managed to place his entire forearm over his eye holes while the other hung on for dear life around his neck.

"Don't look, Aleron!" he yelled, hoping his arm covering his orbs truly hid everything from sight.

Aleron bucked his head, turning it one way and the other, as he attempted to shake him off. "Why not?"

Gideon's eyes darted from one naked and perverse statue of the Witch Owl to the next. He tried not to let a single one truly sink in, merely drifting his gaze around to make sure this was absolutely something neither of them should be witnessing.

Especially not Aleron, her child.

Okay, Weldir. You have now revealed that you are an obsessed sicko. Gideon's ears even heated in mortification, as well as with the discomfort of seeing a woman's body naked and utterly bared to them. *It's like a sex shrine to the poor woman.*

Was she even aware of this?

"Just trust me," Gideon choked out. "This isn't something a kid wants to see of his parent. *I* don't even want to see it."

It shouldn't even exist.

Aleron stopped bucking his head back and forth, and settled. "I should not be witnessing this?"

"Just turn around. Once you do, I'll let you go."

"Okay, I will trust in you," Aleron said, yet the happy note in his tone was obvious. He did as instructed, giving the depraved room their backs.

Just as they were leaving, Gideon did notice one thing. *There is no image of Weldir.* Only the Witch Owl by herself.

Odd, considering many of the positions would require two people to be possible.

Once they were back in the tunnel from which they came, Gideon removed his forearm from across Aleron's bony face. However, before he could slide off, Aleron shoved his arm back and put a supportive arm under his arse, forcing him into riding piggyback.

"You fit nicely between my wings." Aleron had a spring in his step as he carried him forward, and the previous cavern came back into view. "I also felt this way when you were inside them. I cover you completely, whereas Ingram is so big I feel as though I cannot fully protect him."

Gideon's lips tightened in uncertainty as he wound his arms around his neck.

"Hey... can you explain to me what you're feeling towards me? It would make it easier for both of us."

Aleron tilted his skull at that. "Well, you feel warm and light. It would be easy to fly with you like this."

A chuckle passed his lips as his eyes crinkled in humour. "That's not what I meant. I mean in here."

Gideon placed a hand over his fluffy chest.

He didn't expect Aleron's orbs to change to a reddish pink, and Gideon wondered if he directed his skull forward to hide them. He'd stiffened under Gideon, and the tension within his big body hinted at nervousness.

"I do not wish to say," Aleron eventually muttered.

A frown sweeping across Gideon's entire face. "Why not?"

Aleron's shoulders, which had been back and firm, lowered and turned inward. "Last time I did so, you questioned everything."

"Last time?" As soon as he spoke, he realised what Aleron was referring to.

Oh. His head slumped until it was pressing against Aleron's nape. *He said he likes me, and I said it felt a little too fast.*

The sigh that left him was in annoyance at himself.

What he'd said back then was true, and his concerns had been weighty. Gideon still had those worries and fears, but now they were tangled with his own desires – emotions he didn't know he'd begun reciprocating until they became stronger.

"Those questions I asked you... they were important, Aleron. You are learning about everything, and I am learning about you. There are going to be times that we have conversations that are unpleasant, but they are required to ensure an equal balance of understanding. Relationships, no matter what kind, are built on the foundations of communication."

"Says the one who has not shared," Aleron bit back. "You ask me, but I have already told you."

Is that snark I can hear in his tone? Gideon lifted his face to squint his eyes in irritation.

"I already know who I am and understand what I want and feel when it happens. You, on the other hand, are the one who didn't even know where his dick was. Once you figure out what you truly want, you must initiate. When you do, I can then lead."

Aleron parted his fangs to give a huff. "Why? You are the one who knows everything. How am I supposed to know what to do or say? I am not the human."

Gideon released one arm, trusting Aleron to support his backside, so he could grab one of his horns. He yanked it back, forcing Aleron to look at him. Then he jerked back to stop from bashing his own face when he discovered the Duskwalker could twist his neck the whole way around.

"There are terms and labels for it, but what I will explain is that I don't wish to take advantage of your naïveté. You are a big boy, and I can tell you're all grown up, but you lack insight. You even lack insight regarding your own body and desires. What if I hurt or confuse you? That isn't something I want just for my own selfishness."

As much as Gideon had worries that ached his heart, Aleron was the one who lack humanity. His needs and clarity were more important.

"That is a stupid reason," Aleron grumbled in a low voice, ripping his horn from his grip to turn his head forward. "You are needlessly making it confusing and hard."

"That's because it's complicated." He patted him on the top of the skull. "You'll figure it out, and we have plenty of time for you to do so."

Apparently, all of lifeless eternity.

This entire conversation had been enlightening for Gideon. The Duskwalker didn't need to tell him directly. The reminder had been enough.

"But I like you too," Gideon said, knowing he had to give Aleron something. He felt the confidence of that statement so strongly he didn't experience a shred of embarrassment. "Just figure out what you truly want. Make sure it's not because I'm the only human here with you, but because it's *me*."

"I am the only one with you also," Aleron stated back.

"Yeah, but my feelings don't make sense, which is why they make sense to me."

With a growl, and balancing Gideon with only one arm, he lifted a hand to point a sharp claw towards his nose. "You do not make sense, you confusing *fucking* human."

Ha! He's learning how to swear. How fun!

Gideon burst into a fit of laughter, which only made Aleron's growl deepen. "If you don't like it, you can put me down and go pout, you giant, overgrown feather duster."

"No," he barked. "You will stay there as punishment." Aleron did big bird stomps towards the exit of the cave, knees lifting high as his heavy feet slapped against the stone. "And what even is a feather duster?"

His chuckles only grew more persistent.

Hurry up, Aleron. I'll be waiting.

TEN

The feel of the human against Aleron's back popped each bubble of festering irritation with satisfaction. He fit there, slotted nicely between his heavy wings. If he chose to, he could easily cross them and trap Gideon forever.

Unfortunately, he was annoyed. Deeply annoyed, even.

I do not know how to approach him.

Gideon was hesitant. Any chance Aleron had at reaching out to him was often stolen by their conversations, the clumsiness of going around dense forestry, or his own worry. Unsettling worry that had been caused by Gideon, stirring questions he didn't have the answers to.

Why must my partner be female? This seemed to weigh on Gideon, but Aleron just didn't see the problem. He cared not for the gender of his bride, so long as they made him content. And this little human made him very content.

Well... usually. Currently, he was being a massive thorn in the side. Enough so that Aleron wanted to bash him over the head with the arch of one wing, so he could smack some sense into him.

But... he did say it is possible between two males. So why did Gideon have to make it so complicated?

I want to touch him again. He was eager to do so. *What if he pulls away from me? What if he asks all those stupid questions again?*

He was beginning to feel like his affection towards the human was... wrong. Not to Aleron – it just felt right – but from the world's perspective.

'What if I hurt you?' Why does he think this? He is small and feeble. I could easily crush him.

As Aleron continued to carry Gideon on his back while he crossed through the first area they'd ventured, and then up the tunnel to leave, his vision kept changing colours. One minute it was red in anger, then white in worry, to reddish pink in embarrassment – even though he didn't know why – and lastly, blue due to sadness. He didn't think he'd ever had this many sight changes all at once.

All the while, Gideon continued to chuckle on his back. His fur and feathers puffed with an intense thrill, happy to be the cause of it, and yet his skin tightened with strain. Was the human laughing at him or with him?

He ceased walking when something became apparent. *My head and chest hurt.* He wanted to whine at the emotions that toiled within him, as they finally snuffed the enjoyment he'd been feeling.

"Why'd you stop?" Gideon asked, his laughter dying.

Aleron couldn't answer, unsure why his feet didn't want to pass the very last strange lights within the tunnel. He attempted to piece together his muddled thoughts, but they unravelled like fraying twine he lost his bewildered clasp on. He hated the blank spaces within his mind; the missing fragments that made it obvious he was an incomplete creature.

At his silence, Gideon lowered his legs to be put down. He relinquished his hold on the human, letting him slide down when an uncomfortable weakness softened Aleron's muscles.

This unending day weighed on him. These unrelenting questions hammered him.

The source of his disquiet was the human male.

In his keeping, he had a confusing but alluring little beast. Every laugh Gideon produced ached his chest, every smile bruised him. The solemn look he often wore tried to swallow him whole, simply because Aleron didn't know how to fix it.

Gideon's personality often made him bigger than he appeared. Bright and warm, he could also be cool in a calming sort of way. Easy to laugh, willing to teach, and brave enough to fill the quiet when Aleron didn't know how.

He was patient, whereas Aleron lacked that temperament. He didn't know how the human could wait or hold back. Not when Aleron thought his impatience had turned into a parasite that threatened to eat him from the inside out.

He didn't even know *what* craving constantly struck him, yet a wave of *everything* told him to move, touch, taste, consume until he'd satisfied something.

His chest heaved with deepening breaths.

We are so different. He wondered if their differences in heart, mind, and body were the problem. Did Gideon desire him at all? Or was only Aleron lost in all this?

Over time, he'd slowly realised that Gideon had become the most mesmerising creature he'd ever seen. Somewhere along the line, Aleron had turned into a fuzzy moth, ever chasing this human's handsome, transfixing light. He started cherishing him in ways he utterly didn't understand, which hurt his chest. He craved expressing them. He wanted to let his instincts take over and lead him as they had his whole life.

Aleron worried if he were to try to instigate something with Gideon and was pushed away, he'd somehow hurt Gideon's spiritual body here with his claws by trying to keep him close. What if Aleron did something foolish and grabbed the human's soul in frustration and permanently harmed it?

"Hey," Gideon stated softly, attempting to gain his

attention without knowing that he already held *all* of it. He even reached forwards to grab his forearm from behind. "You can talk to me if it helps."

Aleron swiftly spun around as his sight finally chose a colour to remain. A sickening white invaded his vision of Gideon, just as the clogging emotion of it wrapped around his throat like a cord.

As Aleron looked down at the little human, his hands tingled and shook with frustration, his stomach dipping with uncertainty. All his muscles clenched in want, and even his wings tightened against his back.

Gideon turned his face to the side as he scratched his head, making his already messy light-brown hair more tangled. "I'm really not trying to confuse you, I promise. Like I said, communication—"

Of its own accord, Aleron's right hand lunged forward. Before he knew it, he gripped Gideon's entire jaw with his hand, quietened him, and tugged. He lowered his skull.

His heart burned at the startled expression in the male's eyes, the way they'd widened. How his lips parted on a shocked gasp.

But right now, he didn't want to communicate. He didn't know what to say, how to say it. Every fibre of his essence demanded action in order to appease the nasty creature Gideon had caused to grow within him.

Parting his fangs, he messily licked across Gideon's lips. That felt good – it felt *right.* Especially with the way the tiny hairs on his face tickled Aleron's tongue.

"W-wait," Gideon rasped, just as Aleron licked across his moving lips this time.

"No. No waiting," Aleron softly growled.

He told Aleron to initiate. So, here he was, initiating despite not knowing what the fuck he was supposed to be doing!

Yet, his prey backed up – trying to escape, to *flee*!

Aleron followed, incessantly licking at his mouth, his tongue *begging* to sink inside it like before. Within seconds, Gideon's back nudged up against the cave wall, which utterly satisfied the predator in him. Now he had nowhere to go, nowhere to run, and Aleron had happily caught his scampering beast.

"I told you to think about it!" Gideon yelled, pushing against his chest.

Aleron grabbed one of his hands and shoved it against the wall to capture it. The only thing keeping him calm was his sweeping tongue, as though it pacified him against the fight in Gideon.

It would be easier if he could truly sense the human. If he smelled of fear, he would have stopped. If his heart was quick with anxiety, he would have pulled away. Instead, he continued in the hope Gideon would eventually accept him. He wanted to lick away his uncertainty and have him melt again like back in the forest.

"Aleron," Gideon warned, and he noted the serious glare in his piercing green eyes. Their depths struck deeper than normal.

Aleron let out a lung seizing whine, as his sight changed to a deep blue. "You asked me to think, but I have already done so. You asked me to initiate, and yet when I do, you tell me to wait."

"Because I want to make sure—"

Aleron pulled back to stare down at Gideon, while a bubbling growl of frustration thundered in his throat.

"I am doing what feels right to me!" Aleron roared, causing Gideon to recoil in surprise. "I am following my instincts because I do not know how else to be. And this..." He licked across Gideon's mouth once more, and the roughness of hair and the softness of lips both scraped and soothed his tongue. "This feels good. This is what I want, and I desire to do this with you. I have craved it every second since I last did so."

As much as Aleron wanted to lean back down, he didn't. Because, right then, he knew Gideon would be in danger if he was to push away again, and Aleron didn't *want* to hurt him. Even if he could heal, Aleron didn't want to cause pain to the human male before him.

The frustration within him was evolving into desperation. If only he could articulate how he felt, could show it in a way that would make the human understand.

At first, Aleron had humoured the thought of making Gideon his bride simply because he thought it would be entertaining. He'd wondered how Ingram could choose a female over him, why his kindred would come all the way to the afterworld just for her. He wanted to know how he could... *leave* him in here, by himself, *alone*.

He was beginning to understand. He didn't like how heavy this burden weighed already, and yet he couldn't stop himself from wanting to *try*.

Every moment by Gideon's side changed him.

Somewhere along the way, he had inserted Gideon into his heart. Even though they could never actually share that eternal bond here in Tenebris, and it would always remain a wish no matter how much he hoped for it, Aleron wanted this human. By his side, in his wings, under his tongue, and in his hand.

He wanted the essence of a Mavka bond, even if they couldn't complete it. If Gideon were to forget him and disappear, he would search every corner for the male and convince him to be his companion once more.

That was what he knew, and all that mattered to him.

However, if all Gideon wanted was his companionship, then Aleron feared what that meant for himself. He didn't know if he had the strength to be by his side if Gideon didn't return his affection. It already hurt. Would that pain grow into an agonising wound if he gave up and just mindlessly wandered with him?

Aleron would follow, regardless. He'd just rather it wasn't one-sided.

Is this what Weldir meant when he said remaining with an unbonded human would eventually be painful?

"You said you cared for me..." Aleron uttered the words quietly as he watched Gideon's eyes flick over his skull. "But is this only how far?"

Was one touch all he was deserving of? Enough to teach him about his body, show him what desire was, only to scorn any more advances? Yes, he'd wanted to be taught, but hidden beneath that request had been the yearning to be closer to Gideon.

The couple they'd witnessed simply gave him the knowledge of what that entailed.

I want to see his face scrunch in pleasure again...

"No," Gideon finally stated, his shoulders relaxing. "It's not."

He pulled on the fur on the side of Aleron's neck to bring him closer. Even though it wasn't forceful, the Duskwalker clearly let himself be yanked to see what Gideon would do.

With his lips fluttering against one of Aleron's longest fangs, Gideon mumbled, "If this is what you truly want, then go for it."

Aleron's entire body pulsated at once. Just as Gideon opened his mouth to say something else, he darted his skull back so he could part his fangs and sink his tongue into the space between Gideon's lips and teeth.

He needed to be swift, to stop Gideon from changing his mind.

The moment his tongue brushed sideways across the top of Gideon's, and it pushed back in welcome, Aleron let out a contented groan. His orbs returned to their normal pink colouring. He cupped the human's scruffy jaw again and pulled down, parting it further to allow more of his tongue inside.

His invasion was welcomed, and his wings finally eased.

They drooped further when Gideon's fingers dived deeper into his fur as the little human's arm looped around the back of his neck.

Aleron's grip tightened on Gideon's other hand pinned against the wall, making rock chip away under his claws as they dug into the stone. As the textured wetness of their tongues greeted his senses, Aleron's hand slipped from his jaw, caressing his throat, before starting a path lower. He stepped closer, removing the space between them little by little.

I wish I could taste him. Aleron would have liked to drink from his mouth and swallow bits of his essence. *What would he smell like?* he thought, catching Gideon's shirt on his claws as he rubbed down the male's small torso.

He attempted to touch the human how he had once petted Aleron, to instigate desire in the way he'd been taught. It didn't feel as impactful through Gideon's clothes. Aleron was always naked, but even he knew there was a difference between touching over his fur or pushing down to the roots to stroke his flesh.

Just as Gideon's eyes grew lazy and softly closed, they clenched as he let out a hiss. Aleron hesitated, unsure if he'd hurt him by trying to dig his hand under his shirt, wanting to touch him without a barrier.

Perhaps the sharpness of his claws had nicked him.

Aleron tried to be gentler, fumbling with the edge of the material, only to receive a moan. Gideon arched forward into his hand, making the pressure of his claws and fingertips brush more forcibly against the skin between his hips.

He tried a new tactic, instead coming from the side where he could sweep his hand to the right. Once Aleron was underneath the fabric, and had curled his hand over the bare skin of Gideon's waist, he grew curious of the muscles flexing and dipping beneath his fingertips. Aleron traced up his back, marvelling at the dance of them, the way his spine indented.

That was until Gideon chomped on his tongue. Gideon leapt forward and stamped on his foot as a strangling noise broke from him. The sudden pain caused Aleron to flinch.

His tongue retreated as a growl broke from him.

"You bit me." His annoyance quickly deflated out of him, and he nudged the tip of his snout at the human's temple. "Am I hurting you?"

He probably should have ceased gliding his hand up Gideon's spine, but he was just too enamoured with the way he'd been gloriously formed right then to stop. His skin was smooth, cushioned by strong and plump muscles that made the centre of his spine dip in heavily. He'd never thought someone's back could be attractive, yet he was quickly learning just the simplest thing could make his cock twitch behind his seam.

"Your claws tickle," Gideon said with a shudder. "It's making my whole body sensitive."

"Is this a bad thing?" Aleron asked, dipping his skull to the side when he noticed the tip of Gideon's ear had turned pink. He licked over it.

"No!" he barked, tilting his head to the side as though to give him more surface to play with. Or perhaps the human was trying to evade him. "Fucking hell. I just don't think I've been touched this lightly before. Kind of feels weird, if I'm being honest."

His ears are sensitive. Aleron swirled his tongue over and around one of them again, and Gideon let out a low groan. *And he is not telling me to stop.*

Aleron continued to brush his 'tickling' claws and palm over Gideon's back, sliding down so he could come back around. At the same time, he repeatedly swiped his tongue while making a path down his neck.

Was Aleron doing this right? He didn't care. He was finally touching Gideon, and his caresses were welcomed.

Each stifled noise from the male, each choked sound he made as he gripped Aleron's fur tighter, like he attempted to rip it from him, had his cock swelling behind his seam.

"Can you sheath your claws?" Gideon pleaded, arching his chest into his palm before twisting as though to get away. "It's too much. I can't concentrate."

Aleron had figured out how to do this a little while ago, and he happily did as he was told. "Better?" he asked, resuming his caresses of Gideon's muscled chest with his rough palm.

His head fell forward, thumping against Aleron's chest, before he nodded. Tension eased out of him, only to make him twitch very noticeably when Aleron brushed his thumb over a tiny, hard bud.

"Like this?" Aleron asked, brushing over it back and forth, remembering how nice it'd felt when Gideon touched his own nipples.

"Mhm. Yeah." Gideon twisted his head side to side to nuzzle into his fur. "You're so soft. Even your feathers feel nice."

Like he wanted to demonstrate his appreciation, Gideon lowered his arm from his neck so he could rub his hand down Aleron's back. Slowly, Gideon drew it back up, and a surprised growl burst from Aleron. His body dipped forward at his fur and feathers being lifted in their opposite directions. The pressure was light, creating a pleasurable sensation, and he wondered if this was what Gideon meant by being tickled.

It instantly made his sight shift to purple, and the exploration of Gideon's little hand over his body fed desire into his veins. They were just petting each other, and yet Aleron's seam parted as he began to extrude from it. The moment it started, he didn't have a chance of holding himself back, his arousal swift under the power of this human.

Now that Aleron knew it was okay to touch, that his desire for more wasn't one-sided, and that he wasn't hurting Gideon, all his worries disintegrated.

Instead, heat ignited within like a roaring wildfire. One that wanted to set Aleron alight everywhere the alluring male touched him, and it threatened to consume him.

He finally let go of Gideon's pinned hand so he could cup the back of his head. He pulled it back and slipped his tongue between his inviting lips once more. Aleron was rougher this time as he swirled his tongue around Gideon's, more needy with his cock freely throbbing between them.

Perhaps it was to their benefit that neither one of them needed to breathe, as he doubted the human would have been able to. Aleron, on the other hand, let out excited snorting huffs over his cheeks.

More. He wanted more. To touch everywhere all at once, to shower this male in so many caresses that they confused him and left aches in their wake.

The groan that escaped Aleron was loud, intense, and followed by his entire body quaking when Gideon caressed his wing joint. Since both wings had drooped to the ground, that wing suddenly shot back and stiffened under his touch.

Gideon flinched in surprise and pulled his hand away, but Aleron desperately searched for the touch once more.

"Again," Aleron rasped, gliding his hand down his torso. He didn't know his wings were so sensitive. "It felt good, so do not stop."

He cupped Gideon's cock by sliding over it, finding it hard within his trousers. At the same time, the little human grasped the slick head of Aleron's while petting his wing joint, and they both groaned in unison.

He is aroused by this, by me. By his tongue, claws, and touch. Gideon was groping his cock and wing without hesitation, accepting what was different as he did the same in return.

And just knowing that... it had his heart feeling so light

in the freest of ways. It soared, like how he did in the false sky of this world. Aleron wanted it to fly until he came crashing back to land with release.

He shuddered at the thought, at the euphoria already washing over him. He grew more frantic.

"I considered not interrupting," a deep voice stated behind them, making them both freeze in each other's embrace. Gideon let out a startled, muffled yell around his tongue while letting go of his cock and wing to push at his chest. "But I'd rather you didn't do this here."

Aleron's lazy wings shot up when tension jolted him. He ripped his tongue from the bliss of Gideon's mouth, turned his skull to the right, and let out a rumbled warning at Weldir.

Folding his arms across his chest, his appearance like a translucent cloud all over, he narrowed his chalky brows. "Little one, did you just *snarl* at me?"

"Leave us," Aleron barked back, sliding his hand away from Gideon's groin to clutch his hip and draw him closer.

He was finally being gifted what he'd been aching for! He wouldn't let the spirit of the void get in the way of that. It'd been difficult just to get to this point with this human, and now his cock pulsated with deep desire and need.

"No, I don't think I will," Weldir stated, stepping back and gesturing towards the exit with a hand. "You both will quit trying to hump each other and leave this special place."

His answering growl as he shuffled towards Gideon earned Aleron a pulse from the cloudy form. Weldir's lips drew back to reveal sharp fangs.

"Aleron," Gideon called lowly, patting his chest. He turned his skull to him, finding his heated expression had turned cold, and rather panicked. "Sorry, bud, but the mood was just murdered."

How can one murder something such as a 'mood'? Ah, more of that tricky speech of humans.

With an annoyed huff, he made to retreat.

"Wait," Gideon whispered with a shaken voice, gripping the fur at his sides to stop him from going far. He turned his head down, showing Aleron the top of his hair. "Can you like... I don't know, put your dick away first?"

The tips of his ears were redder than they'd been before, and Aleron's sight darkened in its purple hue. The urge to pet them with his tongue again pestered him.

Instead, he looked down as well.

His cock jutted between them as a purple throbbing pole of arousal. The top two tentacles had looped around its girth, while the others wriggled to search for something to hold on to.

With its current engorged state, he doubted that it would go back inside him. Whenever it stiffened within him slowly, it sometimes, thankfully, got caught and stuck behind his seam. This time, however, he'd grown hard very fast. Even now he could tell the pressure of it wouldn't fit.

"It will not go back inside like this," he admitted, since last time it'd needed to soften before it would pull inwards.

"Cover yourself with a wing then?"

He didn't like that Gideon wouldn't look upon his skull and would rather stare off into the empty space to the left. But it seemed he didn't wish to look upon Weldir either.

"Why must I hide it?" Aleron asked, tilting his head.

"Because he knows I'd rather not see it," Weldir butted in, making his fur stand on end.

He wished the spirit of the void would get lost.

Fine. At least the problem was entirely because of his presence, and not because Gideon didn't want to see it.

He wrapped his wing forward, but also brought Gideon into it as well to shield him. With his back against Aleron's chest, he held Gideon tightly, even when the human stiffened from his hardened shaft slipping against his spine.

Just the simple contact had his hips giving a singular thrust. Gideon's back felt so good against him, he considered squeezing them tightly together and pumping his shaft.

"What do you want, Weldir?" Aleron snapped, instead.

Maybe if he got rid of him quickly, they could resume their intimate touching.

With his arms still crossed over his chest, he lifted his head back superiorly. Despite all of him being visible, the misty cloud of his form made it difficult to truly perceive his minor details. Sometimes it'd thicken where there was movement, like how his lips thinned or his eyes twitched.

"I never expected anyone to come here," Weldir stated, his face angling in the direction of the tunnel behind them. "How far did you go?"

"Not far," Gideon quickly butted in before Aleron could speak.

Weldir's eyes squinted mistrustfully. In all the time Aleron had been within Tenebris, Weldir had never been this... standoffish. He was actually rather playful with him.

"Then why am I catching such unsightly behaviour within my personal tunnels?"

Gideon shrugged in his arms. "Our conversation got a little heated, and the lights were distracting. Shit happens?"

Why is he lying?

"But–"

Before Aleron could state otherwise, he choked off his words in surprise when Gideon threw his elbow behind him and straight into his gut.

"Shut up," Gideon quietly hissed.

A few tense moments passed. Weldir sighed as he relaxed his arms before shaking his head. "Follow," he demanded, spinning around to head towards the exit.

Neither of them moved.

"Fucking hell," Gideon eventually stated with an exasperated sigh, his head leaning to the side. "I can't believe we were just cock-blocked."

"I do not wish to stop." Aleron leaned down to draw his tongue over Gideon's nape until he licked over the side of his throat. Then he reached down to cup Gideon's groin, disappointed that his cock had deflated.

His little human hissed through his teeth and flinched with his knees turning inward. "Shit. Don't grip my balls so hard."

Aleron immediately softened his hold, realising there was more to a male human's anatomy than just their dick. He hadn't seen any 'balls' last time, likely still tucked away, but he did feel small ovals against his fingers. A new place on Gideon to discover – especially since his reaction informed him they were sensitive.

Sensitive good, he hoped.

"Better?" he hummed out, refusing to move his hand.

He ground his still-hardened cock against Gideon's pretty back, wishing it had slipped under his shirt so he could have direct contact with him. Aleron's cock remained lubricated, and no matter how much air it was exposed to, it never dried. He'd successfully wetted the back of the shirt.

"This is so embarrassing. I feel like a teenager getting caught by a parent." The back of Gideon's head bumped against his chest as he turned his gaze upwards. "How can you still be hard after that?"

Was he supposed to be embarrassed? He didn't much care that they'd been 'caught,' only that they couldn't continue.

"I said follow," Weldir commanded, much more sternly than before. No longer within sight, his voice wrapped around them as though he spoke from everywhere.

"Let's go," Gideon grumbled, stepping forward. "I don't really want to see what happens when a demi-god is pissed off in his own realm."

Aleron huffed and stepped after him, refusing to let his prey leave the blanket of his wing.

Despite everything, joy did tingle his spine and ruffle his

tail feathers.

Gideon desires me. His orbs shifted to a much brighter pink than usual.

I am not alone in these tender feelings.

ELEVEN

Aleron kept Gideon close as they stepped into sunlight and greeted Weldir. Waiting for them in the clearing just beyond the mouth of the cave, the spirit of the void's expression was too blurry within his mist to make out.

It hadn't taken Aleron long to realise the title Weldir went by to be a grossly incorrect statement. They'd assumed his realm would be dark, like his mist within the Veil. Examining him in the brightness of the world he'd created, he could have been called the spirit of the everlasting day.

Rather cranky with his creator, he doubted his annoyance would fade. His erection had softened, though.

"I'm surprised to see this human still with you, little one," Weldir stated once they were close.

Little one. Weldir always called him and the other Mavka that. It was odd to be called something small, when currently Aleron stood near the same height as him, only half a foot shorter. It'd made more sense before, when he'd walked on all fours.

Aleron gave a growly huff and turned his head to the side dismissively. His claws sunk deeper into Gideon's arms, not in a way that was hurtful – he hoped – but securely.

He didn't know if Weldir intended to rip the male from him, but he wouldn't allow it.

"I slumber in order to recuperate my power, and nearly a month later I find you attached to him." He lifted an arm to give what appeared to be a half-hearted shrug. "In a place you should not have been, no less."

"A month?" Gideon's low voice held a wisp of surprise. "That's..." He brought a hand up to swipe his fingers through his hair. "That's how long we've been here together? Fuck, it feels like it's been forever."

Really? Aleron hummed.

He'd thought it'd been less than that. Then again, he'd already lived for quite a few years, so this passing of time felt minuscule for him. He didn't know how to count, but he'd seen the seasons repeat many times.

The balm of summer evolving into the wilt of autumn, only for the frost to whiten the world. Then spring would come, popping colours that danced on cool breezes. He'd always liked spring.

Spring brought comfort after the cold and dreariness of winter. It brought life and pleasantness.

He tilted his head down to Gideon. *He reminds me of spring.*

Then again, the human also reminded him of a tree with his brown hair and green eyes. He was as stubborn, unmoving, and strong as one, annoyingly so. The idea almost made him chuckle.

Gideon, the tree.

"I guess it does not matter. Whatever makes my child happy within this world," Weldir stated, breaking Aleron out of his ridiculous musings.

If that was his creator's way of stating his approval, it hadn't been needed. Aleron had no qualms about his choice, whether Weldir approved or not – and he wouldn't be moved from it. He didn't care what anyone thought, so long as Gideon remained by his side.

Weldir stood unmoving. He'd never been truly animated,

as though he lacked the urge to behave like a normal person. He even floated just a fraction off the ground, as if his presence here was just as fabricated as everything else.

"I have a task for you, Aleron."

He perked his head up in curiosity. "For me?"

Weldir turned his face to the side, but his expression remained dull.

"I would have preferred to ask Nathair, since he has more humanity than you, but he has been here so long he has lost his ability to speak," he explained, unknowing of how much his words hurt Aleron.

He had not been Weldir's first choice.

"Is this the serpent Mavka? Then why ask me at all?" Aleron snapped with a little more hostility than intended.

He didn't know he had a name, or perhaps he'd been told and forgotten. Either way, he would have preferred to know it before this.

"Because it must be a Mavka who I entrust this task to." Weldir brought his gaze back to them. "The Gilded Maiden has finally awoken, and in her growing strength, has unwittingly allowed me to feel her. I am unable to go to her – I cannot leave my realm or the mists on Earth – but someone must travel to the Elven world in my stead. I have a request of her."

Even though Aleron's body had once more swallowed his shaft, he likely would have stepped forward regardless, even if it hadn't. He unfurled his wing and brought it behind him as he let go of Gideon.

"Are... you saying I can *leave* Tenebris?" he asked in disbelief.

"Yes. You have always been able to leave, so long as I allow it."

At the weight of this knowledge, unbridled rage slashed across his torso like a nasty claw strike. His sight flared crimson, while a growl tore from his throat. Even his wing feathers puffed, making him appear larger and more frightening than before.

"If I have always been able to leave, then why did you keep me here?!" Aleron shouted, digging his claws into his palms. He threw them forward when the desire to slash across Weldir's intangible form struck him – yet he knew trying would prove futile. "I could have been with Ingram all this time!"

Weldir, unfazed by his anger or his swift approach, did nothing but meet his orbs. He looked down at him.

"Yes, you could have haunted your kindred," Weldir stated coolly. "And, in doing so, would have tortured each other."

His skull jerked at that. "What do you mean?"

"I'm not sure if you noticed it or experienced it as well, but Ingram was distressed when he was unable to touch you or Emerie. That is what would have awaited you both had I allowed you to go back to the living world. I can't give you a physical form, therefore you would have been a Ghost who wandered by your kindred's side."

An acute whine whistled out of him. "But I would have been *with* him."

Not a moment had passed in Tenebris that he did not miss his kindred. Every second his chest ached to be by his side, even if he felt other wonderous things with Gideon.

He'd long ago accepted that they could not be together right now, but that didn't stop the cold in his chest. He thought of it like a shard of ice that constantly gave him frostbite in his heart.

"Ingram can touch the earth, but all you would have been given was your sense of sight and hearing. You would not have experienced anything else. You would have watched him grow without you, experience the fullest of life without you, and you would have been the one who was truly tormented."

"I would not have minded," he argued.

He would have accepted any sort of punishment for leaving his kindred behind. His failure to protect him and himself that day often stung him. Had he been quicker... had he been smarter, stronger. Had he been able to *fly*... none of this would have happened.

Had his love for his twin not kept him on the ground, he could have saved them *both*.

Aleron often held regret for that.

All along, he had wings. He could have taken them anywhere, escaped any fight.

Instead, his negligence meant they were apart. He'd hurt his kindred, and himself. They'd lost each other.

Just as another pain-filled whimper threatened to break from his chest, a small and barely warm hand touched at the crease of his palm. He darted his skull down to Gideon, who attempted to poke the pads of his fingers between the large spaces of his own.

Suddenly, the growing ache in his chest softened.

"You would have minded," Weldir rebuffed. "I know better than anyone what it is like to be in that world and not be a part of it."

Aleron glanced back at his creator, and witnessed him stare down at his palms as he opened and closed his misty hands.

"I also know how lonely it is to be by someone's side and not be able to feel them, smell them, taste them. It rots you from the inside out, and it is a special form of agony. One which lingers in a heart you do not even have. A million words can't replace a single, silent action." Then, in a bid to make Aleron truly understand, he lifted his gaze and stated, "Like bringing down the comforting weight of your wing on your kindred when he needs it most."

"But–"

"He's not wrong, Aleron," Gideon added from beside him. "Maybe you don't realise it, but you speak with your wings a lot. If they are an integral part of how you communicate, being unable to use them to express yourself would make things hard."

He thought that may be true. Even now he had the longing to wrap one around Gideon. He'd spent many nights holding Ingram within the cocoon of them, and it had always felt right.

He likely would have missed it and felt the tingling ache to draw him into them. The constant denial likely would have weighed heavily on his conscience.

He remained silent, unsure if this revelation brought him comfort or not. He would have liked to have tried, rather than leaving Ingram completely on his own.

Maybe I could have stopped him from going to the Demonslayers. He could have prevented all the suffering he went through and perhaps continued to guide him – even in an empty existence.

He wouldn't have met Emerie, but Aleron didn't know if he cared. The Ingram he'd last seen was an internally wounded version of his other half. Even if he'd only been a purple spectre, he knew him well enough to know the sad notes of his deep voice, or the unsettled curl of his lizard tail tip.

Then again... I would not have met Gideon either, he thought, glancing at his little human.

And, if he were being truthful, the lack of his scent bothered him greatly. He wanted to taste him, and he knew the warmth they shared between each other to be only a fraction of what it was supposed to be. Things *were* missing, important things that mattered.

He'd just accepted them because there was no other way, but it did nag at the back of his mind. His instincts told him something was amiss, but he chose to ignore it.

Is this what Weldir meant when he told Ingram that being here with his human would eventually feel... wrong? Although their relationship felt the complete opposite of wrong, would these missing things eventually have grown thorns? *I thought he only meant that the human could lose their memories, or that not being able to bond with them would be distressing.*

But was it more than that? How long would it be before Aleron could no longer handle the lack of true life, the depth of it, with another person? The more he thought on it, the more it itched at his skin and twisted his stomach.

He was glad Gideon was next to him for this. The tiny gesture of his hand brought him solace and made it easier to swallow his explanation than Weldir's. Just his presence stopped his skull from lowering in sadness and defeat.

"What I need is for you to ask the Gilded Maiden for a single tear," Weldir stated, bringing them all back to his request. "I have not been back to Nyl'theria since the Demons were brought to Earth, but I will try my best to transport you to Lezokos, the Elven city."

Gideon's brows furrowed tightly and his nose wrinkled on one side. "Wait, so Elves *actually* exist?"

Weldir ignored him. "Once you are at the gate, their ward will not allow you through. Demons will be unable to harm you, so you are able to linger for however long you need until they allow you entry. I have an inkling that Merikh is there, and I have faith he will aid you."

"Merikh?" Aleron asked, cocking his head. "Is this where he disappeared to?"

"Yes. A female Elf took him there."

"You speak of Raewyn." Joy radiated in his chest at the reminder of his Elven friend. Only for it to die when he realised the difficult task bestowed upon him. He pointed a claw in Weldir's direction. "Merikh will not aid me. He is hateful."

Weldir's lips thickened with wisps of chalkiness, making them more noticeable as they spread. He gave a fanged grin.

"Women are powerful creatures. I've watched them enough to know my most bull-headed child can easily be swayed by her."

A small chuckle escaped Aleron. "It is true he was rather protective and possessive of her."

He remembered how the bear-skulled Mavka ushered him and his kindred away with dark-green orbs. A detail he'd missed then, that now became enlightening since his own sight had shifted to that colour due to Gideon.

"If you request that they help you greet the Gilded Maiden on my behalf, they are not allowed to interfere. This is a matter of deities, regardless that I am a demi-god. You are my vassal and messenger, and if they still follow the customs of the old ways, they must let you request an audience with her directly. It will be purely her decision as to whether or not she agrees."

"Why a tear?" Aleron asked curiously.

There was no question of why he should help. He cared deeply for his creator, especially after all he had done for him when he first came to Tenebris.

Without him, Aleron would have been horribly lost. He would have eaten many souls, gained their memories, and let it mingle with his rage and pain until he became a mangled, insane creature.

Weldir let out a small sigh. "The reason doesn't concern you. She will understand, and that's all that matters."

He tossed his skull side to side with a huff, annoyed his question wasn't answered.

"Fine. When will we go?"

"We?" His mist pulsed as he cocked his head. "This task is for you, and you alone."

With a small rumble, his wing whooshed as he extended it and wrapped it around Gideon. He also brought his arm down around him, cupping his hip to draw him deep into his side.

"Then no." The rejection easily fell from him, especially when just the idea of this human's absence left him numb. "I will not leave Gideon here. I will not have him forget."

"I can keep him conscious in your stead, if it is that much of an issue."

"No," Aleron refused again. "He comes, or I do not go at all." Then, just in case Weldir intended to lie, he pointed his claw at him. "If it is possible for me to go as a Ghost, it means a human can as well. Our existences here are the same, and you already told me once that we are anchored to you."

"Yes, but I must sacrifice much of my power to stop myself from calling you back here against my own will. That will be doubled with the human, and I have only just regained consciousness after expending much of it. I am not strong right now."

"Then we will try later," Aleron offered.

For the second time in Aleron's existence within Tenebris, the world violently shook. A result of the silent rage of the powerful being before him, who lowered his head with a glare darkening his blurred expression. His upper lip curled back over his fangs.

He hadn't been the source of ire last time, but Weldir had explained why the world trembled when he questioned him on it. It was difficult to miss when the world quaked and rumbled beneath his hands and feet.

Aleron simply lifted his head up and away dismissively.

Weldir would never harm him. He'd already shown he had a soft spot for Aleron and the other Mavka here. He could growl, hiss, and threaten, but it would be as empty as when Aleron had done those things to Ingram.

Everything grew quiet and unsettled. Then, Weldir let out a huff.

"Impudent child. You are lucky my patience has run its course." He threw his hands up in defeat. "Fine, take the human with you. However, you risk the games of the Gilded Maiden. Don't blame me for your own choices."

"Is no one going to ask if I actually want to go?" Gideon

stated while folding his arms across his chest. "Maybe I don't want to meet some Elven gods."

"You do not wish to come with me?" Aleron asked with his sight shifting to blue and turning to him. He let it deepen.

As soon as Gideon looked upon his skull, his lips thinned and he averted his gaze. "I never said that." His eyes darted back to his skull until their gazes met before he looked away again. His arms tightened across his chest, causing his biceps to flex. "It's not fair when you do that."

Aleron wished he could have kept them blue, but they too easily shifted to yellow as humour struck him. He let out a chuckle. He didn't know he could easily manipulate the male with such a saddened expression of his orbs.

His wings fluttered in delight at discovering that.

TWELVE

Gawking up at the dense canopy above that didn't allow even a shred of light to touch the ground, Gideon couldn't believe trees could be so colossal. Or that leaves could be blue and pink.

How old are these trees? He estimated they were at least three hundred metres tall, maybe taller. He could already tell the ones shading them weren't the biggest. *It'd take me a year to cut one down.* He'd need an infinite number of axes.

His body would give out before a single tree could be cut.

Just one would likely be enough to not only wall off a town, but build the entirety of it.

A 'twig' would be taller than him. A few of the fallen leaves decaying against the ground were large enough to drape over a double bed. If one fell on top of him, he'd likely be crushed under it – if he were not intangible.

The trees mostly had bright-blue leaves, but their bark was such a deep, dark colour of red. All the trunks were covered in thick, melting sap that bled through the scale-like joints of bark. *Sap can be used as sweeteners, teas, and sometimes even glue.*

If strong enough, even the silk within leaves could be used to make clothing, bedding, carpets, and more.

Just one tree alone could vastly increase the livelihood o

an entire town. No one would go cold, without clothing, or a home. Too bad it was within the Elven world.

Gideon couldn't help marvelling at the one nearest him. *I have the urge to climb it. I wonder if I would get above the clouds if I did.*

When he brought his eyes back down, he didn't even need to crouch to examine an otherworldly flower. Spellbinding and *glowing* red petals surrounded an even brighter yellow centre. It looked like a hibiscus flower, just without a pollen stem. Black droplets clung to its petals and the dull-blue stem that held it perky.

The shrub came to his chest height, and a single bloom would have needed to be held in both hands to support it, had he been able to touch anything.

The flower's colouring gave him the impression it was poisonous until a fuzzy insect buzzed closer. It collected its glowing yellow pollen before taking a sip of a black droplet. Fascinated, Gideon watched the creature, a green fuzzy moth with the head of some kind of animal – a cat perhaps – take off to flutter around another flower.

Most of the other plant life, like the leaves and grass, was teal.

They'd been warned by Weldir that he may not be able to take them directly to the Elven city, and they may come across Demons. Of course, they had nothing to fear, but it was remarkable that such a mystical world could exist.

He'd claimed it was even more overrun with Demons than Austrális, yet it appeared so peaceful.

Some type of bird chirped in the distance, and a different kind of insect buzzed its wings just beyond view. Everything swayed with a slow and lulling motion, the wind gentle as it rustled leaves and clacked branches together.

"I see the top of a magical barrier this way," Aleron said, pointing in the distance.

Gideon couldn't see shit, but he trusted Aleron's

instincts. He was a Duskwalker, who likely had superhuman sight, so why should he argue with him?

Like always, they subconsciously reached for each other's hand.

Regardless of the fact that Weldir was using his magic to stop them from teleporting back to Tenebris, Gideon would still lose his memories if they didn't continue to touch. He'd just fall into a trance where he stood in the middle of this world and have to wait for Aleron to complete his task before he was called back. Probably to that dreary and heartbreaking canyon of lost, sleeping souls.

I really don't want to go there. He subconsciously squeezed Aleron a little tighter. *I don't want to leave him.*

It didn't take long to break past the tree line and step into an open field. Long, teal stalks dipped and waved, rippling with the wind, as if the earth had suddenly turned to water. They walked forward, and the grass merely passed through their intangible forms.

Oddly enough, none of this truly... surprised Gideon. A lot had happened to him already, and he'd learnt so much in such a short amount of time. Everything he did now seemed to be new. He'd become resilient in his ever-changing death.

Gideon took in the surprisingly beautiful scene before them. Before them lay a city that looked bleached by the three different-coloured suns that bore down on it. One blue, one green, and the smallest one a yellowish red.

A massive central tree, larger than any other within the realm from what he could tell, stood like a living beacon. Pink-and-purple leaves swayed as they cast dappled light over half the city. The white trunk appeared to be stained with melting grey, similar to how dust and grime did the same to the side of old buildings due to rain.

The architecture had been built within the very branches and roots of the tree. The roots themselves waved in and out of the ground like a network of veins, where buildings had been created as though from the very wood itself, burrowing into and around them.

The rest of the city, further out from the central tree, had been built from bark or a cream stone. The walls around it spanned hundreds of metres tall and detracted from the beguiling beauty of the Elven city.

It looked like a fortress, designed to never let anyone or anything in or out. A pretty cage of stone walls.

Thankfully, colour flirted everywhere. Although some houses had glass dome ceilings, those without had been painted in an array of different colours. From afar, it made the city look playful and festive. Many banners hung from bronze poles, flapping more colour like they wished to hide all the bleached white.

All throughout, as if melted into the side of every home and business, shone molten ore – silver, gold, and more bronze.

At first glance, the city appeared rich in taste, affluent, and even clean.

The central tree cast shade over the middle of the area, and the high walls also created a fair bit around the perimeter, depending on where the three suns were positioned in the green sky. The longer he stared, the more the sky slowly changed to purple, and the shadows moved.

Gideon then took in the sparkling water from some kind of sea or ocean, and the beach that connected to the city itself. At least the water had a normal dark-blue tinge to it, despite the sand itself sparkling as if with some kind of crystal shards.

It was hard to ignore the translucent, oil-slick bubble surrounding the entire circumference of the city. A barrier, which, despite its beauty, revealed their fear of the world beyond.

"To be honest, I half expected the world to look ghostly," Gideon stated with a laugh. "Like we wouldn't be able to perceive it properly."

Aleron dipped his head to him, but said nothing. His orbs were a dark yellow, though. He must be just as deep in thought as they took in this new environment.

"I feel like we stepped onto another planet." Maybe they did. "Everything is so tall – I'm wondering if maybe the Elves are giants."

"Giant? Is that like a human that is the size of the trees here?" Aleron asked, and Gideon nodded. "No, they are not very big."

Gideon hummed at that, a little relieved. He didn't particularly want to be inspected as though he were a tiny mouse.

They walked down a subtle decline parallel to a wide river. Fishlike creatures breached the rushing water, jumping in and out as if they were playing. He couldn't truly identify them, as they weren't close, but they looked rather... furry.

If Elves aren't giants, then why the hell are their gates so damn tall? Gideon thought when they came upon them.

He shielded his eyes from the suns as he looked upwards. It was pointless. They also shone through his hand anyway, making him look transparent, even to himself.

Made of white wood, swirling patterns of gold, silver, and bronze frolicked over the sealed entrance, as if the inhabitants wanted to decorate it and make it less dreary. The design formed a tree with its roots encompassing a seed that had some kind of Elvish writing within it.

"Should we knock?" Gideon asked, pursing his lips.

"We can just pass through," Aleron stated, stepping towards the gate.

With a deep thud, the end of his snout bashed against the barrier, which blocked him from moving through it, then the rest of his face and body impacted. Bouncing backwards, he rubbed at his snout. He shook his bony head, and the sound of dry, rattling bones came from him.

"That hurt," Aleron whimpered.

Gideon stifled the urge to chuckle by coughing into his

fist, mainly because watching his head almost retreat into his shoulders had been rather hilarious. Plus, the pain was sure to fade quickly and wouldn't be lasting.

Aleron then slammed his fist against the barrier. Instead of a thud, it rippled, and Gideon's head twitched when he thought he heard it... ring? Every time Aleron hit it, a gentle, high-pitched tune came from it like wind chimes.

Within seconds, the rich metal ores on the gate sprung to life. Unknotting their interlocking patterns, they receded like water being sucked backwards. The seam of the double doors was revealed as they cracked open, allowing the sunlight from behind them to flood over Aleron and Gideon.

The barrier never disappeared nor allowed them through, even when the doors had fully opened inwards. However, a new bubble grew out from the barrier to surround them.

By Aleron's hand tightening around his own, he figured the big Duskwalker was uneasy about being trapped. Gideon, on the other hand, surmised its true purpose. It was to ensure their safety, had a Demon approached to attack, as it would likely follow the protective shade of the fortress walls to do so.

On the other side of the threshold were two soldiers, who approached holding the strangest spears he'd ever seen. He thought they may actually be some kind of glaive, as the blades came down the first quarter of the poles. At the base of each blade, where it connected to the white pole, was an intricately decorated ribbon – blue on one spear, and the other's was red.

Like the door, swirling and knotted patterns danced along the seams of their armour, which looked more ornamental than battle attire. At first glance, it appeared to be metal painted in muted white. Yet, when one twisted to glance at her companion through a winged helmet, the armour folded and crimpled as though malleable.

The only visible parts of the soldiers were their faces and

the underside of their hands. They both had dark-brown skin, but he noted it lacked any of the pink or olive undertone in humans, and appeared to be grey instead.

I wonder if they have pointed ears, like in storybooks.

They spoke to each other in a language he'd never heard before – and one he could never begin to describe. It was musical, gentle in its tones, and soft-spoken.

"I have a task from Weldir," Aleron explained, stepping back from the barrier. "He wishes for us to speak to the Gilded Maiden."

Gideon couldn't help but peek at Aleron, whose shoulders were tense, and his feathers puffed. Perhaps to most eyes and ears, Aleron would have sounded loud, confident, and even a little... arrogant. Especially with his head lifted up, his shoulders rolled back, and his wings flared, as though he wanted to be daunting.

He's trying to look frightening. His eyes crinkled with humour that mingled with tenderness. *But I know he's a big, soft teddy.*

Gideon could get behind that. He often put up a front when first meeting people. He liked to come across as over-confident and suave, when really, he was actually a giant goofball when given the chance.

After Aleron spoke, their eyes grew wide in unmasked shock, the man's mouth falling. They darted their faces to each other, and their conversation became rushed.

The man ran off, leaving the woman behind, who flattened her hand out as though for them to wait. Apparently, a multi-universal gesture.

Gideon thought about giving a thumbs up, but decided against it in case it was the equivalent of giving the middle finger to these people. Instead, he nodded.

He turned to Aleron and then tightened his features on one side.

"I'm not sure what you want me to do." Gideon attempted to straighten his clothing, even brush it of non-existent dirt, worried he suddenly appeared unkept. He swept his fringe back and grew annoyed when most of it fell forward across his brow. "I don't plan to interfere, since this is your thing. I just agreed to come along for moral support."

"Your presence is all I need to be at ease," Aleron said, causing a wonderfully painful ache of tenderness to swell in Gideon's chest. The Duskwalker lifted his snout in the direction of the waiting soldier before bringing it back to him. "I am... I have not done many things on my own. I always had my kindred by my side. It shames me to admit that I am nervous I will make a mistake."

Gideon's eyes crinkled with humour again. "I thought you only wanted me to come because you didn't want to be lonely."

"This too." Aleron squeezed his hand once more. "As much as I trust Weldir to keep his promises, I wanted to keep you by my side for my own peace of mind. I would like your help if I cannot explain my task properly, or if... I get frustrated that I cannot do so."

Rather than feeling sympathetic to Aleron, pride puffed Gideon's chest. Aleron was honest, whereas most would rather not share their shame regarding the places they thought they were lacking. He knew Aleron's intelligence to be low, yet he had all the internal strength to bravely admit that, even when his orbs turned a reddish pink in either shame or embarrassment.

"I want to be you when I grow up," Gideon stated with a chuckle, hoping to ease him.

Gideon knew he'd only confused him when Aleron tilted his head. "But you are already grown."

His lips parted in a wide grin. "I'm saying I admire you for saying that. It takes a courageous person to admit their flaws. Not even I can do that, but I wish I could. I wish I could be transparent about who I am, without fear of being judged."

"But I would not judge you," Aleron stated. "And I trust that you will not blame me either."

His grin softened into a warm smile. *At this rate, he's going to scoop my heart right out of my chest.* Well, if he had a heart.

To fill in the passage of time as they waited, Gideon attempted small talk with Aleron to distract him from his nervousness. He pointed to the sky, the three suns, and then what they could see further inside the city.

Aleron's shoulders eventually loosened, and he stopped crushing Gideon's knuckles together.

That was, until a daunting creature, as wide as he was tall, made his way down the long hallway of the fortress walls.

Gideon hissed when he thought his fingers would pulverise. *Jeez, Aleron.* He didn't complain, knowing the pain radiating up his finger joints would fade the moment he let go again.

Behind the stomping massive form, a trail of soldiers gallantly followed, all wearing the same armour as the two who appeared earlier.

To his left were two men also dressed in armour, yet one had a dark-blue tunic robe covering his torso with a silver tree stitched into it. The other wore a similar one, although green. Neither wore a helmet, and he only just noticed that their boots were so malleable that they were like a second skin.

To his right, a willowy woman wearing a pale-lavender dress that revealed as much as it hid, gracefully sauntered by his side.

Her cleavage was modest, with most of it hidden in the crossing vee, but her arms were free. Wide, flowing cloth ribbons hung from the backs of her shoulders and danced with the skirt as all the gauzy material skimmed over the ground. Through the tasteful yet daring cut of her dress, her legs became visible all the way to the hip on each step, revealing strange, soleless shoes.

Bronze and golden bangles clinked and chimed together as she moved. Three on her right ankle, and one on her left, while many more adorned her wrists. Golden leaves had been woven into the long fringe of her snow-white hair, which had been intricately braided six times over the crown of her head before falling loose. Half up and half down, tight coils fluttered with each of her steps.

One thing Gideon noticed was the possible Elven quality between all these people. Their ears truly were long and pointed. They all had white hair, and despite the differences in darkness of their brown skin, they all had the strange inhuman grey undertone to it. Yet, their other features were so distinct that it was easy to tell them apart – like the shape of their noses, lips, chins, brows, and eye shape and colour.

Their heights and weights varied, although they mostly appeared willowy except for the man in green.

The woman even had dark freckles cutely scattered across the bridge of her nose and cheeks, with a little beauty mark under her right eye. Other than the approaching Duskwalker in the middle, she was the tallest, and the only one holding some kind of cane.

Her pupils glowed with a white starburst, and were encased by rich, molten-brown irises.

So this is Merikh, Gideon thought, remembering his features from the statue within Weldir's private cave.

He couldn't figure out if he should be disturbed or in awe of him.

His white bear skull looked even more ferocious than Aleron's, with the claw marks going down his right eye hole. His tall bull horns were a sandy brown, but arched over his head like a menacing crown. A bright-red silk tunic rested over his plump torso, but looked perfectly fitted for his rounded stomach and chest. It was sleeveless, and below it he wore black trousers tied just below his knees, revealing bare, humanoid feet tipped with claws.

Short black fur covered all of his body, and unlike Aleron or Ingram, the only bone visible on him was his skull.

Strapped across his forearms, calves, and back were guards like the flexible white metal the Elven soldiers wore.

Surprisingly, he appeared to be half a foot shorter than Aleron, but that didn't stop him from looking any less menacing.

When they all halted just beyond the barrier, a bull tail flicked behind him and he peered at them with bright-red orbs. He folded his meaty arms across his massive chest, assuming a posture that came across as standoffish.

Silence bled between them, heavy and uncomfortable. Everyone waited with bated breath for the other to speak.

Aleron grew the courage to step forward. "Merikh–"

Merikh's orbs brightened in their crimson hue.

"What the *fuck* happened?" he snapped out, his voice even more booming and deeper than Aleron's. He half-unfurled an arm to point a claw at Aleron as his chest rapidly heaved with agitated breaths. "You're pink, like a spectre, like how I started to turn when I visited Weldir's realm. How did it happen? How did you die?"

This is the reaction he has to learning his brother died? Gideon thought with disgust. *What a fucking jerk.* The least he could have done was be gentler or nicer about it. Instead, he'd come across as superior and accusatory.

In his peripheral, Gideon noted how Aleron's head lowered and his shoulders turned inward. "The Demon King ordered for Mavka to be attacked. We were overrun by a horde, and I did not survive it."

Merikh's large, meaty hands clenched and unclenched as tension visibly shook them. Then he slapped one over his skull, snarling, *"Fuck."*

Within the gaps of his thick, dark-grey fingers, Gideon

swore blue flickered in the darkness behind them. Yet, when he lowered his hand to cup the bridge of his snout, his glow was red once more.

He turned to the man on his right, and the man's tied-back, shoulder-length hair swayed as he faced Merikh. With a dull expression, he allowed the Duskwalker to tower over him.

"You! You little fucking shithead," Merikh cursed, jamming at his armoured chest with a claw. "I should bash your skull in for this. Had you not–"

"Merikh, please," the woman to his right pleaded as she tentatively reached out for his arm – only to miss and try again. It was then that Gideon realised she had a visual impairment, when that should have been obvious by the cane looped around her wrist. "Who is it?"

Merikh turned to the woman, and likely noticed her scrunched-up, concerned features. Her white brows were terribly furrowed, her full lips pouting and pressed together in tension. He immediately calmed as he dropped his arm back to let her hold it. The other hand lifted to palm down the length of his bear skull.

"Aleron," he uttered quietly, his tone softening decimals for her.

Her brown eyes, framed by long, curling white lashes, swiftly brimmed with tears. She faced towards them, and the starbursts in her eyes – as though they replaced her pupils – glittered at them.

"Hello, Raewyn," Aleron greeted gently, lowering himself as she approached, with Merikh shadowing behind her.

Gideon released Aleron's hand to let him move towards them without getting in the way.

"I'm so sorry," she sobbed, placing her hand on the barrier while wiping one of her cheeks with the side of her wrist. "We were going to mine some mana stones now that

Merikh is here, but we are too late for you."

"It is okay. It is not your fault, so you do not need to apologise." He placed his hand on the barrier, right where hers was, when a louder sob broke from her. "Please do not cry, little Elf."

"But it hasn't been that long since we left Earth," she stated, before slightly turning her head to Merikh when he placed a comforting hand on her shoulder. "It should have only been seven months since then. I never expected this to... Oh my gosh!" She gasped as she faced Aleron once more. "Where is Ingram? Is he okay?"

Aleron let out a small but weak chuckle. "Ingram is alive, and with his bride. Emerie is very sweet."

"He's not alone?" Merikh asked. "I'm surprised to learn he's found a bride already."

"Much has happened. I did not know you came to this place with Raewyn." Aleron stood and stared down at the shorter Duskwalker, who appeared to be only a foot taller than Gideon. "We thought you went back to the surface."

"Did you two make a mess of my cave?" His tone lacked bite, but there was an inkling of displeasure.

Funnily enough, Aleron lifted his skull up and to the side. "I have no idea what you speak of. Your books and ornaments are exactly how you left them."

Gideon stifled a snorted laugh behind a cough, unable to help himself at Aleron's obvious lie. This only brought attention to his presence.

He would have stiffened, if it weren't for the fact he was insignificant in all this. Gideon was just a bystander and nothing more. He would aid Aleron if he needed it, but there was no point in him inserting himself into the conversation otherwise.

Aleron, being his usual, easily distracted self, leapt towards him. Gideon flinched in surprise and dug his heels into thin air when he was pushed forward to be displayed.

"This is Gideon, my human companion I found in

Tenebris." The joy in Aleron's voice was accompanied by his wings and tail vibrating, his feathers whooshing and flapping. "He is Emerie's brother, and we have bonded during our time together. He has taught me much."

Like an awkward idiot, suddenly wishing he could disappear, he waved. "Sup? Nice to meet you all."

Now that he was closer, he had to crane his neck back to even face Raewyn, who stood over half a foot taller than him. True, she wasn't a giant, but she was a big lady in comparison to him.

Merikh paid him absolutely no notice, directing his skull to the woman at his side. "Since they are Ghosts, I don't see their entry as problematic, correct?"

Raewyn gave a singular nod. "Since they can't harm anyone, I don't see that being an issue. But..." Her full lips tightened. "We must know why you have come here. As a councilmember, I can answer as to whether or not there is a chance for approval."

"Weldir has given me a task. He wishes for me to speak to the Gilded Maiden on his behalf."

"Then no," Merikh quickly snapped. "Tell that useless demi-god to rot in his realm. Whatever he seeks–" He let out a weak choke when Raewyn smacked him in the gut with the back of her arm.

"That's not how it works," she stated with a sigh, rolling her strange eyes.

"But it's Weldir!" Merikh gestured towards the stone hallway where the rest of the city lay beyond it. "The other councillors almost forbid me from staying here due to my tie to him."

"Yes, but this is different. Although indeed concerning." She cupped her chin in deep thought. "There are rules we must obey. One of which is: anyone seeking to speak with our deities with good reason must freely be given the right to formally request an audience with them. Not doing so can result in divine punishment. It has not been unheard of that another god has been locked out of the Nyl'therian realm, so we must allow them to communicate when they desire it."

"I'd rather not give him anything he wants," Merikh bit out. "Damn the rules. I told you how I feel about him."

Raewyn winced before reaching up to hold his skull in her hands. Gideon frowned when Merikh plonked its weight into her awaiting palms. He hadn't expected the aggressive Duskwalker to show any kind of open affection or vulnerability before them.

Instead of being sweet, she giggled as she said, "Too bad." He lightly growled at her for it, only to snort out a huff a second later. "This is what is done here, Merikh. Also, don't you want to spend time with your brother?"

"You should know the answer to that ridiculous question," Merikh grumbled, licking at the inside of his mouth in irritation. "You know the only person I truly wish to speak to is you." Then, he quickly added, "And Lehnenia."

"We still need to work on your social skills."

Once more, he huffed, but he also rolled his head out of her palms – much like how one might have rolled their eyes.

Gideon had intended to stay quiet, but when Aleron's wings drooped slightly at Merikh's reaction to him, a ball of hot iron lit up in his gut.

"The fuck is your problem?" Gideon barked up at Merikh, stomping forward until he was right at the barrier. "In the few minutes we've been here, you've been an absolute jackass to Aleron. He's your family. The least you could do is show a shred of kindness towards your own brother."

Finally, Merikh regarded him.

Gideon narrowed his eyes into a slicing glare, greeting him head-on. At his side, his right hand curled into a tight fist when the desire to clock the bastard across the face struck him.

"I'll have you know, human, that I take great pride in being the biggest prick any world has ever seen. I have little fondness for my own kind, and a deep hatred for yours."

Then Merikh lowered himself so he was leaning on his knees. Somehow, the stance made Gideon feel like he was being spoken down to like a child. As though he were inferior, small, and weak.

His voice was low and quietly unnerving as he stated, "I have no doubt your reasons for being here are less than noble. Are you hoping that if you assist Weldir, he will grant you life? You put your faith in a self-absorbed devil, human. Taking advantage of one of my kind, who has already proven he is rather fond of you and has little humanity to realise your impure intentions, is even more despicable. If you were alive, I would have already ripped your tiny little head from your feeble body."

Before Gideon could yell back to dish out his well-deserved outrage, Aleron's wings and arms were around him. He lifted him off the ground, tucked him against his chest, and jerked to the side to shield him as though he were a stuffed toy. He let out a beastly growl, and the vibration and depth of it rumbled them both.

"You will not threaten my human," Aleron barked, snapping his fangs at him. "I asked him to come here. Even with a bride, I see you have not changed."

Fighting to get free, Gideon yanked a wing down so he could raise his fist to Merikh as he unfurled himself from his feathery cocoon. "If I were alive, I'd hammer a stake through that hard head of yours. Then you could go suffer in the very realm belonging to the father you so obviously hate."

As though the idea of Gideon attempting that truly humoured him, Merikh's orbs flared bright yellow. He gave a deep, dark chuckle.

Sensing he intended some kind of cruel response,

Raewyn stamped her foot next to him and gestured to the soldiers behind them, grabbing his attention. "Stop it, Merikh. There are people watching, some of whom are still getting used to your presence."

He rolled his head. "They cannot understand English, Raewyn. All they know is that we are having a disagreement, one which I can state was in protest of Weldir." He folded his arms across his broad chest. "You know that would work in my favour."

She threw her hands up, her cane attached to her wrist wiggling in the air at her side, before walking away from him. However, the moment she was upon the soldiers, her composure returned, and she spoke to them kindly and with respect.

Gideon figured she was explaining their request.

"You have upset your female," Aleron said quietly.

Merikh hummed as his orbs returned to their normal red, and Aleron's turned to pink.

"She is fine. She knows how I am and how I feel towards humans. She will forgive me later, once I have made amends with her."

Aleron settled Gideon back on his feet, but didn't let him go, as if worried he'd charge forward and verbally assault the Duskwalker some more. He considered it.

"What of Mavka then?" Aleron asked, tilting his head. "What have we done to deserve your anger? You have never truly been welcoming."

Gideon's features twitched when the aggression in Merikh's entire body deflated out of him.

Before he could respond, Raewyn approached.

"Mericato has permitted you both entry." Despite her earlier ire due to Merikh's blatant rudeness, she gave a bright smile in their general direction. "We welcome you into Lekezos City with open hearts. Please do not take any stares that fall upon you wrong; Duskwalkers are a new species to our kind, and none of us have ever looked upon a

Ghost. Their stares will be of curiosity, and they trust that the council would not allow entry to people who would cause hurt or fear."

The bubble over them remained, but the area where it intersected the much larger one opened up to allow them through.

"Once we enter the central palace, we will direct you to a room in which I will need you to wait. I will need to personally inform the other councilmembers of your arrival and why you have come. It shouldn't take long, but I will leave Merikh in your presence so that you have someone who can translate should the need arise, since he has taken well to learning Elysian Elvish so far. You won't mind this task, will you, Sir Grumpybear?"

Her smile was snide as she directed it to Merikh, who huffed at her. "Not at all, *Councillor* Raewyn."

She clapped her hands together once. "Excellent! Please follow Mericato, as he will be leading the way since he is the head of Lekezos security."

When the soldiers took off, Raewyn and Merikh stayed behind a few feet, discussing something quietly. Grabbing Aleron's hand, Gideon pulled him along, since the Duskwalker intended to remain with them – likely due to their familiarity – rather than follow.

However, this situation felt similar to an interaction Gideon once witnessed in Fishket, his hometown. In this case, *they* were the intruders, and it was best to follow the soldiers in order to minimise the chance of any further altercations.

He peeked over his shoulder, hoping to see Raewyn chewing out the Duskwalker. It would have been deserved.

Merikh's orbs flared red as a growl echoed down the fortress hallway. Blinking in surprise, he didn't expect for her to crinkle her nose, grit her teeth, and do it back to him with her head shaking.

Did she really just... growl at him? He considered that rather dangerous.

Yet, the big bear-skulled Duskwalker cupped the woman's jaw with both hands, held her still, and nuzzled her. His orbs were bright pink as he did so.

Her giggle was loud when he licked up her cheek.

She gave in too easily, Gideon grumbled, darting his head forward.

Still, she had already shown that she was very sweet.

If he can win her heart, then I guess he can't be too bad. Not that he planned to forgive the bastard for hurting Aleron anytime soon.

I guess I'm starting to feel pretty protective of him.

Aleron was just so gentle-hearted. It made Gideon want to fight for him, even when facing a monster that would have ripped him in half if he were alive.

"I'm sorry," Gideon eventually grumbled to Aleron as shame prickled the back of his neck. He covered his mouth to hide his grimace. "I shouldn't have gotten involved. I just instigated a fight that caused problems instead of helping."

"I did not know you could be so... combative?"

Gideon laughed at that. "Yeah, I guess. I have an issue with people picking on the little guy, or just being rude to someone for no reason."

A quiet yelp escaped him when Aleron placed his arm around his shoulders and held Gideon as he licked over his ear.

"I appreciate your care. It means much to me." He pointed a claw at Gideon's pinkening face, unsure if it was from his ear being licked, or the bashfulness that stirred behind his sternum at Aleron's words. "However, do not do it again, Gideon. I am still very angered he threatened you."

He threw his free hand up in a half-hearted shrug. "Can't make promises I can't keep."

Still, he'd attempt to be on his best behaviour from now on.

I was supposed to keep Aleron in check, not the other way around.

THIRTEEN

When they had been led through the city's gates, Gideon hadn't expected the joy he saw upon the people's faces. Peace and contentment were obvious by the merry voices, the colours that splashed anywhere possible, and the clean infrastructure they passed.

Many people gaped, but their wide stares held no animosity or hate. As Raewyn had foreseen, curiosity was the cause, and many came closer to get a better glance.

Even as they entered through a doorway that opened into the central tree itself, the trunk apparently habitable, those stares continued.

Gideon mirrored them, trying not to find himself overwhelmed by the white bark walls and flooring, or the molten ore that filled in the gaps. He tried not to rudely look upon the many people with pointed ears, who all stood taller than him by half a foot, if not more.

They passed many open doorways into rooms filled with people doing various things, from eating, to casually lounging and chatting, to those studying. Somehow, it was both quiet and unbearably loud at the same time, as though all attempted to speak in muted tones, but the collective collision of their voices made the constant chatting and movement distinct.

The hallway seemed to go on forever, spiralling subtly as

they ascended further within. The higher they went, the more visible the ore was until they replaced certain sections with glass instead, allowing light to filter in.

In the mass of people, it took him a while to notice something rather peculiar.

Only when they passed a man with brown horns on top of his head, who chanced a glance at them with red eyes, did he realise some of these people had Demon-like features. But that was absurd, right? These Elves wouldn't willingly allow Demons to live among them, wouldn't laugh and talk to them as though they were just any other person.

He doubted it, especially since none of them had that void-like exterior he'd seen back on Earth. Their flesh wasn't glossy, as though stars may begin to twinkle in the obsidian nothingness that kept them together.

They're probably just a different kind of Elf. Who knows, and who am I to judge?

His wide stare connected with another person.

Since they had familiar red eyes to the Demon who had peered into his very being, his very *soul*, as it disembowelled him... it was difficult not to be disturbed.

His gaze shied away. *I haven't thought about how I died in a while.* Gideon sidled a little closer to Aleron, as the hairs on the nape of his neck stood on end.

Once they were halted, and this so-called Mericato gestured to a door, Merikh barged past them. He opened it, then entered without a word. Gideon shared a glance with Aleron, and they silently entered as well, while the others left.

Inside looked like much of the architecture he'd seen so far, the walls matching the hallway they'd just climbed.

Mild sunlight caused the embedded ore to glisten, and turned the disturbed dust from Merikh's entry into sparkles. Sections of glass had been fitted into the wall as windows, utilising the natural gaps in the formation, rather than holes being created for them.

He paused once the door closed shut on its own behind them.

I figured we would be taken to some kind of office or holding room, he thought, surveying the modest and homely décor.

However, to their left was a short hallway that led to two rooms with closed doors. To the right, an opened door revealed a large room with a bed that took up most of the space. It was neatly made, and a pale-blue and green blanket with a pattern like knotted vines was draped over it.

Drifting his gaze back over the entry area, to the right was a large golden table that easily sat four, with chairs that matched. Black cushions appeared to be plush and for supreme comfort.

I guess gold isn't valuable here. One of those chairs could have fed an entire village for a year.

It matched the stout, rectangular table to their left. Behind it, and against the wall, there was a lounge made of a material he couldn't even begin to describe, but kind of looked like tiny feathers. It rested against the wall right next to the doorway they'd just come from.

In front of them was some kind of kitchen, although the stove was quite small and didn't truly look useful for cooking a glorious meal. A mixture of bark, presumably from the tree they currently stood inside of, and more ore, formed a bench around it.

The light above was odd, since it appeared to be made of a green stone, rather than flame. He marvelled at it, as he'd never seen anything like it.

"Where are we?" Gideon blurted out, since this wasn't what he expected at all.

"My home. Raewyn thought it best we brought you here instead." Merikh sighed loudly, while pushing a dining chair back so he could fall into it. "I would offer you something to drink, but that seems rather ridiculous."

Gideon's brows drew together in a frown. It only deepened at the doll sitting upon the lounge, and the picture book on the table.

"This is not like your cave," Aleron said with a light chuckle, probably trying to ease the tension within the room.

"No, it is very different," Merikh agreed. "Much has changed for me, as it has for you. Although, I must admit, I got the better side."

Both chairs opposite Merikh suddenly shunted back, scraping across the timber floor as though he'd kicked them.

"Here, pretend to sit. It'll be more comfortable than standing like a pair of ghostly statues. For me, at least."

Despite wanting to be defiant because... well, fuck this guy, Gideon did as he was told. He floated through the first chair and took the second. They both hovered above their seats, and it took a few moments of waving his hands to settle or he'd lift upwards to the ceiling or sink to the ground. Aleron had the same issue, but at least his tail feathers went straight through the backrest and weren't in the way.

Merikh plonked both elbows on the table, but he laid one arm across it while the other he bent so he could place the underside of his jaw in his palm. He rasped his claws against the surface, his expressionless, bony face taking them in.

"I have decided to take on the advice of my usually right and wise bride," he stated, sounding completely bored.

Great. Gideon rolled his eyes, wondering what this arrogant *shithead* was about to spout.

"You asked me what Mavka have done to incite my anger. In truth, nothing." The lack of emotion in his tone was less than compelling, and the annoying rhythmic thump of his claws pounded in his ears. "The issue lies solely in the fact that I have been the one to suffer the most, while that knowledge was then passed on to the rest of our kind. I am the one that is burdened, and yet none of you have been intelligent enough to be there for me. Instead, you came to my home and destroyed it in your curiosity, or forced me to interact when I would rather be left in peace. I sheltered you within my ward because I did not wish for my siblings to perish, and yet neither you nor Ingram thought beyond yourselves. All the other Mavka lack the intelligence I have obtained, and it makes you all selfish towards any plight I needed aid with. The question I was always left with was: why should I show affection for a family that cannot comfort or support me in return?"

"But we do not know how to be anything but ourselves," Aleron argued, yet his voice was small and held a mingle of hurt and confusion. "We always tried to bring you within our embrace, tried to play with you, and you never wished to do the same."

Since they'd stopped holding hands, Gideon placed his palm on Aleron's knee in case he needed comfort. This time, Gideon would stay quiet and let them talk it out. It wasn't his place, even if he had to bite his tongue.

"I know, and I don't blame you for that. But you must understand this is the first time you and I have truly spoken that isn't barely coherent rambling between you and Ingram. I couldn't even hold a conversation with you, and would have had a better chance of speaking to a child. You were like two idiots that shared one brain. How could I bond with any of you when you all felt like strangers to me?"

"Then what of the other Mavka?" Aleron implored, throwing his hands forward. "Kitty is smart, but even he cautioned we should stay away from you. He taught us much."

"And who do you think taught him?" Merikh snapped back. "*Faunus* didn't understand why I couldn't let go of my hatred towards the world. He wanted me to see things his way, and it made me realise I was an outcast even among my own kind. He likely sees things more my way, now that he has faced true adversity, but it is too late. In my intolerance, I broke the potential for those bonds, and I did so willingly."

Aleron directed his bat skull to Gideon. "Is that fair?"

"No, not really," Gideon answered, breaking his *short* vow of silence. He winced at the reminder of his own behaviours. "But, to be honest, when you don't feel like you belong in your family, it's *easy...* to be resentful. I did a lot of things I'm not proud of." Gideon cast a glare at Merikh. "But I never took it out on my sister when it really wasn't her fault. I would never treat her this way."

"I treat everyone this way," Merikh stated, before he threw his head to the side. "Well, that is not true. I treated everyone on Earth this way. That world wanted to see a monster, so I gave it one. This world, though? A Nyl'therian water droplet has less cruelty and judgement in it than anyone on Earth."

Gideon doubted that, as the people he'd known all his life were kind and caring.

"Still," he grumbled, averting his gaze.

"Listen here, little human," Merikh growled out, pointing his foreclaw at him. "I am the oldest and the wisest Mavka to live. You cannot put your ideologies and morality onto me. As a human, your opinion is biased. You have not suffered what we Mavka endure. We are not hunted just by Demons, but also by humans. You have others to depend on, towns and villages where you can create bonds. We are alone, and even turning to each other can result in a fight due to lacking the capabilities to articulate our wants."

He returned to tapping his claws against the table, his orbs brighter in their red hue.

I guess it would be different for a Duskwalker. His gaze fell to Aleron, only for it to crinkle into a pained expression.

Gideon was aware that Demonslayers had tortured

Ingram. Hell, Emerie had even been the one to capture him before she freed him. He couldn't begin to imagine what life was like for them. If Merikh was indeed the oldest and had the most humanity, it would have been difficult to have a relationship with his fellow kin.

Even as a human, if there was a large age gap between siblings, it could put a significant strain on them. Then, to be estranged by their parents and feel like an outcast... no wonder Merikh had a bone to pick with the world.

He probably felt abandoned by everyone. The world itself.

And yet... Gideon couldn't shake the desire to lean across this table, grab one of his horns, and slam his bony face against the wooden surface.

Even if it's unfair, as the older sibling, you should understand that it's not their fault. Wasn't that what it was to be mature? To extend kindness in the face of pain, so you don't extend that burden onto others?

Then he almost slapped his face into his palm. *Once more, I'm thinking like a human.*

He hated that part of what Merikh said made sense, and how it opened up old wounds within Gideon.

He'd tried to be fair to Emerie, but she had been three years younger than him. Plus, with the loss of his birth parents, the weight of expectations he thought had been thrust upon him, and the lack of self-understanding, Gideon hadn't always been... considerate.

I wasn't perfect...

"Loath as I am to admit it, Raewyn made me realise it has been envy that weighs on me," Merikh said, finally halting the rhythm of his claws so he could fold his arms across his chest. He leaned back in his seat. "Although many traits about our kind bother me, as well as individual personalities, I was not spared the pain others were. I resented it, and I still do. Nothing can change the past, nor can it erase it from my memories. I thought they would fade once I found a place I was accepted, but all this?" He lifted both arms to gesture to their surroundings. "It just makes me question why I hadn't been allowed a single day of peace until I met Raewyn."

Aleron remained silent, likely trying to absorb everything that was said to him. Hopefully in the future, if he had questions, Gideon could potentially clarify most of it.

He did turn his skull to Gideon briefly, though, as if he registered something important relating to Merikh's words. Aleron even tilted his head and gripped Gideon's thigh a little tighter.

Why are my cheeks heating? Gideon thought, since nothing had been said, but he suddenly felt his pulse fluttering shyly.

Thankfully, they faced the bear-skulled Duskwalker again.

The situations Merikh had obviously dealt with in the past must have been difficult to face. His cold and spiteful demeanour gave the impression he was traumatised by it and was still struggling to heal.

Did that excuse his behaviour? Not at all, nor did it make it sweeter to swallow.

Still, it gave light as to why he was doing it, which was at least a start. Other than stating that Merikh was 'mean,' Aleron had never really spoken of him, so he wondered if Aleron was only hurt in the moment.

From what I can tell, he's really forgiving. Aleron didn't seem to hold grudges – or perhaps that was due to his short, and often fleeting, attention span.

"That is not to say I don't care, though," Merikh continued. "I sheltered any Mavka within my ward because I desired to protect you. I still do. Being here has weighed on my conscience when I knew Jabez's wrath was only growing more violent."

Gideon flinched when he bashed a meaty fist against the table while simultaneously shoving his other hand over his skull. He eyed the Duskwalker's hand shaking from suppressed frustration.

"I should have just killed that horned fucker when I had the chance. The fact you're here like this, knowing one of you died, and it's one of you two... it fills me with so much rage that I don't know what to do with it. You and Ingram were inseparable. I can only imagine how difficult this has been for both of you."

With just a few words, that unearthed the truth behind his prickly demeanour, and the burning, barbed anger Gideon had felt dissipated slightly. Not fully, but enough.

He does care.

Enough to take them in when needed, and to feel grief.

"I am... sorry," Merikh uttered quietly, and in the darkness between the gaps of his fingers, blue flickered.

Gideon's lips parted, surprised Merikh would apologise for *anything*. He didn't seem like the kind of person to do so.

Aleron tilted his head and leaned forward. "Why are you apologising?" He waved at his body. "This is not your fault."

"Because I made a choice to stay here, when I may have been able to prevent this." Without removing his hand from his skull, he gestured the other to Aleron. "Jabez offered to cease the attacks on Mavka if I joined him. Even back then... I knew in my heart I would choose Raewyn, even if my absence meant my complicity in the death of one of my siblings. I am sorry because even if I knew the future and foresaw this, I would still choose her and this life over and over again. I am just as guilty of this as he is."

"I do not think so," Aleron rebuffed, placing his hand over the top of Gideon's to squeeze it.

Was it for his own comfort, or to seek strength? Either way, it made his torso swell in tenderness that Aleron would want that from him. He felt needed.

"Yes, I am upset that I am no longer with Ingram, but I have hope we will find a way to be together again. Weldir said there may be a chance I can return, just as he was able to return Ingram's bride to him after she killed the Demon King."

"What?" Merikh asked with unbridled shock, lowering his hand from his skull.

Gideon winced and threw a palm up, gesturing for him to wait. "Tried to," he corrected. "They don't actually know if he's truly dead, but they are hoping he was destroyed by the sun stone they used."

"Sun stone?!" Merikh choked out. Dark yellow filled his orbs, and he cupped the end of his snout in thought, tapping his foreclaw against the side of it. "The Witch Owl... she must have taken it from my cave when we left it behind." He let out a dark chuckle. "You conniving thief. What would you have done if I returned for it?"

The question obviously wasn't intended for them.

Then Merikh turned to them, folded one arm across his chest, and half-heartedly pointed between them.

His voice stern and domineering, he commanded, "Neither of you are to inform Raewyn of this, do you understand? I will tell her of Jabez when we are alone, so that she may deal with it comfortably."

Gideon raised a brow, getting the inkling there was a secret to be told here.

Before either of them could question him as to why Raewyn shouldn't know, the door to their home softly opened.

All three turned to the woman in question, and the tiny hand she held.

Just as Raewyn gently pulled the child forward so they both could enter, their little eyes widened at Aleron and Gideon's transparent, ghostly forms. Their features scrunched up before they ducked behind her, grabbing the skirt of her dress to pull it across their face. They buried into the silky fabric and her leg.

They peeked at Aleron before hiding once more.

"Sorry," Raewyn said with a small giggle in her soothing voice. "She's a little shy with new people, and I'm guessing more so with you, since you aren't what we would normally see in Nyl'theria. Ghosts are uncommon, even beyond the ward."

Raewyn moved forward with careful steps and tentatively placed her hand on the dining table as though to orientate herself within the room. The child stepped to the opposite side of her and then peeked at Merikh.

He tilted his skull down to her.

After giving a wary glance to them, she bolted to his side. Then she proceeded to lift her hands into the air, and open and close them, much like how a child would ask to be picked up.

"Tc'kt, tc'kt," she exclaimed up at his skull, never taking her eyes off it.

Her skin was a medium brown, but that same grey undertone was present in it. Loose, coily white hair cupped around the back of her pointed ears, while the rest of it only came to the tops of her shoulders. Two horns, that appeared too large for a toddler of her size, pointed upwards in a similar fashion to Merikh's bull horns, but were a darker shade of sand.

Tiny black claws glinted in the light from the stones above, while her red irises sparkled as she trustingly faced the rude and frightful Duskwalker.

Within seconds of pleading, Merikh scooped her up with both hands, settled her backside against his inner wrist, and held her back with the other to secure her. She immediately buried her face into the side of his thick neck to hide once more.

Her sleeveless, light-orange dress was simple and came

to her feet. Like Raewyn, the bottoms of her 'shoes' lacked soles, but were like sandals that just decorated the top arches of her feet with loops around her big toes to secure them.

Raewyn stepped closer and placed a hand upon the crook of her little neck before gliding her fingers up. She tucked more strands of hair behind the child's ear, then spoke Elvish to her. The child just shook her head.

"Aleron?" Raewyn asked, directing her face to their side of the table.

"Yes, Raewyn?"

She turned her head more to him and smiled. "I apologise for taking so long. Once I informed the other councilmembers of your arrival, I had to pick up *Lehnenia* from her lessons."

"She is a little Elf," Aleron stated, tilting his head at the child. "I did not know you could be small."

Merikh's sigh was telling. "She is a youngling. People don't start out mature." He patted her back. "She is also not an Elf. Not fully, at least."

"She is a Delysian." When both Aleron and Gideon shook their heads, not understanding, a knowing smile curled Raewyn's lips. "She's a Demon. Most of those with horns within Lekezos are Demons."

"I do not understand," Aleron stated. "Why would you keep Demons here, if you have a ward to keep them out?"

"It's different here," Merikh replied before she could. "Once Demons eat enough people, they take on their features and gain intelligence like us. They stop desiring to hunt, and instead begin to form a society, like with the Demon village."

"Oh. I have never been inside the Demon village," Aleron said, bashfully scratching at the side of his snout. "They never allowed us in."

"There's a village of Demons?" Gideon's lips twisted

into a cringe. "And they act like people?"

"I'm not surprised they wouldn't allow you inside," Merikh said, before turning to Gideon. "And yes, just so. They become like humans, and even eventually start looking like them. It's the same here for the Elvish people. However, because there are almost no Elves beyond the ward anymore, the Demons have begun hunting those who are fully formed to increase their own selves."

"We give all those who have reached the end of development shelter here in our city," Raewyn continued, her hands busy pulling apart the segments of her seeing cane so she could neatly fold it away. "Since they have no desire to hurt anyone, we have no issue with having them inside the city. My species of Elves are called Elysians, which is why we call them Delysians, because they are just like us despite a few physical differences and dietary requirements."

"I questioned it too," Merikh stated, shaking his bear skull like he could read Gideon's cringe of disbelief. "But they really do live in harmony here. The Demons are treated fairly and are welcomed since being accepted into the city means a form of rebirth. Their pasts are forgiven, and they are so trusted that several of them even help lead the city."

Gideon couldn't wrap his head around this. These people allowed Demons into their homes as if they weren't monsters. Demons had terrorised humans for hundreds of years. One had even killed and likely eaten Gideon.

It was difficult to ignore that fact and accept they were capable of change.

Gideon eyed the child resting on Merikh's arm, trying to understand it. He also attempted to keep any loathing or distaste from his features, considering the Duskwalker was holding her with care as though she were precious to him.

"Lehnenia's mother died not long after arriving here," Merikh stated. "Her parents were attacked while fleeing to the city."

That made Gideon's brows furrow. "So you adopted her?"

"I think it would be better to say she adopted us." Raewyn offered him a small smile. "We were not ready for something like this, but she immediately took a liking to Merikh, as you can see."

Oddly enough, a reddish pink swallowed up Merikh's orbs, and he fidgeted in his seat. He didn't deny it.

The child continued to cling to the Duskwalker until he managed to pry one of her little arms from his thick neck. Lehnenia wouldn't pull back, even as Merikh spoke in Elvish to her. His articulation and pronunciation were slow, as though he lacked confidence in his speech.

Raewyn stepped towards the kitchen-like area and began making two drinks. One cup was small, while the other was large and kind of looked like a teacup with no handle.

Merikh tilted his head back towards the Elven woman. "How would I say, 'They are Ghosts who are visiting from the afterlife'?"

She responded without looking back at them, and he repeated what she said.

The child sprung up, her eyes wide. Then she spoke, patting at her chest in excitement. Merikh's orbs flashed blue for just a second, before he shook his head. The girl's features saddened as her shoulders drooped.

Although he couldn't understand the conversation, he figured Lehnenia had asked if her parents could visit, considering what Merikh had asked of Raewyn.

The girl braved peeking at them.

Oh, screw it. She's only a kid.

Gideon waved at her, and her expression eased, then a tiny smile crept onto her features as she waved back. She laughed when Aleron mimicked her.

Shark-like fangs became prominent, but Gideon couldn't help noticing her canines were far too large for her mouth.

They awkwardly pushed the teeth around them to the sides, forcing them inwards so the others were angled into a vee in the centre of her mouth.

Then she pointed at Aleron and spoke.

"She's stating that your skull is like mine, and she likes your fangs," Merikh translated, before a long pause as he listened. "She's wondering why you're pink, and how you came to be a Ghost."

Then he grunted, especially when she turned to Merikh and spoke. She grabbed one of his long fangs with her entire hand and tried to wiggle it with a giggle. Her smile grew bright as she spoke to him, and then shouted at Raewyn, only to come back to Merikh.

Surprised the surly Duskwalker was allowing the child to yank one of his fangs, and then a horn as she rambled on and on, Gideon watched the interaction with fascination.

He's being really patient with her. More than he expected.

Raewyn came over to hand the child a cup, and she enthusiastically took it with both hands, swallowing its contents with big, loud gulps. Then she sucked in a breath as though she'd forgotten to breathe the entire time, just as Raewyn took a seat next to Merikh.

He put the girl on her feet, pointed to a bag, and stated something in Elvish. She shook her head, so he repeated himself. She pointed at him, stamped her foot, then pointed at the bag.

"Raewyn," he stated with a cringe. "Please help."

"No!" She gave a laugh. "If you're going to ask her to do her homework, you know she won't do it without you."

"We have guests." When he turned his skull to her while still leaning towards the child, his orbs once more a reddish pink, her smile grew mischievous. He grunted. "Don't say it. Not in front of them."

When he stood, he wrapped his tail around the child's ankle and hoisted her off the ground so she flipped upside down. She let out a joyful squeal. Grabbing a bag from the doorway, he shook the child as he walked over to the low table in front of the lounge, sat upon the ground, and placed her on his massive knee.

Together, they opened up her bag, pulled out strange, lime-coloured parchment and a writing utensil made from some kind of bark. Then they worked on the child's homework together.

"Don't mind them." Raewyn's soft words forced Gideon's attention forward. "He's still learning how to write in our language, and she has taken it upon herself to teach him."

A light growl rumbled from his left. "I told you not to say anything!"

"Why?" She laughed back. "It's nothing to be ashamed of. You've only been here a few months, and no one expects you to learn all of it so quickly."

He grunted in response before Lehnenia distracted him. Like he couldn't help himself, Aleron rose and walked over. He crouched down and rudely inspected them up close, violating their personal space.

Since Lehnenia didn't seem to be bothered, or perhaps due to her happily attempting to start teaching him as well, Merikh allowed it.

All the uncomfortable tension from their earlier conversation was nullified by the little girl. Even though Gideon had mixed feelings towards Merikh, warmth bled behind his sternum at watching him and the girl interact. He found it even sweeter with the way Aleron looked on.

"Why did you adopt her?" Gideon asked, turning to Raewyn.

It probably wasn't his place to ask, but the unusualness of the situation brought on many questions.

Merikh was a Duskwalker, she an Elf, and the child a Demon; no one could deny the oddity of all this. Plus, if their relationship were new, and it was true he'd been here for only a few months, in Gideon's opinion... it all happened too fast.

She didn't seem like the kind of person to make rushed decisions, considering she was some kind of important councilmember or something. People in governing positions usually had good reasons for their actions, and managed their time and added responsibilities in certain ways. They didn't make brash decisions like this, especially one so life changing.

As someone who had been adopted himself, he had... feelings regarding this.

He hoped they hadn't made a rushed decision that could poorly affect this innocent girl later due to possibly fickle and thoughtless selfishness. If they were to take someone in, he believed they should do so wisely and ensure that the child's needs were the focal point.

"Hmm." Raewyn's expression turned thoughtful. "To be honest, it wasn't really the right time. Lehnenia was four when she was brought to the city, but in the year she's been adjusting to living here and being without her parents, she hasn't had it easy." She gave a very weak smile, mingled with sympathy. "Her horns and fangs are growing in too fast, and she was picked on by the other orphans, both Elysian and Delysian. We think because Merikh is so different, and has big fangs and horns like her, she easily grew attached to him after the few times they interacted. She wanted to come with us and we – *he* – just couldn't say no."

In Gideon's peripheral, Merikh's orbs morphed into a fairly bright reddish pink. He muttered something quietly, like one would do under their breath, as he shuffled himself in his seated position on the floor. His bear skull tilted towards them before going back down to the parchment in front of him and Lehnenia.

Merikh chose to remain quiet, despite his obvious

embarrassment. Gideon figured it was due to something being stated that made him feel vulnerable.

"She is still adjusting," Raewyn continued. "She has only been with us for a little over a week. We are trying to spend as much time with her as we can during the adjustment period. I have also stepped back from some of my duties to do so. No one minds, as I do what is most important."

"I see," Gideon mumbled, looking towards the girl.

She looked happy. With the way Merikh was holding her on his knee and interacting with her, it was easy to tell he was smitten.

The room was filled with chatter between the two Duskwalkers and Lehnenia. Raewyn had her right ear turned to them with a contented smile upon her pretty features, seemingly at peace as she listened from her seat.

Aleron's wings and tail feathers often puffed and vibrated with joy, even when his questions about what they were doing were mostly ignored.

Gideon just remained silent, taking it all in.

I guess this will help Aleron understand what a child is.

Crouched down to observe the Demon youngling, he couldn't help finding her... odd. Her body looked too small and delicate, and he was rather thankful it was impossible to touch her.

Her eyes were large and round, her canine fangs and horns too big and disproportionate to the rest of her, and yet her hands were tiny things. She could barely hold one of Merikh's fingers.

I have not even seen humans this small. And she'd been easily frightened of his and Gideon's presence, making him believe the young were cowardly.

Despite the youngling itself, he actually only came closer because he wanted to see how Merikh interacted with it. Especially after he'd told him it was easier to speak to a youngling than he and Ingram, or other Mavka.

Should he be offended that he'd compared their intellect to this little creature? At first, he had been. However, the more he watched, the more something became very apparent.

She chatted with Merikh, who was quick to respond and show her something with the items in front of them. Up close, he noted how at ease the usually violent and aggressive Mavka acted with her upon his knee. Not an ounce of tension stiffened a single muscle, nor were his spikes puffed beneath his guards.

He'd even sheathed his claws, as though he didn't wish to harm the fragile creature.

Aleron took note of how small her claws were, and how her fangs didn't appear truly threatening. She was a creature that needed protecting, and likely couldn't hurt a Mavka no matter how much she tried.

Is this why he likes her? Because even at whatever young age Raewyn had stated, she communicated clearly with Merikh? Even if they were to argue or fight, the youngling wouldn't stand a chance, whereas both he and his kindred could do – and have done – severe damage to Merikh.

Even the last time they'd fought with him, the bear-skulled Mavka had lost an entire arm, despite winning the overall fight. That was a difficult feat, considering Merikh was the only Mavka that ever won a fight against them.

Merikh pointed to the parchment, and the youngling nodded before writing some squiggles he couldn't decipher. *She is able to learn.*

Up until recently, even Aleron knew he could never have sat like this and been taught anything. He and Ingram would have gotten bored and wanted to play. They'd forget the lesson.

His wings flapped when he figured out *why* Merikh's patience was only present for the child.

"Mavka are like creatures," he muttered aloud. "I have seen small animals following bigger ones. We act more like them, not like this youngling."

Merikh lifted his snout to him. "I'm surprised you were able to surmise that on your own."

Aleron's sight shifted to bright yellow, happily taking the compliment from the mean Mavka. It brightened when the youngling turned her face to his, and she gave him a large, toothy grin. Then she lifted the parchment to Aleron's bat skull, wanting him to take a closer look.

He pretended to do so while nodding. Then she rambled at him.

I like her. She is friendly like Raewyn.

She did not judge him for his skinless face, or his wings and claws. She didn't mind that he was a Mavka, and instead had openly brought him into the fold of their teaching.

Her heart, although likely small, was welcoming. He'd thought this about Raewyn when he first met her, and he'd grown fond of her during the short day he'd been in her presence.

His sight darted up to Raewyn's blue soul flame hovering between Merikh's tall bull horns. It was curled into a ball, and its coily hair gently floated around the back of its head.

After much thought, most of which was broken and difficult to wade through after Merikh spoke of his feelings, Aleron finally gained the courage to share.

"We did not mind that you were mean," he stated honestly, staring down at the youngling, who frowned up at him. "You let us rest, and you saved us once. We remembered these things, so when we thought or spoke of you, it was always conflicting. Mean with your words, nice with your actions. You were safe, even when ripping our arms off to smack us with them."

Merikh grunted, then lifted a finger at him. "That was one time," he snapped out with a grumble. "And you both fucking deserved it after what you did to my tail and back spikes."

"Don't swear in front of Lehnenia!" Raewyn shouted.

"She can't understand me!" he roared back.

"I don't care. Children are intuitive and pick up on things like that."

He let out a defeated huff, especially when the child gave a hissing, playful growl up at him. Yet, her face shined with a grin. He unsheathed his foreclaw, as though to threaten the youngling with it, and tapped her on the nose.

"Don't go taking her side. My pretty starshine is more formidable than she appears. I don't need two of you ganging up on me."

Aleron chuckled before he cut in. "What I am trying to say is: if you hold any regret, please do not do so. Our feelings towards you, although conflicted, were always warm – as they have been with all other Mavka. We did not mean to burden you, so thank you for being a safe place we could return to."

Pleased when Merikh's orbs turned a reddish pink in embarrassment, Aleron chuckled again when he tossed his bear skull around.

"Not like I had a choice. I couldn't shoo you away even when I tried."

Aleron tilted his head knowingly. "But you did have a choice. We knew you could make us leave, but you often chose not to when you were within your ward. You also did not force us away from your side when we followed you."

"You're really annoying, you know that?" Merikh waved his hand through Aleron's intangible face. "Go take your cutesy, lovey words somewhere else. I don't need nor want them."

He said this, yet Aleron thought the opposite.

Aleron could see he and his kindred had been a source of pain for Merikh. Even if he didn't like Aleron, or want anything to do with him, nothing would change the fact that Aleron cared for him in his own way. Not like his kindred, but perhaps similarly.

Since he could articulate that now, he wanted to. He wanted to for Merikh's sake, as well as his own.

Before either one could say anything, the youngling picked up the parchment and threw it. It fluttered through the air, then her writing utensil clacked against the ground. Aleron flinched when she began to scream, and he cringed so hard and fast that he involuntarily backed up in aversion to her.

Just moments before, he'd been enjoying their company. Now, he ran to Gideon's side as she laid back over Merikh's knee and the table, and kicked at his round stomach. She even managed to cop him under the jaw, forcing his head up, and an uncontrollable growl slipped from him.

The child kicked harder and bared her fangs.

Raewyn quickly rose to her feet, but Merikh threw his hand out to her. "Don't," he added sharply, making her pause. "Just stay there. I don't want her hurting you again."

"What is wrong with it?" Aleron asked, his sight white in uncertainty.

Merikh, while wrestling the child who continued to shout, cry, and stamp at his torso, eventually stood. She bashed on his shoulders and pushed at him when he tried to hold her.

"I'll take her to her room," he told them. "You explain while I calm her down."

Aleron placed his hand on Gideon's shoulder, creating contact for two reasons: one, to make sure he didn't slip out of consciousness, and two, so Gideon could just ease him.

He watched Merikh storm off with her while uttering Elvish words.

"She doesn't like being ignored," Raewyn said while giving an apologetic wince. "She doesn't realise that you don't understand our language. Since you weren't responding to her, and because Merikh was distracted by you, she lashed out. She seeks attention since she wasn't treated well by the other orphaned children, no matter if it's positive or not. The guardians tried to make up for it, but they must attend to the others as well, and she didn't like it when they did."

"That sounds complicated," Aleron grumbled, before turning to Gideon. "I do not like younglings if they do this. I liked when she was calm and fun. I do not want to be kicked."

Gideon chuckled, only to cover his mouth when Aleron's sight morphed to red at him for doing so.

"I don't know what to tell you, Aleron," he stated, with mirth and humour in his tone. "That's what kids are like. You can't control them, and they have their own will."

The child's screams eased. Before long, a giggle sounded from a room instead.

In that moment, he understood Merikh.

Mavka couldn't be controlled and had their own will, but they were also dangerous, violent, and couldn't be taught. They also couldn't be calmed so easily, and a tantrum such as this would have evolved into bloodshed.

"I'm sure you're surprised that he is so good with her," Raewyn said, a loving smile lifting on her features, her chin in her hand as she faced where they'd gone off to. "But I always knew he was patient and caring beneath his prickly behaviour. It's moments like this that remind me why I fell in love with him. He's unbelievably gentle with her, just like he is with me."

Merikh entered back into the area they were in. The youngling's face was swollen and wet with drying tears. She looked upon Aleron, twisted up her features in spite, then poked her pointed tongue out at him. Merikh did the same, shoving his tongue out at Aleron, and she laughed.

He chuckled in return as he sat back down in front of the low table and collected everything she'd thrown. Then, as if nothing happened, he started back up her 'homework,' as they'd called it.

Aleron didn't go back over to them, rather put off by what had just happened. Instead, he stayed by Gideon's side, where he felt secure.

I do not like it. Aleron lacked patience for something so chaotic.

Perhaps when he had more humanity, like Merikh, he would be more welcoming. Currently, as he saw it, he was entirely disinterested. It appeared too hard.

A knock sounded from behind.

Raewyn raised her voice at the door as she rose to her feet. They responded, their voice kind and deep even though he didn't know what they said.

"The temple acolytes are ready for you now," Raewyn stated, making both him and Gideon rise and stand fully. She gave a sweet, but sad smile, and it reminded him of the one she gave him when they last said goodbye. "We can't go with you, as only those who are allowed to enter the temple may go. But it was a pleasure meeting you both, and thank you for coming to our home."

A small goodbye was shared, but he noticed the sorrow within her features as she spoke. A coldness swirled in his chest, reflecting that same feeling. He would miss her, his Elven friend, and was disappointed he hadn't been able to spend more time with her.

Merikh, on the other hand, just waved his hand with a grunt, never truly taking his attention from Lehnenia.

FOURTEEN

Aleron was pensive as he walked through halls that often opened up into large, spacious areas. His gaze drifted over the Elves and Demons they passed. He connected with a few green or brown eyes, and once a bright-blue pair, but the reds were the ones he lingered on.

Most Demons seemed to have fangs, claws, and horns, but he only noticed one with a tail. When inspected closely like this, it appeared they could look different. Their horns also varied, some like his own spiralling ones, and others with antlers. They all had shark-like fangs, but like Lehnenia, they could also have big canine ones.

The Elves all looked different as well. Some had straight hair, others wavy or coily. Many had spots on their faces, arms, and chests, and if he remembered correctly, Emerie had told him they were freckles.

The Demons, from what he could tell, were slightly taller, but even some Elves towered over them – like Raewyn.

If he were to take away the Demon characteristics, they truly looked the same. They all had pointed ears, stark-white hair, and brown skin – although in varying shades – with a grey undertone to it.

Even their smiles and kindness in their eyes were the same. Yes, they looked upon him and his companion warily, but before they did, Aleron noticed this.

Demons are not so different. Just like Duskwalkers weren't so different, if they were all to shed their flesh.

They all sought peace, friendship, and the warmth of deep bonds.

He eyed Gideon, who peered back at all the strangers with eyes not as wide as before. He still appeared more concerned than they did, however.

Perhaps Aleron was able to adjust to these people, and this place, easier since he'd seen much in his life. Gideon was a human, who hadn't often left the walls of his home, other than going to some 'Ashpine City' once.

Yet, despite the disquiet in his body language, he still managed to lift his pretty green eyes to Aleron and shine a warm, genuine smile. Then, like he wanted to crush his heart until it permanently ached, Gideon squeezed his left hand.

"Are you okay?" Gideon asked, and the gentleness and care in his voice was unmistakable.

"No," Aleron answered honestly, unable to take his sight from the human. "I have learned much, and it weighs heavily on me."

"That's fair." He turned his eyes away for just a moment as he rubbed at his neck. "To be truthful, I'm a little confused myself. I now understand why you asked me if a person can be both mean and kind. Merikh is a prick, there is no denying that, yet it's obvious he has a good heart. However, to be his brother, and be cared about, but also treated as though you are strangers... I just... I get how much that may hurt and be comforting at the same time."

Once more, Gideon shone another smile at him, one that was much more forced, like a twisted cringe. *I wish he did not do that.* Aleron didn't need him to pretend for his sake.

"I've been trying to figure it out myself so I can say the right thing to you, and I feel really bad that I don't know what to say to help make you feel better. It's why I've been so quiet up until now."

Something about his words made Aleron's sight waver. His whole torso – no – his entire being *ached* in tenderness for his human.

That consideration for Aleron's wellbeing, how his heart may be hurting, showed just how attentive Gideon was. It showed just how deeply he cared for Aleron. He wanted to *help.*

Meanwhile, Aleron had assumed the wary look upon his features was due to the strange people around them.

In that moment, he wanted nothing more than to bring Gideon into his arms, lift him off the ground, and swallow him up in his wings. To express just how much he appreciated his sentiment and wanted to return it.

Had he been thinking of Merikh? Sure, it had been on his mind, along with many other things.

I hope what I said was enough.

Merikh was obviously deeply hurt. He'd wanted to help him shed it any way he could, but also selfishly ease his own misgivings. Gideon had taught him communication was important, so he spoke of what he could understand in order to create that link of healing for both of them.

If it weren't for this human by his side, teaching him all that he could, Aleron would have been lost. He would have stumbled during the conversation. He would have... ruined the chance to connect.

Instead, Merikh stated he was cutesy and loving. Even if those descriptions were uttered insultingly, surely the bear-skulled Mavka couldn't be immune to Aleron's sincere sentiments.

"Is it wrong of me to ask why they would take in a youngling that is so volatile?" Aleron freely asked, knowing Gideon wouldn't judge his curiosity on the matter.

"No, I don't think it's wrong to ask, since I know you aren't saying it to be spiteful," Gideon stated.

Once more, his entire being ached. He absolutely hadn't intended for his question to be filled with spite, and he adored how Gideon recognised that.

"I think they knew she would be – they must have. I also don't think they care how broken that child is, and just want to help heal her. To lose her parents in an unfamiliar environment, and then be bullied... it's a lot for an innocent kid to take in. I can't even begin to imagine the things she's seen outside of the protective walls here."

Gideon's features tightened in thought, his bottom lip pouting forward.

Ever since their tongues had played in the cave back in Tenebris, Aleron had gained a newfound appreciation for a person's fleshy lips – especially Gideon's. He'd like their tongues to touch again, or for his lips to capture him.

He'd liked to rub and pet them, hoping they tingled like his tongue did. Purple flared in his sight as his gaze lingered on his little human.

Gideon lifted his head forward to make sure they were still following the two soldiers who had collected them, as well as some robed individual. Thankfully someone was paying attention, since Aleron absolutely wasn't.

I want him to make those soft noises for me again.

"But," Gideon continued, "after what I've learned and observed of Merikh, it's likely he couldn't turn the child away after everything he's been through. You said he was mean to you in the past, and I'm guessing that meant he was volatile. Perhaps he wants to protect someone who acts just like how he did, to prevent them from turning into who he is now. He probably doesn't even realise he's taken on that child as his way to heal himself of his own pain."

"Is that not selfish?" Aleron asked, tilting his head.

Surprisingly, Gideon's lips curled with mild humour. "A little, but I don't think it's intentional. However, it does mean that Merikh may be the only person who is *right* to parent that child."

Aleron huffed, doubting that. As if he could understand what he'd meant with just the single action, Gideon let out a low chuckle.

"Taking away his rude demeanour with us, he is kind towards his woman – protective even." Gideon waved his hand to the side. "Patience is not enough, but as Lehnenia was kicking him, he showed tolerance and understanding. He demonstrated better parenting than how I've seen many humans act. He will treat that child the way he's always wanted to be treated."

Perhaps Gideon didn't realise it, but Aleron's fondness for him grew with every word he spoke.

He is forgiving, even after he argued with Merikh.

The human didn't hide how much he disliked the bear-skulled Mavka, and yet he still spoke well of him. Rather than trying to incite hatred within Aleron for Merikh, which was possible if guided by someone as cunning as Gideon, he'd instead tried to make him see his brother warmly.

It made him want this little human even more. He craved to tuck him under his wing protectively so no harm could come to something that was so calm, benevolent, and kind. He longed to keep such a tender creature within his clutches, so he could hold that nature as if it were his own.

As soon as he learned what the word 'love' meant, Aleron had long ago realised his heart was full of it. He loved Ingram as his kindred, Merikh as his brother, Raewyn as his friend, and even Weldir and Lindiwe as his creators.

But the sprouting, fluffy feeling of love growing in his chest for this very human was different to all of that.

It was violent as it ran rampant throughout him, flooding his muscles every time he opened his damn mouth. Hot as it seared him where their palms touched until it travelled up his veins. Whenever Gideon said or did something that stroked his essence, he wanted to reach out and *squeeze* him until he popped. It tingled his mind so much that all he wanted to do was lay his skull in those soothing little hands and stare at that beautiful, mesmerising face.

And it had to do with how Gideon viewed the world, how he treated it... and Aleron. His mind was open, free of judgement, and accepting. That was how Aleron wanted to be.

He didn't want to be a menace upon any world, and this human was teaching him how to be better – without even knowing it.

At some point, his sight had shifted to a brighter pink during their walk. *He is lovely.*

At first, he hadn't understood how such a fleshy, furless, weak creature could be attractive to his own kind. *I understand now, Ingram.* He'd needed to see this human's heart first, and only then did his exterior begin to tantalise him.

The growing longing to be near, to touch until he'd given Gideon his all, to thrust them into one being, was born from adoration. He craved watching him, fascinated by his beauty and emotions, desiring to understand his needs and wants so he could find a way to be relied on.

The more he yearned for these things, the more the sharp clip of Gideon's jaw drew his gaze, or the subtle point of his nose. His teeth, and the way his tongue brushed over them. His slightly tanned skin looked soft, smooth, and he'd begun wanting to draw the backs of his claws over every inch.

He wanted to see his chest, his stomach, his thighs, so he could learn what lay beneath his clothes. The longer the little human wore them, keeping his body from him, the more they made his hidden flesh more erotic to him.

Then there was his voice. Deep, masculine, yet always filled with compassion. This male could lull him to sleep, and he thought he may now even have the power to pull him from an enraged state if he purred and cooed at him.

I am pleased I asked him to join me. He would never have known Gideon had a temper, had he not. He liked that he wielded it for Aleron's sake.

Gideon was flawed, just like he was. He'd begun to see him as perfect, placing him into a status of worship within his mind. The fact that he wasn't only allowed fondness to grow.

Unable to keep his gaze off the top of Gideon's light-brown hair, he didn't know they'd arrived at their destination until they were ushered to stop.

Aleron looked around, disappointed he hadn't taken in more of the Elven central palace.

They stood in front of a set of large double doors. Like the gates they'd entered through into the city, molten ore formed a swirling pattern like a tree. However, the material it had been embedded into was of the white bark of the starfir tree they were in. Raewyn had explained much about the environment when they'd first arrived and walked through the city.

He looked up, noticing pink-and-purple leaves rather than a ceiling. They swayed, occasionally letting cold, yet dappled light burst through from two moons. One was much larger than the other and round in comparison to the oval one following it.

Awe filled him as he found a gap through the massive branches. A cloudy, star-filled streak far beyond in the navy night sky spanned across the entire horizon. At the centre of that green cloud, a bright-red light sparkled.

Aleron lifted a claw in its direction. "What is that?"

Gideon followed where he pointed, only to shrug. "No clue. There are theories that there are other galaxies, but if I were to take a wild guess, maybe that's what it is?"

As usual, the human stated something that puzzled him. Just as he turned to him, intending to inquire about this further, the Elf wearing robes halted them.

He began to speak in a different language.

The pale-green clothing he wore lacked any intricate markings, but every time he moved, bronze glittered on his sleeves and skirt. His long, straight white hair had been braided on the sides, but the top and back were left loose.

Bronze markings were painted on his face: two lines coming down from the corners of his dark-brown eyes, as though he'd cried molten tears. His bottom lip had been painted, yet the top one didn't have a smudge upon it.

"Hey, man," Gideon said, waving one of his hands, "we don't understand a word of what you're saying."

The Elf's features hardened, his eyes narrowing, before he sighed. Then his cheek twitched as he gave what Aleron figured was an apologetic cringe.

"Kon, kon," he said, waving forward as a welcoming smile curled his lips and filled his eyes.

He stamped his bare foot, and a stream of green magic flowed against the ground, following a path like tree roots. It spread against the door, up through where the ores swirled their patterns, before metal retreated like water being sucked away from a shore.

"I was wondering why a lot of people don't wear shoes here, but it must be so they can feel with them," Gideon stated. "I didn't realise they could use magic, did you?"

He turned to Aleron, eyes wide and glittering with wonder, and he couldn't help chuckling at the awed human.

"Have you not noticed all the magic?" Even Aleron had been able to tell the lighting stones within the palace used magic and had noticed the small amounts the people here wielded.

Aleron covered the end of his snout in a poor attempt at hiding his deepening chuckles, when Gideon's face scrunched.

"Well, no. I was looking at everything else," he grumbled, turning away to hide his cute face. "But it's cool that they can use their feet for magic. They must need to touch the ground in order to do it."

They were ushered forward by the robed individual after the doors swung open, revealing two other people already within: an Elven female, and a Demon male. Both turned small smiles towards them.

So friendly. He wondered if he should be concerned, but he couldn't sense any hostility in their gazes. Aleron disliked that he lacked his ability to smell; he may have been able to better gauge their intentions, or if they were afraid.

Beside him, Gideon released his hand so he could face both his palms upwards. He opened and closed them as he looked down.

"Bloody hell. It really sucks to be human. I don't have cool wings like you, and these people can use magic. Why can't humans have awesome features like this?"

"I can use magic," Aleron stated, his chest swelling with pride at Gideon calling his wings 'cool.'

He didn't state that he'd never actually done so. Ingram had informed him it was possible, though. One day, he'd like to try.

"Oh fine." Gideon groaned while rolling his eyes. "Just rub it in, why don't you? Next, you'll tell me you can eat the sun and shit gold."

"Shit gold?" Aleron asked, cocking his head before lifting a hand to his snout. He cupped his fangs. "Mavka do not produce waste, let alone gold."

Gideon halted, as though he suddenly froze.

"Excuse me... what did you just say? But you said you eat!" At his yell, the smiles on the faces of the three people around them suddenly died, and instead their expressions grew uncertain. They spared a fidgeting glance among themselves.

Noticing what happened, Gideon's expression paled.

"Oh crap. This is likely some kind of holy place." He slapped his face into his palm. "Never mind. We can talk about this later."

Aleron, not seeing the issue, just nodded.

Gideon shoved a strange smile on his face and walked forward with his hands up. "Sorry for yelling," he stated with a grimace twitching his cheeks.

Their expressions softened, and they awkwardly laughed in return. Then the Demon gestured to a silver disc on the ground large enough to fit three Mavka, if they were to stand close together.

Aleron followed their direction, while drifting his gaze to their surroundings.

The ground was flat in this spacious, roofless room, as though they stood at the very top of this tree. Branches had grown around it, twisting and bending as they made walls before reaching high into the sky. Between the gaps of them, he could just see the world beyond, although deeply shaded by the dark of night. That shade allowed the natural glow of the world to become noticeable, as if certain trees and plants lit up at night. An area where there were no trees, like a long field or meadow, glittered as though stars danced among the grass.

He wished he could see more, but it was difficult to inspect anything between the slivers of gaps.

Yet now that he was aware the world glowed, he finally registered that the stems of leaves above them also had the faintest light. He hadn't realised that was why he'd been able to still see the distinct colours, rather than just darkness.

His gaze fell to the three people who had surrounded them. Their robes were exactly the same. The paint on their faces was similarly drawn, but they each had different metal: bronze, silver, and gold.

The Demon who had gestured to them had gold painted upon them, whereas the female Elf had silver. They all nodded, as if ready, and lifted their arms to reach out to each other. Their hands never touched, the gaps between them long.

The female was the next to speak. However, the moment her eyes rolled back into her skull, revealing only the whites of them, his feathers puffed.

Wrong. Immediately, his instincts told him this.

He stepped back and away from such a harrowing sight, only to duck away from the male who had brought them here. His eyes were the same, as were the third robed individual's.

Yellow magic cascaded from their fingertips before creating a translucent, glowing circle from around the base of the disc they stood upon. It came from a crack, as if light shone from behind it, within the floor and hidden away.

"What is happening?" Aleron asked, bumping into Gideon.

He didn't like this. It felt ominous, despite the enthralling serenity of it all.

He brought Gideon into the safety of his wings and held him tightly as his skull darted one way and then the other.

"You're asking the wrong person here, bud," Gideon mumbled against his chest.

Taking the human with him, Aleron spun in a circle to give each person a bubbling snarl. He did it louder, letting it burst from him menacingly at the woman, warning her since she was the only one chanting.

"Temper, temper," a musical, feminine voice sang from all around.

His chest pounded with growing anxiety and fear for the human he clutched. Aleron stepped forward to flee from the middle of the circle.

His feet came out from under him – or, rather, the floor liquefied. He roared when they swiftly and suddenly sunk into the silver disc.

The world around them disappeared entirely, as if they were eaten.

FIFTEEN

Just as they sunk into the silver disc, their heads emerged from another side like some kind of liquid portal. Eyelids flickering rapidly, Gideon expected his eyes to sting from the silver that swallowed them.

Aleron's roar grew muffled, cutting out as his head passed through the threshold. It died when they emerged, safe and unharmed, on the other side.

Gideon didn't know if the pang in his chest came from sympathy for Aleron who'd grown frantic, or if it came from how he'd acted so protectively.

Even when afraid, the first thing he'd done was bring Gideon into his side.

As someone who had been pushed in front of an unknown noise coming from the forest by a fellow woodcutter, only to find it was nothing, his heart clenched at the complete opposite reaction of the caring Duskwalker. Aleron even cupped the side of his head when he shielded Gideon with his wings, using his entire body to safeguard him.

Aleron's first instinct had been Gideon's wellbeing, which was hard to ignore. Even more so when he could feel the big guy trembling with tension and digging his claws into him by accident.

It hurt a little, but nothing Gideon couldn't grit his teeth through. He had no intention of telling Aleron, not when he found the reason for it so touching.

In truth, the chanting Elven Priestess, or whatever she'd been called, had freaked him the hell out too. The language barrier between them meant they couldn't be informed of what would happen, and asking them as the woman chanted proved less than fruitful. He'd been retreating into Aleron's side, seeking the comfort of his fur and warmth against his back, before the Duskwalker snatched him up.

The swallowing darkness split apart like a curtain when Aleron moved his wings and brought them back behind him.

"Are you okay?" Aleron asked, cupping the side of his head to direct his face up to his skull, leaving his other arm around his waist.

Gideon nodded before taking in their surroundings.

A building, made of what could only be some kind of black stone, but *glittering,* reached up to the blue sky like some kind of pyramid tower. Yet, it didn't take on any form of architecture other than having an open doorway and stairs leading up to it. It appeared to be like perfectly cut obsidian, smooth on all sides, in a near prism shape.

A ring of strange trees circled the rest of the clearing they were in. They were similar to the red-wood trees they'd seen when they first arrived in Nyl'theria, with glowing blue leaves, yet the leaking sap glinted metallic red. Arching roots lifted off the ground before shoving through what appeared to be water. Fizzing red clouds – likely from the sap – dispersed into the water before dissolving.

Casting his gaze downwards, Gideon lifted a foot curiously, since they stood on the surface of a deep lake. They weren't hovering, and their collective feet caused it to ripple whenever they moved.

His drifting gaze didn't make it further around the clearing when he cast it to the left this time.

Gideon stepped back in shock as he tilted his head upwards. *Now that's a big lady,* he thought in wonder.

Standing at least three times his own height, a woman with the same familiar Elven skin tone he was growing accustomed to stared down at them. Yet, within a glance, he knew her to be an entirely different entity.

Her hair was tight with tiny, corkscrew curls, but it was so long it came to her waist. Each strand glittered with gold. The longer he looked upon her, the more he noticed the metal coming from her.

The gold glistened in the vine-like patterns that swirled on her hands and up her forearms, as well as her feet and up her calves. It reflected in the irises of her pupilless eyes, the corners of her lips as though her very saliva was filled with it, and in her brows. At first glance, he thought her to be sightless, but her eyes roamed over them as though seeing.

She stepped forward.

Her black robes, shimmering with rainbow fractures, were plain and simple in design. Considering her striking beauty, she didn't need fancy clothing to aid her. Instead, the sleeveless garment clung to her chest and torso like liquid, silky in its texture, and displayed only a small amount of voluptuous cleavage. Then it danced around her legs, only revealing her left thigh, as the bottom of the skirt caressed the top of the water.

With every step closer, she became smaller. She approached incrementally, appearing to walk a small distance.

Her ears were so long, they poked up an inch or two past the top of her head. A crown made of light hovered above her head like a spiky halo, somehow sharp and menacing, and yet also angelic in nature.

When upon them, she stood about half a foot taller than Aleron.

He shoved Gideon behind him and gave her a soft warning growl. *Why is his first response to everything new... to growl?* Pleasure, a new person, something he didn't understand. Another thing to add to his strange but funny charm.

He peeked around the Duskwalker to stare with stark eyes, mesmerised by the pretty woman.

Two wings made of glowing gold fluttered behind her back at Aleron's threat, finally making their presence known. Oddly, they weren't attached to her; instead, they floated a hand's width of a gap away.

Busty, willowy in height, but curvy, she stared down at them with such gentle features she appeared to be carved by feminine angels. Feminine, because Gideon was aware no man could carve someone so strikingly beautiful.

Her cheeks were high, rounded, and her jawline strong. An ample, button nose sat above full, cupid lips. Her brows weren't deeply arched, but they contoured her eyes delicately. Even with a stern expression, she came across as benign.

Looking upon her, he knew her to be the Gilded Maiden, and the deity they had been seeking.

Gideon expected her to be loud, booming, and commanding. He expected her to raise her hands into the air and speak like some kind of powerful being, throwing lightning as a show of strength and demanding they kneel. He expected her to be arrogant, stating that they should be thankful for her merciful nature as the world rumbled with an earthquake.

He expected to see disdain in her gaze, especially since she had her shoulders back and chin tilted with a regal air. Even her walk had been a saunter.

Instead, she darted forward and cupped the top and bottom of Aleron's skull before he could even process what had happened. Touching him, as though he wasn't a Ghost and intangible, she brought her own face dangerously close to his fangs.

"What a pretty boy!" she purred, rubbing her lips and nose against the tip of his snout. Her voice was moderate in tone, not too high, not too low, and held utter delight. "Look at your skull. What kind of animal is it from?"

Aleron's wings drooped, even though the rest of him stiffened. Gideon didn't blame him for his reaction, as he himself had no idea what the fuck was going on.

He did notice her lips didn't match up with her words when she spoke. She wasn't speaking the same language as them, yet some kind of magic allowed them to communicate – likely hers.

"And you!"

She turned to Gideon, and panic settled in. Oh god, what did this imposing lady want? He didn't get the chance to back up before she placed her large hand on top of his head to still him. It engulfed Gideon completely and was utterly warm.

"Look how small and cute you are." She yanked his ear, as if she wanted to highlight that it wasn't pointed like an Elf's. "I've never had a human in my realm before, not even a dead one."

Gideon yelped in surprise when Aleron yanked him to his chest and hugged him protectively.

"Do not touch," Aleron rumbled, his tone threatening.

She laughed in response, her eyes crinkling with humour.

"Aww, do you want more attention?" She reached down and cupped his skull again, even as Aleron attempted to evade her. "What a good boy you are, coming all the way here with all the challenges before you. I hope my speakers were kind to you, even if you couldn't understand them. When they told me who you were coming on behalf of, and your connection to him, I informed them they should treat you with the utmost kindness. I want the absolute best for one of my grandchildren."

Grandchild? His bottom lip fell until his jaw threatened to unhinge and fall off. *Oh. She's Weldir's mother, therefore...* His eye twitched, wondering when he'd started accepting the strange as his new normal.

Does that mean Duskwalkers are technically... gods?

"Gideon," Aleron whispered, clinging tighter. He stood as still as a statue, his entire being so tense he even began to quake. "Help me."

She visibly flinched and released her hold on him, her features becoming crestfallen.

The laughter that burst out of Gideon was quiet but couldn't be contained. *She fucking scared him.* She'd been so overjoyed that it'd scared the frightening Duskwalker.

She was a new person. He doubted Aleron had been openly welcomed like this upon first meeting a stranger.

"She's just happy to meet you," Gideon stated around chuckles. "She's showing affection."

Her lips flattened in disapproval as her eyes darkened. "I did not realise my actions would require a translator."

That sobered Gideon from his humour. He sighed and slumped into Aleron's strong arms.

"Sorry," Gideon said, meeting her gold, pupilless eyes head-on. "Where we're from, Duskwalkers aren't treated so welcomingly."

Her golden eyelashes tipped, and her lips hardened further. "Why not? Look at him, he's beautiful."

How could Gideon answer that? It was only recently that he'd begun to see Aleron as magnificent; he was handsome in a way that was totally unique.

Why not? *Because humans are stupid.* They had been irrevocably unseeing of the wonder that was Aleron.

"We Mavka are feared," Aleron answered, when Gideon only gave silence. "Our skulls terrify the humans, and they hunt and attack us or flee in fear."

A thunderous rumble vibrated everything around them as sparks fizzled around her. There was the earthquake and lightning he'd been expecting!

"Why? I can't sense any hostility from you."

Aleron tilted his skull to Gideon, flashing white orbs.

Since he didn't know what the Duskwalker silently sought, he shrugged in answer.

I should probably also just stay... quiet. He was a human, and currently the problem species being discussed. In situations like this, it was best just to keep his head down and speak when only required.

"We... have eaten many of them," Aleron explained. "Our hunger is unending, and we often fall into a bloodlust. It is not their fault."

The rumbling stopped, as did the sparks. She cast her eyes to the side. "I see. So the curse extends past Weldir." Her nose and cheeks winced with sorrow. "He experiences no hunger, as he doesn't have a true form, but it appears the Demon thirst for blood is shared with his children. I sense no hostility because you are dead, negating that desire."

She then cast Aleron a wary look, only for it to fade instantly.

"It has always been unfair that my child suffered due to my negligence. Now I have hurt my grandchildren as well."

"It is not a curse," Aleron confidently stated, making her pause.

His statement also caused Gideon's lips to part in surprise.

"Pardon?" she rasped.

"Calling it a curse means there is something wrong with us," Aleron continued, his arms loosening on Gideon. "We Mavka... Weldir said we are not whole and are born with no features. What we first consume becomes our forms, but we are missing an anchor. Once we have it, the hunger goes away."

"I am assuming you speak of soul eating." Her floating, glowing wings fluttered behind her rapidly. "I was surprised when I learned of this trait of Weldir's, as his father was not a soul protector. To be a deity of death is a high honour, and their power is often on par with my own."

"What are you a deity of then?" Aleron asked, tilting his head in the cute, curious way he often did.

"I am the goddess of mana," she answered warmly. "Those with the honour of life tend to be weak, as they are constantly giving away their power for the birth of everything within their realm. Those who take, like those pertaining to death, grow with each soul they harbour, and often will have a contract for rebirth with life."

Aleron moved forward with a single, hesitant step. "Then what of Weldir? He is often weak and must slumber."

Her eyes bowed with what Gideon could only decipher as sadness or pity. "He is not fully formed, so what he collects is barely enough to keep him present. Even now I can sense him, and he has recently weakened to the point he was close to never waking – the equivalent of death, since we are immortal. He should not have destroyed so many souls, or he may never have woken again."

He and Aleron shared a look with each other. Or rather, Gideon shared one with his dark-yellow orbs.

It must have been when they tried to kill Jabez and bring Emerie back to life. If Gideon could, he'd give the guy a father of the year award.

To sacrifice his own life for his children... well, that was pretty freaking neat. Then, in the midst of his weakness, he'd also reunited a child with their deceased loved one.

"I am sorry, by the way," she said, flicking her eyes to Aleron's bat skull. "I didn't mean to cause offense for calling it a curse. It is how he sees it, what he calls it because of all that he has suffered. Weldir considers himself flawed, but I think he is perfect as he is. If it weren't for him, I, and the few remaining deities here, would no longer be present."

Gideon's head cocked.

He never thought he'd meet a higher power, let alone hear one apologise for something so minor. Her benevolent nature was commendable.

Her lips curled into a knowing smile at Gideon. "However, that is not my story to tell. It is also one that spans over many human centuries and your time is limited. I have given Weldir a break from using his power, preventing him from calling you back to his realm, but I have only just awoken myself. I am not at my full capacity, which is why I am not weeping."

"You weep?" Aleron turned his skull to Gideon questioningly. "As in cry?"

"Yes," she laughed, before Gideon could answer. "It is how I naturally feed my mana into the Elven world without needing to think about it. It is also why this realm is upside down and parallel to theirs, as the synergy waters at your feet flow to them directly."

"Why must you be filled with sorrow for this?" Aleron asked, just as his orbs swirled with a deep blue for her. "Is there no one here to bring you into the comfort of their wings?"

She exaggeratedly covered her mouth when she gasped, her eyes widening. "Oh my," she rasped. Then she pointed to him while staring at Gideon. "He's just the sweetest!"

Gideon's eyes crinkled with tenderness and humour. *I think so too.*

She came forward once more, gripping the sides of Aleron's skull, and nuzzled her lips and nose against the tip. He didn't flinch like before, but his feathers did puff.

"As much as I appreciate the sentiment, it is unneeded." She pulled back and turned, her expression coy as she glanced over her shoulder. Gideon followed her gaze, one where she expected someone to interrupt them. "But there is a reason you have come."

Aleron nodded. "Yes. Weldir has tasked me with obtaining a tear.

"I'm sure he did," she said with a hum. "He has been so good, so patient. He likely feels as though I have abandoned him. It's no surprise he has asked me for something as small as this."

Her golden coils bounced and fluttered as she sauntered around the area, the water rippling beneath her feet. Gliding her hand as if caressing the edge of a table, she lifted her face upwards towards the muted sun shining over them.

Then, her head dipped back, her neck craning and arched, so she could glance at them with her lips pouted and her eyes squinted.

With dark humour laden in her tone, she mischievously asked, "The question is: should I?"

Gideon opened his mouth, preparing to spout some outraged statement, but quickly shut it.

Fuck. I've already caused enough problems with Merikh. As much as his heart wanted to fight for Weldir, more so because Aleron seemed to care for him, he didn't. It wasn't his place, and he didn't want to make matters worse.

Aleron tilted his head. "Yes. I think you should."

She laughed at that, especially since her question had been rhetorical.

"That is not what I meant, dear child," she sang. Once more, she turned from them, humming as she thought. "I could give Weldir what he wants, or I can give him more. I shall solely leave that up to the decision you make."

"I do not understand." Ah, Aleron's favourite words.

"Good." She giggled, before swiftly spinning.

She sauntered back over, only to lean her hands on her knees to be at head height with Gideon, her nose barely an inch from his own. Unlike with how Merikh had done this, it didn't come across as superior, but more like she wanted to make them equal.

It felt like a caring mother leaning down to her child.

Just as Aleron reached for Gideon's arm to pull him away, she shoved her hand out between them to stop him.

"Why did you come here, human?"

"Me?" His brows drew together tightly. "I don't know

why you're bothering to ask me. I'm insignificant in all this."

"You did not come seeking power or a wish?"

She leaned her head to the side, causing her long hair to cascade over her shoulder like a waterfall. Her golden, pupilless eyes bored into his own, and looking at his clear reflection in them made him nervous.

He averted his gaze as he rubbed at the side of his head. "No, not really. I don't really need anything if I'm dead."

"What about life?"

He managed to completely stifle his snort of laughter. *Yeah, I considered that.*

But the reason he wasn't going to ask for it was he didn't think it'd matter. Gideon wasn't related to her in any form, and as he'd already mentioned, he was irrelevant. His wants and desires meant little, and he'd rather not state them if they could have a negative impact on Aleron.

He did, however, ask with a sardonic smile, "Can you give it?"

Her full lips formed a conniving pout when she smiled. "Perhaps."

Then she might be able to bring Aleron back to life. He could go back to his kindred, who he deeply cared for.

Aleron missed Ingram like a terrible ache. He never hid it, and frequently spoke of him and their memories together. His orbs were often a dark, swallowing blue because of it, and the colour always made Gideon sad for him.

Eh, so what if that meant he'd be left alone in Tenebris? He'd just forget anyway and go to sleep in that creepy canyon of lost and unwanted souls. He wouldn't even know he'd been left behind.

As if expecting more, she placed two fingers under Gideon's chin and directed his face back to hers. "Well?"

"You already told me what I want to know," he calmly stated back, this time unwavering from her haunting eyes. "I only came here because Aleron wanted me to. Other than that, there's nothing more for me to say."

"I see." Her lips tightened before she stood and turned to Aleron. "And what about you? Do you seek life?"

When he tipped his skull to Gideon, he answered Aleron with a nod. *Go on, man. She's your grandmother or whatever. She'll probably help you.*

"Yes," he answered. "I would like to be returned to my kindred."

Her brows twitched as she frowned. "Kindred?"

"He is my *twin*." He brought his hand to his chest, his claws digging in. "But–"

"Shhh, shhh," she hushed. Her eyes bowed with sympathy as she placed her hand over his snout. "I have heard all I need to."

The Gilded Maiden rose her arms, as if she were about to cast some kind of magic or say something grand. Just as she opened her mouth, a yell had them all turning towards the black crystal prism.

A man with flesh like bright-green scales ran towards them. His Elven-like form, with pointed ears, didn't match the sharp and hard lines of his flat, nearly humanoid, reptilian face. Even with the small distance between them, his yellow eyes were narrowed, and his short, dark-green hair fluttered.

The Gilded Maiden squealed. Fretting, she grabbed an arm of each of them.

"We have to go!"

Gideon thought she was about to run off with them, but the world flashed, and they were transported away. The environment changed. Instead of being surrounded by swampy trees, they were miles in the air.

Stepping back in surprise, it appeared they stood on some kind of glass sheet, or an invisible floor. Below them, lava swirled throughout mountains, flowing in streams before cracking into rivulets.

What must have once been a peaceful plane of the uttermost serenity, had now become violent. He could even feel the heat from high above, like they'd been brought to some fiery pits of damnation.

"That was a close one," she eventually exclaimed with a laugh. "The Evergreen Servant can be rather protective, especially when I've just awoken from a slumber. He won't be able to reach us here."

Evergreen Servant? Well, he was definitely green. He'd almost looked like a snake who ran on two legs, rather than a tail, with claws tipping his fingers and toes.

She tossed her head side to side, forcing her hair back and out of the way. No wind pushed it around, nor his own or Aleron's feathers.

She gave a singular clap of her hands. "But this works in my favour. I now know what I want to do."

She's a delinquent. She'd fled from her caretaker.

"Aleron," she said, flashing a toothy grin. Gideon didn't remember either of them telling her their names. "I offer you a choice."

Great. This couldn't be any good. *I guess she wants to test him or something.* Whatever it was, hopefully he could assist.

She walked around them as she gestured to the world.

"Here, in this realm, life and death do not matter. Here, you are just a being, one who is immortal." She lifted a single finger. "However, falling into one of the rivers below means unending torture, forever drowning in unbearable heat." She gave them a smirk. "You can imagine why no one comes here unless absolutely necessary."

Unable to help himself, his feet moving of their own accord, Gideon stood in front of Aleron and threw his arms open. "If you're asking him to go for a swim, the answer is no."

His chest was tight with fear, unable to handle the

thought of Aleron in pain just for this odd goddess' entertainment. He'd rather throw himself into the rivers of lava.

She pinched Gideon's cheek. "I would never do something so cruel. How dare you think of me like this."

She yanked hard. Although it didn't particularly hurt, and mainly just stretched his skin to the side, he frowned.

"Please leave my human alone," Aleron pleaded, as he gently grabbed her wrist to still her. "My tolerance of your touching of him grows shorter each time."

She let go, unbothered by his interference, and stared down at Gideon.

"You, on the other hand, have no deity essence, human. You are weak, feeble, and as you said, insignificant. You will disintegrate from the heat before you even reach the lava, your soul extinguishing forever."

All her humour, her cheer, and even gentleness faded.

"Aleron, will you choose the human, or your chance at life?" Piercing her icy stare at Gideon, she crooned, "Let's see how sweet *my* Mavka really are."

The ground came out from under Gideon, and within an instant, he plummeted.

Alone.

He gave a yell, scratching at the air, while staring up at Aleron and the Gilded Maiden still standing on the glass platform.

Oh shit!

One minute Gideon was beside him, the next he was just... *gone.*

He'd disappeared so suddenly that Aleron barely had the chance to register he'd fallen. The space next to him immediately felt cold, empty, and barren.

"What will you choose?" the Gilded Maiden asked, causing his skull to raise in her direction in disbelief at what he'd just witnessed. "Sacrifice the human, and I may give you new life. Or go after him, and I will send you back to Weldir as you are."

Ice bled into his pulse, starting from the centre of his torso as it radiated behind his sternum. As it spread, going down his extremities like it flooded his veins, his orbs flared bright crimson. His fingers twitched as he bared his claws, while his maw parted so he could flash his fangs at her.

His snarl came out more like a bark when rage took hold. But Aleron wouldn't linger on her, what she had done, and the icy cyclone of destruction that swirled inside him.

His wings shot back, extending to their full lengths. Aleron dived swiftly, chasing the yell of his little human.

He'd reacted too slow. Gideon had already fallen far, dropping steadily towards the hot lava below.

Except for the day his skull had been broken, and he'd feared for his kindred's life more than his own, he didn't think he'd been this terrified. Dread raced down his spine, stiffening his wings as he flapped them to creep ever closer to Gideon.

For the first time in months, wind cut over his face, bitter and sharp. It rustled his fur and feathers.

The whoosh of his wings was heavier than normal, fighting through the air rather than just peacefully gliding with it. He fought it, that invisible foe, while reaching for Gideon with all his might.

The male had turned, facing his doom like that would save him.

"Gideon!" Aleron roared, just as the temperature began to rise.

Gideon flipped over. His hair rushed around his forehead and temples, while his brown pants and grey sleeveless tunic filled with air and flapped.

"Aleron!" The panicked, fretting crinkle on his brow tightened, yet relief lifted into his eyes.

He looked so pale with fright that it sickened Aleron.

His chest felt bruised when he thought, *Did he not believe I would come for him?*

Gideon flipped, falling feet first, as he shoved his hand up to Aleron. Within seconds, the heat became nearly unbearable. Gideon's small fingertips swiped against the sharp points of his claws, and Aleron's heart squeezed in anxiety from missing.

They swung again.

Aleron flapped his wings hard and grabbed his wrist, then yanked Gideon to his chest. He hugged the male tightly, squishing their torsos together, and the world glowed bright red. All that could be seen was liquid fire.

They were too close to the ground now, and the likelihood of Aleron stopping them from diving headfirst into the lava was low. *I can survive.* That's what the Gilded Maiden said, right?

Although Mavka sunk, perhaps he could figure out a way to swim them to safety – even if it meant clawing his way along the dirt.

So, he wrapped his wings around Gideon, hoping to keep him cocooned within their fluffy feathers, and spun so his back faced danger. Searing heat stung, causing him to wince. The crackling, fizzing, and bubbling of the molten hot liquid filled his ears, and he never realised something could sound so harrowing.

He tucked his head in just when he thought they were about to land.

Aleron faceplanted into something soft, cool, and... not on fire? Actually, the sizzling heat had vanished, leaving only refreshing air swirling around them.

Lifting his head, he noted they were lying upon the invisible platform they had been standing on moments before. With Gideon below him, protected and safe, he darted his skull around, uncertain as to what was happening.

There stood the Gilded Maiden, smiling down at them.

With a deeper, ferocious snarl, Aleron released Gideon from his arms and stood above him on all fours. Wings flared into wide arches to appear more frightening, he parted his jaws to bare his fangs. He shifted into his more monstrous, four-legged form, ensuring he would be stronger and swifter.

As much as Aleron wanted to leap for the Gilded Maiden, he utterly refused to leave Gideon. If she made him fall a second time, he needed to be close. To be near so he could save him faster and then fly them away from her.

When she stepped to the side, her long, metallic hair twinkled in the sun as it swayed. Her smile never fell. Even though he snarled so fiercely that drool seeped from his fangs, and his skull vibrated as he subtly shook it, her eyes crinkled warmly.

Then she dared to inch closer.

He gave her a menacing bark in warning, and his body puffed even further. He had no doubt his feathers from the base of his skull all the way to his tail looked like a fin of aggression.

"Temper, temper," she sang with mirth.

"Stay back," Aleron snapped harshly, knocking his foot against Gideon to check he still remained beneath him.

"For a being that stated he easily falls into a bloodlust, you appear to be rather calm." As she circled them, Aleron followed her, crossing his hands and feet precisely to avoid stepping on the precious creature he protected. "You care so much for that human, you won't even leave his side to attack."

"I wish to leave." He wanted away from her and this odd world.

She tsked at him and pouted. "Before I even give you a gift?"

Mimicking similar words Gideon had spoken earlier, he stated, *"If your reward involves bringing harm to this human again, the answer is no."*

Her eyes widened and her lips parted in shock. Then she laughed. "No. My game has ended. I no longer intend any more playful tricks. You and this human are safe."

When that didn't ease him, instead only deepening his mistrust, he yelped in surprise as he was taken off his feet. A translucent bubble formed around him. It turned him upside down, and he fought to place himself the right way up to orientate himself. Clawing at the bubble did nothing, and when he tried too hard, she spun it to make him dizzy.

His anger deflated as his head swam.

In his peripheral, he noticed she extended her hand out to Gideon. "See?" She stated, looking towards Aleron as he righted himself again.

Gideon rose to his feet on his own. Then, he did that thing he always did, where he brushed off his pants despite them being clean.

"Did he pass your stupid test?" Gideon spat out, eyeing Aleron. "I should have figured you'd do something like that."

The bubble containing him flipped, as did he. Instead of sliding around it and being on his back once more, it popped. He landed on all fours and shook his body to right his feathers so they sat properly.

"Yes," she stated warmly. "He did perfectly, and exceeded my expectations."

Just as Aleron went to stand in front of Gideon protectively, one arm in front of his legs, he noted the way his human's shoulders eased.

One side of Gideon's lips quirked with a smile, while his eyes seemed to bow with some kind of sadness. "Does that mean you'll bring him back to life?"

"No," she answered, grinning widely at them. "I'm a deity of magic, not life or death. I have no abilities such as this."

His expression fell, and he stomped a foot forward. Aleron moved with him, placing himself back in front of his legs.

"What the hell?!" Gideon exclaimed, his hands fisting in outrage. "Then why did you do all that?"

"Because I wanted to see if the heart of a Mavka was selfish. I wanted to know how the offspring of my child really are. Reward him if he does well by saving another, even if it means losing out on what he wants." Her features stiffened, and her golden lashes dipped. "Or punish him by taking away what he cares for if he does evil. The lava below us really would have extinguished you human, and he would have been rewarded with nothing in return for letting you touch it."

"You are rather cruel," Gideon remarked coldly, "and immature."

He inched closer to Aleron and cupped his skull tenderly, gazing at him with trust and appreciation in his green eyes. His anger finally gentled at his human's affectionate touch, and his orbs returned to their normal pink colouring.

Are you okay? Aleron could see the question in Gideon's eyes, even if he never stated it. Aleron leaned into his touch in answer.

"Cruel, immature, insane." She clapped her hands together once. "You try being alive for thousands of years, and have many thousands ask you for a wish. Sometimes it's best to play with them first and ensure you aren't helping those with terribleness inside them."

"You can't even give him what he wants," Gideon grumbled, never taking his eyes from his skull. "So why bother at all?"

"I can't, but someone else can." When they both turned their gazes to her, she gave them a knowing but pitying smile. "And Aleron's actions have allowed me to trust in someone who, until today, was a stranger to me."

Gideon rolled his eyes. "He's your grandchild."

"And my own children have attempted to swallow me for their own power. Blood means nothing."

Tired of their conversation, of her, Aleron stepped between them. *"Will you give us what Weldir seeks?"*

Her pupilless eyes slipped to his skull. "No, I intend to give him something much more valuable."

She waved both hands to the side, and their environment wobbled like a mirage as it changed. Then, once more, they stood on the surface of the lake – or pond – they'd originally arrived through from Nyl'theria.

The two-legged serpent male from before stood near the steps leading to the glittering black crystal that reached kilometres high. With arms folded, a clawed foot tapping against the water's surface and making it ripple, he glared.

She peeked back at him before flicking her hair over her shoulder to show she intended to ignore him. His yellow eyes narrowed further, and he stormed forward.

"Almethrandra," he hissed in warning.

"Oh, shush you," she hissed back. "I am fine, aren't I?"

"You are weak!" he roared, only to smash into an invisible wall when he came too close. He cupped his nose after he bashed it. "You should not have left my mending vines!"

She lifted her nose to snub him, and the sound of him bashing against the barrier turned to quiet warbles. She'd silenced him, or possibly anything beyond where they stood.

"Want to see a deity lose his mind?" she asked with a laugh.

Then she reached up to the floating halo crown above her head. The green male behind her grew more agitated, slamming his shoulder against the barrier. Then, with much force, she snapped a chunk off with a *chink*.

Judging by his open maw, the Evergreen Servant roared.

Aleron paid little attention to him, instead tilting his

skull at her. For just a split second, her entire body...
changed.

The rich colour of her brown skin had turned ashen. The
gold in her hair had stopped glittering and dulled – even the
glossy curls had frizzed as though the moisture in them had
dried up. Her cheeks hollowed, as did her collar bones,
while her lips cracked and dried.

Even the swirling gold on her limbs had turned light
grey, as did her pupilless irises.

She looked haggard and weak, her appearance drawn as
though the very life and blood had been sucked out of her.

Yet, within the span of a heartbeat, she appeared as
voluptuous and lively as they'd seen this entire time...
almost. Now that he'd seen it drop, he became acutely
aware of the glamour she'd placed over herself.

Is this... how she normally appears? The version before
them now looked the same in terms of structure and form,
just stronger. *She is hiding how weak she is...* That must be
it.

Aleron drifted his skull to the reptilian male who had
managed to embed his claws into the barrier. The scales
around his humanoid face became spikes as his eyes
crinkled. He even bared a set of feline fangs, thin but sharp.

He'd stopped moving, but the quiet, unnerving stillness
was more telling of his internal struggle against what she'd
just done. His yellow eyes spared a hateful glance towards
Aleron and Gideon as she approached them.

The chunk of her crown no longer glowed, but it still
glittered in the light when she extended it towards Aleron.
Considering he'd need to hold on to it, he wisely changed
his form back to his more humanoid one.

He reached out for it, and she placed the long, thin spike
in his dark-grey palm. He grunted at its weight, not
expecting it to be so heavy due to its small size. He fisted it
tightly, noting the unusual warmth of it and how it tingled

his hand as though lightly vibrating.

"When I release my hold on you, I doubt Weldir will be prepared for it," she stated, her voice crackly and strained. He lifted his sight to her at the difference. "If you wanted to go back to Nyl'theria, you won't be able to. You'll be transported back to his realm from here."

Aleron nodded, even though an array of emotions swelled in his gut. He would have liked to see Merikh and Raewyn again, especially since it was unlikely he would get the chance to for a long time, if ever. Apparently a portal would be needed, and with the Demon scourge in both worlds, it would be difficult to bridge their realms.

Yet, as he directed his skull to Gideon, he didn't mind.

The sooner they left here, the more at ease he'd feel regarding his companion. The Gilded Maiden's 'test' still unnerved him. He'd jump into any lava she demanded, so long as Gideon was safe and would return to his side.

I also wish to be alone with him again. All these people and gods kept getting in his way.

They'd touched in that secretive cave, and he wanted to know what would have happened had they not been interrupted. After their time in the Elven worlds, his craving to be closer to this male, Aleron's affections for him, had grown.

His anticipation of touching someone who had tried to protect him, defend him with such a fragile and small body, only made him want to worship every inch. To lick Gideon's mouth when he knew it could be rather temperamental and fiery elevated his desire to do it.

Just the thought made a thrill shoot down his spine and tighten his flesh.

Aleron opened his hand slightly so he could inspect the crown shard. Should he thank her? This isn't what Weldir had asked for, not that he knew what he truly desired.

Before he could even speak, the invisible barrier keeping the Evergreen Servant disappeared. He ran forward, but not quick enough to catch the Gilded Maiden as her legs gave out and she fell to the side.

Red glowed from the skin beneath his scales, and scarlet leafy vines shot out from the water. The veins caught her, slowing her fall, so he could slide across the water on his knees and dip beneath her. She landed in the cradle of his arms.

She said nothing, eyelids heavy and gaze fading. He turned his back to them as he stood, his naked shoulders rigid.

"Weldir better be thankful for this," he stated coldly, his voice rough. "This is her way of making up for everything, but it should have come when she truly had strength."

He cast them a glance over his shoulders, yellow eyes hostile and unforgiving. Then they softened when she placed a hand on his cheek. He lowered his head as he walked towards the stairs leading to the crystal.

Beside him, Gideon began to fade. Aleron darted his gaze down to his own hands, finding they were turning transparent as well.

A spike of anxiety struck him, and Aleron quickly reached out. It settled when he grabbed Gideon's arm, hoping that meant he couldn't lose him.

Then everything disappeared.

SIXTEEN

Darting his gaze around the new environment they were transported to, Aleron took in its familiarity.

Like they'd never left, the clearing in front of the cave of Weldir's secretive tunnels hadn't changed. The rest of the mountain cast a shadow over them from the bright, false sun, which sat in the same place it always did. The unusual wind that lacked coolness and any scents fluttered his fur and feathers, while brushing Gideon's light-brown hair.

They had returned to Tenebris in the spot they'd left it.

His grip on Gideon's arm loosened, no longer constrictive now that they were safe. That shard of anxiety, although cruel and panicked, dissipated to its normal soft thrum.

"Guess we're back," Gideon stated, shining a warm and welcoming smile, seemingly relieved to have returned to the afterworld.

His wings twitched, delighted by the contentment of the little human at his side.

Before Aleron could respond, the warm, buzzing shard of metal in his hand was yanked forcibly from his grasp. It floated towards Weldir, who had transported in moments after them.

His form remained a chalky and misty texture, the outline of his body muddled by the cloud that shrouded him.

Staring down at the crown shard, Weldir cupped the end of his chin, which made it difficult to see the rest of his face. It blurred from the disturbance.

"This is far more than I asked for," Weldir mumbled quietly, before lifting his face to them. "I doubt you understand the significance of this."

"The Evergreen Servant said you should be thankful," Aleron said, repeating what had been stated to him.

"I am, very much so," he answered pensively. "I am also thankful towards you, little one, for obtaining it on my behalf. I have no doubt he was rather angry with her." Weldir gave a small but deep chuckle. "He was always overprotective of her, that father of mine. Or rather, *possible* father."

Weldir gripped the shard hard, clenching it, and it disappeared. He waved his fingers as his hand dropped to his side.

"I do not like her," Aleron muttered honestly, slipping his hand around Gideon's arm furthest from him so he could pull the male to his side. "She almost destroyed Gideon."

Weldir's features tightened, and his shroud sucked and clung to his body. A narrow waist became highlighted, as did a leanly muscled torso. It quickly pushed out before Aleron could note any more of his details.

"I see. Although I am rightfully furious she attempted to harm one of my souls, it clears up why she gave me something so precious." He bowed his head, making Aleron tilt his own in bewilderment. "I have much to think on, and much to do."

Then, without another word, he vanished.

Aleron stared at the spot Weldir disappeared from until Gideon stepped away.

"Wow. Well, that was an adventure. I feel like so much happened in such a short amount of time."

"I do not think we were gone long. Perhaps a day."

Aleron was growing tired, as if many days had passed since he last rested right after the canyon of souls.

Gideon lifted his elbow high as he rubbed at his neck, averting his gaze from Aleron's skull.

"I'm not sure if I said it before, but I'm really sorry if I got in the way. I can have quite a temper when something gets my back up." He brought his hand forward and rubbed at his cheek instead, oddly looking tired when he lacked the need for sleep. "It probably would have been better if I hadn't gone. I don't feel like I helped you at all."

Something about the way Gideon held himself, looking off to the side with a pained, furrowed expression, touched at Aleron's chest. It made him feel warm, the vulnerability and insecurity soothing his own misgivings about himself and how he reacted.

It was likely strange, but it only made Gideon appear more... beautiful to him.

Aleron reached out, hesitating part of the way, then braved brushing the smooth backs of his claws down his rough cheek. Gideon flinched and looked up, but didn't pull away.

"Just having you by my side put me at ease," Aleron stated with confidence, dipping his torso to the side so he could be more eye level with him. "I do not think you realise how nervous I was. You helped me understand things I would never have been able to decipher on my own."

Without Gideon, who had grown angered by Merikh's treatment of him, it was doubtful they would have shared the enlightening conversation they'd had afterwards. Aleron never would have learned just how deeply wounded the bear-skulled Mavka was, and never would have been given the chance to apologise in his own way. He would have looked upon the relationship he had with Raewyn and that Demon youngling with confusion, with no hope of being educated on it.

The fact that during the entire time they were there, he

had someone who could touch him comfortingly, or just simply be *there* for him, meant the entire world. He'd needed that. For someone to just be by his side in a place that had felt wrong.

A place where he'd been an outcast, but had belonged within someone's hand.

Gideon snorted a humourless laugh. "I started a fight and almost had you going for a swim in fire."

Although the burn of rage still simmered beneath his flesh at how this wonderful human had been treated, Aleron gently brought his claws forward so he could place two under his chin. He forced Gideon to look up at him as he lowered his skull. He nuzzled the end of his snout against the corner of Gideon's lips, and the scratchiness of the hair on his face tingled Aleron's fangs, sending a thrill down his spine.

The sensation reminded Aleron of their moment within the dark tunnel. The warmth of skin, the tickling sensation of hair, all of which belonged to Gideon, felt wonderful against the smooth bone of his skull.

Aleron stopped paying attention to their conversation. Instead, he wrapped his hand around the side of Gideon's neck to keep him still for his affection.

Prickly. He gave a contented purr.

"Thank you, by the way," Gideon uttered softly, leaning his head to the side to give Aleron more room to play with. "For saving me."

"I will always choose you," Aleron said without thinking, only to pause.

Was that true? Would he always choose Gideon? Something settled within Aleron's mind at the realisation that he might care much more for this human than he originally thought. Enough to balance with his kindred, someone he knew he couldn't truly live without – and was only doing so now due to no longer being alive.

And the afterlife had only become bearable because of this male.

My sight grows pink for him. Not in his normal colouring, but one he only ever shined upon Ingram. Love... was it? A different and wholly special version of it.

"What did you say?" Gideon asked, backing his head away to escape and look upon him. Surprise caused his pitch to turn raspy and go higher.

Aleron refused to let him retreat far.

The growing, swelling, hot emotion behind his sternum demanded he show his fondness.

Aleron parted his fangs and swiped his tongue across Gideon's soft, fleshy lips. Even though Aleron couldn't taste him, the feel of them caused the inferno to swirl tighter, faster, disintegrating everything in its wake. With Aleron's hand around the side of his neck, his fingertips cradling the back of the human's head, he brought Gideon closer.

His tongue was more demanding this time as he licked across Gideon's lips, separating them himself, so Aleron could flick it against his teeth. Just their bumpy, hard texture was enough to send a thrill of delight down his essence.

"I have not forgotten we were interrupted," Aleron purred roughly. "And I would very much like to continue."

It would be a lie to state that he wasn't tired. Aleron hadn't rested in quite some time, but right now, his pestering craving to touch this human nagged at him. It had from the first moment his human hands had brought him 'release,' and the meagre taste of intimacy from earlier nowhere near sated him. Aleron wanted more, wanted to know what would have happened had Weldir not come.

He hadn't truly stopped thinking about it since.

Already his orbs had shifted to purple, and his cock tingled behind his seam.

A small chuckle hummed from Gideon. "A little nuzzling and a kiss, and you're ready to go. You're so easy to provoke that I don't need to do anything."

Perhaps Aleron should have been embarrassed, but Gideon's green eyes staring up at him, softening with each word, allowed him to remain at ease. Even more so when the male hooked an arm around the back of his skull and pulled himself up.

"But yeah, I haven't forgotten either."

His lips and teeth parted, allowing Aleron inside, and the side of his tongue brushed against the top of Gideon's shorter, flatter one. He let himself be lost in the sensation of their textured tastebuds rippling across each other's.

Gideon palmed both his hands up Aleron's sides to dig into his fur.

Wanting to utilise all he'd learned, he slid his hand around to Gideon's back so he could greet the male's spine. Aleron didn't even make it far before his claws caused a hitch of breath to come from him.

Despite the barrier of his shirt, Gideon's back arched when Aleron's fingertips slipped down it, just as he dragged his hands to Aleron's chest. Gideon's fingers delved through fur to the protruding rib bones hidden beneath it, and the bold contact made Aleron's shaft twitch and harden further.

"This is in the way," Aleron muttered, yanking on the back of his shirt.

He wanted to finally see. Hair often peeked out from the vee collar, and Aleron wanted to know how much was truly upon his chest. He wanted to explore this human with his hungry sight, rather than just his greedy fingers.

Unable to speak around Aleron's tongue deep within his mouth, Gideon retracted his hands so he could lift the material off. Following his lead, Aleron assisted, disappointed their mouths had to part at the last moment. Even more so when Gideon lowered his head, only giving Aleron a quick peek at his heated features before he buried his face into the fur on his chest.

But he was pleased at being able to view the lightly

tanned flesh of Gideon's broad shoulders and back. His muscles visibly flexed and danced for him when Aleron brushed his hand down his spine once more. He swirled his tongue against the round shell of his ear, utterly delighted when the male gave a rasping groan.

What else did he know? Where else could Aleron touch to incite such pleasurable, wondrous sounds? He wanted to make this human ravenous.

Just as Aleron wondered what his next move should be, a curt, surprised growl cracked out of him. Something wet slipped against a hard but sensitive nipple. It happened again, boldly. Swirling in a circle, it was completely hidden by Gideon's face buried in his fur, but he knew it had to be his tongue.

Deep purple infiltrated his sight, and his knees shook at the sensation as it sent shocks through him.

Darting his arms down, Aleron grabbed Gideon's backside and swiftly yanked him off his feet. The male gasped in surprise, forced to grip his fur and feathers across his back when lifted until his head reached even higher than Aleron's.

With his cock so engorged that not even his tentacles could hold him back, jutting from his pelvis and wildly thrumming, he licked across Gideon's chest. The sweep was long and messy as Aleron drew it diagonally over his pectoral muscle. He found what he sought, that same firm bud, and the male's legs twitched as they wound around his torso.

"You liked it when I licked your nipple, huh?" Gideon playfully rasped.

"Yes," he hissed back, hoping to return the same cock-tingling sparks.

He held the crook of Gideon's thigh, while Aleron's other arm sat diagonally across his back to ensure he didn't fall.

His tongue was much too big, making it hard to play

with his nipple, but Gideon's head still tilted back with enjoyment. The hard ball at his throat bobbed, his jaw tightened, and little knots of muscle formed at the corners. Gideon's hands slid further back to grip the base of his wings when Aleron nuzzled the dusting of hair that spanned his chest as he made his way to Gideon's other nipple to tease it.

Only when the male groaned and thrust against him did Aleron notice the hard length pressing just below his sternum. Aleron squeezed him tighter, wanting to feel it more deeply – to affirm that Gideon was aroused for him, by him. That the profound throbbing in his cock was not alone, making him momentarily thicken and swell.

Aleron lowered to his knees, no longer wanting to stand when his entire groin felt strained. Then he carefully placed Gideon against the grass, refusing to stop licking at him in the hopes it brought him pleasure.

I want to see. He wanted no barrier between them so he could, for the first time, see this human fully.

Aleron was so desperate for it that he curled his fingers into the waistline of his pants and attempted to yank them down. Gideon grunted, shifting beneath him rather than the material coming away. Annoyed and growing increasingly frustrated, he accidentally nipped the human's entire pectoral muscle.

Aleron yanked again.

Gideon's hands grabbed the sides of his skull and directed his head up.

"If you're going to bite, don't do it so hard." Before Aleron could even react for thoughtlessly hurting him, he needed to support his weight against the ground when Gideon wrapped a hand around the head of his cock, making him hiss through his fangs. "Someone is very eager, and excited."

Was Gideon talking about him or his dick, or both?

Because right then, they were the same, his heart and it aching in unison.

Aleron's stomach dipped, clenching hard, and his cock threatened to disintegrate in bliss when the little human gave him a stroke. He greeted Aleron so readily that his mind dazed as tenderness flooded him.

Yet Gideon pulled away... thankfully, only to undo the buttons of his pants.

Aleron didn't waste a second. He grabbed the waistband once more and tore the pants down, accidentally shredding them with his claws. A snarl tore free – another fucking barrier! The human wore some kind of undershorts.

Enough! No more. I wish to see.

Gideon burst into a fit of laughter when Aleron tore those away too. It died swiftly as Aleron tilted his skull and looked down his body.

Although he'd seen Gideon's cock, he'd been distracted last time. He also hadn't been fully unclothed, and Aleron took in his fill of Gideon, letting his sight learn.

He patted the white raised scars spanning across Gideon's entire torso in a double strike – a cross pattern of claw marks. *This is how he died.* He caressed them, hating them because of the pain and fear he must have suffered, but cherishing them because they brought him to Aleron.

Gideon's shoulders were broad, his chest plump with muscles and dusted in hair, and his waist narrow. Although they were very subtle, and barely noticeable, muscles contracted down his stomach. Seeing the dip of his navel, then gazing lower, he hadn't realised the deep vee of someone's hip bones could be so... erotic, or that they'd lead to such a wonderful place.

A thin, fuzzy trail travelled down the middle of his abdomen to greet his pelvis. Dark hair covered the base of his shaft and what seemed to be some kind of hanging sac.

Sheathing his claws, remembering how the male had reacted when he'd gripped too hard last time and what he'd called them, Aleron gently lifted his *balls*. They were firmer than he expected, and they moved freely under his touch. Gideon's dick jerked, and when Aleron fully gripped them, even stroking them with his thumb, it pulsed a second time.

He is different to me, Aleron thought, caressing his finger pads up the side of his shaft.

It wasn't as thick as he was, not as long, and lacked any purple colouring. The head was partially shielded by skin, while the pale-pink tip peeked out. When Aleron gripped him, nearly swallowing the entire length of it in his big fist, and stroked, more of the pink head became visible.

He placed his other hand upon Gideon's knee and drew it up his hair-dusted thigh. It gave him the response that he wanted, for his legs to twitch and part so Aleron could have more freedom to touch.

"I think it would be better if you go to your back," Gideon said after a long while.

Aleron realised then that Gideon had been giving him time to explore his body.

"Why?" He wasn't too fond of being on his back, considering his wings often got in the way and could be uncomfortable to lie upon.

"Because it's best if I take control for our first time." Gideon's eyes slipped to the jutting erection coming from between Aleron's hips, and the tentacles that lightly squirmed to hold on to something. "You're much bigger than me, in every sense. I'd rather neither one of us hurt the other if possible."

Aleron huffed at that, but couldn't deny his logic.

He trusted in Gideon more than himself.

He dipped to the side, flared his right wing, then rolled to his back while flaring his left. He had to wiggle so he could open his wings slightly, the elbow joints of them bent above his head. His skull was forced forward due to the ends of his horns digging into the ground.

He didn't mind, not when it meant he'd always be focused on Gideon.

He expected Gideon to straddle him like that female he'd seen, but he shoved his knee between Aleron's thighs, forcing them open instead. Gideon knelt on his long tail feathers, but his weight was light enough that it didn't bother Aleron.

Due to their difference in size, the tip of his purple cock was close to the human's pretty mouth. Could he be licked? Considering how his tongue felt against Aleron's, he thought he might like the feeling of it slipping over the sensitive tip.

Disappointment filled him when Gideon leaned back, but that was quickly overshadowed when both his hands gripped Aleron's cock. He subtly thrust when Gideon stroked the first quarter. His joints locked, and his sight deepened in its purple hue at watching Gideon's overlapping fingers play with his girth and length.

Aleron's muscles spasmed when his thumbs played right behind the head, each one taking turns slipping into the deep groove.

Then Gideon dipped a hand into his tentacles, as if exploring their depths. He cupped somewhere sensitive, two ovals embedded into the base of Aleron's cock, and a hiss burst out of him as he thrust hard.

Gideon tried to touch lower, leaning back in search of something.

"Damnit," the male bit out, pulling his hand away from Aleron's tentacles despite their persistence in latching on. He touched lower, outside his tentacles, but nothing happened. "You really don't... There's nowhere for me to enter you."

Even though his sight remained its lustful shade, disappointment seeped into his chest. "Does that mean we cannot... fuck?"

Aleron really didn't care how they would do it, so long

as it was possible. Gideon had stated two males could have sex, and he wished for them to connect somehow. To mingle and mesh.

Gideon's lips pursed, then crept into a coy smile, as though holding back humour. He crawled his way on top of Aleron, making him groan when Gideon's cock slipped up his own. Just as he gripped the male's hips so he could thrust against him, that light contact enough to spur him on, Gideon grabbed his hands and shoved them to the ground.

"No, it doesn't mean we can't fuck," he stated, staring down at Aleron, whose eager cock popped out from underneath Gideon and instead cradled his cheeks. "However, it does mean that you'll have to enter me instead, and I'd been hoping to show you *how* to do that."

I will be inside him. And just the thought of becoming one with this male had his body clenching with want.

"We'll have to go slow, though," Gideon continued, twisting his head to place a kiss against the side of his snout. "I don't mind how I do it, so long as I get to touch my partner any" – Gideon lowered to kiss his neck – "way" – then the little beast bit Aleron's chest – "possible."

Aleron flinched and groaned at his teeth nipping hard.

Then Gideon leaned back on straightened arms, licking at his lips as he stared down at Aleron's skull. The dark heat in his piercing green eyes was mesmerising, and the fact they were so heavily focused on only Aleron had his heart and body clawing for more.

I like him sitting on me like this. Gideon was naked, his dick jutting up while his balls rested on him. Aleron liked the human pinning him down as if he had any chance of actually controlling him. Enjoyed the playfulness of his mouth and his thick, warm thighs cradling his waist.

Gideon lifted and looked behind him as he reached for Aleron's cock. It shoved his chest forward, and Aleron was tempted to push up so he could lick it again.

"You know, it's pretty neat that you have your own lubricant," Gideon said, as he stroked up the length of him. "You were kind of made to do this with a guy."

With the slick he'd stolen, Gideon brought his hand forward and between his thighs. Aleron saw very little and had no idea what he was doing. Yet Gideon's features tightened, and he let out a deep exhale as his cheeks flushed.

When his hand began to move up and down, Aleron's impatience had him shoving Gideon's chest. Aleron swiftly drew his knees up so the male could lie back against them and be exposed, then leaned his head forward. Twisting it so he could see past his snout, he found two of Gideon's fingers had disappeared inside a small hole behind his sac.

"In here?" Aleron asked, gripping Gideon's thigh and pulling it to the side so he could see better. "It looks... rather small."

"Yeah, which is why I'm preparing my ass for you. Anal usually requires a lot of patience, but considering I heal pretty quickly here in Tenebris, I don't think we'll need to worry too much." He glanced behind him again, assessing Aleron's girth, and his lips tightened. "Actually, I don't think I can do that on my own."

Once more, Gideon reached back to stroke Aleron's cock with his free hand, stealing a fair amount of his lubricant. He waved his drenched fingers at Aleron while waggling his brows.

"Want to help?" Gideon gave him a playful grin. "If so, I'll need your hand."

Without hesitation, excited to learn about this, he offered Gideon his left hand since he was more dominant with it. Gideon smeared liquid over Aleron's fingers and then brought them between his thighs. His large palm cupped his sac as Aleron touched right where Gideon was, then he removed his own fingers from his pink hole.

It didn't take Aleron much to realise what he needed to do, but Gideon directed him to insert his middle finger. It was tight, but he'd already stretched himself enough that it went in with ease. Aleron noted the smooth texture inside, how the muscled ring was firm and squeezed the base of his finger, but the rest was snug and warm. Since he'd been pumping his fingers, Aleron tried to mimic what he'd seen, and goosebumps flashed across Gideon's chest.

"Y-yeah, like that," Gideon rasped, placing a steadying palm against his torso. "I think you can add a second now."

Aleron expected it to be even tighter, but the ring opened up slowly. Gideon's nose wrinkled, and he grabbed Aleron's hand when he must have tried to shove in too fast.

"Slowly," he urged with a broken, but reassuring groan. When Aleron eventually sunk both fingers inside, noticing the way Gideon's hole contracted and pulsed, he gently thrust them. "Okay, now push your fingers forward to find my prostate. It'll stop me from going soft and will make it better for me."

He slowed. "It does not feel good?"

"Just trust me, okay?" As much as it worried him, the warmth, trust, and desirous glint in Gideon's gaze calmed him.

Thankfully Tenebris would heal Gideon of any pain or soreness, ensuring this 'preparation' would require little patience from either of them. Gideon had already begun to soften around his fingers, and Aleron enjoyed watching his little pink hole being stretched by his dark-grey fingers.

Doing as instructed, Aleron pushed his fingertips forward, hooking them, as he moved in and out.

Perhaps Aleron did it much too hard for a human's delicate body, since he let out a raspy hitch of breath.

"Oh fuck," Gideon choked out, his knees knocking inwards.

Aleron didn't stop, since Gideon never told him to. The male also moved back and forth with his movements, as if he wanted more.

His cock was hard, his nose scrunched, as he let out a soft moan. Aleron's wings flapped in pride, having once seen him produce such a pained expression and sound while filled with pleasure.

Thrilled that he did good, and that his little human was enjoying his deep touch, Aleron bent forward. He wrapped his free arm around Gideon's waist to hold him still, then lifted him slightly so Aleron could not only lick freely at his chest but also give himself more room.

He thrust his two fingers until the ring of his ass had softened like before.

Aleron worked in a third before he was even told to.

Gideon moaned as his head fell back, grabbing ahold of Aleron's shoulders to keep himself steady. A single hand gripped a horn from underneath, and he adored how Gideon easily accepted and reached for one.

Gideon's hips moved subtly, his skin prickling as though his very flesh waved with bliss. It became more frequent as Aleron moved his tongue in circles, trying to caress his hard nipple. It was so small that he kept swiping it with each draw and lathering it in saliva.

He feels warm inside. Soft, like the inside of his mouth. His tongue enjoyed delving, and he already knew his cock to be far more sensitive. *He will feel nice.*

He panted as drool flooded the cavity of his bony mouth.

Wanting inside, he managed to quickly squeeze a fourth finger in. Gideon's expression tightened. His cheek twitched, his right eye crinkling as he winced, and he released a strained, strangled groan. Noticing Gideon's cock had started to soften, Aleron paused, and a sigh fluttered past his lips.

"Thanks," he croaked. "Just give me a second. I've never had to prepare for something of your size." Then, as though he wanted to release the tension in the moment, Gideon chuckled. "You're very impressive, Aleron, and you're doing really well. You're being very good, going slow for me, being patient."

His talons curled in delight at the compliments.

Perhaps it was the silliest reason for his chest to swell with pride, and for his feathers to puff, but the reassurance did wonders. *I am doing good. He likes it.*

The praise even made his cock, which had been given no attention, swell as he pulsated. Its patience, and his own, was rewarded with just a few words – like Gideon could sense he needed them.

Despite the cringe of pain he'd noted, and that four of his thick fingers were deep inside Gideon, the male had taken the time to care for Aleron. Even after he'd suddenly rushed.

It caused his heart to take flight and soar with adoration.

"Okay, I'm as ready as I'll ever be," Gideon stated.

He leaned out of Aleron's hold and cupped the end of his cock before gripping just underneath the flared rim. He pulled it towards his arse and bumped it against Aleron's knuckles, hinting for him to pull out. Lying back down to give him freedom, and so that he could watch, Aleron held the crook of Gideon's thighs. He slyly kneaded the bottoms of the male's luscious arse cheeks, feeling their plump softness.

Considering he was about to be, hopefully, buried deep between them, he had a new appreciation for the rounded backside of this male.

The pressure against the very tip spread as his body gave way, all the preparation aiding to make it easier than expected – considering the tightness that had first greeted his fingers. Once the end of his thick cock wedged inside, and snug warmth greeted him, Gideon let go so he could press against his torso. The male sat back, his jaw knots flexing as the ball at his throat bobbed.

Aleron let out a curt, but excited growl when the head popped inside. *Tight!* His claws unsheathed and cut into the soft flesh of Gideon's thighs, while his fangs parted slightly to let out a growly huff of pleasure. *So tight. I want him to squeeze me more.*

Aleron absentmindedly pushed him down as he thrust up, his back bowing at the plushness that began to surround his cock. Gideon gasped, just as his fangs parted further in utter bliss. His shaft thickened.

His dark-purple tentacles writhed in rapid succession, nagging him with their craving to latch on to something. They wanted to bring this human down so he mounted Aleron completely until he was trapped.

And the vibrating sensation of Gideon's tight ring slipping over the braided knots down three sides of Aleron had his entire groin clenching inward with violent pleasure. They weren't sensitive, but they tingled the core of his shaft. How would it feel if Gideon swallowed the entire length of him, including the two braids most of the way down?

More lubricant seeped to the surface, making everything wetter and easier as Aleron tried to push him down harder. Grass and dirt crunched beneath his head as his horns gouged into the ground when his head tried to tilt back under the onslaught of this.

A deep groan left him, even when Gideon grabbed his tense hands and shoved them against Aleron's torso.

"Watch your claws," Gideon stated coarsely, his eyes narrowed. "And you can't push me down so fast. Let me do this."

The tightness in Gideon's body faded when his features soothed. Aleron hoped Tenebris had healed Gideon of whatever damage he'd just inflicted.

Whatever apology had been about to fall from Aleron melted away when the determined male bounced on him. Little by little, he fed more inside. Aleron clawed at his own chest when the desire to grab at him gnawed, and he just shook with restraint instead.

By the time Gideon was sitting just above the two rings, Aleron was fighting every instinct to thrust up and forcibly shove him down the rest of the way. *Do not touch. Fuck. I want to.* So badly did he want to, especially since his tentacles had started wrapping themselves around Gideon's thighs.

Gideon was so close to taking him fully.

Aleron looked down, seeing that his cock had been swallowed up by this pretty human. His sight was so dark he thought it was about to disappear, robbing him of the view as Gideon moved back and forth as if to stir Aleron's cock inside.

Yet, when Gideon grabbed his semi-soft cock and stroked it to incite his body to harden once more, Aleron realised the strain this had put on him.

Aleron reached towards him.

"Wait," Gideon grated out.

He ignored him. Instead, he held Gideon's waist, then drifted one palm to his back, while the other ghosted up the front of his torso. Aleron caressed his chest, hoping the roughness of his hand against his pale-pink nipples and his claws tickling up the indents of his spine felt nice.

Gideon's ass clenched around him as he let out a rasp. At the same time, his twisting strokes grew longer as he became erect again.

And the longer Aleron touched, worshipping this male with his palms, his tongue slipping over his snout in interest, the more Gideon moved. His human cock bobbed up and down, while his nails dug into Aleron's furry abdomen, and he panted at the view before him. It was subtle at first, Gideon's body waving back and forth, then his feet slipped to the ground so he could balance with his toes. Eventually, he began to properly move, slipping up half Aleron's cock before pressing back down.

"Fuck," Gideon cursed, letting out his first groan since mounting him. "I don't think I've ever had anything this deep inside me before."

Aleron didn't know how to respond, especially when he had to take his hands from the human or he'd fucking *maim* Gideon the quicker he moved. Right now, Aleron felt like a mess, unsure of what to do, how to move, and the overload of sensations was frying his mind. He wanted to thrust, so, so badly, his hips twitching constantly with the frenzied need.

He wanted to shove Gideon down on him.

His tongue itched to lean forward and lick. His tentacles tried to latch on to flesh, but he wasn't deep enough for them to do so properly. His cock kept swelling, throbbing with a profound ache.

Aleron remembered what that peak of arousal felt like. How his entire body stiffened, went rigid as bliss struck him like lightning hitting a tree – hot, sudden, and violent. He wanted to feel that again.

His talon-tipped toes clenched, and his stomach hollowed out.

Aleron didn't realise he'd stopped breathing, or making any sounds, until a strangled, haunted groan quaked past his fangs. His wings flapped, knocking against the hard ground as every inhuman part of him – fur, feathers, his entire damn essence – radiated in bliss.

"Gideon," Aleron called, wishing his thoughts would piece together so he could truly explain what he wanted to.

"Does it feel good, Aleron?" he asked so quietly, so coyly, around strange breaths, his pretty piercing green eyes fixated on his skull.

But it was Aleron's name... said in a tone that spoke of the male's pleasure, which tore at his control and resolve.

With parted fangs echoing a mild roar, his hands darted forward. Gripping him tightly, just as unfathomable pleasure clawed at his groin, his hips shoved up as he pushed Gideon down. Even before Gideon had managed to fully mount him, his shaft had started pulsating, coming *hard.*

When the two rings popped through, the human gave a

deep squawk. Gideon attempted to escape, but he pushed him back down with his clasping hands and tentacles.

"Nnghn," Aleron grunted and flinched. Every time Gideon tried to flee up his cock, every part of Aleron kept him down, and the subtle movement broke him a little more.

Then Gideon gasped and tentatively swivelled his hips with some kind of realisation. He started to move on Aleron, although barely, as his tentacles trapped him, locked him down, but it was enough to send Aleron into a lather.

His chest caved in as he twitched, his mind and body just trying to survive through this.

Gideon gave him a groan, mirroring the sounds that shuddered out of him.

"Holy shit," Gideon moaned, bouncing on him harder, faster, as his hands slapped against Aleron's torso to steady himself. "Holy *shit*. That feels so damn good."

As Aleron settled back down, his cock ceasing its unbearable pulses, his blackened sight reopened to purple.

He took in Gideon's features. His eyes were closed, the bridge of his nose wrinkled, his lips parted on constant erotic noises. Fisting his own cock, his hips rolled back and forth as though he was thrusting into it, and his head dipped forward.

"Fuck," Gideon muttered under his breath, his hair falling across his brow. "Don't go down, don't go soft."

Any potential of Aleron's dick losing its enthusiastic, excited girth was immediately made impossible by the sight before him. The sounds Gideon made, and how his body kept sucking on Aleron's shaft as it twitched and spasmed, had him rumbling in quickly rekindled need.

Drool seeped between his back fangs, drowning him, but he didn't mind. Not when Aleron focused on his hand placement, finding it still on Gideon's hips. Aleron gave a singular thrust up as a test, a short but deep one, and his little human moaned in answer.

So Aleron finally gave in to the ache in his hips and rocked up and down, greeting Gideon with thrusts. Now that he'd come, everything felt wetter from his lubricant, although nothing else had come from him. A light squelch mixed in with the fwap of their bodies beginning to greet as they both moved hard, grinding, but never going past the two rings.

Gideon seemed content to stay around them, and Aleron was delighted he'd been swallowed whole.

He didn't even care when Gideon gripped and yanked on his fur so hard that he threatened to rip the fibres from his flesh. Not when his hips picked up speed and his half-hidden expression looked... lost, and as crazed as Aleron had been just moments before. His whole face was flushed, his tanned chest and shoulders too.

Then his ass clenched hard, causing Aleron to wince at the tightness that surrounded him, until it pulsed and squeezed repeatedly. But Aleron slowed his thrusts, savouring the blissful feeling as his cock was crushed to its core.

Gideon twitched, muscles flexing at different intervals like his entire body was confused as it leapt. His moan was quiet and shaken, but an erotic caress to Aleron's senses.

It took a moment for Aleron to realise Gideon was coming around him, but he took it in and watched with awe. Experienced it with wonder. Listened with a thrill tearing down his spine that he'd been a part of this, the reason for this human's pleasure.

Mine. My pretty human. He wanted to see this over and over again, wondering if there were different ways to do it.

Gideon eventually calmed. Immobile, leaning on straightened arms against his torso, he lifted his face to Aleron's.

"It really sucks that we don't come properly here," Gideon complained airily. "We don't even produce semen, but I think that was still the most intense orgasm I've ever had."

Aleron, having little experience with sex, tilted his head at that, his horns tearing up more of the grass in the process. "This is not normal?"

"Fuck no," he exclaimed with mirth. "But damn, Aleron. You really worried me there for a moment. I thought that ring at the base of you would be too much, but..." His nose scrunched as he groaned, and his snug hole squeezed him. "It felt amazing inside me."

Aleron's cock pulsated within him. "Gideon..." he uttered quietly, before thrusting his hips up. "I am still hard."

"I guess you're lucky then." Gideon turned his gaze down to his softening shaft. "Since this world is so backwards, it doesn't look like I have to abide by normal human stamina."

Then, his human gave him a wicked grin, one that had his sight flashing bright pink for a moment. Pressing against Aleron's chest, Gideon started to move on him once more. He was learning that Gideon was a lot more teasing and playful than Aleron originally thought, and he'd already been quite intense.

It only made him more enamoured with his little human.

"Let's see how much I can take, now that I'm all warmed up."

Aleron shuddered at the idea, even before Gideon leaned to the side. Worried about losing him, refusing to let them part even a little, Aleron went with him until they rolled.

He was above Gideon, on his hands and knees.

Thighs wide around Aleron's hips, the heels of his feet pressing into his backside to spur him into moving, Gideon buried his face into Aleron's fur.

"Come on, big guy," he said with a muffled purr. "Fuck me. I can tell you've been holding back this entire time, and it doesn't look like we have to worry about me being hurt."

Completely unsure of how Aleron was about to react, as he'd never done this before, he shuddered above Gideon once more. He slammed his aching hips forward until he'd completely and utterly filled the little male. *He wants more. Wants me to* fuck *him.*

All Aleron knew... was that Gideon enjoyed it by his lost groan, and that he was already obsessed with doing this with his little male.

Foolish human.

His claws gouged at the dirt as Aleron thrust hard with all his might.

Gideon shouldn't have given him free rein.

SEVENTEEN

Gideon gave a roar of uncontrolled, tortured laughter. He twisted his body, trying to escape the claws that traced up his side, but instead he faceplanted into feathers. With big black fluffy wings keeping him trapped, along with a pair of elongated, strong arms, he had nowhere to run.

"Stop tickling me!" Gideon yelled, before letting out more screams of laughter. Even his toes curled in repulsion.

The chuckle from his partner was as evil as it was mischievous. "Look at how you squirm," Aleron exclaimed with mirth. "You act like it pains you, and yet you laugh in enjoyment."

"I'm laughing because it tickles! If you don't stop, I'm going to beat the shit out of you." His threat, of course, was empty, but if he'd had the ability to pee, this may have been more embarrassing.

"I would like to see you try, little beast." The mirth in Aleron's tone nettled him, as well as the tease.

In retaliation, Gideon shot his head forward and bit into his pectoral muscle as hard as he could. His teeth clanked against bone before finding something squishy, but he latched on and persisted, even when Aleron groaned.

He didn't get the reaction he'd been seeking.

Aleron shoved Gideon harder against him and ground his hips – his seam – against his thighs. However, he did stop torturing Gideon with his claws.

He released his bite, pulling his head back to face his bat skull.

"I like it when you do that," Aleron purred.

His lips curled in knowing humour. Oh yeah, he knew Aleron enjoyed being bitten as hard as Gideon could.

During the course of... who fucking knew, a day? This Duskwalker had been an unstoppable, pumping force. Gideon couldn't count the number of times both of them came, only to never truly be satisfied nor produce a drop of semen. Pressure built, but never eased. Since Gideon healed instantly, he never ran out of strength. His stamina was as unending as this life.

Considering how much Gideon enjoyed every second of it, he showed Aleron as many positions as he could. The Duskwalker didn't particularly seem fond of being on his back due to his wings, but he did like wrapping them both in them. If they weren't circled around Gideon, they were flared back, arching above them, and occasionally flapping with excitement.

He'd shown Aleron how far his legs could spread, which wasn't too far considering he'd never been overly flexible due to the tightness and mass of his muscles.

Aleron did like lying on him though, to squeeze their bodies together. At one point, Gideon had been taken on his hands and knees, being slammed into wildly, and this big Duskwalker bore his weight down on him. Gideon's knees had slipped out from under him, causing him to lie flat and be fucked into the ground.

The grass, usually scratchy and irritating, had been soft against his cock.

One vital and major detail mattered most, something wholly unique to Aleron.

Although the braids going down three sides of him felt wonderful, the two rings three-quarters of the way down his huge cock had Gideon seeing fucking *stars*.

He wasn't usually the type of person to have his eyes cross, or his head completely numb out, but the thick rings would deeply and intensely massage his prostate. No human dick could do that, and any pain or uncomfortableness was literally overtaken by the knee buckling, back arching, toe curling, groin tingling sensation.

Consistently, he'd been on cloud nine. Euphoria. A heaven made purely of Aleron's cock ramming into him.

If Aleron were only part of the way in, his broad head would shove against that sweet spot, but if he were deep, that's all Gideon would feel.

It absolutely wouldn't have been wise to let Aleron be in complete control of speed, depth, or how hard his hips slammed if they'd been alive. A normal human absolutely wouldn't have been able to handle a fraction of it. But Gideon wasn't human or alive, so he just let the big guy go feral and Gideon enjoyed it as he did.

Gideon did explain that to Aleron, though – just in case in the future he needed it. For some reason, Aleron then slowed and softened his thrusts, as if to experiment with it, which had turned lustful fucking into a more... passionate session.

He'd also grown tired by that point.

Unlike Gideon, Aleron *did* need to rest.

Holding Gideon as though he were a giant teddy bear, Aleron had slept with his wings swallowing them. It gave Gideon time to digest everything, often smirking to himself – or incidentally making himself hard.

Now, though, they lay naked, still intertwined and hidden within the darkness. Just like that human couple they'd spied on, they laughed, teased, and just... enjoyed each other's company. It reminded him of being buried under a blanket on a winter's morning, waking up to the person one cared about most in the world, and spending time with them hidden away.

There was more of this realm to discover, but that could

come later. Gideon was all for this bonding, and happy to remain here until Aleron grew bored and wished to wander.

At least, that's what he'd thought.

Just as he reached down to tease Aleron's seam, hoping to spur him into hardening, someone spoke from outside their cuddle.

"I leave for a few hours, and this is what my poor eyes are blessed with upon my return?" Weldir said, his tone stern but not giving away whether he approved or not.

Aleron squeezed his wings tighter. "Go away," he lightly rumbled.

"Yeah, shoo, Mr dusty man! Or I'll sic my giant feather duster on you," Gideon chimed in. "We've had enough of your interruptions."

Within the darkness, Aleron's orbs flared bright yellow. "He is rather dusty."

They both cackled.

"As much as I would prefer to leave you be, there is something I must discuss with Aleron. It is of great importance."

Orbs fading to their normal pale-pink hue, Aleron blatantly peered down at Gideon. Why did he get the feeling the Duskwalker wanted to know what he thought?

Gideon rolled his eyes and let out a dramatic *ugh*. "Fine!"

Weldir was the ruler of this world, and he'd rather not actually piss him off. He'd only been playful because he didn't actually think he'd care – from what he'd learned of his personality so far.

He lowered Aleron's wing while ensuring he didn't pull it away completely. Gideon sat up as he searched the area, with Aleron following. "Where the hell are my clothes?"

"Gone," Weldir stated, cocking a cloudy brow. "Your soul is naked. Therefore, the clothes you wore earlier were what I conjured. The moment you removed them, they disappeared."

Unlike Weldir's earlier misty formation, he appeared to be made of chalky ribbons. The ribbons swirled, glittered, and coalesced around his essence, and only made up about a quarter of his body. Not much of his face was to be seen, other than his jaw, chin, cheek, nose, his right eye, and a horn. His body followed a similar pattern; only parts of him were visible.

Gideon's lids lowered in annoyance. "Oh." Then, he waved to his naked body, specifically his groin hidden away by black feathers. "Could you conjure some more then?" he *politely* asked.

The only reason embarrassment didn't flush his cheeks at being found naked and entangled by Weldir's son was because of the perverse statues he'd seen. The man, or god, or whatever, obviously wasn't shy about sex. Why should Gideon be?

Weldir waved his visible hand, and the same plain clothing as before snapped into place around his body.

Gideon stood and ignored the eight-foot demi-god as he offered his hand out to Aleron. Gideon appreciated that, although they both knew he didn't actually have the strength to help the big guy to his feet, Aleron still grabbed it and pretended. Gideon flashed him a mild smile, remembering the first time they'd tried that.

Once steady on his feet, Aleron fiercely shook his body, making every part of him quake. His fur and feathers, which had stuck up in odd places in disarray due to Gideon, shifted and lay properly against him. A few stray feathers fluttered out of his wings before disappearing into nothingness. His collar fluffed out, then settled.

He noticed Aleron's chest puffed with a confidence that hadn't been there before.

His orbs flashed bright yellow for a moment, and only faded when he wrapped his hand around Gideon's side.

His tone curt, but kind, Aleron asked, "What is it you want?"

"Hopefully it's not another task," Gideon joked, although he was rather serious.

"No." Weldir stepped closer with his hand out. When his pinkie finger must have touched the other, it also became visible – like spreading ink. "I would like to try something."

A skull appeared from thin air. It was unusually large, but it didn't take much for Gideon to furrow his brows. He darted a glance to Aleron's bat skull and twisting goat horns, realising they appeared *almost* the same.

There were a few differences, like the colour of the horns and how the snout was ever so slightly squarer, but other than that, it was the same. It tilted in Weldir's palm, and sparkled with gold as though glittery dust had been thrown upon it.

"What is this?" Aleron asked, tilting his skull as he closed the distance, leaving Gideon in his curiosity.

He stayed behind, unneeded.

"Lindiwe was unable to find your skull fragments within the rubble of Jabez's castle. So, I asked her to find me a fruit bat skull and goat horns that closely resembled yours." Weldir's head tipped down to it. "She put her all into finding them as quickly as possible for you."

"Why?" Aleron reached forward to touch it, but his intangible hand simply passed through it.

"It is physical, so you are unable to touch it, but..." Weldir lifted his face until he was staring down at Aleron. "With a piece of the crown the Gilded Maiden gave me, I want to use this to give you a new skull. With the combination of her magic and my own binding the pieces, Lindiwe and I are hoping we can use this to bring you back to life."

Aleron's wings slowly drooped. It was all Gideon could see standing behind him.

"Does this... does this mean I can be with Ingram again?" The whispered hope in his voice was so strong it almost became palpable enough for Gideon to gnaw on.

Despite the cold pang that struck across his chest, he couldn't help his sorrowful smile on Aleron's behalf. This is what he wanted, to be with his kindred again. Gideon knew how much that meant to him.

"I hope so," Weldir affirmed with a nod. "I'm going to mould it around your soul so that you may fill it once more, and the combined magic should be enough power to tether it to you."

Weldir lifted it to Aleron's face, and Gideon stepped to the side so he could see what would happen.

"Will... he still be here for a little while before he goes?" Gideon couldn't help asking, rubbing his palms against his pants.

I'd like to say goodbye to him.

Even if it didn't matter for Gideon, who would probably forget him in a damn hour, he'd still like the Duskwalker to think of him fondly in the future. The past month had meant a lot to Gideon, and a big part of him wished he could permanently remember it.

He may even ask Weldir that when he fell into a sleep state, if some of his dreams could be of his time with Aleron. If it were possible, of course.

"Yes, he will have time here. A day of it before I consume him," Weldir stated.

The skull began to bend, minutely changing to take on Aleron's form. He and it seemed to fight with some kind of suction, as though his spirit was truly attaching itself to the skull.

Gideon watched in awe as it started to work and Aleron's form began to change. The ends of his limbs took on a pink spectre, much like how Ingram's had been purple, and slowly grew up them until even his torso took on that colour.

The longer it took, the more his awe was strangled by another emotion.

Seconds felt like minutes, each one thumping Gideon's

false pulse deeper and deeper with longing. Only Aleron's sternum remained white, but it also slowly began to turn transparent.

His own radiated an ache, but he refused to voice his trepidation. Gideon stepped forward but didn't reach out like he suddenly wished to in order to stop them.

I don't want him to go. He said nothing.

At the last second, before Aleron completely changed into a spectre, he ducked away.

"No!" Aleron choked out, stumbling back, with all his fur and feathers sticking up in agitation.

"No?" Weldir asked in disbelief, a single, visible brow furrowing.

"What about Gideon?" Aleron waved his hand to him.

"What about him?" Weldir asked, turning his face to him. He gave a laugh. "Oh. I know I said you may yet steal a soul from me, since I may need the bonding power of a bride to bring you back to life, but I was wrong. With the Gilded Maiden's gift, I am able to do so with this alone. The human is no longer needed."

Gideon's head cocked just as his expression paled. His lips parted slightly as realisation was thrust upon him. *The human is no longer needed.*

A very cruel wave of coldness washed over Gideon's conscience. Then all the tender and pleasant feelings that had bloomed for Aleron suddenly burned in his chest like a searing coal.

With eyes wide, his head lowered so his gaze could slip to the ground.

"Oh," he quietly rasped out. "I didn't realise that was why you kept me around."

Here he thought they'd been glued at the damn hip because of a mutual understanding and desire to just not be alone in this weird world. If he had known Aleron had underhanded intentions to begin with, like using Gideon as a way to come back to life, he may not have allowed all these apparently one-sided emotions to bubble and build inside him.

He clutched at his pants, fisting the material that felt wrong and too fuzzy to be real, realising he'd been an *idiot.*

Good one, dickhead. You decided to grow feelings for a monster, and let him screw the hell out of you, when you didn't actually matter at all. He was just a necessity for Aleron to come back to life, or rather, *had* been.

Gideon lifted his head, turning it to the side as he rubbed at his mouth. *Fucking hell, why does knowing that sting so bad?*

Why did saying goodbye come easier than realising he may have been... used? One brought on deep, understanding sadness, the other a hot strike of betrayal and mortification.

"Gideon..." Aleron called, making him realise he'd spoken out loud earlier.

Without looking at his skull, Gideon gave a dark chuckle. "Hey man, it's all good. We had fun, and you learned a whole bunch. That's all that matters, right?"

Gideon didn't know why he was rambling and shoving a grin on his face. Maybe because it hurt, and he was just trying to deal with it while pretending he was okay, so he didn't come across as pathetic or foolish.

It absolutely wasn't all good, but the only shining light was that he'd forget soon, so it didn't matter. This horrible, sickening feeling in his stomach would disappear, just like his existence. He was about to go to the sad valley of poor, lost souls.

It wasn't like I'd even been thinking of becoming Aleron's bride or anything, since he hadn't actually thought it possible.

That didn't stop his eyes from turning glassy at being lied to or tricked. It never felt great to be the butt of an inside joke, or the only one who wasn't privy to vital and important information that would have been useful to know for self-preservation.

Yeah, saying goodbye to Aleron would have sucked, but at least it wouldn't have been showered in shame and embarrassment. Especially since Gideon usually wouldn't have sex with someone unless he actually *liked* them. Gosh, the mortification of what they'd done over the course of the last few hours! All of it emotionally one-sided!

I'm such a freaking idiot. It would have been horrible to learn it had been done to him by a human, but a monster? He wanted to laugh at himself.

Here he had been... holding his hand because he liked the Duskwalker and wanted to ease his anxieties, when Aleron had just been doing it to not lose his ticket to coming back to life.

He didn't notice Aleron had come closer until a large warm hand cupped the side of his neck. This world couldn't even give him the decency of allowing that touch to feel wrong – for his skin to prickle with goosebumps in repulsion to the affectionate touch.

Gideon was shaking in anger, betrayal, and hurt. He made a fist, hoping to tense his muscles into stillness, which only seemed to worsen it.

"Why are you upset?" Aleron asked, kneeling down so that he was lower, like he wanted to be smaller, for Gideon's sake.

"Upset?" he croaked out, turning his face to his with a false grin. "Who said I'm upset?"

Okay, so the lie came out unconvincing. Even Aleron's orbs flared red for a moment.

"Now you don't need to tie yourself to someone you don't want, and can go be with Ingram," Gideon stated, nodding his head towards Weldir. "This is your chance."

When he recoiled from Aleron, his orbs turned to a deep blue. Aleron darted his hands up and swallowed both sides of Gideon's head in his massive hands, squishing his cheeks and making his lips puff forward.

"I do not understand why you said I do not have to tie

myself to someone I do not want. I have never said this."

Why were they even having this conversation? Weldir spilled the truth, and now Aleron didn't have to have a difficult and awkward discussion about it. Gideon had even given him an easy out to avoid it. So, why the hell was he trying to have it anyway?

It would have been easier for everyone if he'd been ignored until the end.

Now he wished he'd been ignored from the very *start*.

"I'm saying you don't have to force your feelings now," Gideon grumbled through the squish of his palms, frowning deeply.

"But I do not want to go without you," Aleron said, as a little whine echoed from him.

Gideon sighed and rolled his eyes. "You owe me nothing. Even if you got to come back to life, I never expected to be owed life as well just because I chose to be your friend. I did that because I wanted to, with no expectation of receiving anything in return but your company. You don't have to take me with you."

Did Aleron really think his actions had been so self-serving? Maybe he'd shared in Merikh's way of thinking without realising it.

What Gideon had said was true. He'd chosen to be Aleron's friend simply because he wanted to. And he had no one else to blame for the current hurt stinging in his chest. He would have liked to have known the truth, but at the end of the day, Aleron had never been obligated to share his intentions.

Sure, it sucked and was a shitty thing to do, but *oh well*. No point in crying over it. At least he wouldn't be given the time to.

Aleron's hands loosened, and his head dropped. "But I thought you would want to come with me."

A whine echoed from his skull, just as his orbs darkened in their blue hue. The bottoms of them broke. Little glowing water droplets began to float around his skull before growing smaller and disappearing.

Gideon's head reared back in surprise, and Aleron's hands slipped away from him because of it. His wings drooped completely.

When a whimper broke from him this time, Gideon's brows drew together tightly. "Are you... are you *crying*?"

Aleron reached up and scratched at the collar of fur at the side of his neck, while drifting his skull to the right as though he wanted to avoid looking at him.

"I wanted you to be my bride. I thought you loved me, as I do you," Aleron quietly grumbled, through little pain-filled whimpers. "I thought that was why earlier we became one. I do not understand what I did wrong."

This time, when his head reared back, Gideon stumbled because of it.

"Did you just say that you... *love* me?" he asked, dumbfounded that he'd even uttered it.

"Well, yes. Was I not supposed to do this?" Aleron's floating droplets trickled faster and became larger, as if growing in mass from the weight of his sadness. He clawed at his chest. "It is different to how I love Ingram, but I feel it here."

Aleron's honesty baffled him.

Gideon fell to his arse, too busy trying to figure out what was going on to concentrate on standing. With his knees bent and wide, his feet almost touching, he held the soles of his boots together.

"I need your help here, because I'm really confused," Gideon said, leaning his head to the same side Aleron's skull was pointing, hoping to grab his attention and connect their gazes. "I thought you only brought me along with you because you needed me to come back to life, Aleron. That you were thinking of making me your bride just to do this."

The curt growl that cracked from him had a wheezy whine in it. "I would never choose a bride for such a

reason," Aleron snapped out, chomping his fangs in his
direction. "A bride is special, even I know this. It is
someone we must choose within our heart; someone we
love and care for. It should not be meaningless."

"Oh," Gideon sighed out, lifting a hand to rub at his
cheek before digging his fingers into his closed eyes in
annoyance. "I see. Because of what Weldir said, I thought
you didn't feel anything genuine towards me."

"I'm realising I may have added confusion to this
situation," Weldir chimed in, causing Gideon to remember
his existence.

Pulling his hand an inch from his face, he cast Weldir a
dull look. "You think?"

"I was not to know," he answered with a shrug.
"Although I am not pleased to have another soul stolen from
me when it is unnecessary, as I am still rather weakened
after everyone's battle with Jabez. But if this is something
you both choose, it can be done."

Gideon already figured as much, considering he'd helped
reunite Emerie and Ingram.

He sneered at the chalky, ribbony bastard. Mainly
because his chest still ached with residual hurt, and because
Aleron was crying. The ache fully dissipated when he took
in Aleron's ethereal tears once more, as everything he'd said
finally settled in.

Instead, his cheeks and ears warmed, not expecting such
a strong proclamation of affection. It somehow made
Gideon remarkably bashful after the horrible feelings that
had just bombarded him.

Did he love Aleron? He wasn't actually quite sure, since
he'd never really given it much thought. Was he falling in
love with him? It was impossible to deny that his infatuation
wasn't steeped in something more.

His body had responded to Aleron quite enthusiastically.
Gideon imagined these tender feelings would only grow
stronger and stronger by the day. Especially in the real,

living world, where life wasn't meaningless and there was potential for more.

Sometimes a relationship took work. It wasn't always instant, but that was what the point of dating was for – to see if they were compatible.

After everything, Gideon knew they were compatible.

He hoped they weren't perfect for each other, otherwise it'd be boring. Sometimes things needed to be messy to make the good times feel all the better, so long as they comforted and supported each other through those times.

After going to the Elven world, and all the mistakes Gideon had made along the way, he knew Aleron had a wonderful heart. His soul, all this time, had been pure.

Hard not to fall for that.

"Is that how you really feel, Aleron?" Gideon asked, cupping the side of his skull so he could direct it back to him. "Do you really love me and want me to be your bride?"

That would be forever, right? He kind of liked the idea of spending forever with Aleron. It'd be even better with Ingram and Emerie around.

"Yes," Aleron whined out, until his voice strengthened, and he tried to pull away from Gideon's touch. "But I do not want to force you if you do not want this. I did not realise love does not have to be shared, and it is rather hurtful like this."

Ha! Now their situations had been reversed. At least Gideon had the insight to, hopefully, fix it rather quickly and clearly.

"Come here, darling," Gideon cooed as he crawled to his knees and put his arms around Aleron's neck to hug him. "You wouldn't be forcing me at all. If you want me to go with you, then I would like that more than anything."

I didn't really want him to leave. I wanted him to stay here with me. The only reason he hadn't interfered is because he hadn't wanted to be... selfish – even when his whole being had been screaming at him.

Gideon squeezed him tightly and buried his face in his fur. "I've been falling in love with you, too, Aleron."

He glimpsed Aleron's wings lifting through his long fur, regaining their strength at his words. Then, he lightly dug his claws into Gideon's back and shoulder as though Aleron wanted to clutch at him, keep him trapped.

"Really? I am not alone in this feeling?" The sincere hope in his tone pulled on Gideon's heartstrings.

"No, but for a moment there, I thought I was the only one who cared. You can blame Weldir for that."

He received a chomping growl from the dusty bastard.

"No wonder you were upset. It was rather painful to feel alone in this."

"Yeah. I've been pretty fond of you for a while now. I didn't know you wanted more, since you never said so. You should have told me sooner."

"But I did tell you. You said you did not like the term *bride*."

Gideon winced before he laughed brightly against him. "It's a very feminine term, Aleron. You can't blame me for that. But, if that's what you want to call it, then sure. I'll be your bride." Gideon pulled back, only to find that Aleron's orbs and floating tears had turned bright fucking pink, like a beautiful sunset. "You can stop crying now."

"I cannot help it," Aleron muttered. His feathers lifted and puffed, in what Gideon thought may be joy. "I am relieved. I considered staying here to convince you otherwise."

"There's no need. I want to go with you, I really do. I promise." Gideon bent forward so he could land a kiss against the end of his fanged snout. "Let's go find Emerie and Ingram together."

Then they could all be together as one big family. Just the thought had his whole being swelling in anticipation.

Emerie meant the world to him as much as Ingram did

for Aleron. The fact he could share his new life with his little sister sounded perfect. It would have been missing a large and important Emerie-sized chunk otherwise.

After they shared a long and much needed hug, they both stood and faced Weldir.

Aleron grabbed Gideon's hand tightly, almost crushing it. He tried to do it back.

Just as Weldir was attaching the gold-dusted skull to his soul, Aleron asked, "Gideon will be fine, right? He will not forget everything?"

"No," Weldir answered. "I watched over Emerie and Ingram when they reunited, and she managed to retain her memories of Tenebris. I would not be allowing this otherwise, as Mavka and bride are spiritually inseparable once bonded."

Reassured, Aleron shoved the head of his spirit into the skull, and it moulded to him, bending and changing to be exactly the same. The entire time, they held hands until it completed, and they could no longer touch. The space Aleron took up felt empty, considering he'd turned into a pink spectre of himself.

"You look like a real Ghost now," Aleron stated, tilting his head. "You are white and transparent."

Gideon threw his hands up with crooked fingers and shouted, "Boo!"

He just needed to make light of the situation. All of a sudden, nervousness swirled in his stomach. It felt like a piss-poor wedding, and he was about to be married for life. Did any couple not feel nervous on their wedding day, despite their unwavering resolve?

"Are you alright, darling?" Gideon asked anxiously, wanting to make sure Aleron was okay.

"I will be once you are *mine*," he growled back, possessive playfulness evident within it.

An odd shiver ran down his spine.

That proclamation had been rather primal, and managed

to ease Gideon in a singular mental caress. He hoped to get plenty more of that, and *soon*.

Everything will feel stronger on Earth.

Gideon couldn't believe he was going back. He'd never dared to hope for it.

EIGHTEEN

Bouncing from one taloned foot to the other, Aleror impatiently shifted his weight.

Although it had been a long time since he'd felt the true coolness of the wind, and took in the scents as they tangled and fluttered on it, he didn't go sniffing like he may once have. As much as he wanted to rub his neck against the closest tree to feel its rough bark, and maybe even lick at the sap to taste it, he remained where he stood on two legs.

The bright sun cascaded gentle warmth across his shoulders, dawn not long ago risen. It was real, and he often lifted his blackened sight to it to soak it in. The leaves were brown, yellow, red, and green, while many branches were barren. When he'd died, overrun by a horde of Demons that crawled over him like a violent flood, he knew it'd been early autumn.

Now, winter was nearly upon them. Frost attempted to melt, wafting the smell of dew and wet earth into the air.

He darted his skull in the direction he heard a tree snap, excitement wanting to burst his heart.

Weldir said Ingram is nearby.

He wanted to go to him. He wanted to *run* to him. He wanted to find his scent on the wind, chase it down, and tackle his kindred to the ground so he could rub his skull against his scales. He wanted more than anything to surround Ingram in his wings where he should have been all along.

Instead of doing so, his bright-yellow sight drifted across the dirt, sticks, and decaying leaf litter in search of a Ghost.

Where are you, Gideon? It'd been an hour since Aleron first appeared in this spot, and he remained there, waiting for his precious bride.

As much as he yearned to hunt his kindred, Weldir warned him that his human may not be prepared for it. He would be naked, unsure of his surroundings, and may need a few moments to adjust. Apparently humans were uncomfortable being unclothed in front of others, especially the opposite sex.

Even though he had to wait to see Ingram a little longer, he'd rather his bride be content before being introduced to his kindred again and reuniting with his sister.

He'd already waited months, so a few hours couldn't hurt.

Bright pink exploded in his sight. *He said he was falling in love with me.* That meant he loved him... right? Or felt strongly towards him?

He shook his head, making the sound of dry bones rattle from him. *He came here with me—that is all that matters.* Gideon had chosen him, just as Aleron had chosen this male. That was enough.

I cannot wait to smell him. What did Gideon smell like? He couldn't even begin to imagine it, and he'd rather not try to when he could just be pleasantly surprised. *I bet he smells amazing.*

His heart and personality were amazing—so kind, gentle, and warm towards Aleron. He didn't see why his scent wouldn't reflect that.

Then it happened. A transparent white Ghost flickered into the area. He couldn't help letting out a choked breath.

Aleron darted to Gideon peacefully sleeping and curled

up on his side, and knelt around him, ready to lift him off the ground and into the safety of Aleron's arms and wings. Although the chill on the wind didn't bother him due to his feathers and fur, humans did not have these things. He didn't want Gideon to be cold.

Eyelids tipped with long eyelashes twitched, clenching tight, before they flipped open. Gideon lifted his face to him, gasped, and turned solid.

He let out the most harrowing yell Aleron had ever heard. Aleron flinched and skittered back in surprise, as Gideon scuffled out from under him, kicking dirt and sticks in his direction. He fled on his backside.

If Gideon's intense, rapid, and heavy heartbeat didn't give it away, the strong, sour scent of fear that wafted off him did.

Aleron couldn't believe the first thing he smelt from his bride was terror. Gideon's huffing breaths heaved, and his crinkled eyes full of anguish tore at his heart.

"Please. Please don't eat me," he begged – *pleaded* – to Aleron.

Something is wrong... Very wrong.

Aleron reached out to gently cup the side of his face, but Gideon's fear worsened as his pretty green eyes darted to his claws. He hesitated, and drew back, especially when the male threw his arms over his head to protect it.

"Gideon?" Aleron softly called, lowering his head.

"Oh my god." A mangled sob broke from him. "How the fuck does it know my name?!"

Realisation didn't just settle in, it struck him like a stone. *He does not remember. He does not remember me!*

Aleron darted to his feet and backed up, unsure of what to do or how to ease his cowering bride. He... he was terrified of him! *What do I do?!*

"Weldir!" Aleron roared, only to wince at the distressing noise Gideon squeaked in response.

"I know," Weldir stated, his voice echoey as though he

spoke from somewhere distant.

Aleron turned to his voice but found nothing. The space was seemingly empty.

"Weldir?"

"I'm here," he answered in the spot Aleron had turned to. "I cannot use another soul right now; I will not be able to handle the loss of power. You can only hear me, but I am here."

Perhaps to a human eye he may have been invisible, but now that Aleron was aware of Weldir's presence, he noticed something. A humanoid shape blurred everything. It was only a minute shift in his vision, and perhaps only something with a keen eye such as a Mavka would be able to notice it.

Gideon lowered his arms, and with wide, panicked eyes, he searched for where Weldir's voice came from.

"What's going on?" Gideon asked with anxious, huffing breaths. "Who's there?"

"You said he would not forget!" Aleron snapped at Weldir, flashing red orbs at him. He gestured a hand to the trembling creature he adored. "I would have waited longer, until we were certain, had I known this would happen."

"Yes, well... we all wish we had the power of foresight," Weldir snarked, before sighing. "Like I said, Ingram's bride retained her memories." A blurred arm lifted, as though he'd cupped his jaw. "But she only had to remember a day. This human... It has been over a month since he woke from his dream state. Perhaps it was too long."

"That's it! I'm going insane," Gideon chuckled darkly, before staring at his hand. "A Demon is talking to nothing, and the nothing is talking back." The laugh that came from him was high-pitched and unhinged, like a creature that had truly lost their senses. Then he looked beyond his hands and squeaked before covering his exposed groin. "Holy shit! Why the fuck am I naked? Where did my clothes go?"

"This is bad," Weldir stated. "He truly remembers nothing."

"You!" Gideon shouted, pointing at Aleron's skull. "The hell did you do to me? I stop you from eating my sister, so you fly off with me and strip me naked? How the hell did I get here?"

"Fly off with you?" Aleron's wings shifted as he turned his head to glance at them. They drooped. "I am not the Demon that killed you."

Gosh, the fact that Gideon could even mistake him for a Demon... His heart stung.

"As if. You're the only winged Demon I've ever seen."

"I am a Mavka!" Aleron roared at him, beginning to quake as his hands clenched into tight fists. Aleron himself had been destroyed by Demons! To be called one, compared to one... it was so vile that he wanted to lash out. He pointed to his face. "Demons do not have skulls." Then he turned to Weldir. "What do they call us? Duskwalkers?"

Somehow, the colour drained even more from Gideon's face. He looked sickly, and his heart raced as though he was moments from passing out. The tang of his fear worsened.

"A... Duskwalker?!" He threw a hand up and rolled his eyes in defeat. "That's it. I'm dead."

"This conversation is going nowhere," Weldir said, his blurred form moving towards the terror-stricken human shaking upon the ground. "Let me try something. Perhaps I can make him remember."

Noticing the voice was closer, Gideon's startled and stark gaze darted around, unseeing Weldir's approach. It didn't help that the spirit of the void made no sound as he moved.

Weldir crouched down in front of his human and reached out with one hand. Although he placed it on the top of Gideon's head, he didn't seem to feel it. Then Gideon froze, his entire body stiffening as his mouth opened and closed wordlessly. When his eyes rolled back to only reveal the whites, Aleron's fur puffed in aversion to the unnatural sight.

He let out an anguished *scream*.

Aleron tried to accept it, hoping it would bring his Gideon back. The longer it lasted, continuing well past the capacity of his lungs, the more it rippled his wings.

"Stop," Aleron choked out with a shudder, too familiar with the sound of a human's agony. Having it come from his own bride... he found it unbearable.

Gideon clawed at the air before he began to convulse.

"I said stop!" Aleron roared, darting forth to intervene. He clawed at nothing. *"Stop hurting him!"*

With a snarl, Weldir released him and stepped back. Aleron knelt down when Gideon sagged to the side, catching him before his head could touch the ground. The lifeless way the little male lay limp in his big hands, no longer afraid simply because he was too weak, twisted his gut.

Weldir spat out some kind of curse. "He has them. He has his memories – he just can't access them."

"Why not?" Aleron whined.

"I don't know."

"Why do you not know?!" His sight flared white in Weldir's direction when he scented blood coming from Gideon.

It welled in one of his nostrils, but he knew it came out of other places due to how much he could smell.

It no longer caused hunger to clutch at his stomach and mind, making him frenzied to sate his unending starvation. He wasn't given the chance to digest this new piece of himself.

"I am not all-knowing!" Weldir shouted back. "As I said, I thought everything would be fine. I have never done this before today. I have never brought one of my own children back to life, let alone a bride one has chosen. This is new to me."

"Then... what do I do?" Aleron asked with a whimper, looking down at his unconscious bride.

Aleron brushed the male's brown hair from his brow, noticing droplets of sweat upon his flesh. His skin felt like ice when humans were supposed to be warm – he'd eaten enough of them to know that.

"Help him to remember," Weldir stated quietly.

"What if he does not?" He feared the worst. He feared his loving and welcoming bride was lost to him. "What do I do then?"

"He fell in love with you once. Make him do so again."

I do not know how to do that. He didn't even know how he'd done it the first time.

Their first meeting hadn't been ripe with fear. Ingram and Emerie had been there, almost... guiding them to each other. Ingram had taught Aleron much, but it was Emerie who had introduced them, who had eased whatever worry Gideon may have had towards Mavka before they'd even spoken.

Aleron was on his own. He didn't know if he had enough humanity to help Gideon through this.

He mistook me for the Demon who killed him.

Aleron placed his hand upon Gideon's scarred abdomen, the evidence of his past death and how horrible it must have been. He knew this pain, had suffered it many times over, but humans were delicate creatures.

Now that Gideon lay unconscious, and his fear scent dissipated, the anxiety choking him released its grip a fraction, allowing him to take in that his bride smelt like the freshest and loveliest spring he'd ever experienced.

He smells like a purple flower I remember, and... patchouli. Gideon smelt like the herb he had shown Aleron in Tenebris, and the fact his own bride had been the one to teach him its name made his heart swell.

He curled his arms and wings around Gideon, hoping to bring him warmth and security within his embrace. Burying his skull against his glossy hair, he shuddered out a breath.

I will try for you. Aleron squeezed him tighter. *You are my bride. I love you, and you chose me.*

Gideon had been perfect for him. Playful, smart, forgiving.

No matter what he faced, no matter the obstacles before him, he would reflect back on their time in Tenebris. He would be determined to return to that moment in the clearing, where they had been hidden within his cuddle, laughing and teasing.

He is mine. He chose to come here with me.

That was what *he* had to remember.

With short, shallow breaths, Gideon took in the deep aroma of hazelnuts and cedarwood. The familiarity of it lingered in his mind. It reminded him of all the days he'd stop working, and covered in head to toe in cut tree dust, he'd plonk his arse on a fallen trunk around a fire. Hazelnut soup tended to be a favourite among his colleagues, so they always gathered around a hot pot of it – especially in the winter.

Heat surrounded him. It was almost too hot, or perhaps that was due to the splitting headache throbbing behind his eyes. He could barely breathe through the heat, yet he gave a shiver.

I must be coming down with something. Shit, that didn't bode well. He hated taking a single day off work, since it cut into his pay, and he'd been saving to buy his own home.

His nose wrinkled side to side when something super soft tickled the tip of it. At first, he thought it was a sneeze, or maybe Beau's unruly chest hair.

That didn't make sense, considering it didn't smell like his boyfriend. It also didn't feel like he was lying against him either.

When his nose twitched again, he thought perhaps he'd just passed out during lunch and one of his colleagues was messing with him. Wouldn't be the first time Gideon had a mid-afternoon nap, with the aroma of hazelnut soup ensuring he had hungry dreams, and one of the guys woke him by tickling a leaf against his face.

He blinked his eyes open and frowned at the darkness greeting him.

Panic immediately set in. "I can't see!"

Just as he went to cover his eyes to check if they worked or not, light exploded above him. What that revealed almost had him wishing he'd never woken up.

Gideon shoved at the Demon's... wait, no, *Duskwalker's* chest to get away from him. Startled by his sudden movements, the Duskwalker gasped and released him. He flopped to the ground, hissing when his shoulder hit the hard dirt.

Okay, so earlier hadn't been a horrible dream!

Cringing at the Duskwalker, unable to cope with the fact he'd been cuddling into him, he covered his naked groin. A chilly wind wrapped around him, causing shivers to break out across his warmed skin.

Even though a sharp stick stabbed into his bare rump as he shifted back, nothing could stop him from eyeing those massive wings. He'd seen wings like that before, whooshing and flapping above him, as he fought to free Emerie. The sound of them, the sight of them, would forever be entangled with a profound agony that had struck across his stomach and chest, not just once, but twice.

A shiver sliced through him as he drifted his gaze away, unable to bear looking at them.

He'd thought it'd been a nightmare, a cruel joke of his deepest fears. A twisted heroic dream where he was the knight in shining armour for his sister, who screamed as she was let go to safety and Gideon took her place as the feast sacrifice.

"Gideon," the Duskwalker called, so utterly careful with his name.

He couldn't focus on it, not when he cast his gaze down to see the scars marring his torso. They were deep, raised in keloid scarring, and white, as though they'd been carved into his skin years ago.

Did someone heal him somehow?

It was only last night, considering it was now the middle of the day. At least, that's what he told himself. *Did I actually pass out for a few days?*

Then who saved him and where were they now? Did the Duskwalker kill his saviour so that he could eat him?

He didn't realise his hands were shaking in trepidation until he dug his nails into his gut. His eyes crinkled and bowed deeply when he felt so utterly lost.

He looked around, wondering how far from home he was.

So far, the Duskwalker wasn't hurting him, and had spoken to him. Perhaps he could get answers from it.

"What happened? Where am I?" And how could he get away from the monster before him? Which direction would take him to the safety of Fishket's protective walls?

"We are west of the Veil."

Gideon flinched at that, and the depth of his growly voice. No matter that they'd had a conversation earlier, it still startled him that this beast could talk.

West? Fuck! Just how far did that Demon take me? He anxiously darted his gaze to the wings before him. *Or was it he who brought me here?*

Had he taken Gideon as far away from his home and family on purpose to ensure he felt hopeless?

"Why the fuck am I naked?" he asked, refusing to look upon the Duskwalker's skull. He found it unsettling.

Now that he thought back on it, the Demon who had

flown off with him had a wolfish muzzle – which absolutely had skin on it.

Regardless, his damn face heated in embarrassment at being as naked as the day he was born. In the forest, no less. It didn't matter who or what was before him. He could even feel a rock stabbing into his arse!

"Your soul is naked, so you did not have any clothing when you materialised." The Duskwalker placed a massive clawed hand against the ground, inching closer on his knees, until Gideon drew his legs up. He halted. "There is a town nearby. I have been waiting for you to wake up so we could clothe you."

"Clothe me?" Everything this monster stated just added more levels of confusion to his rapid and frantic thoughts. "I don't understand. Aren't you going to eat me? That's what your kind do: kill humans."

His skin crawled when the Duskwalker brushed the backs of his smooth claws against his shin. He shuffled his leg back.

Quietly, and with a hint of sadness, he said, "I would never hurt you."

Could he trust that? He brought his gaze to him, trying to assess skinless features that could never reveal any hint of truth or lie. He took in his twisting, spiralling goat horns and how they loomed above his form like a pair of devil horns. His skull was that of a bat, white, and yet it shimmered in the sunlight with hints of gold.

The rest of him just became a blur as he took in long fur and feathers, his wings and bird-like tail. He looked soft, but he was so damn massive it was like looking at a bear. His claws didn't help, and his bird-like feet were weird to look at.

"Why am I here?" Gideon whined.

His anxiety and fear still remained high and hadn't eased at all. Actually, it grew worse with each huff of breath, his torso beginning to heave with it.

"Because you are my bride. You do not remember, but we bonded in the afterworld."

A callous laugh snorted out of him, and he finally braved standing. *What nonsense is he going on about? Bride? Afterworld?* None of it made sense.

"You have not been alive for a long time," he continued, remaining where he knelt. "You were in Tenebris, a realm belonging to Weldir, the spirit of the void."

Gideon stepped back, shaking his head side to side. *Great. He's fucking crazy.*

"Which way did you say the town was?" Gideon asked, trying to sound casual, hoping to get away from the nutbag of a monster as soon as possible.

He could figure shit out from there. If someone could just clothe him and put an axe in his hand, he'd work to the bone to get back to Fishket.

Gideon suddenly covered his face as dread made it pale. *Shit. Beau must be so damn worried.* Beau was the most soft-hearted, caring man he'd ever met. He'd be pulling his hair out at his disappearance, probably his long beard too.

The Duskwalker tilted his head, the sound of dry bones rattling from him. It was unnerving, and reminded Gideon too much of the taunts Demons made from the shadows.

With his orbs darkening in their blue, the Duskwalker's skull pointed in a direction between two trees. "I smell humans that way."

"This way?" he asked, hiking his thumb towards it. When he nodded, Gideon gave him a two-finger salute, and his skulled head tilted, like a big curious dog. "Sweet. Thanks for the help, but I've got it from here."

Choosing to believe that he truly wouldn't hurt him, and maybe even was the one who accidentally saved him for whatever reason, he strolled off into the forest. The heavy, unnerving crunches behind him made him wince.

He'd been hoping it wouldn't follow.

"Where are you going?"

"To the town, obviously." Glancing behind him, his lips drew downwards in a cringe when he noticed how big he was. Over a foot and a half taller than Gideon's five-foot-eleven height, he was like a menacing wall. "I don't mean to be rude, but for the love of all that is holy, don't follow me."

"We cannot be separated. We are bonded, so you will return to me." Since Gideon didn't respond, the Duskwalker added, "We must talk."

Go find a tree to talk to. It'd be more receptive than him.

When Gideon didn't stop, a soft growl had all the hairs on his body standing on end. "I will not leave you. You are mine, and I must protect you."

"I don't need protecting," Gideon muttered back.

He wants to protect me? Perfect. That meant he wouldn't hurt him, for now. Gideon was sure his giant monster stomach would end up getting the grumbles, and he'd be his next meal if he didn't quickly scamper away.

Right now, the only thing keeping Gideon together, the only thing that was stopping him from losing his ever-living-shit, was his desire to move when deeply stressed. He needed to walk and head in a direction that meant a solution.

The anxiety wasn't going to fade, so he'd just grin and bear it until he was home.

A clawed hand wrapped around his elbow, and it sent repulsive shivers up his arm. He pulled away from it and turned to the Duskwalker.

"Please..." he begged, trying to be nice to not piss him off. "Please, don't touch me."

He was naked, unsure as to why and what that might mean. He'd done a mental check of his body, and absolutely knew nothing horrific had happened to him while he'd been passed out for however long.

He also just didn't trust him.

"Gideon." The Duskwalker's tone was stern. "Talk to me."

He just shook his head and spun away to continue in the direction of the town. *Leave me alone.*

That same large warm hand wrapped around his forearm again, but this time lightly yanked him back. Instincts foolishly, stupidly, thoughtlessly, took hold. *I said don't fucking touch me!* His mind screamed as he spun, raised his enclosed fist, and struck him across the face with all his might.

Rather than the Duskwalker's head twisting to the side, a crack sounded as agony shot down the back of Gideon's knuckles and up his forearm. A howl of pain exploded from him as he cradled his injured hand.

"Holy shit!" he hissed, keeling over as tears stung his eyes. "What is your skull made of, *iron*?"

Considering the force behind his swing and the pain he was currently in, he'd either broken something or at least fractured it.

He probably should have been alert for retaliation, but nothing came. When he looked up at his skull, blue orbs shone down at him darker than before.

"You hit me," he whimpered, cupping the side of his snout. Then his orbs morphed white as his skull dipped downwards. "You are *hurt!*"

He darted forward, as if he wanted to check on Gideon's wellbeing. He hissed out a sharp breath when the Duskwalker cupped his injured hand, and they both darted away from each other in surprise.

"What the hell do you want from me?!" Gideon yelled as rage took hold, his patience lost, agony making him even more stupid. The Duskwalker recoiled in surprise. "Just leave me alone if you're not going to eat me!"

Red flared before snuffing back to blue. His clawed hands clenched and then unclenched, while his fur and feathers puffed in waves, making him appear more menacing.

"You are my bride," he stated again, like that made *any* sense to Gideon. "You asked to come here with me, to be with me, and in doing so, we brought you back to life."

"I don't know who the fuck you are! I've never seen you before today."

"Because you have forgotten!" he snapped, then patted his torso. "I am Aleron."

Fuck me, dude.

"Listen... Aleron, was it?" Gideon said with a sigh and a grimace, squinting his eyes. "Whatever you think happened, didn't. You're a stranger, and I doubt I would have befriended a Duskwalker."

"We met when Ingram and Emerie came to the afterworld, Gideon."

That made Gideon's head rear back and his brows furrow. "Emerie, my sister?"

"Yes, Emerie," Aleron quickly rasped out, his tone growing lighter – eager, almost. "She is a female, with bright-red hair and dots on her face."

His eyes drifted to the side. *Well, that is awfully convincing.* That did sound like Emerie.

"She also has scarring across her face as well."

Gideon stiffened. "She absolutely does not." Still, it was hard to deny that they may have met if he knew her name.

Aleron palmed his skull. "Little human... it has been eight years since you died. This was easier when she was there to explain this, but it has been a long time."

Icy dread slipped down his spine. Cradling the back of his injured hand to his stomach, he spun around and put one foot in front of the other. He ignored his swinging dick for the moment.

Nope. Absolutely not. He refused to believe what Aleron had just uttered. He'd only been taken last night, or a few days ago, or something. It had not been eight years. Impossible.

Because... if he were to accept that it'd been that long

ago, then his life was *over*. His friends, his family, his boyfriend, his job, everything was gone. He couldn't – and wouldn't – accept that.

This delusional monster could go spout this shit somewhere else. Gideon was going home, because his home still existed, just as he still existed.

He was alive, breathing in cool, fresh air, with speckled sunlight warming his skin. The world around him was real.

As he stormed forward, ignoring the sharp rocks and sticks that cut into the bottoms of his bare feet, Aleron continued to follow.

Gideon was not given a moment of peace as the hulking presence attempted to explain some great meeting, followed by a journey, all of which he ignored.

He had not woken up in some afterlife called Tenebris. He had not met this so-called 'kindred' named Ingram, who had a raven skull and short, upwards-jutting horns and scales over his body – apparently.

He mockingly snorted a laugh when Aleron told him Emerie had been a Demonslayer. *That girl would almost piss her pants in fright when there was a rodent or cockroach in the house.* The idea of her being some Demon hunting badass was so damn insane that it was funny.

And it was even funnier that Aleron tried to convince him that Ingram and his easily frightened little sister just magically skipped off into the sunset together. Especially since she would have needed to have died in order to do so, and he was hoping he'd find her back at home with their parents.

She wasn't out in the world with a monster. *Emerie in love with a Duskwalker? Pfft.* That sounded as true as Gideon apparently being this one's companion; therefore, it was utterly false.

All of it was a delusion, a lie.

His life was not over.

It had not been eight years.

"Please wait," Aleron pleaded, grabbing his arm again.

"Don't touch me!" Gideon shouted, twisting his arm and ripping it away from him. How many times did he need to say that? He glanced back over to the town that stood just across a small meadow, like it was a pillar of salvation. "I am going into that human town. I am going to get some clothing so I'm not walking around naked, and I am not coming back out here, so you're better off leaving."

The fact he had to approach the gates in the nude was going to be humiliating, but he'd just grit through it. He'd survive being mocked if it meant he could escape all this. Escape Aleron.

"In a day, you will return to my side."

"Is that a threat?" Gideon sneered, his nose crinkling in outrage. "What? If I don't come back out here, you're going to go in there and kill all the soldiers guarding it just to get to me?"

What a piece of work! Aleron couldn't get his consent to stay by his side, so he was going to kill a bunch of innocent people instead?

"No," Aleron answered in a low voice tinged with... sadness? His head lowered, and his shoulders and wings drooped. "You will see. When you do, I will be waiting for you."

"Yeah, whatever." An emotional Duskwalker was not his problem.

Gideon waved his good hand as he walked away.

He'll eventually get the point and leave.

NINETEEN

Drowning his sorrows in the worst excuse for a beer he'd ever had the displeasure of assaulting his precious tastebuds with, Gideon nursed an aching headache.

He had been through many embarrassing moments in his life, but being paraded through a town like an entertaining show just for a pair of pants may be at the top of his shit list. The only reason it hadn't been any worse, his humiliation not stretched out for too long, was due to the higher ups intervening.

They'd been, justifiably, furious with their underlings.

Not only did the soldiers torment Gideon, the scene had no doubt burned the eyes of every man and woman on the street. Thankfully, no child had been within eyesight as he cupped his junk.

After that, he'd swiftly been given clothes and shoes, and even a small pouch of coins as an apology. Some of the soldiers had taken pity on him, calling him a poor shmuck after teasing his naked ass, and even offered up some of their own coin. Of course, he took it.

So, here he was in some rundown, musty tavern, wasting it on booze.

He probably should have been saving it, but right then he needed a drink more than anything.

Peering down at his own weathered, tired face within the

foul liquid, he couldn't stop thinking about the Duskwalker. He also couldn't stop thinking about his life, the one he was desperate to return to.

He watched himself wince when a strike of pain lanced his entire face, and he rubbed at the side of his head with the heel of his injured hand. Ever since he'd woken up, it felt like someone had taken a mallet to his skull.

I feel like shit. He looked it too. *I wish that bard would stop mangling that poor harp.* Every off-tune, high-pitched note blasted his left eardrum.

At least the black leather trousers they'd given him were clean, and the white tunic they gave him didn't have any frills on it. His brown boots were a little well-worn, but getting a good new boot these days was a hard ask.

I would have preferred a jacket, though, he thought, as he lifted liquid hell to his lips.

At least the fireplace kept the room warm.

Thankfully, no one came to disturb him, since he wasn't in the most sociable of moods. As the night grew later, he eventually groaned and placed his forehead against the sticky bar.

Someone tapped the top of his head. "Hey, you. There's no sleeping here. I keep my doors open, even at night, but that's for the poor insomniacs of this town."

"Sorry, mate," Gideon grumbled, noting how dizzy he'd become. "I don't have anywhere else to go, so I'll try to stay awake and find a place to stay tomorrow."

"Good luck with that." The dark-haired man snorted, narrowing brown eyes at him. "You'll be clawing for an empty home with the rest of the people in the slums. We're short on liveable housing right now."

His lips twisted into a cringe. "You don't force people to sleep on the streets at night, right?"

"No. That would be inhumane with all the Demons roaming around." The lean man then started cleaning the inside of the mugs to remove whatever alcohol residue remained. "There's a shelter, but it's overfilled. You'll likely be sleeping on the floor."

With a solemn sigh, Gideon shrugged. "I'm a strong lad. Just give me a blanket and I'll sleep on dirt. I don't really care, so long as I can lay my head down."

The bartender chuckled. "You've got spirit. You don't see much of that these days."

Yeah, well, Gideon wasn't going to complain when it couldn't be helped. Before long, he'd be travelling back to Fishket. He could rest comfortably there, either in his bed or in Beau's – didn't matter which.

I better get back quick. Even if he didn't know if Gideon was alive or not, he knew Beau would wait a long time for him. A few weeks, a few months, maybe even a year. He would be absolutely devastated, but he knew the burly man would be overcome with relief, likely to weep from it, and pull him into the biggest embrace.

Gideon would hold out for that wonderful moment.

"Another?" the bartender asked when taking away his empty mug.

"Do you have anything that doesn't taste like shit?"

He cast Gideon an apologetic wince. "Not really. Supply has been pretty bad as of late, since we're coming into winter."

His ears twitched. "Winter?" He sat up straight and steadied his hand on the bar. *Shit... has it really been five months?!* "What's the date today?"

"May twenty-ninth," the man answered with a baffled frown. "Lost track of time, have you?"

He placed his forehead into his palm, dragging his hand down his face, through the stubble on his cheeks and chin. "Yeah, you can say that."

Five months? Gideon thought in disbelief, turning his face to the side. *Was I asleep? My scars are fully healed.*

If he'd really forgotten five months, then there was a

chance he'd met the Duskwalker along the way. He doubted they'd truly been friends. Either they'd been using each other for some kind of benefit – Gideon likely needing assistance travelling the dangerous world, and Aleron... well, he didn't know what he could want from him.

I woke up naked.

Nope! Gideon refused to accept that perhaps he'd given up his body for such a reason. He'd never do that, and just the thought made him shudder with disgust. Not because of the monster, but having sex for such a pathetic reason – no matter his partner's species.

Oh gods, I don't know anymore.

Every minute longer in this reality only brought on more questions, more confusion. How could someone forget such a long period of time? Trauma... maybe? Did he suppress everything in order to mentally deal with it until he knew there was a town situated nearby for him to escape to?

From what he could tell, he didn't have a wound on his head – despite his splitting migraine. Then again... if he'd hit it hard enough, he could have memory loss from an old concussion. *My skull feels fine, though.*

He wished he could say the same about his hand. The middle and ring fingers of his right hand were so swollen and black, he knew he'd fractured something. Even trying to tense or move his fingers brought pain.

He didn't know why, but... guilt prickled on the back of his neck. A small part of him felt he deserved to be in pain for clocking the Duskwalker one.

Rubbing the back of his ear in thought, he tried to figure out why.

Aleron was a stranger to him; why should he care for someone he didn't know? No one liked to be handled or grabbed without their consent, so his actions weren't unjustified. Plus, with the fact he was a monster, he'd been defending himself against something that would usually eat his kind.

A carnivorous beast. A human-eating nightmare.

Why did he look so sad, though? Just as he was bringing the fresh mug of beer to his lips, he paused. *Where did that thought come from? He has a skull for a face... a skull can't look sad.*

Perhaps it was the blue colour of his orbs. But he didn't know what the colour signified, did he? Yet, he couldn't stop thinking of them as sorrowful.

Yeah, well, I'm depressed too. A horrible burning sensation radiated in each of his heart beats, bleeding sadness into his veins. He didn't know if he wanted to cry or punch the shit out of something – preferably something not alive.

Wallowing in self-pity, by the time day finally broke, Gideon was an aching being of rage, grief, and self-loathing.

He asked around about work, coming up short at each stall. Due to his own stupidity, he'd avoided asking about labour intensive work due to his injured hand. Unfortunately, all the easy jobs had been taken.

Looking down at his messed-up knuckles, he sighed. *I probably should get this treated.* Instead of finding a doctor, he approached one of the guards, who had been a jerk the previous day.

"Can you direct me to the timber mill or a lumberjack guild?" Gideon asked.

The woman laughed at him, as did the soldier next to her. "You just came from the forest, and now you want to go back to it? Have you got a death wish or something?"

Annoyed, he ran his fingers through his hair to brush it back. "I need work, and that's what I'm good at. I used to be a tree cutter back in my town."

"With that hand," the armoured man stated with a snort, "you'd be lucky to hold a feather, let alone an axe. You'd just be a liability. There are a lot of Demons around these parts. We're surprised you even made it here alive in your birthday suit."

Too tired to even flush in embarrassment, all he could manage was a mental groan.

"Look, the last thing I want to do is go back out there." He worried the Duskwalker would be waiting for him, among other things. "But if I want to get back home, I need coin. I can just use my left hand."

The armoured woman nodded her helmet towards a notice board. "If you really want to work, check the board. There's a lot of dated work that no one wants to do. You'll make good coin fast if you're willing to pick up the dirty jobs."

Although hidden by a crude and bloodied cloth, the decently sized cut across his knuckles could become infected.

"I was hoping to avoid shovelling shit," Gideon grumbled, turning from them.

Stubborn and determined, he approached the board. There wasn't much he could do. Anything that required skill in artistry, such as stonework or blacksmithing, was out of his capabilities. Anything that required the strength of a healthy individual was also ruled out, considering he couldn't even make a proper fist.

He pulled down a job call with a thoughtful hum. "Herb collector?"

Despite his cheeks crinkling in humour because it sounded innocent, he knew the truth. The person would have to go far outside of the town walls and deep into the shaded forest. No wonder the notice was one of the oldest.

They should have the fine print of 'likely to be eaten within the week' *at the bottom.*

Among the pieces of pinned parchment were faces of wanted criminals. He only glanced over them until a name caught his attention.

He dropped the herb collector notice and ripped off the wanted criminal parchment with a Demonslayer emblem stamped into the very top of it.

His hands shook as he took in the name 'Emerie' at the top, and the somewhat familiar face – or rather, half of it. He covered his mouth with a shaking hand, his shock numbing him to the point where crumpling the parchment with his injured hand barely registered to him.

"No," he whispered. "It can't be true."

But it was difficult to ignore this.

The woman drawn had Emerie's nose, her lips, her freckles, and even her wavy hair. It'd come from the eastern sector, from Zagros Fortress, which rung a bell due to Aleron's ramblings the day before.

Clutching the paper, he bolted back to the guards.

Just as he was about to grab one of their shoulders, before thinking better of possibly being accused of assaulting one of them, he hesitated.

"What year is it?" he choked out.

They spared each other a wary look through their helmets.

"You're really odd, you know that?" the man scoffed. "How can you not know what year it is?"

"He did say he couldn't remember how he got here," the woman responded.

"What year is it?!" Gideon yelled. "Stop messing around and just answer the damn question."

"It's two thousand and twenty-three." The man stepped forward. "Look, do we need to take you to a doctor? You don't look so well, and if what you have is contagious, then..."

Whatever the man said after that became inaudible. It felt like someone had shoved cotton inside his ears, his head pounding and throbbing as if all the blood rushed to it.

Sweat dotted his hairline as nausea paled him.

He wasn't lying. As he slapped a hand over his mouth to hold back the strangled, silent sob coming up his throat, someone grabbed his forearm. They led his stupefied body around like a horse, and his feet moved on their own as he followed. *Aleron was telling the truth. It's... it's really been eight years.*

Tears welled in his eyes, and he didn't care to hold them back, nor who saw them staining his cheeks.

She really became a Demonslayer. She really lost half her face. What about our parents? His tears fell faster and faster, and he quietly shed them. *Eight years. What happened to Beau, my dog, my friends? Are any of them alive, or am I the only one that...*

Everything he'd ever feared happening, happened.

His knees gave out, and both soldiers had to carry his pitiful form to wherever their destination was. How could any human stand after learning all this? How could anyone cope with it?

I died. I was really eaten *that night.*

Before long, he was seated inside a room that smelt heavily of medicine and cleaning alcohol. Someone grabbed his hand to check it, but his vision had blurred out as his thoughts took the focus. Their muffled questions were lost to the barrage of his own.

Did they all forget about me? Had the world just moved on as though he hadn't existed?

It was likely due to the human brain not actually truly being able to deal with one's own death, but a part of him thought the world would just... stop. That when he finally left the world, everything too, disappeared.

To come back now, after so long, he couldn't fathom it.

How old am I then? He'd been twenty-three... did that mean he still was? *She would be twenty-seven now.* She wouldn't be his little sister anymore, but his older sister.

Poor Emerie. The last thing she said to me was to get fucked. Right before he'd saved her life. He couldn't imagine how that'd eaten her up inside all these years. *Did she join the guild to get revenge for me?* That shattered his heart.

Her life would have been wasted on his behalf. She would have had no chance for true happiness, to find love, to make a family. To join the guild would be to leave all of that behind.

I ruined her life.

She'd been the reason for the loss of his own.

He could never blame her, would never dare to.

I'm so sorry, Beau.

Sitting on the ground, Aleron stared down at his bride's tiny soul in the rough crease of his palm. Despite his hesitancy to reach for it in case he did something wrong, he'd been unable to deny the longing to peer at it in Gideon's absence.

When he'd first held it, his heart had swelled and his orbs had flared bright pink when it stood and appeared to look up at him. *It looks exactly like him.* From his physique, the bit of hair that curled like someone had licked it out of place, the dimples when he smiled, to his funny, confident stance.

He'd tickled it with the back of his foreknuckles, making it silently chuckle. He'd been surprised by how animated and alert it was, even when it sat in his palm to look up at his skull.

At least his soul wants to be with me.

He hoped that meant his Gideon wasn't completely lost to him.

However, as the day ended and night fell, and the sun eventually shone once more, the whimpers that echoed from him reverberated within the dense forest.

Gideon's soul, which had been bright and fully alight, slowly withered until it looked like charcoal. With only the head still flaming, most of it extinguished. It collapsed to its knees, only to lie down as if... *weak*. No amount of nudging it could stir it to life, no matter how he tried.

By the transformation of his soul, he knew something had happened to his human – he knew it. Aleron wanted to stand and bolt into the nameless town. He wanted to go to Gideon more than anything.

His instincts demanded it, shaking at the cage of his thoughts like a feral beast. Frenzied, snarling for escape.

Aleron couldn't. The humans would attack him, and he worried he'd succumbed to a rage if he was harmed, or if he saw Gideon hurt.

His patience won, and Gideon eventually materialised just beyond his feet as a transparent Ghost. Now that he was by his side, Aleron placed his soul where it belonged: between the security of his horns. Only once it floated freely, their bonding strings attaching to it and his horns, did he let go.

Without moving, he waited for Gideon to wake, giving him space in case he needed it.

He didn't do so swiftly.

Even when he turned physical and opened his eyes, lids fluttering, his gaze was dazed and listless. The loud, boisterous, and agitated male had disappeared. Instead, he lay as lifeless as his soul. When he eventually sat up, he stared at the ground with his legs straight out in front of him. With the backs of his hands lying on the ground between them, Aleron noted the injured one was now healed.

Unable to cope with the way his bride appeared, and the way it burned a cold ache in his chest, he hesitantly reached out. He brushed the backs of his claws against his cool cheek. He didn't flinch or even seem to notice the touch.

But, in a quiet whisper, he rasped, "You were right. It has been eight years."

Is this the reason he is in this state? Was it that...

harrowing to Gideon that so long had passed?

"My whole life is gone," he continued. "There will be no one waiting for me at home if Emerie isn't there. My adopted parents are probably dead, since they were old. My boyfriend probably moved on – if he didn't do something stupid. My dog probably isn't alive anymore either. There is nothing left for me."

Much of what he said was lost to Aleron. It also brought to light that he... didn't know all this. Gideon had chosen not to share much of his past, even if Aleron asked him of it. Was it due to not being able to, or because he hadn't trusted him with his pain?

"But you still have Emerie and me," Aleron offered, palming his own chest. "She is with my kindred, and we can all be together."

Aleron didn't know what hurt more, his hauntingly pale and blank face, or the tears that fell from slowly blinking eyes. Where was the lively person he knew?

"I don't want to go to Emerie. She has her own life – one I am no longer part of. She's probably changed so much, while I'm still the same person as the day I died and left her behind." Then, so quietly, with his voice raspy and croaked, he whispered, "I should have been a better brother. I should have done more to keep her safe."

"It is not your fault," Aleron reassured, gently nudging Gideon's forehead with the back of his hand so he would look up.

When that didn't work, he placed the foreknuckle of his index finger under Gideon's chin to forcibly lift it. Even though his green eyes were directed at him, it was obvious he wasn't truly seeing him.

"I do not know how to help." He wished he did. He didn't like that Gideon blamed himself for his own death, when Aleron knew the selfless sacrifice he'd made for Emerie.

He shouldn't feel terrible for such a noble act.

"Why did you bring me back to life with you?"

"Because I... *love* you."

Gideon's eyelids flickered with life, widening ever so slightly. Yet, the unsettled way his gaze zeroed on his skull made a shiver run down Aleron's spine.

Without warning, the male stood. He turned to the forest and started to walk, and not in the direction of the town.

"Where are you going?" Aleron asked, rising so he could follow.

"Anywhere. Somewhere." He threw his head back halfway, but paused as though he didn't truly wish to look upon Aleron. "*Nowhere.*"

"I told you, we cannot be apart. You already came back to me. Was that not enough to–"

"I know," Gideon interrupted.

He knows I will follow. With heavy steps crushing the forest debris, he tilted his head behind Gideon's back. *Does he want to walk, like how he did in Tenebris?*

The male had been an unstoppable force. A quiet, thoughtful traveller.

When Aleron went to hold his hand to comfort him in the same way he'd done for him many times during their travels, hoping to remind him of them, Gideon drew it away. He hid it in front of himself.

His blue sight darkened, and the cold pain behind his sternum intensified. *He no longer wants to hold my hand or receive my touch.*

He rushed forward to be at Gideon's side so he could look at him, finding he still had the same contradicting pale yet tearful expression. The bottom of Aleron's orbs broke in sympathy for the forlorn male, for himself, and for the way his entire chest cavity ached from the loss of his cheerful bride.

The silence shared between them for the remainder of the day was lonely, and the longer it persisted, the more it ate at him.

But Aleron continued to follow his bride, hoping Gideon would remember. Hoping he would return to him.

I already miss him.

TWENTY

Gideon let out a mangled groan comprised of both pleasure and distress all rolled into one. Heat swelled around him from within him, dotting his brow with sweat as he drew closer to the source. A scent, so earthy and musky, attempted to swallow up his senses until it ached within his lungs and mind, spinning and swirling until he greedily huffed it in.

Images flashed behind his closed eyelids, dreams that were difficult to grasp as they swiftly passed. Sounds echoed within Gideon's conscience, loud for a second before drowning out quietly as a multitude of them blended together. Mild heat swallowed him up, but also radiated from deep within, pounding and pumping until even the images grew murky as his sight wavered.

Seeing through the blurry images left crisp ones that stained his mind.

Something dark, fluffy, and large was below him as he tipped his head to the sky. Suddenly it changed, and he was on his back, gripping fur to stay centred as his legs wound around tighter to make sure the person couldn't escape.

Two purple lights, made of vortex flames that gave an otherworldly glow, peered down at him. A desirous shiver ran rampant throughout his system from gazing into them.

All he saw was grass sticking up around his face. Yet, the lack of motion gave way to what he felt. A clawed hand gently cupping his chin and throat, gripping him from behind. An arm wrapped around his middle to hoist his hips up so theirs could meet, slapping hard against his arse. Something had coiled around his hips, and his cock and balls, gripping harder and harder until the person shook and quaked, as Gideon did so in return. His lust-filled huffs were intense, and his groan of deep-rooted pleasure profound.

And yet, true satisfaction never came. There was no release of pressure. Instead, it built and built, until he thought he'd burst.

A skull came down next to his face. Just as he was being licked across the ear and cheek in what could only be affection, the image faded.

Darkness had taken over, except for those glowing purple orbs, as though he was sheltered within something. The glint of a skull was noticeable, as were the slight reflections on the feathers of the creature not only holding him, but fucking *into* him.

A link within his mind snapped into place, and the images replayed until all the facets of the person were put together.

A purple cock with strange, braided textures, and tentacles that liked to cling. Fur that covered the entire body of a monster he was trying to bring closer and closer with each thrust. Feathers that sprouted all the way down their back, as wings flapped behind them. Then the bat skull and goat horns of a Duskwalker he allowed to lick within the crevice of his mouth.

Shit, Gideon cursed, grinding his hard and throbbing cock into his palm. His eyes flickered open to darkness, and he winced. *I'm so fucking hard.*

He hated it. He hated *why* he'd woken up hard, his dick and balls aching for release, and how he ground into his hand in the hopes he'd achieve it – unlike in his dream.

None of his dreams made sense. There was no context, no rhyme or reason for them. Other than physical pleasure, no emotions had shone through.

A detached, yet insanely perverted dream.

I dreamt of having... sex with the Duskwalker? His features twisted in distress, his heart racing with anxiety and need. *Why?* He had no attraction to Aleron.

Up until he'd fallen asleep, he sincerely wanted Aleron to leave him alone!

I can't breathe. His chest felt so tight with tension, his breaths so raspy, he was moments from passing out. Would he be shoved back into those dreams?

No. He didn't want that. The first set had been torturous enough.

I'm so horny. At least it was a new emotion in comparison to the hollowing emptiness he'd been feeling before he'd gone to sleep. He'd just rather not be in this state at all.

Heat continued to swell within, from around him, enveloping him and taking away the cold that had befallen him when he'd laid down his head. The winter chill had caused him to shiver, but he knew he'd eventually passed out.

He snuggled further into the soothing warmth, huffing in a strange scent that felt too comforting. It reminded him of home, of laughter, and good, hard work.

Grinding into his hand again, wishing his erection would fade, he noticed another heartbeat resonating around him. *So big. So loud.* His eyelids almost shut so he could focus on it, and let it ease his own frantic one.

Something soft, fluffy, and fibrous tickled his nose.

Gideon's eyes flashed open and then grew wide.

He looked up and around, noticing only darkness. Until a gap of light finally caught his attention – daylight.

I'm inside something. That's when he noticed the set of

large arms crossing behind his back. The thing in front of him was a chest that constantly, yet evenly, expanded and decompressed on large breaths.

Horror widened his eyes further, and Gideon struggled. He pushed and shoved with all his might, his breaths growing more constricting. A foreboding shiver ran down his limbs.

Wings parted like a curtain, allowing him freedom. He rushed for air untainted by the tantalising scent of Aleron.

"Fuck!" Gideon shouted, falling to the cold, hard dirt on his hands and knees. "Don't do that! Don't put me in your wings."

"Gideon?" Aleron's voice was higher pitched than normal. He sounded stressed, wary, and unsure.

He didn't need nor want this Duskwalker to be concerned for his wellbeing. His trembling arms gave out.

"I thought I was going to suffocate," Gideon rasped, bowing his sweat-slicked forehead until it rested upon his crossed forearms. Still kneeling, he heaved against the ground.

"You find my wings... suffocating?" Aleron asked quietly.

"Of course, I do! I was killed by a winged Demon!"

That was true, but not the reason for his panic.

Were they suffocating? Gideon wasn't sure.

Had he not woken up hard, he may have been alright with them surrounding him. With his own internal desirous body temperature warming him, his dreams confusing him, and just his life whirling out of control, he couldn't stand the closeness right then. The scent, heartbeat, and softness... it was too much.

Aleron's whimpered response was unmistakable.

Shit. Stop making that sound! He didn't know why, but it gouged at his damn chest.

A soft gust of wind rustled the leaves of the surrounding

forest, and the iciness of it against his skin felt like needles. The longer Gideon dwelled on his current situation, the worse his mind rotted.

The trees were closing in around him like walls, threatening to spring to life and strangle him in their twisted, gnarly roots.

I feel trapped, Gideon cried to himself. His hands curled into tight fists. *I feel so trapped...* By Aleron, his life, where he was in the world.

Apparently another version of himself trapped him in this life, but he couldn't remember it. He remembered nothing, and yet why did he have to be the one to suffer it?

Why did I do it? Why did I bond myself to this Duskwalker... forever? How could he make such a decision? He couldn't comprehend it. No human should bond themselves to a monster, so how could he be so careless?

The groin seam of his pants pressed against the hard length of his dick running down his pant leg, and it hurt. Despite it being crushed, or trying to snap in half, he couldn't find the strength to unfurl himself in that moment.

He wanted to pull his hair out, curse at his past and his dead self. He shook with stress that wouldn't leave him be, and the loss of his life that happened eight years ago, but was only a blink of an eye for him.

He'd had four days to adjust to all this, and he... wasn't. Four days wasn't much time to learn that everything he'd known, everyone he'd loved, and who he'd been, was all gone. Then, on top of that, he felt so trapped and pressured by this Duskwalker that he couldn't handle it.

It felt like his consent had been taken away, his very freedom. His whole life had been stolen from him, and yet he was supposed to just smile and be fucking happy about it?

How am I supposed to do that?

Four days ago, Demons and Duskwalkers were nothing but horrible, terrifying, human-eating, vile monsters to him.

There had been no reason to differentiate between them. They were just bloodthirsty creatures that desired to tear his skin from his muscles and suck on the marrow of his bones.

One had even done so.

"Why?" he whispered, wishing he could have an answer as to how or why past Gideon had done this all to himself. How could he have possibly... loved Aleron? It was too farfetched to believe, and he doubted it completely.

It was a lie, that's what he told himself. Something Aleron said to keep him complacent, to trick him into accepting this bond he was unwilling to be a part of.

It had to be...

"You were cold," Aleron answered him instead. He shouldn't have been expecting his stupid dead self to give him one, but his features crinkled in hurt at the resounding silence from himself. "You were shivering, so I thought warming you with my wings would be better."

Aleron was wrapping what he'd done with apparent kindness? Yes, Gideon remembered shivering to sleep, but he didn't remember being forcibly dragged into his wings.

Only the dream. Flickering images of them fucking like two inseparable, crazed beings.

No, I didn't. He crossed his arms behind his head, squishing his elbows against the side of his face to stop it from touching the ground. He breathed in dirt and grass, finding it settled his anxiety and helped to clear his system of Aleron's scent. *I didn't fuck him in the afterlife. It's not real. Just a dream. Please.*

"Just let me be cold," Gideon stated, his voice cracked and low.

He'd rather be cold than be hard against his will. He wanted to be in control – of his life, his body, his thoughts. They were all he had left.

At least he felt more alert than the disassociating stupor he'd been in for the past day.

I need to walk. Rushing to his feet and stumbling, he balanced against a tree trunk to right his footing. Then he strode forward.

Aleron followed – Gideon knew he would. His footsteps were loud, crunching, and always kept him alerted to the monster that continued to chase him.

He was prey constantly being hunted.

Moving through the forest with a tight chest, his lungs never ceasing to be swollen with his frantic breaths, he didn't care to take in his environment. It didn't matter where he went, what was around him, or his destination.

The only purpose he had was this: to walk.

He had no job, no home, no friends or family. He had nothing, and without a goal, a purpose, he feared he'd crumble. He feared... he'd give up. He didn't even need to *eat,* to pee, since he didn't drink water. Nothing made him feel human or gave him drive now. He didn't need to hunt for food, which gave all people a purpose.

Although he'd been given a second chance at life, if he didn't walk until he sorted through his thoughts, he worried about what he'd do to himself. If he gave up... he'd seek the afterlife again.

And Gideon refused that too.

Despite how low his will was, despite how empty and hollow he felt, despite how imprisoned he was, Gideon held onto life with the last of his strength. He clutched that last thread with a vice grip.

He was struggling. He knew his mind to be deeply unwell, his heart bruised and broken. He was trying to process all the steps of grief at the same time, on his own. Denial, acceptance, bargaining, depression, and definitely anger.

In his own way, he also... *tried* to not take that out on Aleron.

As much as he blamed the Duskwalker for his turmoil, if Gideon had truly given his permission to bring him here...

he couldn't fully blame nor hate him for it. He was obviously hurting Aleron, but he couldn't do anything else but march forward until he collapsed to his knees to sleep.

"I want to go find Ingram," Aleron requested, as he had many times.

"Then go find him," Gideon calmly said back, refusing to look at him.

"It may help. You may remember your time in Tenebris if you meet them."

Gideon opened his mouth to state that he didn't want to remember, but then shut it. It would only be hurtful to the Duskwalker if he said it. He wouldn't needlessly dish out hurt when it did nothing to aid the situation.

"I do not know how to help you, Gideon."

He shoved a branch out of his face, snapping it, rather than walking past it like he had the others. "I don't need help."

Stating he needed help meant something was wrong with him. Which, obviously, there was, but it also meant that he lacked the ability to help *himself*. He felt like prey, when he'd rather be strong and resilient. Level-headed and sound of mind.

He'd like just a small amount of time and forgiveness until he achieved it. He could be patient, considering he apparently wouldn't *die*. Four days, that's all he'd been given so far.

How was that fair?

"If you really want to go find them, go do so. I'm not stopping you," he coldly bit out.

"But I cannot leave you by yourself," Aleron rebuffed. Yet that was exactly what he wanted. "I do not want you to come to harm in the forest. A Demon may come."

"I've already been eaten by one." Gideon kicked a rock, hoping to release some of his anger. "What does it matter if it happens a second time? I'll just return to you, right?"

"I do not wish for you to have to 'return' to me. You are my bride, and I wish for us to stay together."

Gideon wanted to deny being called anything like a 'bride,' but as he glanced over his shoulder and saw his own soul floating between Aleron's horns, he couldn't deny it. Apparently, he was a bride, and his soul looked *awful*, blackened like a dying coal.

He wished Aleron hadn't told him what it was. It made it harder to deny everything, harder to swallow. He found it even more difficult to look at his skull, knowing his own soul hovered just above it.

Maybe... maybe it would be better if I knew everything.

Up until now, Gideon had been ignoring Aleron, and what had apparently transpired between them.

Staring at his soul, though, it made it impossible to deny something had happened. He'd be a fool to. Had been one.

Would it be better if he knew? *What if it brought back those perverse memories?* He hadn't wanted to remember them, averse to the idea, but if he didn't do so, would he be stuck in this wandering state for the rest of their lives?

He's never hurt me. No matter what Gideon said, how he acted, or how he ignored him, not once did this Duskwalker treat him cruelly. *I guess... he doesn't seem* that *bad.* A bit weird personally, and definitely freaky physically, but he hadn't been a villain.

He hated that he was being forced into this, but there was no other way, was there? Either he accepted Aleron, or their future would be steeped in pain and sadness.

What do I want? He needed this constricting pain to end.

He didn't really want to be his friend, but maybe he could try, regardless?

"Hey, Aleron," Gideon grumbled, as he lowered his head and chewed on the inner flesh of his cheek. "Can you tell me about our time in Tenebris?"

Maybe... it would be better to just give in and remember.

If he didn't... If he *couldn't*, he may truly become an

apparition.

He was already halfway there.

TWENTY-ONE

I do not know if he is getting better or worse, Aleron grumbled as he begrudgingly followed his little human.

Every second that passed, he wished to snatch Gideon from the ground and take off into the air. Weldir informed him that Ingram and Emerie had been close by when they first arrived, but that was days ago.

With every step they took in what he believed was a northerly direction, the more he worried they were going further and further from his kindred. Finding them would be harder by the hour, let alone the day.

And yet, he continued to follow Gideon. He continued to do as he wished, understanding that he needed... time. But seconds felt like agonising minutes, and the loneliness was stifling. The crisp air felt raw on his whine-ripped lungs – a noise he'd been trying to hide from Gideon so as to not bother him.

I did not realise I could feel so lonely in another's presence.

He'd thought things were beginning to change when Gideon asked him for their story. He'd been excited to share, detailing every moment to the best of his recollection.

He'd realised shortly that learning of Emerie's suffering, her scars, his home burning, and his parents dying that same night, had brought on deeper pain for Gideon. Aleron had been hesitant to share more when salty liquid dripped down his blank face again.

He had accidentally forced his fragile human back into a hollowed state. He'd even turned transparent against his will and didn't seem to notice that he had. As if... he'd truly grown numb, emotionally and physically.

It was then that Aleron checked on his soul by taking it from between his horns. One fissure of light remained, a barely noticeable crack across his face. It persisted, spurting tiny flames from the crack as though trying to spark the entirety of it back to life.

Despite Aleron's craving to remain silent, Gideon had pushed for more. So, wary and fearful, he obliged and told him the rest.

It had taken much time – an entire day and night, in fact – to explain the duration of a month within Tenebris. During the evening, Gideon laid down to rest before Aleron had finished telling it.

Having to watch his bride cling to himself, shaking from the cold, had been one of the most painful things he'd ever witnessed. Aleron had the answer to his warmth, but his little human's persistent rejection was preventing him from being able to help.

When he couldn't take it any longer, he eventually laid on his side and spread one of his wings backwards so it could blanket Gideon from the cold, but hopefully not suffocate him like the previous night. Rather than being cocooned completely in his tight embrace, arms and wings engulfing him, Aleron did just enough to take away the chill so he might rest peacefully.

He hadn't meant to fall asleep himself near dawn, but some time later, Gideon sitting up shoved him into alertness.

Sitting up as well, Aleron nervously cupped his hands against his stomach. He didn't want to be shouted at again, nor did he wish for Gideon to keel over onto his hands and elbows like the world was ending.

He didn't do either of those things.

Although Gideon shoved the weight of Aleron's wing away, and gave him a distrustful look from the corner of his eye, his reaction had not been the same. He didn't thank him, but Aleron also didn't care – not when the consent to do this was granted silently.

He could keep his bride warm, a meagre blanket of a single wing that didn't cover his head. It may not be much, but it was something.

Aleron wanted to tend to his male, to bring him into his arm and snuggle like they once had, but being some form of shelter from the night and cold was more than he'd been allowed in days.

Perhaps it was foolish, but it allowed hope to bloom.

Aleron stood and unconsciously extended his hand to help the male to his feet. Gideon denied it, getting up on his own, but he hoped every gesture to rekindle a connection was recognised.

Maybe one day, they could play their game again. The one in which Gideon tried to pull him to his feet, and Aleron sat there while holding back his chuckles at the little human's useless struggles.

And so, Aleron waited for Gideon to lead the way on their journey that had no destination. During it, he continued their story of Tenebris – of a time that spanned a month and meant *everything* to Aleron.

He noted Gideon appeared calmer, and not so pale, as he detailed meeting Merikh, Raewyn, and the Elven world. The sombre male even asked questions, starting a *conversation* with Aleron borne from pure curiosity. Unfortunately, he couldn't answer many of them. It forced him to explain that Duskwalkers gain humanity by eating his kind, and that he didn't know much about the Elves, humans, Demons, or even his own kind.

But a small glimpse of Gideon's prior self shone through

because of it.

'How are you supposed to learn anything if no one teaches you?' Aleron clung to those words when they fell from his lips a second time.

Gideon, without meaning to, comforted Aleron about his lack of knowledge and intelligence in a similar way to how he did in Tenebris.

It revealed that his bride was still there, still kind and warm, but was currently swallowed up by mental decay.

Even if he needed to chisel his way through the coal of his inner self, Aleron would make sure he flared bright like lava once more.

Just as he was beginning to explain their return to Tenebris after meeting the Gilded Maiden, a heavy, hard waterdrop crashed against his skull. He paused mid-sentence and looked up.

Through the swiftly rustling leaves, the sky radiated light from grey storm clouds. Another drop hit him, then another, and another, until a light shower drizzled over them.

The foliage was enough cover at first, but eventually the cups of the leaves tipped and poured large droplets on them.

A gust of wind cut through his fur, which seemed to incite the chattering of teeth next to him. Now he just looked wet and miserable.

Aleron partially extended one of his wings and shoved the elbow arch of it forward. Gideon spared him a glance, rubbing his arms, like that would be enough to dry him from the small amount of rain that dampened his clothes.

"Thanks," Gideon grumbled, looking forward to watch his footing. "I left my umbrella at home."

Aleron had never heard of an *umbrella* before. It took him a few seconds to decipher its meaning, coming up with some kind of rain shelter. It took him even longer to come up with a witty response – one which he couldn't think up.

He simply stated the truth. "I am content to be your

umbrella."

As much as he would have liked to state 'always,' he didn't wish to distress Gideon. He always seemed to recede into himself whenever Aleron referenced him as his bride or the longevity of their bond, especially if he mentioned his feelings on the matter. He'd learned not to speak on any of it, if possible.

He barely believed his sight when one side of Gideon's lips curled and twitched upwards, as though a smile fought. It didn't fully take, but he did snort a humourless laugh.

"That was corny." Damnit, he didn't know the meaning of this word to come back with a remark. "I guess I'm just lucky you're tall enough to use your wing for me. I don't particularly want to be cold *and* wet."

A sudden giddiness took hold. He finally had a remark.

"It is lucky that you are rather short," he stated casually, tossing his head to one side in exaggeration. "No doubt you are the same height as an Elven child."

"Excuse me?" His lips drew back on a puzzled cringe.

Aleron cupped the end of his snout as though he were in deep thought. "How is the weather down there? It is rather sunny up here."

Gideon's jaw fell in disbelief, and even his eyes widened. For just a heartbeat's span, Aleron worried he'd made a mistake. His hands curled into fists in trepidation, wondering how he should apologise.

A snort sounded, followed by a small chuckle. "Wow, Aleron. That hurt." Gideon clutched his shirt right over the left side of his chest as though wounded.

A bubble of relief popped in his gut, allowing warmth at the long-awaited and very missed sound of Gideon's humour.

Aleron shrugged. "It is not my fault you did not learn to grow taller. Should I kneel for you, so that we may be at even height?"

"You're big, don't get me wrong, but you're not that tall,

Aleron." Even though the laughter had ceased, the warm, although mild, note of humour lingered in his voice. "I used to be a woodcutter. If you don't watch out, I might mistake you for a tree and cut you down a peg or two."

"Was that a threat, little human?" Aleron hummed playfully. "If you try, I may just *put* you in a tree."

"Alright, you win." Gideon threw his hands up. "I concede."

Even though his handsome face had dulled, he still shone his forest-green eyes upon him. They contained a tiny spark of life that had been absent since they arrived back on Earth.

The urge to reach for his soul and examine it for new flames gripped Aleron, but he refused to break from Gideon's gaze. His bride was finally looking upon him, truly seeing him, and it lacked the fear, trepidation, and uncertainty that had been present.

His sight shifted to bright pink, happy to have this side of Gideon back – even if it might be short-lived, and only slight.

"Were the Elven children really that tall?" Gideon grumbled, looking as though he were about to pout.

"The only one we met was this big," Aleron stated as he gestured to a height that was at Gideon's waist. "She was five. As I said, so close to overshadowing you."

He hadn't expected another snort of laughter, considering Gideon had surrendered and he'd been worried that teasing him further would damage the progress he'd made. Yet, he was rewarded for pushing it.

"You know what? You're actually pretty funny." The compliment was like a balm to all the pain Gideon had incidentally caused over the past few days. "I wasn't expecting it from you."

"You taught me," Aleron admitted. "I had not known... sarcasm before you. You often confused me, and yet you found that rather humorous as well."

"I bet I did," Gideon said, his lips curling up on one side. "I probably had fun picking on you. I tend to do that with all my friends."

He said friends... does that mean he sees me this way again? Hope blossomed even more, and it was light and fluffy behind his sternum.

Even though their conversation eventually tapered off and Gideon reverted back to the expressionless version Aleron had been following, his tail feathers vibrated.

He taught me how to win him back.

In their time in Tenebris, Gideon had taught Aleron what he liked, disliked, and how to reach into the depths of his contentment. Their playful banter, their rough words – he'd failed at first with how to utilise them. Only through this male's patience and willingness to teach did Aleron eventually begin mastering them.

They were new facets to his own personality. Now that he was away from Ingram, Aleron was learning about himself as an individual. He'd been growing, sprouting flowers of uniqueness in the combined garden he shared mentally with his kindred.

And they were the key.

These pieces... they'd only been brought to light due to Gideon. His bride had nurtured growth in him through their companionship. Now it was Aleron's turn to nourish the dying flowers within Gideon until they grew back stronger and brighter than ever.

Like in a field of budding spring flowers, Aleron would be the sun that melted the ice. Gideon already smelled like the prettiest meadow he'd ever had the pleasure of frolicking in.

My little spring... I will thaw you.

As if to demonstrate this, Aleron lightly thwacked Gideon on the top of his head with the elbow of his wing. A gentle tap, of course; he didn't truly wish to harm him.

"Ow," Gideon grumbled, rubbing at his hair as he cast a

suspicious glance at Aleron – one that had life rather than the blankness from seconds ago.

With yellow brightening his orbs, he turned his skull to the side. He hummed, since he couldn't whistle.

When his little human grew unsuspecting once more, Aleron did it again.

TWENTY-TWO

What the hell has gotten into him?! Gideon thought as he pushed up on the small of Aleron's back, trying his hardest to stay upright. His hand slipped, and he faceplanted on one of his wings.

"Put me down," Gideon demanded, refusing to kick his legs bent over the big Duskwalker's shoulder.

"No," Aleron refuted, bouncing him until the wind knocked out of his gut. "Since the little human is so set on marching through the forest, he has lost his walking privileges."

"Oh, come on," Gideon groaned, allowing himself to sway. "I didn't think you'd actually fall on your face."

To be fair, no one could really blame Gideon for purposefully tripping Aleron. The Duskwalker had nettled him for the past day. Once the light rainstorm had passed, Aleron had teased him, knocked his wing into him, and had just done everything he could to disturb him.

When he'd finally had enough, although feeling the flame of humour warming him, he'd just... put his leg out.

He hadn't expected Aleron to actually trip over, since he thought he'd just stumble. He'd fallen like a tall tree that destroyed everything in its descending path. He'd almost taken Gideon to the ground, since his wing caught around him as he flapped in an unsuccessful attempt to steady himself.

Gideon had winced when the crunching and snapping of sticks came from under him, as well as the impressive *thwap* of his entire body hitting the hard dirt.

When Aleron had shone red glowing orbs up at him, Gideon bolted. *'I'm dead,'* was what he'd thought, although somehow knowing he would be perfectly safe. He didn't make it far before he was grabbed around the waist, spun around, hoisted off his feet like he weighed nothing, and tossed over Aleron's shoulder.

As much as all this had... annoyed him at first, he realised that was what had eventually made it *fun*. After days of feeling nothing but numbness, sadness, or anger, he'd been struck with other emotions – annoyance mainly. It also allowed him to stop focusing on his depressed and unsure thoughts and the agonising questions that plagued him.

It reminded him of messing around with the guys. He and his friends liked to bully with affection, play rough, and just get under each other's skin. Of course, they never went too far by picking on sensitive issues, as they were bullies, but they weren't jerks.

He and Emerie also formed a similar relationship.

Sure, this reminded him of home and all the things he'd lost, but they were also new memories. Playful ones he hadn't expected from something like a Duskwalker.

He'd thought his future with Aleron would be bleak and nothing more than solemn duty. To be led around the world like a captive, where his needs, wishes, and happiness didn't matter. That he'd eventually lose large parts of his personality that brought him great enjoyment.

No one was perfect, but Gideon rather liked himself. He tried to be kind, respectful, wise, funny, and just all around a decent human being. He had his failing moments, and sometimes he let his temper get the best of him, but he really did try to be good.

He thought he'd lose all that with Aleron. No more laughter, sensuality, learning, or anything. He didn't want to be isolated from people and had always preferred to travel in a group.

Yet, the idea of doing that with Ingram and Emerie, who were apparently lovebirds, while he was stuck in a miserable mind state... yeah, that had been painful to imagine.

Beau had been mature, composed, and taciturn, but he'd compromised for Gideon by being playful with him in return behind closed doors. In the same way, Gideon had respected his desire to be reserved in public and didn't pick on him like he did his friends. It was a mutual agreement where they both lost and gained in different ways.

It'd always bothered him that he couldn't truly be himself with Beau, whether they were in public or private, but that's how relationships worked. Give and take, and lots of communication to ensure each person's needs were being met to the best of their partner's capabilities.

Aleron... instigated this with me.

The talk of brides, and their future, and everything that had felt like a set of constricting hands around his throat, had stopped. In the silence, he hadn't been alone despite how much his heart had ached.

Then, just when his thoughts were at their lowest point, turning into too many versions of his own voice, and he was ready to crack and embrace temporary insanity to cope, Aleron brought him out of the worst of it.

His heart and head hurt so damn much. Even now, as he bounced from Aleron's heavy footsteps, they radiated agony. Yet, it didn't feel so pressing. Even though a shoulder currently knocked the wind out of him here and there, he felt like he could finally take a damn breath that wasn't laced with the quiet wails of his conscience.

In the darkness, he needed someone to remind him of

who he was. To let him feel like himself for just a few fleeting seconds. To make the unrelenting voice in his head shut up so he could focus on the outside world beyond himself.

He still felt angry, the nasty emotion festering inside him like an infected wound, but at least he'd weakly *smiled.*

"If you don't put me down, I'm going to pluck you like a chicken," Gideon threatened, grabbing a fistful of feathers between Aleron's wings.

"Do not do that, it hurts." Aleron rotated his head a hundred and eighty degrees to look at him. "If you do, I will take you into the sky." He flapped his wings, emphasising his threat.

Letting go of his feathers, Gideon huffed out a sigh. "I'd rather you didn't. I don't know how I feel about flying."

"You will enjoy it, like you did in Tenebris."

Gideon opened his mouth to rebuff him, but closed it. *I... remembered soaring earlier.*

The previous day, not long after Aleron sheltered him with his wing, a memory had rushed to him. It'd been short, only a few seconds, but it'd been vivid. Gideon being cradled, as wind gently pushed his hair and clothes around, while a surreal world opened up. Meadows and a mountain, forests and a large, dark canyon. Below him had been a small lake, with the tail of a creature slipping inside it.

He hadn't been scared, like he thought he would be. Instead, it'd been beautiful and exhilarating.

Other than a murky image of who he guessed was Emerie, since her reddish-orange hair was recognisable, he hadn't regained any other new memories. At least, he didn't think so. They were impersonal, for the most part, but he absolutely remembered the excitement of flying.

He just hadn't known if it was real... or a wild daydream. *I guess it really was something from Tenebris.*

He waited for the fear and panic to come at knowing he

may truly start remembering, but neither did. He felt rather calm.

Does that mean that perverted dream of Aleron was actually real? He winced and clenched his eyes shut, wishing the images that suddenly bombarded him would vanish.

Sweat dotted his brow, and his mouth dried. No, he wasn't ready to accept something like that. He barely considered the living Aleron a friend, and he wasn't ready to think about anything more.

Just as sickly nausea started to seep into his gut, Aleron let out a pained grunt and abruptly stopped walking at the exact moment there was a loud *thunk*. Gideon gasped when he almost fell from his shoulder, but was quickly saved by a tightening grip.

He turned his head up to find Aleron still looking down at him with his neck twisted in an unnatural way.

A burst of laughter erupted from him. "Did you really just walk into a fucking tree?!" He tried to point at him but found it too awkward. Plus, he was forced to cross his arms over the back of Aleron's shoulder when the laughter ended up giving him a stitch, but he wasn't quite able to clutch his stomach. "Watch where you're walking, doofus!"

Aleron's wings twitched, subtly opening and closing with irritation. He grumbled as he stepped back from the tree he'd run into, awkwardly tossing his head. A reddish pink entered his orbs, and it only made Gideon bite his lips shut to stifle the noise that continued to come from him.

Yeah, I bet that was embarrassing.

It hadn't taken Gideon long to realise that he already knew what the colour of his orb changes meant. Even though he had no memory of them, he figured their meanings had passed through from Tenebris to his conscious here.

He'd grown thankful for that, as it made Aleron easier to read. It also made his skull less haunting and creepy, and instead gave it a changing beauty he hadn't realised was there.

Aleron put him down and rubbed at his chest with his head turned away. *Is he actually sulking? That's kind of... cute.*

As per their usual agenda, Gideon walked.

He didn't have the same enthusiasm for it, like his reason for it was waning. He felt lighter than he had for a while, and he peered at Aleron in his peripheral since he was the cause for it.

Strange, that – all things considered.

I should thank him. These past days had been hard for both of them. He should extend some kindness towards the person who had eased him, despite how he'd acted towards him.

Just as he opened his mouth to thank him, a strange sound caught his attention. He'd never heard anything like it before.

Curious about it, since it was sunny overhead and didn't appear to be an approaching Demon, Gideon picked up the pace.

The trees opened up, the forest falling behind them, as vast blue glittered all throughout in the distance. At the edge of the sand, his lips parted with awe at the serene scene before them.

Waves crashed against the shore, frothing and bubbling white as they crawled up the shoreline, only to recede. For as far as the eye could see, water reached into the distance before almost mixing with the blue horizon, as though the ocean and sky blended. A soft wind rustled his clothes and hair as he took in the briny scent.

"Oh wow," Gideon rasped, drawing his gaze from the left, where more beach spanned, all the way to the right, where the land became an incline. Rocks jutted at the foot of a massive cliff that circled the coast. "I've never been to a beach before."

"Do not go near the water," Aleron warned, coming up beside him. "Demons sometimes hide beneath the sand."

Gideon sighed, wishing he hadn't learnt that. It took away from the calming magnificence of what he saw, but it did stop the urge to roll his pants up and go splashing. He wouldn't have cared if the water froze his toes.

He crept closer until he found a spot where sand had gusted onto grass, then lowered himself down.

"Come, sit," Gideon said, nodding to the spot next to him. He took off his boots and dug his toes into the yellow, gritty sand. "Enjoy this with me. I'd like to stay awhile, since I've never experienced anything like this."

As though all he needed was permission, Aleron plonked his butt on the ground with his feet spread out before him. He was forced to lean forward slightly, since his tail feathers made it difficult, but it didn't appear uncomfortable in his slouched position.

He ignored Aleron's weird talon-tipped, four-toed feet shoving into his view, especially when they twitched and closed.

After a while of staring at the beach, Gideon closed his eyes. He took in the rolling crash of the waves, the sound and scent of the wind, the heat of the sun warming his chilled skin. Tiredness overcame him, not physically, but emotionally. In its own way, it was soothing. Each wave that gurgled back to the sea, stealing bits of sand, was like a balm for his spirit.

This is... peaceful.

If the world had permitted it, he may have stayed there forever. Just him, Aleron, and the sea. Only after the thought occurred did he realise that he'd included the Duskwalker in that fantasy.

I guess he's growing on me. Hard not to after the past two days. *People always thought I was happy because I didn't share my troubles.* Only Beau and Emerie discovered just how much life often encumbered him, and were privy to his past mistakes.

They were the ones who knew him to be sombre underneath the mask of his cheer. Aleron hadn't really been sheltered from any of it, and yet... he was still here.

Gideon opened his eyes to take in the world he'd never touched before. Lifting his toes, he watched the sand drizzle off his feet before digging them back under. He never would have guessed sand could sparkle or be so rough. It looked like yellow salt.

"Something has been bothering me," Gideon muttered, turning his head up when a particularly large wave crashed.

When Aleron tipped his head, and then twisted it towards him, he considered deflecting to a different topic. Sharing his innermost thoughts felt odd, but if they really were together forever... would it be so bad if he leaned on Aleron? The idea didn't bring him joy, mainly because he wasn't sure if he could trust Aleron with the wounded parts of himself.

He'd only entrusted two people with his troubles, and even then, he'd only shared parts of them.

A brief glance at the Duskwalker showed he'd looked forward to the horizon. He wasn't pressuring Gideon to continue, now that silence had taken over, instead letting him come to his own decision.

Perhaps that was why he continued.

"I keep thinking back to the day I died." He continued to play with the sand, using it as a way to fidget through his uncertainty. "I keep wondering if I had just not gone home that night, maybe I wouldn't have died. I usually lived between my home and my... *friend's* place."

He didn't expand on his relationship with Beau, simply because he no longer wished to accidentally hurt Aleron with it – if he understood what a boyfriend meant. Beau was eight years in the past.

He wished he knew how to move on from him, from his old life. He was beginning to genuinely want to.

"I only went home that day because I missed my parents and Emerie, but if I'd just stayed at my friend's place, I wouldn't have cornered her outside. We wouldn't have argued in the middle of the night just beyond the porch steps. The Demon may not have tried to take off with her had she just snuck back inside like she'd been intending to. Yet... I also keep wondering if I didn't go home, would Emerie have been taken anyway, without me being able to save her? I don't think I would have been able to cope if I learned she had died. Even now, just the idea of living a life where I didn't save her, hurts my chest so much I'm worried my heart might give out."

"Why are you lingering on 'what ifs' when you cannot change what has happened?" Aleron asked quietly, yet a deep note of melancholy radiated in his voice. "Is being here with... Why do you hurt yourself with these thoughts?"

Damnit. I hurt his feelings again. Shame prickled the nape of his neck, but he hadn't truly meant to hurt Aleron. *He probably thinks I'm saying this because of him.*

"I don't know," Gideon grumbled, rubbing his neck to soothe it. "I honestly can't help them. I guess I would just like to know if I made the right choice or not. I guess a part of it is because I would like to go back to my old life, but also... I get this feeling that I ruined Emerie's life. She was a pretty happy person, but after what you told me we'd learned of her in Tenebris... I feel so guilty that I left her behind. I feel like I failed her and the parents who took me in after the ones I had died. It's hard to let go of those feelings of guilt, and wonder if I could have spared everyone the pain that was caused from that night. So many people would have been affected, like our friends and colleagues. It goes beyond us, and it would have impacted everyone we'd ever come into contact with. Demon attacks have that effect on human towns."

A silence fell over them, one that was weighty and filled with sorrow. Aleron's hand lifted and reached out, but he hesitated and pulled it back. He laid it back between his outstretched legs.

Since Gideon had watched the physical action of his thoughts, he understood that Aleron had wanted to place his large palm on his shoulder for comfort. Once more, shame prickled on the back of his neck as disappointment trailed down his spine.

In that moment, he would have appreciated a platonic yet comforting touch. To feel the warmth of someone's hand against the cold sadness that frosted within. A gesture to show that he wasn't alone, and that it was okay to have these feelings.

He had no one else to blame but himself, and he knew that. He'd pushed Aleron away to the point he couldn't even do something so simple and innocent, for fear it would upset Gideon or he'd shrink from his touch.

His shoulders drooped. *I feel worse than I did before.*

"When I died, it was due to a horde of Demons attacking my kindred and I," Aleron stated. "For over half a day, we ran. They separated us on purpose, then crushed my skull. When I woke up in the afterworld... all I could think about was Ingram. We have never been apart, and we often acted and thought like one being. I was distraught that I could not be by his side, and the space beside me felt remarkably empty. Yet, for all my own selfish pain, I feared for Ingram more. I worried that he would do something foolish, which he did, but a part of me wished he would come join me if I could not go to him."

"Oh, I didn't know something so horrible happened to you." At least Gideon's death had been delivered in mere minutes. He couldn't imagine running for his life for so long.

"But... I never lingered on the things I could not

change," Aleron continued, turning his skull to him. "There was nothing I could do, as there is nothing you can do. I have come to learn that, despite the fact we both died and have been returned, the weight of our time spans is not the same. I also understand that it would not have mattered to me. Whether it be a month or eight years, I would have returned to my kindred's side as though nothing had changed. He will welcome me – I know this for certain. But you? You cannot go back to that life. Too long has passed, and we are bonded."

Gideon hated hearing that last part, but he couldn't deny the truth of it.

"Nothing you linger on will change what happened." Then Aleron turned his skull towards him, and Gideon found himself meeting his glowing gaze. "I have always admired the sacrifice you made that night. I would have made that same sacrifice had I been given a choice."

"I'm a little annoyed at myself that I partially blame her," Gideon grumbled, but he eventually sighed. He averted his gaze by looking forward at the rhythmic waves, watching them froth as they sprayed the sharp scent of brine towards them each time. "But yeah, if given the choice, I would have done it again if it came down to me or her. I just wish it hadn't been necessary."

"Emerie is happy with my kindred," Aleron stated with absolute confidence, dipping forward to sift sand through his clawed fingers. "Ingram is good. He always tried to make me happy, always protected me as I did him, and his heart is big. She could not have asked for a better Mavka."

His eyelids drew down halfway, and he gave Aleron a dull look. "You're making a very big assumption there."

Aleron let out a small chuckle. "I know it for certain, even if I have not seen it. When asked if she wanted to be with Ingram, and knowing what that would entail, she leapt for him. I did not know her long, but she hugged me and showed me kindness. He has chosen a lovely female, and I am happy for him as well. These are the things I choose to linger on. Ingram found contentment even after I was taken from his side, and I am sure it is the same for those in your life."

Somehow, a small smile curled Gideon's lips. "Yeah, I guess that's true. People do learn to heal, especially after so long." He brought his knees up to hug them and placed his chin on top of them. "Thank you. I feel a little better."

"You are welcome. When you are ready, you will see for yourself. We can go find Emerie and Ingram together."

When I'm ready... He examined Aleron from the corner of his eye, noting the usual pale pink of his orbs. *He's not pushing me anymore.*

He was intending to be patient, for Gideon's sake. Even if he didn't say it, he appreciated it. It let him be more at ease in Aleron's presence.

He needed to feel like he was in control, and that he could willingly make this decision. He needed it to not feel forced.

If I go with Aleron, maybe we can be happy too, or something. He was beginning to miss Emerie like crazy. The more playful Aleron had been with him, the more he wished to nettle his little sister until she gave him a sour, but adorable pouty face.

'*We can go find Emerie and Ingram together.*'

Why did it feel like they'd said something along those lines before?

A memory began to resurface, one where he and Aleron were talking on their knees. It popped, but the feelings of relief and... joy swelled within.

A new memory came. One that stung, and instantly made his eyes and nose tingle when he was bombarded by the emotions of betrayal.

The words he began to hear were garbled and inaudible before they became crystal clear. *I know I said you may yet steal a soul from me, since I may need the bonding power of a bride to bring you back to life, but I–*

It faded out, only for the image of a white serpent skull to tower over him with orange orbs. Out of context, the way it twisted its head side to side was eerie, and it didn't help that the last memory felt like a punch to the gut.

When he came back to, nothing had changed.

Aleron still sat by his side. The waves still crashed. The sun still shone down on their backs, but an unholy amount of rage took hold.

Aleron tilted his head at him. "Your heart rate has increased. Is something the matter?"

Gideon rolled to his hands and knees away from the Duskwalker, fisted clumps of sand, then darted to his feet. Anger flushed his cheeks, the back of his neck, his ears, until he thought he'd implode.

"I can't believe I almost trusted you." Gideon chuckled darkly, his hands unclenching to let go of the sand before he fisted them again.

I can't believe I was starting to soften towards him.

"Gideon?" Aleron asked, rising to his four-toed, bird-like feet.

"Couldn't find another soul to trick, huh?" Gideon bit out, turning his head so he could glare over his shoulder. "You made it out as though I came with you willingly, but you forgot to mention the coercion involved."

Aleron warily reached out, only to pull his hand back. He cupped both to his chest while his orbs flared white.

"I do not understand," he admitted. "Just moments ago, you seemed content."

Yeah, well, moments ago, he hadn't known the truth. The fact he'd been content next to Aleron only brought on a more intense anger.

"You didn't want me to come with you. You *needed* me to."

Fuck, just saying that made his chest sting. Hadn't he

suffered enough emotional torture to last a lifetime?

"That is not true," Aleron refuted. "I did not want to leave Tenebris without you."

Gideon began to clap. "So, you developed feelings along the way during your deception. Bravo." Then Gideon turned, opened his arms, and laughed. "You know what? I'm glad I don't remember anything. That way, I don't have to deal with a bunch of feelings I shouldn't have developed in the first place. Our time together should never have existed."

His nose wrinkled tightly in hate when Aleron let out a soft rumble. Gideon's eyes narrowed into a glare, ignoring the red orbs that flashed at him.

"Those memories are precious to me. I did not finish our story after we arrived back in Tenebris, but I cherish what happened afterwards." He pointed a sharp claw, and it glinted in the sun. "I will not let you taint them for whatever reason has come upon you."

He was making it out as though Gideon was being silly!

I'm not the one that lied to him... I don't think. Did I agree to come here with him because there was no other way for him to come back to life?

Had Gideon's feelings been used as a way to manipulate him?

If I truly cared about him... His glare turned into a wince. *Yeah, I probably would have agreed to it, even after learning of the truth.* When Gideon fell, he fell hard. He wasn't a pushover, but he'd bend over backwards for the people he loved.

His glare returned, and he directed it at Aleron.

No one liked feeling manipulated. Thankfully, he didn't have any warmth for this Duskwalker to lean on anymore – only a hollowing emptiness in the pit of his gut. A place he could dig in to grab and throw the muck of this betrayal.

"Since you never shut up about him, go find your damn

kindred and leave me the hell alone. Hopefully if we spend enough time apart, the bond will eventually fade."

"I do not understand," Aleron repeated, this time with a whine. "Just moments before, you... wait, what did you say?" His skull cocked creepily.

"I don't want to be with someone who manipulated me for their own selfish gain," Gideon stated with firmness. "Maybe the fact I don't remember is a blessing for me, since you don't have my feelings to twist anymore."

As much as his anger burned his insides, the mingle of sadness in his voice was noticeable even to his own ears.

The snarl that came from Aleron was menacing and monstrous. Gideon found himself laughing, allowing spite to bubble up inside him.

"Ooooh, I'm so scared." Gideon wiggled his fingers at him. "What are you going to do, kill me? I'll just come back to life. You cursed yourself as much as me."

*"You are **mine**, little human,"* Aleron growled, his voice octaves darker than before as he stomped closer so he could tower over Gideon. "The fact you think I would *ever* hurt you shows just how lost you are. Our bond cannot be broken. And, even if I could, I would not."

His wings flared, as though he wanted to come across more menacing, or perhaps because he was upset. Which, if he was, good! Gideon was fucking upset too.

The soul floating like coal between his horns caught Gideon's attention. It looked like it'd weakly curled into a ball in a poor attempt at hiding from the world, hands cupped against its chest and feet tucked under its backside. Feeling petty, he leapt for it, grabbing a hold of one horn so he could take his soul back with the other. Yet, when he bounced back to his feet, his hand was empty.

"What the...? But I've seen you hold it." His soul no longer belonged to him to the point he couldn't even touch it? "Give it back. I don't want to be bonded to a monster!"

It was his, and should have always been his! *Why the*

fuck did I bond myself to someone like this?!

He ignored the way Aleron gasped at what he'd said, what he'd done, and how his orbs snuffed out to deep blue.

"A *monster*?" Aleron quietly uttered, palming his *monstrous* clawed hand over his fur-covered chest.

Gideon winced, especially with how much he could see that hurt him. Perhaps that was too far, but he'd let the bitterness of his temper get the best of him.

I shouldn't have said that. Even if that was what Aleron was, he hadn't been horrible to him since he'd woken up in his new life.

"Aleron... Look, I'm sor–"

"Is this what you wanted?" Aleron said, as he reached up and took Gideon's soul, and it weakly laid in his palm.

He took one of Gideon's hands, turned it, and gently placed his soul onto it. It didn't lay on him, but rather floated where Aleron last left it.

Then, his wings shuddered when he stepped back, before his entire body followed suit, like a sudden chill crept over him.

"It is yours as much as it is mine, but I cannot do this anymore." The quietness in his tone was haunting, even against Gideon's rage. "I cannot do this by myself. You do not wish to see, nor do you wish to truly *listen*."

After gawking at his soul, he turned his gaze up to Aleron. "What's that supposed to mean? I'm not the one who lied here."

"I have never lied to you, Gideon," Aleron stated, even more dejected than before. "You just do not remember enough to realise the truth. I am hoping Ingram and Emerie can help you, as I do not have the humanity to thaw you of your frost."

"I don't need any help!" He could do this on his own, like he always had. Every time Aleron said it, the more it made him feel so damn weak and pathetic.

"You have asked me to leave you alone, so I will finally do so."

Before Gideon could even respond, his slack jaw threatening to unhinge in shock, Aleron spread his wings. For the first time, he saw the full, daunting lengths of them, and guessed they spanned twenty feet combined.

He shuffled back in surprise.

They whooshed when they flapped. He lifted off the ground – only to fall on his face two seconds later. Dark yellow infiltrated his orbs as he shook his head on a straightened arm. He leapt off, flapping his wings fast, only to drop to the ground on one knee.

"What the hell are you doing?" Gideon asked in disbelief, his lips twisting.

"Trying to fly!" he roared. "I have never flown on Earth before. The air and wind here are different. It is not as easy."

Gideon's nose wrinkled with a sneer. "Thank goodness you weren't holding me when you did this."

Reddish pink flashed before Aleron changed. His form grew more monstrous, his legs bowing and arms elongating to accommodate a four-legged position.

"Holy shit," Gideon rasped, stepping back in surprise. He'd never seen Aleron do this before.

Without another word, although he did give a chomping snarl, the Duskwalker sprinted into the forest in the direction of the incline. Unsure if he felt worse or better by his leaving, Gideon stared off into the space he'd last seen him.

He eventually turned down to his soul.

Whatever. It's not like it matters. Tears of frustration and sadness stung his eyes, even more so when the flames covering the entire head of his soul retreated back to being nothing but a crack across its face. Talk about being hot-headed.

His soul leaned up on one elbow and reached in the direction Aleron had gone. Snapping its face to Gideon's, two solid green slits narrowed into a glare before... giving him the middle finger!

Oh, well fuck you too.

It disappeared, likely going back to Aleron.

I can't believe he... left. He really hadn't expected him to. Rubbing at his chest in frustration, it suddenly hurt.

"Screw this!" Gideon shouted, turning to walk into the forest.

He made it only a few metres before he circled back to the shore, returning just in case Aleron came back. He didn't know, probably to fight with him some more. He *wasn't* going back in case the Duskwalker regretted leaving and came back for him. That's what he told himself, at least.

He also did need his boots, and he swiped them up one at a time to put them back on his feet.

Just as he was shoving his second boot on, to his right, a large black creature jumped off the cliff edge. It started to fall towards the rushing sea. *You idiot!*

Gideon bolted towards the shore like he intended to go save him, despite not knowing how to swim, only for Aleron to spread his wings and glide. He flapped, turned as though he was quickly adjusting, and flew across the sky along the horizon. He dipped to Gideon's left and flew over the forest, back towards the centre of Austrális.

Aleron was truly leaving, and that somehow made him feel even fucking worse.

"He *actually* left." He sat down and placed his face in one of his hands. "How did my life come to this?"

He was arguing with a Duskwalker. In any normal situation, that would be a death sentence.

I just want shit to get better. Is that too much to ask? Just when he thought he could actually accept Aleron, he learned something that would make it impossible. *I feel so trapped.*

"Can the bond really not be broken?" he mumbled, utterly dejected. At this point, he was beginning to truly wish to go back to the afterlife just to escape it.

As much as he wanted to live, he didn't particularly want an empty, shitty life.

"I tire of watching you torture one of my little ones," a deep voice echoed.

I remember that voice, he thought as he lowered his hand to look about at the empty space around him. It was the same voice that had revealed the ugly truth he'd just learned, but had also been there the day he'd come back to life.

"I will not allow my carelessness to be the cause of this miscommunication... *twice.*"

Gideon threw his hands up while letting his head fall back in defeat. "Oh *god*, what now?!"

Wary, Gideon shuffled back at the voice, unable to see him, and wanting away from him. Before he could stand, something took hold of his entire head. It didn't feel like a set of hands, but rather an invisible ball of magic.

"I cannot make you remember, but I can give you my memories of that day."

Gideon let out a strangled choke as he was rendered immobile. A flood of memories were injected into his mind.

From an outsider's perspective, the first image that came to life was of himself and Aleron wrapped in his wings, laughing and goofing off together while he was *naked*.

He wasn't given time to think about it, as the rest were forced upon him swiftly.

Gideon learned his name was Weldir and recalled Aleron telling him that before.

He watched Aleron obtain a skull imbued with magic. He heard the words Weldir stated that had caused this fight, as well as Gideon's paling complexion and hurt features back in another world. He patiently observed Aleron's confession, and Gideon's realisation that none of their time together had been mingled with trickery or betrayal. Then his own confession and how he'd been the one to reach out his hand to Aleron, so they could come to Earth together.

The longer the forced memories were shoved into his brain, the more he convulsed. Even though he couldn't see the real world, his eyes rolled into the back of his head. Liquid tickled as it dripped from both his nostrils before the taste of coppery blood spread across his lips and tongue.

Excruciating pain forked across his skull.

No matter how much he seized, how forceful and violent it became, Weldir didn't let up. There was no Aleron here to interfere. He didn't let Gideon pass out either, keeping him conscious during the injection.

After a while, everything became shrouded in murky red, as if his blood was flooding his brain to the point where it clouded everything.

When it finally ended, he collapsed to the ground. Dark silence swallowed up all his senses. His head felt like it'd been split apart, one ear blocked as though it was filled with the blood that permeated in his mouth.

Hours later, the cold clutched at his bones.

On his side, he shivered before a gasping wince burst from his lips. Gripping his throbbing head, his eyes drifting in and out of blurriness, he curled into a ball.

My head feels like it's on fire.

It burned, a branching pain of lightning sparks that moved like insects crawling across the inside of his skull.

Whatever Weldir had done to him, the pain continued to linger. Dried blood clogging one of his nostrils made it difficult to breathe, and the ear on that same side had gone near silent.

It took him a long while to notice his dark surroundings.

Night had crept in, and it brought a chill and the threat of nightmarish monsters. A black and glittering dome seemed to be covering him, but he was unsure if that was just a trick of his eyes due to his cloudy vision.

Utter disappointment filled his entire being. *He didn't*

come back for me.

Why should Aleron have come back after how he'd acted, treated him, what he'd said to him? All because a fragmented memory came to him, and he clung to it because he was apparently undeniably *stupid.*

Guilt slithered around his essence like a venomous snake, and he covered his mouth to trap his groan of dismay within.

Back in Tenebris... I really did say that I was falling in love with him.

Staring at himself through the gaze of another had been disorientating, but his toothy and beaming grin had been evident. If a passing stranger were to see him in that moment, they would have been able to correctly surmise how *happy* he'd been.

I've been such a fucking prick. He slid his hand up to massage his aching eyes while he silently cursed at himself. He wished he could split his being into two so he could beat the shit out of himself. *Aleron hasn't deserved any of this.*

What Weldir had shown him... it had been damning. It didn't matter that he hadn't experienced it, or his emotions, nor did he remember a single thing from his own perspective. The big guy had been sweet, honest, and *vulnerable,* with broken, crying orbs.

To have gone from that euphoria to their current miserable situation, with a broken and desolate Gideon being the cause of all their suffering... *He's been so strong for me.*

Feelings of overwhelming love hadn't suddenly sprouted for Aleron, but it did bring on a deep appreciation for him. In a time where Gideon had been unbearably weak – mentally, physically, and emotionally – Aleron had stayed by his side.

Gideon had needed someone to wade through the tempestuous oceans of his mind and reach their hand to him. He'd needed them to find him below the surface, already drowning and fading into the dark abyss, and yank him back up, where there was the beauty of light and warmth.

He'd needed someone to force him to take a breath, by sacrificing a little of their own.

He'd needed Aleron to remind him to live, by being his big, goofy, yet sweet self.

Even if most of it had gone unnoticed at the time, he recalled how patient he'd been with Gideon. He winced at much of his own actions and curled up tighter while clutching his head.

Fuck. I shouldn't have called him that. He wasn't a monster, and the damn word shouldn't have fallen from his lips.

Gideon closed his eyes, hoping night would pass quicker if he went back to sleep. He wanted to apologise, to make it *right*. The least he could do was *try* to like Aleron.

If I fell for him once, maybe I can do it a second time.

He just hoped Aleron could forgive him.

Why is it so different this time we met? Was it because Gideon had woken up alive, on Earth, naked as the day he was born? He'd been so embarrassed, having to cover his dick while worrying Aleron would choose to bite that part of him off first, that his mind hadn't truly stopped reeling since.

Everything else was just more and more piled onto his plate.

In the afterlife, had he been calm when he met Aleron? Had the realisation that his existence didn't matter – and there was no point in being upset about the living when he was dead – meant he'd been able to lean on the Duskwalker? He figured the stars had just aligned for them in a way that didn't make sense, but must have felt right for his heart in the end.

Unable to fall asleep, his headache refusing to dissipate and his whirling thoughts worsening it, he peeked open his eyes. He stared out at the sea that gently lapped at the sand. The crescent moon reflecting against the inky water sparkled amongst the ripples, and it was so pretty he felt undeserving of witnessing it.

Groaning in pain, Gideon rolled over to give it his back.

Red eyes illuminated by the white light from above caught his attention. Just before the tree line, he held the stare of the Demon that had been silently watching him. The grass just beyond the protective dome was torn up, as if the creature had tried to get to Gideon while he was vulnerable in sleep.

He tried to take in its features, but the dark of night allowed only the barest of details. The moon made its eyes glow, casting just enough light to reveal it was small, barely humanoid, and had a boorish snout.

"Hasn't anyone told you it's creepy to watch someone while they're sleeping?" Gideon sneered as he rose onto his hip to sit.

That, apparently, was its cue to leap to its hands and feet, and bolt for his protective ward. It clawed at the dome, head-butted it. Squealing and snarls burst from it rapidly, and it just all around sounded like a horrible little cretin.

It was too loud with his headache, too fast for his aching vision.

The rage that had been building and building inside of Gideon finally exploded. Self-loathing and general hatred for everything and anything around him mixed together. He directed every acidic drop of it at the Demon.

Gideon leapt to his own feet and bashed his shoulder against the dome. They fought together to break it.

"Let me out," he whispered, forcing adrenaline to the surface so it could loosen his stiff muscles, fill him with heat, and give him strength. When it didn't let up, he yelled, "Let me out!"

He wanted to punch the shit out of something that deserved it. He wanted to vent all this spiteful hatred, and the sorrowful emotions he truly hadn't been given the chance to release. He wanted to kill, destroy, and maim until he felt better.

He wanted to hurt something that was set on hurting him in return, rather than take out all his pain and frustration on someone who should never have been his target.

The dome popped like a bubble.

Gideon tackled the small Demon to the ground before it even had a chance to catch itself when it stumbled. A grated, cracked roar exploded from him as he straddled its chest to keep it down, while using his knees to lock its biceps to the ground.

Then, as it snapped its gross, drool-covered fangs like a wild animal, its claws cutting and slicing through the air, he grabbed its throat with one hand. He shoved up against its jaw to stop it from biting him. With his free hand, he raised his fist back and launched it across its face.

A *thwack* sounded, as he struck warm flesh and hard bone. The creature grunted, only to let out a horrible hiss as it fought to get out from under him.

He punched it and didn't stop.

Even when its ferocious snapping turned into pathetic wheezes, he unleashed... everything. Even when it clawed down Gideon's face, his biceps, his side, causing ribbons of blood to flow from him, he punched with every bit of his might, his strength.

He wished it was the Demon who had killed him, wished it was himself, wished it was a physical manifestation of his anger and sadness. He pelted its face even when its fangs accidentally cut across his knuckles, and his own blood mixed in with the Demon's. Even when its skull began to crack and eventually caved in, and it stopped moving, he didn't stop until he pulverised it.

Gideon's chest was heavy, as though filled with gravel. His lungs ached as they took in air so cold it sliced his insides like razors. His inhales were short through his nose, but his exhales were long, focused, and foggy through spit-dotted lips.

The salty tracks of his tears stung the slicing wounds on his face and mingled with the rivulets of his own blood.

Only when Gideon couldn't see through his tears, did he stop, and a pitiful sob broke from him as he covered his face. He didn't know what he was doing, or why, nor did he think this was actually helping. Yet the violence had felt so damn good that he didn't know if he was weeping in relief or in shame.

Sand shifted, and Gideon glanced over his shoulder. He rose to his feet to greet the Demon that had slithered from the sea, its tail fishlike, yet its upper body near human.

It looked slow, although not small, like the one he'd just killed.

"I reckon I can take you on," Gideon numbly muttered, reaching down when he noticed a large rock half buried in the grass. His boots squeaked in the sand as he walked across it, stumbling towards danger. "If not, you'll just take me back to Aleron earlier than expected."

With Demon blood tainting his fist, dirt and drying tears upon his face, and his veins flooded with raging adrenaline, he sprinted for the Demon with a yell.

I'll kill everything that tries to eat me.

He wasn't prey, and Gideon was *tired* of feeling like he was.

TWENTY-THREE

Long after day broke, Gideon stayed within the tree he'd climbed to hide. Cradling a shredded arm to his chest to tamp down the worst of the throbbing, he tried to ignore the Demon below him.

The shade cast just enough shadow to allow the Demon freedom even within the day. Hissing whenever it accidentally touched a beam of light, a hint of smoke wafted from it. It spent most of its time clawing at the tree in a poor attempt at climbing it. Rabid, feral, and likely obsessed with the scent of his blood in the air, it never stopped.

He'd ended up struggling with the half-fish Demon, but he did manage to smash its brains out with his rock. After that, he'd mostly been fine until daybreak turned the sky a lighter navy. The little fucker beneath him, although smaller than any of the others, was a fast thing.

His brute strength mattered naught against swift swiping claws and frantic snapping fangs.

Gideon glanced down at his cradled arm.

His sleeve had been torn from him, and the entire length of exposed flesh had suffered deep, gouging marks. The creature had rent skin and muscle all the way to bone. Three of his fingers were crushed, and all round he was just in agony.

His face wasn't faring much better, one eye swollen shut.

His pants were mostly fine, although saturated and kept him freezing. Yet, the numerous purple stains of Demon blood mixed with his own were gratifying.

He'd killed two, which was more than he could say for most humans. For a night, Gideon had been a Demonslayer like Emerie, although she probably had far better skills than him after being a member of the guild for years. He'd started to feel emasculated being called a bride, not to mention knowing his sister could probably kick his ass now. Surviving the night he'd just faced? Pride swelled despite his pain.

Gideon peeked down at the Demon, whose red eyes met his own.

Sure, he could have let it eat him so he could go back to Aleron sooner, but he decided being eaten once was enough. He was willing to be patient, especially if it meant he didn't have to further upset Aleron by returning to him for such a sour reason.

Should I remove my shirt? He'd managed to retain his clothing the last time he'd been transported to him. *It's caked in blood. I don't want him to see it.*

Just as he moved to do exactly that, his body turned transparent. Gideon floated, but he didn't mind feeling weightless. At least the pain faded.

Perhaps he should have figured out how to do it on his own.

Alright. Here I go.

Darkness swallowed him within an instant.

When Gideon opened his eyes, a bright-blue sky appeared, and he squinted against the sun. Reappearing in a curled-up position, as though he'd been lying on his side, he lifted to his hands and knees in his incorporeal form.

Below him, land passed in a blur of greenery.

Miles above the ground, he noted the tops of trees swaying with the light wind, a river sparkling in the distance, and mountains not far to his left. Gideon lifted his head at the whoosh of a large set of wings and took in Aleron's impressive wingspan from behind.

He reached out towards him, relieved to see him.

"Aleron," he called, only to suddenly turn physical.

The yell that came from him was more like a scream as he plummeted headfirst towards the ground. Great! He was fully healed, only to splatter against the fucking ground.

Icy cold wind cut through Gideon's clothes and hair, and the speed of it instantly made his eyes water. His arms and legs flailed, while his horror-struck eyes searched for an answer to stop falling to his painful death.

He tried to revert back to his incorporeal form, but he couldn't figure it out. His panic didn't always allow him to think.

"Gideon!" Aleron roared.

He managed to twist in the air so his back could face his impending doom. Relief clutched his gut when he saw Aleron diving towards him.

"Aleron!" he yelled back, reaching his hand out to his outstretched, clawed one.

His wings flapped faster as he chased Gideon through the air. Then he eclipsed the sun.

His mind and vision split into two as a memory tried to tangle and morph with what was happening in that moment. Aleron diving for him in another world, just as he was now. His hand stretched out with his orbs white, as fear clutched at Gideon's throat.

Aleron eclipsed another bright sun, while heat and the glow of lava shone just below his feet instead of greenery.

For a split second, time seemed to slow.

Emotions, ones that didn't belong to the current Gideon, slammed their way into his chest like a sledgehammer. The intense power of adoration, hope, trust, and reverence collided into him like a ball.

Breathless, Gideon tried to blink himself back into only

seeing one image as Aleron's warm hand took ahold of his wrist. An image flashed of a large lady with golden corkscrew curls and pupilless eyes that peered deep into his own. He saw his reflection in them.

He remembered her – the sound of her voice, her regal saunter, the way she brushed her nose against the tip of Aleron's fanged snout. He also remembered how she'd been the one to drop him off the edge of an invisible platform.

Before any more of that time within a weird Elven deity realm could come back to him, he was shoved into the safe cradle of Aleron's arms.

Gideon panted out strained breaths, his eyes wide. *That was the sharpest memory that's come back to me.* Much of it was missing, but he now had the face of the Gilded Maiden Aleron had told him of. What he'd been told helped fill in the rest.

"You chose me," Gideon whispered, referring to his vision.

Aleron cocked his head but didn't respond.

The Duskwalker hovered them in the air, keeping them in place with his wings. They almost curled around his body as though he was about to be wrapped in them, the tips meeting, only for them to shoot back. Aleron required large flaps to support his heavy weight.

They began a gradual descent to the ground, but Gideon could barely pay attention after his revelation sucker-punched him in the gut.

His eyes bowed in anguish, as guilt once more prickled on the back of his neck.

Aleron chose me, even when he'd been told letting me die in that lava would bring him back to life.

How many times had Aleron chosen him when he hadn't needed to? He'd even halted his rebirth in fear of leaving Gideon behind in Tenebris.

Shit. I said all those awful things to him yesterday. None of it was true or deserved!

The strength of Aleron's body tightly secured Gideon's smaller form to him, and he buried the side of his face against his saviour's hard chest. That scent of hazelnut and cedarwood surrounded him as soft fur caressed his nose, cheek, and chin.

These things no longer filled him with angst, and instead helped to nurture him through his revelations.

Stillness enveloped them when Aleron's feet touched the ground in the middle of a dense forest. The quiet was unnerving, and likely due to the Duskwalker's presence silencing the animals, but Gideon didn't mind it. Instead, the song of Aleron's breaths and heartbeat against his temple filled in that silence – at least, until he was placed on his own feet.

Pale-pink orbs turned blue as he stared down at Gideon. Both hands clenched into fists, but he wrangled a forefinger from his left hand to point at Gideon's arm.

"You were attacked," Aleron stated, and the cold, dejected tone of his voice cut deep. "This is why I did not want to leave you on your own."

Ears burning, Gideon covered his bare arm. "It's fine. I kicked their arses anyway."

"I see, so you do not need me." Somehow, his orbs darkened further, highlighting how much learning that filled him with sadness. Stepping back, retreating from him, Aleron lifted his skull in the direction behind Gideon. "If you go that way, there is a human town nearby. I am sure you want to be with your own kind, which is why I landed here."

A cold crawl of dread tickled down Gideon's spine.

Aleron stepped back, turned, then spread his wings in preparation to leap.

"H-hey, wait!" Gideon exclaimed as he bolted forward with his hand out.

Aleron evaded him and stepped to the side, nearly

causing him to fall. He shoved his wing forward to catch him and then bounced him back to his feet.

"I want to talk," Gideon quickly stated before Aleron could say or do anything.

The way Aleron nervously cupped his hands against his stomach, and how his wings tightened against his back, was like a twisting knife to Gideon's gut. Aleron put more space between them, shaking his head.

"I do not know how to talk to you," Aleron admitted, dipping his snout downwards and to the side to avoid looking upon him. "I am not human. I do not know what it is like to live as a human. Like you said, I am a monster."

"Aleron..." Gideon rasped, wincing in sympathy, in regret and guilt.

"I want to heal you of your sorrow, but I do not understand what it is you need. All I know is that it is not... *me*." His eyes bowed further at how much he could see the big guy was trembling. "You said you wanted me to leave you alone. As much as I do not want to do that, you refuse to come with me in search of Emerie, and I need to find her. Emerie is human; she can help you."

Aleron's wings slowly flared again, preparing to take flight once more. Just a few feet separated them, but suddenly it felt like they were miles apart.

"I'm sorry, Aleron," Gideon stated firmly, staring at him fully in the hope he could see the sincerity of that statement – even if it didn't appear as though Aleron was looking at him. "What I said yesterday... I shouldn't have said any of it. You're not a monster, and I'm really sorry for saying that. If I'm being completely honest, I'm also sorry for how I've acted since the moment I woke up here on Earth with you."

His wings drew in to flatten against his back. "I do not understand. Why are you suddenly saying this?"

"I've been remembering things," Gideon grumbled, rubbing the barely noticeable stubble on his face and cheek.

Even though he turned his head away, he noticed

Aleron's head lift. His voice was so full of hope as he said, "You have?"

"The problem is that it's all out of context, none of it makes sense, and it's often fragments. Sometimes it's just a voice, or a sound, or just an image. They aren't coming to me in a pattern." He lowered his hand to stare at it. "Yesterday, I remembered Weldir saying he thought you'd need a bride to be brought back to life. That's it, nothing else. Not what happened before or after it. In that moment, just like back then, I felt really betrayed by you, really hurt, and very used."

"But that is not why I asked you to come—"

"I know." Gideon lifted his gaze to meet his blue orbs. "After you left, Weldir came and forced his own memories into my conscience. From the moment he found us goofing off in your wings to when I held your hand as he gave you your new skull. He gave me context and made me realise just how... wrong I've been treating you. In the past week, you've shown more strength and intelligence than I was capable of."

He stepped forward, but then hesitated to close the rest of the distance when Aleron recoiled. Gideon didn't realise he'd started trembling as well until he rubbed the back of his neck nervously.

This is a lot harder than I thought it would be. And his damn chest hurt like it was full of gravel – heavy, grainy, and hard to breathe through.

Gideon took in a steeling breath. As much as stating the next words would make him feel weak, he knew he needed to bear it. He needed to explain.

"I'm not okay, Aleron. I've known all along that I'm not okay. I was really angry, and sad, and I felt so hopeless that I considered just lying on the ground and letting the forest grow over me. I hated anything and everything around me, and I felt like the only thing giving me purpose was walking. The thing is... one of the reasons why I wanted you to leave me alone is because a part of me didn't want to take it out on you. But you wouldn't go, and it meant I kept hurting you even if I didn't mean to. I needed time, I needed space, I needed to feel like I was in control of my own life."

His little whimper nearly broke Gideon. "But I am trying to give you space now. Like I said, there is a human town not far from here."

A heavy sigh fell from Gideon, and he lifted his hand so he could dig his fingers into his closed eyes.

"I'm not saying this to hurt you, Aleron." He gritted his teeth, his jaw knots flexing, as he tried to hold back the dam of his emotions. "Fuck, man. I'm trying to apologise to you. I'm used to handling my problems on my own. I'm not used to leaning on people, because half the time it just feels easier to smile, but I just can't do that right now. I'm trying to say that none of this is your fault and I realise that now."

"But it is my fault. If I had not brought you here..."

Why did Aleron saying that finally bring tears to his damn eyes? *Does he regret it?* The fact Gideon could push Aleron to such a thought, after the Duskwalker showed him unconditional support and affection in his own way, was deeply saddening.

"None of this is your fault, nor is it mine. Not even Weldir knew I was going to lose my memories of our time together. I can't imagine what all this must have been like for you. Going from me saying how much I care about you, to suddenly turning into a stranger." He removed his hand from his face so he could look at Aleron once more. "I should have said it from the beginning, but I'm really sorry that I don't remember you."

Aleron's blue orbs broke at the bottoms like glass, and ethereal tears floated around his bat skull. Even though it was heartbreaking, the beauty of this Duskwalker and his bony face, his horns, and even wings, was highlighted by those glowing, ethereal drops.

"I'm ready to try now," Gideon continued. "Instead of fighting any memories that come, I'll try to accept them, as well as you. I'll go with you to find Ingram and Emerie. Wherever you want to go, we'll go."

"You want to come with me?" Aleron asked, palming his chest. "You want to be by my side?"

"Yeah, but I want to go to the human town first." Just when Aleron's wings began to rise, they drooped even further. "I need to buy new clothes, a weapon so I can protect myself, and maybe get a jacket if I can afford it."

A chilly, light gust of wind wrapped around them, and his shivering only highlighted just how cold he was. Somehow, the silence between them seemed even icier.

"I did not want you to come to harm," Aleron grated as he stepped closer, finally closing the gap between them. He danced his claws an inch from Gideon's bare arm, not touching like he could see Aleron wished to. Red flared in his orbs, but at least his ethereal tears began to settle. "I wanted to protect you."

"I don't want you to protect me." Gideon grabbed his arm at the reminder of the pain he'd been in. Yet, when Aleron shied away, he realised he'd said and done the wrong thing. "As much as last night was horrifying, I finally felt like I was strong. I died because of a Demon, and that has been bothering me. Every time you said you wanted to protect me and keep me safe, it made me feel really small and weak. I don't want to be protected, but... I also don't want to fight on my own. I want things to feel balanced between us. I want us to be able to lean on each other, rather than me feeling like a feeble human that does nothing but weigh someone down. Even if my efforts are pointless, and you're worried for me, let me feel like I'm your equal." Then, forcing a small amount of humour, he stated, "So long as I'm holding an axe. Doing it with my bare hands kind of sucked."

"I am sorry I made you feel this way," Aleron said, dropping into a crouch, as though he wanted to appear smaller for Gideon's sake.

With a groan, frustration bubbling, he slapped his hand over his face. "You're not supposed to apologise to me when you've done nothing wrong. I know you didn't mean to make me feel this way."

Aleron stood and once more towered over him. *He's trying everything he can to make me comfortable.* He absolutely wasn't helping, but the Duskwalker's goofy attempts were endearing against the swell of his guilt and shame.

"I do not know what you want me to say or do. Does this mean I should not tease your small stature?" He leaned his head to the side as he peered at Gideon and then obviously trailed his gaze down, as indicated by his skull's movements. "I like calling you little human."

Considering Gideon was just above average height for a human man, he found the notion of being teased for it odd. Usually it was the other way around.

He huffed out a singular, deadened laugh.

"If you stop picking on my height, I think I'll kick you. If I tackle you, though, it'd be nice if you pretend I'm able to knock you to the ground."

"That would be a lie, though."

The corner of Gideon's lips threatened to lift. "Yeah, but it'll make my ego feel better. It's pretty bruised right now."

His heart, too, felt bruised, but it was at least lighter than it had been since he arrived on Earth.

He didn't love Aleron, and he wasn't sure how he was supposed to feel that way towards a Duskwalker, but he hoped he could earn Aleron's forgiveness in the future. That's why he'd braved explaining how messed up his mind was, and how sorry he was about how he'd treated Aleron. He'd try to be better and more accepting.

He'd make an effort to at least see him as a *friend,* and

not some spooky creature that kept following him like an ominous shadow.

Now that everything had settled, and he'd finally gotten much off his chest, he really was cold in his torn clothing. Time to get a move on, and quickly.

He grabbed the coin pouch tied to his trousers and noted how light it was. "While in the town, I can ask if anyone has heard anything about Emerie and Ingram. Maybe they've been spotted nearby."

Just the mention of finding his kindred changed his nervous stance into something more focused.

Dark yellow swirled into his glowing orbs. "I did not think of that."

"It's not like you could have gone to a gate and knocked on it."

Aleron hummed in thought, which Gideon figured was his way of agreeing. He turned and waited for the Duskwalker to come to his side, then they made their way to the town – together.

Let's go find your kindred.

TWENTY-FOUR

With the temperature dropping steadily, Aleron watched his bride run across a small, purposefully made clearing.

He thought the strong, southerly wind would push Gideon off his feet, yet he managed to fight through it. His hair flipped and fluttered, and he pointlessly stopped attempting to shove the hood of his new grey jacket over his head.

In the distance to Aleron's left, light illuminated the sky in flashes across the horizon. Only occasionally would lightning strikes be seen, the cloud cover too heavy to let most of the forking beams be visible. The sky was dancing, rumbling with delay after those shocks, but steadily worsening by the minute.

The clouds had long ago rolled over Aleron, but the thickness of them was only just beginning to truly shield the world in darkness.

Leaves, twigs, and even small branches fluttered on the strong wind, and the fronds of grass laid down under its power. Aleron's fur and feathers rustled along with the trees and shrubs behind him.

Sturdy upon his feet, and holding the trunk of a tree as a way to rest, he waited for Gideon.

In the time he'd been alone, he'd reflected on Gideon over the last two days since they'd properly spoken. His bride was much the same. He still appeared lost, still reserved and spoke little, and the dark smudges under his eyes never softened. It hurt to see his chosen bride so worn down by his mind, but the only solace was that he no longer rejected Aleron's presence.

For now, that would have to be enough.

If there was a possibility he could have the Gideon he'd come to know, the one that was warm, welcoming, and happy to lean forward to kiss the side of his snout... he could wait. He'd wait eons, if need be, for the Gideon that would fully accept him into his heart.

He was worth it, even if it didn't seem so right now.

Their last moments within Tenebris... they had only been the start.

Gideon had only just started fully opening up to him. Aleron had also only just started comfortably expressing himself with the male. How much would their relationship have deepened, how much more inviting and tender could his bride be, if they finally got there again and then surpassed it?

Aleron held onto that hope, even if Gideon's melancholic features burned a hole in his chest as he sprinted closer. His flowery meadow scent, like the purple blooms and patchouli, fluttered to him and warmed the breeze as it met Aleron's senses.

Stopping right before him, Gideon shoved his hands under his armpits to warm them. The blade of an axe looped to his black trousers glinted in the clouded light.

"Sorry that took me so long. They closed the gates because of the coming storm," Gideon stated, just as a large wet leaf splattered across his face.

His lids lowered into a dull look, especially since Aleron laughed at him for it. He couldn't help it with the relief that spread behind his sternum. *He came back to me.* Gideon had taken a few hours to return, and Aleron had started to worry he'd been abandoned again. Even though he had hope, the anxious paranoia that their truce wouldn't last constantly nipped at his being.

"Figuring out this Phantom stuff is a lot harder than I thought it would be," Gideon continued, as if he felt the need to reassure Aleron. "I should have asked you how to turn incorporeal. I would have been stuck in there until either the storm let up or tomorrow came if I didn't figure it out."

"I do not have any answers for you," Aleron said, while shoving his wing forward to block Gideon from the chilly wind. "This is as new to me as it is for you."

"Oh." Gideon spared him a wary glance before it disappeared. "We should move on quickly and seek shelter. Those rain clouds look like they're coming in fast, and I really don't want to be caught in the middle of them."

Aleron's claws dug into the bark of the tree. "Did they not have any information on them?"

Gideon shook his head. "No. I did learn that this place is called Colt's Outpost, though. They haven't seen Emerie or any Duskwalkers in the area. I must admit, though, a few of their soldiers looked at me kind of funny when I asked."

"You said that about the last place," Aleron explained, referencing Slater Town they'd gone to right before sundown the day before. It hadn't been far to the east from here.

"Yeah, but it was an even weirder look." Gideon shook his head once more and came closer until he placed his side against Aleron's torso. "It doesn't matter. Let's go. There might be an empty house or cave nearby we can use to hide from the storm."

With a singular nod, Aleron dipped low so he could place his arms around Gideon's back and behind his knees. He lifted his light weight and securely pressed him against his chest, then crouched, and with a large push of his wings, Aleron leapt. Even before the inertia reached its end point, he'd flapped his wings again, pushing higher and higher into the air.

Compensating for his own weight had been a struggle at first, but adding Gideon's did very little to bother him. Now that he'd gotten used to flying on Earth, it was as easy as breathing.

Once they were above the trees, he took in how dark the clouds were in the distance, despite those above them being quite light. The bright flashes continued, and the soft rumbles reverberated towards them much stronger now. The wind grew more powerful without the barrier of the forest, and he tightened his hold on Gideon when a strong gust shoved him back.

"Maybe we should walk," the little human said up to him, bringing his knees to his chest to hide from the cold. Once more, his arms were folded and his hands were tucked under his armpits.

Aleron shook his head. "No, it should be fine. I am faster flying, and it is easier to see shelter. I will try to beat the storm."

How hard could it be to fly through one? Not that Aleron had ever done so.

He turned to go northeast, but he didn't make it a single wing flap before rain poured on them. He grunted at the weight of his wings, and how difficult it became to fly with water soaking his feathers and fur. Pushing with all his might, he sought a place of safety for his bride while trying to avoid the worst of the storm.

It circled around them, moving from west to east until he was forced to fly north. Just when he managed to escape it, a problem arose.

"Fuck, Aleron," Gideon cursed with chattering teeth. "We have to go back."

Aleron looked out at the large distance, finding only water. They'd reached the land's end and had nowhere else to go.

"I will take you down to the ground," Aleron offered, turning his gaze to the long mountain range below them.

"No!" Gideon yelled. "Mountain ranges are just as dangerous as the Veil. And with the storm sheltering the Demons from the sun, they'll probably come at us like a swarm."

With a heavy heart, Aleron turned to take in the world behind him. It looked dangerous to take his bride through it, but he was right: dropping to the land here would do more harm than good.

A strike of lightning forked across the sky, and he was beginning to feel each one tingling in his flesh. They lifted his fur before they struck, as if it was compelled by the energy they gave off.

He raised his snout. *Maybe up?*

With that thought in mind, hoping to get above the clouds, Aleron flew in a diagonal ascent with great difficulty. Wind pushed him from every direction, and Gideon had long ago buried his face into Aleron's chest with tightly clenched eyes. A small amount of fear clung to his scent, but Aleron knew it must be stronger, the water washing away the worst of it.

Just as he reached the clouds, every fibre of fur, every feather, lifted in aversion. A horrible tingle assaulted his entire body, almost... electrifying it.

He halted his wings and let them fall, to get as far from the clouds as possible. Just as he spread them again, a lightning bolt struck the top of a nearby mountain, and they were far too close. Aleron yelped at the loudness of the sound and banked to get further away from it.

White filled his sight, and the further he flew into the brunt of the storm, the more they were buffeted around. The winds gurgled rather than whistled, and had the chilly force of a Mavka slamming into them at full speed.

An unexpected gust came from the right, rather than the

left.

The roar that exploded from Aleron parted his fangs and was followed by constant whines and whimpers. Agony radiated up his right wing and down his entire back, each flap shunting a pain so excruciating, that he almost stopped moving it.

Had he been alone, he may have. He held his bride tighter, gnashed his fangs, and flew down towards the mountain range.

Fuck the storm, fuck finding a safe place to rest. With the pain he was in, he'd rip a Demon from their cave nest just to escape this weather. He'd spend the remainder of the dark storm protecting his bride in whatever shelter they could find.

"Are you okay, Aleron?" Gideon shouted while sputtering water, peeking his head out from where it was buried. "I can hear cries coming from your chest."

Aleron could do nothing more but shake his head and search.

When he found a lit opening, he dived for it. High on the mountain range, facing east on one of its peaks, he sought the light. Likely it would be a Demon who knew of fire, and he prepared himself for a battle.

Just as he was about to set his feet down in front of the cave mouth, a strong gust shoved them inside. He slammed against the ground, but curled his body around Gideon as much as he could to protect him.

The moment they halted, he sprung to his hands and feet with a snarl, searching for the source of multiple Demon scents that littered the air.

He found three – two females and one male – up against a wall. All three were winged Demons, two large in height and strength, while the last one was small. However, the little one looked more like a youngling than an ill-formed Demon. The male had flared his wing out protectively to shelter the females.

Both females had patches of pale skin spotting through the usual void-like Demon colouring and horns. The male looked entirely human except for his bat-like wings, claws, and fangs, but he lacked horns like them. His hair was dark brown, his skin tanned, and his shape fully humanoid.

He was shirtless, but his pants were a deep navy, whereas both females wore grey-and-brown dresses.

Shifting into his faster and stronger monstrous form, Aleron kept Gideon below him by shoving his chest down. The shivering human stayed where he was.

"Leave," Aleron warned, his voice deeper than usual due to the change.

The male narrowed his red eyes at Aleron. "If you think I will force my family into a storm like this, know I will not do so willingly."

"I said leave!" Aleron roared, stepping a pawed hand forward.

The male stepped closer to them protectively, especially when the female gave a horrible hiss.

"Our daughter can't fly through weather like this!" She tried to shove the male's wing away, so he curled his arm around her side to wisely keep her to him. "She will fall or we will lose her."

"Only a fool would fly through this," the male said calmly. "And by the state of your twisted wing, you already know how dangerous it is."

Aleron braved looking over his shoulder. One of his wings was flared threateningly, while the other drooped against the ground. Resting it only seemed to make the throbbing around the base joint worse.

"We need shelter," Aleron told them, stepping back just enough to reveal his bride. *"I will not permit you to stay with him."*

"I thought I smelled a human," the female said, casting a predatory gaze over Gideon. The hunger in her eyes only solidified that he couldn't trust them.

"Let me up," Gideon urged.

Aleron growled down at him, but instantly quietened at the glare he received. He eyed the axe looped to Gideon's pants before nodding. He promised he would treat them as equals. As much as anxiety crawled inside his gut at allowing Gideon to stand and expose himself, he conceded.

Gideon drew his axe from his trousers and held the handle firm. Aleron couldn't help stepping slightly in front of him.

With water dripping from them, they stood as a united pair.

"He is my priority," Aleron informed them. *"We will not stay where there are creatures who are a danger. Leave and find shelter elsewhere."*

"This is our home!" the female yelled, gesturing her hand to the right.

Deeper within the cave, he noticed more chambers and light. In this area, a small fire currently warmed some kind of meal in a cooking pot. A table with three chairs was situated nearby, with a mass of blankets that smelt recently used, showing the area was lived in quite regularly.

"Daddy," the youngling called quietly, clinging to the back of his pant leg. "He's scaring me. Make them leave."

"You are asking us to face death, whether that is by you or the storm," the male said, his voice low and dark. "The child has done nothing wrong, has never killed for her meals, and has never harmed anyone. She was born with half her human features, and yet you would be willing to make her suffer before she dies?"

Aleron examined the... *family* before him.

Despite them being Demons, was this how a normal family was formed? The youngling did look similar to the two adults, and they were both willing to protect her. He observed their dwelling once more, noting it lacked the general nest-like qualities of other Demons.

The male reminds me of the Delysians we met in the Elven realm. His sight once more found the youngling, who reminded him of Lehnenia with her little horns and red eyes.

Then Aleron turned his head to the entry of the cave and looked into the storm that had worsened terribly. His orbs flared orange with guilt before shifting to white.

Most other Demons had been quite horrible to him. They had clawed him, bitten him, and hurt his kindred. Yet these three were beseeching him to be spared. They were also choosing not to attack him for the meal his bride could be, or the addition of humanity he could see they needed.

The male was fully formed, but both females were not far from their completion.

They would not go from their *home,* but they also weren't trying to harm his bride. They were showing kindness, which was rare for their race.

That kindness was enough for him. He'd never sought to be purposefully violent.

Aleron stepped back and ushered Gideon with him by the use of his wing. *"Fine. We will seek shelter elsewhere."*

There had been other lights, although much lower down the mountain. He'd chosen this one as it was higher, would be safer for his human.

The male's lips tightened as his red eyes darted to the storm. Worry crossed his features as a strike of lightning flashed just beyond it. It was so close the boom of thunder that followed was instantaneous. "I understand your fear. If you promise not to harm us, Duskwalker, I will permit you and this human to stay."

The female gasped, but he cut her a menacing look.

Aleron shook his head. *"I do not trust you."*

The Demon nodded. "Fair enough."

"Aleron?" Gideon asked, tilting his head with a deep frown creasing his brow.

"They have a youngling... I do not wish to hurt them," he

explained, poking his snout in her direction.

The tightness in Gideon's expression fell. Then softness shone in his eyes towards Aleron, and his heart swelled in receiving it. It'd been too long since his bride had gifted him with a look of tenderness.

Those piercing green eyes had felt like a knife since they came to Earth, and now they glided over him with soothing warmth.

"Well, damn. As much as I don't want to freeze, I get it."

The fact he so easily accepted such an answer, rather than wanting to utilise their combined strength to thwart these Demons needlessly, reminded Aleron of why he'd begun to care for Gideon. *He called me a monster, but I do not think he truly meant it.* This alone was enough to prove otherwise.

Gideon tucked his axe back into the loop of his trousers as he turned and headed towards the exit. Aleron shuffled back to keep his sight on the Demons, his four-legged position low and ready to defend them should the need arise.

"If you head due east from here, you will find the northern Demonslayer stronghold. No Demons reside on that mountain, due to the violent humans. You should be able to find shelter there, if you are willing to risk it."

With a grunt, Aleron nodded his thanks. The advice was appreciated, as it would limit their time in the storm. *I would rather take him somewhere with no Demons.* He'd rather not fight with his wing in the state it was in.

When they were at the exit, his tail slipping outside into the wet, he finally shifted back into his more humanoid form. His spine straightened, allowing him to better carry his little human.

"Human," the male called, causing Gideon to look over his shoulder. As he drew his claws up his left thigh, over his pants, he stated, "I remember you."

Nothing more was said, and Aleron shrugged at the Demon's strange statement. Yet, when he faced Gideon, his expression had paled, turned haunted, and his heart accelerated.

Aleron quickly lifted him into his arms. He darted into the storm before the scent of his fear could affect the Demons.

Not even the pelting rain could pull his bride from his slack-jawed stupor. Just when he thought his human was getting better, he looked worse than ever before.

Despite the agony each flap of his wings gave, he worried for him as he searched for somewhere safe.

Whatever the Demon had implied, it'd shaken him.

Gideon didn't think he'd ever experienced a shock so intense that everything became non-existent. Everything disappeared – Aleron, the storm, even the senses pertaining to himself.

To stare one's own death in the face, after it'd already ripped him from the world, was just too much to wrap his head around. Then finding out his cannibalistic murderer had some kind of wife, a child, and wasn't just a monstrous nightmare stalking the shadows for another creepy taste of his flesh was daunting.

In his mind, he'd painted the Demon who killed him eight years ago as something entirely different.

He'd been bigger in his memories, uglier, slimy as he clung on for dear life so he didn't fall to his death. The slashing scars across his torso burned, like he was re-experiencing a shallow memory of them.

The dreams he had of the Demon *every single night* were of laughter he didn't think had ever happened. Of taunting, cruel threats, and a madman bent on eradicating humanity like a despicable villain.

Instead, his killer had been protective of a child. Had held back his upset woman. Had managed to calm and persuade a threatening Duskwalker, without even sparing Gideon a hungry or spiteful glance.

Their eyes had met, but he'd thought nothing of it at first. Yet another Demon, one who just so happened to have wings. A coincidence.

The Demon from eight years ago didn't have any human skin upon his face or shirtless body. His hair had been like a void, not the tan colouring it currently was. He looked so different, to the point even his boorish fangs had stopped protruding past his lips and now sat neatly behind them.

If he hadn't grabbed his thigh, Gideon may not have believed him.

That fateful night, he'd taken his knife from his belt loop and shoved it into the Demon's thigh in order to get it to release Emerie. Then he'd dragged it downwards as he climbed his body. He'd been intending to grab a wing and hopefully crash them towards the ground, with the Demon below him to protect him from the fall.

Instead, his torso had been ripped apart, and he still remembered that gouging agony.

A part of him wished the Demon hadn't said anything. He'd been just fine thinking the worst of him.

But, as Aleron finally touched land and crossed a threshold that ceased the ever-pelting rain, a strange emotion washed over Gideon. A gentle flow of realisation coursed throughout, invading his veins and softening his muscles.

All the lasting hate, anger, and regret started to wash out of him. All of it due to the Duskwalker who just held him tightly in the cold and barren cave, as if he didn't wish to let him go just yet.

If Gideon had any chance of accepting Aleron, he needed

to let go of that Demon. To no longer look back on that
night as an unfortunate event that continued to birth
misgivings, 'what ifs,' and regret. Nothing could change it,
and his killer wasn't as cruel as he made him out to be.

Sure, Gideon was aware that the Demon eating him
meant he probably helped make him more human. That
haunting thought still stung, but he decided to not linger on
it.

He needed to let it go, for Aleron's sake. He doubted
there would ever be a chance for the Duskwalker to gain his
affections if he didn't.

Gideon believed in destiny, and he thought this was the
universe's way of helping him along.

He wished it was easier to let go of all the important
people in his past, but he hadn't figured out how to do that
yet. It hurt too much to think of them, and he didn't know
how to navigate all his pain, regret, love, and guilt to be able
to swim through that vast sea without drowning.

"Gideon," Aleron called, so softly, so breathlessly, that it
shook Gideon back to alertness with its gentleness. He
tipped his eyes up to meet his blue orbs, since he couldn't
see anything else in the dark apart from them. He found that
comforting. "Will... will you tell me what is wrong?"

The laugh that sounded out of him was wrong, dark, and
awkward. A lie, simply because he didn't wish to bother
Aleron when it didn't – shouldn't – matter.

"It's nothing," Gideon stated, peering around them. The
storm clouds were barely letting in enough light to
illuminate the area, and shadows touched every wall. "You
did an amazing job, Aleron. The cave is empty, I'm
guessing."

Then he shifted in his cradle to indicate he wanted to be
put down, but Aleron's grip on him tightened instead. The
Duskwalker's hands shook when he finally put him down
and stepped back, as though to put space between them.

Gideon turned just as a strike of lightning illuminated

everything in brightness. The way Aleron nervously held his hands to his stomach, fidgeting with them, while his skull was turned to the side, told him everything he needed to know.

He didn't want to push Gideon, in case it made him withdraw, but he wanted to know.

A sigh fell from his lips. Shivering, trying to stay warm with the loss of Aleron's heat, Gideon looked towards the ground.

"Sometimes the world is smaller than we think it is," he mumbled. "Of all the places we could have gone, to all the caves in the world, to all the Demons we could have met in the north when I came from the south... tonight, we met the one who killed me. It was a lot to take in. Sorry if I worried you, but I'm alright now."

Gideon believed that, as strange as it was. He wanted to let it go, along with all the negative emotions regarding it. He wanted peace within his mind, even if it was one gruelling step at a time.

He hadn't expected an echoing growl to come from Aleron, or for his orbs to turn such a violent crimson.

"That Demon is the one that haunts you?" The dark and menacing tone of his voice made the wet hair on Gideon's nape stand on end. Was it fear, or did he find it titillating since that rage wasn't turned towards him? "You should have told me. I would have destroyed him for you!" Aleron stamped a foot with a heavy, wet plop. "Once the storm passes, and my wing heals, I'll take us back there for you. If it will help you to heal, I will—"

"Stop, Aleron." Gideon hesitantly stepped forward in the dark, worried he'd trip over something he couldn't see in the dimness. He followed Aleron's glow like a beacon. "It's fine. I don't want to go back and hurt them."

"But it hurts you," Aleron snapped back, more upset than Gideon was over this. "Your face in the storm... I have never seen something so painful."

He placed a palm on Aleron's forearm.

"What you did back there, letting that family stay while taking us back outside, I thought that was really admirable. Not many humans would think selflessly when faced with danger, and yet you did so out of kindness for them, for that Demon child. I would rather that be what I remember than more bloodshed."

Maybe Aleron didn't realise it, but it had exceptionally softened Gideon towards him. A monster had showed exemplary righteousness. He didn't even know he valued that so deeply in a person until just now, because of him. It wasn't a common trait, even among humankind.

"Do you not want revenge for yourself?" Aleron asked, lifting the arm Gideon was touching while looking down at it.

"Before I met him, yes. But not anymore. I wouldn't want to take a child's father from them, no matter what it is. I know what it's like to lose not just one parent but both as a kid, and I wouldn't wish that upon anyone." He stepped back and attempted a smile, only to let it fall when it felt false. A spine-clutching shiver tore through him. "To be honest, I'm more concerned about getting warm. I wish there was some wood here. I bought a small travelling flint-and-steel kit in case I ever wanted to make a fire. Plus, it's really dark. I can't even see your face."

"There is wood," he grumbled. "There is an old Demon nest here. I did not know a human's sight was so poor, but it is just over there."

Aleron's heady scent lifted to right under Gideon's nose when the Duskwalker pointed to a spot just behind him.

He squinted his eyes to better see, noting a pile of... *something*. "If it's not rotting, I should be able to make a fire with it."

If the pieces were too big, he could easily cut them up with his small woodchopping axe. *And then maybe I can do something about that soft whine I can hear coming from him.*

Aleron continued to whimper in pain, even if he was trying to be quiet about it.

TWENTY-FIVE

Creeping slowly forward so as not to be noticed, Aleron watched Gideon strike a tool that gave off sparks. He tried to stay out of the human's way while he worked on starting a fire, but he was enrapt by the task.

Gideon humoured him and answered his eager questions about the process.

"I bought this, but I was also kind of hoping you could spit fire like a dragon," he muttered, before striking his tool again.

When the hemp ball caught little glowing flecks, he fell to his forearms to blow on it. Once it was lit, he used a spare stick to shove it within the depths of the wood he'd placed in a cone shape.

"Didn't you mention that your kind can use magic?" Gideon then asked. "Shouldn't you be able to just click your fingers and make some fire?"

Aleron tipped his head. "I have never used magic before, so I do not know if I can do this."

Yes, he'd mentioned that Mavka could use magic, but he didn't actually know any spells or the extent of his capabilities. The closest he had gotten was changing his form and sheathing his claws, and Ingram had demonstrated those.

Oh, apparently there was body changing magic he could

do to penetrate his partner by shoving his claws into their abdomen, but he didn't know why that'd been necessary to learn. Gideon had taken his cock just fine within Tenebris.

Perhaps Emerie had not been a good teacher, like Gideon. Ingram must not have prepared her properly.

When the wood finally caught fire, Aleron cast it an envious glare of green orbs. He'd been hoping it would never light, so that Gideon would be forced to seek his warmth. As much as he would have liked to draw his little human into his side and blanket him with his wing, he didn't.

His wings meant a lot to him, and being horribly rejected for them once was enough to stop him from trying a second time. He didn't want to violate Gideon's space and make him feel suffocated by his need to embrace his little human with them.

Aleron would like his bride to request it from him – although that seemed increasingly unlikely. He'd rather make fire.

"Ah, that's a little better," he rasped, wiggling his fingers at the heat coming from it. "This should also dry you."

He waved for Aleron to approach, and his heart leapt at the invitation to come closer. That was, until Gideon immediately stood and walked away as he removed his jacket. He spread it out on the floor.

Why ask me to come closer only to leave? Aleron grumbled, his sight flaring red in annoyance. Then it turned dark yellow when Gideon grabbed the hem of his cream shirt and lifted it.

"What are you doing?"

"Getting warm. I need to remove my wet clothes and dry them, otherwise I'll just keep freezing," Gideon answered, grunting as the wet fabric clung to his chest and arms.

Struggling to remove it, Gideon flashed Aleron the muscled plane of his abdomen. The trail of hair from his navel down to his pants had him licking the inside of his mouth.

When he finally removed it, his back was to Aleron as he laid it on the ground beside the jacket.

Aleron hissed out a breath when his wings tightened nervously against his back and the right one shot pain down his spine. As much as he wanted to stare openly at his bride's naked torso, especially since his dipping back muscles flexed and danced, he couldn't.

The last time he'd seen Gideon without a shirt had been the day they arrived back to Earth, and before that... this human had been naked, content, and thoroughly fucked, as he laughed within Aleron's wings. Now just the barest peek felt like too much, and it brought on wildly conflicting emotions and desires.

He wanted to reach out and glide his claws up his bride's spine, knowing he enjoyed it, but Aleron was too scared. When Gideon stood and faced the fire, revealing his chest and the dusting of hair covering it, Aleron wanted to drag him closer and lick at his little pale-pink nipples.

Aleron wanted to play with his bride, but knew he would only be hurt if he tried. He longed to just hold Gideon's hand – what hope did he have for more?

From the corner of his sight, Gideon did something that had his mouth going dry. He reached for the ties of his pants and undid them. Aleron's heart sprinted in his chest cavity. Although he tried not to look, he found his skull turning to him. Gideon lowered his trousers, revealing white shorts that had turned see-through in some areas due to the rainwater.

His fur and feathers puffed despite their drenched state when Gideon bent over to lay his pants down near the fire as well! The shorts were tight against the cleft of his ass when he leaned forward before crouching, and it revealed more than it hid.

Purple flashed in his sight, and he choked back the

sudden saturation of drool within his maw. He turned away, looked up at the ceiling, and just hoped for strength.

Too much had happened since returning to life, and all of it had prevented him from having lustful thoughts for Gideon. Now he was almost completely naked, and Aleron wanted more.

Yet, no matter what he wanted, he... knew it was one-sided. It radiated a coldness within his heart that had his sight returning to its normal pink colouring, cooling the desirous heat that had started to swell. Even his cock stopped twitching.

Gideon's scent warming from the fire, so decadent and lush, made him feel like he was breathing in ash. His smell was always at the tip of his snout, but he wanted it on his tongue for the first time.

He does not want this from me.

Aleron was only truly permitted to touch when he cradled him for flight. It was the only chance he had to embrace his bride, and he did so tightly and with affection, even if the little human didn't know it.

The constant restriction acted like a set of chains around his torso. They constricted him, ached his whole being until he found it difficult to even *breathe*. They were weighty, cold, and made him feel undeniably alone at times, despite his bride being right next to him.

Seemingly unaware of how his near nudity affected Aleron, Gideon turned with his hands on his narrow hips. His thumbs dipped into the hip and pelvis lines that ran lower, and led towards the darker hair covering his groin. Somehow, his wet hair being brushed back made him appear even more handsome than he did just a second ago.

Oddly enough, Gideon flashed him a small smile. "So, how's that? Are you feeling warmer?"

"I was not cold," Aleron muttered, lowering his gaze to the flames to look at something, anything, other than

Gideon.

"Oh," he rasped, his tone dejected. "I was freezing, so I thought you may have been as well. Never mind, I guess. At least we can see each other properly now."

"I do not need the light. Mavka can see in the darkness."

Once more, Gideon rasped, "Oh."

Movement caught his attention, the male an attraction for Aleron like a moth to a flame, and he briefly glanced at Gideon. Shoulders turned inwards, he scratched at the side of his hair, ruffling the wet lengths of it. He combed it back even more.

Aleron's sight shifted to dark yellow as he tilted his skull. Why did he get the impression he'd disappointed Gideon? A shameful knot formed in his gut, since he hadn't meant to upset him. Aleron didn't know why he kept saying or doing the wrong thing.

Even earlier, when he'd stated he'd go back to kill that male Demon, he thought it would make him happy. It didn't; it was a pointless offering.

"You're really independent," Gideon laughed off, but even Aleron could tell it was utterly false. "Alright. Well, could you turn around for me?"

"Why?" Aleron asked, while obediently doing as requested.

"I'd rather be near the fire if you don't need it." Aleron's body twitched with each light tap of approaching feet hitting the stone ground. "Let's check out that wing and see if there is anything I can do to help."

"My wing?" Aleron squeaked, before leaping forward before Gideon could touch him. He spun back around and stood, towering over him. "My wing is fine. You do not need to check it."

Gideon's eyes widened, brows raised in disbelief. "You haven't stopped releasing whimpers since I asked about it in the storm. Let me look at it. Sometimes massaging the muscles around a sprain can help alleviate the pain."

Aleron refused to give this human his back, especially since just the idea had his heart rate spiking until he thought it'd sprint out of his chest.

He shook his head, causing the sound of dry bones to rattle from him. "I will heal in a day. There is no need."

"Turn that feathered rump around right now and sit," Gideon demanded while pointing at the ground, his green eyes sharpening into a glare.

He stepped back with his sight turning white. "No. It does not hurt."

Gideon followed. "The fuck it doesn't!"

Aleron turned to quickly put space between them and found that walking backwards ached his wing. Its current drooping state meant he also almost stepped on it.

Chasing him around the cave, he yelled, "Why are you lying, Aleron?"

He didn't wish to answer. *My wings are sensitive.*

Gideon had shown him this. He worried this human putting his hands over them might cause him to do something foolish. Even just the slightest, lightest touch from him could have Aleron's orbs shifting to deep purple.

He'd never had that reaction with Ingram, only ever this human. Just the thought of this human's hands all over them had desire tensing his seam.

After a while, Gideon stopped chasing him and Aleron finally turned back to him with his chest huffing in anxiety. The male's face was red, his expression tight with irritation.

"I'm trying to do something nice for you, man," Gideon lowly muttered, digging his fingers into his hair to brush it back. "I know I've fucked up a whole bunch, and I'm trying to make up for it in my own way. I just want to take care of you."

Gideon's eyes crinkled as they darted off to the side, and his shoulders fell. Then, with a deep sigh, he gave up and walked back to the fire.

Aleron was as far from the fire as possible, but the flames could never warm him more than Gideon's statement. "You want to... *care* for me?"

With his back to Aleron, he crouched down and put his hands forward to play with its heat. He shrugged. "Yeah, but like, I get it. I wouldn't want me to touch me either after everything." Then he peeked over his shoulder and waved Aleron forward. "Still, come sit by the fire. Even if you're not cold, it'll at least dry all that fur. It must be heavy."

The rest of his rambling didn't sink in. Not when Aleron was too busy cupping both his hands to his chest when a strange emotion fluttered within it. It was so light and fluffy that it made his sight turn bright pink.

He wants to care for me. He wanted to help him, touch him, make him feel good. *He lit the fire for us then?* Not just himself, but because he thought Aleron would be cold and need the light as well?

The gestures may be small, but they meant *so much* to him.

Did this mean they were growing closer again? Rather than avoiding him as though his touch ignited pain, he'd offered contact between them.

He wanted it. Aleron tried his hardest to hide it, but his body was *starved* for affection.

As much as he worried about how he would react to Gideon petting his wings, he did desire his hands upon him – anywhere. He ached for it so desperately it sat like a hungry pit in the centre of his stomach, eating away at his essence.

He hesitantly crept closer.

He gave Gideon's back his own. With his shoulders turning inwards and his head lowering nervously, he sat down.

"I was not avoiding you because of what has happened," Aleron said quietly, not wanting his bride to feel rejected. "It is that my wings are sensitive," he admitted, his orbs flaring reddish pink in embarrassment.

"Oh. Well, it might hurt a lot while I'm trying to massage you, then." A creak of knees informed him Gideon had stood, but he closed his sight in nervous anticipation. "If you're worried about the pain, maybe it's best if I don't."

Aleron guessed Gideon had taken his statement a different way than by what he insinuated. He didn't correct him.

Instead, he flared his wings to gesture to them. "It is fine. Just... be careful."

Do not arouse me, little spring. I do not know if I can take it.

The threat of it paining him actually brought him relief. Hopefully it'd keep his desire at bay, and instead allow them a moment to bond. He sincerely longed for it to bring them closer and would do just about anything for that chance.

"I'll let the heat get to it first. Usually that helps to ease sprains and tense muscles."

Gideon stepped to the side and heat brushed over him from behind. The light wind coming from the cave mouth whistled inside, but it was mostly subtle. The entrance was facing east, so the southerly winds didn't force their way in too badly.

With darkness blocking his vision, he just nodded.

For a few minutes, all Aleron could feel was his feathers drying from the fire. The storm outside rumbled thunderously, while the pelting rain showered his ears in a constant *shaa*. It would never be louder than his bride, not with the way his senses were always so acutely hyper-focused on everything about Gideon.

His breaths were close, his heartbeat lulling. His scent of a purple flower he couldn't name, and the patchouli he taught him of, wrapped around his being.

Aleron heard the shuffle of feet moving behind him and he stopped breathing. Tension shot through him as he waited for the thrill of his bride's touch.

Instead, a yelp shot out of him when Gideon lightly pressed the webbing between his thumb and forefinger against the underside of his wing base. He stopped himself from bouncing forward to escape, but his orbs opened up to white.

"Sorry," Gideon grumbled. "I'll be as gentle as I can."

The next moment, Aleron's back twitched into an arch of pleasure when the male did the same to his other wing.

"What are you doing?" he asked, unsure about the conflicting sensations.

"I, uh, don't really know much about having wings, so I need to feel around both." He drew his thumbs down his back at the same time, tracing the two same muscles on both sides, before returning to prod around the base of each. "You have fur and feathers, so I can't really eyeball you."

Aleron jerked forward at pain only to ease back at pleasure. "Why would you need to put your eye on me? Is that not painful for humans?"

It was an honest question.

The chuckle that fell from Gideon surprised him. "It's a saying. It means I can't see with my eyes, so I have to with my hands instead." He circled his thumb over a rather tender spot, but he didn't yelp this time. "I think I found a fairly large knot. Let me know if I press too hard."

Hissing in a breath, especially since he stopped caressing his uninjured wing, Aleron just nodded. He tried not to jerk and bow his back to flee, but he was unable to help it. He'd never experienced anything like this.

The massage may be unfamiliar, but so was injuring his wing from flying. Both new, both strange, both leading to this moment where he slowly began to relax as the pain dulled. A different kind of pleasure spread across his back, and he took it in.

It didn't stir lust, but it did radiate tenderness within.

Gideon's nimble fingers weren't shy, and they even

rubbed up the arch that drooped until he met the elbow. Aleron's orbs darkened in contentment, and his chest nearly hummed and vibrated with it.

"Does that feel better?" Gideon asked. Aleron just nodded and let out a snorted huff through his bony nose hole, causing him to chuckle. "I'll take that as a yes."

He didn't stop, and Aleron snorted another huff. Eventually, he started to work his way down the muscle pressing against his protruding spine bones, seeking anywhere that could be tense. Gideon dug into his shoulder blade, going below and above his wing base.

Each knead of different muscles softened Aleron further and further until he wanted to turn into a gooey puddle.

"Thank you, by the way," Gideon stated softly. "I kind of like doing this for people." He went back to the areas that originally ached and throbbed, and the pain had dulled exponentially. "Your muscles are really tough though, so you're lucky I used to work as a tree cutter. I have strong hands and fingers from holding my axe and from prying stumps."

Aleron didn't respond, but his contentment increased at listening to his deep voice cascading around him. Gideon was filling in the silence with rich tones, and each word sounded marvellous against his essence right then. He'd always liked Gideon's voice, but Aleron just enjoyed that he was speaking with him, rather than remaining silent like he often chose to be.

Pretty male. He didn't need to be looking at him to think this. His face and body may be beautiful to him, but there was so much about him that attracted Aleron.

The smell of petrichor, dirt, rock, and burning wood was hidden by the earthy musk of Gideon. It swelled in his mind and almost made it throb with delight.

Even just his breaths and little heartbeat lulled Aleron. His body grew heavy, sleepy even, and he took it all in while his bride roamed his strong hands over his aches.

My pretty human.

A mild smile curled the corners of Gideon's lips as he took in Aleron's slumping form. *He likes this.* It was evident by how his firm muscles softened and his posture drooped, combined with the soft hums he constantly made.

Stealthily peering over the Duskwalker's shoulder, Gideon took in that his orbs had turned black like he was falling asleep.

Aleron didn't seem to notice it, or maybe he did, but the more Gideon worked the muscles surrounding his wing, the more upright it lifted. He liked that he could observe the strength returning to it.

I still can't believe he put up such a fight. His gut had tightened into a horrible ball of guilt when he thought it was because Aleron didn't want Gideon to touch him. Finding out it was just because of the pain brought on a reassuring wave of relief.

He tried not to hurt him further, and always gentled his touch when Aleron flinched or arched away. The longer he did this, moving away from painful spots only to return, the less the Duskwalker's body tried to subconsciously flee.

I'm glad this seems to be helping. He really did want to reciprocate with a caring gesture; it was a way to say he was thankful for everything, and to show in his own way that he was sorry for a lot of it.

Every time he stopped digging his fingertips in, Aleron's wings twitched as though silently begging for more. So, Gideon continued.

If he had a few love languages, whether that be romantically or platonically, Gideon knew for certain of two. Physical touch was a big one, and usually only reserved for those he was very close with. Deep down inside, he was a massive love bug, and he enjoyed showing that with one-arm wrestle hugs, cuddles, or even just leaning his shoulder against the person he sat next to.

It was why he didn't like people he didn't know or trust touching him – and one of the reasons why he'd often shirked from Aleron's touch before this.

Another language was acts of service. This had fewer restrictions, as he enjoyed helping most people.

Feeding Emerie soup when she was sick as a teenager, helping their dad fix the roof, helping the little old lady down the street move her market items from her house to her store as free labour. These were things that brought him pride, especially when he was able to have a good laugh with them along the way, or even just receive an appreciative smile.

Sure, his and Aleron's friendship may be a little rocky currently, but it brought him pleasure to do this.

Although he felt bad that Aleron had hurt himself, a selfish part of him was kind of thankful for it. It allowed an opening for him to try and return the kindness this Duskwalker had shown him. A way for him to make amends, even if it was small and may go unnoticed in the long run.

Aleron told him he would heal tomorrow, so technically, all this was pointless. Still, if he could make it more bearable until then, it was worth it.

Plus, the moment he started doing this, he became fascinated by touching him.

I didn't realise his feathers were so silky. He slyly caressed a few between his thumb and fingers while his other hand massaged. *They're also really beautiful.* Now that they were dry, they caught the light from the campfire and glistened with blue and purple while still retaining their general blackness.

And his fur is really soft. He felt it down his sides, having to manoeuvre past its substantial length. *He's like a giant teddy bear.* The long fibres usually tickled his nose and cheek while Aleron was carrying him, but feeling them with his hands made his palms tingle.

When he'd been digging down to find muscle, having to be careful of the stems of his feathers, he'd found protruding bones when he lifted them to see. Rib bones, the vertebrae of his spine, and even his shoulder blades: all these were hidden within the depths of exterior fluffiness.

He also smells really nice. His cheeks heated at that thought.

Whenever he was close to Aleron, his scent of hazelnuts and cedarwood penetrated his senses. It reminded him of home. Although it bothered him at first, he was beginning to find... comfort in it.

Gideon missed home terribly, but it was nice to somehow have a piece of it with him.

He was appreciating these parts of the Duskwalker while he massaged him, but he didn't particularly care to be bothered about it. He liked them, even if that made little sense.

His muscles are really firm, though. They were plump like his own, but dense. No wonder Aleron was so freaking strong. Or was that Duskwalkers in general? The muscles almost felt like stone, or perhaps that was just Aleron, since he came across as really lean under all his fluffiness.

Gideon, doing a last check over the areas that had been particularly sensitive, pressed his thumb into the last hard knot remaining. Aleron let out a quiet groan, but it didn't sound of pain. He'd stopped yelping and whimpering a while ago.

"You seem to really like this," Gideon mused with humour.

"I have craved you touching me again," Aleron croaked out.

He paused, his eyes widening slightly, and Aleron stiffened. Just as he began to fidget nervously, Gideon continued in order to show him what he'd said was okay. Yet he couldn't stop his ears from heating along with his cheeks.

He hadn't expected him to come right out and say something like that. It brought on a wave of bashfulness Gideon wasn't prepared for.

Now that his right wing was as good as he could get it, and Gideon didn't want to overwork the tender muscles, he moved over to the left one slowly. Being gentler, since it wasn't injured, he glided his thumb over the base and up the length of it.

Aleron's feathers lifted all over his back, and even his tail ones vibrated like a shiver had run down his spine. When he dipped forward as if to escape, Gideon reflexively grabbed the base and yanked him back.

"Where do you think you're going?" He frowned when Aleron's entire body went stiff at his hand placement. "It's not good to only work one side of someone's back. I need to do both, so it feels balanced."

Aleron obediently allowed him to fully drag him to his rump. He got back to work, digging into warm feathers and fur with a lighter touch. Feeling for knots, he didn't find any, but did press out small areas of tension. Now that he fully understood where all the muscles were, and how they were supposed to feel, Gideon pressed with confidence.

That was until he caressed both hands up his wing, from its base to the first arch, and Aleron's entire body quaked. He let out the strangest, strangled groan, and his left hand shot down like he was clutching his abdomen.

Once more, Gideon's brows drew together as he rubbed back down, but even lighter. "Am I hurting you?"

Nothing feels twisted like the other wing, though.

He was actually only doing this as a precaution. Backs

were a funny part of the body, and healthy parts often became sore due to overcompensating in order to alleviate injured areas.

"No," Aleron practically growled out. "Not hurting."

He darted his head to the side to look at Gideon over his shoulder, only to hastily cover his skull with his hand. He swiftly looked forward once more.

But what Gideon had seen was enough to make his eyes widened and his jaw to go slack until it parted his lips. He dipped his head, hiding his expression behind his drying hair that fell forward. He absentmindedly grasped and groped.

His orbs are purple. And if those erotic dreams he'd had of Aleron were actually broken fragments of his memories, then... *Am I turning him on?* His eyes darted side to side as he watched his suddenly clumsy hands. *Is* that *what he meant by sensitive?*

So why wasn't he stopping?

Shit. Why am I blushing so hard? His entire head felt like it was about to combust into flames hotter than the ones at his back.

Suddenly his heart was stammering, racing through his veins until it throbbed in his ears. They became more responsive, and he noticed that Aleron's breaths had quietly become more panted and breathier.

He felt warmer than he did just seconds ago. Gideon no longer knew if that was because of his own internal body temperature rising or not.

Aleron let out a soft, but obviously stifled groan. His body shivered until both wings twitched and flapped slightly.

Should... I stop? Not because of the Duskwalker's reaction, but because his own was alarming him.

By the time he realised his groin was tingling, his dick had already started to lengthen over his hip. And each time Aleron let out another stifled noise, or his wings twitched, his own cock hardened further until he'd grown a full-blown erection.

Why am I getting hard? An aroused, yet shy blush had even spread across his nape.

Like he couldn't help himself, truly wanting to double-check, Gideon leaned to the side. His teeth clenched as he took in Aleron's parted fangs and purple orbs. He even appeared to be drooling slightly, his tongue poking just past his fangs, while he clutched his groin with digging claws.

He ducked back, hiding so Aleron didn't know what he'd seen. *Definitely turned on.*

A mixture of emotions bombarded Gideon.

A sense of empowerment that such a minor touch could elicit such a visceral reaction in this Duskwalker. Satisfaction. The foolish, likely stupid, desire to deepen it. A small amount of uncertainty tangled with curiosity.

Before he knew it, his touch had gone from perfunctory to sensual.

Gideon should have known better than to lightly caress him by doing nothing more than lifting his feathers. Dancing the pad of his thumb between the stems, he barely ghosted his warm flesh. Aleron's fangs clomped shut with a sharp clip, and he produced a wet, frothing snarl.

The hairs over Gideon's entire body lifted in reaction, while his cock pulsated until he knew he'd released a drop of precum.

"Gideon," Aleron warned, dipping forward until he rested his free hand against the ground. Then his voice turned dark and deep. ***"Stop."***

He yanked his hands back and put them in the air as if surrendering. "Yep. Fair enough."

He'd pushed too far, especially since he actually had no intention of doing anything with Aleron. The idea still freaked him out a little, and it wasn't until this very moment that he'd ever even considered anything remotely sexual with Aleron.

His wings pushed forward to block his sides, and his skull lowered as if to hide it. But Gideon could see the Duskwalker trembling, could see how agitated his fur and feathers were. Aleron almost looked like a giant fuzzball, and Gideon didn't know how dangerously close he'd been getting to the edge until he'd stepped back to see it.

Holy shit. What the hell was I just doing?

Suddenly feeling too exposed, he spun to collect his clothes. Until now, it hadn't registered that he was prancing around someone who could desire him, while he was in nothing but his underwear.

Gideon had just been thinking of them as two dudes platonically hanging out. There'd been no reason for him to be ashamed of his body, and most men weren't interested in him. Being half naked with other men generally wasn't an issue that fazed anyone. Not even his friends – who were straight while knowing he wasn't – cared about their combined nudity.

Only when Gideon dragged his shirt on did he notice how hard his nipples had gotten and that his skin tingled all over. Then he shoved one leg into his pants. *Fuck, I need air.* Especially when he had to yank the flaps of his trousers forward to fit them over his raging erection that didn't want to go down.

"Where are you going?" Aleron asked when he headed towards the exit.

Gideon glanced at him, only to look up at the ceiling when he connected with his purple orbs. Somehow, his damn face heated further.

"I'm just getting some fresh air."

"But it is still raining. You will get wet again." Aleron's voice was so damn hoarse that it made his ears tingle.

"I'm not made of sugar. I won't melt," Gideon argued. Then he forced out a laugh; it came out shaken, likely due to his awkwardness. He felt like he'd been caught red-handed doing something he wasn't supposed to. "I'm just feeling a little warm. Hopefully I'm not getting a fever."

Maybe he was growing delirious and sick.

As Gideon exited the cave, he walked against the outer wall of the mountain, thankful the shallow alcove there gave enough shelter to keep him mostly dry. He pressed the back of his wrist to his forehead. Sweat lightly dotted his brow, but he knew straight away that the constant cold hadn't made him ill.

He silently laughed as he slipped his back down the wall and landed on his arse. Then, with one knee propped up, the other bent with his foot between his backside and his other foot, Gideon put his face in his palm.

I turned us on. By accident, he'd aroused them both. *And yet... I'm not actually upset by it.* Instead, he had half a deranged mind to pull his cock out and ease the pressure in it by jerking off.

He covered his mouth since it felt dry, as he turned his gaze to the dimly lit entrance.

Is that what Aleron's doing in there now that he's alone?

His cock jerked in excitement at the idea, and Gideon groaned at himself. A reaction to the deep, groin clutching throb, and in dismay.

It'd been a long time since Gideon had been hard like this. His heart raced like he had a stupid crush, his body flushed in bashful embarrassment, his dick hard even if he didn't particularly understand why. His mind, heart, and body felt like a mess.

Fuck. Go down. Gideon pleaded at his dick, gripping it through his trousers, as he let his head fall back until it *thunked* against the wall. *Does this mean I'm actually attracted to him?*

Before all this, he hadn't felt this way towards Aleron at all. If the Duskwalker hadn't gotten aroused, neither would have Gideon. It would have just been a platonic massage between two people. A play at being a doctor for a few... *It's almost dark out. How long was I doing that for?*

He took in the cool, unfiltered air, letting Aleron's scent leave him. His own heated pants grew stronger with each breath he took.

Waiting for his body to calm down and catch up with his brain, Gideon dwelled on what just happened. He waited for shame, or to be angry with himself, but neither came. So, he tried thinking on what that meant for him, for them, and what he was supposed to do now.

Is there a chance that my emotions from the afterlife are trickling through? Or... was this perhaps all his own doing? He wanted it to be new. If he didn't have his old memories to give his feelings context, he'd rather they be birthed from what happened between them now. To be real.

Gideon's tingling and throbbing cock said it was all real. That, although he hadn't expected this, he desired Aleron even if his heart wasn't completely open to him.

With his eyes crinkling and his teeth digging into his bottom lip, he pulled aside one of his trouser ties. *Maybe I'll be able to think straight if I cum.*

Just when Gideon thought he fully accepted his desire, the reminder of someone important flittered behind his blinking eyes. The fact he felt guilty that he thought of that person while being hard for another messed with his head.

It wasn't Beau he felt bad for, though, but *Aleron*. A strange turn of events, considering it should be the other way around, but Aleron was the one who had stirred this reaction in him. The stiffness in his pants was for the Duskwalker, and the Duskwalker alone.

I need to get over him. Beau was in his past. Eight years in the past. He was no longer his boyfriend, but his ex, and it was likely that Beau had someone else now. *I don't know how to do that.*

Gideon dug the pads of his fingers into his closed eyes. *No matter how long it's actually been, it feels like it was less than two weeks ago for me.*

He wished he could disconnect it. To unlink them in his mind. Gideon wanted it to be quick, and so sudden that he couldn't even process it and just moved on with a clean slate.

He had Aleron now. A very broken and one-sided relationship, all due to his own faults. *He apparently loves me, but... I don't know how to really open my heart to him. Gideon* needed to drain it of everyone else so he could give it to Aleron. He'd like to do that with it undamaged, because he'd rather give himself over to someone fully.

I don't want to confuse or hurt him, just because I might be horny. Gideon didn't want to use someone like that.

He was also nervous about Aleron's possible size, considering he was a freaking giant to him. Then, there was his experience level, his strength. *Would I have to teach him? Or did I already do that?*

He drew his shaking hand down his face to stare out at the heavy rain. *Why am I even thinking about this?* A few days ago, just the thought had filled him with suffocating dread. *At least... the idea doesn't freak me out anymore, I guess.*

Gideon had wished for many things in his life, but he thought this may be the first time he truly desired something with his entire being.

I wish I could just... remember everything.

I wish I could remember him.

TWENTY-SIX

Curled forward on his knees and a single forearm, Aleron covered his sides with his wings to hide his body. Then, with his head hidden beneath the arch of one, he shut off his purple sight to focus on steadying through his lustful need.

He clamped his seam shut with his other hand, and blood welled where his claws were embedded into his own flesh. The pain of them was nothing in comparison to the unbearable pressure within.

Aleron's cock was too hard to be inside his seam. It felt jammed, uncomfortably stretching him from within. Even his tentacles were squashed, unable to move within the tight crevice.

He refused to unlatch his claws, no matter how much it ached. No matter how much his fur and feathers lifted in aversion to him doing this, he wouldn't release his throbbing cock.

I can still feel his hands on me...

The press of a thumb digging into the muscles of the uninjured side of his back, so gentle and light in comparison to how the little human had massaged the first. The impression of Gideon's alluring fingertips tracing along the arch of his wing, the way they tickled him by lifting his feathers *one by one* in a slow motion.

Each touch sent tingles down Aleron's spine, spreading

pleasure all throughout. They pierced his groin until he'd been forced to stop himself from extruding.

He'd needed to make Gideon stop before he lost control. His snorted pants had become so heated they'd started strangling him, his heart racing until he thought it'd give out. His mind had fogged until he'd turned into a desperate, needy ache, seconds from reaching out and shoving his precious, fragile, beguiling male below him. Any longer, and he feared what he would have done to this little human.

Aleron groaned when his abdomen clenched.

His cock ached, but the little embedded ovals at the base of it somehow felt swollen and so full he worried they'd burst. He'd never experienced anything like that within Tenebris, the sensation utterly new and profoundly intense.

I want him to touch me all over. From head to toe, wing tip to tail tip, he wanted Gideon to run his soft palms all over every inch of him, until the male took Aleron's cock into his welcoming, rough hands. *I want him to stroke me.* Like the very first time, within one of the many forests of Tenebris.

I ache to be inside you, little spring. Aleron didn't care how. If the male was below him, above him, on his hands and knees, or on his back. Aleron would hold him in the air while he stood, if need be, but he wanted Gideon's body snuggling his cock as Aleron blissfully pumped into him. *I want to fuck him so bad it hurts.*

He'd wanted that male from the moment they'd stepped foot on Earth, but the emotional lows had been too damaging to his desires. His bride's tired and distressed expressions had not aroused him at all, and only made his heart shrivel in his chest in sympathy.

But now that some kind of truce had settled between them, and they seemed to be agonisingly slowly growing closer, it'd been nagging him in the back of his mind. At every turn, the more his bride's features unwound from their tightness and hardness, the more Aleron wished to reach out.

To touch the beauty of his human face, the softness of his light-brown hair. To draw the curved and smooth side of a claw just below one of Gideon's piercing green eyes that sliced him into tangled ribbons, only to brush over a soft lip. Even the strong point of his nose, the high arch of his full brows, and the sharp lines of his jaw and cheeks stirred his fingers, nagging at him to caress.

Aleron often stared at the ball at the front of Gideon's throat, his pulsing jugular, and his collar bones that peeked out from the neckline of his vee-cut shirt. Such delicate but mesmerising places which Aleron wished to brush the pad of his thumb against, knowing he was trusted to do so.

His scent itched Aleron's tongue to taste him, tease him, while every fibre of his being desired to rub against the alluring male until he shared that aroma all over his own body.

His bride was so beautiful, from his tousled brown hair down to his feet, that Aleron wished to dole out endless affection. In any and every way possible, whether it be his tongue, his hands, his sight upon his bare body, to even his fur and feathers caressing over him until he'd stained Aleron in his pretty spring scent.

Yet, as much as he wanted to, he couldn't even hold the male without there being an ulterior motive. Up until now, what he'd longed for, what he'd been craving, was just to innocently embrace his own damn bride, and have him do so in return.

He wouldn't risk damaging whatever broken bond they currently had, where his bride would be willing to touch him as he had today, by revealing his growing need for him.

He thought his body would give out if he didn't ease himself. Despite the torture, he clamped tighter and shuddered through it.

I do not want to... frighten him. He didn't wish for his

bride to see this part of him in case he showed fear, disgust, or anger. He didn't want to see that kind of look upon Gideon's face, so he'd rather suffer by holding himself back.

His patience only drew strength from hope.

A thousand rapid and frantic heartbeats later, the pressure began to ease. Only to reignite into an inferno when Gideon re-entered the cave, and the soft breeze fluttered his earthy, flowery musk to him.

Aleron grunted and then shuddered harder, wanting that scent in him, on him, touching his entire essence until it eroded his own smell. Aleron drew his wings tighter around his body to block him out, especially as drool seeped through his fangs.

"Hey, just thought I should let you know that it's dark out now," Gideon casually stated, his feet padding against the stone of the cave as he strode towards the fire.

How could just his voice cause his cock to swell painfully behind his seam? *I need him.* He dug his claws under the base of his skull with the arm he was leaning on, while covering his snout with the crook of his elbow.

"Are... you alright? I wasn't expecting to still see you there like that." His voice was quiet, and almost coy.

"Tired," Aleron grated, the lie sour upon his tongue.

"Fair enough." The grumble in Gideon's tone said he might not believe him. Thankfully he didn't press the issue. "I'm tired too. I guess the storm really took it out of us. It was nice to watch, though, but it was too cold to stay outside."

Aleron didn't respond, not when he was resisting every urge to walk over to him. If he moved even a single muscle, he just might do something foolish.

The only sounds within the cave for a long while were the shuffling around of Gideon, the patter of rain, booms of thunder, and the crackle of fire. A certain area slowly, but

constantly, dropped water into a shallow puddle, and he
tried to focus on it.

Aleron already began to ease when light snoring
reverberated off the walls of the cave. If he hadn't been –
annoyingly – hyper fixated on him right at that moment, he
may not have heard it. At least knowing Gideon was asleep
allowed him to deal with his insufferable erection alone.

A sigh of relief flittered past his fangs when it softened
and the stiffness in the rest of his body relaxed.

Finally, he unfurled himself and sat back to stare at the
wall.

I... miss him. He missed the Gideon that had laughed
within his wings in their final hours in Tenebris. The one
who had played with him, jumped on his back to tease him,
and had simply taken up all the space within his thoughts.

Aleron hadn't thought it was possible to achieve
happiness without his kindred, but he'd felt it in their last
moments of the afterworld.

With his sight blue, he braved peeking over his shoulder.

Facing the flames, Gideon lay on the other side of the
fire. He'd bundled his jacket under his head to cushion it,
with his arms folded across his chest and his hands tucked
under his armpits. Hair sweeping over his forehead, lips
parted, and eyelids twitching as though dreaming, he looked
peaceful.

Aleron *longed* to share that peace with him.

He turned and lowered to his hands so he could walk
upon them. Slowly, and hesitantly, he crawled forward,
closing the distance between them. He made sure Gideon
didn't wake, pausing when he stirred, just in case. Then,
Aleron knelt on all fours above him, one hand on either side
of his resting head, while keeping the rest of his crouched
body behind him.

Usually Aleron left the human be when he slept,
knowing he felt vulnerable like this. Yet, Aleron's mind,
heart, and body had been in turmoil this day, and he was

struggling to deal with it on his own. He missed this mesmerising creature, and it gnawed at his essence.

He sought comfort, needing closeness more than ever. He wanted solace from the one being he craved it the most from.

He lowered his skull until he was able to very lightly brush the end of his snout against Gideon's hair, taking in the briefest feel of it, and his scent. A groan of satisfaction nearly rumbled out of him, but he managed to stifle it. He smelt so nice Aleron was tempted to nibble on his hair.

Before he knew it, Aleron laid down behind him. He made sure Gideon didn't stir by monitoring his constant quiet snores and regular heartbeat as Aleron rested the underside of his jaw against the top of his head. He brought his knees up until they tucked into the back of Gideon's, finding his little bride fit perfectly within the nook of him.

He wanted to bring his wing forward and blanket him in it, but he only brought his arm over the little human. Aleron didn't lay it completely on him, worried the weight would wake him, and he didn't clutch tightly.

Gideon's heart thumping against his chest, the warmth of his body, the pressure of him, felt sublime. It quelled the worst of his loneliness.

Sad contentment radiated through him. *Thaw for me, little spring.* His chest burned, and Aleron wished it would melt Gideon.

For a long while, he basked in the feeling of this human pressed up against him. The fact guilt niggled in the back of his mind for doing this, and he feared Gideon waking to discover this, told him he was probably doing the wrong thing.

He couldn't help it right then. His *bright*-yellow sight ensured he held on just a little longer. It'd been so long since he'd seen this colour and felt the joy of it – although muted.

He denied the urge to squeeze. He resisted sniffing him. He just softly hugged until his heart and mind realigned and reminded him of what he was waiting for.

Aleron held back his whimper, trying to ignore how this also... *hurt.*

He retracted his arm and drew back until he was on all fours once more. Then he moved to the other side of the fire, assuming Gideon would want him as far away as possible. Lying down, he placed the hand that had been upon Gideon's chest over his snout so the lingering aroma on it could soothe him.

It kept the chill from within at bay and allowed him to rest peacefully.

When Aleron woke a few hours later, he hadn't expected to see Gideon sitting up and looking into the fire. Night still blanketed the world, and he usually slept through the early hours. Restlessly, usually twitching with groans and the scent of mild fear.

Aleron sat up, nervous when he noted the other male's paleness. The dark impressions under his eyes were more alarming than the way he stared dazedly into the flames.

He often looked sickly when he woke, but not like this. At least, not for the past few days.

"Gideon?" he called, shifting to his knees and a single hand to move closer, only to pause in case he didn't want him near.

Gideon cast him a tired, weak smile with his eyes closed. "Hey."

At least he responded, when usually he didn't.

Even though Aleron doubted he'd receive an answer, he asked, "What is wrong?"

Gideon drew his knees up and hugged his calves. "I had a bad dream." His lips tightened, his brows furrowing, until he sighed and released both. "No, I don't think that's right. I think I remembered something from Tenebris."

"You do?" Aleron didn't know whether to be relieved or

distressed, considering Gideon's state.

"Yeah." He rubbed at his cheek before palming his mouth. "I remember meeting Emerie. I don't know. Maybe it's because of the fire, but I vividly remember her scars and her telling me that our parents died in a house fire from her dropping her oil lamp. It kind of shocked me awake. I just can't imagine what that was like for her, to lose everyone and be in so much pain at the same time."

Aleron remained silent for a long while, wondering what he could say to help. Nothing truly came to mind, except... "Despite everything, she was very kind to me."

"Yeah, she was always kind, so that doesn't surprise me." Then Gideon looked off to the side. "I'm sure I probably already told you, but my birth parents died when I was eight, so her parents adopted me since our families were close friends. It was a really hard time for me, but one thing always stuck with me."

True mirth filled his eyes, and colour returned to his features. Even his tiredness waned as he brought his gaze back to the fire.

"Emerie was only five at the time, and she apparently wanted to cheer me up with a cake. Our mother helped her, but she must have turned her back for a few minutes because it ended up being the most disgusting thing I'd ever eaten. I found out much later that she'd accidentally added salt, thinking it was sugar. At the time, I thought she'd purposefully sabotaged it to get back at me for being so sad all the time. So, from that day forward, I'd add salt to her honey milk as a prank. I did it for years, but she never got upset with me over it. When we were teenagers, she admitted it was the only reason why I'd laugh or smile, even though that kind of makes me a jerk as a kid. It just reminds me of how much of a good person she is."

Gideon shone him a smile and then laughed as if thinking back on it fondly. Aleron didn't know what to say, but was just happy he appeared much better than moments before.

That was, until his features fell, and he dipped his head forward. "Sorry. I've probably told you that story already."

"No," Aleron rasped, reaching forward despite the distance between them. "I do not mind. I would like to hear your stories again, as they are important to you. You did not share very many with me, and you may tell me new ones."

Gideon was speaking with him. This was the first time they were told by *this* version of him, and Aleron would be content to hear them over and over again until time ceased. He would never tire of them.

He would never tire of *him*.

Gideon lifted his head with a frown, seeming unconvinced.

"Please do not stop," Aleron quietly muttered.

"I don't know," Gideon said with an empty laugh, scratching the side of his head. "That was all I have on that." Then he turned his face towards the exit. "But it doesn't look like we'll be leaving any time soon. The storm is still really heavy. I guess I can figure out something else to talk about. I have a lot of pranks Emerie and I pulled on each other, or our friends. They're all pretty funny when you think about all the planning we put into our schemes."

Aleron's sight shifted to bright yellow, pleased that Gideon intended to share more with him.

"She and I could be pretty similar people at times. We both often put a foot in our mouths, so it got us into a lot of trouble. There was this one time–"

"That is odd. You put your foot in your mouth?" Aleron interjected, humour tickling his chest as he raised a foot and gnawed on his ankle between his fangs. "Why would you do this?"

"What?" Gideon's eyes widened in shock, before his features crinkled tightly as he laughed. "No! I don't mean literally!" His pretty green eyes, like a sun soaked, mossy forest, lit up with life in his direction. "It's a saying, Aleron. It means we often speak before we think."

I know, Aleron thought warmly, lowering his leg. He just wanted to re-enact the first time Gideon had said it to him, and Aleron had misinterpreted it. *I just wanted to see you laugh because of me.*

Aleron would do anything to make this human grow to like him as he once did, even if it meant replaying the conversations and things they'd already done.

He didn't mind if it made him appear foolish, not when his heart clenched with tenderness from the warmth he received.

When, exactly, this Duskwalker had turned up the charm, Gideon didn't know. But it'd sent him into a few laughing fits and made him smile.

He peeked out at the entrance of the cave. The rain had eased, and in its place, snow fell. The clouds weren't as dark and angry, and thunder had long stopped vibrating the world.

Wind still whistled, but after the second day, every hour it settled.

Maybe it's a good thing the storm happened. They had been stuck in this cave with nothing but sticks, rocks, and each other to keep themselves entertained. *I learned a lot about him.*

Gideon tried to share as many stories as he could, without touching on things like Beau. He'd started referring to him as his... friend, rather than his boyfriend. As much as talking about Beau hurt, Gideon had been in a relationship with him for three years, and much of his adult life revolved around him and Emerie. To not speak about his past, simply because of that, would have left him with little to talk about.

In some ways, sharing all the good things from his life made him feel a little better.

He also encouraged Aleron to speak of Ingram. And, once the Duskwalker started, he didn't shut up. Which, to be honest, Gideon didn't mind. It allowed him to sit quietly and listen, rather than share until his tongue dried.

He... Gideon chewed on his bottom lip when his chest gave a deep pang. *He's laid down with me both nights.*

The first night, he'd been unaware of that fact until Aleron disturbed him by moving away. The light drape of a comforting arm being removed brought him out of sleep. With his eyes barely open, he'd watched the Duskwalker move away to lie by himself on the opposite side of the fire. The second time... he'd already been half awake when Aleron snuck over.

He'd remained relaxed, waiting to see what the Duskwalker would do. Then, he just... cuddled Gideon from behind. He held Gideon in the most innocent, yearning of embraces with his hand over his heart, like he wanted to feel it. Like he wanted to capture it.

Gideon never pulled away, even when it seemed to span an hour. Instead, he laid awake, allowing Aleron to fulfil this need and *savouring* it himself.

A mixture of hurt and tenderness had flooded his very being. Hurt because he'd forced Aleron to only be comfortable doing this while Gideon was 'unaware,' and tenderness because it showed just how much Aleron cared for him.

He also hadn't realised just how much he *needed* a hug, and had been disappointed when it ended too soon.

When Gideon slept, he'd been hoping to remember more – something, anything – but nothing new came to him. Only the distressing dream of Emerie, and often nightmares of his own death, although those had started to ease and not be so frightening now that he'd met his murderer.

It also helped he had a pretty funny and sweet

Duskwalker constantly keeping him company, helping to remove the negative emotions regarding winged monsters.

At least he seems to be enjoying himself now.

When the conversations dulled, Gideon showed Aleron how to play naughts and crosses, and scissors, paper, rock. Not the most intellectual games to play, but they had little else to use. Just anything to fill in the time as they waited out the violent rainstorm that turned into blizzards throughout the nights.

By the second day, Gideon had taken it upon himself to teach Aleron how to read and write when he discovered he couldn't do either. It took up time, and he kind of liked teaching people new things. Aleron was also very receptive to learning.

When he found a decent rock, he carved the alphabet into the smoothest wall he could find. He taught Aleron how to say each letter phonetically and then worked on teaching him to write his own name.

Watching the Duskwalker clutch his stone and write with the bottom of his fist had been kind of cute.

Aleron had been very interested in learning how to spell Gideon's name, then Emerie and Ingram. Gideon didn't know how to spell many of the other Duskwalkers' names since he'd never heard of them before. Merikh was a tricky one, as phonetically sounding it out was 'Merr-ick,' and he doubted that was correct.

Then he watched Aleron pick his own words to spell – ones that would be more meaningful for him. *Maybe in the future, I can find us a book. Something easy to read for a beginner.*

At least he learned faster than a human. Much faster.

I figure he just needs someone to show him. He took in the sound of rock scratching against stone. *Can't learn if no one teaches you.*

"Human?" Aleron asked, tapping a claw at the ground to

grab his attention.

He peeked at what he'd written and shook his head. "Human has a 'u' and not two 'o's.'"

He snorted a huff through his nose hole, making Gideon stifle the urge to smile with humour. "I do not understand why letters and words must be so complicated," he argued as he attempted it a second time. "It looked right to me."

When he'd written it correctly, Gideon nodded. Aleron continued on with a new word. *I'm just glad he doesn't feel bad about getting words wrong. I wonder if it's because he knows I won't judge him for it.* Gideon hoped his past self had at least given Aleron that confidence in him.

"Mavka," Aleron stated confidently, as if he wouldn't budge on it being incorrect even if it was.

"I'm not sure how to spell that," Gideon stated with a shrug. "I'd never heard the term before I met you. We call you Duskwalkers."

"Duskwalker is wrong. Mavka," he rebuffed, pointing at his carving. "It means forest creature."

"And Duskwalker means a creature from the Veil that can walk in both the day and night," Gideon argued warmly. "Unlike Demons."

"Hmm. I guess both can be correct." Aleron stood and walked over to where he'd previously written words until he took up all the room on the floor. He pointed to Gideon's name. "What does Gideon mean?"

Staying where he sat, he shrugged once more. "I'm not sure."

"Emerie?" Gideon shrugged again. "Why do they not have meanings? Ingram means raven of peace, and it was given to him because of his skull. Aleron means the winged one, to fly."

"Maybe I'm called Gideon because I'm so giddy."

Aleron swiftly turned his skull to him and snorted out a deliberate huff as if disagreeing. Gideon cast him a coy grin; he kind of liked playfully bickering with him. Then he looked over the Duskwalker kneeling before him, and a question crossed his mind.

"I've been wanting to ask, since I don't really know all that much about your kind. Can all Duskwalkers fly?"

"No." Aleron shook his head, which caused a light rattle to come from his skull. "I am the only Mavka I know with wings."

"Oh cool. That's pretty badass then. I bet you're one of the strongest and fastest Duskwalkers since you can just fly and use your wings for extra momentum."

Aleron's tail feathers vibrated in what he figured was joy from his compliment, then he lifted his skull with thought and... hummed. Gideon's ears pinkened, having realised a little while ago that whenever Aleron hummed, it was a sign he may have said something like this before.

He'd grown a little self-conscious about doubling up on conversations.

"I guess it's lucky you didn't know how to fly before. You would have been able to get into towns really easily," he rambled, rubbing at the side of his neck when Aleron drew closer.

He plonked his butt where he'd been sitting in front of Gideon earlier. It was a little far, but gave him plenty of space to write.

Suddenly Gideon's gut twisted. "You're not planning to do that anymore, right? Eat humans... I mean."

Since Aleron had never been violent or cruel towards him, he'd forgotten what he was, what he could be. A human-eating Duskwalker. He'd started seeing him as just Aleron, the person who had a bat skull and spiralling goat horns for a face.

Seeming to note the difference in his body language, or perhaps his spiking heart rate, Aleron tilted his head.

"No, I do not plan to do this," he confirmed, sitting up and facing him. "Because of you, I no longer feel hunger."

Gideon lowered his hand from his neck with his lips and brows tightening. "Because of me?"

Aleron placed his hands in his lap and scratched at his writing rock as if fidgeting. He looked nervous and unsure.

"Mavka gain humanity by eating humans, and anything we eat makes us bigger and stronger. Yet none of this makes us feel whole, content, or satisfied. I was always filled with this insatiable hunger, but that disappeared the moment we bonded. Mavka are soul eaters, and what we seek is our..." His orbs flashed white, instead of finishing his sentence. His skull turned to the left, then twisted and twitched as he fidgeted further. "Sorry, this is not a conversation you are comfortable with."

The fact that Aleron felt the need to apologise made shame itch at Gideon's nape. He let out an awkward, false laugh.

"It's all good. I did ask."

I also don't need to eat. It hadn't taken Gideon long to realise he no longer felt the desire to consume food or drink water. He also didn't need to piss, since he put nothing in his body.

He'd found it strange at first and hated it, but now that he was used to it, he preferred it.

His body didn't seem to be changing. He didn't lose any of his hard-earned muscle, but it also meant his hair wasn't growing, nor had his barely noticeable stubble grown into a beard. He already summarised that he was frozen in time, and that he'd look this way for the rest of his life.

Gideon wasn't all that broken up about it.

He didn't mind the way he looked, except for the thick keloid scarring across his torso – mainly because it reminded him of his death. If he were to change anything about himself, it'd be his dishevelled clothing and his lack of earrings. He missed having rings dangling from his earlobes, and he hoped the holes he could feel in them meant he could wear them in the future.

Like a saving grace, a bright stream of sunlight shone into the cave and stole their attention. It washed over them and made the gold in Aleron's skull glitter. He often forgot his skull did that, since it was near impossible to see it without the light.

"Looks like the storm is completely gone," Gideon stated, rising to his feet.

A small part of him filled with disappointment at that, considering he'd... *enjoyed* his time in this cave with Aleron. He held his hand out to Aleron to help him to his feet.

"Come on. Let's go."

Aleron's skull lowered from his face to his outstretched palm. His orbs flared bright yellow, and he tentatively reached for it.

Then he did nothing.

Gideon struggled to pull the heavy fucker to his bird-like feet. He used all his strength, all his might, to no avail.

By the time he had to grab his thick wrist with his other hand and tug with both, he grunted out, "You're supposed to help m– AH!"

Aleron suddenly stood, and Gideon went flying back.

Before he could fall to his arse, a strong arm wrapped around his back and kept him to his feet. Dipped backwards, resting all his weight on Aleron's forearm and hand, he huffed through the rapid drumming of his heart.

"I have you," Aleron assured him, the end of his snout barely inches from his nose.

Unsure if it was due to embarrassment, or just Aleron's presence so close to him in an intimate hold, his cheeks heated. Gideon had even gripped the long fur of his chest to hold on.

"Nice catch," he grumbled.

Almost like Aleron had expected Gideon to fall on his arse, he'd leapt straight away to grab him. He'd moved so damn fast... Realisation struck when Aleron let out a quiet, rumbling chuckle as he pulled him to his feet completely.

You sneaky bastard. You knew that was going to happen.

To his dismay, Gideon found that ridiculously charming.

TWENTY-SEVEN

Aleron halted when they'd reached the very east of Austrális and had passed over the tapering point of the Veil's canyon crack. It had taken them the entire day to get to this spot, since he flew slowly in order to scour the ground for any sign of his kindred.

Night would fall soon, making it difficult to see anything dark moving within the shade of the trees. Up this high, he could barely scent the earth, let alone a being.

They hadn't long passed a mountainous fortress, one in which he knew held vicious Demonslayers. Gideon had pointed to it from a distance, calling it Zagros Fortress. He knew this name only because of Emerie.

This is the place my kindred suffered... He had half a mind to turn to it and destroy it for harming Ingram. For chaining him deep within its bowels and torturing him. The only reason he didn't was because of the human he wished to keep safe.

He also didn't wish for them to rest near it, but he found himself hesitant to move forward.

"What's wrong?" Gideon asked from within the cradle of his arms.

"I do not know where to go," Aleron admitted, feeling them bounce in the air with each of his wing flaps. "I do not know where Ingram is, where he could be. I do not know if we should go south, or if we should go back and check the north. I may have missed them due to the storm."

"I've been meaning to ask, but don't you guys have, like... a home?"

Aleron searched the distance, wishing he could see a trace of Ingram's shiny iridescent scales, or Emerie's bright-red hair.

"We were each other's home. There was never a need for us to find shelter anywhere else."

"That's kind of sweet." Gideon bravely peeked over the side to look at the ground. In Aleron's peripheral, he noticed Gideon chew at his bottom lip; he didn't do it often, so Aleron found it odd. Gideon's tone was low, his words slow, as he grumbled, "We're in the east, right?"

"Yes." He nodded his head to gesture forward. "I am unsure if your measly human eyes can see it, but the southland wall is that way."

He rolled his eyes, like Aleron knew he would. "Look, I ate all my carrots as a kid."

"Then you should have eaten more," Aleron answered with a chuckle, despite not understanding what that meant or knowing what a carrot was.

He was thankful to be able to say these light-hearted things once more with his bride. They warmed him, made him feel closer to Gideon, and Aleron hoped it was the same for him.

A small silence fell on them as they both thought.

In the meantime, the blue sky morphed to have a hint of orange when the sun dipped to the edge of the horizon. Aleron turned, preferring to double-check the north before going south.

If need be, he'd go in circle after circle over this land. *I will find them, no matter how long it takes.* He'd just rather it be sooner than later.

"W-wait," Gideon yelled, grabbing the fur of his chest. "I have a favour to ask of you."

"Of course, anything." He truly meant this. He would give or do anything for Gideon if it would make him content.

"Could we go south?" Then, with a small voice and looking down at his arms crossed over his stomach, he added, "To Fishket."

Aleron momentarily lost height when his entire body stiffened. His sight flashed white as worry pierced his gut.

"Why do you wish to go there?" Aleron asked nervously.

Just seconds before, he'd meant what he'd said about giving Gideon anything, but Aleron never thought he'd ask to take him... *home*. Aleron feared if he took them there, the male would never want to leave it again.

Sure, that would mean Aleron would be forced to take him from it after a day when Gideon returned to his side as a Phantom, but he didn't wish to see the disappointment upon his face. He didn't wish to be the cause of it.

He didn't want Gideon to have to plead and beg for Aleron to take him back there every day. To create a cycle of longing, Gideon clawing to return, as Aleron clawed to keep him by his side.

Aleron feared losing him, and whatever progress they'd made. Just the idea of it stung him all the way to his core.

Back in the cave, Gideon had reached his hand out to him.

It may not have been offered in affection, but Aleron missed the roughness of this human's hand. He craved to feel the strength of it, and how it was so little within his own. So he'd let the solace of it brand his very soul, prolonging it in a game of tug-o-war, unsure of when he'd be able to feel it again.

"I just want to see for my own eyes that it's... different," he uttered so quietly, that Aleron doubted anything but a Duskwalker would have heard it. "That it's *gone*."

Aleron shook his head and subconsciously flapped them

further from it. "But it is not gone," Aleron rebutted, resisting this request.

"That it's gone to me." Gideon sighed, tightened his arms across his stomach, and then... leaned the side of his head against the fur of his chest. "*Please?* I know what I'm asking for is unfair, but I just can't see it as anything but my home."

Already he pleaded to go back, and Aleron's heart couldn't take it.

Despite his misgivings, Aleron banked to the left to spin around, and headed towards the south. Each whoosh of his wings tightened the invisible chains wrapped around his torso until it felt constrained. His lungs shuddered, squeezed by the anxiety that filled him.

"Thank you," Gideon whispered.

"I do not know where it is. You will have to direct me," Aleron told him, trying to minimise the dark, solemn note of his tone. "First, we will rest somewhere safe."

It was an excuse to be with Gideon a little longer, in case he reverted to the pale, hollow version of himself.

Gideon's heart fluttered nervously when they quietly flew above Fishket.

They'd reached it in the mid-afternoon, but he'd suggested waiting until nightfall for them to get closer. Hidden in the forest, his whole chest had burned during the agonising wait.

Aleron's wings drooped in disbelief, not expecting Gideon to ask him to come with him.

Although Gideon didn't say it aloud, he didn't particularly want to do this alone. He was asking the Duskwalker for a lot by requesting this, and he didn't want to hurt Aleron needlessly when Gideon could just bring him along.

He hoped it alleviated the worst of the Duskwalker's anxieties.

So, when night could shroud their approach, they flew over it. No humans dared to walk the streets, but many candles lit the insides of homes and glowed through thin curtains.

Gideon pointed in the direction he wanted them to go and immediately saw a rundown home on the outskirts of the town. He asked for Aleron to land, and they found a flat rooftop to softly descend on top of.

His taloned toe tips and feet were surprisingly agile and silent.

Just as Aleron was about to put him down, Gideon clutched his dense biceps and shook his head.

"There's no need. I don't want to stay here long."

He pointed to a house pressing against many others, which actually had a second level that was separated from the first. Like most of the poorer side of town, families lived closely cluttered together. The dilapidated building was in even worse condition than when he'd last seen it, which was over twelve years ago, if he counted the eight he'd missed. He'd tried not to come to this part of town often.

Grime stained the outer walls. Many bricks had started to decay to the point it completely leaned against the house directly next to it. It was falling apart, unloved, but too used to be demolished and rebuilt.

The houses next to it weren't faring any better.

"That's where I lived with my birth parents."

Aleron said nothing and allowed Gideon to take in its deteriorating state. At least the last time he'd seen it, it'd been standing upright on its own.

It's changed so much.

Even the street leading it to look filthier and rundown.

When he was done, he gestured for them to leave.

He directed for them to go more towards the centre of the town. One minute they were travelling over buildings that had seen better days, then the houses became nicer. Many had been freshly rebuilt or painted, and not a single one had a hole in its straw or a clay tile missing from its roofing.

It took him a while to find the house he wanted to see, and he made Aleron circle a certain area a few times. When he finally did, they landed on a balcony where the house lacked light – either it was unoccupied, or everyone was on the first level.

It's really gone.

The house he'd grown up in, which had been in near immaculate condition when he'd died, no longer existed. The houses it had once sat between had char marks; the evidence of being next to a house in flames, but being far enough away from it that they didn't burn along with it.

What stood there now was a completely new building. Candles lit it from within, the evidence of a new family residing in it.

"This is where I died," Gideon muttered, wanting to explain what they were looking at. He pointed to the ground where he knew they'd argued before pointing to the new building. "Mine and Emerie's home used to be here, before it burnt down."

As much as seeing it weighed on his conscience, it allowed him to finally feel... disconnected from this place. His home no longer existed, and therefore, his presence within this street and part of town didn't exist. The past was real, the evidence of time passed, and he hadn't been alive for any of it.

He and his home disappeared the same night.

When he absorbed all this, guilt prickled his nape as he gestured for them to go to another location. He made Aleron follow a set of streets, only knowing the way from how he'd walked to their destination. Once they were in an odd

section of the town, where the better off and the poor
sections began to blend together, he found the last place he
wanted to visit.

Aleron landed on a slanted straw roof, and in the security
of his arms, Gideon mulled over what he wanted to do. The
house looked the same, well-maintained and cared for. The
lights were on, but the question was: did the same person
live here?

Something caught his eye – a cat statue sitting in a tiny
strip of garden that lacked any flowers.

Upon seeing it, he knew for certain the same person
lived within this dwelling.

With his voice hoarse and thick from emotion, he rasped,
"Aleron, can you quickly drop me onto the street below?"

His claws dug into Gideon's arm and leg as if he didn't
want to let go, but he eventually nodded. Aleron quickly did
as he was asked, and Gideon barely had the chance to catch
himself when Aleron flew down, dropped him off, and lifted
off without ever touching the ground.

Gideon looked back from where they'd just come from
to find Aleron had returned to the same roof. Gideon waved
at him, hoping to quell his anxiety while being riddled with
it himself.

Then, like a thief stalking low, Gideon crouched his way
to the house to get a closer look. He went down the side
between the two buildings where there was a window. The
window wasn't entirely pointless even though it faced a
wall, since it allowed fresh air to drift inside on hot summer
days.

When he heard deep voices, he clutched the windowsill,
but couldn't bring himself to look inside just yet. Even
though the air was cold and fresh, it felt like he was choking
on gravel as it rattled in his lungs. He felt strangled, like he
had rope braided around his throat.

For a little while, he just listened and tried to make out

the voices.

"...She's not doing well in class," an unfamiliar, high-pitched yet masculine voice stated. "I've spoken with her teacher, and she said that Cassidy doesn't pay attention like the other students."

"She's only six, Nolan," a gruff, older voice grated out. Gideon covered his mouth, disbelieving how much it had aged in the years he'd been gone. It'd even deepened. "What do they expect from a child? All she does is learn her ABCs and colour in."

"There's more to kindergarten than that, Beau," *Nolan* responded. "I think she's really struggling being away from us. I think she's worried that we're going to leave her there and not come back one day."

Beau gave an irritated but loud grumble, and Gideon braved peeking through the window just in time to watch him put his forehead in his palm.

He looked the same, and yet... so different.

Beau still had his muscular yet heavy-set build, his gut a little rounder than he remembered. By the creases on his forehead and corners of his eyes, Beau looked much older than the twenty-nine Gideon remembered him being. A beard, which had once barely been an inch from his face, now hung down to his sternum. An unruly mane, still as long as ever, had fully receded like he'd thought it would. White and grey had begun to pepper his black hair and beard.

Gideon still thought Beau looked handsome, even if it wasn't the face he'd known.

Then, with a gawking stare, he took in Nolan. He was thin, tall, and lacked facial hair. His eyes were brown, but they were warm and kind as he looked over at Beau, despite being exasperated with the older man.

Even Gideon could see Nolan was pretty, despite being a little sour towards him.

"You know I'm not the best at talking with her. She likes

you more," Beau admitted. "But I'll walk her to school in the morning and reassure her."

Nolan's features softened, obviously appeased, and he smiled. "Thank y–"

A scream cut them off, and they both looked towards the ceiling where the second level was. Seconds later, a small girl with blonde hair came bolting down the stairs with wet eyes.

"Daaaddddyyy!" she cried, running straight to Nolan's legs, just as a second cry sounded from up the stairs. It grew louder by the second. "G-Gideon p-pulled my hair again."

"He's only three, sweetheart." Nolan sighed, before carting her towards the second level. "Come on, let's go check on him and see if he will apologise." Beau went to rise and follow, but Nolan gestured with his hand out. "It's okay, I'll handle this. Could you take the water from the stove and put it in the bath for them?"

Beau did as he was told, walking over to the small kitchen. He grabbed a large steaming pot by the handles on each side of it and lifted it as though it weighed nothing. He held it out from himself as he carted it through the dining area, before turning left to head up the stairs himself.

A fire continued to burn from within the stove hearth, crackling with life in the silence that came from their absence.

Gideon, frozen where he knelt, let everything sink in.

Beau had found someone else. He wasn't alone, and they had a family. A daughter named Cassidy, and a son they'd named after... *him*. They'd adopted two kids, just like he'd always wanted, or perhaps Nolan had his own children before meeting Beau.

Regardless, this was proof that his old life was gone.

It stung. His eyes watered and Gideon struggled to hold back the tears, but this was what he'd wanted to see. Beau looked happy, even if his permanently grumpy face didn't come across that way. Their house was warm, full of love, affection, and support.

It was everything he'd wanted, and now couldn't have.

I'm just glad he's okay. He'd needed to know that. Needed to see that the man hadn't turned to an existence that never looked beyond the bottom of a bottle. He'd needed to see that Beau had moved on, and that Gideon's death hadn't irrevocably ruined his chance for a good life.

The guilt of those fears had been *eating* at him constantly. The gnaw of them finally eased, leaving only relief in the release of their fangs.

Just as he was about to back away, a brown weathered case caught his eye. The long neck of it poked out from under the stairs, dangerously close to being in the way of an unsuspecting foot.

No way. Is that my...?

In a split-second decision, Gideon reached higher and placed the pads of his fingers against the cold glass of the window, intending to lift it. He knew the lock was busted, unless Beau had finally fixed it, even though he'd nagged him repeatedly about it.

He paused when it opened a crack, and the smell of warm stew filled his nose. *I shouldn't... I should leave it.* Yet, he couldn't take his eyes off that brown case.

Longing to take something of his own back, he lifted the window. Wincing every time it creaked and squeaked, he opened it slowly.

He quickly climbed inside, ducked down, and headed over to it. He made sure to pay attention to the thudding footsteps above, just in case he needed to make a quick exit so he wasn't caught.

Just as he grabbed the smooth handle of the case, a whine from down the hallway sounded, coming from what Gideon knew to be a lounging room with a warm fireplace. Little claws pattered against the distressed timber floor as a dog slowly made its way up it.

Fuck! If it started barking, it'd give him away.

Heart in his damn throat, he turned to it as he gripped the case to his chest. His feet were ready to bolt, until he watched it hopping its way down the hallway, ears flopping as it did.

Black and grey all over its face and back, with brown eyebrows and feet, its tail wagged excitedly as it drew closer.

"Holy shit," he whispered, kneeling down to greet the dog. "Hey, boy."

Before the black-and-grey Cattle dog even got to him, his whines turned into acute cries. Dex jumped up to place his paws on Gideon's shoulders, and gave frantic, wild licks to his face, hair, and any part he could reach. With a long, fluffy tail wagging, his dog from eight years ago greeted him as if he'd been missed dearly.

"I can't believe you're still alive." Gideon kept his voice low, and scratched at the back of his neck, then his furry cheeks where he used to love it. "Has Beau been treating you good?" He leaned to the side to take in a missing back leg. "I bet you've been doing your job well, huh? You taking care of everyone for me?"

A creak far too close to the top of the stairs snagged his focus.

"Dex?" Beau's booming voice yelled. "What's got you crying?"

Before Beau could even stomp a heavy foot down on the top step, Gideon was fighting Dex's love as he headed for the window. He shoved the large and awkward case through it before ducking his head outside. Dex clawed at his pants, jumping up and down on one leg, desperate to keep him inside.

"Sorry, boy, but I have to go."

He gave him a last pat, then dropped down to the ground just as Beau's shadow crept to the lower level. Dex continued to whine with his head out the window before barking at him as he bolted.

ShitshitSHIT! That was too close.

He clung to his precious case, disbelieving he'd actually stolen it without getting caught. Then again... he didn't technically steal it since it belonged to him.

Adrenaline pumped in his veins as the cold air chilled further at his speed, whistling over him as he sprinted. His feet echoed and sounded far too loud as he rushed down the side of the house before exiting onto the street.

Needing a quick getaway, he waved at Aleron as he ran, about to make him the partner of his crime.

Within seconds, the Duskwalker landed in front of him, and Gideon almost faceplanted into his damn chest. Just as Aleron collected him into his arms and was about to lift off, the front door of Beau's home slammed open.

"Get back here, you fucking thief!" Beau roared, braving the dangerous outside world.

Gideon winced, knowing the man rarely swore unless truly enraged, and never shouted unless absolutely necessary. Especially at night, where Demons could be lurking – no doubt his neighbours would be enraged for making such a fuss in the dark.

Beau looked like a woolly mammoth as he shook his fist.

Aleron flapped his wings and jumped up before Beau could land his sights on them. With his heart beating like crazy, Gideon stared down at Beau as he ran further outside. Beau frantically searched for the person who had stolen Gideon's precious guitar, never knowing it was him that had taken it.

Sorry, Beau, but you knew how much this meant to me, he thought, hugging it to his chest like his life depended on it.

He was sure it meant a lot to Beau now as well, and likely had all their memories attached to it. Gideon couldn't believe he'd kept it, or named their son after him, but he didn't wish to linger on it.

It was selfish of him, but it was time for them to *both* let go.

I can't believe I did that. A bright smile curled his lips and crinkled his eyes. *And I'm really glad I was able to see Dex again.*

He'd loved that dog. He'd given him food scraps under the table even though Beau told him not to, unable to handle how his hazel eyes looked up at him, begging, *pleading* for just a little taste. Dex had been a great dog, and a wonderful protector, who had saved his life twice from Demons loitering in the shade of trees in the day.

"Who was that?" Aleron asked as he flew away from the street Gideon had walked countless times.

"Nobody important," he stated, before laughing – although quietly since he didn't want anyone to see them. In some ways, despite the pang in his chest, he felt a little freer.

He sniffed at Gideon's cheek and let out a low, snorted huff of deep annoyance. "You smell funny, like another creature."

His smile grew. "They had a dog. He was pretty friendly." Aleron banked to the right, circling the town, and a spot caught his eye. "There's one last place I'd like to go."

It hadn't originally been on his mental list of destinations, but he wouldn't mind checking it out. He pointed to a walled-off area that stuck out in this part of town, since it didn't have any houses within it.

Aleron banked to the left and headed that way.

"Could you land in there?" Just as they began to lose height he added, "Be careful not to break anything. It'll be really disrespectful if you do."

The area was dark, with a tree barren of leaves due to the early winter. Its branches looked like gnarly, long fingers, frightfully ready to trap unsuspecting prey in their clutches.

Roots had emerged from the ground, the tree large and daunting as it cast webbed shadows upon the dirt.

It was eerie, only because of where it had been planted and what this place signified.

Each one of Aleron's wing beats disturbed the wet fog that hovered throughout the stone slabs. When they were on solid ground once more, Gideon grabbed his wrist when he looked like he was about to take off.

"Stay with me?" He dragged him along, and Aleron stumbled but readily followed.

"What if someone sees me?" Aleron asked, following him even when he let go.

"No one is going to come here, trust me." Gideon gestured to the wall blocking out the rest of the town and then the many stone plates surrounding them. "It's a cemetery, although no one is buried here. It's just a place we keep so that people can go somewhere to remember those that passed."

Like it'd been just yesterday, Gideon found the plaque he wanted. He carefully placed his case down as he knelt. After brushing the grime from it, he let out a growl of annoyance. Anger flushed his neck as he looked at his birth parents' plaque.

There were many names carved into it, but he only had an issue with one: his own.

"You're fucking kidding me," Gideon bit out, snatching his heavy case before rising to go find his adoptive family's plaque. "I barely knew my birth parents, and they carved my damn name on it?"

He struggled to find the plaque he wanted, since he'd never been to it before. He just searched the list of plaques in each row for their last names, before finally coming across the one he thought was correct. It was clean and pristine, as if someone had tended to it recently – unlike the prior one – and his anger deflated out of him.

Tenderness filled his eyes before he let himself fall to his backside to stare at it. He dusted the dirt from his hands as he folded his legs.

Thanks, Beau, Gideon thought, taking in his name crudely carved into it as if someone had used a knife on the stone, rather than a chisel.

He placed his hand on top of his guitar case next to him, while Aleron leaned over the stone plaque.

"This has your name carved into it," he stated, thumbing it before brushing over the many names above it. "But it is not like the others."

Gideon gave a sad smile. "Yeah. Someone who cared about me a lot knows that the people who took me in when I was little were my family. They carved my name here for me when I died, since the officials did it on my birth parents' plaque."

Aleron stood and tilted his head at it.

Gideon patted the ground next to him. "Could you sit with me? I think I'd like to stay here for a bit, if that's okay."

Although there wasn't much room in the narrow dirt aisle, Aleron sat right where he'd patted. They stared at the stone together.

The air was cool, but Gideon felt warmed by all the excitement, emotions, and just general thoughts that swirled around in his mind. He had much to reflect on, but he knew deep down inside, he needed this night more than anything.

Gideon had needed to see that his first home was decaying, and that his second home had truly burnt down. He'd needed to see that the person he'd once loved had aged, moved on, and looked happy even after his death. He'd needed to know that life had truly moved on without him, so he could move on without it.

For the first time since he'd woken up in this new and confusing life, Gideon took in a full breath that wasn't laced with regret and guilt. A sense of calmness settled over him, and it'd been forever since he'd been allowed to feel that way.

I feel better.

With his chest, mind, and shoulders lighter, Gideon went to lean back on his hands. Hard, textured warmth greeted his palm, and he darted his hand away in surprise, since he'd been expecting cold dirt. It took him a moment to realise it was Aleron's hand already resting on the ground.

At Gideon's sudden retreat, Aleron's claws dug into the earth. For the briefest second, his orbs flashed blue.

Once the shock faded, Gideon placed his hand back down... on top of Aleron's. Then, as if that wasn't enough, with his ears heating nervously and his heart pounding, he dug and curled his fingers over the webbing of Aleron's large hand to hold it.

A strange, almost strangled noise came from Aleron when he closed his big fist and clamped Gideon's fingers within the depth of it. With his other hand covering the end of his snout, he turned his head to the side, away from Gideon, as bright yellow lifted into his orbs.

A gentle and sweet emotion trickled into Gideon's conscience as the Duskwalker showed bashful joy at simply holding his hand.

Minutes ticked by as Gideon took in his crudely carved name. He'd thought coming to stare at it would make him sombre, but he suddenly couldn't keep his mind off the person next to him. Especially since his heart seemed to flip upside down in his chest, acting all shy and out of sorts as well.

In the cold darkness, with the lightest gusts of air brushing his hair back and forth across his brow, he took in Aleron's presence.

The subtle scent of his hazelnut-and-cedarwood aroma no longer instilled homesickness, but instead the comfort of being where he needed to be. Aleron's warmth spread along Gideon's fingertips and up his arm, linking them in a way he didn't fully comprehend. The points of his claws just lightly pressing into him were like sharp little trappings, but Gideon found himself wanting them to press harder until they'd burrowed under his skin.

Even just the sound of Aleron's large lungs working out heavy breaths was lulling and tingled his ears.

In this place, surrounded by the plaques of those who had died, Aleron looked like an angel of death with his imposing, feathered wings. Gideon didn't think he'd ever looked more beautiful.

"Thank you for bringing me here," Gideon said quietly, refusing to be loud so he didn't completely steal the serenity of this moment. "I also want to thank you for being with me during a time of my life where I felt really confused, scared, and very lost. It hasn't been easy for either of us, and I'm sorry I took most of that out on you, but it really means a lot to me that I didn't have to go through it alone."

"I care for you deeply, Gideon," Aleron stated firmly, and with unwavering conviction.

His wings twitched, like he wanted to say more, but Gideon spoke quickly before he could. He worried Aleron would try to apologise for his part in all this, which is the last thing he wanted right now.

"Yeah, but that usually isn't enough." Gideon turned his face up to the crescent moon, similar to the one that had shone brightly the night he died. "Thank you for still being here for me, even after I gave you my absolute worst. Not many people would have remained."

He squeezed Aleron's big, clawed hand a little tighter. *Thank you for forgiving me, even if I don't really deserve it.*

Then, a small, humour-filled smile curled the corners of his lips. "Hey, Aleron... I have another favour to ask of you."

"Anything, little spring."

His eyes crinkled at that, since the affectionate name was

rather cute.

"When we find Emerie, can you please not tell her about what happened after the first week we came back to life?"

Aleron tilted his head and dipped forward like he wanted to fully take in his expression. "Why not?"

"Because I know she'll try to beat the ever-living daylights out of me." He chuckled and tipped his head towards Aleron's skull so he could see the mirth in his eyes. "She'll punch first and ask questions later."

Since Aleron had still been holding the end of his snout, he tapped the side of it with a claw in thought. "Can you not just punch her back? I punch Ingram all the time." The completely dumbfounded note in his tone set Gideon off.

He gave a mild laugh. "Yeah, but it's not nice to hit your sister. I'd rather not argue with her if I don't have to. No matter how strong she's gotten, it appears my body is the same as when I died. I don't want to hurt her since I'm bigger than her."

Aleron's large shoulders lifted as if to shrug. "If that is what you want, then okay."

"Thanks."

Then, once more, Gideon lifted his gaze to the moon. He found it prettier than usual, only because out of the corner of his eye, he noted it made the gold glitter in Aleron's skull sparkle. Gideon squeezed his big hand tighter.

I think I'm ready to move on now.

TWENTY-EIGHT

A campfire lit the undersides of the leaves above, giving the forest canopy an earthy glow. It crackled, sparking with life, and billowed soft, steamy smoke into the air.

After quietly holding hands in the cemetery for a little while longer, they'd eventually left Fishket. They were only a small distance away from it, impossible to see, but likely an hour for Gideon if he were to walk back on his own.

He didn't feel a single desire to go back. All the longing, his homesickness, his attachment to that town faded at the same time as it faded from view. It was no longer important, a place he didn't need to think about anymore.

The spot they'd chosen to set up camp was a decently cleared area within a ring of trees. A small gap in the centre allowed cool moonlight to shine down, and stars glittered and peeked through the thin clouds shrouding them.

Gideon disturbed the quiet by plopping down the last branches he'd found in their direct vicinity. Aleron also returned, doing the same, but with much larger branches. The Duskwalker broke them into smaller pieces for burning with nothing but his bare hands, whereas Gideon would've needed to use his axe.

He squatted next to his brown case so he could open it, brushing his hands of dirt and debris before he did.

Just as the last latch unclipped, he spared a glance at

Aleron, who chose to sit a few metres to his right. Annoyed and rather disappointed he didn't sit next to him, Gideon was at least glad he'd chosen to be there rather than on the opposite side of the fire, like in the cave.

He's still cautious of being close to me. As usual, shame prickled the back of his neck. *I thought he'd be a little more comfortable after the cemetery. Guess I have my work cut out for me.*

Except... Gideon was an awkward fucking idiot at the best of times.

He could be a great leader, but he found it hard to take a leap of faith when it came to urges of the heart. He often acted boldly while his hands, and even knees, shook wildly.

Before his thoughts could run rampant with how he could get closer to Aleron and bridge the gap naturally, they dissipated when he opened his case with bated breath.

His guitar was in great condition, since only some of the edges had started to deteriorate – but it shouldn't affect the sound at all. He gently ran the pads of his fingers down strings that lacked rust from disuse; they had to be new, as if recently replaced. He smiled, once more thanking Beau for attending to the things that mattered to him, even though Gideon hadn't existed anymore in his life.

Giant sap, he thought with a snort of laughter.

"What is that?" Aleron asked, revealing he'd been staring the entire time.

Gideon grabbed the neck to eagerly pull it out before finally sitting down. "It's my guitar. If you pluck the metal strings, it plays music notes."

Before he could continue his explanation, a cream-coloured aged envelope was revealed underneath it. His face dropped and grew cold as he reached for it.

He knew he hadn't left anything like this in it, and when he flipped it over, it wasn't addressed to anyone. His heart sped up when he lifted the flap, pulled out a letter, and opened its folds.

Two rings, both golden and plain, slid to the bottom fold, and he had to stop them from falling to the ground. He fumbled when one slipped to the side, but managed to catch it.

He gnashed his teeth at the ring he'd hidden away in the side pocket within his guitar case, a place Beau never would have looked. He'd been intending to give it to him in the autumn... as a marriage proposal. The other ring was one he'd never seen, but it didn't take a genius to figure it out.

Gideon covered his face so he could dig his fingers into his eyes, stemming whatever tears threatened to well. *Damnit. He'd had the same damn intentions as me.*

Once he quelled the worst of his emotions, he finally looked at the letter.

Dear Gideon,
It's the anniversary of your death, and I still can't get over you—

He flipped the top fold down so he couldn't read further.

Gideon had a choice.

He could read this tragic, romantic letter, and let all the emotions – all the feelings of love and longing he'd just let go – come back. He could let himself fall back in love with the man he'd planned a massive future around, knowing it wouldn't be unrequited since it was obvious he still held a place in Beau's heart.

He could do that, or...

Gideon looked up at Aleron.

He took in talons, claws, and black fur. His eyes roamed over pale-pink orbs glittering in a bat skull that sparkled with gold from the fire. He looked over the dark, feathered wings that hung behind him like he was a flying omen of death. Then, finally, his spiralling goat horns that held an almost fully flaming soul – his soul, which looked much healthier than it had before this night started. It looked more relaxed than he'd ever seen it, like it was at peace.

Next to him wasn't a human, or a normal person. Instead, there sat a human-eating, dark entity, with a skull for a face – a monster, as most would say. Yet... he'd never been more at ease.

All his life, Gideon had been afraid of the dark. He'd been wary of the sharp fangs and red eyes that could be lurking in it, but he had no need for that anymore. He had someone bigger and more frightening protecting him.

Aleron could also be endearing and sweet. The Duskwalker obviously lacked humanity, yet he'd been supportive even when not knowing how to. He'd been patient, understanding, and kind towards someone who was always moments from imploding. He'd been unbelievably *loyal*.

What more could a person ask for?

Well, there was the need for sexual attraction, of course. But, after the first night in that cave, where he'd tended to Aleron's wings, Gideon knew for certain he could be aroused by this Duskwalker.

The idea no longer frightened him. Instead, it stimulated him, invoking lustful thoughts at random. How would those feathered wings feel brushing up the backs of his naked thighs, or his back, tickling him in their softness?

The strange stomach quivers in the cemetery at just holding his imposing hand had not gone unnoticed; they were shy flutters of a growing infatuation.

He'd had many goals in his life, but it was time to make a new dream: Aleron.

Without reading it, Gideon tossed the letter into the fire, rings and all.

He didn't need it, nor the affections for someone in the past. In front of him was someone new. Not better or worse.

They were different, Aleron and Beau. One a Duskwalker, the other human, but both... possible of capturing his attention, so long as he left himself open to it.

It'd happened once; a time he didn't remember. He already felt the trickles of it happening again. He didn't care if it was old emotions from the afterlife, or new ones anymore, only that they existed.

The way his heart had flipped shyly in his chest in the cemetery. Their days in the cave where it had squeezed. Without realising he'd woken Gideon, this Duskwalker had tried to sneakily hug him from behind, and he'd found himself wanting Aleron to hug him tighter.

He couldn't ignore these signs, and he wouldn't.

I'm starting to really care about him.

Gideon cared if Aleron was anxious or nervous around him, becoming hyperaware of the way he cupped his hands to his chest, or how his wings would tighten against his back. It deeply bothered him when Aleron's orbs would shift blue.

The space between them was beginning to feel barren, cold.

Looking at him from afar meant Gideon always took him in fully. There was no denying what Aleron was, but when one looked past the veil of normality and human ideology, there was definitely much more to be seen. He looked like a deity of death, but there was beauty in dying. Just like there was beauty in Aleron's skull and ethereal, glowing orbs.

Gideon frowned at himself. *Why do I feel like I've had that thought before?*

But it was more than that.

Aleron's personality was kind. He was gentle and understanding towards a creature that had been *dying* inside.

Gideon would take that Demon eating him repeatedly, rather than experience any more of the internal suffering he'd gone through the first week he'd come back to life. The urge to lie down and let the forest grow over him, unable to move forward in a pointless life, had been so harrowing and draining.

Throughout all of it, he'd never been alone. If he had been, if Aleron had abandoned him as he'd demanded multiple times, he didn't think he would have survived his own dark internal thoughts.

Gideon needed someone to distract him, to fill in the space around him. The silence, the coldness. He needed someone to make him *laugh* again.

Aleron had cared for him when no one else would have, not even Beau. A human could only take being beaten down by another for so long, and this Duskwalker had shown more selflessness and love than anyone else could have.

What he'd done to be gifted that level of devotion... he didn't know.

"Gideon?" Aleron called, making him realise he'd just been staring at the magnificent creature before him.

He hated how Aleron cupped his hands to his chest because of it.

"Oh, sorry." He laughed awkwardly, darting his gaze from the burning letter before looking down at his guitar. He grabbed the neck of it and fully pulled it from its case. "Here, let me show you what it does."

He thrummed the strings and instantly grimaced.

"Shit, it's out of tune. Give me a second."

He checked the saddle and bridge pegs, then twisted the tuning pegs one by one as he thumbed the strings attached to them. Once it sounded in tune, he thrummed all the strings, happy with the cascade of notes.

Just when Gideon started playing, he paused.

"I would like to apologise in advance if this is horrible," he stated. "I didn't actually have this guitar long. It took me years to afford it with my pay, and a bunch of my friends chipped in the rest for my twenty-first birthday to help me get it."

And, for the two years he'd had it, he'd played it nearly every day to learn. He couldn't afford lessons, but he'd borrowed music books to teach himself. His parents had wanted to help, but Gideon had been set on doing this on his own, so he could say with pride that he was self-taught.

With the apology about his skills out of the way, he played a light, heartfelt song, with a touch of melancholy underlining it – one of the many he'd made up. He enjoyed playing from his soul, rather than following a sheet of music from someone else's. He felt the song, the music, and each note that vibrated as he moved up and down the fingerboard.

It felt like he'd been transported to eight years ago, but in a way, that was uplifting.

He had to pause a few times when he played the incorrect note, or accidentally played two instead of one. Still, he felt his chest swelling, and his mind emptying.

Words threatened to bubble past his lips, but he kept them at bay. He liked to sing, but was utterly tone-deaf and one hundred percent aware of it. He wouldn't subject Aleron's sensitive ear holes to that unpleasantness.

Plus, this moment was meant to be between himself, Aleron, and the guitar.

It took him a while to notice it, since he kept needing to look down at the fingerboard, but wings twitching captured his attention. When he looked up at Aleron, his orbs had flared to bright yellow.

The smile that pulled at the edges of Gideon's lips, and crinkled the corners of his eyes, was a reflection of the lightness that came from his hurt and internal struggles lifting away.

Until now, he hadn't realised how important this guitar was to him, nor had he known just how much he needed Aleron to enjoy him playing it. Perhaps it was a small thing, but it made Gideon feel closer to him by knowing he accepted this.

Not wishing to draw it out for too long, he finished after

a couple more minutes, then settled the instrument in his lap.

Aleron's tail feathers vibrated in a pronounced manner, and combined with his joyous eye colour, Gideon took that as his version of applause. "That was very good," he added, confirming Gideon's guess that he enjoyed the music. Aleron shifted like he wanted to come closer, even lifting a little before sitting back down. "I have never heard anything like this."

"Want to have a go?" Gideon offered coyly, lifting the neck of it in his direction. He wiggled his eyebrows playfully. "You just can't break it."

Aleron shook his head. "No. I do not trust I will not harm it."

Dammit, he just wanted the big guy to come over.

Since his excuse didn't work, he rose to his feet and walked over. Facing him, Gideon sat in front of Aleron with his legs crossed and placed the guitar in his fur-covered lap.

"Just sheath your claws," Gideon stated, turning it so the strings were facing him. "I'll show you how to play. It requires very little pressure."

When Aleron refused, still hesitant, Gideon grabbed his massive hand and forced it to cup the neck of the instrument from underneath. Then he grabbed Aleron's other hand and made him strum the strings. None of them snapped as a mess of notes cascaded from it.

"See?" Then Gideon showed him each string on its own by using his fingers, letting him hear each one individually. He quickly discovered a problem. "Your fingers are a little too big. One second."

He stood and walked back over to his guitar case to go rifling through the inner pockets. Two earrings clinked together, but he ignored them for now; the Duskwalker was his priority. Once he found what he wanted, he moved back over to Aleron.

"This is a guitar pick," he explained, holding it between

his thumb and forefinger to show it. "You use it to pluck strings individually."

He placed the blunt, triangular pick in Aleron's hand, taught him how to hold it, and then waited for him to experiment on his own.

His finger pads were still too big for the fingerboard, but that was fine. This was still fun, even though Aleron seemed hopelessly lost with it all.

It also gave him an idea – one that had his head bowing forward so he could poorly hide his reddening cheeks under his brow-length hair.

"Here. It's hard to get a gauge of how to play since it's from an odd angle for me." Gideon grumbled the lie as he pushed the guitar up into the air.

He crawled underneath it, turned around, and sat between it and Aleron's torso. A strange shiver ran down his spine at the heat that pressed against the small of his back. Now that he was sitting between his legs, Gideon's heart raced like it wanted to come up his throat – especially since Aleron didn't lower the guitar to secure him in place.

He clenched his eyes shut when the urge to bolt itched at him.

Aleron finally lowered his arms, locking Gideon in, and somehow his pulse went fucking faster.

With a shaking hand, he grabbed Aleron's to show him how to use the fingerboard. He explained how notes worked, what each one of the six strings was, and helped him play.

Slowly, bit by bit, Aleron's chest pressed more and more firmly into his back. Gideon thought his entire being shuddered all the way to his soul between Aleron's horns, when the end of his bony snout pressed against the side of his head as he sniffed. Aleron's exhale brushed through his hair, tickled his scalp, and had goosebumps trailing down his arms and legs.

His mouth dried, and suddenly Gideon became tongue-tied as he tried to teach him about the instrument. It became obvious that Aleron wasn't listening anyway.

"You play it," Aleron grated behind him, his voice gruff and deeper than usual. Hearing it directly in his ear almost had a groan falling from Gideon. "You are better at it, and I liked the sound of your... *music.*"

Gideon did as he was requested. He played the same song as before, a little more confidently now that he fully remembered how to play. Or perhaps he didn't care what or how he played, since he was waiting with anticipation to see what would happen now that they were so close.

Which was nothing.

Aleron pulled his head to the side to watch, rather than sniff him further. He didn't try to touch him, and only moved by bringing his knees up to give the guitar space in front of them so Gideon could play it freely.

He didn't know what he wanted, what he'd been expecting, but disappointment flooded Gideon's veins. He attempted to keep playing, occasionally stopping to throw more wood onto the fire, then settled back in while hoping for more.

Still, it'd been a long while since he'd felt at peace like this.

As time passed, the moon reached its highest peak and his cold fingertips radiated an ache up his hand from playing for so long. His eyes grew heavy as the emotions of the night bled from him, the high and adrenaline fully waning.

What time is it? It'd been a few hours since night had fallen, but the air didn't feel cold – not with Aleron surrounding him from three sides.

Gideon stopped playing and stared at the flames with his thoughts quietening.

Before he knew it, his eyelids drooped as he squinted with tiredness, then they closed of their own accord. He tried to keep himself awake, but as the weight of the night sapped the last of his energy, he found himself slipping to the side.

The guitar fell from his hands and slid off his lap, but never clanged when it hit the ground.

Aleron darted forward to grab the length of the musical instrument before it could hit the dirt. He gently lifted it to the side, so it was out of the way, and placed it down with care, already summarising it was important to this human.

Then, he dipped and tilted his head forward so he could see that his bride had truly fallen asleep and now rested against the inner wall of his bent leg. His light-brown hair softly swayed in the breeze, brushing back and forth across his brow as he took calm, even breaths. One of his hands had fallen to the ground, while the other rested in the middle of his crossed legs.

He fell asleep on me, Aleron mused, lifting the knuckle of his forefinger to brush it down the thick, corded muscle on the side of Gideon's neck. He gently flicked it forward so the smooth, curved part of his claw traced down the male's firm jaw.

What does this mean?

He wanted to believe it was because Gideon wanted to lie with him, and be embraced by him, but Aleron couldn't shake the uncertainty that lingered. The male had wanted to play the instrument and teach Aleron. Did he only come closer to do that, or was it to be within his presence like this?

His heart yearned for the latter. Every piece of him longed for his bride to seek his attention, rather than dismiss Aleron when he tried to give it.

I do not know why he did this.

Right before Gideon had started playing, he'd pulled out

some kind of parchment and had grown awfully pale. His pretty eyes had turned glassy, stark, and even from a distance, Aleron had been able to smell a tangle of *fear*.

He'd stared at Aleron's skull for an uncomfortable length of time, only to then toss the parchment into the flames as if it were meaningless.

Does it have something to do with the male I saw chasing him? Gideon had taken the case from the human's dwelling, so this made sense.

Aleron wanted to ask him further about the human, and the one who had cared enough about Gideon to carve his name on the death stone of names. The only reason he didn't was because he doubted Gideon would tell him. Even in Tenebris, he only revealed the surface of what lay within his mind.

Aleron had discovered enough, and almost everything pertained to Emerie and their family. He hadn't learned much about his other companions.

He'd already told Gideon everything he could remember about his life once. He didn't mind doing so again, since much of it seemed to make the male warm to him. However, coming to Earth made him realise just how complex and complicated humans were.

Having a bride is hard. He wrapped Gideon's throat in his palm, and caressed his jaw back and forth with the side of his thumb. *I do like this one, though.*

In the back of his mind, he constantly pondered the past few weeks. How it felt for him, the loneliness, rejection, and dejection. None of it had been easy, most of it unpleasant, and he'd rather not relive it.

This wait was painstakingly long. He thought it may be worth it just to have Gideon trustingly and peacefully resting against him like this.

Noticing the way the hair on his jaw tickled his thumb, he braved lowering his head. Aleron's entire body quaked, his wings flapping and fluttering behind him, when he gently brushed the side of his snout against his stubble. He almost groaned in satisfaction at the spikey texture scraping against his bone.

Aleron placed both his arms around Gideon and nuzzled repeatedly, wishing for his beard to score him.

His pretty scent, just at the tip of his nose hole, was gulped down. Hot, fresh, and decadent. The urge to lick him itched his tongue, and the only reason he didn't was because he doubted he'd stop.

He didn't mean to lift Gideon's shirt, but the moment bare skin touched his fingertips, his hand ducked underneath it. Aleron palmed his lightly muscled abdomen, feeling the keloid scars there.

Just the merest contact, the smallest of embraces, and already Aleron's sight flashed purple with desire. *I want to touch him, lick him, eat at him so he can't get away.* He yearned to see Gideon desirously cling to him again, desperate to keep him close, so Aleron was the one who couldn't escape.

A groan fell from the male's lips, and Aleron stiffened.

He wasn't doing anything inappropriate... he didn't think. One of his hands may be under his shirt, but it was upon his stomach, and the other had tightly gripped his inner thigh.

Aleron considered it. He considered bringing both his hands higher to touch at Gideon's groin and chest, wanting to wake his bride with pleasure. Aleron was tired of holding back. He longed to bring them closer until they'd meshed into one writhing creature of adoring need.

But, when Gideon put his knees together and slid his feet under his backside, and turned so he could place his cheek against the middle of Aleron's sternum, he let a sigh flutter past his fangs. Instead, he wrapped his arms around the little human's torso, and gave into a different urge.

He shoved his wings forward and wrapped them around

his arms and knees. Although he couldn't feel Gideon with them, his own body in the way, it still felt remarkable to enclose him like this. Aleron squeezed with all his might, letting himself be content that his bride was sleeping on his chest for the first time.

Ready to remove his wings in case Gideon woke, this was more than enough to quell the worst of his need.

Something white landed on the tip of his snout before melting. He looked up to find fluffy little snow puffs falling. They instantly melted against him and the fire, but he shielded Gideon from most of them. A few stuck to his light-brown hair, and Aleron found that rather cute.

A tiny heartbeat fluttered, as soft breaths made the fur on his chest dance. The itch to chuckle came when Gideon screwed up his features as some of the longer strands tickled his nose and lips.

A crack from the fire drew his attention to it, and something glinted from within its embers. Something golden, but he couldn't make out what it truly was before a stick fell on top of it. The fire jumped and crackled again.

He threw metal into the fire? Aleron thought hard on this, unsure of why Gideon would do this. *But is this not important to keep?* As far as he knew, humans used such items for trade, especially if they were of that metal colouring.

Maybe he did not know it was within the parchment?

It was the only logic Aleron could come up with, but he shrugged. There was little he could do about it, unless he wished to stop selfishly holding his bride.

Which he didn't. *Mine. My pretty bride is lying on me. He chose this.*

He'd hold this human until the sun rose, or the fire gave out. Then Aleron would lay him down and let him rest properly.

A few minutes – hours – more couldn't hurt.

TWENTY-NINE

Gideon's face twitched and stiffened before he hunkered down under the draping warmth.

He didn't remember falling asleep, nor when he'd chosen to lie on the ground on his side. He rolled onto his back, and with his arms crossed over his chest to keep them from touching the grass, he scooched over. He wiggled until he found what he wanted and then rubbed his face into the fur and feathers of Aleron's back.

To say he was disappointed that this was how he'd woken up was an understatement.

He opened his eyes to near darkness; the only light peeking through was a small gap just above his head. Aleron's wing blanketed him, as it did every night, but he'd been hoping for a little more. Maybe to be blanketed from the front? He wouldn't mind being pressed up against his torso and having the Duskwalker's arms secure him.

Gideon imagined it'd be even warmer – and sweeter.

He'd be able to take in Aleron's big heartbeat better.

Instead, as per usual, they were back-to-back like an unspoken but distrustful truce.

He's still being closed off with me. Even after Gideon held Aleron's hand, thanked him for everything, apologised again for the past, and even sat between his legs. He pouted as he thought, *He didn't even want to hold me when I sa with him.*

Other than being sniffed, Aleron didn't even casually place his hand on his side or thigh. Nothing.

Since he'd rolled over, he pressed his forehead against Aleron's back and let out a solemn sigh.

Given Aleron's response in the cemetery, Gideon knew this Duskwalker still felt... *something* for him. He worried it was too late. Had he completely lost all the potential of receiving free affection from Aleron?

Gideon had chosen to let go of his past completely last night. He'd smashed his own heart to pieces on purpose, and now planned to rebuild it, bigger and better than ever, so something like a giant monster could fit in it. But he couldn't do that on his own.

He didn't want someone who felt too nervous or scared to be affectionate with him. He'd always wanted to be the king of his own story, not the *villain* in someone else's.

Aleron had been a stranger to me. His anger, spite, and callousness hadn't been towards a friend or partner, someone he was supposed to care for and protect. A stranger was no one, and they usually meant little to him.

Worse still, not only had Aleron been a stranger, he was something Gideon had been... terrified of. A creature of nightmares, who then followed him with a set of claws and fangs, threatening to never let him go.

Any human in his position would have freaked out.

But it's different now.

He wanted Aleron to be... himself.

Gideon didn't want him to hold back anymore, so that Aleron could win his heart naturally. Even with the distance between them, he'd already started doing so. Aleron, in his own way, could be rather endearing and charming, even while acting all shy and nervous. That, too, was cute.

He wanted to see what it truly looked like to be loved by a Duskwalker.

Right now, Aleron just felt like his friend.

But what if he no longer... wants me? This thought had started pestering him.

He'd started worrying that Aleron was putting up with his presence, simply because he was forced to through their bond. In the same way Gideon had forced himself to accept their relationship at first.

Maybe Aleron no longer wanted anything more than distant friendship. Gideon wouldn't blame him for that, since it was his own fault.

Aleron had obviously wanted more in the beginning, considering he'd woken up wrapped in his arms and wings. There were also the dream memories of this Duskwalker... *inside* him, in a different world. Aleron's purple tongue slipping across his neck, his lips, and inside his mouth to brush against his own. Ravishing him inside and out.

Now that they no longer alarmed him, Gideon was growing curious about doing all these things with him. Was the licking Aleron's form of kisses? He wouldn't mind receiving a few to see if he liked them – his dead self seemed to.

I guess I need to be brave. He needed to lead and accept where that may take them.

"Aleron," Gideon called, hoping he could start them with at least a cuddle.

The wing blanketing him swiftly pulled away as Aleron rolled to his front to escape. With a quiet scream, Gideon rolled over when his other wing slipped out from under him. He'd thought he'd been lying on the ground!

"Was it too much?" Aleron quietly asked, before looking around apprehensively. "It began to snow, so I did not wish for you to lie directly upon the ground."

Annoyed that Aleron was being insecure and meek, he sat up and placed his elbow on his knee. Gideon scratched at the side of his scalp while averting his gaze, and ruffled his hair in the process.

How can someone that big act so unsure? The moment

he asked himself that question, he knew he wouldn't like the answer.

"No, it was fine," Gideon stated, looking around at the thin layer of snow. "It was actually really warm. Thank you, I really appreciate it."

He forced his negative emotions to leave him as he let out a deep exhale. He braved a glance at the nervously fidgeting Aleron. *One step at a time.*

Unfortunately for Aleron, he was about to learn that when Gideon set his mind to something, he could become very bold. A nervous boulder rolling down a hill, taking a leap of faith, even if it was a poor mistake.

Every opportunity Gideon had, he would bridge the gap between them. He would like to do this in a way that didn't overwhelm the Duskwalker. He wanted Aleron to be comfortable, and to only have Gideon's touch if it was something the Duskwalker desired.

I could ask him... He snorted a laugh at himself. *But I also want to take it slow because I'm also kind of unsure.* Not of Aleron, but of what he wanted to do with him.

Gideon didn't want to kiss him and then for Aleron to get over-excited and suddenly try to ram whatever kind of cock he had in his ass. He was human, and it had been... years since he'd been penetrated by something bigger than a finger. Beau was usually the receiver, and although Gideon had absolutely no qualms in being below someone, he'd need patience after so long.

Apparently Rome wasn't built in a day, and his hole wouldn't be able to take a seven-and-a-half-foot Duskwalker in a night.

But the fact I'm thinking about it... means I want to try now, right? An idea lit in Gideon's mind. His ears grew hot as he peeked at Aleron again, who stood and flapped his wings to dust off the snow, blissfully unaware of where Gideon's thoughts had gone. *Unless I can take him.*

All his blurry, fragmented memories were of himself

being pumped into. Was Aleron just opposed to it being the other way around?

He frowned. *But why do I get the impression there's another reason?* A memory tried to arise, a conversation, but it was so damn murky their voices were inaudible.

Ah, screw it. I'll figure it out later.

He stood and brushed off his pants, since forest debris collected on them. In the meantime, he noted their campfire still burning, as if Aleron had thrown more wood onto it before laying them down. There were only a few glowing coals of wood left, but Gideon still rounded up some snow and dumped it on top of them.

Last thing they needed was to start a wildfire not even a kilometre from Fishket.

He turned to Aleron, finding him standing there more awkwardly than usual. His skull was partly turned to the side, and one of his wings had come forward to hide his arm.

Before Gideon could grow more curious, he realised something was missing.

"Shit, where's my guitar?" Gideon spun in a circle, only to find his case was right next to where the imprint of their bodies remained, where they had stopped the snowfall from touching the ground. He walked over to the case, opened it, and found his guitar safely tucked away inside it. He looked up at Aleron. "Did you put this away for me?"

"Yes. It is important to you, so I laid it within my wings next to you."

Gratitude crinkled the outer corner of his eyes. "Thank you. That was astute of you."

Aleron's orbs flashed bright yellow, only to quickly sink back to their usual pale pink. Yet, within seconds, they morphed to white, and he averted his skull to the side once more.

"Are you ready to leave?" Aleron asked, his wings shifting slightly. "I would like to continue searching for

Ingram."

"What's wrong?" Gideon asked instead.

"It is nothing." He said this, yet his orbs flared... orange?

Gideon couldn't remember if he'd ever seen them turn that colour, nor did he know what it meant.

His chest tightened in uncertainty, and he rubbed the side of his neck. *Something is obviously wrong, but I don't want to pressure him.* Staring at the Duskwalker whose shoulders were turned inward, looking unbearably uncomfortable under his gaze, Gideon sighed.

I think I only find it cute when he looks like this because I feel so bad for him. He was a Duskwalker! He could literally rip him in half with the smallest amount of effort, and yet he looked so damn awkward that Gideon found it sweet. It made Aleron feel... human, almost.

He'll hopefully tell me when he's ready. Or maybe Gideon could figure it out on his own. He'd just add it to the list of things he needed to make up for.

Just as he was about to close his case, he remembered something. His eyes lit up, and he started fishing through the two pockets inside it. *Come on, I know I felt you last night.* Metal clinked, causing a grin to curl his lips. *Yes!*

He yanked out two earrings – a spare set.

"Please fit," he pleaded under his breath, as he unlatched the thin hook and poked it into the hole in his ear.

When he slipped it through, although tightly and with a wince, and was able to close the ring, he let out a breath of relief. The bottom of the ring was thicker and had a golden colour despite actually being low quality. It matched the second one, which had an easier time going in.

Once they were in, Gideon shook his head, happy with the weight of them and the way they tapped against the sides of his neck.

Then he shut his case and stood.

"Alright, let's go," he stated, coming closer so Aleron could pick him up. Aleron tilted his skull, obviously inspecting one of his earrings, but didn't comment on them. "I'm glad you're okay with carrying me and the guitar."

Gideon would clutch it while Aleron held him. Hopefully, in the future, they could acquire a strap big enough to sling it over Aleron's back, so long as it didn't get in the way of his wings. If not, they'd get one to strap across his own, and he could hold on to Aleron's neck from behind.

Aleron crouched so he could reach around him, and Gideon managed to get a glimpse of his hand – although not a good one. Then the Duskwalker lifted him off the ground and to his chest. As per usual, his right arm crossed Gideon's back, with his hand grasping his biceps. The other was behind his knees, but instead of holding him, his hand was curled into a tight fist.

The fact Aleron wasn't gripping him securely was enough to draw his gaze to it. The moment Gideon took in the state of his hand, his face didn't know if it wanted to go cold and pale in dread, or heat and flush with fury.

"Holy shit!" Gideon squirmed to be put down, shoving at his chest. "What the fuck happened to your hand, Aleron?"

Aleron fought him, trying to keep Gideon in his arms. "It is nothing."

"The fuck it's not!" When he struggled to no avail, he cast Aleron the filthiest glare he could muster. "Put me down. *Now.*"

Not even Aleron's quiet whimper could lessen his anger after being placed on his feet. Gideon darted for Aleron's wrist, but he pulled it away.

"Give me your hand."

He placed his guitar on the ground, held his hand out with his palm facing upwards, and waited.

"I do not want you to see," Aleron grumbled, tossing his skull from side to side.

Gideon wiggled his fingers to show he was waiting as his eyes narrowed further. Aleron's wings lifted up and down, his fur and feathers puffed and raised. Likely seeing that Gideon wasn't going to give up on this, he eventually placed the back of his hand in Gideon's palm.

"What happened?" he asked quietly, his stomach knotting at the pain he must be in.

The entirety of his hand was burned to the point skin had started to peel away from his protruding knuckle bones. His fingers looked worse, but Gideon couldn't fully inspect them with Aleron refusing to uncurl his fist.

"I do not want to say," Aleron answered, before his orbs brightened in their orange hue. "I do not want you to be... upset with me."

"Upset with you?"

His brows drew together, unable to understand how this could have happened during the night. Then it hit him, and Gideon let out a sigh while shaking his head. He petted his wrist, wishing to soothe him when it likely wasn't helping.

"I'm upset with myself," he grumbled, inspecting Aleron's hand with annoyance. "You don't have to tend to the fires I make. If they burn out, then don't worry about them. You always throw your wing over me anyway, and the fire is just to make light and keep me warm until I go to sleep."

The fact he would do that... it just shows how damn sweet he is. How much he cares for me. If Gideon had known that Aleron would hurt himself, he wouldn't have made the campfire. He'd rather stumble through the dark than Aleron be in pain. *I could just use the lack of warmth as a way to get closer to him.*

"Can you open your hand so I can see how bad the damage is?"

"This is not why I think you will be upset." Aleron looked down at his own fist. "I broke one. I am sorry."

Hesitantly, Aleron finally opened it.

Sitting in the centre of his big palm were two golden rings, the same ones Gideon had thrown into the fire the night before. The smaller ring, which had been intended for

Gideon, was perfectly intact, while the larger one had been mangled and bent out of shape.

Dread crawled down his spine, paled his features, and he drew his stark gaze up to Aleron's skull.

"I did not realise there were two, but the pain made me squeeze them and one bent in my palm. I thought they were coins, but once I saw them, I knew your kind wear them as decorations." Aleron fidgeted on his feet, and once again said, "I am sorry. I did not mean to ruin them."

A thousand words wanted to fall from Gideon's mouth. He hadn't wanted to see these again, didn't want to touch them. He would rather forget their existence.

Instead, he grumbled as he took them and shoved them into his pocket. Aleron had fucking fished them from the fire. He absolutely refused to explain how much he didn't want them.

"Thank you," Gideon forced out through clenched teeth, then patted the uninjured part of his palm. "But don't do that again. Humans have a rule: if it falls into the fire, it's gone."

"But your instrument and case were important enough for you to take them. I did not want you to discover something missing from them because you did not realise you threw it into the flames."

Gideon's features crinkled into a grimace, his heart squeezing with painful tenderness at Aleron's considerate words and gesture. Yet, the lukewarm rings in his pocket felt heavy and hot, as if they threatened to burn a hole in his clothing.

"You're so kind to the point of silliness," Gideon mumbled, not meaning anything cruel but just stating the fact of the situation.

He took in the melted tips of Aleron's claws, his destroyed fingertips, and the purple muscle Gideon could see exposed when it really shouldn't be.

Unsure of what to do or say, he lowered his head and pressed his forehead against Aleron's inner wrist.

"Don't hurt yourself for me again, okay? I've hurt you enough, and I already feel terrible."

How the hell did I ever think so badly of him? He wished he'd known Aleron was like this when he first opened his eyes on Earth. More than anything, he wished he hadn't forgotten everything, so none of the past few weeks would have happened.

He was beginning to want to go back in time and start over.

"But I did not mind doing this for you," Aleron stated with assurance. "You do not need to feel bad."

It twisted his stomach more.

Gideon was getting tired of the way shame trickled down the back of his neck. He didn't deserve this much consideration from Aleron, not when there were still so many things he needed to apologise for.

The things they still needed to discuss festered inside him daily. *I made so many mistakes.*

Gideon lifted his head to shout out, "I punched you in the fucking face, Aleron!"

He let Aleron's wrist go, stepped back, and ran his fingers through his hair in annoyance at himself. This was just one of the many things he thought about and didn't have the bravery to bring up yet. *All the things I did to him... said to him.*

The way I made him feel. The way he made Aleron... cry ethereal tears, silently as he followed behind Gideon, who also couldn't contain his own tears.

"But it did not hurt me." Aleron dipped his head as he lowered into a crouch, trying to make himself smaller. "Instead, I hurt your hand and it bled. I am–"

"Don't you dare." Gideon's tone was dark as he narrowed his eyes into a tight glare. "Don't you dare say sorry for something I did to myself. I'm glad that I busted my hand and not your face. I've considered it instant karma ever since I realised you were telling me the truth."

Aleron cupped his damn hands to his chest, and Gideon wanted to explode. Even more so when he said, "I have upset you."

I wish he'd just get angry with me, rather than be so nice all the time. Gideon could accept anger, since it would be deserved. He could accept being threatened or treated coarsely, as a reaction to his own mistreatment of Aleron.

But this? Where this Duskwalker, who was meant to be a terrifying, ferocious monster, appeared beaten down? How he seemed to recede into himself?

It was breaking him. And the deeper he felt towards Aleron, the fonder he became of him, the more it *hurt.* Gideon didn't want to see this side of Aleron anymore.

How the hell do I fix this?

Gideon lifted his face to the sky, trying to pull strength from it, to seek an answer from it. If only some kind of deity would take pity on him and give him the answers he needed.

Gideon was still trying to heal himself, and he now had to heal all the damage he'd done along the way.

His eyes drifted to the corners of his lids so he could take in his soul, noting that it appeared fully flaming and full of life. Something had changed last night, enough to affect it, but he still felt altered within.

Sure, his chest no longer ached for the past and the people in it, but now it was heavy because of the person beside him.

He was wise enough to know that *meant* something.

Once Gideon managed to cool his anger, he let out a foggy sigh. He walked over to Aleron, and crouched down so that he was smaller than him – mimicking him. Then he placed a hand on top of his skull.

"I'm not angry with you. It may seem that way, but I'm not."

"You humans are so complicated," Aleron grumbled. He sounded annoyed, yet he pressed his skull upwards, so Gideon's hand pressed more firmly on it. "You yell and shout, and then say you are not angry at the person. It makes little sense."

"That is an absolutely fair statement, all things considered." Gideon stared into his orbs, hoping Aleron could see his earnestness as well as hear it in his voice. "I don't want you to apologise or feel bad for anything that has happened in the past. None of it is your fault. Very little of how I acted towards you was deserved, and I want you to understand that I am sorry for a lot of it. What happened to my hand means little compared to the action that caused it, and you proved how much you didn't deserve me swinging one at you by this."

Gideon carefully reached down and grabbed the wrist of Aleron's injured hand to gesture to it.

"Yes, I am upset that you hurt yourself on my behalf, but I don't care that you bent one of the rings. I know you will heal in a day, much like your wing, but I don't want you to suffer needlessly on my account, even if any injury or illness is temporary."

Even if Gideon had to repeat himself in the future, or apologise a thousand times, he hoped one day Aleron believed him.

Gideon stood and reached to the side to grab his guitar once more. The tension between them was so thick it would have needed a saw to cut through it. Still, he tried to smooth his features, then offered a smile as Aleron picked him up and launched them into the air.

He would have liked to say he was nice and friendly for the remainder of the day, but he wasn't always amicable. Rather, he stayed quiet while he thought deeply, reflecting on the recent past. Hugging the body of his guitar case, with the long neck of it between his knees, he tried to ignore the rings burning a hole in his conscience.

Gideon hoped they rolled out of his pocket, so he didn't have to deal with them. He'd feel guilty if he were to toss them, considering what Aleron had gone through to get them. He could get away with 'accidentally' losing them.

Maybe I can sell them? The extra coin would be nice, even though he doubted he'd get much for them.

Thankfully, flying with any kind of speed made it difficult for them to have a conversation. The wind meant Aleron needed to shout for Gideon to hear him clearly, so they often travelled in silence.

One thing he knew with absolute certainty: he needed to better their relationship before they found Ingram and Emerie.

Things were going poorly, and he'd rather do this on his own. As much as he loved Emerie, missed her and wanted to see her, he didn't think he'd be comfortable being as forward as he was likely about to be with Aleron in front of her.

Some things were easier than others.

When the sun went down once more, they set up camp. Gideon made Aleron promise he wouldn't touch the fire before he lit one, which was needed because of the light snowfall.

Then, he laid down, but forced himself to remain awake.

As soon as Aleron laid down behind him, with his back to his, Gideon immediately got to his feet. Without speaking a word, and ignoring how Aleron flinched and receded into himself, Gideon walked around him. Then he knelt in front of the Duskwalker, lifted his heavy arm, and laid down so they were torso to torso.

Just to make certain Aleron knew it was okay, Gideon draped the Duskwalker's arm over his body himself, while placing his head on Aleron's firm biceps as a pillow.

The embrace felt forced. *Come on...* He clenched his eyes shut tight at the stillness that greeted him.

Aleron held tension for a long while, even when he tightened his hold on Gideon to bring him closer. Even though it was only his forehead pressing against his furry chest, Gideon could feel and hear how frantic Aleron's heart was by the proximity and their new position.

I hope that's in excitement and not apprehension.

His own seemed to match it, but it settled as Aleron's heat bled into his body. He closed his eyes when the Duskwalker curled around him even more, growing more confident as the seconds passed.

"This is nice," Gideon stated, verbally letting Aleron know of his approval. However, he shoved his hand under the arm on top of him so he could pat Aleron's back. "But can you bring your wing forward? My back is freezing."

The snow had melted, which meant a layer of frost now coated everything. The wind, although light, was chillier and wetter than usual.

"I do not wish to suffocate you."

Gideon winced at that. He patted Aleron's back hard, slapping him. "Give me the damn wing, Aleron, or I'll bite your chest."

Aleron let out a deep, rumbling groan and almost seemed to... *thrust* against him. "No," he rasped hoarsely. "Do not do that."

Aleron threw his wing forward and draped it over his body, leaving his head free. Gideon appreciated it, since he'd gotten what he wanted, but now... he couldn't think about anything but the way Aleron had reacted.

With his eyes open wide and his teeth nipping at the inside of his cheek, he thought, *Does... he like being bitten?* The biggest and most mischievous grin Gideon had ever produced curled his lips until it bared his teeth. *That's handy to know.*

Not even the wariness that the Duskwalker might bite back could temper his excitement of what that meant.

I guess it's time for me to grow fangs.

THIRTY

Aleron noticed his human seemed cheerier than normal when he woke. He also had more colour in his skin, and the dark smudges under his eyes had started to fade. Considering how much Gideon had snored with his face squished against Aleron's chest, and how lax his body had grown, Aleron wondered if he'd properly rested.

With his injured hand holding Gideon's back as he slept, he'd reached between his horns to gently take his bride's soul from between them. When he'd opened his fist, he hadn't expected it to be so bright and beautiful, with not a single bit of charcoal to be seen.

Aleron didn't know why he fisted it and hugged Gideon closer with his orbs flaring bright pink. Perhaps the relief of knowing it now flickered the way it was supposed to overwhelmed him, or maybe it was even in hope.

He put it back where it belonged, and wrapped his arms completely around the soul's owner.

Somehow, in the back of his mind, he knew the desire to anxiously check it would wane from then on. He'd only look at it because he wanted to marvel at his bride's soul, knowing it belonged to him, was his to cherish.

Sleep came peacefully to Aleron as well, even if they weren't resting as closely as he wished them to. He wanted to bring both his wings around Gideon protectively, but would be satisfied if this was all he could do. A single wing, loosely keeping out the world but allowing his head freedom.

That mild contentment radiated through him for the duration of the next morning, aided by Gideon's increased mood. He couldn't quite put his finger on the difference, since they spoke little and did nothing more than usual.

Aleron pondered on if it was due to the warmth in Gideon's eyes, or how his lips weren't so hard pressed. It may be because his bride had subtly turned to him as he flew, pressing against his torso rather than away from it. On the odd occasion, Gideon even turned the other way – a movement that required trust – so he could search the ground with Aleron.

Although he doubted Ingram would have taken Emerie within the border of the southlands, Aleron chose to check it thoroughly.

Minimal clouds allowed for the sun to wash over them. His human seemed to appreciate it, and he enjoyed the way the male's eyes closed as he lifted his face to bask in its light.

They passed a few towns, landing in each only long enough for Gideon to quickly run inside and ask about Emerie, but not a single person he approached seemed to have seen her. Aleron liked that he now knew what Ashpine City looked like, as Gideon had often spoken of it and its great *library*.

They also passed over a small bandit encampment, which had spikes protecting them – not that it would truly do much if multiple Demons chose to attack.

Eventually, they found themselves near the only set of mountains on the southwestern side. Just as they circled over them briefly and started to fly north, Gideon nearly fell out of his arms.

"Wait. Wait!" Gideon pointed at something; it was the only spot where snow didn't cling to the ground. "I think I know of that place. Could we go down there?"

Aleron bit back his annoyance with a huff, since Gideon kept stopping their search. There were the rest stops every night. Their stay in his hometown. The cave where Aleron thought they may have been able to fly through the rain once the worst of the storm dissipated. And the very beginning where Gideon refused to help him search.

I want to find my kindred. His mind constantly obsessed over being reunited with his twin. His thoughts were always split evenly between trying to care for Gideon and the longing he had for Ingram. His heart twisted in his absence with how much he missed him.

The urge to deny Gideon just this once fled out of him at his bride's grin. With teeth bared, gaze alight with an emotion he didn't understand, and his handsome dimples prominent, the effect had Aleron's wings fluttering in delight.

They fell from the sky for a second. *I have missed that, missed the way he smiles.* A true one that wasn't steeped in sadness or falsities. He wanted to see more of them and spared a glance at the pools that had instigated it. *If I go down, will he smile so brightly for me instead?*

Aleron promptly took them back to a section of rock where trees refused to grow. The forest backed little pools that flowed constantly with steaming, fresh water. The air, warm and moist, kept the lingering snow at bay. A mingle of scents fluttered in the wind, like dewy stone, overripe plants, and a hint of... something tangy – a mineral he wasn't used to. He was unsure if it was unpleasant or not.

When they landed at the edge of the forest, Gideon wriggled to be put down.

"These are Sunnet Hill's headsprings," Gideon stated, awe radiating in his voice. His green eyes spanned over the lush greenery growing up the mountain behind the pools, then the rocks that housed them, before he brought his gaze to Aleron. "They're hot springs."

"I do not understand why this matters," Aleron stated honestly. It was water, and they'd passed many lakes and rivers. "Why is this place so special?"

"Because it's warm!" Gideon gently placed his guitar down, and immediately reached over his head to grab the back of his shirt and jacket at the same time. "So many people have travelled here just to bathe in them, and rumours state no one has ever made it back alive."

Aleron didn't doubt that, as he could smell the evidence of Demons who had recently come through the area.

"Hundreds of years ago, there used to be some kind of establishment here, claiming the water had healing properties. Even though many think it's a myth, people with ailments will brave the possibility of being eaten by Demons just to come bathe in the springs."

As he spoke, Gideon removed his tunic and Aleron nervously shifted his weight between his feet. Aleron wished he'd keep his clothing on, since just a glance at Gideon's rippling back had his insides tightening.

Just as Gideon lifted a foot to remove a boot, he halted. Then he walked over to one of the pools as he said, "I should probably check that this won't boil me alive."

Be too hot. Not enough to scald him, but to deter him into stripping and hopping inside.

He tentatively touched the water's surface before shoving his entire hand in.

"Nope. Perfect," Gideon stated, then retreated to where the grass lacked dampness. He removed one boot at a time. "I know you probably don't want to get your wings wet, but you can lay them on the ground and sit in it with me."

"Me?" Aleron asked, stepping back. "No. I do not wish to do this."

Actually, Aleron was intending to turn around and sit with his back to Gideon, so he couldn't view his body. As much as he wanted to take in his bride's tantalising form and admire it, he also knew he would want... more. He avoided anything that could stir desire.

This human had allowed him to hold his hand *once*, and had only just let him embrace him properly the previous night.

These were slow steps, much like in Tenebris. It'd taken them over a month to fully embrace, but their time together had never been steeped in... sadness and pain involving each other.

Things are changing... Bit by bit, Aleron noticed the spaces separating them growing smaller. *But I must be patient, yes?* He needed Gideon to accept this, him, *them*.

Ugh. I don't wish to wait. Why must humans be so complicated? He hadn't fully understood this one in Tenebris, let alone everything that had happened since.

His love had been met with hatred, but it was now being returned with a strange, tense fondness. Aleron had never taken change well, and the last few weeks had been a mess of them.

"Your loss." Gideon shrugged and reached for the ties of his trousers.

Aleron, slowly and slyly, turned around with his snout already lifted so he could avert his gaze. He didn't wish to be noticed, didn't want to be questioned on his avoidance.

"I'll be honest, the whole not needing to eat, drink, or piss thing is kind of a benefit, but I have been hammering to be clean. How long have we been travelling? Three weeks, almost a month? Not once have I had a bath that isn't rainwater. Just because it's winter and I'm not sweating, doesn't mean I don't feel dirty. I hope these springs are healing for the mind as much as the body."

Water sloshed behind Aleron, and each kick of feet had his wings twitching. Was Gideon fully naked? Just the thought had him cupping the end of his snout to hide the groan that wanted to escape through his gnashing fangs.

Unable to bear not knowing, he peeked. Gideon's arse was covered by his undershorts before they disappeared into the water as he waded deeper. Still, Aleron had taken in the rounded muscles of his backside, and how soft and squishy they looked as his shorts clung to him.

His tentacles shifted behind his seam, wishing to cling to Gideon's smooth skin instead of that cloth.

He let out a choked noise and darted his head forward when his orbs flashed purple. *Do not look.* His entire body itched to turn around.

Even more so when Gideon let out a loud, deep, and satisfied groan. "Fuck *yeah*. That feels so good."

He'd said those very words to Aleron before, while his cock was deep inside him! He squeezed the end of his snout to stifle his groan as best he could with his hand, more afraid of his desire for the human than crushing his skull.

"You better be ready to save me." Water splashed, as if he lay on his back and was floating. "This pool is pretty deep and I've never swum before. I might drown if we're not careful."

A harrowing crawl of dread slithered up his spine. It puffed his feathers and fur, and now his heart accelerated with worry.

"Then get out of the water!" Aleron growled. "Mavka sink. We cannot swim."

"Eh, don't worry." The shrug in his voice only made irritation ruffle his feathers. "The deep end only looks like it'll come to your head height. Too tall for me, obviously, but you should be okay."

That did not make him feel any better whatsoever! *Why would someone go into the water if they cannot swim?* He and Ingram had avoided deep lakes for such a reason.

"You should join me, Aleron," Gideon stated firmly. Then his tone became almost aloof as he cooed, "You know, just in case. To keep me safe."

He ached to. Aleron longed to be near him, to keep

Gideon in his sights, to watch him flit around doing any task.

He shook his head. "I cannot."

My bride is almost naked, wanting me near. And he was too busy shaking, resisting, because he wanted to fucking touch! Just knowing Gideon was there, barely clothed, teased his thoughts more than he could handle.

Last night, as they'd cuddled torso to torso, Aleron had needed to hold back every urge to stop himself from touching Gideon then. Inch by inch, his hand had uncontrollably slipped down his back until he grabbed his bride's backside, and his cock had nearly extruded in utter delight. It'd been so soft and round in his large palm, perfect for him to knead and hold.

Even just the bulge of Gideon's softened shaft and balls nestled against him had his pulse racing with want.

It'd felt wrong grasping his bride in that manner while he slept unaware – even more so when he had to shove Gideon against his seam to keep his shaft at bay. Aleron's control was slipping.

He is not ready. At least, Aleron didn't think so. Not that he truly understood when it was appropriate to fucking try.

The more Gideon smiled, the more life that shined in his eyes, the more Aleron felt himself falling under some kind of spell.

I wish I had more humanity. It'd be easier without the blank spaces in his mind. The way his thoughts unravelled made him even more uncertain than their past already made him. *I wish I was... smarter.*

He wanted to be able to recognise when the right time would be. He'd like to be able to... communicate what he wanted, what he needed, but just like in Tenebris, his body demanded actions rather than words. To use his instincts because it was easier.

But I do not trust myself, my instincts. The few times

he'd let them be in control, he'd made matters worse.

Aleron hated how he felt that way about himself.

Quick, noisy splashes interrupted his stressful musings, just as gurgling bubbled.

"Shit! Help!"

His feathers puffed, his claws ready to maim the water as if it was an enemy. With his heart about to come up through his maw, Aleron turned, ready to jump in. He'd subjugate himself to drowning just to save him from harm.

He halted.

There Gideon lay, on his back, while he gently floated. A giant, evil grin curled his lips, and his piercing green eyes glinted with humour.

"Got you," Gideon playfully hummed.

Aleron's sight flared bright crimson, and he let out an explosive snarl. He stomped a foot forward with his lethal claws bared. "That was not funny!"

Gideon rolled his eyes. "I got you to turn around, didn't I?" Then he knelt on the stone, showing the depth of the water only came to the bottom of his chest, as Gideon reached his hand out to *him*. "Join me, Aleron. I promise it feels good."

A small, quiet whimper tickled his chest at Gideon beckoning him closer. The sun shining down made the water sparkle around him, causing his bride to look more mystical and tantalising than usual.

He was the most mesmerising creature Aleron had ever seen.

With his hair wet and darker than usual, it'd been swept back. It revealed his entire face, pinkened from the heat, and Aleron didn't understand how viewing it in full could cause him to think his bride even more handsome. It radiated an ache behind his sternum, and that pain only deepened at the warmth, tenderness, and trust in his softened eyes.

Water clung to the dark hairs on his arms and chest, making them glitter, but it was the droplets falling that dried

Aleron's tongue. Suddenly he felt thirsty... when he'd never experienced that sensation before.

The sun shone down on half of Gideon's face, highlighting the point of his nose, his sharp jawline, and the ball at his throat Aleron often found himself wanting to lick. It even made the dips between his pectoral muscles, his biceps, and his ridged stomach more prominent, shading the lines of his body in cool shadows and hot light.

His thick thighs beneath the water drew Aleron's gaze. He knew them to be soft enough to mould between the gaps of his fingers, and he longed to touch them, knead them with appreciative squeezes, or have them cushioned around his waist.

Even when Gideon's arm began to shake from exertion, his thick fingers open in Aleron's direction, he didn't lower it as he waited.

His bride was reaching out to *him*. His little human wanted Aleron to join him, but his insides were so knotted and unsure that even a single step forward was too hard.

"You don't have to come in all the way, if you don't want to," Gideon stated with a reassuring smile, his dimples just barely peeking through. "You can just put your feet in."

Just my feet? One hesitantly stepped forward. He found the next one easier. His wings twitched nervously, and his pulse skipped a few beats when he put a foot into the water and then the other.

He wanted to take Gideon's hand, but he was too far away. Aleron sat on the edge when he thought it would help to hide the bewitching human better from his sight. He also didn't want to tower over him, in case it came across as menacing.

But the water did feel nice surrounding him all the way to his knees, and he looked down so he could put his hand into it. In his peripheral, Gideon walked along the shallow bottom of the pool with his hands, before diving under momentarily to wet his hair.

How can one's back be so alluring? Aleron thought as he chanced a glance at his alluring form.

His shirt often hid the deep vee where muscles puffed around his spine. Aleron thought the dip that travelled from the top of Gideon's back all the way to his rounded backside looked like the perfect place to nestle his tongue as he licked up. Or down, depending on where he wanted to go.

His undershorts are see-through. He cupped the end of his snout as his orbs deepened in their purple. He closed them, both to hide the colour from Gideon, and to block his bride from view.

For a few moments, everything was quiet, other than Gideon popping in and out of the water. Aleron followed the sound, and occasionally peeked at him – only to shut his sight once more.

Be calm. He could do this. Hopefully this would be over soon.

Humans like to bathe. If things ever became better between them, he would like to do this with Gideon properly. Aleron thought he may enjoy soaking in its warmth while his little human was upon his lap, naked and easy to touch, tease, and soothe. Perhaps its heat would make it easier for Aleron to steal deep little groans from his firm lips, and he would soak up each one.

Only the subtle rustling of leaves and pleasant sound of trickling played in his ears until it was interrupted by a violent *shaa* of cascading water... right between his legs. Weight settled on his knees, and he flinched and opened his sight to look down.

Gideon's face was less than a foot from the end of his bony snout, his arms resting upon his thighs. Aleron took in a full view of the plane of his stomach, his chest lightly dusted in hair, his little pale nipples.

Fuck. His heart nearly exploded.

"How's the spring?" One side of Gideon's lips lifted into

a crooked smirk. "I told you it was nice."

Too close. He is too close. Aleron froze, seconds from grabbing so he could do... he wasn't sure. Shove his tongue past Gideon's spread lips, dip it into the shell of his ear, grab his chest or round arse?

"Come deeper," Gideon rasped, grabbing his ankle and pulling as if to drag him in.

There *had* to be a name for creatures that could lull unsuspecting Mavka to their watery demise. Suddenly his alluring bride had turned into one, and he was helpless to deny the call.

Aleron let his tail flip forward so he could slide into the water with it between his legs, and laid back against the rock with his wings resting upon the ground. Hopefully now that he'd gotten in, Gideon would leave him be. Hopefully he went to the other side of the pool – but not the deeper area, since there seemed to be a sudden drop into darker blue.

Since Aleron had never sat in warmth like this, he did find it remarkably soothing. Too bad his bride swimming around like a carnivorous fish kept him too tight with tension to truly enjoy it.

Aleron let out panted breaths and lifted his snout to the sky. The sun was bright, but the heat meek in comparison to the water. Somehow, they'd found a piece of summer in the middle of winter.

A bird flew over, snagging his attention.

It squawked, reminding him of all the times he and Ingram used to watch them fly overhead. *If only I had learnt to fly before.* Things would have been different for them.

He managed to snuff the desire in his sight, and it dulled back to its usual pale-pink colouring.

Yet every time he tried to look away to ease himself, that's when Gideon attacked. A set of hands rested on Aleron's knees and then crawled up his straightened legs.

His entire body stiffened, and he looked down just as a light weight settled on his thighs.

Kneeling on top of him, Gideon tilted his head when their gazes connected.

"What are you doing?" Aleron grated out.

"Getting to know you? What better way to do that than when we're both almost bare."

What has gotten into him? Gideon had never been like this with him. He'd been bold, but other than their final intimate moment within Tenebris, he'd never been so forward.

Gideon even grabbed the sides of his snout, and... brushed the pads of his thumbs over his fangs.

"Your teeth are so sharp." Then he tried to pry his mouth apart! "You don't open your mouth much, so it took me a while to learn that your tongue is purple."

Aleron's tongue curled in apprehension as his head lifted, trying to escape him and the oddity of this.

"Can you feel with the bone of your skull, or does it lack sensation?"

Something soft and warm *moulded* against the underside of his jaw, but he couldn't see past his snout to determine what it was. All he knew... was that Gideon had ducked underneath it.

His heart stammered in his chest and became the only thing that moved as he froze, daring not to believe what was pressed against him.

"Can you feel that?" Gideon asked, as hot breath whispered against him and tickled in subtle waves.

Did he just... kiss me? Was it really lips he could feel against his skull?

Alarmingly, his orbs flared purple and remained. Aleron ducked his hand between them to clutch at his seam, worried he would extrude within an instant. His cock throbbed, swelling as blood rapidly filled it and caused him to pant in need.

"Yes," Aleron grated, lifting his snout higher.

"Really?" Gideon's lips fluttered over the bone as he brushed them down the underside of Aleron's jaw. "That's good to know."

Wetness flicked at the corner, a firm, caressing tongue, just as exploring palms slipped up his chest. Aleron's muscles leapt at the foreign touch while a shudder coursed through him.

Aleron gripped Gideon's narrow waist with one hand, unsure if it was to bring him closer or shove him away. The other tightened on his seam until claws bit through his flesh.

His smooth stomach pressed against the back of Aleron's arm as Gideon shifted closer until their chests touched.

Frozen, growing dizzier with each time his bride's lips gently caressed bone, Aleron melted under the foray. Then the male's hands slid higher up Aleron's chest, wound around his neck, and nails scraped his flesh as they dug into the feathers of his back.

"Gideon," he rasped, his mind clouding and his body growing weak.

Why is this happening? Aleron's breaths grew horribly strangled.

Fingertips danced over the base of his wings to ghost up them, and they flapped against the ground before buckling. *Fuuuck.*

A gut clenching, groin quivering, seam twitching shudder ripped through him. Every fibre of fur, every feather, every bit of his flesh tingled. The inhuman parts of him ruffled and puffed, and he desperately wanted to let go of his groin so he could release the unbearable pressure that had shot behind it.

"Stop," Aleron pleaded, feeling too dizzy, suddenly too hot. His pants were so deeply laced in need that he was moments from choking on them.

I cannot breathe. Aleron couldn't think even with his

limited humanity, not with this human lying on him like this. His warm breaths wrapped around Aleron's mind as much as his sweet spring scent.

He was afraid of hurting Gideon, and worried that all this was... misunderstood on his part. *He said getting to know me, as in exploring?* He considered this torture then.

Gideon leaned back with a tight expression. An endless number of unspoken words were shared as his eyes shifted side to side, seeming to search his skull.

The male sighed and pushed off his chest to float backwards. "Fair enough. I just thought since your orbs had turned purple, you wanted me to touch you."

Without thinking, Aleron snatched his wrist. Since he'd been looking away, Gideon brought his gaze back to him, and somehow his chest tightened further.

"You know what it means?" Aleron asked, wondering how that would be possible. He'd done everything to hide his desire for this male in worry of being rejected, or putting needless pressure on their shaky bond. "How?"

Gideon's expression softened. "I remember a few things." When Aleron's grip tightened on him with a whimper, he quickly added, "But not a lot. Just enough."

For a long while, they remained unmoving; Aleron refused to let go, and Gideon willingly stayed.

He knows what it means and yet... he touched me, pressed his lips to me. Aleron wanted it to mean exactly what he hoped it did. That this male... wanted him, in the same way he desperately, achingly, needed him in return.

His heart gave out, his pulse stuttering, when Gideon seemed to sense what Aleron silently pleaded. *Please... touch me, want me.* He crawled back over and placed himself exactly where he'd been just seconds before.

Aleron tensed once more, but this time with nervous anticipation, rather than cold apprehension. His blood boiled when Gideon tentatively placed his palms against Aleron's chest, then dug his fingertips into his fur. The long-awaited sensation caused him to shiver in delight. His lips quirked, then he leaned forward and pressed them to one of Aleron's two longest fangs, not seeming to be put off or wary of them.

"Your heart is beating really fast," Gideon whispered, slipping one hand around his neck again, while the other traced down his abdomen. "And your breaths are short. You sound very excited for me to touch you here."

Gideon cupped the back of Aleron's knuckles where he held back his engorged cock, which was threatening to shove through his seam and knock his hand away.

Leaning forward so his lips were near Aleron's jaw, this seductive little human whispered right near his ear, "I need you to let go if you want me to touch you, Aleron."

Aleron bit back a groan as he lightly shuddered under the weight of his irresistible lure.

For the briefest of seconds, he wondered why Gideon suddenly wanted to be intimate with him. That was only until he realised he didn't *fucking* care, only that his bride was the one asking for it. His reasons didn't matter, whether they be pure or malicious, so long as he was allowed a taste of his little spring.

He often thought of Gideon as a beautiful meadow. However, currently he was a spring of water, slowly eroding away the trepidation of Aleron's worries like rock and earth. If he allowed it, he'd let this human turn into violent, frothing rapids and drown him.

But Aleron knew he'd go willingly, even if it suffocated him.

Unlatching his claws, he parted his fangs in relief when the hard pressure finally escaped him... right into Gideon's awaiting soft palm. Gideon encompassed the head, fully greeting him, and all tension bled out of him.

I want to hold him. That should be allowed, right? All things considered.

Aleron had just enough sense to sheath his claws before he dug his fingers into the smooth, soft skin of Gideon's back at the merest explorative graze he received. Upon his chest, he felt Gideon turn his gaze downwards, and knowing he was watching himself stroke Aleron's throbbing cock caused it to swell.

Aleron buried the end of his snout against the crook of his neck to sniff him, pleased when Gideon tilted his head slightly to give him more surface. The urge to lick pestered Aleron, but once he started, he doubted he'd stop.

"It really is purple," he uttered quietly, surprise rasping his voice.

Quaking with need, Aleron allowed his thoughts to grow quiet as he gave himself over to the little exploring hand. He let his bride do whatever he wanted to Aleron, and say whatever he needed to ensure he kept stroking.

He is touching me... And already it felt wonderful.

Aleron also took the freedom while it was available and traced down Gideon's entire back so his claws and callouses could tickle him. His back bowed, his muscles flexing, and Aleron rumbled with satisfaction when Gideon let out a sharp breath. Gideon lifted his head, and Aleron brushed the side of his jaw against his, so the male's stubble could scratch at the bone of his skull.

As soon as Aleron began nuzzling him affectionately, he lost the ability to cease. All he could do was nuzzle and thoughtlessly let his hands roam, his mind focused on the long-awaited sensations overwhelming him.

The strengthening strokes of two hands going up and down his cock, as they slowly began to squeeze with tightening pressure. The feel of Gideon's facial hair, his breaths rolling down the side of his skull, and the way his skin felt under Aleron's touch starved fingertips.

His shaft swelled, like he was rapidly drawing closer to bliss. Too quickly, but it'd been so long.

Yet a heavy weight laid over his subconscious, one

where he didn't wish to be... alone in this need. Aleron tried to look between them. Gideon's shoulder and his own cock-blocked his view to see if the male was hard as well.

In his peripheral, he noted Gideon's ears had reddened. Just as Aleron brushed one of his hands around the human's side and descended, following the line of his body to Aleron's destination, his eyes averted to the forest. Gideon's hands upon his cock slowed, and even softened the lower Aleron went.

Right before Aleron could brush past his navel, Gideon leant back slightly as if to escape. Aleron halted, desire thickening in his mind, but worry nibbling at it. *Does he not want me to touch him?*

It was too late for Aleron; his cock was hard, freed, and swollen with arousal. He needed release, even if he had to achieve it himself. He just... would have preferred to pleasure his bride in return.

"Since you seem to really like this, I, uh, have an idea." Then Gideon stopped moving altogether before releasing him. "Could you sit on the edge of the pool?"

He grabbed one of his bride's hands and placed it back against the side of his ache. "Do not stop," Aleron pleaded, nudging the tip of his snout against his temple encouragingly. "I will not touch, if that is what you want."

"I'm not stopping." He bit at his bottom lip, before the high arches of his cheeks seemed to pinken. "I just... want to try something."

Aleron did as he was told, simply because he didn't want to deny Gideon, in case he stopped altogether. His tail flicked over the edge, but as he moved to sit, he noted how wide Gideon's eyes became with Aleron's cock less than an inch from his face.

The male recovered quickly, came forward, and lifted up. Aleron didn't even have time to grow nervous, not when Gideon immediately wrapped his hands around him once more.

"You are not following?" Aleron asked, disappointed he'd remained in the water.

He was further away now. *Is he only doing this... for me?* He didn't know if he liked the idea of being pitied.

A wicked glint shone in Gideon's eyes as he angled them up to his skull. The sly smirk that curled his lips looked mischievous, and Aleron shuddered under the power this human somehow had over him. Suddenly he didn't care if it was pity, especially when his bride licked at the seam of his lips as though hungry.

"No," Gideon stated, coming closer. "I'm fine down here between your thighs."

At first, he thought Gideon weirdly just wanted to examine his cock and tentacles. He didn't mind, enjoying the perverted image of his bride's gaze and face so close to them, while his hands gave long and hard strokes. The curious male came so close that his breath wrapped around the head, and a groan fell from Aleron's parted fangs.

He looks nice there.

He parted his thighs so he could get a better view, needing to twist his head so he could see past his snout.

Gideon struck.

Brushing his tongue over Aleron's cock from the groove right behind the flared rim of the head, he darted it to the rounded tip. The sweep was made up of a textured wetness, and Aleron thickened as a deep thrum radiated up the length and clutched his entire groin in pleasure.

"You licked me," he grated hoarsely.

Aleron couldn't believe it.

He licked– Gideon encompassed the sensitive tip with his entire mouth. Hot softness greeted Aleron when his tongue lapped forward, while his lips pillowed him.

A growl tore from his throat, and his hand darted forward to fist what he could of Gideon's hair. Aleron kept him there as shudders wracked him, his wings tightening against his back and quivering. His other hand dug its claws into the rock of the ledge, threatening to crack a chunk off.

"I did." Gideon's eyes peeked up at him, his little tongue darting out. "Did I not do this before?"

"No," he stated with a gruff pant.

Something akin to giddiness seemed to take over his features. Gideon swirled his tongue and moved his lips back and forth over what he could, being messy as he wildly lapped at Aleron. Each twirl had his talons twitching until his feet curled inwards in profound pleasure.

At the same time, Gideon's hands worshipped up and down the sides of him, until one drew up and the other descended into his tentacles. Gideon cupped deep as he explored, then gently grazed the two ovals at the base that forced a bliss-filled yelp to burst from Aleron.

For the longest while, even before this, Aleron had been wondering why everything felt so much more intense. His cock hardening here had a completely different and more extreme feeling than in the afterworld.

In Tenebris, Gideon's touch had elicited pleasure, but the *pressure* deep within was muted in comparison. His thighs hadn't shaken like this as his muscles leapt and twitched from even the lightest of intimate forays. His tentacles had gripped, but they hadn't ached to hold his bride down as Aleron's pleasure built and built until the need to ease it had his brain melting.

Breathing in the afterworld had been easy, but now each one stung – like he couldn't take in enough air. There had been no scent to wrap around his senses, leaving Aleron panting wildly through drool. Gideon had felt so soft and warm, yet his tongue and lips felt hot in comparison, scalding him with pleasure.

And, as Gideon bobbed his head, stroked up the thickened length of Aleron, and caressed his embedded ovals, Gideon had Aleron clenching hard. The mind-numbing pressure suddenly eased as something travelled up his shaft, yet it filled his entire body with violent heat, need, and desperation until Aleron thought he was moments from disintegrating.

A pearly, thick liquid bubbled at the tip of his cock, just as a pant exploded from him.

"Your cock self-lubricates," Gideon mumbled against him, feathering his lips so he could nibble down the side of Aleron's cock. He even sucked here and there.

He stole some of it, leaving patches that quickly re-moistened from his deep, ground-clenching arousal. *More.* He wanted Gideon to lick and suck him clean, only to do it again and again.

"And your cum kind of tastes nice, like your scent." Then he licked just behind the head repeatedly, dipping his tongue into the groove. A new, tender spot had been discovered. His skull tilted back while his sight blackened and faded from existence under the onslaught. "Looks like your frenulum is sensitive like a human's. You're really not that different."

"Fuck, little spring," he pathetically whimpered.

He'd wanted to thaw his bride, not have him evaporate Aleron with his damn mouth and hands.

"These are different, but they're kind of cute." Gideon pushed his stroking hand into his tentacles so they could latch on. Then he laughed as he said, "Your dick is pretty. Like a purple flower."

Aleron's snout fell to his chest as he shook his head. His bride was rambling, complimenting him, as he petted his cock. Each word damaged his heart in the most blissful way, leaving it tender and bruised.

It was all too intense, so he gripped Gideon's hair tight and shoved his mouth back over the end of his cock to shut him up. He was close, dangerously close, and he wanted this to end. Pent up and needy. For so long, he'd been deprived of this, and he ached.

If I had known he could lick me... I would have made him do it in the afterworld. He would have done it back. *Pretty male, with pretty lips on my cock.*

Aleron didn't realise what he was doing wrong until Gideon bit down hard. He snarled at the pain, his sight flaring red, even as it made his groin clench from the sharp thrill of it. He pulled the naughty human's head back with the intention of warning him.

"Don't push," Gideon choked out, his glare hard. "You'll break my jaw doing that." Then his features softened, and he gave the tip a gentle kiss. "Let me do it."

Distrust was obvious as Gideon untangled Aleron's clawed fingers from his hair and placed his tense hand on his shoulder instead. Aleron had made a mistake and had been hurting his precious bride. He caressed his thumb over his smooth skin of his collarbone to show his appreciation for still being permitted to touch – and that Gideon wasn't stopping.

Yet, the closer Aleron got, the more his hand inched up to grab Gideon's hair again, only to remember the warning and brush through it in a caress.

I want deeper. He wanted Gideon's mouth to swallow him whole until he disappeared. *I want inside him.* Like in Tenebris, where he'd pumped into Gideon until he collapsed in tiredness and thrust until he fell asleep, not truly satisfied but utterly content.

I want to fill him again, have him moan for me again. Aleron wanted to hear Gideon plead for his cock not to go soft as he pleasured himself until they both came.

Aleron didn't know what shoved him violently over the edge. If it was the memory of that time, or what Gideon was currently doing to him. Perhaps it was his bride's eyes raised up to Aleron as he did this, looking at him, seeing who and what he was tasting and stroking without hesitancy. Something caused a trickle down his spine, one that clutched at his groin until everything clenched.

Aleron bit out a groan so choked it came out silent.

His head shot back, his maw parting on a deep exhale, as liquid climbed up his cock. Fuck, that didn't happen in Tenebris either. Euphoria smashed into him when his girth swelled repeatedly and that hot liquid expelled straight into Gideon's mouth, blackening his sight again.

Yet, his damn heart soared at the same time, and he wondered if it was possible for it to gain wings and flap out of him. It'd stopped, gone missing, as he quaked through his pleasure. Whines broke from him, his body tense, as more liquid climbed, only to burst from his constantly pulsating cock.

All the while, a tongue lapped at Aleron and a hand petted the clenching ovals at the base of him, currently causing him immense rapture. It felt like the human was trying to completely drain them.

Gideon let out a grunted choke, but kept teasing until the last drop came from him.

Gideon pulled back, just as the arm Aleron used to support himself threatened to cave in. Shocks twitched his muscles as his pants came out frantic, trying to catch those he'd lost from seizing lungs. His sight fell, and his head shook in confusion at the bliss that had threatened to kill him.

White liquid trickled from Gideon's lips and he reached up to catch it before it dripped from his chin. "Holy shit. I didn't expect so much."

"Something came out of me?" Aleron rasped, looking down at his softening cock.

It lay between his thighs, dangling, and he'd never seen it be anything but a hard, jutting, pulsating rod. He'd also never experienced the deflating satisfaction that gripped it before, either.

Gideon paused, eyes widening, and he lifted them to Aleron's orbs. "Why are you surprised by that? Didn't it happen before?"

"No."

"That was your first time producing semen?" When Aleron tilted his head, never hearing the word before, Gideon mimicked him. "Cum? ...Seed then?" He shook his head, and a slight rattle came from him. "Well, that was my first time swallowing so much of it. It's a little odd to think that the only thing I've eaten in nearly a month is your cum."

Aleron gulped down a copious amount of drool. Why did hearing that satisfy him so much? A piece of him was inside this male, a substance he brought forth and willingly gulped down.

Aleron could also smell it staining his face, mingling with Gideon's scent, and the strange... possessive marking had a dark emotion striking across his torso. It even made his orbs flare dark green, a colour that had never penetrated his sight before. The more Gideon wiped at his chin, and even licked at his lips, moving it around and tasting Aleron's scent, the deeper the hue became.

His semi-soft cock jerked, just as his gaze darted down when he realised Gideon was kneeling upright.

Almost completely see-through, his undershorts clung to a jutting erection that tented them. Hair pressed against the inside, cradling his balls, and the pink head was easily noticeable. Since his skin tended to shield him when he was soft, Aleron had only seen Gideon's tip when he was fully engorged – like now.

He is turned on. By this, by Aleron, and by what he'd just done.

"Now I'm hoping you won't be so shy," Gideon admitted coyly with a hum, just as he shuffled back on his knees to sink into the water.

Something about seeing his arousal, while he marked in Aleron's release, snapped the last tether of his mind. Right after his bride erotically sucked his very essence right out of his cock, he intended to flee with *that* in his pants?

His hold on his control withered away like ash.

A dangerous snarl tore from Aleron and then he pounced.

I will not let you escape so easily.

THIRTY-ONE

A surprised yell bellowed from Gideon when he was grabbed and flung forward, only for it to cut short with a gasp when his back hit the ground. He barely had time to register what happened before Aleron knelt around Gideon on his hands and knees, trapping him.

A soft, rumbling growl vibrated the air. It sounded dangerous, a menacing, lustful forewarning. Goosebumps trailed down Gideon's chest and through his scalp before a shiver tightened his flesh as a drool-coated tongue slipped across his jaw and over his ear.

Yet a stifled chuckle burned the bottom of his lungs.

There he is. I wondered if he'd snap out of it. And by that, he meant when this Duskwalker would finally lose his shit and do something!

Sure, Gideon hadn't appreciated his jaw almost unhinging when Aleron tried to shove his face on his dick. He chose to think of it as evidence of his lust-addled mind being filled with passion.

It was better than the alternative: disinterest, or... restless cautiousness.

So, he pushed and pushed Aleron's boundaries.

Stroking him clearly hadn't been enough. Aleron had still been too calm, so Gideon wondered if he could unravel the Duskwalker with his mouth instead. Learning it was

Aleron's first experience with it... he'd amped up his playfulness. Gideon tried to be perverted and erotic with his words, caressing Aleron not only physically, but mentally.

Anything to see if he could break down the barrier between them. He'd needed to be daring. He knew this Duskwalker desired him, and if Aleron wasn't going to act on it, then Gideon needed to be the one who did.

Gideon needed to show him that he *was* wanted.

Which is why, when Aleron incessantly licked his neck, Gideon didn't fight him. He also arched into his touch when Aleron ran his rough palm down Gideon's chest, abrading his hardened, sensitive nipple in the process. His sharp claws made Gideon want to burst out of his skin with how gently they caressed him, but the snap of his body twisting had been from the excited thrill of them.

Gideon was a big boy. Perhaps not a smart one, but he chose to believe he could protect himself if need be; that he'd be able to control the situation should the need arise.

For now, he would let what happened, happen.

Aleron wouldn't intentionally hurt him. Gideon would allow this Duskwalker to do whatever he wanted, to a point, if it meant he could finally see the real him.

He'd be open to Aleron, even if it was a little confusing and strange.

Gideon did squirm slightly when Aleron folded his tongue against his ear, leaving a trail of saliva his warm breath rolled over afterwards. His stomach rippled with tension when claw tips brushed down through the hair between his navel and pelvis. Gideon thrust into his massive hand when he gently cupped his cock and then his sensitive balls, thankful the Duskwalker seemed to know not to squeeze too hard.

"You are hard for me," Aleron grated with a rumbling growl. Gideon flinched when his purple tongue licked across the entire bottom of his face, and his short stubble scraping against it tingled his ears. "You like the taste of me?"

When Gideon parted his lips to respond, he let out a huff of surprise when Aleron took the opportunity to stuff his mouth. *Nhn. His tongue is huge.* Long and tapered, it licked from one cheek to the other.

Oddly enough, his saliva was sweet, like the lubricant that had been covering his cock. He didn't mind drinking it down, especially since Aleron was being considerate enough not to care that the remnants of his seed still lingered.

The probing, flexible muscle pulled away and left his lips tingling afterwards until Gideon was forced to run his tongue along the seam of his mouth to ease the sensation.

Aleron licked at Gideon's neck while deeply burying his nose hole against his jugular. Gideon's breath deepened, and Aleron seemed to come closer until his furry spread thighs brushed the sides of Gideon's closed ones.

"Why do you have to smell so good?" Aleron said on a low whine. "Do you know how hard it has been not to drink from your skin?"

"I didn't know I smelled nice." To be honest, Gideon thought he'd smelt like forest, dirt, and sweat up until his bath. Still, he entertained it, letting the Duskwalker be his beastly self. "What do I smell like?"

"I am not completely sure," Aleron whispered, tasting his neck, his collarbone, and then chest. "You smell like patchouli, and purple stem flowers. I have seen them, touched them, smelt them, but I do not know their name."

Aleron carefully nibbled Gideon's flesh with his front fangs before striking his tongue across the nipple he hadn't abraded earlier. Gideon flinched and lifted his chest slightly in welcome.

That sounds like maybe... lavender? Then again, the world was big, and he didn't know all the plants.

Before he could linger on it, a gasp shot out of him when his underwear was *torn* from him! He didn't even realise

Aleron had ripped his claws into them.

Gideon had no urge to cover himself, even when the Duskwalker made a trail down his body. Although precious blood, and therefore sense, was exiting his brain to pump heavily into his cock, he was remarkably calm.

I wasn't originally going to let him do this. He'd wanted it, but had also just wanted to give. *But if this is what he wants...* Then of course he'd be happy to lie there and let Aleron enjoy himself.

Water sloshed when Aleron backed up and stood, moving around Gideon's body rather than shoving it across the rough rock beneath him.

Gideon let him lift a leg and draw his tongue down the inside of it, playing and tasting. The sight of it was erotic with the way Aleron's skull glinted with gold in the sunlight, his purple tongue trailing a line everywhere it went.

This Duskwalker had earned his trust to do what he desired.

Emphasis on *had*. He considered rescinding it when the fucker licked between his toes and nearly had Gideon booting him in the head. It tickled, felt wrong, yet his dick tapped against his pelvis anyway.

Gideon threw his arm across his face when it heated in embarrassment as a drop of precum welled from those particular ministrations.

I'm starting to feel really weird.

Everywhere this Duskwalker explored, he left behind a trail of sensitivity. Even Gideon's thigh twitched open further when he licked up the length of it this time, and his dick throbbed in anticipation. Aleron caressed the other leg with a rough hand, wanting to stimulate both of them, and it left Gideon panting.

With heavy lids, Gideon lifted his arm up just enough so he could peek underneath it and watch his skull come closer to where he hoped Aleron went next.

He tried to remain relaxed, even when Aleron pushed his knee up and to the side. Gideon was strong for a human, but he wasn't all that flexible since he had a decent amount of muscle. It did make Gideon feel as though this Duskwalker was less likely to break him when he grabbed the back of his thigh too hard and lowered his skull.

Before today, the idea of a fanged maw coming so close to his privates had been concerning. Now it seemed to excite Gideon to the point he let out strained huffs through damp lips.

Gideon's head shot back, his back arching, when Aleron's firm, drool-coated, warm tongue slipped between the cleft of his arse, over the tight hole, and his guiche. He hadn't expected Aleron to go straight for his asshole, so by the time he was licking across Gideon's balls and up his cock, he'd already become a trembling mess.

"Holy shit," Gideon groaned out, pushing on Aleron's snout with both hands so he had something to hold on to.

Why did that feel so good?

And when the Duskwalker did it a second time, his lungs seized, and he spread his legs wider.

"You seem to like it when I lick here," Aleron stated with a pant, before tonguing his hole repeatedly. "I want to teach my tongue all your favourite places."

It wasn't his first time receiving a rim job, but it sure as hell felt entirely freaking different. Aleron's tongue was more textured, hotter, wetter, and much longer than a human's. The sensation was odd, wrong, and yet he couldn't deny how much his body was responding to it.

Gideon even groaned as Aleron dabbed harder, and harder, until he felt it opening the tight ring. *Fuck. Thank goodness I just had a bath before he–* It shot forward, an inch or two sinking inside him, and Gideon tensed.

"Shit! Fuck, wait," he pleaded, pushing on his snout. His hands shook, body trembling as Gideon kept him from sinking deeper, yet Aleron didn't back away and Gideon was forced to throb around his tongue. "W-wait."

At least it was lubricated, but it still felt like he'd just had one of Aleron's big fingers inserted into him. It was tapered but quickly thickened.

His whole body flushed, goosebumps breaking out across his chest and arms. The suddenness of it brought mild pain and uncomfortableness, but there had also been a spark of... pleasure.

"You are much tighter than before." The fact Aleron could fucking *talk* while his tongue was buried partially within Gideon caused him to clench.

He looked down, only to find a fanged maw parted around his pelvis and purple orbs looking up at him. Somehow, Gideon found the colour comforting, and it eased the tension that had locked his muscles. It helped that his white skull glittered with gold, and it kind of sweetly dazzled him.

"Slowly," Aleron reassured. "Gentle?"

Aleron pulled his tongue back, only to press it forward and a little deeper than before. Gideon wasn't entirely sure how he felt about this, but if this was what Aleron wanted to do...

Dammit. I told myself I would just welcome it.

He tentatively nodded.

Since Gideon didn't eat, there was nothing unseemly for Aleron to taste. He was clean, empty, and he realised in that moment he probably wouldn't ever willingly swallow anything in the future – except maybe Aleron's cum. It did taste rather nice, like his scent with a hint of salt.

The deeper Aleron went, the easier it became. *It kind of feels like a finger, but softer.* He liked that it was soft and malleable, gently coaxing him to accept it rather than forcing it upon him.

His body adjusted to the foreign sensation and then melted for it when Aleron thrust it back and forth. Aleron twisted and swirled that strong, flexible muscle, and Gideon was so sensitive that it felt amazing. Aleron kept rubbing it against a spot Gideon hadn't been familiar with in a long time, one he forgot could clutch his groin until precum constantly dribbled.

Seed clung between the tip of his dick and his abdomen as Gideon subtly rocked his hips.

You acted all cute and shy... Gideon's lips parted as he tried to breathe through the twisted pleasure shuddering his lungs. His eyes crinkled with deepening arousal, his head hot and growing dizzier by the second. *But just look at what you're doing to me.*

Gideon let out a few soft groans, trying his hardest not to come from simply this. Thankfully the sun was beginning to go down, otherwise he thought it would painfully pierce his dilated pupils.

Huffs fluttered out of Gideon as he watched from behind his forearm, while his other hand remained shaking as he steadied himself on the end of Aleron's snout. *Holy hell. Why does that feel so damn good?* A meek groan fell from .him when that flexible muscle continuously flicked against his prostate, making his cock jerk and jump each time.

By the time Aleron finally pulled away, Gideon was a puddle of need. His balls felt fuller than before, his cock so hard it hurt, like he'd turned to stone, and the aching need to come pestered him. Gideon considered pushing Aleron's snout back down so he could keep going.

The only reason Gideon hadn't started stroking himself was because this was the first time he was experiencing all this with Aleron.

His past self didn't matter. What he could barely remember wasn't important. Right now, for him, it was their first intimate moment, and he wasn't going to rob either one of them of it just so he could get off as fast as possible.

Oversensitive now, when Aleron licked over his balls, he

hissed out a sharp breath. But it was the Duskwalker *sniffing* him and hunting a scent that almost had Gideon shutting his legs. Even if he wanted to, Aleron placed himself in the way and dabbed his tongue against his... stomach?

He looked down to find Aleron was licking up the little puddle of pearly white precum from his abdomen.

For some stupid reason, he found that more perverted than what Aleron had just been doing to him. It felt more primal, more beastly, and just reminded Gideon he had a monstrous Duskwalker between his thighs.

He also got to witness the way Aleron's wings snapped back in reaction, and how his purple orbs darkened in their hue. Aleron released a harrowing groan, and his entire body shook like he was trying to shake out a shiver racing down his feathered spine.

Then Gideon's cock was gone from view.

Parting his fangs and shoving down, Aleron's tongue swirled completely around the length of Gideon's shaft. The strange sensation of being wrapped up in a firm, flexible limb, one that moved up and down while moving his foreskin, twirling as it did, had Gideon seeing night in the daytime.

Aleron's tongue somehow managed to squeeze him, flicking over the rim of his head. It wonderfully abraded the tip and even slipped over his frenulum.

"Aleron," Gideon groaned out, unable to mistake the feeling for anything or anyone else. No human could do this, touch him like this, and he fisted both the Duskwalker's horns to root himself through it.

Gideon used them to thrust, his hips desperate to move as if that would help him achieve orgasm. Rather, Aleron's claws sliding down his trembling inner thigh, teasing him even further, shoved him much closer. He squished his skull with his thighs when they shut, only to open them, and then close them as he began to mindlessly thrust.

He was already so close, and Gideon chased his orgasm.

Seeming to sense he needed more friction, Aleron coiled his tongue faster. Drool spread over Gideon, making the glide slippery. His stomach dipped, and his nose wrinkled on one side as he gritted his teeth through a pitiful moan.

"I'm about to come," he rasped, fisting Aleron's horns tighter until Gideon worried he'd crush them in his firm grip.

Aleron went faster still until Gideon could barely make sense of the movement, only that it felt fucking *sublime*. His hips jerked and twitched, and his back bowed and tensed repeatedly. His eyes crinkled as he looked down, his lips parting on a strangled groan.

His balls drew up tight. *Fuck, I'm coming.* They pulsated, as did his cock, and his eyes became dazed. Goosebumps danced across his flesh as they burrowed down to make his muscles twitch.

Aleron's skull grew blurry, but he knew with absolute certainty... he was releasing ropes of semen up his purple tongue.

He was coming inside a Duskwalker's dangerous maw, and with the way it burst from him, Gideon knew it was the hardest he'd ever released. He was likely hitting the roof of Aleron's mouth, or the back of his throat, and yet Gideon could do nothing else but ride the waves of his bliss.

His shaft jerked with each spurt, and his lungs seized in time with the pulses. On and on, white-hot pleasure burst within his mind, and his groin, nibbling away at him.

When it finally ceased, Aleron was slow to release him. His tongue smacked inside his mouth as he tasted him and then slipped across his fangs.

His frenetic growl afterwards should have sent fear through Gideon. He should have taken it for the warning it was. Instead, it tingled every nerve and cell of his body until he just shivered in response.

With his heart racing, his oxygen-starved lungs rapidly

heaving for breath, and his satisfied muscles lax, Gideon didn't move an inch when Aleron crawled up his body. His tongue seemed to go everywhere. It roamed like it wanted to taste every inch of Gideon's skin: the vee line of his hips, between his abdomen muscles, up his sternum, and over a nipple.

He figured the Duskwalker would have another raging erection jutting from between his hips. If Aleron wanted to use Gideon's torso as a masturbation tool right now, he was too sated to mind. So long as this ended with them both much emptier, he'd be content.

Aleron slipped his hand underneath Gideon's head to cage it in a set of claws, and buried the end of his snout into the crook of his neck.

"Gideon," Aleron rasped, and Gideon heard the desperation in it, the need and craving he'd been denying.

The way Aleron's snorted breaths wrapped around his throat as he licked across his Adam's apple had Gideon gulping for air. Gideon tried to nuzzle him, to show Aleron he was accepted.

Only for him to clamp up when the head of Aleron's cock nestled against the tight ring of his ass. *Not what I meant!* His knees buckled inwards, and he shoved against his chest to separate them when Aleron tried to push it into him.

"W-wait," Gideon whispered hoarsely. "I'm too tight. I won't be able to take you."

He'd need more than just his tongue as preparation!

Aleron had been so thick in his hands that he'd needed to utilise both of them to handle the girth. He couldn't even fit in his mouth without breaking his jaw. It'd been far too long for Gideon, and Aleron was just too big for this to even be possible right now.

The excited Duskwalker above him didn't seem to be listening. He twirled his tongue into the shell of his ear, as if he knew it would disarm Gideon.

Aleron purred, "You have taken me before, little spring."

With Gideon's hands on his chest, he could feel how fast Aleron's heart was beating, how rapid his breaths were. His body was so hot it felt like fire, and every inhuman part of him was ruffled until the Duskwalker almost looked like a giant fuzzy ball.

Aleron wasn't just excited; he was delirious with pent-up lust. And finally given freedom to touch Gideon.

When Aleron pushed a little harder, realising he needed more pressure, Gideon was just thankful his cock had its own lubricant, so Aleron didn't tear him already.

Gideon did the only thing he could think of to get through to this horny Duskwalker.

He brought his hand up, and with the bottom of his fist where it was padded, Gideon landed a singular hard punch downwards on his damn bony forehead. That got him to stop. His orbs flashed bright red, before turning white, and then fading back to the purple of before.

So many emotions. It just made it obvious that Aleron wasn't thinking straight. His heart was likely all over the place, and Gideon was aware he was the reason for it.

"You punched me," Aleron whined, placing his hand on his forehead, even though Gideon doubted it hurt.

Grabbing the sides of his head, Gideon held Aleron still so he could kiss the end of his snout. "You're hurting me. I need you to calm down, okay? Sex isn't going to be possible."

He'd always known this may have been a possibility, and he'd had other ways to bring Aleron back to sense. Gideon just hadn't wanted to boot his big dick with the heel of his foot and possibly hurt them both.

Then Gideon reached down and grabbed the Duskwalker's cock to push it out – since the head was wedged partially inside him.

"I am sorry," Aleron rasped, shuddering at his grasp but

still backing his hips up. When Gideon pulled and directed it, Aleron thrust forward. His slime-coated cock slid up Gideon's, and tentacles wrapped around his thighs when they were hip to hip. "I do not want to hurt you."

"I know," Gideon whispered back, burying his face into his furry neck when Aleron began to move his hips back and forth. Gideon held onto Aleron's cock with one hand, giving him something to thrust into.

I'm just glad that worked. He was immensely enjoying this and didn't want it to end sourly.

Aleron moved his hand from the back of Gideon's head to cover his palm where it still lay on the ground. His claws dug into rock until he managed to fist Gideon's hand, to hold and capture it. Aleron's other hand came down to wrap around Gideon's as it stroked, clamping it to his cock.

His snout pressed into the side of Gideon's head, sniffing on every groaning inhale, as Aleron started to fuck the thick head wildly into their combined hold.

Although Gideon's shaft wasn't being stroked by their palms, the bottom half of Aleron's hot cock constantly slid over him. The longer it happened, the more he twitched and began to harden. The groove underneath kind of pillowed Gideon and kept him in place, rather than slipping side to side. He liked how wet everything had grown, which stopped any chafing friction. The two rings three-quarters of the way down were firm, but it added to the strangeness that had him panting with rekindling desire.

Gideon didn't mind having this Duskwalker's massive body bearing down on him. More and more, he liked it, especially since Aleron gave off heat and his fur was unbelievably soft – it tickled him all over. Aleron felt strong, masculine, and his growly groan had tremors running down Gideon's back.

His scent showered Gideon in a new sense of home, and he nuzzled into his fur to take it in deeply.

"Gideon," Aleron groaned against his ear, messily

licking the same spot at the corner of his jaw repeatedly. His hips quaked and jerked as Aleron fucked into their hands harder, faster, until he'd turned into a rutting beast. "You smell so good. *Feel* so good. I just want to eat you whole."

Aleron had completely lost his mind and started babbling his way to his orgasm. Aleron told him how much he wanted inside Gideon, how soft yet tight he'd be. How he wanted Gideon's body to hold him. Aleron even pleaded for it, without trying to take action.

Aleron had, for now, let go.

I wouldn't have been able to accept any of this before. Aleron's intensity was a lot stronger than Gideon had anticipated, and it would have freaked him out. But now? He just let Aleron do or say whatever he pleased, so long as it brought the Duskwalker closer to his impending release.

It all felt good for him too.

"Come for me, Aleron," Gideon rasped, trying to help him along. "Cleanse me in your pleasure."

His torso was absolutely about to be washed in seed, so he just embraced it. There was a bath at their feet, and he planned to put them both back inside it once this Duskwalker was content.

Aleron shuddered, but didn't come. Gideon didn't like that.

Gideon bit through the collar of fur to dig his teeth into the side of Aleron's neck as hard as he could muster, hoping it would be the answer. Aleron's entire body clenched, the elbows of his wings slammed against the ground, and his skull snapped back. Aleron's fangs parted as he let out a violent roar, one that pierced Gideon's eardrums and made him wince.

Yet the heavy, thick, and hot ropes of cum shooting between them were all that mattered. Gideon moved his hand up and down to help Aleron push it out as it covered his chest and throat.

Every stroke seemed to have this Duskwalker quaking wilder and wilder, deeper tension locking his muscles.

There we go. Come nice and hard for me.

When nothing was left, Aleron partially collapsed on top of him, softly thrusting to nurse himself through the striking aftershocks. They rattled Aleron, and had every part of him twitching.

Aleron eventually fell to the side, still gripping both of Gideon's hands like he didn't wish to let go of them. His chest heaved quickly, his breaths so hot Gideon felt the billow of each one across his scalp.

"Feel better now?" Gideon asked with a sly smile, curling his lips as he ignored his current erection.

The cute little whine that echoed from Aleron while his legs softly kicked had him beaming.

I bet you do.

With both of them huffing, the Duskwalker a sated heap next to him, Gideon turned a grin to the dusk-filled sky.

A colony of bats chirped, squawked, and chittered as they lifted from the trees like swarming clouds. They fluttered across the sky, darkening it even further, and they somehow reminded him of Aleron and his magnificent skull.

Gideon had a new appreciation for bats, since he had his own fluffy sky puppy.

Hopefully everything is easier between us from now on.

With the last of his twitches finally dissipating, Aleron softened his grip on Gideon's hands.

When they both released his cock, his tentacles swirled halfway up its length protectively. He'd never felt satisfied like this before. He'd never wanted to just simply lay there as a huffing mess until he eventually succumbed to sleep.

With his bride covered in his scent, the taste of him upon Aleron's tongue, and his heart swollen for what this all meant, he thought it may have been peaceful.

Instead, movement brought him back to full alertness.

"The sun is almost gone," Gideon said, his voice hoarse and weakened. The male sat up, incidentally pulling out of the last of Aleron's hold. "We better wash up."

"Why?" Aleron asked, raising himself on straightened arms before shifting back to stand in the water.

Before Aleron could stop him, Gideon slipped neck high into the water himself. "In case a Demon comes?" His tone said that should have been obvious.

That was not what I meant, Aleron thought, as he turned to Gideon, who had ducked beneath the surface to wash his face and head. *Why must we wash?* He'd been mollified at having his bride covered in his marking, like some strange, unknown need had been accomplished.

He didn't like that Gideon immediately wished to remove it.

Did I do something wrong?

When Gideon came up for air, swiping back his hair as he rubbed at his face, Aleron's sight shifted to orange.

Yes. Now that Aleron thought about it, he had done something wrong.

Unable to contain the desire, he reached out to the little human currently on his knees and washing his chest with his back facing him. Did he not wish to look upon Aleron anymore, like before? He didn't want that to be true.

Aleron hesitated at the last second, crouching slightly until his tail slipped against the ground, which stopped him from going lower. Deciding to just brave it, he brushed the back of his knuckle over the rounded top of his bride's ear.

"I am... sorry," he stated softly.

With his brows drawn, Gideon swiftly twisted to face him. Then he let out a sharp breath. Water splashed as he turned completely and launched forward to cup the sides of Aleron's head.

"Holy shit. Why are your orbs orange?"

Concern was evident in every one of the lines in his furrowed forehead, the tightness of his lips, and even the muscle ticking in his jaw.

Surprised by Gideon's expression, the oddity of him asking about his sight colour change, and the way he held his bony face, Aleron reared back slightly. Only to hold Gideon's wrists to keep his soft hands against his skull as Aleron peered into piercing green eyes reflecting his own face.

"I did not mean to hurt you." Not just once, but twice.

And that was only what Gideon had been vocal about. Were there other times Aleron had foolishly harmed him? He'd bitten the male a few times, not enough to break skin, but he could see the bruising imprints of his fangs on Gideon's leg, even through the water.

What I almost did... If Gideon hadn't stopped him the many times he'd needed stopping, Aleron would have hurt his precious bride.

He'd been so excited, finally receiving some of the attention he'd been starved for, that Aleron acted thoughtlessly. He'd let his instincts take over when he should have wisely held back.

A mild chuckle fell from his lips. "It's fine, Aleron. You stopped when I asked."

Grumbling, as he wasn't satisfied with that answer, Aleron only released Gideon's hands because it was obvious he wanted them back. Gideon's lips parted to say something, just as Aleron intended to apologise more.

A hissing squabble from the other side of the mountain rendered them both silent. They simultaneously looked into the shade of the forest.

Currently where they stood, the last of the day's light shone over them. Not much longer, and the entire area would be shielded in shadow.

"There are Demons nearby," Aleron informed him. "There are not many, but their scent lingers here, as if they live within the mountain."

Aleron pointed to the peak behind Gideon. It wasn't a large mountain, but it would be plenty of cover for those that didn't wish to go back to the Veil.

"You're kidding me," Gideon bit out. His nose crinkled as he let out a disgruntled groan. "I was hoping we could camp here for the night. We better hurry up then."

Then the human cupped some water and brought it to Aleron's chest, and he tilted his head at him for it. None of Gideon's scent was upon Aleron, only his own. It clumped the fur on his stomach and pelvis, and even coated his shaft currently slipping back inside him.

His head tilted the other way when Gideon's ears reddened as he proceeded to wash Aleron as well.

He is cleaning me? Perhaps his original assumption of Gideon rejecting his marking was incorrect. He'd like it to be. *Is cleaning afterwards a human custom?*

Then he remembered a time from Tenebris.

When a human male had helped to wash a female with a wet cloth, soothing her and giving 'aftercare' as Gideon had explained. *He is caring for me?*

When the worst of it was rinsed off by the handfuls of water sluiced over his chest, Gideon stood. Then a dimness slipped over them, and Gideon bounced out of the water and rushed to his clothes.

"We're cutting it close." Hopping around on one foot at a time, he shoved his legs into his pants. "Maybe if we head towards the border, we can find a good spot to camp for the night."

Aleron watched him for a few moments before standing fully and looking down at himself. The orange in his sight faded to dark yellow as he touched his wet abdomen. *We touched.*

Of course he hadn't expected it. In Tenebris, Aleron had needed to be the one to instigate such intimacy. *Does this mean he feels the same way as me?* He wanted to ask, to know.

Aleron brought his gaze back to Gideon, who was slipping his arms through his shirt sleeves. *But in the afterworld... even after we touched, he asked all these silly, confusing questions.*

He'd still been hesitant with Aleron.

Cupping the top of his skull, he dug his claws in, wishing he could think clearly. Why did all the answers seem obvious, and he just couldn't grasp them?

The male picked up his guitar case and swiftly turned to him. "Well?" Gideon offered a small smile, and it was like a balm to Aleron's aching mind and heart. "Are you going to hop out of the water, or have you decided you want to become a fish?"

That smile, that humour... just his bride being his old self, let Aleron know it would be okay. He needed that more than anything right then.

He found himself chuckling as he lifted a leg out of the water to step up onto dry land. "Only if fish can fly."

I can ponder later. For now, I must keep him safe.

THIRTY-TWO

Holding a rolled-up piece of parchment, Gideon ran up a small hill of swaying grass. He looked over his shoulder and narrowed his eyes at the town just behind him with a large cornfield right beside it.

Greenshire had been less than friendly.

When he made it to the top of the incline, he ran his fingers through his hair in annoyance, shoving it back – only for some of it to flick forward. He lacked the sap gel that used to hold his hair the way he preferred it.

Crouching to stay hidden in the daylight, Aleron met him.

He's annoyed with me. Gideon's lips tightened. *I can't say that I don't blame him, even though it's not my fault.*

At least things between them seemed less tense after yesterday. Sure, it meant Gideon often blushed when he remembered what they'd done to each other – that neither had chosen to speak of since – but he could tell the air between them no longer seemed to be laced with wariness.

Instead, at times, he thought it may be charged with something else, something *more*.

Whatever it was, it often caused his heart to flutter bashfully in his chest. It'd softened him to Aleron immensely.

Gideon scanned his gaze over his twisting goat horns to

his glittering bat skull, until his eyes fell onto his fangs. Fangs that had parted so Aleron could nearly lick him from head to toe, nibbling along the way.

Shit. He quickly looked away when his chest and groin lurched at the same time. *Every time I look at his fangs now, my body gets weird.*

"Sorry that took me so long," Gideon stated, pushing a pout into his voice in an attempt to be cute – despite knowing he wasn't a very adorable person. "When I asked them about Emerie, they detained me and questioned why I wanted to find her. Apparently, she's not only a wanted criminal for deserting the guild, but she also stole from a few of the markets here."

Orbs flaring bright yellow, the irritation in Aleron's stiff muscles softened. "Does that mean they have seen them recently?"

Gideon winced at the hope he heard. Since Aleron was crouching, Gideon brought his eyes to his skull near the same height as him.

"No. This was nearly two months ago." He cast Aleron a sympathetic, crinkled expression. Then Gideon punched the parchment he had upwards. "But I do have this. They were polite enough to give me a map, so maybe we can figure out a plan tonight to tackle where we'll go?"

It'd taken a fair while, with Aleron scouting and flying at the same time, to even make it here to Greenshire from the hot springs. Half a day, in fact, despite them being rather close to each other since they were only separated by a little distance and the southland wall. Sure, they were being thorough, but searching without any rhyme or reason would likely take too long.

It'd taken too long already.

"Night is almost upon us," Aleron grumbled with a snorted huff, turning his head away. He was sulking. "You also stink of the other humans more than usual."

"I know, I'm sorry." Gideon sighed and knelt down to

attach the strap he'd bought for his guitar, since he'd left it with Aleron. "Like I said, they detained me for questioning. If I hadn't managed to think my way out of it, I'd probably be locked up right now. I also bought a few things."

The rings in his pocket had been deeply bothering Gideon. He should have sold them sooner, but he hadn't wanted to stay long in the villages or towns they'd visited along the way here. Just enough to ask the guards for some information and then leave.

He'd hoped they would disappear at the hot springs, since they'd stayed there the night, but he'd woken with them in his pocket. Yet his torn underwear had gone missing, and he hadn't appreciated donning his leather trousers without them.

He'd bought a new pair after selling his rings for a decent amount of gold. His coin pouch was rather hefty.

Strapping his case over his back, he waited for Aleron to pick him up. "Alright, let's go find a place to camp for the night where it's not out in the open."

Aleron took them west, seeming to want to scout the area just in case they'd come back this way. They hadn't.

Just as they were landing, Aleron hovered them above the ground. He turned his head in a certain direction, while sniffing the air.

"There is a Mavka who has made a nest nearby," he stated, tilting his head with dark-yellow orbs of curiosity. He slowly lifted back off, taking them into the air. "I do not know their scent. We cannot rest here. They will not like us lingering in their territory."

Gideon never expected Aleron to have that type of reaction to one of his own kind, considering the intimate brotherly bond he had with his twin. Gideon thought they would all be pleasant and familiar with each other.

Is that why he's never taken us to one of them? He placed a fist against his temple, uselessly trying to force memories to the surface. It'd never been that easy, nor had it ever worked. *Didn't we meet one in the Elven world, though?* That's what Aleron had told him.

By the time they found a place to camp, night had long fallen. Making a campfire in the dark wasn't the most optimal time, since finding dry kindling was difficult. A layer of sleet covered everything, but they both worked together to ensure it was done efficiently.

We're starting to really work as a team.

He'd like them to act as a unit, wordlessly communicating to get a task done. The thought made him smile.

Once Gideon had light, he unfurled the parchment against the ground, with stones weighing down the corners to keep it open.

The chill wind blew softly, but he didn't find it too bad with his jacket. He leaned a little to the right until Aleron's shoulder pressed against his own, and the heat that came off the big guy instantly had his muscles relaxing in contentment.

"I'm guessing we're around here," Gideon stated, pointing just below the southwest region of the Veil's canyon. Just above their rough location, and little more to the left, were three villages – he thought one may be where he'd done his mortifying naked march. "I don't know exactly where we came to Earth, but I think we kind of did this."

He slipped his finger north. He hated how guilt nagged his stomach, sickening it, as he went west towards the beach – where he'd unfairly told Aleron he wanted to sever their bond.

Shit. Was that really three weeks ago? In such a small amount of time, so much had changed. *And yesterday...* A shiver ran down his spine at the memory of them at the hot springs.

Gideon didn't realise how fast things were moving until

he looked at the evidence of their path and how long it'd taken them to get to this spot.

His cheeks drained of colour, but he tried to ignore the regret that simmered beneath the surface as he drew an estimated path. He circled the map, going far north, then east to where the cave had been, right behind the northern Demonslayer stronghold called Hawthorne Keep. Then, he moved further east to Zagros Fortress, where Emerie had likely enrolled to become a Demonslayer, before pointing to Fishket.

They'd spent a lot of time in the southlands, scouting it with not a single trace of their siblings. He scanned over the hot springs and then pointed to Greenshire and their corn crop they'd visited today.

"I'll be honest with you, Aleron, I don't know where they could be. If I were Emerie, I would stay away from the north," he stated, lifting his gaze to Aleron, who had crouched closer to the map. "If it hasn't changed from eight years ago, the north has a heavier presence of Demonslayers due to their mountains."

"So they are likely in the south?" Aleron asked, tapping a claw against the parchment. He darted his hand away when he poked a hole in it. "But we have checked the south."

Gideon palmed his cheek in thought.

"Look, if I were Emerie, I'd stay away from the east as well." He pointed to Zagros Fortress. "This is likely the guild she deserted, and she wouldn't risk travelling through regions that would know her face. Plus, both the north and east snow more than the southwest. She would hunker down for winter. I don't know where, since the only place I've been to, besides Fishket, is Ashpine City."

Well, that wasn't true, as he'd technically been all around Austrális now.

The giant, crudely drawn crack that spanned the entire continent kept drawing his eye.

He asked the question he didn't want to.

With a beseeching expression, Gideon turned to the Duskwalker. "Could they be in the Veil, Aleron?"

Seeming to forget that he'd just poked a hole in the parchment, Aleron tapped at it again. This time, he held the end of his snout as he pondered.

He kept tapping the same spot, an area far east. Gideon pointed to it.

"Here?" Gideon asked.

"I do not think he would take his bride so deep where Demons dwell," Aleron explained, his skull jerking in his direction as though he glanced at him. "He would not wish her to come to harm, but... Merikh's cave is here. It is often unoccupied, although you and I know he will never return to it. He is in the Elven world with Raewyn. But... it is a safe place to rest, and we have lingered there many times."

Merikh and Raewyn? Those names sound familiar. Gideon recalled no memories of them, per se, but he was sure Aleron spoke of them a few times. *That must be who I was trying to remember earlier.*

"Should we start heading to Merikh's cave then? We can fly back over the south again, and we may end up finding them along the way."

Aleron nodded, agreeing with his plan of attack. It also seemed to soothe Aleron, whether that was because Gideon was wholeheartedly trying to aid their search, or because having a plan eased him.

Rolling up the parchment, Gideon moved to his case to tuck it away carefully for safekeeping, then sat next to it. He also took his new underwear out of his pocket, planning to put them on in the morning. Then, he waited for tiredness to begin clutching at him, as he did most nights.

Plucking a string of his guitar here and there, without pulling it from his case, he wasn't sure if he actually wanted to play it or not. Honestly, just having it brought him joy. It'd meant a lot to him, so just being able to look at it and touch it placated him.

Sometimes it was the simple things in life.

At the same time, his hyperaware senses soaked in Aleron.

Difficult to truly tell where Aleron was looking, Gideon thought he may be staring at the fire. His wings twitched, flapping while closed and resting at his back.

Gideon had the impression he was unsettled when his orbs seeped into blue. "What's wrong?"

"I miss my kindred," Aleron answered in a low voice, almost whispering it. "I thought we would be with him by now."

Damnit, Gideon thought with a curse, looking away as he rubbed at the back of his neck. *We probably would have been if it weren't for me.*

But he couldn't go back in time.

"We'll find them soon," Gideon promised, before pulling his guitar from its case.

Now that he was unsettled as well, he'd rather distract himself. Hopefully it'd pull Aleron away from staring at the fire.

Letting his fingers rather than his mind do all the work, he just played whatever came to him. After a little while, the Duskwalker moved in his peripheral, inching closer and closer until he'd crossed half the short distance.

His pulse raced a little, overjoyed that Aleron was finally bridging their physical distance on his own. It didn't matter that he stopped before he made it the entire way.

Aleron picked at the grass with his skull turned downwards to watch, fidgeting nervously. Like before, his wings twitched.

"Can I sit with you?" he murmured quietly.

Gideon snuffed the grin trying to fill his face, acting casual in the hopes of not making him feel awkward. However, Gideon knew his eyes would have glinted with warmth as he stopped playing and turned his gaze up to Aleron.

"Yeah, of course."

Quickly closing the distance, Aleron eventually went behind him. Before Gideon could ask where he was going, a surprise gasp shot from him when he was pulled into Aleron's lap. His backside slipped into the nook between Aleron's crossed legs, and he hugged his guitar so he didn't drop or damage it in the process.

A chuckle fell past his lips. This wasn't what he thought the Duskwalker intended, but he didn't mind. *This is more than he's ever done before.* He'd really been hoping that instigating intimacy would help connect them, and it looked as though he'd been right.

He's not very talkative, so maybe doing feels more natural for him?

Gideon leaned back against his furry chest, and tension bled out of Aleron. The Duskwalker eased into the seated cuddle and said, "Keep playing. I did not mean to interrupt."

Gideon was supposed to be making himself tired, but suddenly he was more awake than ever. *I can't remember if I've ever sat in someone's lap like this.*

He was almost six feet tall and built like how a novice wood cutter should be. More athletically muscled rather than overtly bulky, though, since he'd only been in his career for a few years. He'd never had someone be nearly two feet taller than him, or twice as big in leg and chest width, so he'd been uncomfortable with a position such as this.

He was heavy and hadn't wanted to crush the person.

It's kind of nice. I can feel his warmth, his heart, his very breaths. And Aleron was strong enough to hold him, and may actually be the only person he would have ever allowed this with. *It makes me feel small, but not... weak.*

Maybe cherished?

With the end of his snout barely an inch from the side of

Gideon's head, Aleron released warm breaths over him as he stared down. Being peered at with an unwavering gaze, as if Gideon's face held the most interest in comparison to the forest, flames, or even the clear sky, had his heart flipping in his chest.

Aleron's voice was soft and whispered as he asked, "Can I touch you?"

Gideon winced when he played an incorrect note, his hands trembling with an odd emotion. *Shit. Why am I so nervous?*

"Yeah." He nodded, unsure of what he was actually agreeing to.

His ears grew so hot he worried his earrings would melt from his lobes. Even more so when Aleron tapped the back of a claw against one, causing it to flick forward each time he did.

"I like these. They are pretty on you."

Gideon laughed at that. "Thanks. Getting my ears pierced started off as a dare from my friends, but I ended up liking them once I saw myself in the mirror."

That claw then sifted through the sensitive hairs on the back of his neck before drawing down the corded muscle. The long hairs on his arm lifted when his skin prickled in reaction. Aleron looked over Gideon's shoulder as his large hand drew down his arm, wanting to explore it.

Aleron grabbed Gideon's hand and took it from his guitar, lifting it when Gideon moved his instrument away with his other, since it became impossible for him to actually play it with only one. It appeared Aleron no longer cared about interrupting him – and Gideon was just thankful he could stop pretending to care to play it.

Now with freedom to move, Aleron wrapped both his big paws around Gideon's entire hand. Running the pad of his clawed thumb over his knuckles, Aleron played with them, caressing them so lightly that it tingled. It made Gideon look down as well.

"Your hands are so little." Those words had never been uttered to Gideon before, considering his fingers and palms were meaty from years of swinging his axe and manual labour. "Soft, and yet they do not feel delicate."

His claws are really long.

The curved backs of them were so glossy they reflected the firelight, the tips so sharp they almost turned into needles. Yet Gideon had never been hurt with them. Aleron's touch was always gentle, but looking down at his large, calloused hands, it seemed impossible for him to be considerate. Impossible, yet the Duskwalker proved otherwise time and time again.

The dark grey of Aleron's flesh was stark against the fire, whereas it gave Gideon's tanned skin an orange glow.

The protruding white knuckles drew Gideon's curious attention until something else caused him to bite the corner of his lips. The way Aleron's tendons moved as he explored Gideon's fingers showed utter strength, as did the thick, pumping veins that played across them.

From walking on them for years, it'd seemed he'd trained his hands to be massive, muscled, and fierce.

Underneath all the fur and feathers, was Aleron hiding an attractively muscular body? Right now, he just looked like a giant fluffy teddy. He even felt like it with how cosy Gideon was nestled against him.

Cute but dangerous. That was how Gideon had begun seeing him.

But that hand... he found it far more enticing than he should have. Gideon even wondered what it would look like wrapped around his cock in a tight, claw-tipped fist. He bet he'd nearly hold him from base to tip, with just the head popping through.

Holy shit, Gideon mentally cursed, covering his mouth with his free palm and looking away. *Why the hell am I the one having perverted thoughts right now?* He peeked at

Aleron's orbs, finding them to be bright pink, rather than purple with desire.

Annoyed that he seemed to be the only one growing aroused, his dick jerking and thickening in his trousers, Gideon lifted a knee to hide it.

It's just a hand. Okay, a pretty nice one, but *still*.

Something was wrong with his heart. It shouldn't be acting up over this, thumping in his chest frantically. Just the day before, he'd had this Duskwalker's cum in his mouth. Innocently holding each other's hand shouldn't even make him bat an eye.

Aleron finally moved away to wrap his arms across Gideon's torso. It didn't escape his notice that one large palm had snuck under his tunic and jacket to cup underneath his pectoral muscle, the length of Aleron's fingers wrapping around his ribs. The other hand just held his hip.

Then Aleron bumped the side of his jaw against his own, and the big guy let out a little quake. He did it harder, like he wanted to score the bone with his short facial hair.

"Spikey. It is like you are scratching and tickling me at the same time."

The pure innocence of this embrace, what the Duskwalker was doing and just said, touched Gideon's very being. It petted his mind in a way it'd never been caressed before.

It made his chest tighten with tenderness, but his gut clenched with a painful knot. *Is this all he's wanted to do this entire time? Just fucking hold me and rub his skull against me?* Once more, the overwhelming feeling of guilt tried to wrap around his throat.

Before he could linger on it, Aleron's claws had Gideon bursting out with laughter. He wriggled and twisted his back.

"That tickles!" he hissed through clenched teeth, trying to escape the fingers moving up and down his side.

"You smell nice, and your hair is a nice colour," Aleron stated, ignoring Gideon as he lifted and began gnawing on some of the strands.

When he realised the Duskwalker was purposefully messing with him, Gideon went to get up. He was pulled back down, and Aleron stopped tickling him and nibbling his hair.

Yet Aleron's light chuckle deflated any irritation, and he ended up laughing with him.

"I will stop. Just stay." Then the Duskwalker tentatively licked across the side of his neck. When Gideon didn't stop him, Aleron did it again more confidently until he became incessant. "I just wish to hug you."

Aleron was doing more than that, and yet... not enough?

It's like he's trying to pull me in every direction. Wringing his emotions until he'd twisted out all the ones Aleron didn't want to remain.

When one of his clawed hands dipped down Gideon's stomach to graze his flesh, it brushed over his scars. He thought that would bother him, as he hadn't liked being reminded of them before. However, all he could think about was how Aleron just placed his palm low but didn't go any further down.

The heat of it sent a tingle down to his groin, like the mildest, incidental tease.

All his life, Gideon usually let his feelings be captured before his body, but all this just made him internally ache. His dick was hard, seeming to tell him what his brain couldn't, and it almost felt... easier to use his body. To give into it and let it lead the way. Give instincts and need the reins.

It had done far better already than his stupid mouth had.

They were both already confused, and he really *did* want to be touched. Or perhaps that was because all his valuable blood was flooding his dick and making it throb to the point his balls were tight.

Go lower, Gideon mentally pleaded at his damn hand.

Gideon lowered his knee, trying to make the outline of his erection more obvious, but Aleron seemed too distracted with licking his throat to notice. Each swipe had little goosebumps prickling down his chest that made his nipples harden.

"Your skin is so smooth."

Fuck it. Gideon placed his palm over Aleron's knuckles and slowly pushed his hand down until he made the pads of Aleron's fingers graze over his hardness.

The licking paused. The only movement for a few seconds was Gideon's rapidly huffing chest. Then Aleron squeezed his cock and a groan of relief shook past Gideon's teeth. He even thrust against the Duskwalker's hand, only to hiss out a breath when those sharp claws danced up the length of it.

"You are hard?" Since he asked a pointless question, Gideon lifted his head back and to the side to give him a bland look. Aleron peered over Gideon's shoulder to watch himself trace up and down the hard length of it, and purple immediately bled into his orbs. "Can I touch it?"

Holy shit, this Duskwalker was killing him.

"No. I only put your hand there so you could feel it," Gideon stated sarcastically, while lowering his hands to undo the ties of his trousers. Then he winced when he realised he'd allowed his pent-up and sexually frustrated self to say something that could *actually* be taken the wrong way. "What I mean is–"

Before he could finish, Aleron had sheathed his claws and shoved his hand into the opened pocket of his trousers. He twisted his wrist so he could grip Gideon properly and dragged him free.

"If you are going to tease with lies, then I will do this."

He brought his arm up, cupped the side of Gideon's head, and tilted his face. Then he licked across his lips for the very first time. Sure, it'd been *inside* his mouth, but never swiped across it. His lips parted in surprise, finding he liked the texture of Aleron's tongue slipping against his lips, only to let out a raspy groan when Aleron started stroking him.

What do I do? Do I lick it back? Did he open his mouth further and let it in? The hell was he supposed to do? But as his eyes dazed when Aleron's fingers flicked up and down over the rim of his cockhead, Gideon just found himself... panting against it.

Aleron showed him anyway by sinking it within the well of his mouth. A soft growl bubbled as Gideon brushed his tongue back and forth against Aleron's. It grew more ferocious when Gideon let his body take over and he sucked on it, and the big Duskwalker shuddered out a groan as a reward.

His back arched when something wet, hard, and thick slipped under his lifted shirt and jacket. Nestled between his back muscles, it pushed up his spine until eventually little limbs swirled against his back. Everything was hot, and he leaned into Aleron's strange, inhuman cock rather than away from it.

Then Aleron pulled his fist from his shaft, and Gideon shook his head. He tried to ask him not to stop, but was muffled by his tongue swirling within his mouth.

Aleron fisted his own cock, and his knuckles gouged into Gideon's back as he stroked. Then Aleron brought his hand back. Layered in a copious amount of lubricant, he smeared it all over Gideon's cock as he pressed deep within his trousers.

"Gideon," Aleron groaned, slipping his fingers down until he found the tight hole just behind his balls. "I want inside here."

As soon as Aleron touched it, Gideon knew he wanted to push the finger he was dabbing against it inside. With precum welling at the tip of his cock at the lightest touch, he quickly made his decision.

Holding the back of Aleron's hand, Gideon helped him penetrate to show he accepted it, while lifting his knees to make it easier. Bracing himself, he winced, but forced himself to soften against the thick digit entering him.

He grabbed Aleron's wrist when it was all the way inside, halting him so Gideon could adjust. Thankfully, after his tongue yesterday, it was a little easier than expected. Uncomfortable at first, he loosened his grip to let Aleron thrust his finger so he could prepare Gideon for the future.

He didn't have the heart to tell him it probably wouldn't happen tonight either, but the more they trained him, the more likely they could.

Unless... He pulled his face to the side to dislodge Aleron's tongue. "I could always fuck you," he offered, his cock jerking at the idea.

With how hot Aleron was, and the fact his cock was self-lubricating, he thought burying himself inside him would feel amazing.

"We have already discovered I do not have this," Aleron explained, angling his finger forward as he moved it. "I absorb all that I consume."

He doesn't have an–?

With eyes and mouth snapping open wide, Gideon stopped listening, stopped paying attention. Fuck, he may have stopped *breathing* when Aleron attacked his prostate with an unbelievable amount of pressure. A jolt of pleasure had his back arching.

"Oh fuck," Gideon rasped, grinding his ass into Aleron's palm.

He released such a thick drop of precum it instantly overspilled. Even when Aleron quickly stretched him with a second finger, he barely noticed when it anchored right where Gideon needed him to. Gideon gripped his cock to drown out any uncomfortableness by stroking himself.

He felt bad that he wasn't touching Aleron in return. Yet, Gideon couldn't do anything else but brace through this when his whole body sparked lightning beneath the surface of his skin. Flushed, pulse stammering, he stared wide-eyed at his groin.

He'd thought Aleron would fumble through this, but it felt amazing. For the first time since he'd woken up in his second life, he thanked his past self. He'd at least taught Aleron how to do *this*.

"You look needy like this," Aleron grated with a groan. He forced Gideon's face up so he could look down at the dazed expression that had fallen over him. "It is different to Tenebris, but better. Your noises are more erotic, your body hotter and softer, and I can scent *all* of you."

Then, as though overcome with passion, Aleron darted his head forward to sink his tongue into Gideon's mouth once more. Aleron began to rock against his back, groaning over his face.

"I have *missed* this," Aleron rasped.

Gideon winced when he tried to add a third finger, his body tightening against the uncomfortable sting. The fact his hand was so big was half the problem, and Gideon already knew he'd never had this much girth inside him.

It's too much. Gideon didn't think he was ready for this much, but he couldn't pull away from Aleron's mouth, even if he wanted to. At least him pressing against the right places aided to spark bliss, and Gideon stroked his cock to help.

He was also so turned on, and so fucking close to coming, that he just tried everything he could to achieve release. His mind and body obsessed over it, his balls constantly drew up like he was about to, only for it to escape him.

The head of Gideon's cock was drenched in precum, and he shuddered all over. His thighs shook and his abdomen muscles dipped, his entire pelvis radiating with painful bliss.

Then it clutched him, and he let out a harrowing groan... just as Aleron stopped. His fingers ceased moving, as did his tongue.

Fuck! No! Gideon yanked his head back.

"Don't stop," he choked out.

Before he could shout that he was about to come, Aleron covered his mouth.

He removed his fingers a little faster than Gideon appreciated, his asshole snapping back to a smaller state, as he said, "A Demon is coming."

I don't care. Probably not the thought to have. Thankfully he never said it, as he would have expired in embarrassment later if he had.

Gideon also didn't have the chance to react. Aleron yanked his hand from Gideon's trousers, wrapped his arms around his torso, and Gideon bellowed as the Duskwalker jumped metres into the air. Gideon had just enough time to grab his trousers to stop them from falling to his ankles.

Snorting rabid huffs echoed beneath their feet. A Demon leapt into the tiny space between the trees they'd just been sitting in. They'd only just escaped it.

"I thought you said you'd smell or hear them coming!" Gideon stated in disbelief, clutching the waist of his trousers tighter.

"Distracted," Aleron grated out hoarsely. "I have never had you squirming like that before."

Gideon's face heated in mortification of being told he'd been *squirming*. Of course Aleron had been distracted. He'd had his fingers knuckle deep inside his bride for the first time – on Earth.

A chime of notes stole his attention, and Gideon darted stark, wide eyes to the ground. He reached downwards, not caring in the moment if he fell.

"Fuck, Aleron. My guitar!" The Demon was shoving it around, sniffing right where they'd just been sitting.

At his shout, it even stood on it with one hand as it looked up at them!

Sensing the emergency, Aleron acted quickly. He stopped flapping his wings and fell to the ground, landing right on top of the Demon. With his bird-like feet, he clamped his talons around it to keep it down as it flailed and screeched. A long tail flicked, but that was the only definable feature he could recognise of the wretched creature.

Gideon jumped from his arms.

Sprinting, he tied his pants while ignoring his still semi-hard erection, then grabbed his guitar and shoved it in its protective case. Just as he was closing it and flicking the latches to lock it, Aleron let out a hiss and yelped.

At the distressed sound he made, he thought, *Screw the guitar.* He pulled his axe from his belt loop so he could aid the whimpering Duskwalker.

The Demon was still in the same position, trapped and unable to do anything. Yet, Aleron clutched at his exposed dick with his orbs white.

His orbs only ever turn that colour when he's afraid or in pain.

"It stings," Aleron hissed out with a shudder wracking him. His wings flapped and kinked, showing just how much agony he was in. "It has never stung before." Then he turned his snout towards the forest. "Hurry, Gideon. Another is approaching."

Two? Is it because we're so close to the Veil?

Unsure of what was happening to Aleron, and just thankful he'd considered Gideon's feelings by bringing them back to the ground, he hastened his steps. He grabbed the case handle and bolted back over.

Aleron didn't cradle him.

Instead, he wound a single arm around his torso while still protecting his exposed shaft. He lifted him like a football nestled under his armpit and pushed off the ground once more. The Demon made a sharp choking noise below his heavy weight as it was crushed during Aleron's take off. Then they were in the air once more, Gideon cringing with the weight of his case at the end of his dangling arm.

In the distance, branches snapped and shrubs rustled as a much larger Demon sprinted to what had been their campsite. *Fucking hell. That one sounds like a bear.*

As they fled the area, their altitude bobbed and dipped erratically with each of Aleron's pained hisses. It was only once he managed to shove his shaft back behind his seam that Aleron stopped letting out whines and started flying straight.

Wind cut through Gideon's hair, cooled his desirously heated skin, and billowed inside his shirt and jacket.

As bad as Gideon felt for Aleron, an uncontrolled laugh burst from his lips. His eyes wetted with humour-filled tears that turned ice cold in the chilly air.

"Why are you laughing?" Aleron bit out, snapping his fangs at him. "You could have been hurt."

"Do you not realise how fucking funny all that was? We were too busy fooling around, and I..." His chuckles deepened when he almost stated hadn't cared a Demon was coming so long as he *came.* "Aleron, you have to understand... this is all new to me. I've been so afraid of the dark, and being outside the walls of Fishket, that I never would have dreamed of a night like this. Even if it was scary, I knew you'd get us out of there safely."

A normal situation during all this for a human would be all of them even more terrified of the forest. They would be checking their wounds and making sure none of their friends had just died.

Instead, now, with Aleron... *All I can think about is how we didn't get to finish.* There was a twisted humour in that.

Gideon had also never felt more *alive.*

THIRTY-THREE

Aleron had never expected once his bride thawed of his iciness, he would be annoying. Cute, but chatty.

Perhaps it could be blamed on his foul mood, but Aleron found his constant shouting, in order to speak over the wind, grating. Or maybe it was due to every night they landed to rest, he'd been permitted to touch, only to be interrupted by Demons!

Ever since deciding their path, they'd shared two nights of touching, tasting, and Aleron learning his bride's favourite places. Only for it to end with him needing to swiftly collect the male and his precious case, and leap.

In the day, Aleron gained no rest. He didn't know what sparked this human turning into a bold, perverse little beast, but Gideon tried teasing him in the air. He touched Aleron's chest, lifted up to kiss at his jaw, with his trousers hiding away his hardness. Then the male muttered words that didn't seem erotic, but absolutely were for Aleron.

When he'd chosen to land in the daytime, the sun making his bride's eyes appear even more heated than usual, a Demon lurking in shade came near. Such a rare occurrence, and apparently only for when Aleron was hard and needy.

Gideon then promised he wouldn't do it again, and Aleron didn't know if he was relieved or not. *Perhaps if there are no Demons...*

They'd gone most of their travels without seeing the horrible, nasty vermin, so why suddenly now? Just when Aleron could finally grasp this human and drink from his lips?

His seed sacs now constantly ached, and his need was growing violent. Aleron wanted release, and the denial of it seemed to be warping his thoughts. In Tenebris, there had been no pressure within his seed sacs, only the bliss of release. Release that had been *mild* in comparison to releasing with liquid expelling from him.

Now it built and built until Aleron felt overfull.

He'd even considered tearing the human's pants from him and shoving him down on his cock while he flew. Where they were safe. Where no one could interrupt them.

Considering how his wings and body reacted under the lightest touch from Gideon, Aleron knew he'd crash against the ground before he even reached orgasm. They'd fall, but he'd be too busy rutting his body to care.

Aleron didn't know if Gideon was ready for him to unleash that. His bride was set on making Aleron prepare him without giving him the bliss they both sought.

He could land to try again in the day, but Aleron was split between two desires, both important, both strong, both tugging him in different directions.

One was to connect with his bride, consume him on nearly all levels. The other was to find his kindred.

The balance of that, his longing never tipping one way or the other, weighed on Aleron. He wanted both. Not tomorrow, but now, this very second. He ached so acutely with these needs that they mangled him.

Now that Gideon had slowly begun to open up to him, Aleron's focus on him waned and only grew stronger towards their search. His anxieties transformed, evolving into new worries.

Then, today, he'd discovered Gideon to be a chatty little thing.

He... *loved* it – even if it annoyed him right at that moment – mainly because he smiled for a lot of his ramblings, especially when talking of his old friends, his job, Emerie, and his family. Aleron learned more this day than he ever had before.

I want to smother him in affection while he speaks to me.

Instead, Aleron was stuck holding him as they flew closer to Merikh's ward. In the distance, a bright-red dome glittered right against the Veil's canyon wall.

He also had questions, but was unsure if he wanted the answers.

Why did his Gideon suddenly... *change?* Of course he appreciated it, but he went from a pale, lifeless being to someone who had so much colour he sometimes turned pink. His dimples were prominent, his mossy-green eyes alight with emotion. He'd started to play with him again, like in Tenebris, returning to the wonderful creature that had captured Aleron's heart to begin with.

As much as he adored learning about him, it still felt like Gideon was holding back much.

There were times Gideon appeared tired not long after waking, or he looked off into the distant horizon with a sombre expression. When Aleron asked about them, Gideon would either smile and tell him nothing was wrong, or he'd talk about something that didn't seem relevant at all.

Gideon didn't realise how much that hurt.

Aleron wanted his pain, to share it with him, so if in the future Gideon succumbed to it once more, Aleron could bring him out of it. He wanted to discover and consume his bride on every level, not just the ones the little human had figured out brought Aleron contentment.

He wanted to be... trusted with Gideon's most vulnerable self. In the same way he wished to share his own disquiet, but refused to because Gideon wouldn't.

Perhaps this is what truly brings me discontent.

His mind was in a million places; a number he couldn't even count and yet it dotted within his conscience as a festering swarm.

Aleron also didn't want to go to Merikh's cave.

A part of him had avoided it even when they flew past it over a week ago, due to unpleasant and distressing memories. He only came here for the chance to be reunited with his twin.

As if to make matters worse, his whole torso filled with hateful disappointment when they started to descend past the Veil's edge and into Merikh's ward. Without needing to land, the area smelt empty of his kindred's scent.

Ingram is not here. Every day that he wasn't reunited with him brought on a deeper, frustrating desperation.

He tried not to feel resentment towards his bride for it. However, the happier Gideon became, the more Aleron wished he'd just remembered everything when they arrived here. He wished the male had just trusted in Aleron and had come with him when he asked.

He would have been with his kindred within a day.

Ingram had been nearby. Not close enough to take in his scent, but enough that if he went in the direction Weldir had pointed, they would be together.

It had been almost a month since then. As time passed... as days ended and began, he grew more afraid. Austrális wasn't small.

What if we never find them?

Restless, Aleron carefully placed Gideon on his feet with his wings shifting behind him.

His sight morphed to red as he took in the lake that glistened, despite the late-afternoon shade cast over them from the rock wall. The waterfall he usually found soothing did nothing but irritate his senses. Everything smelt clean and fresh, but because it was empty of his kindred's scent, it aggravated him.

He drew his enraged sight over the area: the tree that rustled with two large boulders beneath it, the grass, the entrance to Merikh's cave. It settled on the back of Gideon as he placed his guitar on the ground.

Aleron snapped his skull away from him, angered with himself that he could shine such a colour upon his precious bride.

It is not his fault.

It wasn't his fault he couldn't remember. It wasn't his fault Aleron had been separated from his twin to begin with, and that was why he wasn't with Ingram now. Gideon was not to blame for his death.

No, that was due to Demons and the Demon King.

His sight shifted to a deep well of blue as he drifted it towards the Veil's forest. A certain direction captured him.

Only a few months ago, he and Ingram had been fleeing to this very place – only for Aleron to perish not even a few metres beyond the tree line.

For so long, he'd been trying to push those thoughts from his conscience. He'd ignored them, shaking his head when they tried to emerge, but being here, in this place, it was hard to keep them at bay any longer.

Inaudible rambling fell on his unlistening ears.

Aleron was too busy being overwhelmed by the memory of dozens of feet chasing him. The yelps and cries that filled the air, unsure if they were his own or Ingram's. The scent of Demon blood and Mavka blood blending together into a disgusting coppery mixture.

The utter darkness that shadowed Aleron on a night he could see clearly in, blocking him out from the world as he was overrun by writhing bodies.

We were so close.

He didn't know if it was the present or the past where his chest rattled with agony until soft, warm fingers slipped against the inside of his own. Shocked by it, he darted his hand away. The foreign touch didn't belong in his memories of sharp fangs and claws.

He looked down to his side as the little human frowned up at him. "Aleron?"

He realised then that the rattling in his chest was due to him whimpering. He'd also ruined the chance for his bride to hold his hand, like he often longed for, by recoiling away.

"I'm sorry they're not here." His apology bothered Aleron, simply because he didn't wish for his human to do this.

He didn't want Gideon to apologise anymore. It only made the male recede into himself whenever he did.

This is why I did not want to come here. Aleron knew he'd be unsettled in this place. Merikh's ward had once been a beacon of safety, and now it felt like a dark spot within his subconscious.

I should have known Ingram would not bring his bride so close to where we were separated. But he was... desperate.

Aleron didn't know where else to go, where else Ingram could be.

A sigh parted his fangs, as a heavy weight seemed to lie over his very essence. It was cold as it wrapped around him like a wet cloth of clinging sadness and pain.

"I am upset that they are not here," he admitted, unfurling his fist before looking back into the Veil. Part of him wanted to go to where it all happened to see if he could find pieces of his broken skull fragments. "But that is not why I am unsettled."

"Do you want to talk to me about it?" Gideon offered, his bowed eyes filled with concern. "I'd be happy to listen."

Another whimper fell from him. *I want to.* More than anything, he wanted his bride to comfort him. Aleron desired to lean on him, as he would have his kindred.

"It is because I died not far from here. Ingram and I... We

were trying to make our way here, knowing we would be safe once we were inside this ward. It is just beyond the trees, a short distance in. A few minutes. If we had made it..."

Before he could continue, soft fingers tickled the inside of his once more. The solace of them as they tentatively slipped over his roughness warmed him. Aleron didn't shy away from the contact this time, and Gideon attempted to poke his fingertips through the large gaps.

The gesture meant much and quelled the worst of his sorrow. He was thankful the little human braved trying again, despite how Aleron responded the first time.

It was also a reminder.

If we had made it... he would not be here with me. Aleron tilted his sight down to Gideon. His handsome face, filled with so much worry for *his* sake that it was all crinkled and screwed up, gazed up at him almost expectantly. *I would not have him, and Ingram would not have found Emerie.*

They would have continued playing in the world, none the wiser that they would shortly find brides of their own should they painfully part ways.

For a moment, he'd regretted his death. In doing so, he hurt his own consciousness and immediately felt guilt.

Because... if he chose to regret it, it would mean that Gideon was never meant to be his bride, and he'd chosen wrong. Their chances of meeting would have been impossible. Without Emerie to guide them, without Aleron dying, he never would have met this human who had already left this world.

He didn't wish to think this way.

"I am sorry," Aleron said, turning to him. "This is not a pleasant conversation."

Gideon rolled his eyes with a scoff. "I don't care if it's pleasant or the most depressing thing I've ever heard." He lifted Aleron's hand and pressed his free palm on top of it. "This is the second time you have really spoken to me about how you feel about when you died. I want to be here for you through it."

Tenderness swelled in Aleron's chest, even as he shook his head. "I am burdened by this, yes, but I do not want to think on it. It is in the past."

A small gust filled with leaf litter wrapped around their shared silence as they gazed upon each other. Despite the chill, all Aleron could feel was the warmth of their hands touching. Then, understanding that Aleron truly wished to leave it be, Gideon sighed. Gideon released him and stepped back while rubbing the side of his neck.

"Fair enough. It'd be hypocritical of me to force you." He poked his thumb over his shoulder. "You said this guy is gone for good, right?"

"Yes. Merikh is in the Elven realm."

"Excellent! Let's go see if he has any good shit to steal."

His mirth and immediate redirection of the conversation was welcomed. However, Gideon then turned and bent over to pick up his guitar case. The rounded cleft of his backside now on display in front of Aleron reminded him why he'd been frustrated to begin with.

He wanted to leave this *shitty* place and knead every inch of his pretty human's body to pacify himself until he felt better.

Now he was just sad and horny at the same time; two emotions he was well aware shouldn't coincide.

Even just his hair swaying over the arch of his little ear made Aleron want to reach out. He'd rather it be Aleron's tongue brushing over such a sensitive area that always caused him to shiver.

My mind is all over the place, he reiterated as he followed Gideon to the cave entrance. The cloth flap, that was usually tied down to keep out forest debris, currently fluttered loosely. Merikh had obviously left swiftly and without warning.

It'd once been a barrier for him and his kindred.

They could have easily torn their way inside, but they had been worried Merikh would hunt them down if they did. They had been permitted within his ward, just never within his cave.

Inside, Gideon placed his case down and started rifling through Merikh's abandoned effects.

Much of it had already been disturbed, as Ingram and Aleron had both pawed through his belongings when they were last there together. They hadn't been able to contain their excitement at getting to explore within its secretive walls, only to discover it was utterly *boring*.

Merikh's bed shoved into the very back of the long, oval area was unmade. The hide-covered armchair to the left had leaves and dust coating it from the flap being loose, and more forest debris lay over the ground and the hide rug in the middle. A few tools lay on a stone bench not far from the entryway. A shelf of some kind up against the opposite wall to them was filled with books, tools, and various other items: animal skulls, crystals, and glass bottles of dried herbs.

Gideon looked over the only place of interest: the shelves.

"He has a bunch of books. Maybe we can take one and continue your reading and writing lessons?"

"I would like that," Aleron admitted, watching him rifle through a few before eventually taking one and placing it in his pocket. It was too big and threatened to fall out.

Aleron liked that Gideon wanted to spend more time with him, to teach him. He liked that there would be little judgement if he stumbled in learning, and it was one of his favourite qualities. He didn't want to be judged or shamed for something that, as Gideon had once stated, he couldn't help.

Gideon moved on to a different shelf.

"Holy crap. How big was this guy?" he asked, pulling

down a shirt to open it. Not only did it come to his knees, it was wide enough to fit three Gideons, if not more. "What was he, a freaking bear?"

Aleron mildly chuckled at that, despite the heaviness radiating behind his sternum. "Well, he does have a bear skull."

"Oh really–" The male's voice cut out, just as the shirt slipped from his hold. It crumpled against the grey stone at his feet.

Immediately sensing something was off, Aleron's sight flashed white. He dived forward when Gideon swayed. His right knee buckled inwards, and he collapsed to the side. Thankfully, Aleron caught him before he could hit the ground.

"Gideon?" Aleron's pulse sped up when the little human's suddenly became eerily slow.

Sweat instantly broke out across Gideon's forehead, his lids low as he panted weakly. Unresponsive at first, he only came out of the trance when Aleron cupped the side of his face and gently stroked his thumb across the little human's broad cheek.

Gideon's nose scrunched and his upper lip twisted. The disgust in his features was harrowing, only because Aleron thought it was aimed at him.

"Wow. What a dick he was."

His skull tilted sharply at that. "You remembered something?"

"Yeah. It was brief, but I remember sitting in their home or something and Merikh was saying a bunch of heartless stuff about all Duskwalkers." Gideon looked around and his brows furrowed as he took in their position. "Did I fall?"

Being gentle with him, Aleron helped him back to his feet. Gideon was quick to recover, the colour returning to his features, but Aleron couldn't help finding it odd. *He is not startled by this?* It's like... it wasn't the first time memories had returned to him while he was conscious and awake for them.

The moment he was steady, and he no longer needed support, Gideon bounced forward to do a final look over what remained here. Aleron made a fist until his claws sunk into the flesh of his palm.

Why does he remember Merikh and Emerie, but not our time together? Restless once more, he let out a sigh before palming down his skull. *No. That is not true. He has regained some memories of us.*

Enough to know of his orb changes, bits of their conversations, and apparently bits of them walking while in comfortable silence. Aleron just wished he'd remember the important things. Or, at least, told Aleron of what he *did* recall.

Gideon spun to him. Then with a grin and his eyebrows wiggling up and down, he hiked his thumb over his shoulder. "There's a massive bed here."

"Well, yes. It is Merikh's." That should have been obvious.

When his features and hand fell, as if displeased by Aleron's response, he realised he was ruining his bride's unusually cheery mood. Just when he'd achieved it.

Something is wrong with me today, Aleron thought as he left the cave.

Perhaps it was being in a place that he often frequented with his kindred. It felt wrong to be here without him, and it made him miss Ingram terribly.

Aleron eventually sat in the open clearing and turned his head up at the darkening sky. The waterfall gave a continuous *shaa* to his right, while the gentle winds softly rustled the trees in front of him. With a defeated slump in his shoulders, his sight shifted to blue.

I do not know what to do.

And he was getting tired of seeing dusk. It signified the end of another day, once more without Ingram.

"Alright, so this was a bust," Gideon stated as he walked out, slapping his hands together to dust them. "Look, why don't we find the other Duskwalkers? One of them might know where they are."

Aleron had already considered this.

He shook his head. "I know the whereabouts of three, but I do not know if they will be helpful. Orpheus is also not welcoming of us, after what we have done to him and his home. I doubt he would have gone there."

Gideon came to Aleron and crouched between his feet so they were close to eye level. Then he placed a soothing hand on top of his skull.

"Yeah, but didn't Emerie fight alongside all their brides or something? My memory is fuzzy on the details, but I could have sworn she said something about meeting a bunch of women and their Duskwalkers."

"Did she?" Aleron cupped the end of his snout in thought. "I did not know this. I thought the Witch Owl was the only one to help her kill the Demon King."

The male's brows furrowed deeply. "Really? Didn't Ingram tell you this in Tenebris?"

"No." Then Aleron rolled his head when he thought back on what his kindred had informed him of.

Since their time had been brief, they'd spoken of Emerie, of what magic he could utilise if he learned it, and... sex. Aleron hadn't even known he had a dick until Ingram informed him, and Emerie had gotten in the way of that.

Now that he thought about it... he didn't actually know how Emerie came to be in the afterworld. *I thought she was eaten by the Demon King.*

"Oh. I thought you had a reason for not wanting to go to them, and not because you didn't know they'd formed a relationship with them. I remember Emerie telling me about the other brides."

See? He remembers such a conversation with such

clarity. Aleron wanted to be remembered with the same lucidity.

Gideon looked off to the side and covered his mouth as he rubbed his jaw. "If I had known this, I would have said to go there first, rather than a last-ditch effort."

Aleron went to stand. "Then let's go there. I know where Orpheus' territory is."

"Hold on there, big fellow." Gideon fell into his lap to prevent him from rising. "Night will fall soon, Aleron."

Not meaning to growl at him, Aleron snapped his fangs to quieten himself. "Yes, but I will not need to search the Veil." His sight morphed to the orange of dusk, mirroring the colour of the very sky above them. "If we are to leave now, I can fly there by tomorrow."

A Mavka could sprint to the centre of the Veil in a day. With how fast he could fly, Aleron thought he may be able to cross it *entirely* in that time. Especially if he flew with all his strength and might.

Anything to be closer to his other half, his kindred. Even if it may *endanger* this human a little.

"But we're safe here for the night, right? The ward will keep Demons away."

Unsure of what Gideon was trying to say, he snorted out an irritated huff.

"But I want to leave now," Aleron bit out. "If we are fast enough, we may even be able to find them tomorrow if the others know where they are."

Just the idea had his wings tightening in joy.

Gideon dabbed his tongue at the seam of his lips before biting at the bottom one. An emotion glinted in his eyes, one filled with tenderness and heat. "I want to stay here for the night."

Why does he always want to stay, and rest, and go to other places?! Why did Aleron's wants not matter?

The longing he felt, how his heart twisted with the desperate need to find his twin, caused another deep growl to burst from him. Even his orbs reddened.

He wanted away from here! This was the last place he wished to linger. Even if they didn't have a destination, he would have made them leave, regardless.

Aleron was shoved to his back, and the shock of this little male doing so immobilised him. Then the hue in his sight turned crimson, even as the human sat upon his chest and poorly attempted to pin him down by his shoulders.

"Gideon," he rumbled, his voice twisting into something dark.

"I'm trying to have sex with you, Aleron," Gideon stated with a nervous chuckle, ignoring his aggression. "We have been literally cock-blocked by Demons for the last three days and I'm starting to *ache*. I even got excited at the sight of a real bed."

His growl died in the back of his throat, and Aleron tilted his skull down when he swore he felt something... hardening against his sternum.

He is growing aroused? At the mere sight of a *bed*?

"We can go find them or... we can have a go at seeing if you fit inside me." Then his features twisted. The humour in them faded and turned into something much more agonised. Gideon bent forward, gripping Aleron's shoulders tight to stop himself from slipping forward, and placed his forehead against his bony one. "Every night you've been preparing me, and I now can't stop thinking about it."

What had been a heavy heartbeat, slow but dangerous, suddenly quickened to fill him with heat.

All his thoughts, and the mess of his emotions, untwisted at the words that lingered between them.

He wants me inside him... And Gideon sounded so breathy, like he desperately ached for it. He even began placing soft little kisses over Aleron's skull, lathering it in affection, and each one soothed him in ways he didn't understand. The male's lids were so low his lashes tipped, and he gazed at Aleron with unhidden desire.

So swiftly, his bride had handled him until all his aggression faded and left him numb under a set of lips. They felt like little fluttering moths, so gentle and leaving a fuzziness behind. His mind quivered under their foray until Aleron thought he'd dissolve into a puddle of goo. *So soft.*

He pulled away too soon.

Gideon leaned back to pant over him, his gaze soft and his lips wet. "What do you want to do?"

With a groan, Aleron hooked his hand behind the back of Gideon's head to bring him back down. "More."

Aleron wanted this pretty male to keep kissing his face. They left tingles in their wake and evaporated all his frustrations. All except one, and he hoped it would be eased shortly.

He no longer cared where he was, so long as he received more touches. They could stain his mind instead of his memories.

"I was hoping you'd say that," Gideon whispered against his snout. Only to reach down between them as he lowered, nipping and kissing at his chest. "I'd like this, if you don't mind."

The tips of his fingers tickled his seam, and it clenched from the sensation. Then Aleron's back arched sharply. His fangs parted in a gasp as Gideon *deeply* pressed inside it. Aleron grabbed his wrist, halting him as he shuddered and let out a woofing growl.

A thunderbolt of pleasure struck him to his core at having his bride's fingers suddenly inside his seam like this.

Gideon already achieved what he'd wanted, and he circled his hand around his semi-soft cock. He pulled it from Aleron's seam and leaned back to sit just behind his tentacles. Thumbing behind the head where it was most sensitive, teasing it, Gideon bit his lip as he looked down.

Aleron twitched at what he'd just done to him.

He... he yanked my cock from me!

Within seconds, his entire body had been shoved into desire. His orbs morphed to such a dark purple that it suddenly became night.

I have needed him for so long.

Wanting to speed this along, and just hungry to see the human bared to him, Aleron grabbed the back of his jacket and shirt at the same time to pull them up and off him. Gideon leaned forward and pushed his arms up to help, giving him a toothy grin once his head popped through.

He started this, wants me. Aleron twitched when violent lust flooded his veins and muscles until his fur puffed when it burned just beneath his flesh.

Just the sight of this male's hair-dusted chest, little pinkish nipples, and his green eyes staring down at Aleron's shaft with want, had him licking at his snout. His purple tentacles wriggled to reach for him. Gideon willingly greeted them as he stroked until Aleron was fully erect.

Watching him, especially after what he'd done to obtain his prize, had drool coating his fangs.

His bride was much bolder than he ever could have imagined. *I cannot take it anymore.*

It just made him hungrier.

He is mine.

And he was tired of pretending Gideon wasn't his beast to tame.

THIRTY-FOUR

With Gideon's right hand wrapped around what he could fit of the Duskwalker's broad cockhead, he greeted two of his four wiggling tentacles with the other. They swirled around his fingers, slithering up the lengths of them, and tried to pull him down.

He wanted to chuckle when they incidentally made him place his palm against the middle of Aleron's shaft.

It's probably wrong of me to find them cute. They felt firm and playful. *But this part of him really does remind me of a flower.*

Dabbing his tongue at the seam of his lips, Gideon bit down on the bottom one. It really had tasted nice, and he knew having the Duskwalker's lubricant on his tongue, wetting his lips, would just make him even hornier.

He gave into the urge when a pearly white drop welled at the eye of his cock, and Gideon slipped back until Aleron had to part his thighs for him. He licked the very tip, tasting Aleron's diluted scent, only to suck on it a moment later. *Mmm, so sweet.*

Clawed fingers fisted what they could of his hair, and Aleron's hips jerked up. He kissed downwards when Aleron's dick slipped over his lips from the action, thankful Aleron didn't try to break his jaw this time.

Gideon's eyes flicked up, taking in the hulking

Duskwalker whose head was bent forward. Aleron was watching very intently, his orbs such a dark colour of purple Gideon found them terribly erotic. Gideon brought his head back up so Aleron could watch him poke his tongue out and circle the tip, earning himself a wolfish huff.

Although he was used to the aching in his cock, the deeper throb in his ass – where he hoped to have stimulated – was new.

In just a handful of nights, Gideon had gone from nervous about having Aleron's huge girth inside him to needing it. It probably wouldn't be so bad if he'd been allowed to come, but now he felt built up, pent up, and so fucking horny that he would sport an erection at the most basic of perverted thoughts.

All their touching had helped to ease both their physical restraints. Aleron was cuddlier, more confident about being affectionate, while Gideon was just growing comfortable being touched by a Duskwalker.

His claws no longer made Gideon unsure, but rather titillated him as they danced across his flesh. Aleron's fangs nipped him and made Gideon want to bite back in fondness. Gideon adored that he could dig his teeth in as hard as he wanted, and instead of pleading for him to stop or be gentle, Aleron would sometimes cup the back of his head for more.

He'd always liked Aleron's fur, but his fingers dived into it more just so Gideon could feel the heat of his flesh directly.

He'd started wanting this Duskwalker to trap him to his chest, or desiring to be crushed beneath his weight. He wanted his heat, scent, and body all over him. His purple tongue trailing to places he'd never been licked before, his fingers ghosting over every inch.

Gods, I want this inside me, he thought with a groan, lightly biting at the side of Aleron's cock to see if he enjoyed it.

Gideon also pulled at the ties of his trousers when he knew he wouldn't be able to wait much longer.

Aleron had been... off today. Moody, cranky, and just not himself. Gideon knew it was deeper than just unreleased lust, but he couldn't aid him if he wouldn't talk about it. He hoped giving them both something they obviously desperately ached for would help.

There were other reasons, but one had started to be more important than the rest. *I want to be... closer with him.* Fooling around with their hands and mouths was one thing, but to Gideon... sex was more than just fucking around. It often mattered to him, and usually meant he cared about the person.

And, considering Gideon was about to jam this monstrous thing inside him, even if his body wasn't ready... well, shit, that had to mean something right?

He not only wanted to connect them, but mesh them together until his erotic memory dreams were reality.

Lowering his trousers caused an eager bubble of precum to well at the tip of his cock. Just a simple action proved how much he craved this Duskwalker right then.

As much as Gideon wanted to keep sucking him, especially since Aleron had placed a hand on his shoulder to keep him still as he thrust, he couldn't stand waiting any longer.

Face flushed with arousal, nipples hard, and his erection jutting up eagerly, Gideon climbed on top of him. Their dicks glided over each other's as he passed over Aleron's, and Gideon placed his hands on Aleron's broad chest when he was far enough forward.

Goosebumps trailed up Gideon's legs when the Duskwalker traced his clawed hands over his bare thighs.

"We have been in this position before," Aleron grated, lifting up so he could slide his tongue underneath Gideon's sharp jaw.

Aleron's left hand disappeared before coming back to

swipe over the cleft of his backside. Smothered in lubricant, Gideon grunted when a finger pushed inside him. Soft enough to take it after the last few days, he sunk back onto it greedily.

Looks like I'm not the only one who is impatient.

"I thought I would need to ask for your help," Gideon said with a nervous chuckle. Then his nails bit down into Aleron's shoulders when he grazed the spot that instantly made Gideon's shaft jump.

"You have already taught me how to prepare you," Aleron rumbled, nipping at his skin, which had him lifting his head back for more.

It was still so strange to imagine that this wasn't Aleron's first time, or that Gideon had been the one to take his virginity in the afterlife. This, for Gideon, was their first, so it was incomprehensible.

His breath hitched when a second finger joined in. It was only uncomfortable for a second, and Aleron's arm helped by wrapping around his torso and cupping one of his pectoral muscles. Aleron grazed his fingers up and down over Gideon's nipple, like he wanted to distract him.

Pleasure sparked, and Gideon grabbed his own dick. He just held it, putting pressure around it, as if that would help to ease the throbbing need he felt in it. His hips twitched at each slow pump of Aleron's fingers, and his nose wrinkled, a groan falling from him, as they wiggled and moved.

Gideon clenched his jaw, making the muscled corners knot, as a third slipped inside. Pain and pleasure coiled together. Just as he was trying to grind back to help, Aleron played where he needed him to.

"Okay. I think I'm ready," Gideon hoarsely rasped, only to clamp up when a fourth was pushed inside!

"No. Last time you made me do this."

Shuddering, the uncomfortable trickle up his spine began to soften him. Gideon stroked himself, trying to keep his erection so it would aid him. The harder he stayed, the more lax his body would be for this.

Aleron was being far more patient than Gideon was, but he couldn't be more thankful. He probably got ahead of himself, but having this many moving digits inside him just felt weird.

They were too hard, and not round. He needed an equal stretch, with a velvet soft outside and a firm centre. It'd feel better, even if the size was truly daunting.

With a moan, Gideon planted his forehead against the top of the Duskwalker's shoulder. Aleron's heat, along with his panted breaths rolling over Gideon's ear to brush into his hair and over his scalp, helped to loosen him. He moaned against Aleron's shoulder.

"Gideon," Aleron whimpered, before bumping his bony snout against his sweat-slicked forehead.

Now that he'd adjusted, and was no longer focusing on what was happening inside him, he realised just how much Aleron was quaking.

"This should be enough," he whispered.

Aleron slowly slipped his fingers away, being gentle with him. Then he grabbed Gideon's hips and pushed him down until the head of his big cock slipped between the cleft of his backside. He didn't push inside, waiting for Gideon to take over.

More lubricant than usual smeared over him, and he looked down to see a small puddle of Aleron's precum had drizzled onto his own stomach. Gideon stared at how much he'd leaked just while fingering him.

Oh. He's a lot more excited than I thought.

"Gideon, please," Aleron begged quietly. "I cannot wait much longer."

Big hands gripped his hips, and they shook with restraint. His claws were wisely sheathed, otherwise their hard grip may have caused them to sink beneath his skin.

Just how much was Aleron holding back? The fact he'd

taken the time to prepare him just showed the power of Aleron's self-control, and how much he *cared* for Gideon.

Lifting up, he gripped the head of Aleron's purple cock and nudged it against his hole. He opened up over the tip easily, but Gideon shook with exertion to get the flared rim through. He bent his head back, resting it as he bounced – just trying everything to make it go in without hurting.

Bit by bit, he worked it in until it popped through. His toes on the ground pushed up as his knees buckled, and he let out a hiss through his teeth. His skin crawled now, and his breaths stammered as he shoved both hands forward to grip Aleron's fur.

Fuck. It's in. And he needed a damn moment.

His body *could* accept it. He knew he would eventually soften around it, but right then, he felt like he was seconds from splitting in two.

If we didn't prepare me over the last few days... Gideon knew this wouldn't have been possible at all. First Aleron's tongue near the spring, and almost a new finger each night. Without all that, Gideon knew he'd be clawing to get away with the snugness that lingered even now.

It was probably too soon, but Gideon... just wanted Aleron more than anything. He was finally giving them both what they yearned for, and he hoped it soothed all the tender aches that remained within their chests and hearts.

"You're huge." He bit out the compliment.

When Gideon received no answer, and his partner had been awfully quiet for too long, he opened his eyes – he hadn't even realised he'd clenched them shut. He also hadn't noticed that Aleron's hands had come away from him, and one was wrapped around his snout. The other dug its claws into his abdomen, drawing purple blood, while his whole body quaked.

"Aleron?" he asked softly, tension easing out of him.

"You are so tight," Aleron choked out, before his hand

slipped away from his snout to grip Gideon's thigh. "And so hot inside." His claws dug into his skin when he gripped the other leg, no longer able to keep them safely sheathed. "Soft, and warm, and better than before. *Finally.*"

With a deep, shuddering groan, he pushed Gideon down halfway. A gasp ripped from him, just as Aleron's head fell back and his spine arched.

"W-wait," Gideon stated when the Duskwalker subtly started thrusting into him. His cock was getting bigger, thickening before going down like it was swelling repeatedly!

Aleron's wings buckled inwards beneath his weight. He didn't stop moving, but it stopped mattering when heat spread within Gideon.

With his lips parted and his eyes wide, Gideon looked down as if that would help him see through his own body. Yet, he knew without a doubt that hot, thick liquid was flooding his insides.

The feel of it rekindled his erection, hardening it.

"Are you... coming already?" Gideon asked in disbelief.

A whimper was Aleron's response as his abdomen rippled and contracted. His long arms quaked while he held onto Gideon and softly rocked himself through his orgasm. His skull tossed to the left as he wildly huffed through parted fangs.

Holy shit. Do I really feel that good for him?

Why did knowing that help to unwind the last of Gideon's tension? He found the heat soothing as well, and knowing that Aleron was this crazed for him had Gideon wanting to be naughtier. Bring Aleron to greater heights so it would be more overwhelming.

It stroked him in a different way – in his subconscious, where he didn't mind the uncomfortableness in his own body so long as it brought Aleron bliss. Gideon even started to rock with his hips, hoping the last of his release would be stronger.

When his cock finally ceased twitching, Gideon waited for Aleron to go lax beneath them.

"Did that feel good?" Eyes alight with mischievous desire when his skull drifted back over to look upon him, Gideon licked at the seam of his lips. "Feeling you come made me hard again." He wasn't lying either. His dick had been soft until he felt it. "You weren't even the whole way inside me, Aleron."

A sly grin lifted his cheeks as Gideon raised up and off Aleron's cock. The Duskwalker's snout dropped to his chest, so he could look down to where they were joined, until he popped out. Gideon didn't mind that he would have to work it back inside, not when he was pleased that Aleron's cum drizzled out and on top of his purple shaft.

"Look at how much you came just from putting it in. Did you want me that much?"

Gideon did wince at how much came out, but the satisfied growl that burst from Aleron was utterly worth it.

Just as another lewd remark was about to fall past his lips, hoping to play with and rile this Duskwalker up, he shortly realised it was entirely unnecessary. It was also far too late to take back what he'd just done, and it may have been a poor decision on his part.

Whether it be the sight, or the fact Gideon had taken his cock out, one had worked Aleron into a lather that bubbled over into action.

A yell clogged in Gideon's throat when he was tossed to the side. It hadn't been careful, and he barely had time to register what happened before he was rolled onto his knees and chest. His right thigh was grabbed and then used to yank him backwards across the grass. Gideon pushed up against the ground, but Aleron shoved him back down as he knelt behind Gideon.

"Wait. I haven't completely taken–" He couldn't finish explaining that he should be on top until his body had fully adjusted.

A tongue slipped from between his hips, over each of his vertebrae, until it was gliding over his neck. He let out a fucked-up squeak when it pushed into the shell of his ear.

"I will be slow," Aleron rumbled, gripping his girth to steady it as he prodded at his entrance. "I will be gentle with my human bride and his cute little hole soaked in my cum."

Instantly groaning at the perverted image those words brought forth, Gideon found that was so much more titillating being spoken in his deep, gruff voice.

Gideon decided to just... trust him. *He knows what he's doing... I hope. I've already taught him.* Rather than tightening up in uncertainty as Aleron started feeding him his massive cock, Gideon focused on breathing through it, and even pushed to help accept it. The head popped through faster, Aleron's strength and all the adjustment from before making it easier.

Fisting stalks of wet grass, Gideon braced himself.

Aleron pumped with long strokes, and each one gouged his abdomen. They abraded Gideon's prostate with mild friction, enough to make it feel good despite the strangeness of his body moving and adjusting to something this big... and long. The deeper Aleron shoved, the closer he came until his fur started tickling Gideon's back, causing shivers to rush over him.

His head tilted back when Aleron got to a certain point and remained there for a moment. Gideon had thought it was over, that he'd taken all he could, until a hard ridge nudged against his tight ring stretched around this Duskwalker's cock.

Aleron pushed, as if he wanted to work it inside him as well.

Gideon tensed up and darted his hand down to grab Aleron's shaft. His tentacles had started gliding over Gideon's hips, proving how deeply he was taking the Duskwalker.

"N-no more," he pleaded through huffs. "You're so deep. I can't take any more."

By the two braided rings he fingered, he knew he'd taken him three-quarters of the way. Most humans couldn't reach this depth, and Gideon's insides already felt like a mess just by taking this. He was full, stuffed, and already struggling. He wanted this to feel good, but it was starting to hurt his gut.

Aleron took Gideon's hand from where it was wrapped around his cock and pinned it against the ground near his head. Then Aleron curled his strong, furry arm underneath him, hugging Gideon to his chest while his palm stroked down his bare stomach.

Aleron's fangs were parted when he buried his snout at the corner of his jaw, and let out pants that wrapped around Gideon's throat. They were wet and hot, and smelt like hazelnuts and cedarwood – so soothing and pleasant.

"But you have not taken your favourite part of me yet, little spring," Aleron purred against him.

With a small amount of slow force, Aleron shoved both those rings inside him, and Gideon tensed around them. His knees tried to buckle inwards as his back bowed. He let out a grunted yell as his eyes clenched when they popped through.

"Aleron," he whined.

"Good, little human. You feel so good around me already." Aleron nibbled at his neck as he stroked up Gideon's stomach so he could cup his chest. "You are so close to taking all of me, but I will wait until you see."

Gideon didn't know if Aleron did it on purpose or not, but his nipple slipped between two of the Duskwalker's fingers and they pinched it. Aleron gave him time at this depth, and just seemed content to tease Gideon with his fangs and tongue while his hand petted.

At least the mixture of cum and lubricant made

everything feel nice. And having hard heat penetrating all the way inside him like this softened his muscles from within.

Aleron pulled back, only to push forward to the same spot. The movement was subtle, not too far that the rings popped back out of him, but not going any deeper. Gideon was thankful for that; he still didn't know how he felt about this depth.

Aleron moved again before starting a slow rhythm. This time, a tiny moan slipped out of Gideon as pleasure sparked, one he hadn't expected.

Then Aleron spread his knees slightly, pressed down a touch more, and Gideon's eyes shot open wide. The spark morphed into a jolt that spasmed through his balls and up his semi-hard cock, which hardened more and more each time Aleron rolled back or forth.

After only a few thrusts, bliss radiated within his entire groin until his pelvic bones vibrated with it.

"See?" Aleron rasped when he clenched around his thick cock, licking over his cheek and coating it with wetness. "You like me right here."

Gosh. Having a Duskwalker say that about him, seeming to know more about his body than Gideon did, twisted his thoughts. And yet, Gideon couldn't respond, not when he was too busy moaning each time those firm, pliable rings pressed hard against his prostate. Back and forth, over and over again, shoving against it in a way that had him seeing stars.

Stars that blended with the ones that were beginning to twinkle through the darkening dusk. Everything got brighter, his pupils dilating while his vision blurred in euphoria.

Aleron's arm was wedged into Gideon's armpit and spanned across his chest, preventing him from gripping his own cock to stroke it, so Gideon reached up with his free hand to grip the fur on Aleron's shoulder. The grass Gideon had been fisting had ripped, and he needed to grab ahold of something sturdy as his mind fizzled and crackled.

Gideon tilted his hips until he found a position that intensified it. White-hot pleasure struck him.

"Oh fuck," he moaned out on parted lips, his features tensing up.

Why does that have to feel so damn good? It took away all uncomfortableness, all the pain, and only radiated pleasure that bordered on agony. Suddenly he needed more, needed faster, needed to be pumped into until he turned into a twitchy puddle.

He started grinding with Aleron, his body trying to take over, until Gideon just shoved back hard and mounted him the entire way in one swift motion. He choked out a sharp gasp as his lungs seized.

When he clamped up, Aleron let out a deep growl. Hips shoved harder, his strokes became longer and deeper. The moment Gideon relaxed around him, Aleron held him tight and thrust faster.

"Do you understand how much I have longed for this?" Aleron snarled, suddenly slamming into him. "You have made me wait so long."

His balls drew up constantly as precum bubbled, each clench shooting pleasure throughout his body. His abdomen muscles twitched and tightened, his parted thighs quaking between Aleron's. The Duskwalker's low snorts and deep huffs tingled his senses as he shoved into Gideon. They grew louder, more ferocious, each time his hips nestled tightly against Gideon's arse with a wet slap.

The sounds that came from Gideon were lewd and strangled, but he couldn't stop making them. His eyes flickered, only to shut tightly when his body began to stiffen.

Still pinning Gideon's hand to the ground, Aleron grew frantic. Harder and deeper, where no human could touch, yet Gideon rocked back for more, needing that depth so Aleron's rings could play with him.

"Oh god," Gideon choked out when his spine tingled, his cock aching to be touched. "Oh fuck, Aleron." His stomach clenched, his balls drew up tightly, and his eyes rolled back hard. "Ohfuckoh–*nngh*."

He flinched as white-hot pleasure jolted through him.

Gideon twitched and spasmed as his balls began to empty against the grass beneath him. His bobbing cock pulsated wildly, while his ass quivered and clamped around Aleron as he violently came. Squirming, thrusting back and forth as one of the most intense orgasms of his life was ripped from him, Gideon ceased existing.

For a few moments, all he knew was complete and utter euphoria. It radiated throughout his entire body, from the crown of his head all the way to his arching feet.

The intensity of releasing from this stimulation was tenfold compared to coming through just his dick. He felt it in his blood, in every muscle and cell of his body. He was boiling over until he thought he'd evaporate.

The Duskwalker shuddered in reaction, letting out a broken groan as he snugly held Gideon. Aleron braced Gideon's body as Gideon came for him, because of him, in the most profound and startling way.

His aftershocks were made more powerful by Aleron still pumping, never ceasing. His cock continued to jerk because of it, and his eyelids fluttered.

"I felt you come, smelt it," Aleron whimpered. "You felt so good clamping around me. I like knowing you adore me inside you like this. I missed it."

Aleron released the grip he had on Gideon's hand and tickled his claws down his abdomen, his pelvis. Every inch he brushed down had Gideon gulping for air until Aleron gripped his deflating cock.

Breaths cutting short, Gideon shakily covered Aleron's fingers with a pathetic groan. "I just came. I'm really sensitive." There was little fight in his body, too weak from his orgasm to have any strength. The ring still moving inside him further drained him, causing his lungs to squeeze almost every time. "Not both at the same time."

Aleron's hand fisting his cock felt too amazing right now while he fucked into him. No human should take this kind of pleasure. It was even rapidly hardening him, despite having just released.

He wondered why it was so slippery, until he realised that some of Aleron's cum and lubricant had leaked from his ass, trickled down his balls and onto his shaft. Now, it was being used as a thick, sticky lubricant, squelching as he cuddled him within his massive hand.

"But I want to feel you come again. I want you to milk me of my seed while I'm deep inside you. Have you spasm like you did before, and make that cute little noise again." Seeming to excite himself, Aleron's hips picked up speed. A quiet growl vibrated against his back as Aleron deeply, darkly rumbled, "I want to see you fucking lost for me, Gideon. I have needed you for so long. To be inside you, fucking you, and have you needy beneath me."

The more he spoke, the more his growl softened, and a pleasure-laced whine echoed from him instead. Aleron started pounding into him hard. Each slap against his arse cheeks shoved Gideon's cock into his fist while tentacles drew him back. Aleron lowered some of his heavy weight onto him, as his slams made Gideon fuck into his clawed fist.

In that moment, Aleron released his pent-up frustrations on Gideon's body. Yet the bliss that clutched at his groin forced little more than weak moans to spill from his lips. With his eyes rolling back constantly, Gideon happily welcomed it, his mind flicking over into a thoughtless, lust-addled tempest of chaos.

His brain throbbed at the sensation of being struck deep.

His skin tingled until he was sure it'd melt from his muscles, rendering him even more bare than his naked body up against Aleron's furry, feathery one.

The pleasure was too much. He became a sensitive bundle of nerves beneath this rutting Duskwalker, his whole body turning into an erogenous zone. Gideon dug his nails deeper into Aleron's wonderful fist, unsure if it was to pry it off or clamp him until Gideon came again.

He couldn't even speak, and the only two words that could reach through his conscience were 'please' and 'Aleron.'

His head lolled. Grass tickled Gideon's lips before he turned his face to the side, just so he wasn't breathing in dirt. The only things holding him up were tentacles and the arm crossed over his chest.

Without them, he would have collapsed long ago.

When he was close, Gideon tightened. Despite the overbearing intensity, he started thrusting into Aleron's hand, his hips jerking back and forth frantically of their own accord. Gideon desperately chased his release.

Two wings *thunked* against the ground and drew in tight against his sides, trapping him, but never wrapping around him. They flapped and shuddered, and it took him moments to understand they were in reaction to each of Gideon's ass spasms and clenches around his shaft.

Sweat had long ago drenched his entire body, and his hair clung to his cheeks, his brow, and the back of his neck. Aleron's heat was too much bearing down on him, yet he wanted – needed – more.

In that moment, Gideon felt so vulnerable that he wanted to be covered up head to toe as sparks flashed behind his clenched eyes. Especially as his entire groin tightened, and all Gideon knew was unfathomable pleasure, unable to do anything but let it consume him.

No sound came from his spit-covered lips as seed spurted from his cock into Aleron's tight fist. Orgasming inside something warm and tight, while he was pounded into, was so intense Gideon thought he'd burst from his tingling skin. He stopped moving when it felt like his heart had given up and ceased beating. Then his knees tried to spread when Aleron's cock started thickening, pulsing over and over again as a copious amount of cum filled him deep within.

It was warm, that's all he could tell.

The Duskwalker's quaking roar parted his fangs and tilted his head back. With his tentacles locked around Gideon so tight they were bruising, Aleron's hips stayed snug against him. Other than their combined shudders, neither moved. It allowed Gideon to experience them achieving release in tandem, and somehow it felt... beautiful.

Then, when it finally ended, his hands dropped to the ground. After the tension that had locked up all his swollen muscles, Gideon couldn't lift a single finger. Sweat coated him to the point where it dripped down his temples. All he could do was rapidly chase the breaths he'd lost, willing his heart to stop thrumming in his head and making it dizzy. It beat so fast, like it was about to burst through his ribcage.

When had night fallen upon them? *I feel like I'm about to pass out.*

Sex had never been this insane before.

He'd been a heaving huff many times, but he'd never been *feeble*.

Gideon couldn't even open his eyes as blood and oxygen rushed back to his brain. Blots of light flashed behind his eyelids, and nothing he did helped to aid him. He felt too hot, too empty and full at the same time. The level of satisfaction he'd achieved bled contentment into every capillary in his body, washing through him in the most heart-warming, blissful way.

He'd never been so calm before, or this at ease.

With Aleron jammed inside him to the absolute hilt, he drifted off as images of another world began to flicker behind his eyelids.

As content as he was, Gideon knew one thing with absolute certainty: something was... *missing*.

Aleron wished his feathers would go down, or that he could do more than be frozen as he held his lax bride.

It is warm inside him.

A little heartbeat fluttered all over him: around his cock, in his arms, his hand, and against his chest. It felt like a moth flapping fuzzy wings against his skull, so delicate, pretty, and cuddly.

The yearning to speak drizzled through him. The longing to tell this male how much he meant to Aleron, how much he cared for and adored him, simmered within his mind. He wanted to call Gideon his bride and let him know he would be utterly cherished for life.

But Aleron held back, as he did with his wings, not wishing to overwhelm him.

They'd truly connected this night. They were one, as he'd so desperately craved. Gideon had gifted him this – a moment where most of his fears and worries evaporated into utter serenity.

Aleron didn't wish for it to be cut short by his own foolishness. Gideon was currently full of life in his arms, his features pink from their fucking, his skin dotted in salty liquid.

He didn't want to see it pale.

Eventually that fluttering beat settled, as did Gideon's expression. Aleron lifted his skull so he could lick his cheek, doting on Gideon with his tongue if he couldn't use his words.

Aleron received no response, not even a twitch of an eye.

His tentacles loosened their hold, their nagging desire to clutch until he spent finally satisfied. Upon their release, white filled his sight when Gideon slipped halfway down his cock until the ground stopped him from going any further.

Leaning back a bit, he sheathed his claws and lifted his bride's handsome face off the ground to direct it towards him. "Gideon?"

When he didn't respond again, his chest tightened. *Oh no. Did I break him? I was too rough.*

Aleron had been trying to be gentle with him! Well, he tried.

Is it possible to fuck a human to death?! If so, he would have liked to have known that before he did it!

Carefully, so as not to hurt him, Aleron pulled his hips back until he no longer mounted Gideon's small form. Too worried to be disappointed that the little male was no longer cuddling his dick, he turned Gideon to his side so Aleron could check on him.

His sensitive hearing meant he registered Gideon's steady heartbeat without needing to press the side of his head to him. He was breathing fine – actually, it was rather deep and even.

Aleron took in his closed eyelids flickering, then a light snore, and a small, relieved chuckle fell from him.

He is fine, just asleep.

Aleron wished he'd figured that out before he took his shaft from Gideon, but that was okay. With his cum-drenched hand, Aleron patted his own chest to smear Gideon's scent on him, wanting it to stain. He then collected the little male into his arms until their bodies meshed against each other, and draped a wing over him so he would be warm.

Face to face and lying on their sides, Aleron supported

the back of his head so he could gaze down at his slumbering bride.

Such a pretty, handsome male, Aleron thought with a hum, brushing the pad of his thumb down his broad cheek. He flicked the golden ring dangling from his lobe, as his sight turned bright pink. *I like these. It is like we are matching now.*

Aleron knew his skull glittered with gold, and he adored that they now both sparkled.

We connected. It'd felt better than Tenebris. Stronger, more real, and even more precious. *We finally became one again.* The thrill of that shone behind his sternum, radiating tenderness. There was no need for hope, not when his bride had so sweetly called his name all throughout.

You are mine, little spring, and I am yours. The gratification of being able to finally show that made his heart feel swollen, while his deflated cock pushed up over their snuggling hips.

He brought his snout down to nuzzle Gideon's sharp jaw, letting it scratch at his bone. Then Aleron licked his forehead, returning the sweet kisses he'd given him earlier. He gave the male many, uncaring of the salty taste that greeted him.

Aleron hoped Gideon could feel his doting actions, trusting he wouldn't reject them.

He hoped they gave him pleasant dreams.

THIRTY-FIVE

When Aleron woke from his slumber, he did so with his
arms empty of a soft and alluring human, and night still
present. His body lacked an external heat source – one that
didn't even tentatively press against his back.

Fur and feathers lifting in apprehension, a lance of
disquiet pierced his gut. *Where did he go?*

Lifting his head to dart it around, he searched for the
male who smelt like the freshest, dewiest forest. Aleron
didn't have to look far. Relief immediately washed through
him, and he let out the breath he'd incidentally been
holding.

Gideon sat a few feet away. Close enough to show he
had remained by his side, but far enough that they weren't
touching.

Immediately he sensed something was wrong.

The hard and heavy pound of Gideon's pulse, the sharp,
shallow breathing, and the tension in his shoulders was all
alarming. With his knees up and one arm crossed over his
lap, while the elbow of the other leant on his right knee,
Gideon covered his eyes and appeared to be pressing his
fingers into them.

I have only seen him do this when he is deeply distressed.

Aleron shifted to crouch, then cautiously crawled over to
him on his hands and feet.

Considering what they'd done before this human slept, he'd expected him to wake... well. Aleron had held him, petted him, gave him soft licks so as not to disturb Gideon until he himself had drifted off hours later. Aleron thought he'd wake up peacefully, contentedly, with this human still in his arms.

Aleron always woke before him. Being Mavka, he only required a few hours of rest close to dawn, whereas Gideon slept the whole night – often restlessly.

He'd actually been hoping to wake up and replay their time in Tenebris, where Aleron had teased this male right after they'd been intimate. He'd been trying to stay alert to do this until Gideon's soft breaths and heartbeat had eventually lulled him asleep as well.

To find Gideon sitting by himself instead instilled worry.

I did not feel him leave me.

Aleron also hadn't heard him slip into Merikh's lake and wash, considering the mingle of their sexual marking scents had softened. Gideon had even fully donned his clothing.

Yet... rather than coming back to Aleron's warmth, he'd chosen to lightly shiver with nothing but his jacket to keep out the winter night air.

"Gideon?" he called softly, reaching out to brush the backs of his claws against his exposed cheek.

With a sharp gasp, Gideon darted his hand away from his face and turned to him. His eyes were glassy, with a small amount of pinkness at the edges. He didn't appear to have cried, but he didn't look well. Sweat dotted his brow, and he looked less colourful. Not pale, but not tanned like usual.

"You scared the shit out of me," Gideon muttered, averting his gaze. "How can you be that big and so quiet at the same time?"

"Did... I do something wrong?" It was all Aleron could think, since nothing could have happened between their intimacy and now.

Gideon's eyes widened with mild panic and shot to his

skull. They softened, and a small chuckle fell past his lips as he rubbed the back of his neck. His ears pinkened.

"What? No," Gideon reassured, casting him a smile that didn't reach his eyes. His arm shook, and the trembling in his pinkened fingers was even more noticeable. "I had a great time."

Why did that make him feel *worse,* somehow? Aleron couldn't tell if it was a lie or not.

Aleron lowered onto his hands so he could be the same level as him. He dipped his skull underneath his gaze. "Then what is wrong?"

Aleron's heart told him to scoop this male into his arms and hold him, but his mind said to give him space. Always space, always the opposite of what *he* wanted.

Gideon's brows furrowed and his gaze hardened. He opened his mouth, only to shut it like he couldn't decide what he wished to say. Avoidance, most likely. He rarely spoke about what lingered in his mind, no matter how much Aleron silently pleaded for him to.

Then the male covered his mouth as he looked away, only to scratch at the side of his scalp. Fidgeting and restless, he appeared to be fighting with himself.

"I had a... dream," Gideon started, his quiet revelation surprising Aleron. His head bent forward to stare at the ground near his feet. "I remember a bunch of stuff from Tenebris."

Fingers twitching, Aleron brought them closer to his abdomen and cupped them. "Were they not *good* memories?"

As far as Aleron was concerned, almost all of their time in Tenebris had been pleasant. There had only been a single conversation he'd found terrible, and it had been when he asked Gideon to come back to life with him.

But Weldir gave Gideon his own memories. There should be no reason for another misunderstanding regarding it.

"No, they weren't bad," Gideon stated warmly, with a note of humour. "They were actually quite lovely." Then he leaned back on his hands to look at the sky, inspecting the many stars and the setting crescent moon with deep interest. "However, I remember us walking through a town full of cats, and you being veeery interested in what a man and woman were doing together in private. That's quite improper, Aleron. You shouldn't peek while people are having sex."

His wings shifted nervously as his orbs turned a reddish pink. Yet Gideon granted him a sly smirk, showing that he actually wasn't all that bothered by it.

"Mainly, I just remember us walking through different forests." His expression fell then, as he tilted his head at a star. "Lots of you talking about Ingram, but I think you've repeated much of it. I can't believe all that witty sarcasm you have is from me teaching you."

"I like it. I find it funny," Aleron grumbled.

He didn't want Gideon to think this newfound trait was done only to appease him.

It wasn't. It was like a game, one which Aleron enjoyed playing – he just hadn't known that yet. He *adored* teasing this human. Even more so when Aleron caught him stumbling, rather than the other way around.

It often filled his chest with humour.

"Some of it is just flashes or long moments. Perhaps a week of it, but it felt so long. I don't think I really remembered anything important. Or... maybe it's all important, I don't know." Then Gideon ran his fingers through his hair like he often did. "You slept a few times, but I never did. We held hands almost the entire way, but I remembered why I first reached out to you."

Then Gideon, with a bent elbow, lifted his hand up. He covered his face with the other and went still. When too long passed, he wiggled his fingers.

Aleron realised Gideon wanted him to place his own into

it.

As soon as he did, Gideon wrapped his fingers around his thumb, and Aleron swallowed his whole hand up. He tried not to put too much weight into it, since the small human never lowered his arm to relax into the hold.

"Aleron... what does this *mean* to you?"

Tilting his head at where they were touching, his sight morphing to dark yellow, he didn't quite understand the point of this question.

Not when his little hand felt perfect in his.

"That you are with me, and wish to remain so," he answered plainly.

The entire time they had done this in Tenebris, Aleron had thought Gideon had done this to remain by his side. That he would rather be with Aleron than fade into his happiest dreams like all the other humans.

Aleron had chosen him. To ease his loneliness and eventually steal his heart along the way. Gideon had been his companion, his first human friend.

Aleron always knew he did not *need* to choose him as his bride.

But, when given the chance to go back to Ingram by himself, all Aleron could think was that he didn't wish to leave Gideon behind. He'd wanted this human just as much as he longed to be with his kindred, and he couldn't picture his future without him.

Gideon's humour and cheer had brightened him, just as his seriousness and sternness stiffened him. His sadness touched his own, but it meant they were the same and could deeply understand each other better than anyone else living. Gideon had been patient with Aleron as he taught him all he could. Gideon reassured him when he felt lacking, making Aleron think fondly of himself despite the blankness within his thoughts that still lingered.

And, despite all the ugliness of their return to Earth, not

once had Gideon made him feel less. Yes, he'd made him feel deeply unwanted, but not once had he been cruel. He'd never truly verbally assaulted him, called him ugly, or stupid, or annoying.

Even when deeply lost, the heart of his bride had still remained. Kind, even when crying. Gentle, even when ripping away from his touch. Loving enough to *try*.

Hope was what had guided him.

The male who had giggled within Aleron's wings during their final hours in Tenebris was still a part of him. Already, bit by bit, Gideon's true nature was revealing itself from behind the invisible veil of his sadness.

He would not blame Gideon for how he acted while blanketed in hopelessness. Aleron, when suffering and unsure of how to cope with it, had been violent towards his own kindred. Yet, he'd always been forgiven.

He had already done the same for this male currently holding his hand.

That you are with me and wish to remain so. That would forever be its meaning to him.

"That's what I thought," Gideon muttered, before slipping his hand away despite Aleron wishing to hold on.

A coldness swept through him, unsure if this was the wrong thing to say or not.

Gideon immediately warmed that cold sensation by shifting to his knees and lifting to place his arms around Aleron's neck. He hugged Aleron tightly to the point his shoulder dug into the front of his throat. Aleron didn't mind. This human had the urge to embrace him, and he swiftly curled his arms around Gideon's torso to bring them even closer.

For a long while, they just held each other.

It felt... sad, even when it radiated with tenderness. Aleron couldn't explain it, but it brought a heaviness.

"You can put your wings around me," Gideon whispered so softly it tickled his senses.

As much as he wanted to, Aleron hesitated. They twitched behind him, nagging and begging to take his offer.

He gave in and placed them around the lower half of his body. Enough to partially bring him into them, but not in a way that would cover Gideon's head.

Uncertainty clawed down his spine when Gideon's nails bit down through his feathers to dig into flesh. Did Gideon clutch him in joy, or was he uncomfortable with the tightness that now surrounded him?

Gideon buried his face into the fur of his neck.

Unsure of what to do, or what any of this meant, he just held the male. Aleron did rapidly sniff at the air when he scented the tiniest hint of salt, but he didn't know where it came from. *Tears?*

Gideon leaned back, releasing him as he did, and swiftly turned. Aleron didn't have the chance to assess his face to know if he'd been correct.

The sky had lightened, the world waking and the sun beginning its crawl.

"Alright. I guess it's time to go find these other Duskwalkers." Gideon trotted over to his guitar not far from them and came back with it quickly. He grinned, but at Aleron's chest and not his skull. "Is it weird that I'm excited to meet more of your kind? I bet none of them are as cool as you, though, since you can fly."

I have no idea what just happened.

Aleron had an inkling that he'd made matters undoubtably *worse.*

THIRTY-SIX

Hovering in a beam of moonlight, Aleron clutched his precious human tighter.

"Is that the Demon King's castle?" Gideon asked, peering over his arm. "Looks like he needs to remodel it."

Aleron didn't know what to feel regarding the stone rubble that lay in waste before them. The entire castle looked as though it'd crumbled from the inside before falling on top of itself. Nothing had managed to stay upright.

It'd been so long since it was destroyed that dust had settled around it like a grey pool of ash.

"Yes. This was where it was."

Should he be relieved? Perhaps it was due to his nature, but he'd never hated the Demon King. Even when he'd been the reason for Aleron's death, it was just something that happened in his life.

The pain and fear he'd suffered had been intense, but it was over, and he was alive... again.

Aleron didn't care if the Demon King lived or died. So long as he left him, his kindred, and their brides in peace, he could do what he wanted. His war was not Aleron's.

Emerie did this. His chest puffed in pride for his twin's chosen bride. No matter the reason, it was still magnificent that such a tiny creature could cause this kind of devastation. *She is a formidable human.*

In the distance, the Demon village looked similar to how he last saw it. A few of the large trees facing Jabez's castle were a little bare, but they were mostly intact. From the outside, he could tell something like cloth was blocking it from within to stop the sunlight from filtering in.

Not wishing to linger in the centre of the Veil, Aleron moved them on.

Thankfully his ability to fly allowed them to swiftly cross the land in comparison to sprinting, but he didn't move at full strength due to his poor bride. Aleron didn't wish to chill Gideon too badly, and his eyes often watered when battered by too much speed. However, they were moving faster now that he wasn't searching for his kindred. He truly believed they wouldn't be within the Veil, since Aleron wouldn't even dare take Gideon into it.

Which was why he never landed, even when his human grew tired and fell asleep in his arms.

The Witch Owl visited us.

Since a large, yet white creature had approached them in the air, Aleron knew instantly it hadn't been a Demon. Still, he'd never expected her, in her barn owl form, to fly next to them with the tip of her wing almost brushing against his own. Many of her feathers had turned brown, as if her cloak of them had changed since he'd last seen her this way.

Oddly enough... he hadn't minded her presence. In a way, it had been comforting to not be alone in the air.

After Weldir spoke with Aleron in Tenebris, and explained who and what she was, fondness had grown in Aleron's heart for her. She'd also played with him and his kindred, toying with them from the air to invite them to chase her. They could never harm her; she was too quick for them and seemed to know their next actions as if she could see the future.

She'd also rested just outside their kindred cuddle. Never

inside it, as they wouldn't let her, but she'd inserted herself into the warm bond as best she could.

He'd never understood why until Weldir. *She is my creator.* The one who had given the Mavka life, and had tried to guide them as best she could.

Since Gideon never woke during their short flight together, Aleron refrained from speaking to her. Yet her yellow owl eyes communicated silently – she was relieved about his return. She also looked towards Gideon in his arms, as though she'd truly approached to check on their progress.

Aleron just held him tighter and nodded. Then she banked to the left and disappeared into the mist.

Tranquillity fell over him after she left, only for it to be broken when they were attacked in the air by a curious winged Demon.

Aleron was able to grab ahold of it with his talons, spin in the air, and throw it towards a tree below them. He quickly flew and evaded from then on, and flew higher, hoping to avoid a second one noticing him in the air over the Veil.

The interruption startled the human awake.

Gideon spoke even less after this, if at all, and Aleron found that... alarming after the day before where he'd chatted non-stop. He wanted to believe it was just due to tiredness, but he couldn't shake that something was amiss.

Where was the annoyingly chatty, cheerful human from the day before? He missed that side of Gideon already.

When Aleron asked him about it, he mentioned his backside was sore while laughing. He didn't find that funny whatsoever. He didn't want Gideon to be in pain, nor did Aleron wish for him to deflect what truly bothered him with humour.

Then Gideon had receded further into himself.

Yet he terribly confused Aleron. Gideon would respond to Aleron's attempts at stirring him, and would smile warmly up at him, with emotional exhaustion evident in his gaze. At one point, Gideon even placed his palm over the back of Aleron's hand where it gripped his thigh, grasping it like Gideon wished to silently comfort him.

He became a contradiction – tender towards Aleron, but otherwise subdued and withdrawn.

Aleron hoped he wasn't the reason for his troubled mind, since Gideon kept reaching for him. It did leave him wondering... *why*.

Musing on this was pointless, as he'd gain no answers within his stunted thoughts.

Just as dawn tinted the sky with purple, the glow of multiple domes glittered into view. Aleron ducked inside the closest, a yellow one, before dropping to the ground.

"This is new," Aleron stated. Although the magical dome above wasn't, the small clearing surrounded by dense trees was. His gaze drifted over the freshly built house that hadn't been here last time he'd seen this ward, but the scent here was familiar. "It is heavy with Kitty... I mean Faunus' scent. No one is here, though."

There were also many others' scents here, but he only knew who one of them was. The wolf-skulled Mavka had frequented here regularly, as well as three humans – he couldn't tell their genders by the faded scents.

Even Ingram's scent lingers. But it was weeks, perhaps even months old.

It was Faunus' that remained the strongest, and he gazed up at the dome. *This is his magic? It is the same colour as his orbs.*

A ripple rushed down his back, shuddering his wings. He swiftly lifted off without warning.

"Whoa!" Gideon yelled, taken by surprise.

As soon as Aleron was high enough, he took in the two other wards he could see. One green, like the fox Mavka's orbs and the other... purple! Like his kindred's!

Aleron shot for the purple one barely a few minutes' flying distance away.

All the hope that flooded his veins with fiery adrenaline bled out like cold poison. As soon as he landed, Aleron knew it to be empty. There was no building, and his kindred had spent so little time here that not even his scent remained.

It bordered directly with the fox-skulled Mavka's ward, and he walked through them. Ingram's dome half sat over the top of it, as though Ingram hadn't wisely planned where he placed it.

Another house came into view, this one empty like the last. The scents here were stronger, as if those that occupied it only left within the last few days.

A deep growl tightened his lungs as it bubbled up his throat. He could not question the other Mavka if none of them were here! And if he struggled to find Ingram, Aleron doubted he'd have any luck finding these Mavka either.

Only one last house remained, and he'd been rather hoping he wouldn't have to greet Orpheus. Although Aleron liked him because he was of his kind, Orpheus did not return that affection.

That is, if he is even in his territory!

Aleron lifted off.

Since the sun had nearly fully risen now, he was able to locate the house surrounded by a clearing. Not a single tree swayed within the salt border, as if Orpheus had wanted the area to be showered in sunshine throughout the day. Already, light peeked over his territory, highlighting it in warmth.

Relief coursed through Aleron when he noticed the wolf-skulled Mavka sitting within his makeshift ward carved of salt. He did, however, tilt his head at the little blonde human seated next to him, who let out a wild giggle.

She wore a simple pink dress, from what he could tell, and Orpheus had donned some kind of black trousers. His chest was bare, as were his humanoid feet, and his curled deer tail stuck out as it rested upon the ground.

Aleron circled them, and Orpheus' skull darted up towards them.

He correctly assumed Orpheus would swiftly pounce to his hands and feet. Still territorial as ever, Orpheus brought himself closer to the blonde human, tucking her seated form into his side to shield her.

Aleron made sure to land in front of him, and some distance away, so as not to encroach too heavily upon what Aleron could now see to be his bride. Even if the soul between his twisting horns hadn't been obvious, the possessive markings covering each other were. They had recently been entangled, although hers smelt... different to Gideon's. More feminine, sweet, and subtle.

Thankfully Gideon remained unmoving in his hold as Aleron waited for Orpheus to take them in. The female poked her head around his shoulder, wary but not shy, with bright-green eyes. Her loose, blonde hair swayed down her cheek to curtain one side of her head.

The wolf Mavka tilted his head sharply before slowly unfurling himself from his protective stance. He did so sooner than Aleron expected, but perhaps that was due to Gideon and his soul floating between his own twisting horns.

"Aleron?" Orpheus said his name hesitantly, lowering his hand to help the female to her feet. "You've returned?"

With orbs shifting dark yellow in curiosity, Aleron's skull reared back in surprise. "You know of my name?"

"Who doesn't?" the female stated with a laugh, her sharp features softening. She placed her hands on the swell of her hips. "Ingram speaks of you quite a lot when he and Emerie are here."

Her laughter caused him to flinch, unused to such a feminine voice producing the sound. He much preferred

Gideon's warm chuckle, finding its depth and familiarity soothing and alluring.

"Is it safe to put me down now?" Gideon asked in a low voice, his hand beside his mouth as if to hide it from them. "My back aches and my case strap is killing my shoulder."

"Oh, sorry." Aleron promptly placed him on his feet, and the male was quick to move the strap so it crossed his torso in the opposite direction. Aleron lifted his skull to Orpheus. "I am searching for Ingram. Has he been here recently?"

Neither came forward to close the space between them, but Aleron could tell that his apprehension was unneeded. Orpheus' orbs were yellow rather than blue, and his stance lacked the aggressive, threatening tension he was used to.

Placing an arm around his female's side, showing his affection for her, Orpheus stated, "They were here three weeks ago."

Aleron's wings drooped as his head lowered in defeat. *Three weeks?* His hand clenched into a tight fist, just as red flared in his orbs. *Then where are they?*

Why must he wait? Why must this task be so difficult? He and his kindred were bonded on a spiritual level. He'd always thought he'd be able to follow his instincts to Ingram, that the strings connecting them would steer them closer.

Yet Aleron's sight lacked his kindred's scales, his raven skull, his very presence, even after a month of searching.

As if reading his thoughts, the female gave a little mischievous hum before looking down to an unmoving black *blob* tucked next to her breast. "We know where they are, though."

His body stiffened and his head lifted. "You do?" This time, bright yellow filled his sight, and Aleron stepped forward. "Please. Which way? We have been searching for a long time."

Perhaps over a month wasn't a long time in the grand scheme of his lifespan, but it had felt like an eternity. He'd already been parted from his kindred before this, and now that they were on the same plane of existence, he found the separation nearly unbearable.

She put her fingertips together, while keeping her palms separated. "I'll tell you in exchange for a *favour*."

Her lips curled coyly and with mirth, as she flicked her green eyes to Aleron in a mischievous manner.

They weren't the same kind of green as Gideon's.

Whereas his appeared like the freshest, dewiest forest showered in bright sunshine, a colour so light that he found it pierced his soul every time Gideon looked upon Aleron, hers were darker. His were like spring, hers like summer – almost... warmer.

His fangs parted in disbelief, and Gideon's jaw dropped as well. Orpheus tilted his head at his female, seemingly just as perplexed.

"I'm Reia, by the way." Her smile turned into an evil grin – or perhaps he only saw it thusly due to her withholding information from him.

"Reia," Aleron lowly growled out, acknowledging her with a nod. "What is it you seek?"

Despite the excitement alight in her eyes, they hardened as she looked over Gideon. "You have a bride. Groom? I don't know what to call him, to be honest."

Groom? Gideon has stated this word. It truly did appear to be a human term. Aleron peeked at the male at his side. *Does this mean I should call him something different?*

But he liked bride. It felt right to him.

"Yes, I have a bride," Aleron confirmed, placing a hand at Gideon's waist to tuck him into his side. "What of it?"

"It means I can trust you. Well... as much as I can trust a stranger. But! It means you won't be dangerous unless you *choose* to be, which I doubt because all you Duskwalkers seem to be sweethearts."

"Reia, what is it you seek from him?" Orpheus pushed

while turning to her, his fur lifting. In a way, he looked untrusting of his own female.

"He has wings!" she exclaimed. "I want him to take me into the air. I can't imagine how exhilarating it would be."

"But we don't know him." Orpheus waved his hand in their direction.

She greeted the wolf Mavka with a bright expression.

"Please, Orpheus? Who knows when he'll be back, and he has a bride. It's unlikely he'd hurt me, right?" She'd turned to Aleron when she asked her question, as if she'd actually been questioning him rather than Orpheus.

Despite how much Aleron wanted to leave, something about her cheer and expression suddenly warmed him.

"In exchange for information, you want me to take you into the air? Why? You just met me."

The mirth in her gaze deepened. "You Duskwalkers are quick to move. Whether it be on your journeys, or to take action, your attention spans are kind of... brief and ever-changing. I've learned its best if I go at your speed and ask for what I want directly. And the moment Ingram told me you had wings, I always knew I would ask you to take me for a flight." She turned back to Orpheus and reached out to clasp his wrist with both her hands. "Ingram is so nice that his literal twin has to be as well."

I like her. She spoke clearly and was easy for him to understand, as if she understood his mind already. She was also quick to trust him, to trust Mavka, as if she could tell they weren't horrible, violent creatures.

In the span of a few minutes, she'd showed just how deeply she cared about all of his kind – even one who was a stranger. She even spoke fondly of his kindred, which was the absolute best way to soften his resolve and birth tenderness in his heart.

Ingram is nice. He is a wonderful kindred.

But he knew Orpheus. The territorial male, who was often grouchy, would never agree to such a thing.

"If that is what you wish, my little doe," Orpheus responded with a chuckle. It cut short when his fangs snapped in Aleron's direction. "Would you agree to this? And promise not to harm her?"

Taken aback by Orpheus' allowance of this, especially since Aleron understood how much a bride meant by having his own, his wings twitched in realisation. His sight drifted over the female at Orpheus' side, and Aleron was unable to help his chuckle.

She has changed him. Or rather... *healed* him.

"I will not do it in exchange for Ingram's whereabouts. I would do it simply because she asked so enthusiastically," Aleron stated cordially. Still, he lowered his gaze to Gideon. "Would this be okay with you?"

"Of course," he said, shrugging. "I don't mind. I'd like to rest a little bit anyway."

Aleron searched his features to make sure he was being honest. When he saw no misgivings in Gideon's expression, only the dark impressions under his eyes from his two nights of poor sleep, he nodded.

A *horrible* squeal came from the woman as she stamped her feet. She leapt, throwing her arms around Orpheus' furry neck to hug him. Quick to catch her, he lifted her into the crook of his elbow with her arse seated upon it.

Aleron tilted his head when she looked like a bird that had perched on a branch.

"I will have to take this one, though," Orpheus stated, reaching towards her stomach.

The black blob from earlier lifted a featureless face towards his claws, sniffed them, then grabbed the sharp ends of them with two tiny, pliable hands. Orpheus took the creature from her and placed it against the fur of his chest, where it latched on.

Its mouth opened, and a purple tongue curled, before burying into his fur until it blended and almost seemed to disappear.

"Before you ask," Orpheus started, looking down at Reia's cheerful expression. "It is a baby Mavka. Our youngling. I will explain, if need be."

Although Aleron was rather curious about the youngling, he tipped his gaze to Orpheus' skull instead. He tilted his own in surprise.

"You have changed." He couldn't help commenting on it.

"I am aware," Orpheus grumbled, tossing his wolf head side to side lightly, like admitting that came with difficulty. "It has taken me a long time to feel at ease. Much has happened, especially in the last few months. And even more so in the past two weeks."

Unable to contain the urge, Aleron petted Gideon's back with the inside of one of his wings.

Much has happened for me as well.

Aleron would have been envious of the harmony of their relationship if he weren't just overjoyed for this Mavka.

All this time, there had been a sense of brokenness within Orpheus. He'd always known something was *deeply* wrong with this Mavka.

Even though his orbs were naturally blue, there had been a swallowing darkness within them. Longing and sadness that transpired past the natural hue and had almost been so palpable that Aleron could have drunk from the well of it. Peering into them had overwhelmed him with coldness, as if his very soul couldn't stand the melancholy in them.

Orpheus had never been warm, nor inviting. He had never been calm, as if restlessness seeped into the very ground he walked on and poisoned it.

Aleron had seen this home many times in his long life, but it had always been foreboding due to this Mavka's pain. Yet, no matter how much remaining here hurt Orpheus, he'd always stayed and protected it with all his might. He'd cared for it, maintained it, and grew enraged if anyone but himself stepped foot on his land.

But today... not once had his orbs been blue.

The cold melancholy in his voice, in his stance, in his very breath, was gone. Perhaps not completely, but enough that he had so willingly agreed to Aleron temporarily taking his bride away from him.

Again, he brought his sight to Reia.

It is because of her.

For her, as well. He wished to appease her, and her utter excitement was bleeding into him, and Aleron too, like a contagion.

She was brave enough to want this, and Orpheus was brave enough to give it to her. The unity and strength of their bond shone radiantly in this moment.

Aleron would not be envious of it – he refused to.

He just hoped to one day experience something as beautiful. Their bond gave him hope... even if it pained him a little to witness it.

Before he could linger any longer on this, an elbow knocked into his side.

Once more, Gideon had covered the side of his mouth. The male stared at the couple before them, while leaning to the side to be closer.

"You know what kids and babies are... right?"

Aleron mimicked the hush of his voice as he lowered his head. "Yes. I have met another youngling, although she was a Delysian – one Merikh has taken under his protection."

I did tell him of the Elven child I met. Aleron thought that would make it obvious he knew what they were.

Gideon nodded. "Okay, good. *Good.*" Then his eyes flicked up to his skull, but they held a strange beseeching emotion within them. "And you understand I can't give you one, right?"

His head cocked at that. "Well, yes. You are male, as am I. We do not have a place within us to create life."

Although, he must admit... he wasn't completely certain

of the details regarding the creation of life.

Aleron just wouldn't tell him that.

"Perfect." Gideon gave him a relieved smile, and even stuck his fist with his thumb up towards him – not that he knew what it meant. "Just wanted to make sure."

Aleron was baffled as to why he needed to.

His kindred had fully accepted a bride who couldn't produce younglings, and Aleron had no qualms about it either.

They would create their own *family* – just all four of them.

That would be all he needed.

Gideon watched as the other Duskwalker relinquished his woman into Aleron's arms. Sensing this was some kind of unspoken trade, he ventured closer to Orpheus – although not daring to touch him.

He turned to Reia and eyed the sword and dagger at her waist. She had only recently put them on after venturing inside the quaint little log-cabin home situated in the middle of the clearing they'd landed in.

He had a funny feeling she'd donned weapons for Orpheus' sense of security rather than her own.

They'd all been properly introduced before all this. He'd even shaken this Duskwalker's hand, and surprisingly, he hadn't shaken him face first into the dirt. There had only been a brief period of small talk, as Aleron obviously wanted to end this quickly so they could move on. Which is where the sense of urgency regarding her ride had come from.

Safely cradled by a monster, Reia flashed a beguiling smile at Orpheus, utterly refusing to place her gaze on Gideon.

Gideon mused over his interactions with this woman.

His attempts at trying to talk to her, since they were both humans who had bonded with Duskwalkers, had gone poorly.

Even after pasting on the most welcoming expression he could muster, her lips had tightened. Her gaze narrowed into a steely glare. Then she'd shrunk into Orpheus' side and wrapped both her hands around his thick wrist while hiding behind his arm.

What she'd done was obvious.

She had very plainly, and sternly, informed him that she wasn't interested in him. That her heart completely and utterly belonged to the Duskwalker she was with. Or maybe she just wanted to show that her eager trust was only for those who weren't human.

Gideon was sure there were other reasons as to why she didn't like him, since there had been a hint of deep hurt and lack of faith. He figured human men in the past acted rather unforgivably towards her.

It was also likely his face.

It's always the handsome men that end up being the biggest cretins. Even Gideon had dealt with attractive males who utilised their temporary looks for their own gain.

For most of his life, his friends had teased him about being a 'pretty boy.' Apparently he had a face women wanted to date, and men wanted to carve out and place over their own. Gideon had always known he was attractive, and it tended to incite many uncomfortable conversations he'd rather have avoided.

Women tried to cling to him because he was pretty, had a good job that paid well, and a decent personality. They'd just never known he'd rather date their brother.

The whole situation with Reia was silly, considering he was bonded to a Duskwalker as well.

Regardless of her reasons, Gideon had become

platonically smitten with her for it.

He adored her loyalty. Already he could tell she was brash, did what she wanted, and gave no shits unless it involved herself, Orpheus, and their Duskwalker child.

A woman who strongly expressed herself.

He liked that in a person, even if it wasn't always welcoming.

However, when Gideon tried, he could be rather charming. He'd win her over, and he'd bet he could do it by the time they left.

She may even think I bonded with Aleron to use him to come back to life. Especially since her behaviour worsened when she learned he was Emerie's brother, who had met Aleron in the afterlife. *Or that I wanted immortality, no matter how I achieved it.*

He did find it strange that she was completely at ease with Aleron, though. She'd immediately showed him kindness. With a bright smile, she even playfully threatened that if he dropped her, she'd shank him with her dagger when she came back to life.

Ballsy. Aleron had been taken aback and fidgeted nervously.

Gideon had laughed to help defuse the situation when it became obvious Aleron didn't understand she was only joking with him. Then he'd let Aleron know, regardless of the truth in her threat, it was mostly empty – simply because he knew Aleron wouldn't harm a single blonde hair on her pretty head.

"Be safe, Reia." Orpheus's warning was soft but serious as he fully stepped away once she put her arms around Aleron's neck for extra security.

Aleron's snout tipped in Gideon's direction, showing he was looking at him, so Gideon waved. "Don't worry, I'll be fine."

With a nod of his bat skull, he lifted off. Kicking her legs, Reia pelted out a horrible squeal as they climbed through the air, and the stupidest lopsided grin lifted his cheek.

I can already tell she's going to have a ball up there.

Then he was alone with Orpheus and the baby Duskwalker that still clung to his chest.

With his wolf skull tilted to the sky, watching them, Orpheus' fur puffed in agitation before he seemed to turn to stone. It was like he'd intended to become an unmoving statue that did little more than wait to be reunited with her.

Unsure of what to say to Orpheus, Gideon unslung his case to unburden himself. The light *thunk* of it hitting the ground pulled the Duskwalker from his trance, and Orpheus tilted his skull to look at him.

"Do you wish for food or water?" He gestured towards the log-cabin house behind him, and a silver bell dangling from each of his horns jingled at the motion. "I can take you inside so you may be comfortable."

"Nah," Gideon rejected, shaking his head. "I don't really feel the desire to eat or drink, nor do I want to."

His lack of bodily functions was a benefit. Even if playing pretend at being a good guest would have been kinder, he had priorities.

"Perhaps a chair, then?"

"No, I'm fine. Thank you." Gideon sat on the grass and folded his legs under himself. "You can join me, though, if you want. We might as well wait together."

Orpheus hesitated, but did eventually sit across from him.

Their silence was filled with awkward tension as the weak sun shone down upon them. The subtle wind barely swayed the short grass stalks; it appeared someone, likely Orpheus, regularly cut them with a scythe.

The area and the cute log cabin all looked well-maintained and loved, as if the person living in it cherished its existence.

Summarising he'd need to be the one to break the quiet, Gideon said, "I like your house. I never expected to see a human house in the Veil."

Though, as he roamed his gaze over it, he noted it *did* look a little taller than a normal house.

"I built it a long time ago," Orpheus answered, eventually lifting his snout to the sky again.

Reia and Aleron had long disappeared, but he seemed content to watch for any sign of her. At the same time, he lightly pet the tiny, furless Duskwalker against his chest until they eventually stirred. After a small while, they reached out to cling to his hand.

Orpheus moved his wrist in a certain way that allowed them to crawl over his hand without falling. One moment he was palm up, the next they roamed over his knuckles. With one arm up and the opposing foot mirroring it, they stomped over his hand with curious but trusting steps.

It was a simple action, but it appeared to be natural and pleasant for him. Like someone rolling a coin back and forth across their knuckles or, even more daring, a spider.

Gideon found himself unable to tear his gaze away from the creature, a little curious about them. *Would it be rude if I asked about it?*

"She does not like you," Orpheus eventually said.

He let out a small chuckle. "Yeah, I gathered that already."

"She made me fulfil a promise, one which saw a male of your kind dying at the fangs of another Mavka."

His lips tightened. "She made you feed a human to your kind?"

"She was not treated well. She has been mistrustful of every human we have met, and it took her a while to grow relaxed with all those we have befriended."

Gideon cocked a brow, as humour twitched his mouth. "Are you telling me to be patient with her?"

"She will either befriend you if she sees you are worthy,

or she will shove a sword through your chest. The choice is entirely up to you, but know she can be merciless when provoked."

Gideon noted the hint of admiration in his tone.

They both peered up at the sky when the shadow of Aleron and Reia glided over them. She was pointing east, in a certain direction, and he figured they'd both finished their initial flight to go further exploring.

Choosing to direct the conversation elsewhere, Gideon stated, "I noticed you aren't completely comfortable with this."

"I'm not," he admitted.

"Then why did you allow it so easily?"

Orpheus looked at his hand, but this time to catch his child when it began crawling down his arm. They let out a weak and quiet shriek when he placed them back within the safety of his palm.

When Orpheus spoke, he did so with quiet pride. "She cannot be restrained, even when I will it. She will fight with Demons to protect our home, and venture to see her human companions when I wish to remain alone with her. She will find a way to make me see her side, so why fight her on it?"

These are all negative qualities, Gideon thought, with his brows furrowing deeply.

"That doesn't sound like a fair compromise," Gideon muttered.

A small chuckle fell from Orpheus, as he cupped his hand around his child when they remained seated in his palm. A small hug was shared between them.

"Reia is brave, foolishly so. It's something I adore about her. She has shown me how to be at ease, even when I am wary. Without her doing these things, we would not have our friends' companionship, nor would our home be as safe as it is." Then, Orpheus finally directed his wolf skull to him. "Reia doesn't ask for anything for herself. She doesn't seek pretty things, or to travel when she once told me she wanted that more than anything. Yet, she does everything in her power to make me happy, so the least I can do for her is trust her instincts. She trusts Aleron, so I will do so as well."

Gideon blew a strand of hair from his brow. "Are all you Duskwalkers nice? Until I met Aleron, I thought you were all bloodthirsty."

Orpheus sniffed in sharply, then let out a heavy huff. "Before Reia, I was much more violent. Although less so than others. Your original assumption is correct for unbonded Mavka."

Gideon pondered on this, on Orpheus and what he'd said. Despite the negative aspects he'd revealed about his woman, he'd done so with affection, as if these traits weren't flaws to him.

He hummed out a harrumph. "You seem to really love her."

"My little doe is perfect." Orpheus brushed his clawed forefinger under what Gideon assumed was the baby Duskwalker's jaw. "She is everything I need, even when I don't know it, and she has given me everything I have wanted."

Aleron mentioned earlier that he'd changed. He wondered how Orpheus had been before this woman came along.

He'd make a mental note to ask Aleron later.

"I didn't know Duskwalkers could produce children with humans," Gideon stated, staring at the featureless creature. "Are they a boy or a girl?"

Orpheus chuckled. "Mavka are born androgynous."

"Ahkay." He rubbed at his neck, oddly embarrassed when there would have been no way for him to have known that. "What's their name then?"

"Reia has named them Kevin," Orpheus stated with humour. "It brings her great enjoyment whenever she calls them."

Gideon immediately drew his lips into his mouth when the urge to burst into laughter hit him like a boulder. He never expected such a basic human name for a Duskwalker.

"She is not good at giving names," Orpheus continued. "She couldn't even give Magnar his name. This was the best she could do."

He turned his head away and covered his mouth. *Now I can't stop picturing her running after them, screaming, 'Kevin!'*

"The other females laughed as well. You are not alone."

"Could you not think of one?" Gideon asked with a laugh, finally letting it out since he could tell it wouldn't offend him.

"I had many names, but I wanted them to be named by her." His orbs shifted to bright yellow as his wolf skull cocked in his direction. "Reia is never afraid, but she was nervous about them. I was beginning to worry that she would never be ready or want a youngling with me. I am happy with their name, little human, because it means that they *exist*."

His features tightened at the sudden turn of their conversation. "You were worried she didn't want a child?"

Orpheus' shoulders fell as he looked up to the sky once more, almost as if he was seeking a glimpse of her. They hadn't returned.

"It was not something I desired until her, but the moment I discovered she could hold life for me, I craved it. She kept saying no, until I stopped asking, but it... bothered me that the other Mavka were able to do this with their brides and we had not. I thought perhaps she did not love me as intensely as they did. If she could not have them, I do not think I would have minded, but the fact she could but refused to... I began to worry she did not want to make something with me. She gave me her soul, so I thought I had all of her heart, but I grew uncertain."

"Having a child with someone doesn't equate to a person's love," Gideon sternly told him.

Perhaps Orpheus was talking to the wrong person, but Gideon couldn't suddenly grow a womb. He'd been born a man, so even if it was something Aleron wanted from him, having a child of theirs was completely impossible. Then there were women who just... couldn't have one, for a myriad of reasons, and people who didn't want them out of their own volition.

"I knew this," Orpheus quietly uttered.

He lowered his skull when Kevin gave a squawk and started biting at his thumb. Not hard enough to draw blood, but in a pacifying, nibbling way.

Oddly enough, Gideon found this conversation enlightening. He could tell Orpheus had far more humanity than Aleron, so it was interesting to speak with a Duskwalker who could clearly articulate their words and formulate intricate thoughts.

Aleron sometimes came across brutish with the way he communicated. It meant Gideon had begun learning how to read his body language, rather than truly taking what he said to heart.

He'd grown in tune to Aleron's feelings, to the point where he knew that in the past day, with how Gideon had been acting, it hadn't been taken well. He had his reasons for it, but he didn't know how to approach Aleron.

In some way, he was hoping speaking to Orpheus would eventually help him figure it out.

So, despite that it probably wasn't his place, Gideon pushed their conversation. He hoped it revealed more of the inner workings of a creature, who, just a month ago, had been unapproachable in his thoughts.

"If you knew a child doesn't equate to a person's love, then why did it bother you?" Then, just to make sure he didn't appear too prying, he added, "If I may ask."

Orpheus hummed, seeming to think on how he may

answer, or if he even would.

"I was hurt deeply by someone in the past, and that suffering had lasted for a hundred and eighty years. I wanted that person's soul, but they didn't wish to be by my side and chose to torment me in their hatred instead. Then, when Reia gave me her soul, and her love, all the things I had wanted, I desired something that I had never wanted from anyone but her. I wanted more because it meant that Reia had claimed all of me, *including* my past. The moment she gave me this youngling, and I held them, heard them, saw them, something changed within me. I am no longer... *scared*."

Gideon averted his gaze, once more rubbing at the side of his neck. Not in embarrassment, but because of the seriousness of what he'd just heard. *What a large amount of weight to place on something like having a child.*

"Do you wish to hold them?" Orpheus offered, the excitement in his voice thick. "They do not bite unless provoked. They will only nibble."

Gideon brought his gaze back to him with eyes wide, then turned down to Orpheus' outreaching hand.

"Are you sure? I don't want to hurt them." He could only imagine how Orpheus and Reia would react if he did!

Gideon wouldn't lie and say he didn't want to when he was rather curious. But Orpheus had just stated how much they meant to him. He hadn't expected for Orpheus to so willingly offer for him to touch them.

Actually... he kind of reminds me of a proud dad wanting everyone to come see his child. His eyes crinkled with humour at the thought, finding it rather sweet.

"They are indestructible, see?" Then, to demonstrate, he shoved his claw through their back until it came out through the other side! Sitting on their rump, the baby Duskwalker let out a squawk at Gideon, seemingly unaware they'd just been stabbed through the gut. "You cannot harm them."

Fuck, he wanted him to stop doing that as quickly as possible. Gideon took the child with both hands and held them in the air. Unsure of what to do with them, he attempted to cradle them like one would a normal human infant.

They struggled at first, wriggling to get free, until he tickled their stomach. Instantly, they stopped moving. They went lax in his arms, and he would have thought they'd died if their chest wasn't moving.

"How old are they?" Gideon asked, trying to hide how awkward he was.

Had it been a human child, he would have been rather content with them on his arm. He liked children and had wanted to adopt a few himself.

The creature had a weird, jagged maw that looked rather sharp. He didn't wish to irritate them in case they bit him. *Will they fall into a bloodlust, like Aleron told me of?*

"Eight days," Orpheus stated casually.

He nodded. "Uh huh, eight days." His head shot up, and he snapped his gaze to Orpheus. "Eight days?"

But they were so active! He'd expected a few weeks at least.

"You are the first to hold them apart from myself or Reia. Magnar and Delora left before they knew Reia was carrying my youngling, and Mayumi and Faunus left with Ingram and Emerie."

"They left with Emerie?"

Watching intently as Gideon held his child, he stated, "Their entire family has left to show Emerie and Ingram where Mayumi's home is in the north. Emerie wished to find somewhere safe and warm until winter is over."

Distracted, Gideon almost had his hand bitten when he stopped petting the child. Luckily, he yanked his hand away in time.

"Be careful. If they bite you, it will trigger the bloodthirstiness in them." Well, that answered that question.

"I will be able to heal you, though."

Too much was being stated at once, and he didn't like the idea of holding a tiny ball of potentially violent chaos. Gideon handed them back to Orpheus, and he enthusiastically took them.

Emerie is in the north? I thought with the guild after her, she would have avoided it. Then again, he'd always known she'd find a place to hunker down until the snow season passed.

"Duskwalkers can heal? I didn't know you could use magic in that way."

At least that was handy to know.

"You didn't? But you have bonded with Aleron. I assumed he would have used healing magic with you, especially since you carry his marking scent."

It took a moment for Gideon to understand what he meant. Once he did, his whole head heated and the desire to shut his legs itched his knees. He didn't, only because he doubted that would help.

"No. He's, uh, never done any magic around me."

"I see." He cupped the end of his snout and tapped the side of it with a claw. "Actually, since you are both males, I have questions about this."

"Questions I absolutely will not answer," Gideon quickly stated with an awkward laugh.

"Why not? I am curious about how two males can fuck, since you do not have a pussy."

Gideon almost choked on his spit at how honestly and abruptly he'd spoken. "Sorry, man, but that's kind of private. I'd prefer not to explain it." With his cheeks reddening, Gideon tried to look anywhere else but his bony face. "Maybe ask Reia?"

"Fine." Orpheus snorted an annoyed huff. "Since Aleron does not know how to use his magic properly, I will try to teach him all I know before he leaves. Much of it is helpful in taking care of a human. Healing is actually rather easy once we know how."

"Thanks. I'd really appreciate that." He offered Orpheus a small, appreciative smile, thankful he'd dropped the sex topic. "You said Emerie went north roughly three weeks ago?"

"This is correct."

I see, Gideon thought while patting the side of his bent pointer finger against his lips. *That's roughly when we were caught up in the storm. They were either in the Veil, or making their way there, which is why we didn't find them.*

"Where were they before that?"

"The south, mainly the western side before the southlands border. Less people."

So... while we were in the north, they were in the south, and vice versa.

Then Gideon's eyes grew wide. "Did you say the west?"

"Yes."

He winced. *Shit. Didn't we first arrive back in the west? We would have been close to them...* His thoughts trailed off before he threw his face into one of his palms. *Damn, Aleron knew it. He had to have known they were close by. And instead of going after his twin, he chose to follow me.*

The gut-wrenching knot within him, the one that had turned into lead last night and had eased during this conversation, tightened. At this point, he was beginning to feel so ill from it, he feared he'd throw up his emotions despite his empty stomach.

"Your heart rate has increased, and you are sweating. Are you okay? Aleron will be angered with me if you become unwell."

Gideon would never get used to how easy it was for Duskwalkers to pick up on something so minor.

"Yeah, I'm fine." The lie tasted sour.

He wasn't fine, and he hadn't been fine for a while.

While he was trying to get closer to Aleron, something

had been nagging in the back of his mind. He'd never been able to put his finger on it, but it'd been there, constantly eating at him.

His chest felt swollen with an overdose of too many confusing and conflicting emotions. Sometimes painful, other times tender. Hot and cold, soft and then barbed. The backlash of them was driving him insane.

At this rate, he'd start yanking his damn hair out.

Sex with Aleron had been wonderful. He'd deeply enjoyed it, perhaps far too much than what could be deemed normal. The fact his whole brain had turned off, and he'd turned into a horny puddle of goo while he'd been thoroughly humped... He'd never experienced anything like that before.

It'd been... easy, even though Aleron was so much bigger than him in every sense. Once he'd given Gideon *all* of his cock, he hadn't been able to stop thinking about how much it felt like Aleron had been *made* for him. Sure, it'd been painful at first, but once he adjusted, he'd been on fucking cloud nine.

Hell, he'd even passed out from extreme satisfaction.

Only to be plagued with the sweetest of dreams.

Memories of some of their time together. Most of it had been mundane and useless, but there had been a few that finally pieced together the puzzle of why he may have started growing fond of the big silly Duskwalker.

He'd held Aleron's hand because Gideon had wanted him to stop being anxious of Gideon disappearing. He, himself, hadn't wanted to fade to what the other Ghosts would turn into, living their happiest memories, but it also wouldn't have really mattered to him in the end if he did.

He wouldn't have remembered anyway.

But he'd known then that it had a different meaning to Aleron. After a little while, Gideon had begun to see it the same way as him.

He tried to hold my hand when we first came here. And he remembered ripping away from Aleron every time.

He couldn't even begin to imagine how much that hurt Aleron. To go from constantly entwined in the most innocent sense, to being denied something so simple, yet so reassuring.

Although this had been damning to learn, nothing could have prepared him for the chest burning he regretfully felt at a different memory.

"My heart is telling me to hold you," Aleron had softly stated, embracing him with all of his being. *"My wings are precious to me, but they ached to bring you into their close and protective hold. I have never felt this for anyone but my kindred. It means much to me to feel this for you."*

Shame trickled down his spine.

I stopped him from finding Ingram when they were close. I refused to hold his hand. I told him I didn't want him. And... Gideon's jaw clenched until he thought he'd shatter his teeth. *And I said I found his precious wings suffocating.*

It hadn't taken Gideon long to realise that Aleron frequently spoke with his wings. They sometimes nudged against him when they shouldn't have. They twitched nervously or in excitement. Sometimes Gideon didn't even need to look at Aleron's orb colour changes. Instead, he just needed to see how his wings were sitting – if they were tight or drooping, fluffed out or smooth.

His heart told him to hold me, so he put his wings around me. I can't believe I rejected something so important to him.

Gideon understood why his own soul had given him the middle finger. Now that he'd come to know him, and feel deeply for him, he'd rather eat glass than hurt Aleron like this.

I wish I could go back in time. Gideon wanted to go back to when he first woke up on Earth... and shake himself to sense. To instil in himself all the memories he had now, from their time together in the living world.

"Has Reia ever hurt you deeply?" Gideon asked, his throat so clogged his voice croaked.

"Yes," Orpheus slowly stated with a thoughtful hum. "But her actions helped destroy the Demon King. My hurt did not last long."

Well, that didn't help.

Gideon drew his hand from his face and pushed his messy fringe back, so he could rest it against his forehead.

"I've hurt Aleron in ways I didn't even understand until recently," he admitted, hoping that maybe talking to a Duskwalker about one would help. "I don't know how to make it up to him."

I told him he could put his wings around me, and he still wouldn't. Gideon could have begged and pleaded, tried to explain and excuse himself, but he hadn't just rejected his wings – he'd punched Aleron repeatedly in the damn heart.

How the hell am I supposed to make up for everything?

"Hmm," Orpheus mused. "Aleron's humanity is low. You have to be direct, speak plainly, and be curt. It may hurt him to learn the truth of why, but it is better than being confused."

"I'm scared that if I tell him why, it'll only hurt him further."

Orpheus waved a single hand forward. "Then show him."

Gideon lifted his head towards Orpheus. "I've tried that. You even said you could... *smell* it." He was too ashamed right then to even flush in embarrassment at that statement. "I've been trying to show him I do care, but it doesn't seem to matter."

Aleron refused to hold him the way he knew the big Duskwalker wanted to. He also never spoke of Gideon as his bride, or their future, or even their feelings when it was outside of anything sexually intimate. While they were in the thick of it, he couldn't seem to contain himself, but outside of it... Aleron was reserved.

He acted nervously – skittish even.

That was not the Duskwalker in his memories.

Aleron in Tenebris had been bold, even when uncertain.

"Is there no other way for you to show him?" Orpheus asked, tilting his head and making the charm bells dangling from his horns jingle.

When one of the silver bells sparkled in the sun, it caught his eye.

His horn type is interesting. What kind of animal is–

A memory arose. A gentle and heart-warming one.

Despite the dizziness and how his mind swam, it came to him clear and hyper focused.

Aleron, with orbs bright yellow in joy, stroked the fawny-brown fur of an impala antelope. Experiencing parallel emotions, his heart gave a pang at how sweet the memory was, and how gentle Aleron tended to the creature. He looked like a monstrous beast, yet awe radiated from him with a sense of innocence.

Aleron shined that yellow at Gideon, and it brightened. In his memory, it warmed him even further. He'd trusted in Gideon's guidance, even when his own hand released the protruding white knuckle bones of Aleron's and he continued to pet it.

The deer's horns had been large and imposing on such a slim creature, and Aleron had dominated it. Yet it remained, despite its wariness of the monster stroking it, as if it could sense Aleron wouldn't harm it.

Because, like Gideon now knew, Aleron would never willingly harm anyone. He was kind, gentle, and wonderful.

His mind flittered back to the present as he took in the same horns before him. *Impala antelope horns. I've seen sketches of them.*

A choking noise burst from him, and he grabbed at the collar of his shirt. When Orpheus darted forward to pat his back, likely about to ask him if he was okay, he threw his hand up.

"Don't worry!" he managed to get out through strangled breaths. "It happens. It's normal."

Normal for him, at least.

Whenever he dreamed his memories, they drifted to him peacefully. If he was awake, they tended to rip from his conscious like a cyclone. It often made him breathless and lightheaded, but it'd quickly pass.

"W-what were we talking about?" Gideon asked, lifting a crinkled and beseeching gaze at him. "Show him some other way I care? I don't know your kind well enough to know how I could do that."

His breaths quickly settled, and the final frantic one shuddered out of him when his heartbeat slowed to its natural rhythm.

Seeing he was unneeded, Orpheus settled back into his seat on the grass and sighed. "It does not need to be Mavka related. We often do not even know what we want. What is a human gesture you could do?"

"A human gesture?" He cupped his mouth in thought, trying to think of something he could do. "I don't really know what I could–"

His face paled and turned cold when an idea came to mind, only for it to suddenly heat in embarrassment. The only thing he could think of... wouldn't be easy.

At least, not for Gideon. He'd probably be a shaking, trembling mess through it.

But damn... He covered his mouth in bewilderment that made him nervously grin. Even his damn heart, which had calmed from his memory returning, fluttered shyly and with longing. *Now that I'm thinking about it, I kind of really want to do it.*

The wolf-skulled Duskwalker tilted his head with his orbs glowing dark yellow as he took in Gideon's sudden emotional change. Gideon didn't doubt he looked odd, since his eyes had probably turned glassy and yet his face was heated with an awkward blush.

"Orpheus!" came Reia's excited squeal as she and Aleron shot to the ground.

Aleron halted their dangerous falling speed right before they touched the dirt, only to place his feet gently. She threw herself out of his arms and ran straight for Orpheus, who had already risen to his feet to greet her.

Just before they could embrace each other, Kevin leapt through the air, impatient to be against her.

"Aleron took me close to Ackermeadow Village," she said as she hugged him.

"That is where I took you from," Orpheus answered, nudging the end of his snout against her blonde hair.

"Yeah, I know. I could see your ward still in place, even from a distance." Then she leaned back to stroke the baby Duskwalker shoving their face against her generous chest. "How was Kevin? I missed you both while I was gone."

While they began to have a deep conversation, Gideon rose to meet Aleron. His wings shifted, likely wanting to embrace Gideon when he came closer. However, Aleron only slid his arms around him, since Gideon had been the one to instigate their hug.

It just further proved how much he'd broken this compassionate and affectionate being.

Before we find our siblings, there's something I want to do.

Gideon didn't think he could handle witnesses for what he was planning.

THIRTY-SEVEN

With the ground blanketed in inch-deep snow, Aleron shuffled his feet back and forth, wishing Gideon would hurry. It crunched and squeaked until he patted it down into a dense layer.

I can smell Ingram. Aleron would know his scent anywhere; it was like a balm to his aching soul. His kindred was near. So close, in fact, that the northerly wind had pushed his familiar scent to him during Gideon's absence.

A soft growl bubbled from his chest. *And I cannot go to him yet.*

Instead, he stood at the fringes of a forest, staring at the timber stakes of a town's protective walls.

Gideon had pleaded with him to be dropped off here. Now, of all times, when they both knew how close they were to their family.

For the first time, Aleron had denied him. Tried to, rather. When he refused to land, Gideon had wiggled like he wanted to fall from his arms, metres in the air no less! The male's safety was the only reason he'd landed, immediately snapping his fangs at him.

He'd run off. Shouting over his shoulders as he left Aleron dumbstruck at his sudden departure, he promised he'd return shortly without further explanation.

Aleron had considered leaving without him to search

He'd come back to his side within a day, so it wouldn't be permanent.

He couldn't, *wouldn't*, do that, and felt deeply ashamed that he'd even considered such a terrible thought.

Even when Ingram's fresh scent fluttered to him on the wind, Aleron found his feet frozen when every other inch of him longed to chase after it. His claws dug into the tree beside him, gouging it until bark cracked and flung off as he impatiently waited.

Hours had passed. They'd arrived here near noon, Aleron flying fast from Orpheus' ward. Now, the sun steadily dropped.

There would be no rest for them, even if night came. He and Ingram would be reunited this day, no matter what this human said or did.

I wish he would stop doing this. Why did he need to keep going into human towns? He didn't need to eat or drink, and his clothes were surely fine. What more did he need? Gideon also returned with the smell of others on him, and every time it had Aleron wanting to rub against his body to remove the evidence of their brief touches.

When Aleron finally spotted him leaving the town's gates, he was so irritated that another growl rumbled from him. Gideon headed straight to him, his case jiggling behind him as he did.

He unslung it from his shoulders as soon as he reached Aleron, and they moved deeper into the tree line to hide in case human eyes saw them from afar.

"Sorry for taking so long," Gideon forced out around deep, fogging huffs of exertion from sprinting. He turned his head away as he rubbed his hands together for warmth. "Thank you for being patient."

The fact he refused to look upon Aleron's face deepened his annoyance. Ever since he'd taken Reia for a flight, Gideon had not brought his eyes to him.

If he was so upset by it, he should not have told me it was okay. He'd much rather have denied the female if it meant keeping this human happy.

Their relationship was constantly strained. One minute Gideon appeared content, then he looked deeply unnerved. He'd rather not add to it.

"I can smell Ingram," Aleron snapped out, despite trying his hardest to sound calm. "They are not far."

With urgency, he went to grab Gideon, but the little human swiftly stepped away from him.

"Wait," he choked out, looking at Aleron's chest as he put up a hand. "Please wait."

His wings fluttered with agitation behind him, dusting loose snow and causing it to flurry behind him.

"I *tire* of waiting, Gideon," Aleron stated honestly, with a bite in his tone. "I wish to see–"

"I know." His eyes flicked up to his reddening orbs before darting away. "There's something I'd like to do first. Please give me a moment."

Crimson flared into his orbs as his growl deepened. "Gideon."

"Please? It's important and I'm really fucking nervous." His cheeks heated to the point that even his ears and neck went red. "I don't think I've been this nervous in my whole life, if I'm being honest. I made this decision really quick and there is a bunch of stuff I want to say, and I'm worried I'm going to mess it up."

As he spoke, Aleron stepped back when he noticed how... fidgety Gideon had become. With his side to Aleron, he could see how much his hands were shaking, and that sweat dotted his neck and forehead.

His anger cooled when he took in how fast his little human's heart was beating. It was too fast, like it was moments from either bursting out of his chest or just... giving out. Aleron's own began to sprint, mirroring it, when tangy fear began to cascade into his flowery forest scent.

"What is wrong?" Aleron asked, his tone decibels lighter than moments before.

He went to reach out but hesitated halfway. *He is afraid...* Did that mean he did not wish for Aleron's comfort right then?

Gideon palmed his face and then dug his fingers into his closed eyes. "I'm worried I'm going to look like an idiot? I don't know. I'm just feeling really sensitive."

With every second that passed as he watched this male tremble, the more nervous Aleron became. Cupping his hands to his stomach, he was growing unsure of what Gideon was about to do. Aleron would follow this human to the ends of the Earth if need be, but he was starting to grow... tired of being hurt. He was so sore inside from the constantly changing waves of their relationship.

Gideon was afraid of what he was about to do, and now Aleron was as well.

"If you are this worried, then do not do it?" Aleron asked, offering a clear solution.

He let out a terrible laugh. It didn't sound sincere whatsoever. "Not an option. It's happening either way." His eyes flicked to Aleron's skull, then to his hands cupped at his stomach, and he winced. "Shit. Sorry, I'm freaking you out. Okay. *Okay.*"

Gideon took in a deep, long breath, held it, and turned to Aleron fully. Then he suddenly ducked down, and Aleron tilted his head at him for it. He hadn't expected Gideon to drop, nor kneel on a single knee and thrust a tiny wooden case at him.

"I feel like asking you to marry me is literally pointless, all things considered, but I would still like to present this to you like this because it's what I would have done with a human."

He opened the case, and two rings sat within some form of cushion. Both were silver, one much larger than the other.

Utterly baffled by what was happening, Aleron stared at

Gideon silently for a long while. That seemed to distress him further, since his fretting heart sped up even more and his breaths turned shallower.

It appears to be some sort of important human custom. So Aleron got down on one knee and presented his hand out, mirroring him.

Gideon just looked so frightfully nervous that Aleron didn't wish for him to do whatever he was doing alone. Aleron also didn't like how he towered over and dominated his small bride, when he had presented himself in some kind of submissive position with fear in his scent. Gideon looked so feeble, since his hands trembled while holding the case.

Aleron did wince when Gideon's expression widened in horror. Then he burst into a fit of laughter as he snapped the case closed with one hand, covered his red face, and shook his head.

"I didn't even think about the fact you likely wouldn't understand!" The foot that had been placed firmly upon the ground slipped back, and he knelt on both knees. Gideon peeked at Aleron from behind his fingers, a broken grin shining before he lowered his hand to fully reveal it. "But thanks, Aleron. I kind of feel a little better since you did it back to me."

Aleron's wings drooped, feeling as though he'd done the wrong thing. "Gideon, I do not understand," he whined.

"It's okay."

Wrestling to his feet, Gideon offered his hand out to Aleron to pretend he could help him to his own. He took it and played this game because it made his human feel better.

"Here, I'll explain it to you while I put them on."

He held onto Aleron's left hand as he opened the case again and placed the large ring on the finger next to Aleron's pinkie.

"Marriage is the human equivalent to me giving you my soul, although far less permanent if we wish it," Gideon explained, as he placed the smaller ring on his own hand. "There are many things I wanted to do in my life. One of those things was to get down on one knee for the person I loved, and wanted to spend the rest of my life with, and ask them to marry me. It wasn't a decision I would have made lightly, and I had planned to put my all into it."

He cupped the bottom of Aleron's hand and placed the other on top while he stared down at them. Their rings clinked together.

"I probably haven't proven it to you yet, but I'm actually a really loyal person. Once someone steals my heart, it's pretty hard for me to let them go. You have stolen mine, Aleron."

"I have?" he asked as a thrill tore down his spine, ruffling his tail feathers.

"Yes, you have," Gideon stated warmly, brushing his thumb back and forth over the smooth metal circling the base of Aleron's finger.

Aleron's sight shifted to dark yellow as he brought his sight down to the silver rings. *This is the way humans bond?* He didn't truly understand the significance of a piece of metal, but he did like the heartfelt words that came with them.

Aleron liked they were being said to him.

"These rings aren't pretty since they are plain. Yours was made today, but I asked the blacksmith to make it with iron because it is stronger than gold or silver. It should stand the test of time much longer, just like we hopefully will. It's why I wanted to stop here today."

Finally, Gideon lifted his eyes to Aleron's skull. They held unwavering conviction, and his bride shone that upon him with utter strength.

"This is my way of showing you, in the biggest gesture a human can do for another, that I deeply care for you. That I fully accept you for all that you are, and that I want to be with you."

His gaze has never looked so... soft before. The remaining pinkness of Gideon's cheeks just made his dimpled smile more radiant than the speckles of sun twinkling over him. His expression was filled with warmth, tenderness, and affection – all of it directed solely on Aleron.

It instantly made his orbs shift to bright pink as his heart clenched with a wonderful emotion.

He said he wants to be with me. His wings drooped heavily as words from earlier fully registered. *Wait. He said he wanted to do this with someone he... loves?*

"When I think we are both ready, I would like to fully explain to you why things were so hard for me in the beginning. There were important people in my life that I had to abandon, and I would like to share my fond memories of them with you one day." Then Gideon placed his forehead against their hands. "I have hurt you deeply, Aleron. The more I know of you and remember of Tenebris, the more I realise it. None of it has been deserved, and the more I came to understand that, the more I hated myself for the way I treated you."

With his sight turning blue, Aleron reached forward and placed his free hand against the side of Gideon's face. Aleron lifted it towards his skull as he drew his thumb down his soft cheek to the corner of his lips.

His voice radiated with the sadness present behind his sternum. "You have hated yourself?"

He never wanted Gideon to feel this way.

"Yeah," he stated, yet he shined a genuine smile towards Aleron. Then Gideon reached up to cup the side of his snout. "But I didn't know how to tell you that because I didn't want you to blame yourself for something that is my own fault. I've been trying to get closer to you and show you how sorry I am, but I just kept failing. Nothing I did felt like enough, except for this."

Gideon turned his face down towards their hands and fiddled with the ring around Aleron's finger again, twisting it side to side. It didn't fit perfectly, but it was loose enough to likely still fit him should he shift into his more monstrous form.

"I want you to be open with me, Aleron," Gideon continued. "I don't want you to be nervous anymore. I'm not going to run away or be upset by anything you do. I want you to hold me completely and tell me how you really feel, knowing I will accept it. That I accept all parts of you, from your colour-changing orbs, to your skull, claws, fur, and even wings. You are the person I got down on one knee for, and put this ring on, and in my heart, we are as connected as two humans can be, as well as a bride and a *Mavka* can be."

Cupping both sides of his bat snout to pull him down, Gideon lifted up to press a singular kiss to his front fangs.

"If I go into towns, everyone will know I am taken. I will wear it proudly because I am happy to be yours. I want you to know that and feel at ease." He drew back, just as he softly said, "So please, just be yourself. Do what you want, whenever you want. No more hiding. I won't hide either."

Before Gideon could back away completely, a rumbling growl bubbled in Aleron's chest. "You want me to do what I want?" Aleron put his arms around his bride's waist, and lifted him so Gideon was not only closer, but needed to go to his toes and be higher. "Whenever I want?"

Did Gideon truly understand what that meant? Did he truly... mean that?

"Yes," he answered, leaning into Aleron's hold.

"What if I want to *kiss* you?" He parted his fangs and swept his tongue across Gideon's lips. "Can I do this whenever my tongue itches to taste you?"

Aleron flinched when Gideon's tongue pushed forward and greeted his own right before he could finish licking him.

He didn't need an answer; that had been enough.

Aleron cupped the back of Gideon's head with his free hand, and swept across his lips again, hoping his tongue would greet him once more. The groan that tore from Aleron shuddered his whole body when Gideon's saliva-covered tongue teased up his own.

They repeated the kiss, and Aleron grew more obsessed and incessant each time.

He said he is mine. Just the possessiveness, willingly asked of him and encouraged, had a violent wave of adoration crashing over him. Gideon had even stated he was proud and happy about it! *He accepts all of me.*

"More," Aleron pleaded, wanting more kisses, more freedom to touch in the ways his heart begged him to.

He shoved Gideon against him and found that wasn't close enough. Aleron pressed him against a nearby tree so he could utterly squish him, wishing to have his bride so close he would seep beneath his flesh.

He said he would do this gesture for someone he loves and chooses to be with. Does this mean he loves me in return?

Just the thought had his sight trying to mix with bright pink and purple. Both love and desire tangling together in a tender mix that ached him all the way to his bones.

Aleron needed him higher, closer. He picked Gideon up by the backs of his thighs, so he no longer needed to bend to his height and could press his tongue more firmly.

Wrapping his legs around Aleron's narrow waist, Gideon parted his lips, allowing him in. The groan that fell from Aleron was deep and shaken from their tongues grazing, and Aleron immediately sunk his within the dampness of his bride's mouth. Aleron tasted him as overwhelming emotions swelled within him, all of them pleasant, all of them clawing away the pains he'd held for far too long.

A wincing moan burst from Gideon just as the sweet scent of blood perfumed the air.

Pulling back, his gut knotted and white filled his sight at his claws embedded into Gideon's thigh. "I am sorry," he whined, realising his excitement had caused him to hurt his precious male. "I did not m–"

"Come here," Gideon demanded, and the pure possessiveness of it rendered him quiet. Then the little human yanked Aleron's head forward and gave a heavy, hard lick across his fangs. "You can claw me all over, destroy me, bite me – I don't care. Just don't stop."

The intensity of the thrill that tore down his back vibrated his tail feathers until they were fully splayed. His hand slipped higher to grab Gideon's arse and push the male's hips against his torso more, as Aleron dived back in to fill his mouth. Deep purple took over his sight as desire clung to every fibre of his being.

Desire Aleron no longer felt the need to *hide*.

"I want you so badly, little spring," Aleron groaned.

He wanted to connect with his bride until they were one, while his heart felt so content and light after so long. He wanted to shower Gideon in all the affection he'd been restraining and hoped to be given back.

His body felt starved of love and attention, and he longed for Gideon to cradle him the way he desired. To cling to Aleron, want and need him, be desperate and craving to make up for all the time they'd lost.

His kindred was so close he could scent him in the air, but his bride's taste on his tongue felt far too important right then to matter. Right now, the balance of his love for them tipped towards Gideon, his whole being wanting to remain here with him if it meant they could become one. Meshing their bodies until he and Gideon were two inseparable beings was all he could focus on.

Gideon's narrowed but heated gaze returned Aleron's yearning, and it ignited his blood. His green eyes were sharp and focused on Aleron's skull, while his nails dug into his shoulders like Gideon, too, wished to seep beneath his skin.

The hardness pressed against Aleron's torso sparked delight. Even more so when Gideon rocked it against his abdomen, showing his need, and accepting Aleron's at the same time.

The throbbing in his own cock had already taken over his mind, and his tentacles' poor attempt at holding him back lost their pathetic fight. He extruded, his erection jutting from his hips just below Gideon's backside.

Aleron moved his hand up slightly to hook his claws into the back of his trousers and undershorts. Gideon gasped as he tossed his head to the side.

"Don't rip them!" he yelled, darting a hand between them. "I refuse to do another bare-arsed walk through another town."

Gideon undid the ties of his trousers, and Aleron separated them long enough to yank his pants down once they were loose, while the little male grabbed a boot to get it off before removing the other. Awkward to do in the air, Aleron refusing to put this human down, but they managed to remove a single leg from his pants.

Aleron caressed the other leg, removing the dangling clothing completely, so it didn't get in his way. It was just an excuse to touch him and let the hairs on his body tickle his palm. Then he gripped Gideon by the backs of his muscular thighs, making sure to have a secure hold on him.

Lowering the male meant Aleron couldn't push his tongue back within the delicious well of his mouth, but grinding his cock between the cleft of Gideon's arse cheeks made up for it. He let out a strained huff, finding even Gideon's sac rubbing over him felt wonderful.

A small amount of heat deflated out of him. "I need to prepare you," Aleron grated out, thrusting against him.

Fogged pants fell from Gideon's mouth as he looked down, and his features seemed to flush even more at what he saw. "No, I don't care. I'm cold, and I think you have the perfect thing to warm me."

Damnit, as Gideon would often say... *I did not think about how the snow would affect him unclothed.*

Aleron found he also selfishly... didn't care right then. Aleron wanted inside him, so, fuck the cold and snow.

He did mind if he hurt his precious bride, though. "But–"

With a cute little human snarl, Gideon let go of one of his shoulders. Then he reached between them and grabbed his purple cock right behind the thick head. Gideon shoved it against his tight hole.

The moment their bodies met and just the tip sank inside, nothing could have prevented Aleron from slowly pushing deeper with a gut-clenching shudder. Gideon widened his thighs at the snugness that greeted them both, while Aleron's skull tilted back as he involuntarily swelled in delight.

"Nhnn. It's so big," Gideon moaned, his ass clenching and rapidly softening the further he pushed.

Gideon was still soft from the last time Aleron had been inside him, but he'd shrunk enough that Aleron feared hurting him. Orpheus had told him he could heal, and all that was required was the determination to take the person's wounds for them – a sacrifice.

Aleron tried to heal him after the head popped through, pausing to focus. Because, with how swollen and overfilled his heart currently felt, once he was seated deep, Aleron knew he wouldn't remember to do it. Gideon already felt amazing, and it was dizzying, causing his thoughts to haze and his sight to darken rapidly.

Pride fluffed his feathers when a pinch wrapped around the base of his spine where it attached to his tail. The sting mattered little in comparison to the profound throbbing in his cock. Gideon did, however, soften completely, from hand grip to hole, and even let out a deep sigh.

Aleron was surprised it was so easy.

"Did you just heal– *Ohhh.*"

Gideon's words trailed off when Aleron pulled back so his lubricant could collect inside him and make the next pump easier.

Aleron didn't mean to shove all the way to the two rings three-quarters of the way down his cock, but Gideon ground against him at the same time.

Oh fuck. Aleron's mind began to fray at the edges, his fangs parting at the heat that greeted him. Their groans mingled, but Aleron's hips started to thrust uncontrollably at the warmth that sheathed him, the snug cushion of his bride cuddling this much of his cock.

Already losing the control on his craving to be gentle, he was so close to slamming himself all the way to the hilt every time Gideon's tight asshole pressed against that braided ring. He wanted to be swallowed completely and utterly whole.

"Deeper," his little human pleaded with an airiness.

A thrill racing down his spine made his wings flare and his fur lift. His tail vibrated, his grip on the crooks of Gideon's thighs and backside tightened, and Aleron darted his head down to him.

With Gideon's back curved and resting against the tree, his bride's glistening green eyes were focused on where they were joined. Knees up, Gideon tried to dig the heel of a foot into the back of his side to bring Aleron in.

"Please, deeper." Gideon let go of one shoulder to undo the buttons of his jacket and parted it as if wanting a better view. "Put it inside me. I need it."

The snarl that tore through Aleron was beastly as it reverberated off the snow and trees surrounding them. He shoved Gideon down at the same time as he thrust hard. The two rings popped through half a heartbeat before their hips slammed against each other's.

With a strangled squeak, Gideon's back arched as he threw his head back. His knees bent, and his feet arched.

Barely able to feel Gideon pulling his fur out, Aleron was too busy shuddering wildly at being fully gloved. Blackness muddled his purple sight, yet his chest felt like it was glowing with warmth and lightness, like the pretty flaming soul between his horns.

He rocked himself within Gideon as a bliss-filled whimper echoed from his throat.

"Mine," Aleron whined, human blood thickening the air as his claws dug. "Mine?"

"Yours," Gideon rasped out.

"I can touch and hold whenever I like?" Aleron tipped his head forward so he could swirl his tongue against Gideon's cute pink ear. Gideon gave a squirming shudder while nodding. "I can lick however I like, and ask for kisses from you? I want your lips all over me, little spring."

Reaching up to grab a horn and keep himself steady, Gideon messily kissed at the side of his snout. It was obvious he wasn't paying attention to where, especially since his eyes flickered back as though they were rolling in pleasure.

Each press of his lips was followed by a soft and airy moan as Aleron pumped into him.

"I felt so lost without this side of you. I wanted your affection so badly that I felt cold inside, but now my chest feels radiant. I want to hear you moan for me, Gideon. I missed your little cries, and your smiles, and the way your eyes began to light up at me. I crave to see your face hazy with need for me."

Planning to have exactly what he yearned for, Aleron's thrusts quickened. He buried his snout in his bride's hair, ignoring the slickness of sweat, and searched for his sweet scent. His fangs parted to let out a contented huff when he found it, and he shoved harder.

Aleron nearly released one of Gideon's legs so he could brace himself against the fucking tree when the little male tightly spasmed around him for it.

"Oh fuck," Gideon cursed with a whisper, burying his forehead against Aleron's chest to look down. With a solid, fur-clutching grip on the back of his shoulder, Gideon pushed at Aleron's rippling stomach. "Oh gods. It's too much. Let go."

Let go? Aleron leaned back to separate their torsos, trusting that his hands and the tree could support Gideon.

His heavy-lidded gaze was already riveted down on his own body. His green eyes were crinkled with pleasurable anguish, his lips parted on constant lewd moans that he didn't even try to contain.

Aleron immediately knew why, and was rather fucking pleased by what he saw.

Since his control of his tentacles was rather weak, he couldn't always feel them.

Currently, the bottom two had wrapped just in front of his fingers to cling to Gideon's backside. The top two, however, had coiled themselves over his hair-dusted balls and up the length of his cock.

One coiled just beneath his bride's sac to push it up and tight against the base of his shaft, before twirling halfway up him. The other wrapped the other way until the tapered end clung to the side of his pink head. Each time Aleron pulled his hips back, the tentacles would stroke downwards on the loose skin of Gideon's cock, only to slip forward when he thrust deep.

Instead of letting go, seeing his human liked them despite his words otherwise, Aleron attempted to tighten them. His little bride's cock was very hard, to the point thick blue veins had risen to the surface all over.

The excitement at watching another cock being stroked by his tentacles, and seeing his own spreading his bride as it pumped, bled amorous lava into his veins. The sight just made him more ravenous. All gentleness eroded, leaving him through his drooling, frothing maw.

Perhaps Aleron should have been more careful with Gideon's sensitive core, but nothing in that moment could have stopped him from rutting this human wildly. His hips sprinted alongside his racing heart, while his lungs let out huffing whines in feverish anticipation.

With the change of speed, Gideon was rendered utterly speechless. His eyes grew wide, as did his lips, and the only noises that came from him were gasping hitches of breath.

"Lift your shirt," Aleron demanded. "I want to see the body that's mine. I wish to see you coming apart at my every touch."

Pulling his shirt up, Gideon bit down on the bottom of it to keep it up. Even just his easy obedience seemed to twist Aleron's thoughts.

Aleron gazed at his hair-dusted chest, then his pale nipples that were hard and just begging for his tongue. His muscles were hidden away, all squished together, but they were slick with sweat.

Pretty. All of it was pretty, all of it tantalising. All of it *his.*

And then it happened. What Aleron sought started out as magnificent clenches and spasms around his thick cock, just as Gideon's sac tightened against his tentacles.

His bride's eyes rolled back, eyelids flickering, just as his back drew tight like a string. His shirt fell from his teeth to crumble above his exposed chest as he let loose a loud moan, just as erotic-scented white liquid spurted up his abdomen. Gideon's first release of seed was so strong it splattered across his own lips, while the others that followed left puddles against his sternum and abdomen. Just the sight, the sound of his cry, the scent of this male coming, all while his ass massaged Aleron all the way around, nearly broke him.

His wings shot forward until the arches of them punched the tree just above Gideon's head. Aleron shuddered as his hips slowed, bracing himself through Gideon's orgasm. The longer it went on, the more his wings slipped closer and closer until they were hugging the sides of this male with all their might.

Aleron wanted to bring Gideon into them more than anything. He longed to hold him fully while Gideon cuddled his cock like this. His entire being yearned for them to be one. To shelter his little bride until Aleron had completely swallowed up and consumed him in his feathery embrace, and the world could no longer perceive him.

But he couldn't.

Even if Gideon had fully accepted all of him, humans easily perished. He didn't wish to harm Gideon or make him feel anything distressful in an embrace that meant so much to Aleron.

He'd just rather not do it, but would satisfy the urge as much as he could. To... *compromise*, something Gideon stated was important when they were in Tenebris.

Content with Gideon sheltered from the sides, Aleron slowly thrust to let Gideon gently ease his way down from coming. It didn't seem to help, considering the male frantically twitched each time his rings rolled over a certain spot just behind the entrance of his hole.

He's going lax. Even his drained cock was trying to deflate, which caused Aleron's tentacles to squeeze him in protest. They were enjoying strangling his cock.

Gideon's shaking legs lost their tension, as did his grip.

A growling groan fell from his parted fangs as Gideon's bright gaze roamed up him, especially when it had a softness to it that was rare. His crooked, sated grin caused Aleron's hips to immediately pick up their rhythm once more.

Aleron hadn't come on purpose. He'd slowed his thrusts when he'd been drawing too close to his end and took a tight hold on his control. Just enough to hold back. He wanted this to last as long as it could.

His bride was around him, in his arms, looking all sweet and cute. The lust ignited in his veins could never compare to the fondness Aleron held for him, and was purely a byproduct of it.

Aleron was getting what he wanted, and he wanted it to last.

"You didn't come?" Gideon asked, his deep voice hoarse.

When he shook his skull, Gideon's head lolled to the side. He planted his face against one of Aleron's wings, yet Gideon's eyes darted to the corners of his lids to gaze up at Aleron. Gideon huffed against the tickling feathers before burying into them with his nose.

Then he whispered softly, "You can put your wings around me."

At just the offer and mention of them, the tips crossed below him. Aleron shook his head, refusing. Yet, his heart clenched, and his hips slammed against him a little harder.

With a glare, Gideon turned his face to him. "Put your wings around me, Aleron."

"I do not wish to—"

Gideon's nose wrinkled tightly in rage. "Just do it!" he shouted, yanking himself up. Then he bit into the side of Aleron's neck so hard it was as if he was trying to tear a chunk from him.

His bride's bold act shocked him enough that he stumbled back a step, but they were little flat teeth – the perfect kind of sting. His wings snapped shut around Gideon.

A shiver rippled across Aleron's entire body and his knees gave out at finally being able to do this. Falling to his knees, his cock utterly buried to the base, and his arms coiling around Gideon's shoulders and hips, he clung to the male. Aleron clung so tightly the human let out a squeak at being crushed, but his wings continued to squeeze and spread until they wrapped against his own back.

His wings forced the heels of Gideon's hidden feet down until it changed their position. Still torso to torso, Aleron craned his head back from Gideon so he could dig into the sheltered cavity his bride was nestled in. His snout slipped across Gideon's warm back and nuzzled the side of his head.

"Gideon," he whimpered within the darkness.

His forest scent had quickly filled the small space. It lulled Aleron so completely he began to greedily pant it in, rapidly licking at his drooling fangs. He was choking on it. Yet the strangulation was the sweetest thing he'd ever experienced, especially with the saltiness from the release of his pleasure now clinging between them.

Despite the joy that swelled in his chest, his claws sunk into his bride's flesh in fear. The delicious coppery scent mingling with the rest of him just made him dizzier, his mind heavy.

Had Aleron been able to take Gideon in like this while he wasn't his bride and hadn't removed his hunger... Aleron doubted he would have been able to contain himself. The space was too small, too tight. Despite the lack of bloodlust, his gut clenched.

Cock thrumming, it called for Aleron to satisfy that old urge by manically thrusting into this male. To consume him with pleasure, rather than with fangs.

"Mmm, so *warm*," Gideon hummed softly with his chin planted against the fur over Aleron's pectoral muscle.

Suddenly his bride didn't feel close enough.

Aleron loosened his wings just enough so he could create a pocket for his arm. Grabbing the back of Gideon's shirt and jacket, Aleron lifted them until they slipped over his head. He sightlessly tossed the clothes out of their embrace, not giving a damn where they landed or if they were ever found again.

Being cuddled by Aleron's wings once more, Gideon

shivered in the wake of his feathers gliding over the skin of his bare back, his shoulders, and even his forearms. His hairs caught on the fibres of them, and Aleron wondered if it were possible for them to entangle permanently.

"They are so soft and warm," Gideon whispered, twitching as they tickled him all over. "I can feel your heartbeat all around me. They feel lovely, darling."

The acceptance of them, spoken so tenderly, gnawed away at the last of Aleron's anxieties. Gideon even welcomed his claws, and the way they cut through flesh.

"Come here," Gideon purred.

Nudging at the side of Aleron's skull with his nose, Gideon grabbed a horn to gently pull it back. The purple in his sight was too strong to let the pink that flickered linger long, but it flashed at Gideon when he pressed his lips against Aleron's fangs.

A small amount of seed transferred during the tender contact. Aleron licked at his fangs before swiping across Gideon's soft lips and spikey chin to steal the rest. Aleron shivered in delight, his cock swelling deep within the damp warmth of him.

I have never felt so close to another.

He'd never been deep inside someone while they were inside him. He'd not only sheltered Gideon with his wings, but his very heart.

Aleron felt so painfully vulnerable in that moment. Yet Gideon's lips and tongue greeting his in return left security and safety in their wake. His warm little hands gliding over the back of Aleron's neck, his shoulders, and down his chest left him raw in the most wonderous way.

Then the male tilted his hips wantonly back and forth, moving Aleron inside him, and his fucking brain split in two. His cock was hardening against Aleron's torso, and the crawl of it thickening and lengthening tingled his mind and stroked his body. His tentacles began to wriggle to clutch it, wanting to hold it in their clasps.

"Are you going to finish fucking your bride or not?" The devious beast nipped at Aleron's chest as his hands glided across his sides to touch at his back. His fingers dug into his feathers, dangerously close to brushing the base of his wings. "You can kneel and worship me later, or I can do it with your cock in my mouth."

A choked huff punched out of Aleron.

He'd known the male could be devilishly bold when he chose to be, but he didn't know he could be *this* erotic.

His hips started to rock, moving in tandem with Gideon's grinds. *He called himself my bride.* He'd never done that before.

Kneading Gideon's arse with one hand, and keeping a firm grip across his shoulders, Aleron groaned as he licked Gideon. Then the tantalising creature grabbed the base of both his wings and put his all into his movements.

Blood pulsated up them in reaction to being touched, and his hips lifted upwards until he knelt higher.

Before Aleron knew it, he was ramming up into Gideon with quick, hard slams. The speed of his jarring movements, combined with a lack of balance from his wings weighing his back down, caused him to start falling.

Instead of landing on his fragile human, Aleron managed to land on his side, using his elbow to create a pocket between him and the ground for Gideon's leg to fit through.

Aleron's body pulled taut.

With everywhere sensitive being kneaded – his back, his cock, his conscience – he fucked his bride with all his might.

He smelt blood from his claws, but he was too lost to heal Gideon, too broken to think about anything but the way he felt in his embrace.

"Gideon," Aleron called, again and again, wanting to say his name as bliss stroked him all over. Shivers danced down all six of his limbs, and his hands and talons clenched along with them.

He was so soft, so warm, yet his massaging tight ring was robbing him of breath.

Gideon kept moaning. "Don't stop. Fuck, don't stop." He could do little else but hold on now, their positions stuck unless Aleron let go of him.

His human was utterly trapped, his arms, legs, and even head forced to remain still while Aleron rutted into him.

And then Gideon repeatedly called his name so beautifully, 'Aleron' whispering from his lips like it was a coy secret. It broke his heart and mended it all at the same time.

Letting go of his shoulder, Aleron grabbed the back of his head and yanked it back to force Gideon to look up at his skull. He immediately knew his little spring couldn't see anything but the glow of his purple orbs with the way his pupils had blown, his eyelids drooped and barely flickering. Gideon's mind was gone, his face pink, and his body lax in welcome for Aleron.

But Aleron could see his pleasure, his need, all of it for him.

"I love you," Aleron whimpered. Gideon's gaze flickered, registering it. "I *love* you."

Fuck, just saying it was pushing him ever closer to his end. For so long, he'd yearned just to say those three words again without seeing this male's face pale.

Instead, now it grew redder, and he soundlessly tried to mouth something back to him.

Aleron wanted to believe it was to return it, but he also didn't care. What mattered was that this human heard it, finally accepted it, and that he was allowed to say it whenever he desired.

So he repeated it. Even when his legs began to quake and shivers traced down his spine. Even when Aleron couldn't think and he let his body completely take over, he said it – his entire being, all the way to his essence, at peace and in agreement with that sentiment.

Aleron received no warning when Gideon's ass began to strangle his cock in spasms, crushing him all the way to the core. He scented more cum. He felt it spurting between their meshed torsos while Gideon's cock fluttered and twitched against him.

It ripped his own release from him violently, a mindless, haunted groan gnashing his fangs tightly shut. He thrust harder, faster, letting Gideon draw every drop from his cock until it felt like Aleron had completely drained his embedded seed sacs inside him.

As he spilled the last of his release, Aleron found himself thoughtlessly pumping through aftershocks. He couldn't stop moving, the pleasure of it curling his talons and rippling his wings constantly.

Aleron couldn't imagine what he looked like from outside their erotic cuddle. He'd probably appeared as a lonely, squirming, tormented creature upon the ground, the world unaware he was losing his ever-loving mind within this male.

Gideon didn't seem to be faring any better, although he lacked tension, whereas Aleron couldn't seem to shed it.

With messy hair and eyes shut, his head bounced from Aleron's gentle thrusts as it lolled to the side. Gideon frantically panted through wetted lips. He even looked to be drooling slightly, but perhaps not as much as Aleron's rabid maw did. Redness blotted his cheeks, and flushed his neck and chest.

Only once Aleron stopped moving did Gideon attempt to open his eyes. They rolled before shutting again.

His small, fragile human heart sprinted alongside Aleron's much larger one. Both frantic, both going far too fast.

The bridge of his nose scrunched as his brows furrowed.

"Air," Gideon managed to huff out through shallow,

choked breaths. "I can't breathe."

A cold slice tore through his chest. *I am suffocating him.*

Before he could react, a hand slapped onto his bony jaw. "Not all the way. I'm just really hot. I need a little fresh air for a second."

Aleron opened the top arch of his wings to let an icy breeze wash over his face, ready to fully release him if need be. But he didn't want to, hoping this was enough.

Lifting his face to it, Gideon greedily gulped in air, the ball in his throat bobbing as he did. The redness in Gideon's face became less blotchy and instead faded to his normal heated flush. The dim light Aleron let in highlighted just how much the little male had been sweating.

But with each breath Gideon took, his chest calmed, as did his pulse. Eventually dipping his head down, he nodded for Aleron to close his wings again.

When Aleron didn't comply immediately, he managed to glare without even opening his eyes. "Close them."

At the sternness in his tone, Aleron obeyed his command.

Bright pink flooded his sight at doing so.

THIRTY-EIGHT

Still lying within their tight cuddle, Aleron watched Gideon
lay his head against his wing in his special darkness.

Tranquillity fell over them within the peacefulness of
their unspoken silence. All that could be heard were their
harmonious huffs and pulses. At least for Aleron, who had
sensitive hearing.

The stiffness in Aleron's muscles eventually waned, and
Gideon moaned in reaction to it. He reached between them
when Aleron's tentacles finally unlatched from his softened
dick and moved to sway over his abdomen instead.

"You're not allowed to do that again," Gideon rasped,
touching them.

Aleron hoped he was joking.

"But you came so hard from them," Aleron teased,
nudging the end of his snout against his brow. "You crushed
me until I thought you'd pulverise my cock."

He didn't know if the shiver that tore through Gideon
was due to his words, or Aleron's claws trailing up his
spine. Gideon's back arched and twitched in enjoyment, his
thighs tightening around his waist, but lacking the energy
for anything more.

Aleron adored... this. This cuddle, one that was so
similar to the one they shared back in Tenebris. Yet, it was
so much better. The scents, the sounds, the true satisfaction;

none of these had been present before. He hadn't made Gideon his bride yet either, and Aleron could feel that connection, could feel Gideon's warmth within him from his soul – as if he'd truly eaten it.

His thoughts lingered on his utter contentment, until his little spring, fully thawed of his frost, broke their silence.

He never opened his eyes as they spoke.

"Maybe it's because you're still inside me, but I wanted to ask you something." He touched Aleron's pelvis, right along the edge of where his tentacles and shaft were coming from. "Did it feel good when I put my fingers inside you here?"

Aleron shuddered. "Yes. It felt *very* good. It was like you were stroking everything all at once."

"I'll be honest, I was nervous about entering you here at first. It kind of reminded me of a pussy, and it made me uncomfortable."

White flared in his sight as he grew unsure as to why Gideon was saying something so hurtful in such a tender moment.

"But," he continued, gliding his hand up through the fur of Aleron's abdomen, "now that I've seen what comes out of you, I can't seem to think of it as anything but a... cock pocket." His dimples peeked at Aleron as he let out a little chuckle. "It makes me horny whenever I think about it."

"My seam arouses you?" Aleron asked, both confused and very pleased about this.

His bride was being truthful with him. Gideon was being open even if it meant digging through a small amount of hurt to get to the wonderfulness. This is what he'd longed for, and he hoped he continued to be this way in the future.

"Yeah." The pink in his ears deepened, and they were so cute, Aleron nibbled one. The fact Gideon shivered from it only made him want to do it again. "Since it feels good, I was wondering if maybe I could... fuck it."

"You want to fuck my seam?" Aleron asked in disbelief,

tilting his head.

"I-if you don't want to, that's fine. I don't mind."

It wasn't that he was against it. "You will not be able to. When I harden, it pushes everything forward."

"But before that," he grumbled. "I just think it'll feel really good, and I'd like us to bond as much as we can in different ways."

Aleron pondered on this. He wasn't sure how he felt about it, since inside his seam was rather sensitive. As he'd previously stated, just his fingers felt like he'd stroked Aleron all throughout his groin. He knew penetration would feel good, but he didn't know if he could handle the intensity.

"Can I think about it?"

"Of course." He smiled before it quickly fell. Gideon's breaths truly settled, just as he started a new conversation. "Hey, darling..."

Look at him. He is being all chatty again.

"I like it when you call me this," Aleron stated, lifting a hand to brush the back of his curved claw under his jaw. "Is this your heart's name for me?"

His smile returned. "Yeah, it's your little spring's pet name for you."

The joyous thrill that tore through him engulfed his chest. His wings attempted to flap around him.

"Hey, Aleron."

"I thought it was darling," he rumbled playfully, brushing his claw again.

The chuckle that exploded from Gideon tingled his mind – only for him to wince a second later.

"I-if it's not too much trouble... could you heal me like before? Now that I'm not overcome with need, all your claw marks are really starting to sting."

The orange of guilt blasted into his sight and Aleron gnashed his fangs. Without wasting another second, he

ᴏcused on trying to take his bride's wounds from him –
something he *should* have done sooner.

Like before, it was slow. This was only the second time
in his life using magic consciously, and the first time had
only been within the last hour.

The transference caused him to flinch.

Pain lashed over his right shoulder, the left side of his
backside, and across the backs of his thighs. Blood welled –
his own – and he instantly knew he'd sliced deep. The
pinching at the base of his spine was different, but not as
prevalent.

"I am sorry," Aleron grated, nuzzling his snout against
him apologetically. "I did not mean to hurt you."

"It's fine. They actually felt really good in the moment."
His lips puckered with thought. "Then again, I don't think I
really registered them through everything else."

Aleron didn't know how to respond to that, so he didn't.
Aleron just let himself be content that he could have such a
power over Gideon to steal some of his senses.

Patting his hand around, Gideon searched behind himself
until he found what he sought. Bringing Aleron's palm to
his thigh, Gideon fisted his fingers and played with the ring
he'd placed on him.

Aleron had not forgotten about it.

A strange sensation had clutched him, and he had a
feeling it was entirely nonphysical. Ever since Gideon had
slid it onto his finger, he'd felt like he was trapped and
possessed. Aleron didn't think it was possible, considering
he held Gideon's soul, but he felt further bonded with this
human.

Perhaps not as much as his cock currently buried to the
base, but in a way that was far more subtle, yet more lasting.

Once he finished playing with it, Gideon just held his
hand.

"I'm... I'm really tired, and you're so comfortable right
now," he stated softly.

Aleron already figured, since he hadn't opened his eyes once during their entire conversation. The compliment was nice.

"You also did not sleep much last night."

Gideon had only drifted off for a short while before they were attacked by a flying Demon. Perhaps it hadn't been wise to fly above the Veil with the dark of night giving them freedom.

He hadn't cared in the search for his kindred.

"I haven't been sleeping well since we came back."

"I know," Aleron uttered with a hint of sadness.

"I kept having nightmares. I often remembered when I died, or I'd dream of Emerie burning. And then... my other dreams terrified me."

"Other dreams?" he asked, despite being worried about the answer.

"Yeah. My memories were so confusing, and they weren't always clear. But then..." All of a sudden, his features grew exhausted. "I don't know anymore if they are old feelings or new ones, but I've been falling for you in *this* life. The more I did, the more I wanted to see the memories, but I also grew scared of learning everything because of how I hurt you." Gideon squeezed his hand. "I feel better now, though. I'm glad you like your ring."

"Sleep, little spring."

"But there was more I wanted to say before you interrupted me with this." He ground against Aleron's hips, stirring his softening cock within him.

"It can wait."

As could his reunion with his kindred.

He opened his wings just enough to peek at the outside world, finding it was still bright even in the shade of the trees. Faded, but they had time before the sun truly began to set.

His bride needed rest. A small nap was deserved, and

d like Gideon to rest with them as one.

Honestly... after so much longing, Aleron just wanted to soak up as much of this as possible. He hadn't felt truly content since they arrived on Earth. His essence needed this healing moment more than he'd like to admit, and he savoured every second of it.

"Thank you," Gideon whispered so quietly, so airily, Aleron knew he meant more than just the offer of sleep.

When his bride finally, and rather swiftly, passed out, Aleron licked away the stray tear that fell from the corner of his eye. He stopped the droplet from falling onto his wing and removed the salty evidence of it.

In this embrace, filled with adoration and tenderness, there was no room for sorrow.

THIRTY-NINE

"Oh gods... where are my pants, Aleron?!" Gideon yelled, walking around with nothing but his shirt and jacket on.

Arse bare, dick swinging, he searched unsuccessfully, and Aleron was being utterly unhelpful. *My feet and dick are fucking freezing!* At this rate, his balls were going to shrivel up and recede inside himself just to escape the damn cold. *Snow hadn't blanketed the ground the last time we came to the north.*

Aleron pointed to the tree he'd fucked him against. "Over there."

"I already searched there, though." Gideon threw his hands up when a second search failed. "Can't you just... sniff them out?"

With a huff that was done only to poorly hide his chuckle, Aleron stomped over to the location in question. "But I prefer you without them. They get in the way. Taking them off is difficult."

It was only when Aleron clawed and yanked Gideon's trousers from underneath the snow, which had fallen from a branch above, that Gideon noticed the nose of his boot was actually not a stick like he'd originally thought. Aleron shook everything out and passed it to his shivering form.

"Yeah, *no.* I'm not walking around buck-naked like the day I was born. What if something bites me?"

He probably shouldn't have bent over with his backside in Aleron's direction – he just didn't think about it with the rush to clothe himself.

A set of claw tips tickled over his rounded cheek. "The only thing likely to bite you is me."

Gideon shot Aleron a withering glare as he pulled his undershorts on, before doing the same to his pants and tying them. Ignoring the shiver of cold that ran up his spine, hoping his body heat would thaw his clothes, Gideon hurried to put on his boots.

The glare had been empty. He actually rather liked this side of Aleron, and was relieved he was finally allowed to see it.

"You know I bite back." Gideon threw a hand up to stop him from responding. "And before you say anything, I'll find somewhere on you where you *don't* like being bitten. You're not afraid to lick me everywhere, so don't think I won't go exploring everywhere too."

After Gideon wrestled to put his second boot on, he didn't have a chance to straighten up before an arm wrapped around his waist.

Aleron lifted him, far higher than he normally did. With his backside resting on Aleron's forearm and his back supported by the other, the side of his bony cheek rubbed against his own. Aleron squeezed them together with their heads at the same height, when usually he cradled him lower. Bright pink glowed from Aleron's orbs, more passionate than Gideon had ever seen, as the big Duskwalker let out a deep chuckle.

Even his wings came forward to hug Gideon from one side, as the tips of them crossed beneath his feet.

"I hope you bite me everywhere, little spring." Aleron nuzzled harder against his prickly five o'clock shadow. "We can make a game of it."

Gideon chuckled back, and even tried to return his nuzzle by placing his hand under Aleron's long jaw to bring him closer.

It felt like it'd been forever since his heart had been this light and lacked any painful aches. He also couldn't remember if it'd ever been this... full and content.

For the first time in his life, Gideon didn't feel like he had to hide. He could be himself, which could often change since he was an ambivert. With Aleron, he didn't need a filter, and could just express himself in any way he desired – physically or verbally. Both were accepted, no matter how ridiculous.

Aleron took the doting as just that... adoration, even if it was Gideon threatening and picking on him. He liked that Aleron did it back, showing him just how playful he really could be.

After his short nap, they'd both been slow to leave their cuddle. Gideon had done so begrudgingly, but willingly, since Aleron wanted to leave.

But even just those minutes had been amazing, full of the warmth and love Aleron seemed quick to dole out. If that was what his future would be like, he'd be smitten with this big Duskwalker forever.

Gideon cherished physical touch, and the fact Aleron wanted to touch him everywhere constantly fed it. In just a short amount of time, Gideon not only consumed it until he was full, but to the point he was near bursting.

It was hard to keep his hands off someone like that.

He'd nearly fallen back asleep within the span of a breath when Aleron ran the points of his claws up through his hair and across his scalp. The action almost made him catatonic.

Those claws were dangerous... for all the right reasons.

Sure, Aleron's nipping fangs stung, but he didn't mind having a few love bites. Each one was worth it.

Gideon's softer touches, like his kisses, seemed to touch Aleron on a spiritual level. He'd like to see how docile this beast could become if Gideon lathered him in them from head to talons.

A grin formed across his features, widening until his teeth were revealed. *I don't think I've ever wanted to do that with anyone.* Likely because Aleron might be the only one who would truly, utterly, and completely relish it.

"We are losing the light," Gideon noted, gesturing his head to the fading dusk. Seeming to come to his senses, Aleron flared his wings and lowered Gideon into his normal cradle. "Wait! Don't forget my case."

Gideon reached for it, and Aleron lowered him until he could grab the handle. Awkwardly, he strapped it to his chest before pushing it behind him. He nodded that he was ready.

With a quick swoosh and flurry of snowflakes, Aleron leapt, only to flap them higher. He flew lower than normal, swaying side to side, ducking tree after tree as he followed Ingram's scent.

Gideon held the strap of his case and gazed at his silver ring glinting in the sun.

I'm glad I didn't have to sell my guitar. He'd taken it into the town in case he needed to trade it for the urgency he'd requested.

Asking someone to drop all their current orders on his whim was a hard sell. The blacksmith had fought him on it, claiming he didn't have enough coin for him to drop everything he was doing right then to make them. No one liked to assist a customer who came across bossy and impatient, despite not realising there may actually be cause for urgency.

But the burly bloke had quickly changed his tune when Gideon said he'd be back after he sold his guitar. Only when he'd made the offer to sell his prized possession, did the tradesman understand that Gideon really just didn't have time to wait, and that it was important to him. Before that, the blacksmith had just thought he was being rudely entitled.

He would have liked to have nicer ones made, but he just didn't have time. While the blacksmith had been working to make Aleron's from iron, Gideon ran off to an actual jeweller. His own ring was pre-made and of silver.

However, he didn't walk on his hands, nor could he crush silver. Both were plain, looked identical, and had meaning. That's all that mattered.

When he got down on one knee for this Duskwalker like an idiot, his emotions were so high and chaotic he hadn't even thought that Aleron wouldn't understand. He'd just had the urge to do it, and it'd gripped him so damn tightly he thought he'd break apart if he didn't.

Because Aleron had mirrored him, he'd stolen even more of his heart. Gideon had been so scared doing it that the laughter that had burst out of him had been much needed and soothed his anxieties.

He lifted his gaze to Aleron's skull.

I'm really glad he didn't figure out that the golden rings were another set. Although he hadn't purchased the one Beau had been intending for him, Gideon had been a nervous wreck at the thought of presenting his rings to Aleron.

He didn't want him to put two and two together.

I'll tell him when we're both ready. When Aleron understood Beau no longer mattered and was completely in the past. That he no longer pined after or wanted him because he'd found someone who, funnily enough, suited him much better.

The compromises between them were much smaller, and he was reaching for different goals.

Yes, he'd wanted to have a good-paying job, buy his own home, have a husband, and start a family.

His priorities were different now.

His home would be Aleron because in their own weird,

wacky way, they were husbands now. He didn't know about having a family, but maybe they could find a way to adopt some lost child in the woods that didn't want to live in a town. He didn't need a job, since he didn't need to provide food for a belly that no longer required feeding, and he had a set of fluffy wings to keep him sheltered.

Gideon had always been adventurous, but he had denied that urge for many reasons. Beau didn't want to risk leaving their town, and the Demons had kept his feet from truly itching to leave.

Fear? What was the point in having such an intense emotion when he had the biggest, baddest monster protecting him? Hell, even if Gideon was fatally wounded, Aleron could heal him, or he'd just come back to life.

So, when they were both ready, Gideon would completely reveal his past. Being fully open meant honesty in all regards, and he'd like Aleron to know who he had been. He'd like the chance to explain... why he'd been dying inside when they arrived on Earth.

He wanted to tell him the truth, no matter how painful it may be, knowing that he'd be forgiven.

And that certainty of forgiveness meant much.

Gideon finally felt like he could accept it.

"We're almost there." The excitement in Aleron's voice was palpable.

Gideon looked forward and smelt subtle smoke from a chimney hidden within the forest long before he saw it. Night came, just as a wooden house came into view with a small clearing surrounding it. A wooden stake was sticking up from the ground a few metres from a set of porch steps. Odd.

Just as the last bit of light was about to snuff out, bright reddish-orange hair caught his attention. Wearing a blue dress, a woman crossed the clearing with a basket of herbs – that likely came from the garden partially buried in snow.

"Emerie!" Gideon shouted, knowing that long, wavy hair

anywhere.

Just as he went to wave and Aleron started dropping to the ground, Emerie looked up at them.

The harrowing scream that came from her pierced the air as she tossed the basket. Emerie backed up, immediately fell on her arse, and covered her face with both arms.

Aleron, confused and shocked, clambered to halt his descent due to her reaction.

"Oh shit," Gideon muttered in disbelief.

A ferocious, beastly roar from the right tore a gasp out of Gideon's throat, only for his eyes to widen when something with glowing red orbs leapt for them.

"*Oh shit!*" Gideon bellowed, just as they were tackled in mid-air.

It was too late.

Wings shielded Gideon and tightened their hold on him as all three went crashing to the ground. Aleron let loose a bellowing roar of pain and nearly crushed him to fucking death. His case creaked, his guitar jingling within it, then he was tossed to the ground when Aleron managed to wrangle himself free from their assailant.

On his hands and feet in his monstrous form, Aleron stood above Gideon protectively.

It wasn't hard to guess who'd attacked them. Gideon knew it was likely Ingram, who had just acted on instinct to protect Emerie when she let out a scream. He didn't need to see through Aleron's bowed chest to know that.

He also didn't need Ingram to curiously ask, "Aleron?"

But Gideon knew something was horribly wrong when liquid with a strong, coppery smell dripped onto his face. In the darkness that had fallen over them, he tried to wipe it away and inspect the purple blood on him.

Shit. He's hurt pretty badly.

A shiver of dread traced down his back like a ghastly cold finger, when a menacing snarl radiated from Aleron's drooling fangs. Hot breath puffed out like fog.

"Aleron, wa–" He didn't even get to finish before Aleron lunged.

Within the span of a heartbeat, Aleron tackled Ingram to the ground with a hard thwack of their dense torsos colliding. Ingram let out a horrible yelp, right before their bodies writhed as they mindlessly fought.

Two sets of crimson orbs glowed against white skulls, but the rest of them were just dark shadows clawing and beating against each other.

"Oh shit!" Gideon repeated, rushing to his feet.

Backing away, he didn't know what to do, how to help. He wasn't dumb enough to get into the thick of two Duskwalkers raging.

His head whipped towards the house. *Emerie.*

Gideon sprinted over to it, hissing between his teeth as he pulled up short, forced to limp the last few metres due to some injury. He found her on the ground, sliding along her arse against the snow as she crawled towards the porch steps.

Her eyes were fixated on Ingram and Aleron as she subtly shook her head.

"Emerie," Gideon rasped, heading straight for her.

He attempted to help her to her feet by grabbing her forearm, but she ripped it away from him. She turned a pale, fear-stricken face up at him, and he winced at the webbed burn scars marring the left side of it. With the whites of her eyes visible, her irises moving back and forth over his features, she looked... petrified.

Even her breaths were short, shallow, and panicked.

He knelt, trying to ignore the distressing sounds of two giant monsters fighting behind him. Fangs chomped, and a beak snapped as rabid, wet snarls radiated between them. Trees groaned after hard thuds, while leaves rustled. He occasionally heard a snap and just hoped they were branches breaking or shrubs being crushed.

"Emerie, I need you to get up. We need to stop them," he told her, placing a hand on top of her head.

Tears instantly welled in her blue eyes as she choked out, "Wings."

She didn't need to say more.

I'm not the only one who has had nightmares about them.

Gideon wondered if he handled them better because he'd died. Emerie had suffered years of them tormenting her dreams, after they had taken everything away from her.

For Gideon, he'd died, and woken back on Earth with Aleron, who had used his wings to comfort and protect him. To warm him from the cold and mesmerise him with their little flutters.

As much as he felt for her, he understood right now she was having an intense trauma response, so he grabbed her face with both hands. With her cheeks squished, and her nose pointed up to him, Gideon... licked her face from chin to forehead.

She let out a squeal, her lips twisting with disgust. Ingram let out a roar in reaction, but it suddenly cut out. He chanced looking behind him, sucking in a horrible gasp, when it looked as though Ingram had leapt to attack Gideon, only for his back legs to be snagged by Aleron.

Shit. That could have been bad.

"Ew! You did not just lick me!" She pushed at his chest and even started kicking him. At least it'd snapped her out of it, as he thought it would – honestly, it'd been the only solution he could think of. "The hell, Gideon? What's wrong... with... you?" Halting halfway through wiping her face, her arm dropped and her lips parted so far he thought her jaw would unhinge and fall off. "Gideon!"

She leapt forward and put her arms around his neck to force him into a tight hug. She let out a broken, relieved sob.

As much as he wanted this reunion, he grabbed her biceps and pushed her back.

"Yes. Hugs and kisses. I missed you too," he quickly stated, and hurt dulled her features. "Now... if you don't mind. Help me with the fucking Duskwalkers!"

She gasped and shoved her head to the side to peer over his shoulder. Her eyes grew wide once more. "Oh fuck."

"Tell me about it!" he yelled, rolling back so his heels could touch the ground and he could stand. He took her with him. "I think they're in a bloodlust or rage or something? Aleron was hurt. I don't know how to stop them."

If Gideon got hurt in the process, he feared Aleron wouldn't calm down at all until he returned.

Unslinging his guitar case from his torso, he placed it safely on the snow-covered ground.

Cheeks wincing, guilt radiated in her crinkled face. "Sorry. Ingram probably heard me scream and thought the worst."

"No shit." He gestured to the wrestling twins, one trying to get above the other. "What do we do? I've never seen a Duskwalker's rage before."

Her eyes flickered over them before darting to his face. "My advice? Stay the fuck out of it. There's nothing we can do. One will win, and the other will come back tomorrow."

His lids lowered in annoyance. "Weren't you a Demonslayer or something? Surely you have something that can help."

Averting her gaze, she rubbed the side of her neck. "I have some enchanted rope, but it won't do much with both of them."

"Good enough. You handle Ingram, and I'll deal with Aleron."

Her hand came away in shock. "What?"

"I've already been mauled to death – a second time can't be worse."

Her face paled, and she looked moments from stamping

her foot in outrage. "Gideon!"

With an irritated groan, he threw his head back to sigh. Then it fell forward so he could grab her shoulders.

"Aleron has been looking forward to seeing his brother for over a month. This is not how he wanted to greet him." He squeezed her shoulders with his brow creasing beseechingly. "Please. Just trust me."

She absolutely should not trust him right now. What he was about to do would be stupid, but he really didn't mind if he got hurt.

Gideon couldn't be trusted, but he absolutely trusted Aleron with his whole heart. Even in the midst of this... he didn't think Aleron would hurt him. Ingram, yeah, absolutely.

A Duskwalker would never hurt their bride even when enraged... right? He may be narrow sighted on this, but he was choosing to have faith.

"Ugh, fine!" Emerie shouted while stamping a foot.

She uncoiled a whip from one side of her weapons belt situated over her blue dress, and a loop of rope from the other. Then they both turned to the Duskwalkers.

They launched forward.

The moment Emerie snapped the end of her whip around Ingram's neck, she ran up his back to quickly loop her rope around it as well. Ingram didn't notice her there, but she was bucked off the moment Aleron managed to get out from underneath him.

Aleron jumped back, just as Ingram did. Emerie flung one end of her rope around a tree, and the other end around itself, tethering him to it. The action seemed practised, as if she'd done it before.

Gideon took that as his chance. Especially since Aleron had stalked closer on limping hands. Running between them, Gideon threw his hands out while facing Aleron.

A small amount of doubt stabbed his gut when his friend

and lover sprinted for him like a rabid creature. A snapping snarl chomped from Aleron's fangs, just as he lunged.

Within seconds, Gideon was below Aleron, with the Duskwalker's chest pressing him against the thin layer of snow. Claws crunched into the earth, one wing upright in aggression, the other drooping from an injury. Blood coated Gideon, and the heat coming of Aleron was so intense, he thought it'd fry his skin.

Gideon knew what was about to happen when Aleron's fur and feathers lifted. Instead of letting him leap for Ingram, who struggled at the end of his tether to attack his own brother, Gideon grabbed the thick furry collar around Aleron's neck. Gideon yanked himself along the ground until he was below Aleron's skull, sat up, and threw his chest against his bony face.

He clung to his horns when Aleron tried to bring Gideon back down to safety underneath him. Hoping his chest blocked Aleron's sight and the ability to smell by being pressed against his nose hole, he refused to budge.

"H-hey darling," Gideon grated out, trying not to grunt from the strain of being pulled. "I need you to calm down for me, okay?"

Gideon pressed his face against the feral Duskwalker's bony forehead and rubbed against it. Gideon attempted to tickle him with his stubble – a strange and animalistic desire Aleron seemed to be obsessed with.

Aleron fought to get Gideon below him. Claws nicked him, but they never dug hard enough to truly do any damage. Even when enraged, this Duskwalker's desire to protect him was just too strong.

Snap out of it, Aleron. Cloth tore as his shirt and jacket were ripped apart at his back and sides.

Just as his arms were about to give out, both quaking against Aleron's strength, the Duskwalker stopped tugging. A rippling, full body shudder wracked Aleron and even his wings flapped – although the damaged one barely moved.

Then short, sharp whines echoed from his chest and between his fangs. They twisted Gideon's gut, and he wrapped his arms across the base of Aleron's skull to hug him comfortingly. Gideon continued to nuzzle him with his cheeks, chin, and nose, hoping to ease him a little.

A shaking, obviously injured hand gave out.

"Gideon." Curling his elongated arms around Gideon's torso and arse, he lowered to his belly. Aleron cradled him while placing his bony head on top of Gideon's partially straight legs. *"It hurts."*

"I know it does, darling," he cooed, eyeing down his spine.

Difficult to see the true extent of Aleron's injuries in the dark, he could mostly tell by the thick clumps of fur and feathers – many of which were missing. The slowly rising moon made the blood covering him glisten.

Ingram continued to struggle with rabid snarls and a chomping beak. Peeking over his shoulder, Gideon watched Emerie slowly approach with her hands up in order to calm down her own Duskwalker. Ingram never attacked her, and tried to pull her under him as well.

As Aleron's whines grew louder when the aggressive tension truly seeped out of him, Gideon patted his neck, only to immediately regret it. He touched wet wounds, so instead he quickly focused on the part of Aleron that was unharmed – his beautiful skull.

"Did we hurt you?" Aleron asked, trying to shift his head back enough so he could look up. *"I was holding you."*

"No. I'm alright." A small lie, but whatever was wrong with his right ankle and knee was nothing in comparison.

As if he'd known Gideon wouldn't be truthful, the pain dulled and eventually faded.

Gideon let out an annoyed sigh. "You didn't have to do that."

Apparently pleased with himself, Aleron held him tighter and subtly rubbed against his stomach.

A similar conversation happened behind him, and he peeked to see Ingram had collapsed to his knees to hold Emerie. Even his tail wrapped around her ankles as he let out his own whines and whimpers.

"Not quite the greeting we were expecting, were we?" Gideon said with a soft, yet saddened chuckle.

Aleron just shook his head and squeezed tighter.

Humour spiked in his chest. *Five minutes ago, he was a mindless, rabid beast, now he's being a giant sook.* Gideon found that so endearing and cute that a cyclone of tenderness swirled within.

"Aleron?" Ingram called, coming forward since Emerie must have released him from the rope she'd placed over his neck.

Aleron let out a small, half-hearted, growling huff. *"You attacked me."*

"You frightened Emerie!"

"I'm really sorry. I didn't mean to scream and ruin this," Emerie grumbled, her words heavy with regret.

"Eh. It's not your fault," Gideon said back to her. Only to smile as he brought his hands back to cup under the sides of Aleron's jaw and direct his snout upwards. "You didn't have someone to make wings comforting like I did." Aleron's orbs brightened in their pink hue, which made him grin. "Come on. You ready to forgive and meet your kindred?"

A snorted huff echoed from Aleron's snout in a foggy cloud before he shakily lifted to his hands and feet. Gideon stood as well, just as Ingram came up next to him.

Then Aleron leapt for his twin. *"Ingram!"*

If it weren't for the joy in his shout, Gideon would have thought they were about to start fighting again when Aleron tackled his twin.

The two Duskwalkers rolled around as they attempted to bring each other into the tightest hug possible. Using injured tails, wings, arms, legs, and even their skulls, they meshed their bodies together until they were one heap. Someone purred, while another groaned in relief.

Gideon backed up to give them space, wishing globs of purple blood didn't stain the white snow everywhere they went. Never mind the intermittent light whines that could be heard.

"I feel bad that I started a fight," Emerie stated, coming up beside him to watch them as well.

"Don't be." He refused to allow Emerie to berate herself for something she couldn't control. "I honestly doubt this will be the last time we have to separate these two."

Considering the level of post-traumatic stress she had, that had continued over the last eight years, his death, her burns, and just her life in general, he guessed none of it had been easy for her. She couldn't help her reaction, and he just hoped that his return helped to heal her.

Maybe Aleron can soothe her nightmares in the same way he inadvertently did mine.

"At least they're together now," he added. "Aleron always spoke of him."

"Same with Ingram. I'm so glad they're reunited."

A small smile curled his lips. "So are we." He turned to her slightly and found her own smile had formed. "Sucks to be you. You're stuck with me for eternity now."

Her nose scrunched up in disgust. "I forgot how annoying you are."

"Just you fucking wait!" he exclaimed, letting a chuckle out. "I think Aleron's going to make me worse. He seems to find me humorous."

"That's because he doesn't know any better," she teased. "I think we should give him a hundred years of your crap and he'll be looking for a way out."

Throwing his hand over his heart, he clutched at his jacket. "Ouch, Em. That hurt."

A laugh exploded from her. "No, it didn't. You'll just try to be even more annoying." Then her laughter died, and her smile grew small. "You really are the same. It's just so hard to imagine."

"If that's your way of calling me immature, I did die at twenty-three," he said in his own defence, a scowl furrowing his features. "Now, if you don't mind... can I have that hug?"

"I thought you'd never ask."

She threw her arms around his neck, and he circled his around her waist. They both squeezed with all their might, pushing years of missed time – mainly for her – into just a short hug.

Gideon took in the familiar smell of her, and the colour of her hair. Wanting to deepen it, he turned his cheek and placed the side of his face against the top of her head. He had to go to his toes a little to do so.

"I remember you being shorter."

"If a single joke about my height falls from your mouth tonight, I'll show you how the guild taught me to punch right in the kidney."

Gideon chuckled. "That's not fair. You have an advantage over me now. Don't tell me my brute strength will become meaningless."

"I wised up and learned how to fight so I can finally kick your butt." She buried her face against his shoulder as she mumbled, "Had been planning to do it in the afterlife, but at least now I know it'll actually hurt."

Just as Gideon opened his mouth, likely with some smartarse comment falling from him, he closed it. Two deep huffs blew over them, billowing their hair in one direction, just as the chill in the air seemed to ominously... disappear.

They loosened their hold, neither truly wishing to let go, to face the two Duskwalkers who towered over them in their more humanoid forms. One with the skull of a raven, the other with a fruit bat skull, and both with different goat horns. Both had bright-pink orbs as they looked down at them.

"You are also reunited with your kindred," Aleron stated, reaching out to place a hand on Gideon's side.

"I wouldn't say kindred..." He eyed Emerie, who smiled knowingly. "Our bond isn't as close as yours. Family, not by blood, but by choice."

Aleron lifted his snout to Ingram. "I do not understand why it matters."

"It doesn't," Ingram responded.

"Let's go inside," Emerie said, letting her remaining arm drop as she turned to the log-cabin home. "There's a fire going. It's too cold to be out here."

Gideon turned to follow, his palm racing down Aleron's arm as he let his side go, so he could hold his Duskwalker's hand. He led the way, only to stop at the porch steps as Emerie climbed them.

"This is where you're staying?" he asked, his lips drawing tight with thought.

"Yeah," she faced them just as Ingram came to her. The poor guy had to bend his body awkwardly just to fit his raven skull and upward-jutting goat horns under the roof of the porch. "Mayumi, a friend of ours and another bride, said we can stay here since she no longer occupies it. It was her family's home."

Taking in the height of the entryway, just compared to Ingram, Gideon's features twisted in uncertainty.

"Aleron has longer horns, and I don't even think his wings will fit through the doorway."

"I know it's not the most comfortable, and we already take up a huge amount of space, but we need somewhere warm to stay during winter. It's only going to get colder, and the storms are starting."

One of his cheeks twitched at that.

She wasn't wrong. If given the choice, Gideon would

prefer to settle somewhere they could stay warm and dry until the snow season passed.

But this? Sure, it looked suitable for them, but Aleron... give it a day or two and he'd feel claustrophobic. The arches of his wings sat a foot higher than his skull, around eight and a half feet in total. And Gideon, who was nearly six feet tall, could tell his hair would scrape the top of the doorframe as he entered.

This place was obviously designed for shorter people in mind.

Whatever. I'll figure something out.

For now, he wouldn't complain. He didn't wish to sour their reunion further than it already had been.

Ingram and Aleron chose to remain outside to sit on the porch steps, where they were both comfortable. Gideon went deeper inside, only to be further disheartened by the size.

"I was really hoping you two would bond, if I'm being honest," Emerie stated as she walked across a long area that appeared to be the entirety of the house. "When we left you two in Tenebris, we both hoped you'd come back. I'm so glad you did."

With a grin, she leaned her backside against a dining table that sat on the other side of the room and on the left. A long kitchen counter sat next to it, with a door on the other side of it behind her, leading to what looked to be another room. At the back of the house, two cushions sat on two different armchairs, with a low coffee table between them.

Everything had a homey feel, since much remained, like ornaments and decorations, the person having chosen to leave it all behind for their new life. It looked lived in, loved, and somehow... abandoned.

The fireplace to their right was lit and warm, and his feet instinctually moved to it. He breathed in its heat, shivering in delight at it curling around his half-frozen form.

The only time I've been this warm since coming to Earth

is... A small but fond smile settled as he stared at the flickering flames. *Since today, when I woke in Aleron's embrace.*

"Gideon," Aleron called, as if summoned by his thoughts. "You left this outside."

He spun around to find his Duskwalker crouching at the doorway with his case. Aleron blocked it completely, and already Gideon could tell he'd struggle to shove his way through it.

Walking over, Gideon took it from him with a thanks, and Aleron retreated back outside to sit with Ingram.

He placed it next to the entrance, crouched down, and opened it. Inspecting the contents, he was relieved to find his guitar had survived being thrown. The case, however, had a massive dent in the body of it.

"I can't believe you have that." Emerie nodded her nose at it. "It looks exactly like your old one."

Gideon spared her a solemn glance. He remained silent at first, unsure if he should tell the truth or not. A deep, annoyed sigh fell from him.

He wished she hadn't mentioned it. At least, not so soon.

"That's because it is." He grabbed the neck, pretending to double-check it, when really he was avoiding her gaze.

"What do you mean, it's the same one?" The frown of disbelief was obvious in her tone. "How the hell did you get it?"

"How do you think?" he coldly bit out, glaring at it, and hating the way shame prickled on the back of his neck.

"Gideon... you didn't," she rasped. "How could you do that to him? To go to... *his* home just to get it."

His lips tightened. "I didn't know he'd still have it."

In his peripheral, he noted she threw her arms forward. "Then why?"

"Because, Emerie... I forgot everything." His posture slumped, and he finally looked at her from over his shoulder. "I lost all my memories of Tenebris. Of meeting you, him, and accepting that eight years had passed without me, and..." One knee thudded against the ground, unable to hold its crouched position any longer. "I needed to figure out a way to let go, and fast. I needed to see that everything had changed, so I could break away from that life and accept this new one. That's why."

Then he closed the case, clicked the latches shut, and stood.

He turned and narrowed his eyes at her.

"If you're wondering, no. I didn't take it to remember him. I took it because it's mine. I died, and this guitar was my consolation prize. I plan to make new and better memories with it, and Aleron." He walked closer to her and placed his hands on the table on either side of her. "But if you don't mind, I'd like this conversation to *end*. He doesn't know what I left behind yet, and I will tell him when *we* are ready. Okay?"

Thankfully the two Duskwalkers outside were too busy getting to know each other again to pay attention to what they were saying. They'd also kept their exchange vague enough that he didn't think Aleron would understand.

She gave him a cute, pouted glare, only to roll her blue eyes at him. "Fine. Fair enough."

Surprised by her response, his head cocked.

For a moment there, he'd forgotten this wasn't the same woman. *Look at how much she's aged.* She sported a tiny wrinkle here and there at the corners of her eyes, lips, and even her forehead.

She still looked as beautiful as he remembered. She was still Emerie, just... different.

The nineteen-year-old he'd known would have thrown a tantrum at him by now. She would have spat venom with her words, throwing her hands up and giving him a disapproving growl, likely through bared teeth.

She may have even childishly stomped her foot.

Her flushed, freckled face of confrontation wouldn't have softened and then eased back to the gentle tan that he knew.

She'd matured.

Her features soothed, her shoulders relaxed, and her gaze returned to him with understanding.

So much has changed.

In some ways, she felt like a stranger to him. Their roles were reversed. She was five years older than him now, becoming his older sister, who was wiser, more experienced, and had survived the test of life in the cruellest of ways.

How could he swallow the truth that was so blatant before his very eyes? He guessed he'd have to get used to it and try not to feel inferior for it. They were supposed to grow up together as siblings, hand in hand, and that had been robbed from them.

Neither was to blame, and he'd spend forever ensuring she knew that – regardless of what had happened in the past, or why.

Gideon smiled appreciatively that she'd let it go, and backed up.

Feeling a little silly for cornering her now, he turned away.

He walked back over to the front door, this time to fold his arms across his chest and lean his side against the doorframe. Rather than fight with her, he wanted to watch the two Duskwalkers so he could witness Aleron's excitement, and let it soothe him from his sudden disgruntled emotions.

Tenderness washed over him.

Already, Aleron had wrapped his uninjured wing around the back of Ingram, just as he had slung an arm over Aleron's shoulders. Even their tails had crossed, Ingram's lizard one on top of Aleron's raven one to curl around his waist. They were chatting, both trying to shove into and interrupt each other's conversation, eager to be the first to tell all of what they'd been doing for the last few months.

"Would you like something to eat or drink?" Emerie offered.

"No," he answered without looking at her. "I'm pretty content with the idea of not consuming anything. What's the point anyway?"

"I don't know? It makes me feel human. But yeah, you're right. Sometimes I question why I still do it, and honestly... half the time, I don't either, since doing my business in the forest while travelling with Ingram is a bit of a headache."

"Being a Phantom comes with its struggles, I guess."

"Yeah. I'm still trying to wrap my head around the whole half human, half spirit – half alive, half dead thing."

He nodded to show he understood. As Emerie came up beside him, he lifted his arm. She slotted herself underneath it, tucking herself against him with an arm around his back. He settled his on her shoulders.

Then, the cretin sniffed in his direction, and her lips pulled downwards sourly. "You need a bath."

The urge to shove her face into his armpit was strong, but he denied it. However, what Emerie said did cause him to narrow his eyes in thought.

"On our way here, we met another Duskwalker. Orpheus."

"How was he?" A chuckle fell from her. "Last time I saw Orpheus, Reia was pregnant, and he was following her around like she'd break in half from a gust of wind."

One side of his lips curled in humour. "They're fine. So is Kevin, if you're wondering."

"She didn't actually call them Kevin, did she?!" She gave a horrendous laugh, making him wince. "I thought she was joking!"

He joined in, only for his laughter to quickly fade. "Before that, though, we went to some other houses. I noticed the Duskwalkers left protective dome wards down."

"Yeah. Ingram accidentally made one." He didn't know why her cheeks heated in embarrassment at that, which only made the scarring on her face more prominent.

Gideon ducked his head down to her. "But he can show Aleron how to make one, yeah?"

She shrugged. "Sure. I don't see why not."

"How long do they last for?"

"I think around ten years. Why?"

"Perfect. I think I just figured out where we can go that'll be better than here. We can use it as our winter base for the future."

"Where?" Emerie asked, her brows knitting as she finally turned her face to his.

A mischievous grin lifted his features. "You'll see."

FORTY

When movement shifted from inside his wing, Aleron was softly brought to alertness. It'd happened a few times already, so he thought nothing of it and began to drift off again.

Snow surrounded them, as did an unknown forest. Once he and his kindred had healed their wounds, they'd moved on from the home they'd stayed in.

Aleron was still getting used to holding so many within his wings, and all of them moved periodically. It'd take time for him to adjust, but the contentment in his heart meant any disturbance only deepened his joy.

Gideon had already explained Emerie's fear.

It'd bothered Aleron that something so important to him could frighten his kindred's bride. Gideon had assured him that with time, she'd grow comfortable with them.

Yet, despite this, Emerie had shut her eyes tight and bravely let herself be settled into their cuddle within his wings. Aleron, who held Gideon to his front, and Ingram, who held her to his front, placed their brides back-to-back in the middle.

She shook like a leaf at first, but managed to be soothed by her Mavka and brother until she fell asleep. Remaining quiet and stiff, Aleron tried not to jostle the part of his body encompassing her, nor speak – since he doubted he had the humanity to assist.

It wasn't difficult to make the cuddle, since his wings were so long and large. The elbow arches of them sat next to Ingram's raven skull, and the rest of them crossed over his back. The important thing was that their little humans were sheltered, hidden from sight and mostly scent, and everyone was included.

He didn't even mind when Gideon rolled over to cuddle Emerie in his sleep, only to shift back around. However, he did mind occasionally being kneed in the seam when he tried to slot a leg between his thighs, but Aleron just bit back his choke. He also brought his wings in tighter to stop Gideon from moving.

Just as Aleron was about to fall back asleep, more movement shifted. Ingram's arm moved, then something large and strong – his lizard tail – smacked against Aleron's foot. This time, he woke a little more, and opened his sight.

Gideon stirred when Emerie must have shoved against his back.

Ducking his head out from under his stretched wing, he took in the beginning light of morning. Early daybreak, the groggiest point of the day, but sometimes the most peaceful. He could still remember Ingram and himself resting similarly to this with entwined limbs, choosing to remain on their sides long after they woke before truly rising.

Bright pink lifted into his sight, changing it from its normal hue at knowing he now did this with his whole family. Four bonds, linked together totally through their own interwoven strings.

Weldir had once shown him his bond strings. How they connected to his father creator, the other Mavka in Tenebris, and all the human souls he'd eaten and brought there. He wondered what those same strings looked like now with the four of them; he hoped they were knotted and entirely incapable of being untangled.

Emerie shifted before giving a small moan. It sounded groggy, lazy, and breathy.

"Not in the cuddle, Ingram," she whined softly.

"It has been forever, little butterfly," his kindred responded with a deep groan.

"It's only been two days."

Aleron ducked his head back underneath his wings to investigate. Ingram's orbs were their normal purple, so nothing was the matter. Well... perhaps they *were* a little darker.

A few new scents from them drifted within the space, hers turning a little sweeter than normal.

Ingram jostled Emerie, who let out a gasp. "I said not in the cuddle!"

With an annoyed growl, Ingram backed out from under his wing, dragging his female with him like prey from underneath a bush. Before Aleron could even bring his head out, Ingram started carting her away, deeper within the forest.

He tilted his head, unsure of what had just happened.

It started off as small movements, but eventually Gideon's torso heaved.

"Pfft," he let out a muffled chuckle against Aleron's chest. "Talk about an emergency."

A little disappointed they'd escaped when Aleron would've preferred they'd remained, he tried to stay positive. At least he had his little spring all to his greedy self now.

Rolling to his back, he took Gideon with him so he could lie upon Aleron's body while he wrapped his wings entirely around the male. His light weight was nice, and Aleron pulled him down in a tight hug. His bride's short arms attempted to wrap around him, only came to where Aleron's back met the ground.

Gideon shoved his face against Aleron's chest and rubbed against his fur. "I'm glad you washed in the outside bath back at that house. You're no longer covered in blood and smell nice again."

Sliding his claws through his bride's short hair, Aleron tilted his head slightly. "I smell nice to you?"

Gideon ground his hips against Aleron as he nuzzled deeper. "Yeah. Like hazelnuts and cedarwood. You smell like home to me."

A warm bubble formed behind his sternum at such a wonderful compliment. "You smell nice as well. Like purple stem flowers and patchouli."

Sliding his chin up, Gideon rested it against that warm bubble so he could frown up at Aleron. "You know, I've been trying to figure out what kind of flower that is for you, since patchouli also has purple flowers. All I can come up with is lavender. To be honest, I'm surprised you know what patchouli smells like."

"I do not mind what it is called, only that you smell like fresh spring." Aleron continued sifting his claws through his bride's hair. "You taught me what this herb smells like, back in Tenebris. However, you did say there was a vinegar undertone to everything."

Gideon shone a small smile at him, only for his nose to crinkle. He shifted higher, coming just that little bit closer to his skull, and something hard slipped against Aleron's pelvis. Gideon shoved his head against him again, only to chuckle.

"I think I just realised what's going to happen. One couple is going to start and then the other probably will too."

Aleron's sight morphed to dark yellow. "What do you mean?"

Sitting up to straddle Aleron's hips with his hands just below his pectoral muscles, Gideon's ears appeared a little pinker than normal. "They've gone to have sex, Aleron."

"Did they?" Aleron asked in surprise, turning his skull in

the direction they'd gone.

Small noises fluttered over to him, as well as scents. Now that he understood what the others were doing, they made more sense.

"I see," he rasped out, turning to Gideon. His gaze drifted down when Aleron thought he noted stiffness within his trousers. He curled a claw over the top of it. "Oh. You are hard."

His little human's brows drew together in apparent puzzlement. "You're not?"

His sight shifted to a reddish pink, a little embarrassed that he hadn't managed to put together on his own what had happened. Should he be aroused? He felt a little behind now, more than usual.

It hadn't escaped Aleron's notice that his kindred seemed to be quicker witted than him. Which had never been possible before, as they'd always shared everything they'd ever eaten – gaining humanity and intelligence at the same time.

He chose to ignore it.

His bride was hard, sitting on him, and *that* made his cock jerk behind his seam despite his insecurities.

"Can I see?" Aleron asked with enthusiasm, drawing the back of his claw down the length of it.

"We don't have to," Gideon offered for some reason, despite his body's readiness.

His bride wanted his touch, and Aleron didn't think there would ever be a time where he wouldn't want to give it. He also liked that Gideon was aroused for him, even without Aleron trying to bring that forth.

It made it all the more worthwhile.

Sheathing his claws, he fumbled with the little ties of his trousers.

Gideon took over when his thick fingers were too cumbersome with such tiny strings. Then Aleron wiggled a fingertip into the band of his undershorts and flipped them down to reveal this male's jutting cock.

Licking at his fangs in interest until his tongue tip slipped over the top of his snout, he traced the pads of all his fingers up the length of Gideon's erection until they glided over the head. Gideon let out a quiet rasp for Aleron, and pinkness finally spread over his cheek bones.

He is very hard. Yet Aleron was only just stirring.

He thought for long moments, trying to make his mind up about something. *He did say he wanted to try.* And he wanted to see how this human would react.

With purple rising in his sight, he released Gideon's shaft so he could put his arm around the eager male's shoulders. Aleron brought his clothed chest down until it pressed against his abdomen, forcing Gideon to lie down, then grabbed his little human's arse to knead it tightly.

So squishy. Aleron forgot what he was doing as he played with it.

"Aleron?" Gideon asked, his brows crinkled with confusion, snapping him out of his distraction.

With his palm, Aleron pushed Gideon's arse down, forcing the male's body to slip down his own. The head of his cock prodded and glided between Aleron's hips.

"Shit, w-wait," Gideon choked out.

Aleron had done exactly what he'd been seeking. He shoved Gideon's hips against him harder as Aleron lifted so the tip of his bride's cock could prod deeper. They both shuddered wildly as a confusing growl rumbled past his closed fangs. Shaking tension stiffened his muscles, just as Gideon's head tilted back and he let out a wonderful, lost little groan.

"Oh, *fuck*," he hissed out, his eyes rolling back slightly. Gideon ground his hips, helping to bury his cock all the way inside Aleron's seam. "It's so hot inside you."

Dark purple blasted into his sight, and he let out a whimper of sudden need. "Hurry, Gideon."

With how deeply pleasure pierced his groin, his own arousal would harden Aleron swiftly. Just having his bride buried like this within his seam was already too powerful. He could feel it bulging his flesh.

Palming Gideon's arse to push him out, Aleron dug his fingers upwards to shunt him back inside, trying to stir the male into action. Tightness was forming, but thankfully his little human started to move.

With his hands pressed against the wide span of Aleron's chest, Gideon lifted up onto straightened arms. Then he thrust his hips against Aleron's, starting slow, then gaining speed with each one.

It felt odd – wonderful, but odd. Gideon stroked against the top, the side, and even underneath Aleron's cock. Since his tentacles were moving, trying to swirl around his growing erection, sometimes Gideon slotted between them.

Gideon lifted his shirt so he could see what he was doing, could watch himself be buried within Aleron like this, and even he thought it was perverse. Gideon soon let the garment go, only so he could pump harder.

Aleron tried to help, staying still beneath him while his hands on his round cheeks drew Gideon in and out. He felt each glide of being penetrated, the back-and-forth motion, and his claws bit deeper and deeper as he shuddered and groaned.

But it was his bride's face, tightly crinkled as he let out a groan through gritted teeth, that ignited Aleron like a wildfire. His expression as he fucked Aleron, a little hazy, but more focused, more determined, and more aggressive than when Aleron took Gideon, appeared fierce and hungry.

The quick little pants and huffs falling from his lips sounded so heated and pleasure-filled, they tingled Aleron's ears. He answered them with sharp intakes of his own, taking in the mesmerising sight of his bride fucking him like this, witnessing how much he seemed to enjoy it.

"Oh gods," Gideon groaned loudly when everything

suddenly tightened.

Aleron, desperate to prolong this, tried to hold back.

It was too late; his own cock began to extrude with heavy throbs. The intensity within him gentled at releasing some of the held-back stiffness. Gideon's hips picked up speed, as if he could feel it, and his nails dug into Aleron's chest. Sweat dotted his brow.

"Wait," he pleaded, just as all of Aleron shoved forward and pushed Gideon out. Gideon groaned, rocking his cock within the groove underneath his own, only to settle. His hands trembled against Aleron's chest as he said, "I almost came inside you. I knew that would feel amazing."

"I am sorry," Aleron offered, lifting his skull so he could lick under Gideon's jaw, wanting to taste him while they ground against each other.

"Don't be." Gideon yanked his horn to pull his head back, just so he could lather Aleron's skull in kisses as he softly moved. "Thank you for doing that with me. I'm really horny now, though."

Joy lit up in his heart, only to feed into his veins as hot lust. Aleron ground upwards harder, squishing their cocks when his tentacles tried to swirl around them both to trap them together.

Gideon's kisses slowed, became messier, and even his tongue joined in. Then he rasped out against Aleron's forehead, "Can we try something else?"

"Whatever you like," he answered, since he'd thoroughly adored everything else they'd done so far.

Actually, Aleron was rather ecstatic to learn more new and exciting things. *He said he wants to bond with me in many ways.* After this, Aleron knew he'd want to try everything, so long as it brought them both unfathomable pleasure.

"Can I come over your skull?"

Aleron paused at that. "Why?"

His lips curled against Aleron's bone before Gideon pulled his head back to show his lust-filled humour. "Because I want to jerk off to and come on the face of the person who is turning me on right now."

A thrill raced down his spine at such a proclamation. It tingled his entire body, ruffling his fur and feathers, when Aleron took in the devious, heated gaze of his bride looking down at him. His need looked deep, yet it was also filled with feverish passion.

Gripping the backs of his thighs, Aleron dragged him higher until he straddled the top part of his chest.

Aleron would like to see his bride pleasure himself. He'd like to watch, knowing it was for him, because of him, and being able to reap the reward of that straight across his skull was an exhilarating thought.

"Can you hide me? Just in case," Gideon whispered down as he towered over Aleron on his knees and wrapped his hand around his cock.

Aleron brought his wings up to shield him from view from three sides, leaving his front open since it would be too difficult to bend the arches like this.

Drenched in Aleron's glistening lubricant, Gideon stroked his cock. It started slow, his hips subtly rocking back and forth to help. He twisted his wrist as he moved his loose flesh back and forth, spinning his palm up and down the length. His body waved and twitched whenever he went over the head.

Keeping one hand on Gideon's thigh, Aleron shoved the other under his shirt. He cupped his soft pectoral muscle, playing with his chest, and caressed his hardened nipples. The hair tickled his fingers, and he liked diving into it as he crossed over to the other side.

He wanted to help, to be more of a reason for his release in hopes he'd come harder for him.

"Nhnn," Gideon shuddered out through tightly clenched teeth, his jaw muscles bunching. "I'm already close from fucking your seam."

His hand moved faster, his hip pumps becoming stronger. As much as Aleron enjoyed watching him pleasure himself, what he liked the most was that Gideon's pretty green eyes never left his skull. Instead, they were riveted to it, never shying away, as though what he saw truly excited him.

Unable to take it any longer, Aleron released his bride's thigh so he could grab his own cock. After swelling in reaction so many times to Gideon, it was soaked in lubricant, sensitive, and so hard that it took him a bit of strength to squeeze.

A quake rippled him as his fangs parted slightly in bliss.

He mimicked Gideon's movements, copying the way his wrist twisted. His bride's lips twitched with a smirk, giving away that he knew what Aleron was doing. It was kind of obvious when he bounced the human with each of his strokes, his arm moving swifter and swifter and jostling him around.

His excitement caused him to pant frantically up at him.

He'd never pleasured his own cock before. Although he'd rather it be any part of Gideon touching him instead, he was too busy enjoying this to care.

"You like watching me masturbate to you?"

He released a hissing growl. *"Yes."*

"Next time, I'd like to watch," Gideon stated, before his body dipped forward. Suddenly, his arm was moving faster. "I'm about to come, Aleron."

Aleron crushed his cock when it swelled in anticipation.

The noise that came from Gideon was strangled as he tried to suppress and hide it. Then, the right side of his face crinkled as his lips quivered and parted, just as white ropes of seed burst from the tip of his pink head. They landed straight across his skull.

He parted his fangs so that just a drop could touch his

hungry tongue.

The sight, the liquid warmth, the salty scent and taste caused him to swell so powerfully he thought he was moments from joining Gideon. Aleron halted. Instead, he squeezed his cock with a deep, shaken groan as *multiple* bubbles of precum welled and eventually dripped down his groove. Even his tentacles coiled downwards, desperately wanting something to latch on to.

He truly thought he'd spill his seed.

Only when Gideon stopped raining cum upon his skull did he cease crushing himself.

He huffed above Aleron as though his lungs had seized. A self-satisfied grin lifted his cheeks, making his dimples rise to the surface. "I hope you lick all that off before Ingram and Emerie come back, but I really like it."

"No, it will stay." This male had possessively marked his face, and he'd like to keep it that way. "My turn?"

He grabbed one of Gideon's legs to straighten it and drag him down before he dug his claws into the back of his pants and undershorts. He lowered them until Gideon spread his knees to stop them going any further.

He let out a quiet snarl of annoyance. Currently, Aleron was feeling very, *very* impatient.

"I don't think it's a good idea if you come on my face right now," Gideon stated with a chuckle, putting up no fight. "We can experiment with me drowning in the fountain that comes out of you when we have a bath nearby. But what about this?"

Gideon lowered and clamped his purple cock between his closed, muscular thighs.

Aleron immediately shoved upwards, needing this human's body to stroke him any way possible – he didn't care how. He thrust, just as Gideon bit hard against his chest, drowning him deeper under the waves of his need and riling him further. He grabbed his bride's arse with both hands, claws digging to hold him hard against him, as his skull tilted back.

His pants were loud, each one drawing in the tantalising scent covering him. He unconsciously licked across his snout.

"That's it," Gideon whispered. "Show me how much that turned you on."

It is not enough. But right now, he was so hard, so excited, so fucking desperate, Aleron feared he'd hurt him.

Without preparing him, which Gideon didn't have the patience for right now, he was worried about inflicting undue pain on his precious, naughty bride – the one who had sent him hurtling into this crazed state. He couldn't even sheath his claws right then to try.

Aleron whimpered when his groin clenched, pumping between Gideon's lubricant-coated thighs faster. He needed more friction and warmth.

His tentacles latched onto the sides of the male's muscular legs, trying to circle them. *"Gideon, please."*

With a coy, seductive purr, Gideon hoarsely rasped, "Use your words, darling."

I made a mistake. Gideon internally groaned, pushing his groin upwards to slide Aleron out of him.

Still letting out twitches and shudders, Aleron pushed him back down until Gideon's arse firmly pressed against the base of his tentacles. He fisted the fur behind his Duskwalker's head harder, letting out a soft gasp.

Unfortunately, due to the wings blanketing everything from below Gideon' neck while leaving his head free, he couldn't look down at his body lying atop Aleron's. Maybe that was a good thing; he couldn't imagine the mess.

He threw the back of his head against Aleron's chest. "No more," he pleaded.

I shouldn't have come first. He'd been so fucking turned on after being balls deep in Aleron's cock pocket that he'd just let his lust-crazed brain lead the way, dick first. He hadn't thought about the repercussions, only about getting off in the most perverted way possible.

Coming over a Duskwalker's skull? *Without* having his dick bitten off for trying? Despite the utter safety and trust he had in Aleron, it'd felt dangerous, depraved, and shamelessly immoral. Each staining streak of Gideon's cum had been a worship to his own deity of death, who had parted his damn fangs for a taste.

Gideon thought he could get away with just using his thighs afterwards, letting them fool around without actually having sex. That did *not* happen. Instead, still buzzing from what he'd just done over his skull, Gideon let Aleron turn him over and enter him from behind.

Big guy was so pent up that Aleron ended up penetrating Gideon with the head repeatedly, releasing swifter than he'd expected. Only to then slam him all the way down and just keep going until Gideon became mindless and an over-satisfied, twitching mess.

Even his damn toes curled while his feet started kicking in a feeble attempt to escape after the last time he came.

Gideon pushed his hips upwards once more, a little firmer now that a small amount of strength had returned. This time, Aleron helped to lift him off his cock.

The loss of soothing heat and the copious amount of liquid that came from Gideon caused him to cringe. At least his pants were around his ankles and away from getting saturated.

Hopefully now that Aleron was no longer jammed inside him, he'd put that purple snake monster away.

A false disgruntled moan fell from him. "Aleron... You don't have to completely drain my balls every time we do this. I'd like to walk afterwards."

Shit. I don't even know if anything came out of me by the

third time. Human men weren't meant to come this much back-to-back! *He's going to rail me to death one day.* His heart would give out, or his lungs would completely seize and he'd pass out from the lack of oxygen.

An evil, sinister sort of chuckle rumbled from Aleron as he bumped his snout against Gideon's sweat-coated brow. "Maybe I do not want you to walk. I rather like you docile for me." He slid his rough palm down Gideon's abdomen, tickling it with his claws. "You are very naughty, little spring."

Before Aleron could go any lower, Gideon shot his hand down and shoved his fingertips between the fingers to stop him. Then he only gripped a few so their rings could *clink* together.

His cheeks would have heated in embarrassment at what Aleron said, but he wasn't ashamed of it.

Gideon had never felt freer than being entangled with his Duskwalker. His perverted thoughts and desires? They only seemed to excite Aleron. There was no judgement. It likely would cause Gideon to want to do some questionable shit with him, all of it in the hopes of it feeling good for both of them.

Plus, who was going to judge him... Emerie?

Her own cries were still going, echoing through the forest. Gideon had tried his best to stay quiet. Considering her crescendo only seemed to be getting louder, it appeared she'd forgotten her surroundings just as much as he did in the end.

Of course he'd rather not see or be seen, if given the choice. Not being heard might be out of the question, though, unfortunately.

Gideon mentally shrugged; it'd be something they'd both just have to accept.

With his body so relaxed, he barely tensed a muscle when Aleron brought Gideon higher up his chest while he continued to lay back. Aleron pulled Gideon into the crook of his arm until his head rested against the ball of Aleron's shoulder joint and his arse fell into his large palm. His feet tucked between his furry thighs as Gideon's legs rested over his hip, finding a place to be comfortable.

Aleron held him off the ground like he barely weighed anything.

With how gentle he can be, I sometimes forget how strong he is. Yet... he didn't feel weak or inferior to Aleron, just small.

Together, they stared up at the dappled light glittering through the canopy of leaves above. Their chests eventually softened their heaves, their breaths lulling to normal rhythms. A fluffy white cloud quickly floated past, highlighting the bitterly cold wind Aleron was shielding him from.

Not once had Gideon ever laid back in someone's arms and just stared up at the sky before. Not even in the day. He'd been too busy rushing through his short life, trying to reach all his goals, not knowing it was about to end prematurely.

Now that his brow had dried, his damp hair swayed across his forehead. He rested his arm across Aleron's stomach.

I've never been at peace like this.

It was made even better by the subtle scent of hazelnuts, cedarwood, and their strange mix of sexual musk.

I think it was fate that we were meant to meet. Whether some higher power was out there directing all beings in the world, or it was a random, chaotic cosmic event, there had to be some kind of destiny at play.

As he pondered over their story, it became apparent their chances of meeting were slim.

Gideon had needed to die eight years ago to be here now, and Aleron needed to find a way to meet him in the afterlife. Even then, they'd been there together for a few months,

never passing, never knowing to reach out for each other –
like the moon unwittingly chasing the sun. Emerie had
needed to suffer all that she did, remain pure hearted despite
all the adversity she'd faced, and then bring them together
once she sacrificed her own life for Ingram.

Without all these things, and probably many more
unknown interferences from fate, this tranquillity he
experienced in this monster's arms would never have
happened.

I can't believe I almost... missed this.

"Hey, Aleron," Gideon called with a clog of emotion
stuck behind his Adam's apple. His mouth grew sticky, and
he thickly swallowed. "I know I've never said it, but thank
you for bringing me back to life with you."

Aleron placed his palm over the back of Gideon's hand
where it rested on him, gripping the entirety of it in a tender
hold. Since his ear was against the left side of Aleron's
chest, he witnessed the moment Aleron's heart seemed to
stutter before beating frantically.

When Aleron didn't respond, Gideon turned his gaze up
to see his pink orbs had brightened in their hue. *He doesn't
know how to respond.* But it was obvious his words had
overwhelmed him with joy.

"Do you know what will happen to us if you die?"

"No. I do not think a Mavka with a bride has died
before."

A thoughtful hum vibrated his lips, and he placed his ear
against Aleron's chest so he could look within the shade of
the forest. Everything had gone quiet. Since they were
above the surface of the Veil, a few birds chirped, but
mostly everything had gone into hibernation or left the
north.

"Can you do me a favour?" Gideon asked, once more
trying to battle the clog in his throat. "If we return to
Tenebris, and we're not together, can you come find me?"

Aleron squeezed his hand – and his arse – comfortingly. "Of course, Gideon. I will always come for you."

A small smile twitched his lips, only to fall. "If I've forgotten you, can you make me fall in love with you again? No matter what it takes? I don't want to have a future without you, no matter where it is."

Aleron's big chest shuddered, just as something sparkled in Gideon's peripheral.

Once more, Gideon looked up to his bat skull, only for his eyes to glisten. With a streak of sunlight making Aleron's face glitter with gold, floating drops of the brightest pink he'd ever seen hovered around Aleron's empty eye sockets.

I've seen those ethereal tears before, he thought, as a soft and tender expression bowed his eyes.

"I love you, Aleron." Gideon lifted up just enough to press a kiss to his longest fang. "And I know I'll love you no matter how many times I forget."

"I love you as well, little spring." Aleron lifted his free hand to cup the side of his face. "I have, deeply, since Tenebris."

"I know," Gideon whispered, leaning into his big palm, just as Ingram and Emerie came out from the trees.

He tried to ignore that she looked half-dead within the cradle of Ingram's arms, her eyes barely peeking open. She didn't even have the strength to blush or pull the leaves and twigs from her hair.

With bright-pink orbs as well, Ingram snorted a strange huff at them, the colour brightening. Then Ingram laid down next to them just as Aleron turned away and placed Gideon in front of him so they could cuddle with their torsos facing.

The kindreds pressed their backs to each other's.

A truce of no contact between them and their brides was silently made, and Gideon figured this was due to the scents. Neither wanted to spread them between them.

Yet, it was obvious they wanted to touch. Gideon felt

Ingram's lizard tail bump against the underside of his foot as it coiled around one of Aleron's calves.

We'll move on in a bit. They had forever, after all.

He hoped for many lazy mornings just like this one.

EPILOGUE

Patting her hands together, Emerie exited the cave situated about two metres behind Gideon.

"Well, I think that'll do for now." With a harrumph, she sat next to him on the natural ledge of rock that acted as a stair. "We should get some bedding we can lay on the floor, and maybe figure out some sort of makeshift table."

"I'm happy for you to doll it up to your heart's content," Gideon offered, before he cast her a sly grin. "But only if you admit this was a great idea. I'm down for some boot kisses as forgiveness for your impudence."

She scrunched her face up. "Ew! Grow up, would you?"

"You know what? I would, but I'm all out of growing up. You're stuck with me like this... forever." He turned to her and wiggled his fingers like he was some kind of spooky Ghost.

"Oh nooo, the horror," she fake whined, rolling her eyes. They both let out a soft chuckle. "But sure, you're right. I just didn't know if I should trust you, since you were making this out to be some kind of big secret. I never even considered Sunnet Hill's headsprings as a place to settle down for winter. How'd you even come up with it?"

Drifting his gaze over this section of hot springs, a small smile curled his lips.

"Aleron and I found it while searching for you guys."

The main springs were around the other side of the mountain's base, and were more open to the elements. This section was far smaller, with only four pools and a grassy clearing just before them. The forest intersected it, hiding certain areas from each other.

Not far from his feet, perhaps four or so metres, was a pool large enough that both Duskwalkers could stand at the deepest edge and be fully submerged. It ran into a smaller one that had two others flowing into it, but they were private and a little further away.

They'd searched the entire mountain base and decided to stay here due to its layout. The last two remaining pools sat within the forest on either side and gave each couple privacy if they wished. They bled into the bottom pool, meaning any questionable liquid flowed away from the main one at the very top.

The cave behind them was shallow but comfortable.

Since Duskwalkers could heal in a day, including their claws, they planned to dig it out further. It wouldn't take long, with Ingram and Aleron working fast together, while they, as the humans, would help by scooping out the smaller chunks of rock they broke away.

They'd work as a tightly knit team, and Gideon figured that would continue for their rest of their unending lives.

Just as he was admiring his grand idea, Ingram let out a beastly roar, causing them both to startle in surprise.

Digging his claws into the earth, Ingram tore up grass as he was dragged across the clearing. Gideon couldn't hear it, but he knew Aleron would be snickering as he used his taloned feet to hold on to his twin's leg and tail. Aleron was trying to fly off with him, and Ingram wasn't having it.

Ingram grabbed the edge of a rock ledge and kicked his free foot to battle his twin.

Emerie tipped her head down, going out of her way to avoid watching Aleron fly. Gideon noted the paleness in her cheeks, but he couldn't help laughing at them playing.

"It's not fair that he can do that," Emerie muttered. "Aleron has an advantage over him."

"What do you mean?!" Gideon asked in mock outrage, throwing his hands forward. "I've seen Ingram beat the shit out of Aleron with his tail and trap his wings to him. It's all about who can one-up the other before they use their advantages."

A small laugh escaped her. "Yeah, that's true."

Aleron made the mistake of landing so he could unlatch Ingram's hands. He was instantly tackled, and they rolled across the clearing until disappearing into the forest. Destruction would likely occur in their wake, especially since he could hear trees rustling from a distance.

Gideon wasn't used to seeing Aleron in his monstrous form regularly, but he was quickly adjusting, since it happened more often with Ingram around. It still startled him when he saw Aleron walking on elongated arms with his back curled like a four-legged animal, but he found he actually didn't mind it.

Just another new facet of him to fall in love with.

He liked watching Aleron be completely free as he played with his twin. When he got to know Ingram a little better, Gideon planned to see if he could find a way to insert himself into their wrestles. Especially since he enjoyed doing so with Aleron, although that tended to lead to other, more nefarious and erotic playfulness.

I'm glad everyone likes it here. Gideon lifted his gaze to the pink dome surrounding them.

For the next ten years, this hot spring would keep away the snow and chill during winter, and Aleron's magic would stop the Demons from tainting it. Perhaps they'd find a new place afterwards to temporarily call home, or they might settle down permanently within Ingram's ward in the middle of the Veil.

They may even eventually place their wards side by side

with each other. Who knew?

Whatever makes them happy.

That thought stiffened his features, and he drifted his gaze to the corner of his eyes. He fidgeted nervously.

"Em, there's something I want to tell you." Leaning forward, he clasped his hands together and rested them between his spread knees, staring down at them.

"Oh, boy. Here we go," she teased, unprepared for the seriousness of what he was about to deliver.

"I want to tell Aleron about Beau. I want to do so before he remembers I had another pair of rings." He flicked his gaze to her briefly, without moving his head, and took in her furrowed brows. "I don't want him putting that together on his own."

He didn't want Aleron coming to his own conclusions, and then have to deal with the jealous or agonising emotions that may arise with them. Gideon would rather get it out of the way so he could reassure him. He wanted to explain that Beau no longer mattered – nor was he settling for Aleron because he had to.

If Gideon really didn't want to be here, or found Aleron so distasteful, he really would have sought a way to break their bond. He wouldn't have cared if it killed him, since he'd already died once and his life was over.

Everything was gone: his home, his friends, his old lover.

No. Instead, he had chosen this life, and he was happier with it than the one he'd been living before. He was overjoyed by it.

"Then tell him?"

"I can't. I love him, I really do, but I know his humanity is low." Gideon clenched his teeth, causing a jaw muscle to pulse before he quietly said, "He knows it, too."

He spared her a glance, and her lips tightened knowingly. She didn't deny it; it was too obvious. It also meant she knew she couldn't convince him otherwise.

"Aleron won't admit it, but I know Ingram having more intelligence bothers him. He feels behind, and doesn't like being lost in conversations his own twin can keep up with. It hurts me to see him recede into himself when it happens."

Aleron always cupped his hands to his stomach, with his wings drooping ever so slightly. It was subtle enough that Gideon didn't know if anyone else noticed it, or perhaps he was just more hyperaware of Aleron's wellbeing. Even if his orbs didn't change colour, Gideon knew him – knew when he was distressed and anxious.

Gideon also understood how he felt on a deeply ingrained level, since Emerie was now years of experience and growth ahead of him. It bothered him as well that she was brighter, wiser, and more mature than him, but there was little he could do to change that but wait out the years.

His darling Duskwalker, on the other hand, could be aided.

Her orange brows drew together. "What are you trying to say?"

"I know there is a small bandit camp not far from here. I noticed it when we flew over and originally found this place." He looked away from her when Aleron went roaring across the clearing, with Ingram hot on his feathered tail. "I'm going to take him there."

"If you're implying what I think you are, I won't agree to it." In the corner of his eye, she sat up straight while her hands curled into tight fists on her knees. "I was a Demonslayer, Gideon. I spent the last eight years valuing human life, no matter who they are or what they've done."

He clasped his hands tighter with his eyes darkening at nothing. "I wasn't asking for your blessing, Emerie. I'm asking for your forgiveness."

"It's wrong, Gideon!" she shouted, throwing her hands forward in disbelief.

"I don't give a fuck what it is," Gideon answered coldly.

"*He* is all that matters. Well... all four of us. But right now, I'm thinking about him. I know it may not make sense to you, but the moment I put that ring on him, he became my husband in the most unconventional sense. I would fight for him, I'd die for him, and I'd kill for him – just as he would me."

Their bond would be built on unity and equal footing. What Aleron brought forth, Gideon would try with all his might to do – no matter what it cost him or what unholy, deplorable thing he had to do to achieve it.

Sighing, he leaned back and ran his fingers through his hair.

"I'm not going to take him on a continent-wide massacre, Em. I just want him to catch up to Ingram, that's all. I don't want him to feel left out, and I want to be able to talk to him about important things without him getting lost or... *hurt* because he can't understand."

The last thing I want to do is hurt him, he thought. *I've done enough of that.* But he'd like to give the truth, and all of himself. He didn't think that was asking too much.

Her silence was heavy, but he refused to be crushed by it.

"Fine," Emerie eventually bit out. "I get it. I already accepted that one or two humans may get eaten by Ingram if they attack us. If this is something you think you can stomach – how wrong and immoral it is – then I'll try to forgive you."

He cast her an awkward glance. "Thanks. I know he'll appreciate it too. He's trying so hard not to upset or scare you, so it'll make it easier if I tell him you'll forgive him."

"Ingram is going to want to go with him, you know that, right? He's not going to let his twin go off into a battle by himself."

"I figured, but if he could please not eat them so Aleron can, that'd be just dandy. They don't experience hunger anymore."

Her lips tightened, and her blue eyes became steely. "When?"

"Soon." He shrugged a single shoulder. "A day or two, if possible."

She took a deep inhale and let it out defeatedly. For a moment, she, and everything, was silent, as the weight of his request hung between them.

Then she placed her hand on his shoulder, rudely using him as a leaning board to stand.

"What have our lives come to?" She shook her head as she went down the hill and around the main pool. "You're lucky I love Ingram just as much, Gideon, and understand why you're doing this."

He watched her go, probably hunting down Ingram to have a sulk about her feelings... or something.

Still, he appreciated that beautiful red-haired woman more than words could ever say. He also loved his little, yet older, sister more than life.

He was glad she'd find a way to forgive them.

Gideon knew his life was complete with them both in it, and he'd rather there not be abrasive tension between them if possible. There would be times when they would part, although likely rarely, but he wanted them to always come back to each other's presences with a collective unity.

Sitting by himself, he rested his elbow against his knee and placed his chin on top of his enclosed fist, wanting to take in his new family from a distance. Aleron and Ingram's playful brawling was interrupted by Emerie. Her orange hair and plain-brown dress glowed in the bright light as they fluttered to the right due to the direction of the wind.

A mild, but affectionate smile lifted his cheeks when his Duskwalker immediately directed his bony face towards him. Crawling on all fours, Aleron made his way up the hill, as if he didn't wish for Gideon to be alone for even a second.

He didn't move, and just waited.

I don't care if I remember him anymore.

He'd welcome each memory that *did* come to him, since most of his time in Tenebris was still missing. It just didn't bother him anymore that he couldn't remember.

Gideon had new memories to create. And they were livelier and lovelier than any that could have been created in the afterlife. Filled with real air, sensations, a working pulse, and a world they could truly touch. They were no longer stagnant and non-existent, but were moving towards some unknown future.

When Aleron was almost upon him, he shifted to his more humanoid form. The sun shining over the side of him caused his bat skull and spiralling goat horns to glitter, and the sight never ceased to be transfixing. Gideon's fully flaming soul only added to the beauty of his bony face, simply because of what it represented: their everlasting bond.

"Why are you alone, little spring?" Aleron asked curiously, his gruff voice soothing, warm, and filled with utter adoration.

Gideon gingerly reached forward with his left hand, knowing what he sought would be silently given.

Their rings sparkled in the sun together when Aleron's claws tickled against the inside of his hand until their fingers touched each other's palms. With overwhelming tenderness, he gazed up at his Duskwalker, who was beautiful in his own way, inside and out.

Gideon gave him a loving smile. "I'm never alone with you around, darling."

My soul was his to steal in the afterlife, but it was my heart he took in this one.

Also by Opal Reyne

DUSKWALKER BRIDES
A Soul to Keep
A Soul to Heal
A Soul to Touch
A Soul to Guide
A Soul to Revive
A Soul to Steal
A Soul to Protect *(TBA 2024)*
(More titles coming soon)

WITCH BOUND
The WitchSlayer
The ShadowHunter
(More titles coming soon)

Completed Series

A PIRATE ROMANCE DUOLOGY
Sea of Roses
Storms of Paine

~~THE ADEUS CHRONICLES~~
This series has been **unpublished** as of
20th of June 2022

If you would like to keep up to date with all the novels I will be publishing in the future, follow me on my social media platforms.

Facebook Page:
https://www.facebook.com/OpalReyne

Facebook Group:
https://www.facebook.com/groups/opals.nawty.book.realm

Instagram:
https://www.instagram.com/opalreyne

Twitter:
https://www.twitter.com/opalreyne

Discord:
https://discord.gg/opalites

TikTok:
@OpalReyneAuthor